# THE NOVELS OF

# FRANCIS BRETT YOUNG

---

## SEVERN EDITION

# THE
# NOVELS OF
# FRANCIS BRETT YOUNG

UNDERGROWTH
(with E. Brett Young)

DEEP SEA

THE DARK TOWER

IRON AGE

THE CRESCENT MOON

THE YOUNG PHYSICIAN

THE TRAGIC BRIDE

THE BLACK DIAMOND

THE RED KNIGHT

PILGRIM'S REST

WOODSMOKE

COLD HARBOUR

SEA HORSES

PORTRAIT OF CLARE

MY BROTHER JONATHAN

BLACK ROSES

JIM REDLAKE

MR. AND MRS. PENNINGTON

THE HOUSE UNDER THE WATER

THIS LITTLE WORLD

WHITE LADIES

FAR FOREST

THEY SEEK A COUNTRY

DR. BRADLEY REMEMBERS

FRANCIS BRETT YOUNG

# PORTRAIT
# OF
# CLARE

LONDON: WILLIAM HEINEMANN LTD

*First published March* 1927
*Reprinted April, June* 1927
*Cheap Edition June* 1929
*Reprinted October* 1929
*January* 1931, *April* 1932
*April* 1933, *June* 1934
*First published in the Severn Edition* 1935
*Reprinted May* 1936, *August* 1937
*October* 1938

Printed in Great Britain at
The Windmill Press, Kingswood, Surrey

*To*

**The** *Countess Beauchamp*
*because of her love for*
*Worcestershire,*
*and mine for*
*Madresfield*

PREFACE

# PREFACE

THE planning of *Portrait of Clare* during the winter of 1923 arose from two sources. The first was an ever-increasing nostalgia for the shapes and colours and smells of my own country, the inevitable result of having been forced to live in Italy. The second was an instinctive reaction on my part against the kind of heroine who had become fashionable in the fiction of those strained and excited years which immediately followed the great war. To many of us who had known in our own not very recent youth a coolness and quietude of life with which those writers who had grown up during the war were impatient, the kind of existence they portrayed appeared even more revolting than pitiful. The idea of inventing a woman who did not 'live on her nerves' to an accompaniment of negroid music made as strong an appeal to the contrariness of my nature as did the prospect of writing a romance of Victorian dimensions at a period when novels generally were tending to become shorter and shorter.

Thus Clare Lydiatt was conceived: a normal and (possibly) a rather silly woman moving quite unimportantly across the West Midland landscape which I loved and which had already established itself as my chosen scene; and the book, begun at Anacapri on April the First flowed on smoothly enough through spring and autumn until the first part was finished. At this point the disadvantages of its subject and its dimensions began to appear. An American friend, who had asked to read the manuscript, returned it to me in an ominous silence and admitted, on being pressed, not only that she had found it boring but also that she was sure that if the book had been written by an unknown writer no publisher would print it. This was life, she said, seen through the eyes of a shy young curate: it was not, in fact, a 'modern' novel at all, and for the sake of my reputation as a man of letters she begged me to abandon it.

To me, who am constitutionally unable to judge my own work, her verdict was a heavy blow. But when, having taken courage from my wife's staunch approval, I went on with the book in the following December and finished it in May 1926, an even heavier discouragement awaited me. The publishers who were under contract to publish it protested against its length. No book, they maintained, of nearly three hundred thousand words could possibly 'pay': the only way out of the difficulty was to publish it in three volumes issued at intervals of three months. That, of course, was a mutilation I could not accept. However loose its form might be, *Portrait of Clare*, in my eyes, was a single book and indivisible. At a pinch, the publishers said, two volumes might do; but even in that case there must be a long interval between them. I was supplied with figures which proved the precise degree of loss with which the firm was faced; and, to cut a long story short, they finally refused to produce the book in one volume and the contract was cancelled.

It was published, at length, and in one volume, by Heinemann's: the first book in a lengthy partnership which neither the publishers nor I have had cause to regret. In 1927 it was awarded the James Tait Black Prize.

# CONTENTS

# CONTENTS

# BOOK ONE
## CLARE LYDIATT

## PEN HOUSE

HALF a mile above the village of Wychbury the convex
windows in the lower storey of Pen House returned the
lurid reflex of a sun sinking to extinction among the
mountains of Wales, and surveyed, with the dispassionate
indolence of age, the darkening expanses of the Severn Plain
four hundred feet below. In front of them, screening the
precipitous foreground, inviting, as it were, the perpetual
contemplation of sombre distances, lay the shrubberies
which Dr. Weir had planted in the days of youth and
activity many years before. In house and garden alike the
only shapes that suggested vigour or aspiration were two
gigantic Wellingtonias, whose tall pyramids stood etched in
immobility against the sunset. These also the doctor had
planted in the first year of his ownership and the last of the
Crimean war. Sometimes, on sunny evenings, the old
man would stand rapt in admiration of these two prodigious
children of his fancy : and more rarely, when he ventured
out with Jabez in the old victoria, he would slew round
his thin shoulders to see, from a distance, their twin spires
dominating the low-browed stucco façade of the little
Georgian house in whose shadow he had planted them.

It was an old man's house, and the spirit of one old man
inhabited and informed it. Dr. Weir was now in his
seventy-eighth year. For nearly forty he had lived at
Pen House, and, but for the incalculable accidents of age,
seemed likely to go on living there for many years to come,
so warily, and with such meticulous moderation his present

mode of life was planned; so jealously was he guarded from all adversity by the attentions of his daughter Catherine and the devotion of Mrs. Rudge.

In fifty odd years of practice he had gathered to himself the reputation and respect that old age, of itself, acquires; his great gaunt height, his magnificent eyes, which seemed to penetrate no less deeply as the fire within them failed, his ruthless common sense had impressed his own generation and gained the reinforcement of tradition in the two that followed it. A hard man, whose hardness was often tempered by sudden surprising kindliness; a just man, whose judgments rose above the prejudice of the local bench; a skilled physician, unorthodox but weighty with experience; a sceptic, illuminated by mystical intuitions: a wealthy man, but generous, and one whose riches nobody envied.

In his seventy-second year the doctor had retired from the active practice of medicine; but no idle retirement could satisfy his zest for living. From those high terraces, like an old eagle, he still contemplated the life that he had been forced to abandon; nothing that happened in the village of Wychbury escaped his attention; and the village itself was conscious of his scrutiny, his very aloofness creating a legend of supernatural knowledge and power. For a long time his old patients persisted in climbing the hill and pestering him for advice that his agreement with his successor, young Dr. Boyd, would not allow him to give. Catherine stood guard over him and turned them all away; all except George Vigors, the sexton, for whom, in spite of his clerical associations, the doctor always had a weak spot.

"It's as well to keep in with George," he said grimly. "You never know when I may not want him to bury me."

In spite of these prognostications he still clung obstinately to his office as chairman of the bench. Each Thursday morning the old victoria took him down to Wychbury, his lean legs cramped to a conventional attitude, his dark eyes devouring every detail on the roadway as he passed. Not even Sir Joseph Hingston, with his challenging crest and the new magnificence of Stourford Castle behind him, commanded such veneration. And then, one day, at the end of a weary licensing session, the court-room swam in front of him, the strength faded away from his limbs, a black pall descended, and he awoke to find himself dazed and weak in the arms of the magistrate's clerk.

" It's heart," he told himself. " The heart muscle's good for so many pulsations and no more. It's no good flogging a tired horse. I must give in."

His daughter tried to force him to a consultation. Why shouldn't his old friend, Lloyd Moore, run over from North Bromwich and see him in a friendly way ?

" Lloyd Moore ? " he snorted. " I know Lloyd Moore, and he knows me. Lloyd Moore was once my dresser. Now his time's worth six guineas an hour, and I'm not going to rob him of half a day to tell me something that I know better than he does. Besides, he's a surgeon, and mine is a medical case. Still, he's in a position to sign my death certificate, if that's what you're after."

She wasn't after that. The harshness of the suggestion made her cry. He took her hand and pressed it. The gesture was unusual. He had never shown himself so tender to her as to Sylvia, who had gone and married that rascal Lydiatt ; but, for all that, Catherine was a good girl who might show more sense when she came to years of discretion. At that time she was only thirty-two.

" I tell you," he went on, " there's nothing to worry about. I'm going to take care of myself, and you'll have to help me. See ? "

It wasn't as easy as it sounded. The denial of this last means of self-expression made him restless and occasionally fretful ; the proposal that she might help him was a mere form of words. He had always prided himself on his independence ; and though, professionally, he knew women better than most men, he had very little understanding or use for them in domestic relations ; for he had married in middle age and lost his wife within five years of their marriage, leaving his two daughters to the care of Mrs. Rudge, and treating them with the alternations of roughness and intimacy, unexpected and therefore embarrassing, which had endeared him to his women patients. It was clear, as Catherine found to her cost, that the whole nature of a relation which had lasted for over thirty years could not suddenly be changed. A habit, so fixed as to be superior to circumstance, forced him to resent the attentions that he invited. His irritability made her dread the sudden harsh judgments and humiliations that she daily suffered at his hands. Mrs. Rudge, providentially, was blessed with a thicker skin.

In those early years of the doctor's retirement Catherine Weir knew little happiness ; only the strength and obstinacy that she had inherited from the old man himself could have sustained her through them ; for her life, apart from one tragic incident in the early twenties, still passionately remembered, had been barren of beauty or emotional experience. It is true that the childhood of Claerwen, her niece, had absorbed her ; but mingled with the vicarious maternal tenderness that Clare awakened in her, ran a deeper strain which, struggle as she might, she could not conceal or suppress. For Clare was the daughter of her sister Sylvia, and all of Sylvia that showed itself in the growing Clare renewed the pain of a wrong she could never forget.

It recalled to her the memory of Clare's father, Ambrose Lydiatt. Lydiatt was a musician, organist of the parish church at Stourton. He came to Pen House to give piano and singing lessons to the doctor's young ladies ; but in his worn leather portfolio, like some new Prometheus, he had carried into their almost monastic seclusion something more than music. Twice a week the sisters took their lessons in turn at the old Broadwood, faced with pleatings of maroon silk, which still stood in the drawing-room at Pen House. There Catherine Weir had lost her heart. It was natural enough that Lydiatt should make love to her in circumstances so intimate and in a scene so obviously set for passion ; it was natural that a creature so young and generous should be thrilled by this adventure ; it was prudent, in view of the doctor's known and violent prejudices, that their love-making should remain secret, sweeter for its secrecy and for the subdued and luscious tenderness of Schumann's music that enveloped it.

In the ecstatic humility of the *Frauenliebe und leben,* freely and mawkishly translated, Catherine's devotion found its liturgy. Not even Sylvia her sister must know. She and Sylvia sang Mendelssohn duets, with words that for her and Lydiatt had meanings that poor Sylvia couldn't guess. Nor did she guess that, with an equal enthusiasm, Lydiatt was making love to Sylvia.

For many months the double intrigue went on. Lydiatt, it seemed, found it easier to make love than to make up his mind ; for though Catherine undoubtedly possessed more absolute beauty, Sylvia was younger, more pliable and infinitely more sensitive. Not till the very day of her sister's elopement did Catherine dream for a moment that Lydiatt was not wholly hers. It came, and her life was broken. It withered away like a bough of lilac broken in full flower, and her beauty withered with it. She grew bitter with a desolation that found its only comfort in her father's anger ; for the doctor was old-fashioned in his ideas of filial duty and exaggerated the contempt of the scientist for those who practised the arts without material success. All the fervour of her love found new expression in an inclusive hatred for Lydiatt, for her sister and for the human race ; a hatred so persistent that when, a few years later, Sylvia died in the poverty that she had chosen and

Catherine had escaped, and Lydiatt, emigrating to Canada with a new wife, had left to their mercy this child with the fantastic name, she could not look on it as anything but a reminder of her own humiliation. Not even the helplessness of the small creature touched her heart.

All this was many years ago, and with the passage of time, made swifter by the endless monotony of life at Pen House, her attitude towards Clare changed. From the first day of its arrival Mrs. Rudge took the child to her heart. Catherine watched her jealously, and from a distance, learning, against her will, the barrenness of a life devoid of love. Within a few years she had begun to be interested in Clare, to envy the devotion which Thirza Rudge, without effort, inspired. So she crept nearer. She loved Clare hungrily, passionately, yet always, to her grief, with an awkwardness, an obstinate spiritual inhibition, that the child's instinct infallibly divined. She couldn't help it. Always, even in the moments of her most passionate will to love, the image of Sylvia, which year by year defined itself more clearly in Clare's features and tricks of expression, rose between them like a barrier transparent but impassable, denying all completeness of confidence.

Then, with the doctor's breakdown, came the care of another child, one more wilful and obstinate than Clare could ever be, and in the absorption of this new charge, the raw wound healed. Yet, in the scar, as in old wounds that itch and burn with changes of wind and temperature, there remained a focus of potential pain, ready to be stirred into activity by agencies unsuspected and unforeseen.

Another and a greater anxiety arose. In the third year of his retirement the doctor had a stroke ; a small affair it seemed at first, no more than a sudden numbness and loss of power in the left leg. Lloyd Moore came out from North Bromwich to confirm the verdict that the old man already had delivered. For a few weeks his ancient obstinacy asserted itself in a painful renewal of energy. He persisted in pacing his terrace with a stick, dragging the weight of the dead limb behind him. To and fro he went along the level ground, seeing nothing of the flowers in which he delighted or the wide prospect of the plain, his face lined, concentrated, as though he hoped that by sheer force of will he could drive the power of his determination into the degenerate nerves.

Catherine watched him in an agony ; for she really loved him, and particularly that part of him which compelled him to this martyrdom. At times, standing behind the lace curtains of the drawing-room window, she could almost feel in her own limbs the fierce effort of his will, forcing life into blind channels that would no longer contain it. At last he gave in. He knew, as well as she did, that this was the beginning of the end. He had told her as much in his harsh, challenging way : " This is the first. Some day there'll come a second. And the third will do for me ! " The time for joking about death certificates had passed. At any moment the second blow might fall, and then the next, and then . . . She dared not think of it.

Only she knew that, with the first dimming of that central fire, a curious gentleness was born in him that made him more lovable. All through those years of suspension that marked Clare's adolescence his nature was taking on a mellow patina, through which the brightness of the original metal gleamed, on occasion, with a hard and devastating brilliance ; but, for the most part, he had grown submissive to his fate and to the attentions of his two nurses. To those of Thirza in particular ; for Thirza was now an old woman, only ten years younger than himself, and, like himself, admitted to the pains and privileges of age. It was she who trimmed his beard for him : an operation that, even in his most submissive moments, Catherine would never have dared to undertake.

Gradually he settled down into a routine of artificial peace. His old study, adjoining the dining-room, was converted into a bedroom ; a little chamber of the barest simplicity with no furniture but his bed, a few books, his dressing-table, an articulated skeleton, and a single arm-chair ; the whole impregnated by a faint odour of carbolic acid, the old fashioned antiseptic to which, since the days of Lister, he had given his faith. From this room he issued every morning at ten precisely, leaning on Thirza's arm. In summer his chair was placed beside the open window of the dining-room facing his Wellingtonias ; in winter at the fireside. There he would sit all day, reading or dozing for hours on end, only moving to take his seat at the head of the table at meal-times and to wind up the clock in the hall on Sunday mornings. Little by little his rugged face became softened to a curious unsubstantial whiteness, so frail that it seemed as if the least shock might shatter it.

And yet his mind was clear, as clear, in most ways, as ever before, with a still, sunset clarity. The absence of a future, or rather the sense of its calculable definition, turned his thoughts backward into unusual channels. He began to read history with an almost youthful eagerness, as though he had suddenly attained the wisdom of a new perspective. With equal enthusiasm he returned to the writings of Comte and the religious sceptics who had most deeply influenced his youth, violently reaffirming his distrust in all religious systems, satisfying himself, again and again, of the rightness which had set him in opposition to the vicar, Mr. Pomfret, and all his tribe. With politics he had finished for ever ; he had no faith in politicians. Even Gladstone had failed him, not only by the establishment of a Catholic Maynooth, but by the enormity of conferring a peerage on that scribbler Tennyson.

One other thing, surprisingly, absorbed his interest. Money. And this was strange ; for in all his active life he had scarcely given it a thought. Perhaps he had always been too busy; but now that he had leisure to survey his possessions he found that, almost insensibly, he had become a wealthy man; wealthy, at least, for his own modest station in life. His own needs had been infinitesimal, the demands of his small family never exacting; and since the day, more than forty years ago, when he had bought Pen House, he had never been forced to any capital expenditure. In that half century his original possessions had more than quadrupled in value; and the steady stream of his earnings had deposited a delta of rich alluvium which it amazed him to contemplate. Unconsciously a strain of carefulness, almost of avarice, asserted itself. To his daughter's astonishment, he began, for the first time in his life, to preach economy and to complain of extravagance; to read financial journals and watch the markets; to find an endless fascination in the casting and recasting of his will, a document which he always kept in a drawer of the dining-room bureau within reach of his left hand.

It was by reason of this new development that Dudley Wilburn had lately become a frequent visitor of Pen House. Wilburn was junior partner in the old firm of Wilburn and Wilburn, the most reputable solicitors of North Bromwich. In earlier days the doctor had been contented with the services of the lawyer in Wychbury who practised in the court over which he presided and on rare occasions collected his debts; but Mr. Mayhew, he feared, was hardly competent to deal with graver matters; and Wilburn, when he presented himself at Pen House for the first time, turned out to be an old acquaintance, whom they had all known as a boy. A fellow with all his wits about him, the doctor soon decided; and, though he disliked the intrusion of the magnificent Hingstons into his own corner of the county, what was good enough for the Hingstons was good enough for him. He respected the air of clean strength, the keen.

calculated soberness that Wilburn carried with him. He approved the way in which Wilburn kept his end up in their many subjects of disagreement ; he liked his tact, his kindness, his diffidence ; he liked the man himself ; and so did Catherine.

For, with the arrival of Wilburn, the first man of her own —or nearly her own—generation with whom she had been brought into intimate contact since the days of Lydiatt, Catherine Weir experienced a curious rejuvenation. He filled her consciousness with airs of a world outside Pen House, the very existence of which she had taught herself to disregard. He brought with him the breath of life which she had consciously, and, later, half-unconsciously, denied herself. He flattered her, from the first, by accepting her as coequal and coeval, in a category definitely removed from that of the old man and the old serving maid with whose life she had identified herself. His coming roused her from the fatalistic resignation which she had gradually accepted ; it suggested to her that, perhaps, her life was not quite finished. Her body, her mind, awakened to a new and surprising sensibility that responded eagerly to the stimulus of physical contacts and whispered confidences. She saw that Wilburn and herself were partners in a kind of benevolent conspiracy, with pass-words and understandings and secrets that nobody else understood ; and in this partnership he deferred to her wisdom more completely than he ever deferred to the wisdom of her father.

But that was not enough for her. She discovered that in spirit, at least, she had scarcely aged since the days of her first romance ; that, through all the time between, her life had remained suspended in a kind of wintry trance from which it was now awakening. It seemed, indeed, as if the ageing of her body had been retarded beneath the same long hibernation ; that it, too, had emerged from sleep into a similitude of youth. In certain aspects she could still persuade herself that she was handsome ; as a girl she had been pale ; now she had more colour in her cheeks, though the colour was fixed, not fugitive. Whenever the days of Wilburn's visits came round, she found herself trying to set that beauty to its best advantage.

She would wake in the morning with a queer, fluttering elation ; she would go about the work of the house with restless benevolence. Nothing was too much trouble for her ; she seemed to be mistress of her own life, to carry with her such abundance of gaiety, hope and vitality that she was able to shoulder other people's problems as well as her own. The morning's work melted away before her consuming energy, so that she had time to spare. Time for the complete performance of her toilet. Time even to play the piano. Before Wilburn's arrival on the scene nobody but Clare had ever touched its yellow keys since the day of Sylvia's elopement. Now music seemed to flow from her fingers like the flowers of a blackthorn breaking into bloom. The memory of Lydiatt no longer haunted that room.

And then the evening. It had its climactic moments, like a ritual. Wilburn invariably came out of town by the six o'clock train and returned to North Bromwich by another that left Wychbury at nine-thirty-five. At half-past six, precisely, Catherine could expect to hear the carriage approaching. Neither Ellen nor Mrs. Rudge must ever open the door for him. She went to greet him herself. In the narrow, ill-lighted hall, where, twenty years before, Lydiatt had kissed her, their hands met. Only for one moment ; for the doctor also was impatient for Wilburn's company. Nothing but a smile and a whispered word about the old man's health while she took Wilburn's coat from him. Then, for the hour before supper, she would sit silent on the other side of the fire, listening to their business discussions, admiring the strength which Wilburn had succeeded in impressing on her father's mind, pretending to be rapt in the popular drawn-thread work, but rarely working ; because, without spectacles that tried her eyes, and she could not bring herself to wear them in his presence. They seemed to carry a suggestion of maturity that was not fair to her.

Sometimes, when Wilburn was ready to go, Jabez would be behindhand with the carriage. Then they would stand for long moments in the hall, talking of things that related to the doings of their own generation, in which the doctor was no longer interested. At such times, perhaps, their conspiracy seemed most intimate and enthralling. They were as much alone as they could have been on any mountain top. Sometimes, unexpectedly, he would call her by her Christian name. Precious moments . . . moments to live for.

And now, by some peculiar malice of fate, the latest of these ecstasies had been complicated by the coincidence of Clare's return from school and the inexorable onset of one of those periodic headaches which devastated Catherine's life and had become such commonplaces that nobody at Pen House—not even the motherly Thirza—took any notice of them. It was always like that. The tenor of her daily life was so automatically subdued that any unusual excitement had power to precipitate this scourge. That morning, as luck would have it, the wind had set in shrewdly from the East, and though they had reached the middle of April, she knew well enough what the sudden chill portended.

So, equally, did Ellen, the village blacksmith's daughter, who shared with Mrs. Rudge the heavier domestic labours of Pen House, and suffered from her mistress's headaches as acutely as Miss Cathie herself. Together, in an atmosphere of tense irritability, they had fallen on Clare's bedroom and submitted it to its second spring-cleaning in six weeks. At the end of the morning Ellen had retired in disorder to Thirza's bosom, Catherine to a darkened room in which she lay for hours on end, fasting, tormented by the prospect of some imperious disturbance on the part of the doctor, and the ruin of an evening to which she had eagerly looked forward for more than a month. In the painful activity of her bewildered mind it seemed to her that Clare was personally responsible for all her troubles : and this, too, distressed her, for she knew that it was unjust, and prided herself upon her sense of justice.

At five o'clock Ellen knocked diffidently at her bedroom door and handed her a telegram which confirmed the hour of Wilburn's arrival. Still sick and giddy, but nerved by the approaching excitement, she dressed herself with care. Before Wilburn's appearance she had always contented herself with the art of the Wychbury dressmaker ; but on her last visit to Clare at St. Monica's she had tremulously entered Milton's the mantle-makers, and ordered the very latest example of North Bromwich elegance : a bodice of purple velvet with inflated shoulder-of-mutton sleeves and a high, stiff neck-band edged with white frilling, and a black cloth skirt, gathered about the hips with bunches of material that resembled nothing so much as the folds of a curtain above a theatre's proscenium. The pain that she had suffered in purchasing these expensive garments and the shyness with which their magnificence had oppressed her were magnified a hundred times when she put them on. The frilled neck-band frayed her throat like a saw, the waist stifled her with its constriction ; and yet, when she stepped back to survey the effect, a flush of excited pleasure lightened, for one moment, her splitting head. Nothing, she knew, could give her back her youth ; but nobody, thanks to Milton's artistry, could deny that she was a handsome woman. Secure in the consciousness of a new dignity she examined her fine, dark eyes ; her cheeks, a thought too highly coloured for beauty ; the firm, if faintly bitter, formation of her lips.

When she had finished her toilet she hurried, quite needlessly, downstairs.

Through the closed door of the dining-room she heard the soothing West-country drone of Mrs. Rudge's voice occasionally broken by the old man's answering grunts. She did not enter. She feared the acid comments which her new finery would provoke, and hoped that later, under the cover of Wilburn's presence she might escape them. Aimlessly she opened the hall door and stepped out on to the gravel drive. The sun had set. Now even the tall pyramids of the Wellingtonias had lost their definition, but though the dank air of the Spring night made her shiver, she knew from the stillness of the shrubberies that the wind had changed. The very silence comforted her. If only Clare had not been coming home !

## II

## ST. MONICA'S

THAT morning at St. Monica's, Clare had wakened early, her mind taut with excitement. For a long while she had lain quiet with eyes open wide drinking in the new strangeness of her familiar room ; its four beds with coarse twill sheets ; the sleeping figures of the three girls who shared it with her. Ever since she had come to St. Monica's six years before, a shy and lanky little creature of eleven, through more than half of her conscious life, that room had been the fixed point round which her slow-moving world revolved ; this day would dislocate the whole system with the ruthlessness of a stellar convulsion. Probably she would never see it again. Even if she revisited it, it would be no longer hers. From this day forward she would be no different from the other occupants whom she remembered or had forgotten. She would be whirled away into space like Marion Prosser, over whose loss she had cried so bitterly ; like Hope Harvey, who was now married ; like Esther Reeve. Esther Reeve was dead. . . . Dead, but in no way more lost than those two others, more lost than she herself would be.

It was incredible ; so disturbingly incredible that she wished to goodness the other three would wake and distract her thoughts with their chatter. She couldn't bear to approach this crucial day so solemnly. Soon, thank Heaven, there would be plenty of distraction. A morning of packing, of laughter, of strained, hurried farewells ; and, in the afternoon, the prize-giving and the school concert. Not that the prize-giving meant much to Clare herself ; but the concert was another matter. In this she would perform a small but terrifying part ; in this she would know the pride, the glow, the exultation of hearing her own, her darling, her worshipped Miss Boldmere play. For the last time.

Unless the others wakened she felt she would be forced to cry. She mustn't cry. To cry would have been unworthy of Miss Boldmere. Instead of crying she forced herself to dwell upon the vision of the reseda shantung dress designed by Liberty in which Miss Boldmere would perform. Two nights before Miss Boldmere had shown it to her. It was the most lovely thing on earth, and nobody else at St. Monica's, not even the mistresses, had seen it. The thought of this exclusive knowledge made Clare shiver with ecstasy.

One morning, six weeks before, Clare had been working at the tinkling Schubert *Impromptu* which she was to play at the school concert when Miss Boldmere had stolen quietly into the wintry practice room. Even though her eyes were concentrated on the music, Clare knew that it was she. She had felt the blood rising in her cheeks, her red, numbed fingers refused to obey her ; a tide of the White Rose scent which Miss Boldmere and no other used enveloped her.

She fumbled and came to a stop. Miss Boldmere took her hands in hers, Miss Boldmere was speaking to her :

"Clare, my dear child, your fingers are like ice. The temperature of this room is impossible ; I must speak to the headmistress about it ! " Miss Boldmere's hands were warm and soft, chafing Clare's numb fingers ; and then, in a moment of incredible ecstasy, Clare heard her speaking of things that had no relation to music ; of Christ, and the love of Christ and the calm beauty of Mary.

"We don't often talk of these things at St. Monica's," she had said, " but you, Clare, seem to me different from most of the others." How had she guessed it ? " I want you," she whispered, " to know the wonderful happiness that is within the reach of us all. This is your last term, Clare, and soon you'll be leaving us and forgetting us."

As if she could ever forget ! But Clare could not speak, and in a few moments, the Schubert *Impromptu* forgotten, she found herself kneeling on the linoleum floor of the practice-room, praying, with one cold hand in Miss Boldmere's. For a moment some faint sense of the ridiculous made her feel shy ; but a sudden reaction of shame humbled her. She was overwhelmed by the wonder of such unexpected intimacy. This was the crowning glory of her long adoration ; her heart melted into a warm ecstasy.

Even when Miss Boldmere rose and laughed shyly as she brushed the dust from her skirt, her pale cheeks flushed, her grey eyes swimming behind the lenses of her pincenez, Clare's chilly fingers tingled with an infusion of the warmth that filled her mind.

"Now you had better make up for lost time," said Miss Boldmere, " though ' lost ' is hardly the right word." She spoke in her ordinary scholastic voice, still a little shaken with emotion. She stood at Clare's left hand. Clare went on playing in a dream. " Take off that pedal ! How many times have I told you ! " said Miss Boldmere. " One

—two—three—four : mind—the—same—touch." Then, like a mouse, she stole away.

But that wasn't the end. Miss Boldmere lent her books. Two or three times she entered the sanctuary of Miss Boldmere's bedroom. Secretly. It wouldn't do to talk about such mysteries. Miss Boldmere burnt incense in her bedroom ; odours of paradise. And once, on a Sunday morning, she found herself detached from the double file that trailed soberly to Matins at Alvaston Parish Church, penetrating, in Miss Boldmere's company, strange areas of bricky slum on the way to the Anglican chapel of St. Jude. There, once again, in sweet ambient incense, they had knelt side by side, and Clare's heart had fainted in the confused warmth of two adorations. That evening Miss Boldmere gave her a copy of *Thomas à Kempis* in odorous Russian leather. It lay beneath her pillow and perfumed her dreams. Inside it was written : "*To dear Clare from A. B.*" Agnes Boldmere. St. Agnes. Clare pressed it to her warm heart as she lay that morning waiting for the others to wake. The wan sun faded into a grey sky. A harsh wind troubled the sooty shrubberies. A bell clanged on the landing.

So the day passed in uneasiness and frustration. Nothing could assuage the ache or fill the central emptiness ; not even the assumption of the frock, of white silk, which Aunt Cathie had authorized for the occasion. The hour of the concert came. Miss Boldmere, elegant and serious, in her green shantung, played the *Moonlight Sonata*. Joyce Barrat, clumsily, turned over. Clare sat with her prize, a red, quilted Tennyson, on her knees. Her own turn came. Hurriedly she thrust the Tennyson on to a neighbour's lap and walked to the platform as to a scaffold. As Clare passed her level with flaming cheeks Miss Boldmere's eyes were turned away from her. The perfume of hothouse flowers and scented clothes rose as from a swamp. Her fingers, obeying a habit stronger than volition, began to move. The first phrases of the *Impromptu* tinkled in the air, though she could hardly believe that her hot hands were playing it.

It was over. Amid a silly clapping of hands she rose and retired. Miss Boldmere sat in the front row with lowered eyes. Clare knew what that meant. It meant that she had made a fool of herself, and that was Miss Boldmere's fault. She flushed with anger near to tears. But, as she hurried clumsily down the steps and into the alley between the blocks of chairs, Miss Boldmere raised her eyes and smiled, and it was paradise.

But the joys of the seventh heaven were reserved for the moment, two hours later, when all the guests and most of the girls had gone. Clare was standing in the hall, her luggage at her feet ; the four-wheeler which should take her to the station waited outside. Miss Cash, the head-mistress, came out of her study to give her the little stereo-typed farewell that she kept for departing pupils ; and as Clare answered : " Yes, Miss Cash," and " Thank you, Miss Cash," and " Oh, of *course* I will ! " her heart grew wretched and more wretched wondering if Miss Boldmere, who had run upstairs to change her dress, had quite forgotten her. She need not have wondered. A rapid step on the stairs brought her heart into her mouth. Miss Boldmere, in a high-necked tailor-made dress, with sleeves puffed at the shoulders, a constricted waist and thirty or forty jet buttons down the front, stood beside them. She spoke with a pretty breathlessness : " If Clare is going to the station, Miss Cash, I think I'll ask if I may share her cab. May I, Clare ? "

The head-mistress smiled and left them. Clare found herself alone with her divinity in a musty four-wheeler that smelt of straw. Down all the grim and windy length of the Halesby Road the cab passed slowly ; its interior was dim and sepulchral, as if it had habitually been used for funerals ;

the wheels growled, the windows rattled so incessantly that it was impossible to talk. But Clare's heart was too full for speech ; in a rare, exalted silence they sat close together. She was conscious of nothing but the pallor of Miss Boldmere's tired, sweet face above the goffered frilling, the cold gleam of a wintry sky reflected in her eye-glasses, the warm pressure of Miss Boldmere's body. Clare put out her hand. Miss Boldmere took it in hers and held it until they jolted over the cobbles of the station yard.

The platform was a pandemonium of people hurrying for trains bound westward ; the great glass vault a sounding board pitilessly returning echoes of their steps, of shrill signal horns and the shrieking of locomotives. Barrows of milk-tins clattered by them. A train from the North roared in with snow on the roofs of its black coaches. In such a tumult they could not even think. Like wisps of straw held together by capillary attraction the current swept them in the direction of the backwater in which the local train stood waiting. They walked up and down until they found an empty second-class carriage.

" But I won't wait, dear," Miss Boldmere shouted. " There's nothing so distressing as protracted good-byes." Her voice sank to a husky whisper scarcely audible : " I want you to take this little gift to remember me by," she said. " Every night when you go to bed you read what it tells you. . . . I shall be doing the same, you see. Reading the same words. A kind of spiritual communion. And so . . ." she hesitated. . . . " You understand ? God bless you, my dear."

Clare understood. A small book with a blue cover, and on it in florid gold lettering : *The More Excellent Way*. She could not summon a single word of thanks. Then, suddenly, Miss Boldmere raised her veil. She took Clare in her arms. At last ! For one exquisite moment they clung together. On her young mouth Clare felt the faint downi-

ness of Miss Boldmere's upper lip ; and then, a second later, she was gone, carrying with her all the grace and joy and loveliness of life.

## III

### FIRES OF SPRING

SHE was lost, and yet the memory of her kiss remained, penetrating Clare's body and mind like the perfume of Spring hedgerows and windless woods ; a perfume so faint as scarcely to be perceived, yet so potent as to sweeten all her blood and stir within it intuitions of hope and passionate happiness. In those last moments when they had stood together on the roaring platform she had felt that she would need all her courage not to cry ; she had even, prudently, prepared for the emergency by making sure that her handkerchief was ready ; but now that the end had come she knew that, even if she wanted to, she couldn't cry.

She smiled at her own fears, smiled for a joyousness which she could suppress no more easily than the blackthorn could deny its blossoming. Her mind was thrilled with a tenderness that seemed, once generated, to go on distilling sensual beauty of its own accord ; and as the train clanked slowly through that wilderness of slag and cinder the flame in her heart laughed back at the dark flame-lit pennons of smoke and steam that the East wind blew along with her, at the blood-red afterglow of sun or furnace that brooded above the lips of the basin in which the Black Country lies. She glowed, she burned, she was consumed. And she could not understand it. She only knew that no other kiss could have kindled such a flame.

The kisses of Aunt Cathie, for instance, or of her grand-father. Ever since she could remember living at Pen House

Aunt Cathie and Dr. Weir had bidden her good-night. Aunt Cathie generally kissed the air in the neighbourhood of her left ear ; the kisses of Aunt Cathie were associated with the sensation of a cool, flaccid cheek. Those of her grandfather were bored and bristly ; for in later years his feebleness had compromised mid-way between a beard and a clean shave. On festive occasions, at Christmas, on her birthday, on departures or arrivals, old Mrs. Rudge embraced her. The kisses of Mrs. Rudge were wet and lingering, as though in the middle of them she forgot what she was about. They tasted, or smelt, of the caraway seeds which the old woman had a habit of chewing. Then Marion Prosser's . . . But Marion's were of a jolly, unemotional frankness that made it doubtful if they should be counted at all. Wherein, then, lay the magic of Miss Boldmere's kiss ? Partly in the virtue of Miss Boldmere's divinity ; more, perhaps, in the sweetness of the mysteries that they had shared. *Your sister in Christ :* that was what Miss Boldmere had signed herself in her one, her treasured letter. Spiritual communion. That was the meaning of this serene, expansive joy. And in the little book, the devotional calendar which now lay in her lap, reposed an inexhaustible store of this unique ecstasy. How to conserve it ? How to be worthy of it ?

Her mind descended abruptly to the practical plane. *Do unto others*. . . . That should not be so very difficult. Of course Aunt Cathie was incalculable, particularly on the days when her headaches exploded, and the day after. Once a fortnight. Everybody except Aunt Cathie herself could always tell when they were coming ; an unusual heartiness at breakfast, irritability towards mid-day, then tea, toast, and a hot-water bottle. This period of irritability was one in which allowances must be made. Clare determined to make them. Aunt Cathie's life was not easy, for the doctor, as she always called him, grew always more and more exacting. On some days his bell kept up a continuous tinkle. Now, she, Clare, was no longer a child; she must take her share of the irritation and inconvenience if only they would allow her. She must make herself useful in the house-work too. She must live for others. Obliteration of Self, Miss Boldmere called it. So much for the duty toward her neighbour.

But that was only half of it, and perhaps the least important half. Even if she had not made her promise to Miss Boldmere she was determined to be confirmed. That would be difficult, for nobody at Pen House, except Mrs. Rudge, in furtive moments of what the doctor called superstition, ever went to church. Her grandfather and Mr. Pomfret, the Vicar, were not even on speaking terms. Through all Clare's childhood she had accepted this situation as a natural phenomenon; now it seemed to her inexplicable and sinister. She would have to question Aunt Cathie about it, two days after the next headache; for she couldn't believe that Aunt Cathie's irreligion was more than an unfortunate habit, or that the feud with the Vicarage arose from anything but misunderstanding. For a moment her imagination flattered her with a vision of herself as a missionary in that godless household. She saw herself kneeling with Aunt Cathie at the foot of her bed, as she and Miss Boldmere had knelt beside the piano. She saw tears of repentance in the eyes of Thirza Rudge. But she couldn't see herself converting her grandfather. And yet he is such a good man, she told herself.

Mawne Road. This windy junction clung to the very lip of the coal-basin; an enormous pit-bank rose sheer behind it, a sterile mound of mineral, black as a night sky, in which coruscations of fire revealed themselves at dusk. The wind that swept it was charged with a smell of fire; the wooden platform sagged, the offices tilted helplessly above subterranean strains. Here the engine stood waiting for its signal;

the up-train from Dulston was late ; and Clare, gazing out on to the desolate platform, heard the voices of a group of men who had emerged from the first-class carriage next her own.

One she recognized at once as that of Sir Joseph Hingston, the iron-master baronet ; the other belonged to Mr. Willis, of Mawne Hall. They were talking, without concealment, about developments at the Sedgebury Main Colliery and of a certain Mr. Furnival, the new manager, of whom Mr. Willis disapproved. In the background, like aides-de-camp on a battlefield, stood their sons, Edward Willis and Ralph Hingston.

Clare had known the Willises for years and liked them ; in the days before his retirement her grandfather had doctored the family at Mawne Hall, and she herself had always been invited to the children's parties that were part of their lavish Christmas programme. Everybody liked Walter Willis ; he was so natural and generous ; Mrs. Willis was a darling : and Edward, in spite of his shyness, had always seemed to her a nice kind of boy. And yet when the two young men tactfully detached themselves from their parents and strolled up the platform together past her carriage window, a sudden access of shyness compelled Clare to withdraw herself into the shadow.

This queer instinctive withdrawal surprised her and made her go hot with embarrassment. She knew that it was ridiculous to avoid Edward Willis. Perhaps her shyness had something to do with the mood of devotional exaltation in which Miss Boldmere's kiss had left her ; perhaps she was anxious, unconsciously, not to break that spell ; perhaps, she thought, as the train restarted with a jolt and shook another pattern into her kaleidoscopic brain, perhaps it was the presence of Ralph Hingston, whom she had never seen since the old man had sent him to Oxford five years before.

There was no reason in the world why she should be frightened of the Hingstons except that the whole country-side was full of stories of their wealth and magnificence since Sir Joseph had established himself behind the stucco battlements of Stourford Castle ; and Ralph, as she remembered him, was the least formidable of the family : a fair, sanguine, clean-cut boy, with none of the devastating timidity of Edward Willis nor the aloofness of his brother George, the heir. She knew that she had behaved like a giggling school-girl, and was ashamed of it ; for now she was a school-girl no longer. She was seventeen. At eighteen her mother had run away to be married. By the time that her mother was nineteen Clare herself had been born. Something must be done about it.

But, for the moment, she had time to do nothing. The black dome of the Mawne Road spoil-heap fell away on her left into the tree-softened contours of Mawne Bank, among which, as Mr. Willis proudly maintained, nightingales were still to be heard. On such a raw and windy evening as this no nightingale would dare to sing ; and yet, as the train swung round beneath the cover of the hills, it seemed as though the air grew softer ; the smell of baking bricks and fire no longer scorched it. She threw open the window ; she leaned out into the darkness and let the wind stream through her dark hair till her skin glowed in reaction and her heart beat faster. In the rush of the wind her religious preoccupations, her instinctive self-consciousness, all the habitual inhibitions of life at school were blown clean away. She emerged from it new-born as from a rite of baptism.

Stourton Junction. She wondered suddenly if Sir Joseph and Ralph Hingston had rejoined the train when Mr. Willis had left them at Mawne Road ; for this was the station at which, in the ordinary way, they would leave it. It must be so ; for there, on the platform, stood the Hingstons' cockaded footman. She resolved to be stupid and shy no longer.

She stood at the carriage window with her wild wind-blown hair and called " Good-evening " as they passed. Sir Joseph did not hear her, but Ralph turned suddenly and raised his hat and smiled ; it was a very charming smile : a smile that dawned in the blue wide-set eyes before it reached his big, good-humoured mouth. That mouth, whose full lips disclosed a row of square and regular teeth, as white as a healthy animal's, was shadowed now by a fair moustache, which showed her that the boy of her acquaintance had become a man. A tall young man, loose-limbed, too heavy-shouldered, whose clumsiness as well as his strength were scarcely hidden by his peat-smelling Harris tweeds. As he stood smiling at the carriage window those masculine smoky odours of turf and tobacco enveloped her. If Clare had known that he was as formidable and grown-up as that she would never have dared to speak to him.

" Hello ! " he said, " home for the holidays ? "

" I'm home for good," she answered breathlessly. " I've left school ! "

" Good luck. I must tell Vivien. Au revoir ! The guv'nor's in a hurry."

Sir Joseph, who had handed a dispatch case to the footman, stood waiting for him at the door of the booking office. The stationmaster bowed them out. With a flush of achievement on her cheeks Clare returned to her corner. How wonderful it must be, she thought, to live at Stourford ; to have a footman waiting to carry things that you could perfectly well carry yourself ; to be a baronet. But Ralph would never be a baronet unless George died. And George, four years ago, had married Eleanor Pomfret, a sort of cousin of the Vicar whom her grandfather disliked. In another five minutes the train was due at Wychbury, where Jabez Bean would be waiting to drive her home in the victoria. She stood up in the swaying carriage and tried to tidy her hair by the help of a glazed photograph of the

Wyndcliff at Chepstow. It was no good; the wind had entangled it hopelessly; and so she jammed on her wide-brimmed sailor hat and collected her scattered luggage, just as the brakes shrieked on the gradient falling to Wychbury station. The little platform received her with indifference. At the rear of the train a single porter leaned against a pile of milk-cans. From his office door Mr. Hemus, the station-master, considered the train and any possible passengers impersonally in the light of four miserable oil-lamps set on wooden posts. Clare hurried up to him.

" Has Jabez come with the carriage, Mr. Hemus ? " she asked.

" That I can't say, Miss," he answered. " I shouldn't wonder if he has."

As a concession to politeness he shouted down the platform to the porter, who was now rolling milk-cans into the van : " George ! Have you seen aught of the doctor's Jabez ? " But the porter, deafened by the noise that he and the guard were making, could not hear him.

" It doesn't matter a bit, Mr. Hemus," Clare said. " Please don't bother. Of course I can see for myself."

" That's true enough, Miss," said Mr. Hemus. " If he's there, he's there. I suppose you've got that ticket ? "

Clare, in her eagerness, had forgotten all about it. She couldn't even remember in which pocket she had so carefully placed it. She put down her bag and began to search. It was no good; her gloves encumbered her fingers so that they could not feel. " I shall have to take them off," she said, and while Mr. Hemus watched the process sympathetic-ally, she was suddenly startled by a firm grip on her arm from behind.

" Hello, young woman," said a deeper voice.

" Good-evening, Mr. Wilburn, good-evening, sir," said the stationmaster, suddenly deferential.

Clare turned quickly. " Oh, Mr. Wilburn, I've lost my ticket."

Wilburn laughed. " Your ticket ? Travelling without having paid your fare ? That's a serious matter, isn't it, Hemus. And I can't defend you, I'm afraid. You know we represent the Company. Isn't that so ? "

Mr. Hemus assented. Hence his surprising deference. He knew better than to ask Dudley Wilburn for his. The Wilburns always travelled " on pass."

" Well, you won't have to," said Clare, triumphantly producing the blue slip of pasteboard. " I knew it was there all the time. Thank you so much, Mr. Hemus."

Wilburn stooped and picked up her bag. " Is this all ? Nothing in the van ? "

" Allow me, sir," said Mr. Hemus.

" No, that's all," said Clare quickly. " The rest is coming by the carrier. But please don't carry it. Jabez is sure to be outside. . . . I hope so anyway."

" So do I," said Wilburn.

" Why, have you come to see grandpapa ? "

" Clever little girl ! "

" Oh, then, he's sure to be there," said Clare. " What fun ! "

Again Wilburn laughed ; her frankness amused him. He was even a little surprised, for since he had last seen her, the child had developed enormously. As they passed toward the victoria on the box of which old Jabez sat hunched in his seedy livery, he couldn't help looking at her face under the broad-brimmed hat. This face aroused in him a peculiar poignancy of emotion, for in its poise, its purity of feature and in the dark wide eyes he could recall another, the face of the exquisite, the unapproachable Sylvia Weir which had enthralled him in his boyhood. Now he was thirty-five, a widower with two children, and yet the memory of this adolescent passion, rarefied in its remoteness, had power to make him restless, to renew the wistful atmosphere of another Spring more than eighteen years ago ; the flush of young larchwoods on the southern slope of Uffdown, the heavy scent of may. Sometimes he had surprised the ghost of some such remembrance in the company of Clare's Aunt Cathie ; but with her it had been fugitive, while here, walking at Clare's side, it swept over him suddenly, sweetly, like the perfume of wild white violets. An April madness, he told himself, and yet, as he stepped into the victoria and settled upon the cushions, aware of Clare's soft presence at his side, he found himself saying : " Clare, do you know that you grow more like your mother every day ? "

" Do I ? " she whispered eagerly. " Oh, do tell me how."

" Her voice, her colouring, the tilt of her head," he told her.

" But she was lovely, you know," said Clare.

He laughed, and the laugh made her feel that she had said something silly and had better hold her tongue. It was the first time that anyone except the devoted Marion had ever spoken to her of her physical attractions ; but all regret for the bold innocence of her reply was quickly lost in a thrill of pleasure at the comparison. What thrilled her was not that her mother had been beautiful, but only that she was like her ; for the image of her mother, eagerly reconstructed for want of memory from the reticences of Aunt Cathie and Mrs. Rudge's meanderings, had been her principal imaginative idol before the advent of the more tangible Miss Boldmere.

As they drove through the lanes that climbed toward Pen House, this romantic image, with its faint airs of passion and tragedy, was as near to her as to Wilburn, and so sweet that she dared not break the devotional air of their silence. She hoped, indeed, that her quietness would tempt him to say more ; but when he next spoke she knew that, as usual, the subject had been dropped. His words were an echo of Ralph Hingston's on the platform at Stourton : " What are *you* doing here ? " he said. " Home for the holidays ? "

" I've left St. Monica's," she told him. " I'm coming home for good."

" Does that mean that you're grown up ? " he said. " If I'd known that I should have treated you with more respect. I suppose the next thing is to put up your hair."

" It's up already," she said ; " only the wind's blown it to bits."

" And what are you going to do ? "

She became serious. " I suppose I shall help in the house. There are always lots of things to do at home. And I shall work at my music. Oh, you've no idea . . ."

" I don't suppose I have," he said. " When my daughters are as old as you I expect I shall want them to keep house for me ; but I've a long time to wait for that."

" They're darlings," said Clare.

" Yes, I suppose they are ; but I don't see much of them. I'm a hard-worked, middle-aged business-man, Clare. I get older and older every year."

She said : " Yes, of course you do." He laughed. It wasn't exactly the answer that he had expected, and yet its directness pleased him. It had never occurred to Clare to consider him anything but middle-aged. For years and years she had always thought of him as a member of Aunt Cathie's generation who came to Pen House occasionally to advise her grandfather on legal and financial matters. Definitely he belonged to their world, not to hers, and to that part of their world which was associated with money and mortgages and serious decisions. The fact that so wise a tyrant as her grandfather deferred to him in these matters only emphasized the distance between them. Everybody at Pen House trusted Dudley Wilburn and everybody seemed fond of him. Clare liked him too His strong, square, rather swarthy face, his straight mouth and his slow smile.

That evening she was liking him more than ever before, principally because of the romantic interest of his reference to her mother, a little because of the implied compliment to herself, and more than a little because of his stable, solid composure as he sat beside her, and the concession which his friendliness implied. Not so much a concession, after all ; for, as he had said, she was now nearly, if not quite, grown up ; and to be admitted to such a friendship was one of the privileges of her new status. She liked the smell of him too ; it reminded her of Ralph Hingston ; a composite odour of homespun and of the cigarette which he had asked her permission to light. It was strange and potent and masculine in its suggestions. By the time they had climbed the hillside to Pen House she was getting used to it and talking to him so naturally that it surprised her to hear the wheels of the victoria grating on the gravelled drive. And when the carriage stopped before the porch he dismounted before her and offered her the support of his hand : a broad, long-fingered hand in which her own was almost lost. " Oh, thank you, so much, Mr. Wilburn," she said. " Thank you for your company, Miss Lydiatt," he answered. Perhaps he was only making solemn fun of her.

## IV

### A GHOST WALKS

CLARE ran in front to open the door within the porch, for Wilburn's hands were encumbered with her luggage, and as she reached it the shadow of Aunt Cathie loomed against the frosted glass. The door opened in front of her, and Aunt Cathie appeared. Never had Clare seen her so magnificently dressed. The new purple velvet bodice took away her breath. In addition to the turquoise ring that always mysteriously encircled her engagement finger, Aunt Cathie wore a long gold chain attached to the watch in her waistband, an amethyst necklace and a silver chatelaine. This was not all. In the three months of Clare's absence Aunt Cathie's hair had not only grown glossier and darker, but was cut above the forehead in a fringe. Undeterred by this transformation Clare hurried forward to kiss her ; but Aunt Cathie's eyes, which shone with an unusual brightness in keeping with her attire, avoided her, and the flushed cheek that Clare's lips approached was quickly averted. Aunt Cathie had eyes for nobody but Mr. Wilburn.

" I'm so glad you've come," she said. " The doctor has been fidgety all day expecting a reply to his telegram. It only reached us an hour ago."

" I'm sorry," said Wilburn. " I didn't get it till late in the afternoon and only just managed to catch the train. Luckily Clare was on it, and gave me a lift in return for my services as a porter."

" Oh, you shouldn't have done that," said Aunt Cathie, suddenly aware of Clare's luggage. " Clare shouldn't have let you. Jabez would have carried it in. Hurry up, Clare, and take your bag from Mr. Wilburn ; I can't imagine what you're thinking of."

" It's not her fault," said Wilburn with a smile. " She tried to stop me, didn't you, Clare ? "

Clare blushed. She couldn't answer him. As a matter of fact she had done nothing of the sort ; but the lie sustained her, as evidence of their new and unexpressed alliance. Aunt Cathie did not wait for her reply. " Young and thoughtless ! " she went on. " You'd better take it up-stairs yourself. If it's too heavy, leave it. Ellen's busy with supper now ; she can help you later. Do come along, Mr. Wilburn."

She turned and Wilburn followed her into the darkness of

the inner hall. Clare heard them talking in lowered, confidential tones. Her mood of exultation had given way to one of vague distress. She picked up the bag that Wilburn had left on an oak bench and dragged it upstairs. Of course it was heavy ; but its very weight seemed to offer a contest into which she might lose her unhappiness. Young and thoughtless ! She had not been thoughtless ; and as for youth—youth was not a thing to be despised. Aunt Cathie herself didn't despise it. If she did she certainly wouldn't have darkened her hair and had it cut in a fringe and got herself dolled up in purple velvet. It was just like Aunt Cathie to go discrediting and belittling her in front of Mr. Wilburn. If she wanted to be rude she should keep her reflections till they were alone. " And anyway, I'm not young," she thought, " or at least not as young as all that. I'm seventeen."

She lit two candles on the dressing-table—the doctor objected to the smell of gas, and Aunt Cathie comforted herself by declaring that it ruined the silver—and began to brush her hair violently ; and when with this she had exhausted the spurious energy of indignation, she sat on with the long tresses spread over her shoulders, half conscious of her reflection in the Chippendale mirror and of the objects, familiar but newly interesting, that Ellen had arranged on her dressing-table : the lacquer glove-box, the pin-tray, the antlered china ring-stand which always stood there empty. There, too, hung a yellow photograph of her mother, the only one in the house, which Aunt Cathie, in one of her queer moments of kindliness, had given her on her birthday. It reminded Clare how kind, on occasion, how bewilderingly familiar, Aunt Cathie could be ; and this made her suddenly doubtful of her own right to be angry.

Only an hour before she had formed sacred resolutions to make allowances, and now, at the first moment of contact, she had not made them. Perhaps Aunt Cathie was suffering from one of those headaches—the unusual excitement of Mr. Wilburn's visit might easily have precipitated an attack ; perhaps some sudden change in her grandfather's health had made this visit necessary ; Clare hadn't, for one moment, considered the possibility of excuses for Aunt Cathie's behaviour. Thoughtless : the word was justified. It was not enough, Miss Boldmere would have said, to repent. She must make amends. The thought of the humiliation to which she would subject herself gave her a certain savage satisfaction.

The clock in the hall struck a leisurely seven. Her grand-father couldn't be as ill as all that, for he always insisted on winding it himself on Sundays. To-day was Monday, and yesterday he had evidently wound it up. Supper was always on the table at seven-thirty ; she had half an hour to waste before she appeared in the room in which her elders were now talking business. It struck her that the most appropriate symbol of repentance would be to change her silk frock for something more modest ; but this could not be done ; for all her every-day clothes were now lumbering out to Wychbury in the carrier's van ; so she sat on at the dressing-table in the comfort of a good motive frustrated, idly surveying her own reflection and the faded image of her mother's photograph.

Out of this dream she seemed to hear Mr. Wilburn's voice : " Clare, do you know that you grow more like your mother every day ? " The words awakened her with a return of the old excitement. Could they be really true ? She took down the photograph and compared its details with that of the reflection before her. Yes, it was true. Feature by feature she verified the likeness : the same fine, dark eyebrows that gave to wide-set eyes a look of earnest concentration ; the same straight nose, too insignificant for absolute beauty ; the same firm, small mouth ; the same challenging, expectant tilt of the head. The hair, of course, was all wrong ; for while hers fell in disorder about her shoulders, the hair of the portrait was swept backward above the ears like that of the ladies in du Maurier's drawings.

But this was easily remedied. She set to work, with an absorbed and half instinctive mimicry, imitating with careful accuracy the photograph's coiffure. How fortunate that she now had hairpins to do it with ! How strange and how exciting that she should be able to reproduce everything so exactly ! The colour came into her cheeks, her eyes glowed ; everything of the actress in her was on fire. She stepped back to survey herself at a distance and shivered with delight. The hair was a little fuller. How lovely her mother was ! She'd said that before to Mr. Wilburn, and he had only laughed ; but now that the dead woman had come to life it was true . . . true ! Something was lacking. She realized triumphantly that the lack could be remedied. On her fifteenth birthday Aunt Cathie had given her the chain and the oval locket with Clare's own hair in it which her mother was wearing in the photograph. It lay, together with Lydiatt's poor little garnet engagement ring, in the small box of olive-wood from Jerusalem in which she kept her treasures. She passed the chain of the locket carefully over her head. Why not the ring as well ? She had as much right to wear it as Aunt Cathie had to wear hers. Miss Boldmere, who was not engaged, wore one too ; but that was a symbol of her mystical union with her Redeemer. The ring was rather tight. What tiny fingers her mother must have had ! So tight that when once she had slipped it on she was overwhelmed with panic lest it should have to be cut off by a jeweller, like Mrs. Rudge's wedding ring. Such a disaster would give her away hopelessly. She struggled with it ; but her fingers were moist with excitement, and the ring stuck. And then the dinner-bell clanged in the hall below.

It was hopeless. Punctuality was a foible of the doctor's

to which Aunt Cathie subscribed with the bigotry of a convert ; and this was an occasion made exceptional by Wilburn's presence. Even if she took down her hair and discarded the locket that obstinate ring must remain to give her away. In this divided mind a helpless panic seized her. She ran downstairs, hurried along the passage and opened the dining-room door.

For all the rest of her life she was to remember that moment and that scene. Before her lay the low-ceiled room with its heavy shadows of mahogany furniture. The beams of a hanging lamp fell like limelight on the linen cloth and three figures sitting round it. At the top of the table her grandfather ; a big man, bowed with age. She saw his bald head bent over the plates in front of him, a white wrinkled dome, too desiccated to shine ; the frowning eyes above his thin nose, and that sparse growth of beard and whisker that gave an ashen pallor to the flesh surrounding his bluish lips. In one hand he held a game-carver ; in the other a steel with which he whetted the blade to a surgical acuteness. On his right sat Dudley Wilburn, upright, well-knit ; his dark eyes fascinated by the twinkling blade ; on the left Aunt Cathie, her cheeks still flushed, the string of amethysts glancing on her bodice as if they were an index of the emotion within. All three were so absorbed that they did not notice Clare's arrival. Their silence perturbed her ; and, even more, the empty chair at the foot of the table which proclaimed her unpunctuality brought an excuse to her lips. " I'm so sorry," she said and hesitated, petrified with shyness.

Suddenly all three were looking at her. Her grandfather stared fixedly, unmoved, above his suspended steel. Then Wilburn started backward : " Good lord ! " he said. " Good lord, it's Clare ! " Aunt Cathie drew her breath in a quick gasp. Her cheeks went suddenly white, wrinkled, old. Then back came the colour in a flood. She pushed away her

chair, rose to her feet, and spoke in a shrill, unnatural voice:
" What is the meaning of this ? " she flamed. " How
dare you, Clare ? How dare you ? "

" Auntie," Clare stammered, " Auntie ! " The voice
frightened her.

" Go to your room. How dare you ? Go to your room
at once ! "

Clare went. Aunt Cathie, tall and trembling, followed
her to the door and shut it behind her. Clare waited,
dazed with astonishment at the unexpected fury, in the
passage outside. Something terrible, of which she herself
was guilty, had happened. Inside the closed door a sinister
silence brooded, until she heard Aunt Cathie speaking with
an uneasy laugh.

" I'm sorry, so sorry," she was saying. " It took my
breath away."

" After all the child couldn't help it," Wilburn answered
calmly. " I was only thinking this evening . . ."

" Couldn't help it ? " the other voice repeated. " No,
it was deliberate. And she isn't a child. She's seventeen
. . . nearly eighteen."

Her grandfather grunted. " Mustard, Wilburn ? Catherine, pass Mr. Wilburn the mustard."

Clare stole on tiptoe along the hall. The furniture, the
very walls seemed aware of her passing as though some
ghostly memory had stirred them in their sleep. The broad
brass face of the grandfather clock regarded her. The
staircase creaked under her feet as she hurried back to her
bedroom where the two candles still flared in the draught
from the open window. She sat down again in front of the
mirror and began to take down her hair ; mechanically,
out of sheer bewilderment. Then tears filled her eyes, so
that her own image became blurred. Still crying, miserably
and for no reason, she continued to undress. She guided
the locket over her head and tugged at the ring. Now it

slipped easily from her cold fingers as though it knew that its malicious work was over. Then, like a punished child she blew out the candles and crept into the cool sheets ; but even their comforting stimulus could not check her tears ; and brown owls, hunting in the shrubberies, mimicked her with their faint, wild whimpering.

Gradually, under pressure of the darkness, her scared mind grew more sober ; her breath became soft and steady, unchecked by the convulsion of sobbing. The whole incident now appeared to her fantastic and Aunt Cathie's outburst a thing to be resented. But even so she could not forget the transformation of Aunt Cathie's face. It troubled her tranquillity, accusing her of failure in all the righteous resolutions she had made. She thought to herself, " What would Miss Boldmere do ? " and the question carried with it the suggestion of a duty neglected, which set her groping in the dark for a box of matches with which to relight her candle.

The blue gold-lettered book lay on the dressing-table where she had left it. She turned the pages eagerly, thrilled by an unreasoning hope that some mystical power might present her with a ready-made solution for her distress. The heading of April the nineteenth referred her to an obscure passage of dialectic in the Epistle to the Hebrews. She read it through three times without understanding one word of it. She grew angry with her own ignorance and stupidity, determined to wrest from it the consolation which it was warranted to contain. And slowly, miraculously, that consolation came, not through the persuasions of St. Paul, but from the consciousness that, in this very moment, Miss Boldmere was doing the same. Spiritual communion. Once more she felt that she was going to cry, but this time with happiness. Distantly, as she fell asleep, she heard the wheels of the carriage that was taking Wilburn to the station grate upon the gravel beneath.

V

# STILL LIFE

WHEN Clare had gone, Aunt Cathie, still flushed and palpitating, returned to her seat at the supper-table. She could not eat. On these days of headache it was wiser to starve. She knew that she had made an exhibition of herself; that one rude gesture had humiliated her for ever before Wilburn, in whose eyes, particularly, she wished to appear at her best. The words: "How dare you? How dare you?" kept on reforming themselves mechanically in her mind, even while she knew that it was her duty to apologize for her loss of control. But she could not trust herself to speak; and so she sat on, staring at the willow-pattern on her empty plate, listening to the business consultation which her father would not allow so small a matter as a woman's temper to interrupt.

She could only listen; for in these matters, or even in others of which she was more qualified to speak, the old man would not have respected her opinion. However long she lived she knew that he would never regard her as anything but a child. It was an attitude which the childishness of her outburst justified; and yet she couldn't help resenting it when she saw the reliance that he seemed to place in Wilburn's judgment; for Wilburn, after all, was even a little younger than herself.

Dr. Weir, with the disinterested asceticism of age, ate nothing; but all through the meal he kept the visitor busy with his shrewd questions and commentary on the new developments at the Sedgebury Main Colliery, to which Wilburn, in his capacity of friend and lawyer, had advised a transfer of investments. He crouched above the head of the table like an old, bald vulture; his eyes piercing the darkness beyond the lighted supper-table, his gruff voice rasping like a file.

" So Hingston is in it, is he ? "

" Up to the neck."

" Hingston's a bounder."

" Possibly. But Hingston's a shrewd fellow."

" The concern's over-capitalized, like everything else hereabouts. The same thing's happening all round us. Walter Willis at Mawne's another. Willis is a good fellow ; but none of them can see a yard in front of their noses. No sense of history."

Wilburn smiled ; he had heard all this before ; and yet, usually, he had his way.

" No sense of history," the doctor repeated. " This country's been at peace ever since the Crimea. You don't remember that. Human nature can't exist without wars. Plague, pestilence and famine : history's a disciple of Malthus. Huh ? We're too thick on the ground. Sooner or later that means labour troubles. You're too cocksure like all the rest of them. Ignorant, if you prefer it."

Wilburn shook his head :

" Sedan changed all that. Modern weapons make war impossible."

" Impossible ! " the doctor grunted. " Look at South Africa. What's this monkey game of Jameson's ? Suppose the Dutchmen want to fight ? "

" They don't," said Wilburn. " But if they did, so much the better for the Black Country and Walter Willis : so much the better for the Sedgebury Main. You can't make guns without coal and iron. With or without war, the Black Country's going to boom."

" I like to see my money on the top of the earth, not under it," the old man growled. " I tell you frankly, I don't like mining shares."

" But then you don't know Furnival. The fellow's a

genius. Of course you can do what you like ; but Sedgebury Main Preference at twelve and six is a thing that you'll
never see again."

So they went on ; and through it all Aunt Cathie's heart
beat violently, driving the blood in throbs to her tormented
head. They talked endlessly of things that she had neither
the will nor power to understand; and by nine o'clock, when
Jabez drove round to take Wilburn to the station, and she
herself followed him out to the dark drive to say good-bye,
she was almost glad to think that the visit that she had
anticipated so eagerly was over.

She stood on the wide terrace fronting the house and
watched the lights disappear into the shadows of the shrubberies. She followed them to the first turn of the drive.
Behind her two greater shadows, those of the hill that gave
the house its name and of its twin dome of Uffdown,
thickened the northern sky. Southward not a light was to
be seen but the intermittent glow of a goods train grinding
down toward Worcester with its iron freights. Even by
daylight those wide, green levels held little that suggested
distraction or surprise ; for though the jagged outline of
Malvern, black and imminent above the elm-tops in days of
storm, might conjure aspirations, their appeal was so remote
and so modified by the intervening expanses that it seemed
to be related to some future life ; and now this dark monotony oppressed her.

She turned back from the corner to which her feet had
carried her in pursuit of the victoria's lights, toward the
house. That sombre Georgian building, its low-browed
stucco front unbroken by the impetuous gables of periods
more restless and romantic, contemplated her serenely
through eight uniform windows. That night she hated its
sleepy, rectangular complacency ; but even so, she knew
that it was as essentially part of her life as is the shell to the
snail ; without its habitual shelter she would be vulnerable,

naked, defenceless. For thirty-eight years she had known no other ; now she would never leave it.

She had looked forward so happily to Clare's arrival. She loved Clare ; and she did not love Wilburn. In their relation, as she had told herself a thousand times, there was nothing but a frank, admiring, ideal friendship. And yet, that evening, what with her headache and the excitement of their appearance at the same moment, she had lost her sense of proportion and her temper together.

Now, in the soothing darkness of the drive, she couldn't bear to think of it. Poor little Clare ! It wasn't Clare's fault that a natural instinct had prompted her to this devilish trick. Clare didn't know what it had meant to her ; she hoped that Clare would never know. But for this ghastly head nothing would have happened.

· Entering the hall she heard the mumble of Mrs. Rudge putting the doctor to bed. She could hardly bear to say good-night to him. Not that he would mention the humiliating subject ; his mind was far too full of money for that. As soon as his head touched the pillow he would fall asleep like a child, waking automatically at four o'clock in the morning to concentrate once more upon the prospects of the Sedgebury Main. But Aunt Cathie knew that she would not sleep until the fierceness of her headache had spent itself. Flat on her bed she lay, a handkerchief soaked in eau-de-cologne spread over her beating temples. Her head ached continually ; before her eyes, or somewhere at the back of them in that inferno of pressure, there glowed and faded roses of blue flame and coruscating tracks of fire, jagged, like lightning.

If Catherine had only known it, these heartburnings and sympathies were wasted on Clare. Her youth had power of itself to pierce the age-bound hardness of Pen House as surely as the spears of daffodils break soil that is sealed with frost. For in that single night the full Spring burst upon them. Next morning, out of the watery brilliance of the South, clouds came driving ; clouds of a high and dazzling brightness, blown like white pollen from the flower of the sky. The rich plain seemed dusted with this fallen bloom ; in the walled orchard at the back of Pen House plum-trees made drifts of their snowy blossom. The shrubberies woke to the timid voices and rustlings of chiff-chaff and willow-wren, first-comers of the winged clouds migrating northward. In the garden at St. Monica's only loud chaffinches had flung their hard, challenging cries from the forks of the smoke-blackened apple-trees in which they were to nest. Those, and the blackbirds, whose harsh stutters of alarm seemed more frequent than their songs.

As for Aunt Cathie : according to her new rule of life Clare had made allowances. Next morning she kissed her at breakfast as though no harsh word had been spoken. It wasn't difficult ; for Aunt Cathie, despite her morning frostiness, had moved half-way to meet her in an affecting reconciliation that troubled them both, since the elder acknowledged her fault, the younger had nothing to forgive, and neither realized the other's pathetic anxiety to make amends.

In another week Clare had forgotten all about it. These were days not only of Spring but of holiday. Released into this month of sweet, dazzling weather, she feasted on all the beauty that Alvaston had denied her. It was not merely that she was free, standing, with St. Monica's behind her, on the brink of a new life ; she had reached, for the first time, a point of spiritual development at which she could appreciate her freedom. It carried with it a sense of power and of possession. The hills were hers ; all that green flank of Pen Beacon up to the standing stones ; all Uffdown's dome of furze, an almond-scented wilderness. There, on the windy summit, she could command the dominions, of fire and water : the scorched basin of the Black Country and the moist Severn Plain. Into the tender sky above them her heart fluttered like a rising lark. Hers too, with a softer emotion, were the red-banked lanes of primrose and white violet that drained the valley, falling to Uffdown Manor. For her, descending at evening time, the trout leapt in the Sling fish-ponds between flats of swimming water-lilies. On her way home she gathered to herself the secrets of the meadowland below the mill-race, imprisoned in the viscid stems of king-cups, the pungent leaves of horse-mint growing clumpy in the marshland, the airy, moth-like flowers of lilac lady's-smocks. By these possessions she was possessed, till all her heart was Spring ; so brimmed with vernal loveliness that she must give, give, give of its over-flowing. And then the cuckoo came.

In a while the first ecstasy of freedom passed. Clare did not grudge its passing ; her heart still sang, though its song was attuned to the tenor of life at Pen House and modified by its smooth, unchanging rhythm. Duties were assigned to her by Aunt Cathie, all leisurely and soothing. In the early morning she helped Ellen to make the beds. All through this business of stretching, folding and tucking in sheets, subdued sounds of human activity stole up like a slow smoke from the village beneath them. And Ellen would tell her all the gossip of Wychbury as she punched the pillows into shape, in words that lent an actuality to those homely sounds : the tinkle of her father's anvil, the creak of cartwheels in the lane, the faint voices of women and birds and beasts subdued, by their remoteness, to a hum that was like that of bees buzzing in lime-blossom.

After a little time, Ellen, emboldened, began to tell Clare things that she would never have dared to mention to Aunt Cathie ; for Ellen was walking out with a young man who worked at the Uffdown mill, and it pleased her to ask the advice of Clare, a contemporary if not an equal, on nice matters of conduct. " There now, I knew you'd think that ! " she said. " It's a proper treat to have you here, Miss."

No doubt she spread Clare's fame among the villagers ; for now, whenever she went down shopping into Wychbury, people whom she did not know gave her their smiles ; and once a red-faced young man whose back was dusted with flour as a bee's velvet with pollen, pulled off his cap and beamed at her. It was jolly for Ellen to be in love. A right and natural state, in keeping with the rich, languorous expectancy of those days. For now the meadows were alive with calling cuckoos. It was right and natural for Ellen to interpret the impulse of the season in a way that could not conceivably touch Clare herself. She smiled at Ellen's love-making and thought little of it.

It was strange that a life so static should seem so crowded. In the first week of it Clare had wondered, with a mild rest-lessness, if she were ever again going to see a human being apart from the inhabitants of Pen House. She had left St. Monica's with the expectancy of new and surprising human contacts. She remembered how gaily Ralph Hingston had called back to her on Stourton platform that he would tell his sister Vivien of her arrival ; but weeks passed, and she heard nothing of the Hingstons but her grandfather's habitual growls at their magnificence. Prob-ably Ralph had forgotten all about her ; and really it didn't matter, for there was no room for the Hingstons in her routine. Duty came first, and after that there seemed too little time to spare for her particular pleasures.

Toward the end of the morning she could generally snatch her half-hour's practice at the piano. The old Broadwood was more worn than the worst of the practice-room pianos at St. Monica's ; its keys seemed flat and unresponsive, their ivory streaked with yellow like the teeth of an old horse ; the bass notes were tinny, the treble out of tune ; and yet it enabled Clare to transport herself to heights of

emotional experience that she could never otherwise attain.
Her own school music slowly became stale and too familiar ;
but in the lockers of an ebony cupboard, fretted with gilt
arabesques and smelling of must and pot-pourri, she discovered, one day, a pile of yellow sheet-music, most of which
bore her mother's name.

It was a curious collection, reflecting the superficial
brilliance of a young lady's accomplishment in the eighteen-
eighties ; show-pieces of Heller, Henselt, Mendelssohn and
Moscheles ; dead operatic arias festooned with tinkling
arpeggios ; Field, and Rubinstein, and Sterndale-Bennett.
But though she knew that they were trivial, she played them
all, not realizing that their echoes might have awakened the
furniture of the drawing-room, whose life had stopped short
before the period of blue china, peacock's feathers and
enamelled milking-stools to a ghostly renewal of consciousness.  Only Aunt Cathie knew.  For her the tinkling
triviality of Clare's arpeggios raised ghosts enough.  But she
suffered their haunting silently, telling herself that the child
had talent and must be allowed to express it.  An inheritance :
Lydiatt, she had imagined, in those old days, was a master.

So Clare played on :  not so much because the old-
fashioned music pleased her as because mere contact with
those yellow pages seemed to connect her spiritually with
her mother.  At such times that image, mystically adored,
grew, not clearer, but definitely more near.  This cult was
new to her.  In earlier years her mother's history had never
aroused her curiosity ;  but ever since that dark drive up from
Wychbury in which Mr. Wilburn's words had set her quivering with delight, her mind, eager for new devotions, had
fastened on the idea and pursued it.  Now, for the first
time, that story seemed to hold a personal significance, since
she herself, at the distance of twenty years, was following
like a phantom in the footsteps of that frail romantic figure.
These ivory keys her mother's fingers had touched in the

same series of co-ordinate movements : no one had touched them since. Over these stairs and through these lanes her mother's feet had passed. She saw herself not as herself but as a reincarnation, mysteriously following on ghostly guidance. And when the gong sounded for lunch and she found herself again in the presence of Aunt Cathie and her grandfather she felt confused, as though she had emerged from a dream whose figments still seemed real.

For them, Clare knew by instinct, and by the fact of its avoidance, the subject was forbidden. She realized, vaguely, that her mother's career had ended in some event which was distasteful to them both. The effect of her apparition at the supper-table had shown her that ; but this, indeed, did nothing but make her dear phantom more pathetic and beloved, and herself more eager to penetrate the mystery.

One afternoon in early May, when the plum-blossom had fallen and cherries and pear-trees stood in snowy pyramids, Clare went up to sit and talk with Mrs. Rudge. There, like a pale pink fondant, the face of Thirza rose from the white apron that covered her voluminous bust, above it a white cap with a gophered frill. Her cheeks were lax and downy, puckered by age to a childish softness ; her lips, too, were soft, and always rather moist. Habitually they smiled in the peace of an assured Nirvana, and the words that issued from them still kept the burr of the West Country from which, fifty years before, she had come to Wychbury. She sat there placidly, surrounded by awkward-postured portraits of her family. Several of them had died ; but, dead or living, she still rejoiced in their possession. She spoke of them all as though they had remained for ever fixed in the state in which they were portrayed. The stories that she told of them were trifling, but never tedious, for her slow tongue had the power of communicating to the thoughts it uttered something of its native languor. All

Thirza's stories smelt heavy with the scents of summer noons.

As she spoke she waddled heavily about the little room, as though the volume of her skirts swayed her from side to side ; and while she busied herself with the making of tea, a ritual as strict in its detail as the consecration of a sacrament, Clare tried to coax or startle the old woman into talking of what she sought.

" Was mother as tall as me, Thirza ? "

" Why, no, Miss Clare. Miss Sylvia must have been an inch or two shorter than you since you've shot up so. Miss Cathie was the taller. I can see them now, standing up again' that wall to measure it. Slight you'd call her, rather than thin. But that was before the days of wasp-waists, my dear. Many's the time I've laced them up. I ought to know ! Then the bustles came in. No need for bustles when you've a'passed forty. Now, my dear, us'd better warm that pot. Ah, my dear life, this was a gay house in they days when the doctor had his strength ! You should have seen them playing croquet. That was the croquet lawn, over there where Jabez has got his currant bushes now. You could have watched them out of this very window. Lovely and graceful they looked. That Mr. Wilburn now ; I can remember him coming up here as a lad from school. All the gentlemen wore whiskers in those days, and properly handsome they were, I can tell you."

" Did father play croquet, Thirza ? "

" Two for you and me and one more," Thirza murmured. " This brown pot, I wouldn't lose it for a fortune, nor trust it in that Ellen's hands. But we never get the tea now we used to get. It used to come in boxes with red dragons on the outside. Croquet ? No, not your father, Miss Clare. He never came for that. Only for the music-lessons Tuesday and Fridays he used to come. The doctor never took to him that way. Not his class, you might say. But there ! Love-making takes no count of other folk's likes or dislikes nor money either. If there was any choice you'd have said Miss Cathie was the beauty; though a gentleman, mind you, would always look twice at your mother for once at her. Just like my Alice, the one that passed away ten years come June. There she is, poor Alice too, leaning up against that marble banister. Now she went for a housemaid at Mr. Loxton's up to the Manor. Seventeen she was, and a poor pale little toad, never picked up rightly from the ear-complaint after the measles. You could never a'guessed she'd get married afore our Jane. Jane was a quiet one, like Miss Cathie. She came on later. And I always said that Miss Cathie had her eye on your father too . . ."

" Aunt Cathie ? " Clare gasped.

" Three and a half minutes by the clock," said Thirza. " So now we're ready to pour out."

" Aunt Cathie ? " Clare repeated. " Do you think Aunt Cathie was in love with him too ? "

" Well, no, Miss Clare. I couldn't say that. Miss Cathie was very upset, as was natural. Ah, she's a good girl, too, Miss Cathie. Nobody but me and the doctor knows how good she is. Time after time she puts me in mind of my Lucy that died of the consumption. Poor soul, too ! The doctor always said you could read it in her face. The eyes he'd got in those days ! One look was enough for him. When first she took ill I had her up here for a bit. If anyone's going to cure her, I said, it's our doctor. But you couldn't make her take a morsel. Pecked and pecked like any bird. Port wine, he ordered her ; but you might as well have gived her water for all the good it done in spite of keeping her in a warm room away from draughts. Now, Lucy, I used to say . . ."

So Clare sat and listened, casting her net into the flowing deeps of Mrs. Rudge's memory, holding, for a moment, some gleaming capture that flashed its sides and vanished into the dark current of older memories, memories, for the most part, of a youth and childhood incredibly remote which unfolded itself against the outline of savage western hills.

The hint of a thwarted passion on the part of Aunt Cathie troubled her. It explained so much. Even as the words escaped her Thirza had denied it ; but if it were true . . . Clare had never thought of Aunt Cathie in any passionate relation. The picture filled her with a certain awe.

That evening, when she sat, as usual, reading aloud to her grandfather, whose eyes were now incapable of bearing the strain of lamplight, she became aware of Aunt Cathie poring over her frame on the other side of the fireplace, and found herself wondering, beneath the surface of meaningless words which her lips formed and emitted, into what strange ecstasies Aunt Cathie's heart might have flowered. For if father had married Aunt Cathie, she thought, Aunt Cathie would have been my mother : which seemed ridiculous, since Aunt Cathie had never been anything, could never have been anything but Aunt Cathie, a figure so different in all its outlines from that of the tenuous and evanescent image of motherhood which she treasured. Aunt Cathie could not have satisfied this ghostly love. A wave of sentimental compassion, not only for Aunt Cathie but for all the inhabitants of Pen House, herself included, sent tears into her eyes, so that the print became dim and she stammered and stopped.

" What's that ? What's that ? " said the doctor.

" I'm sorry," she said. " I thought I was going to sneeze." Aunt Cathie looked up and smiled at her kindly. She's a darling, Clare thought. I don't love her nearly enough ; I'm a selfish brute, that's what I am. She went on reading in a hurry : " The directors of Hingston's Ironworks intimated to the last general meeting that the eighteen ninety-six results would be unsatisfactory, and they now report that after providing five thousand pounds for depreciation, as they did in the last two balance sheets, that there was a loss of nine thousand one hundred and twenty-seven pounds."

" Too big for his boots," the doctor grunted. " Go on."

" They now report . . . oh, I'm sorry. The position is better, however, than it has been. The loss in the second part of the year was only three thousand and twenty pounds ; and, better still, the aggregate value of orders in hand at the end of the year was more than double that of a year before. Important coal-mining developments are in progress . . ."

" Sedgebury Main ! "

". . . and in view of the general conditions of trade, which, in spite of the increase in German competition, show steady signs of improvement, the directors feel confident in proposing an issue of debenture shares to the extent of twenty thousand pounds."

" Huh, the man's mad," said the doctor. " Catherine, what did I tell Wilburn the other night ? Is that all ? Then you'd better ring for Thirza."

Clare sighed, folded the paper, and kissed him good-night. It seemed curious to her that evening how little this formal salutation meant. As the stubbles of the doctor's beard grazed her cheek she wondered if the old man really ever thought of her as anything but a normal encumbrance which couldn't be avoided. That evening, as she went to bed, she felt very lonely and strange.

## VI

### MR. DARNAY

ONE day, tremulous but resolved, Clare went down to Wychbury and rang at the Vicarage door. Mr. Pomfret was out. She waited for over an hour in his study, a room that proclaimed his prowess as oarsman rather than as scholar or divine. At last he entered, in riding-kit, for he had hacked over to one of the last meets of the Woodland Stourton. Although he knew her by sight, he eyed Clare suspiciously. " I'm Dr. Weir's granddaughter," she said, " and I am anxious to be prepared for confirmation." " For confirmation ? " he echoed, as though the word were unfamiliar to him. " Ah, yes, for confirmation. Quite so. Now let me see . . ." He rubbed his blue, shaven jowl with a massive hand, and begged her to sit down with the consideration that a Harrod or Whiteley might have shown to a customer who asked him personally for a yard of elastic.

" I think," he said at last, " that under the circumstances I had better give you a note to Mr. Darnay. He usually deals with these matters for me." He sat down at his desk and wrote a letter, glancing at Clare from time to time, as if to assure himself that she was real. A retriever scratched at the door and was admitted. The diversion seemed to relieve him. The dog sniffed at his riding-breeches as he wrote. " I'll also speak to Mr. Darnay myself," he said, as he handed her the letter and showed her out. " Heel, Nell, heel ! Good dog, then ! "

Mr. Darnay was his curate. Clare found him living at the lower end of the village in rooms which seemed far more homely than the vicar's study. In one corner there was a Bechstein piano with Bach's " Matthew Passion " open at the Sanctus. She was devouring it when Mr. Darnay entered : a gaunt, young man whose clothes hung loosely about an angular figure like garments on a clothes-horse. He had lank red hair and a long nose, like that of an ant-eater ; his face was clean-shaven and blistered by the Spring sun ; it went redder as he perused the vicar's letter.

" You are Dr. Weir's granddaughter ? " he said ; but when she admitted the damning circumstance he smiled : " A magnificent figure. I've seen him. A good man, too. Nobody could go about among the poor people in this parish without realizing that. I've often wished that I knew him, though in some things, I gather, we shouldn't agree. Not that this lessens my respect. Supposing we sit down and talk ? "

They talked, and as they did so Clare felt curiously relieved of all the constraints that lay upon her at Pen House. She spoke of her life at St. Monica's, of Miss Boldmere, her music, her visits to St. Jude's. " A charming little church," said Mr. Darnay. " Father Shiplake and I were up at Oxford together." Not until the very end of their interview did Mr. Darnay make any mention of personal religion. Even then he spoke in passing, without impressiveness, as though the subject were one on which they were so completely in agreement that no words from him were needed. His attitude put Clare at ease ; it seemed so liberal, so human, so friendly, so free from any insistence on the solemnity of her mission or the sanctity of his. All those things were taken for granted as the assured basis of their friendship.

At parting he spoke more seriously.

" I wonder if your aunt and your grandfather know that you have come to see me ? "

She admitted that they did not. He frowned ; his pale eyes were fixed in vacancy.

" Do you think I ought to tell them ? " she said.

He considered. " Perhaps, for the moment, you had better say nothing," he told her. " In the end, of course, your profession must be made public, and then, sooner or later you are bound to meet with opposition. Better, perhaps, later than sooner. At this stage there is no need to testify openly. The early Christians, even St. Peter and St. Paul, were forced to hide themselves in Roman catacombs. I don't think," he said, " you need even excite the general interest of the parish by going to church on Sundays. Every morning, at seven o'clock, I say Low Mass at St. Chad's. If you will come to hear me it will be far better than any formal preparation, though first, of course, you must make sure that you are in a state of Grace by performing the sacrament of Penance. Whenever you feel ready to make them, I will hear your confessions. To-morrow, half an hour before the Holy Sacrifice ? "

He lent her a book which dealt with the process of preparation. Later he lent her music : that very copy of the " St. Matthew Passion " which she had seen open on his piano, and another of the great Mass in B Minor, in the gay *Laudamus* of which she seemed to find the expression of liberty and exultant youth that her mother's mid-Victorian fantasias and Miss Boldmere's *Schwärmerei* denied her. And solemnly she played to herself the mighty contrapuntal choruses which, as Mr. Darnay told her, rose like mountains of granite above the alpine meadows of the solos. The Broadwood was a poor, spent thing ; yet, from its twanging strings grandeur flowed like a dark, slow-moving river on whose surface her soul was carried out to a vast sea that knew nothing of Pen House, nor Wychbury, nor even of Clare Lydiatt. Mr. Darnay had judged her well ; his weak eyes had rightly probed the fluidity of her spirit and gauged the depth of her untroubled imagination. He found her fit for the annunciation of mysteries ; his heart warmed to her.

Every morning, early, through the misty air of Spring, she walked over the fields to St. Chad's. There was no danger of discovery ; the life of Pen House took its hours from the feebleness of her grandfather, who often fell into a doze at the time when other people were waking. The path to St. Chad's was familiar and beloved : past the mill, where Ellen's sweetheart worked, through flats of mare's-tail and king-cup steeped in moist, marshy odours. At this early hour the mill-pool lay tranced as in the quiet of evening. On its glassy flats the roach rose lazily with sucking dimples that spread to rings. Sometimes the burning blue of a kingfisher that haunted the willow-roots passed with a flash that brought her heart into her mouth. Above the pool a field of cowslips. The low sun raked their pale clusters with a keener fire ; their gusty vinous odour mounted to her brain. Then the edge of the larchwood, piercingly green, younger than anything on earth. Within its curved shadow dew lay late ; the cropped turf was bloomed with it ; and there, unconscious of her coming, crouched the little huddled shapes of rabbits nibbling against time. It was almost as if they could hear her smile. Suddenly the nibbling ceased ; the warm bodies lay like scattered stones. One drummed with his feet, and all vanished with a clumsy, unhurried reluctance. They did not seem very much afraid of her. She was sorry that they mistrusted her at all. Couldn't they see, the silly things, that she loved them ?

The little church took shelter under the hillside on a shelf of red soil bastioned by pagan yews. It cowered there, that fortress of an earlier faith, retired in timelessness, as removed from the tides of life that set southward down Severn, or northward toward the iron magnet of North Bromwich, as the standing stones on the summit of the beacon. That was how Mr. Darnay thought of it ; for St. Chad, as he told Clare, was a Mercian Saint, an Englishman, as English as herself, canonized in the days when the Catholic Church in England still maintained the purity that Rome had bartered to the Franks. Mr. Darnay liked to think that the continuity of worship at St. Chad's had never been disturbed. Nobody from the outside world visited it but a few archæologists who stopped to stare at the Saint's grotesque image above the southern porch. Nobody in Wychbury took count of its existence but a few devout women who followed the older way under Mr. Darnay's guidance and a number of Nonconformists incensed by Mr. Darnay's practices. Certainly not the Vicar ; for Mr. Pomfret was an aristocrat and a man of the world. As long as the bishop did not object there was no reason in the world why Mr. Darnay should not have his way. The ritual of a church, in his judgment, should conform to the ideas of its congregation. Wychbury was Latitudinarian, and so was he. St. Chad's was a nuisance in any case, and the people who went there could have what they liked. He only drew the line at incense, because it made his head ache. An odour of decadence, he called it, comparable in religious surroundings to that of patchouli in a theatre. Mr. Darnay was an admirable curate, who relieved him of the bulk of the parish work and allowed him to carry the odour of sanctity into the more exalted surroundings in which he was at home. As for the reservation of the Sacrament . . .

So, in St. Chad's, Mr. Darnay daily said Low Mass, and Clare, humbly hidden in the west-end among the woolly bell-ropes, came to hear it, compassing, in that short half-hour, the rarest emotional experience she had ever known. Why this was so she couldn't really say. Perhaps her generous nature demanded the sacrifice of some complete surrender. Mr. Darnay had given her minute instructions as to the state of mind in which each stage of the Sacrament should be received. In spirit, and to the letter, she obeyed them. From the moment when he passed with his long eager strides from the sacristy to the altar, carrying the vessels hidden by the chalice-veil, and removed his biretta, Clare concentrated all her thought upon the progress of the ritual. The Mass, Mr. Darnay had told her, celebrated a mystery in a series of symbolical acts. The thing that mattered was not so much what was said as what was done. He had begged her to dissociate him personally from the ceremony ; and yet, since he was the celebrant, and since all the great acts of ritual were performed by him, she found it difficult to separate the idea of his personality from her devotions. In that little sanctuary his was the dominant figure. She could not subdue it. Even when she made her confession, in the form that he had taught her—*to God, to the Blessed Mary, ever Virgin, to Blessed Michael, the Archangel, to all the Saints*—the words: "*and to thee, father*," aroused in her an emotion more poignant than all the rest.

She knew that it was wrong of her. In any case this gaunt, red-haired young man with his sunburnt cheeks and high sloping forehead was a strange substitute for the handsome father whom she had never seen; yet she did not regret him; in place of that lost guardian God had given her a new paternal love; she returned it with a piety which was more than filial. So, in the moist and stony odour of St. Chad's, she knelt and waited, with closed eyes, for those rare moments of exaltation: the summons of the Sanctus bell, the Consecration, the Elevation of Host and Chalice, the ceremony of Fraction and Commixture. So, when the Mass was ended, she passed out into the sounds and scents of the Spring morning, newly awakened and revivified, it seemed to her, by the passage of that sweet mystery. *Coo-oop, coo-oop, coo-oop !* Ellen's young man was calling up the cows. The busy cuckoo mimicked him. Joy and gladness. The God, she thought, who maketh glad my youth. Those words she carried in secret over the enchanted fields, alone, yet bringing with her all the company of heaven.

And nobody at Pen House guessed. Or rather nobody but Ellen, whose sweetheart saw Clare as she passed by the roach-ringed mill-pond. But Ellen did not tell Clare that she knew. Only in Ellen's attitude toward her there arose a new, mysterious comradeship which held them in long converse over the bed-making upstairs. Ellen could never have made a confidante of Aunt Cathie or Mrs. Rudge or anyone else in that house of age. It was Clare's youth and the sharing of a secret that drew her toward her. When once this freedom was attained Clare listened to her with a sort of tolerant wonder.

The idea of love, curiously aroused in her by the contemplation of her mother's story, held, as yet, no definite place in her thoughts. It did not thrill her to hear Ellen's hushed stories of kisses, of strained partings and long embraces. Her heart was full to overflowing with a rarer love. She couldn't, for instance, imagine Mr. Darnay in any passionate situation. Darnay himself had taught her that celibacy was the ideal state enjoined by the Apostle Paul and Christ himself. And yet, in the modest ecstasies which Ellen confided to her, blushing above her folded sheets, she could not help feeling a gentle sympathy ; not because she dreamed that Ellen's debased conception of love could ever mean anything to herself, but because, in that ecstatic Springtime, all life seemed so drenched in the spirit of love that her heart could not refuse to recognize its least manifestation. She saw that Ellen was happy, in some ways as happy as herself. And happiness, all happiness was divine. Sometimes she felt that Ellen was telling her too much. Even though she was not competent to reject them, she felt herself compelled to put a brake on Ellen's enthusiasms. Then Ellen, reduced to silence, regarded her with a slow, subdued, confident smile.

" You wait a bit, Miss Clare," she said. " You wait a bit, and then you'll see for yourself."

" Oh, don't be silly," said Clare, blushing.

Ellen shook her head.

## VII

### MASS IN B MINOR

So May passed into a dry and brilliant June, and always Clare was happy ; but poor Aunt Cathie did not share her happiness. For her the seasons rolled on a relentless wheel. Bound to its felloe she was carried onward, hopelessly conscious of the approaching moment when its career would precipitate her into disaster. She told Clare nothing of these dark preoccupations ; it was better that Clare should not know. In any case her growing anxiety for the doctor, over which she and Mrs. Rudge and Wilburn could shake heads together, was not to be shared with a creature so irresponsible as her niece. She was grateful to feel that Clare had found out a way of life for herself, and was not adding to her troubles by making demands upon her interest or her time.

To her these dawns of early summer brought nothing but uneasiness and dread. Solemnly, each morning, she met, in the pier glass at the foot of the stairs, the image of her own strained face unsmoothed by sleep. She knew them so well, those features ; daily she saw them reflected again in the puckered eyes of Thirza. With a sinking of dread she knocked at the doctor's door ; and when, impatiently, he called for her to enter, the reassurance that she felt when she heard his living voice was shattered by the frailty that she saw before her.

During the last few months the texture of Dr. Weir's gaunt body seemed to have changed ; it was translucent, like a figure of brittle, delicate porcelain ; blanched, like a growth to which light has been denied. Beneath his overhanging brows the eyes burned with remote, inhuman blackness ; his pugnacious mouth pushed itself forward as if in it were concentrated the whole of his will to live. And, as his body weakened and grew cold, his mind seemed to glow with a more condensed, malicious brightness, as though it had succeeded in consuming the physical burden by which it had been stifled. All the old tenderness which had shown itself in the first days of his surrender was gone. Together with human weakness, that spirit, almost disembodied, seemed to have rid itself of human sympathies. It stood out naked and untrammelled, no longer a man but an intelligence free to assert itself in unreasonable prejudice and ruthless reasoning.

Aunt Cathie schooled herself to bear with him. At times the task seemed impossible. She could not look for sympathy to Mrs. Rudge, for Thirza, though equally a victim, was less sensitive than herself. She had no longer any friends in Wychbury ; for with the doctor's retirement she had acquiesced in the isolation that his illness demanded, and misunderstanding had estranged them.

Clare could not share her troubles. The whole of a generation, and more than a generation, lay between them. Aunt Cathie had no friend in the world but Dudley Wilburn ; and though Wilburn's visits were rare and brief, she made the most of them. To him she confided the most of her misery. He listened gravely, and with that air of respect and gallantry which had changed her outlook on life when first he came. With his hand on her arm he gave her brotherly counsel, which was only part of what she needed ; he praised her, he flattered her, and yet she sometimes felt that his sympathy was that of the tactful lawyer rather than of the human being whose sympathy she so passionately desired.

"I'm not sure you don't exaggerate," he said. "Of course he's weaker ; but his mind, you know, is extraordinarily clear."

"It's not the clearness of his mind," she tried to explain to him. "It's the nature of it. Can't you see that he's different ? He's a sort of changeling, not a bit like himself, different from the father I've always loved."

He couldn't see it. "I think the change is in yourself," he said. "You're worn out. I'm not surprised at that. And yet, honestly, I don't see why he shouldn't go on for a year or two like this. You ought to be proud of it. It's you who have made it possible."

"Sometimes I wish it were over," she said. "Ah, there

you are ! Now you're shocked at me. You think I'm inhuman. But I can't go on much longer. I can't. I know I can't.'

" I'll tell him I think you ought to go away for a bit. You're on the edge of a breakdown. There's no reason, under the circumstances, why you shouldn't get a nurse in."

" Oh no, no, no ! " she cried. " For heaven's sake don't say anything. It's really nothing but silly weakness. I shall be all right to-morrow. You see . . . I suppose it's just the fact of having somebody to speak to. It's a relief ; you've been too sweet to me ; only—I don't know—I simply can't stand it."

" What about Clare ! " he said suddenly.

At that word her self-control melted away in the disconcerting, blinding manner which had lately puzzled her. If anyone else had suggested Clare's possibilities she wouldn't, probably, have minded ; but on Wilburn's lips the name had power to wound. In its inflection she detected a tenderness that enraged her and tumbled together in a cumulative rush of memory all the occasions for grudging or jealousy that she had so rigidly repressed : Clare's youth, her music, her happiness, Sylvia. A hundred times, by sheer force of suggestion, she had convinced herself that she didn't grudge Clare anything ; now, under the scrutiny of Wilburn's straight blue eyes, she knew that she did, and was less ashamed than angry, for, in the same moment, she realized that however skilfully he might flatter her or she might flatter herself, this man cared nothing for her . . . nothing. She had to find words to show her unconcern.

" Oh, Clare's no good," she said. " Clare's nothing but a child."

Still the vindictive memory pursued her. In these very words, once before, Wilburn had made excuse for Clare, and she had contradicted him. Would he remember ? He left her in doubt, with an embarrassed laugh. Confused and suffering she led him without another word to the doctor's room. She wondered, hopelessly, how it was that Clare, in her innocence, should always show her at her worst. At any rate she need deceive herself no longer. Now she suspected that the magnet which drew Wilburn so often and so dutifully to Pen House was not respect for her father or regard for herself, but Clare's youth, Clare's passive beauty.

From that moment she forgot her preoccupations over the old man's health, the agony of self-pity which she had disclosed for Wilburn's sympathy, in an intense examination of Clare and Wilburn as they sat together at the supper table. She watched them in vain. Not a word, not a glance that passed between them betrayed as much as his earlier question had given her. But this did not satisfy her. That night, deliberately, she denied herself the treasured privilege of seeing Wilburn to the door. " Clare had better see you off," she said. If he wanted the foolish child he should have her. It was a triumph. It proved, as nothing else could have proved, that she wasn't jealous ; and Clare assented with an easy, bright naturalness that would have deceived any woman less acute than herself. When they had gone she sat staring in front of her, intently listening ; and not a sound reached her but the sharp slam of the hall-door. Which was worse than ever.

For the next few days she threw herself into an artificial fury of activity, embarrassing to Mrs. Rudge and Ellen, who were used to the routine of a house that ran like clockwork, and mildly astonishing to Clare. It was only by incessant occupation that Aunt Cathie could subdue her agitated mind. She embarked on a third spring-cleaning that swept the house like a whirlwind from end to end, sparing neither herself nor Clare nor the bewildered servants.

" This morning," she told Clare with a peculiar satisfaction, " I'm going to ' do ' the drawing-room, so you'll have to give up your piano-playing for once."

Clare found herself enrolled in the forces of invasion that stripped the walls of pictures and furniture, revealing grotesque unfaded patches of the figured paper that were like ghosts of the shapes that had been torn from them. Finally, with a swoop of exultation, Aunt Cathie pounced upon the contents of the ebony music-cupboard. Red, dusty, flustered, she stood above the piles of music that it disgorged.

"This cabinet," she said, "has never been cleaned properly since before you were born. It's a perfect scandal. You'd think we had no servants in the house. All this old rubbish"—she pointed to the yellow sheets of Clare's mother's collection—"it's no business here. It ought to go up into the attic instead of breeding dust and moths and spiders."

It was a challenge, and Clare accepted it.

"But Aunt Cathie," she said, "I love these old things of mother's. I often play them."

"I know you do. I've heard you. Haven't you got music of your own? This stuff is nothing but a silly waste of time. You'd better put them all together, Ellen, and carry them upstairs," she added, returning to her old trick of suggesting that Clare disliked doing things for herself. "Now do, for heaven's sake, pull yourself together, Clare. Don't stand gaping at them like that!"

But Clare's spirit was roused. Her eyes brightened. She knew that she must assert herself.

"You can do what you like with your own music, Aunt Cathie," she said, "but mother's is mine, and I want it."

For a moment the issue hung undecided. Ellen stood sheepishly waiting in the background. Clare crouched protectively over the beloved pages. Aunt Cathie hovered, a bird of prey waiting to strike. Then, abruptly, she changed her mind.

"There's no need to be dramatic about it," she said.

" At any rate you might take the trouble to keep the cupboard dusted. Moth-eggs ! Cobwebs ! Really . . ." She threw her energies wildly on the lower shelf where Clare's own music reposed. She picked out an armful and flung it in a heap on the floor-boards, as though she hated every sheet. Then an unfamiliar title caught her eye. " Mass in B Minor ? " she gasped. " Mass in B Minor ? What are *you* doing with Masses, pray ? Where did you get this from ? " She snatched up the volume before Clare could lay hands on it. Destruction was in her eye.

" Give it to me," Clare cried. " It's mine, it's mine ! "

It wasn't hers ; yet it was hers a thousand times.

" Yours ? " Aunt Cathie sneered. " Then what's the meaning of this ? Michael Darnay. You needn't lie to me, Clare."

" I'm not lying," Clare protested. " I mean that it goes with my music. Of course it belongs to Mr. Darnay."

" Then what are *you* doing with it ? "

" He lent it to me."

" Mr. Darnay ? I'd no idea that you were acquainted with him. I don't know Mr. Darnay and don't want to know him. Perhaps you'll kindly explain."

" You've no right to ask me, Aunt Cathie."

" No right ? My dear Clare . ."

" No right at all. But I'll tell you all the same. Mr. Pomfret sent me to him when I told him I wanted to be prepared for Confirmation."

" Mr. Pomfret ? Mr. Pomfret ? My dear child, I think you must be mad. You know perfectly well how we're situated. Do you want to kill your grandfather ? "

Aunt Cathie always said that when she wanted to be most impressive.

" Oh, Aunt Cathie, don't be so silly ! " Clare said. " You know you needn't tell him unless you want to."

But Aunt Cathie was determined to be silly. She swept

across the room toward the fireplace and possessed herself of a fan of moth-eaten peacock's feathers which she swished through the air like an angry bird spreading its tail.

" I don't know this Mr. Darnay personally," she went on, " but I've heard enough about him to form an opinion. These rubbishy feathers ought to be thrown away. Full of moths and dust. Besides, they say they're unlucky. Mr. Pomfret, indeed ! Mr. Pomfret ought to have known better than to send you to a Romanizer, a Papist, who hasn't the courage to ' go over.' A bachelor, too. That's a fine thing to do with a young girl ! I know that Mr. Darnay is a great favourite with the women. No doubt he enjoys their confessions. Spiritual flirtations : that's what I call them."

" Aunt Cathie," Clare cried, " I won't allow you to speak about him like this ! "

" You'll have to, my dear." And Cathie spoke with a bitter laugh. " Now don't excuse yourself. You know as well as I do how scandalously Mr. Pomfret has behaved to your grandfather. You know that we, in this house, have nothing, absolutely nothing to do with him. You know what our opinions are, how strongly the doctor feels ; and when he's on his dying bed off you go, sneaking over to the other side. You must be mad. *You're* not a member of the Church of England."

" But I *am*, Aunt Cathie ! That's where you make a mistake. Whether you like it or not, I was baptized into it. At Stourton, where I'm going to be confirmed next week."

" Confirmed ? " Aunt Cathie spluttered. " Confirmed ? "

She began to pat her chest nervously, as though by this method of correction she could reduce her heart to order. Evidently it had the effect that she desired ; for, when next she spoke, it was with a grim and injured resignation :

" Please go and see what Ellen is doing," she said, " and tell her to come here at once. You needn't bother to come back again. We can manage perfectly well without you."

Clare went, carrying the precious music with her. Aunt Cathie was standing alone in the midst of the dismantled room, with the moth-eaten fan of peacock's feathers in her hand. Her heart was so hot with irritation and resentment that, if there had been a chair, she could have sat down and cried. She knew that it was unreasonable ; she knew that she was powerless to bend or break Clare. The child was a match for her, fashioned out of the same hard stuff as the doctor and herself. The only thing which could console her was a just indignation that she, an older woman, to whom Clare owed a kind of filial submission had been scorned and insulted ; and even here she could not be quite sure of her ground.

Ellen, with a scared face, returned. They worked together in a dreadful, tense silence. Dust was in Aunt Cathie's eyes and throat. A blackbird, on the lawn, mocked her with the delicious ease of its song. Clare had got out of this dusty turmoil far too easily. Clare was in her high, cool bedroom, or in the garden, lazy as a blackbird. As usual ! That was the root of the whole trouble. The child had not enough to do. She'd been running wild. Running wild. Whatever the words might mean, they gave Aunt Cathie a partial satisfaction. She knew that all her life had been one long sacrifice. Clare had never made a sacrifice of any kind since she was born. That was the trouble. Running wild !

And as for Mr. Pomfret . . . Why, only that week, she had felt herself compelled to refuse one of the Vicar's overtures ! This Diamond Jubilee that everyone was raving about. Mr. Pomfret had written her a friendly letter, a letter so friendly that it could only be regarded with suspicion, inviting her to serve on the Ladies' Committee which was to arrange the Jubilee festivities in Wychbury.

She had wanted, most awfully, to serve on this Committee ; it didn't look well for a person of her importance to abstain from it. Yet, out of consideration for the doctor's feelings, she had refused. She had made her usual sacrifice, only to discover that Clare, behind her back, had entered the enemy's camp.

It would serve Clare right if she abandoned her spring-cleaning, or left it in Ellen's bungling hands, and went straight in to the doctor to tell him of this vile perfidy. She hesitated to do so : partly because, although she knew it wouldn't kill him as she had extravagantly suggested, he would be upset, and partly because life was already too complicated to admit the disturbance of a scene. She tried to put the idea of this obvious and easy revenge out of her mind ; but when, that evening, she sat over her work exhausted with the day's activities, when she heard Clare reading to the doctor in Sylvia's voice, and saw, in Clare's, the mild reproachfulness of Sylvia's eyes, the desire to wound, to crush, to humiliate, gathered in her body like a storm and made her fingers tremble.

Quivering she rose from her chair and came to the old man's elbow.

" Father," she said, " I think you ought to know what Clare has been doing."

" What's this ? What's this ? " said the doctor. " What's the matter now ? "

He looked from one to the other with the eyes of an animal disturbed in the middle of a meal, for the teeth of his mind were already fixed in Sedgebury Main Preference. And Clare stood before them in the composure of a mute humility, with a cool, pale quietness that was worse to Aunt Cathie than any scarlet of indignation. It spurred her into ruthlessness !

" I think you ought to know, father," she said, " that Clare has got into the hands of our friend, the Vicar. That

Mr. Darnay has been preparing her for confirmation. She's going to be confirmed in Stourton this week."

The doctor's eyes glittered savagely. Aunt Cathie stood waiting for the sky to crack and fall. It did not fall. From his thin lips and nose there issued a sound that was between a snort and a laugh.

" Ha ! To be confirmed ? What else do you expect Catherine ? Like father, like daughter. Ha ? "

Not another word.

" I thought you ought to know," Aunt Cathie weakly repeated.

" Ring for Thirza," the doctor snarled.

She hurried to the bell. She heard it tinkle in the kitchen-passage. Even that futile sound seemed a relief, for, though Clare had not spoken, she knew that Clare's eyes were on her, and that this silence concealed a reproach that would never be spoken. She deserved it. She was so ready to admit her baseness that she accused herself without pity of meanness and disloyalty, to Clare, to herself, to her sex. And as she waited awkwardly for the relief of Mrs. Rudge's arrival another question troubled her : What would Dudley Wilburn think of it ? Once again the dreadful passive power that was in Clare had compelled her to humiliate herself in Wilburn's eyes. There was no peace, no happiness in life since Clare's return ; she was no longer mistress of herself ; some spiteful devil possessed her. And once again her soul cried for the revelation of some means by which she could make amends ; if that were possible, if Clare could ever forgive her. Even now she could not calculate the consequences of her betrayal.

The first of these was easily to be anticipated. Next morning, when she met Clare at breakfast with troubled, penitent eyes, she realized that she had lost the child's confidence for ever, that all the pretences of sisterly love and intimacy which duty and desire had compelled her to imagine had been swept away. She knew at once that the shamed tenderness which she was prepared to offer would be rejected ; that the melting reconciliation, which she had planned as a preface to begging Clare not to tell Wilburn what had happened, was out of the question.

What troubled her even more was the uncertainty of the doctor's attitude. She knew that he had fiercely approved her rejection of Mr. Pomfret's overtures in the matter of the Jubilee fête ; indeed, she had extracted virtuous satisfaction from his approval ; she wondered in what light he would consider Clare's defection.

She need not have worried herself. On the surface, at any rate, his behaviour toward Clare was, as usual, that of an impassionate patriarch performing his bare duty toward the stranger within his gates. He was too old, too careful, too absorbed in cold calculations, to show the active intolerance of his middle-age. Only, as a whimsical penance for Clare's heterodoxy, it now amused him to inflict on her, in the intervals between pages of the *Financial Times*, the reading of those old destructive, sceptical writings which had inspired his youth, and a new book which curiously fitted the occasion. It was called *The Secret Records of the Oxford Movement*, a spirited, and occasionally lubricious attack on the activities of Mr. Darnay's kind.

Clare read this exposure aloud from cover to cover. The old man spared her nothing. She read of the scandalous indecencies of the confessional, the lusts of celibate priests, the enormities practised in the convents of Protestant sisterhoods. The doctor grunted over them and licked his lips ; for they confirmed his theory that all mystical religions were nothing but manifestations of sexual suppressions. Aunt Cathie sat listening in her chair and blushed. This torture, if torture it was meant to be, recoiled upon her, its instigator, rather than on Clare. For Clare did not understand.

All through those first blue days of summer, when wild hyacinths flooded the copses and apple-blossom swept, like the foam of a tidal wave, up the basin of the Severn sea, Aunt Cathie was forced to endure the reproach which she imagined in Clare's quiet eyes. There was no reproach in them ; for Clare had soon forgiven her. In the overflow of joy and serenity which her confirmation had given her she could not help being at peace with all the world. Her happiness separated her from the older woman more surely than any enmity could have done. The gates of her heart lay open ; but Aunt Cathie would not enter, and Clare could never imagine why. She thought, in her new humility, that she herself must be at fault, never realizing that what Aunt Cathie's shyness demanded was a particular occasion, a full-dress setting for the act of reparation and forgiveness.

It came, and from an unexpected quarter, in one of the heavy square envelopes which Lady Hingston had affected since her translation to Stourford Castle ; an invitation for the Misses Weir and Lydiatt to be present at a dance to be held at Stourford on the evening of Jubilee Day. It was many years since an invitation of this kind had reached Pen House. When Clare came down to breakfast it was prominently displayed on the dining-room mantelpiece, a gleaming white copper-plate pasteboard, surmounted, like the cards that summon to municipal luncheons, by the Hingstons' crest. Aunt Cathie, who usually acquiesced in the doctor's depreciation of the Hingstons as social climbers, was visibly flattered. With a carefully modulated satisfaction she showed it to Clare.

" But how awfully nice of them," Clare said. " I wonder what made them think of asking us ? "

" My dear child," said Aunt Cathie, bridling, " on an occasion of this kind they couldn't very well leave us out. Please remember that the Weirs are a much better and older family than the Hingstons. We've been here, in Wychbury, for hundreds and hundreds of years. Sir Joseph Hingston's father was only a collier from Halesby. I've heard that Sir Joseph himself worked as a boy in the Great Mawne pit."

Clare scarcely heard this vindication of family pride. She was thinking how Ralph Hingston had smiled and waved to her on the platform at Stourton a few months before. He had promised to speak to his sister Vivien about her. She wondered if this invitation were the result of that promise. In any case she couldn't grudge Aunt Cathie the pleasure of a little self-flattery.

" Of course," Aunt Cathie was saying, " at a house of that kind the company's bound to be very mixed. Since my day there are a lot of people in Stourton and the district who go everywhere. People that the doctor would never have let us know. He hasn't been able to reconcile himself to the changes of the last ten years."

" And in any case," said Clare, wistfully, " we couldn't go, could we ? "

" Naturally, I couldn't," said Aunt Cathie, " even if I wanted to. Lady Hingston must have known that perfectly well. But I don't see any real reason why you shouldn't."

" Oh, Aunt Cathie, how nice of you ! " said Clare.

" Your dancing-lessons were an expensive extra. It seems a pity that they should be wasted. This is the first chance you've had of using them."

" I don't quite see how I could go alone," said Clare.

" Of course you couldn't go alone. My dear child, what are you thinking about ! "

" I wasn't thinking about it. That's what I said."

" Though in these days," said Aunt Cathie, scraping the surface of cinder from a piece of Ellen's toast, ' young people are allowed a licence such as we never dreamed of. Still, I think it can be managed. You see Mr. Wilburn is bound to be invited. He's their solicitor. He's coming over to-night, and I shall take the opportunity of asking him if he'll be kind enough to take you with him. It's bound to be a late affair, so it might suit him to dress here and come back to sleep afterwards. Jabez could drive you."

" Oh, that's a wonderful idea," said Clare. " How clever of you to think of it ! I should love to go with Mr. Wilburn," she added tactlessly.

" No doubt you would," said Aunt Cathie, bridling. " The only question is whether Mr. Wilburn would love to go with you."

A question that Clare thought she could have answered : but already another was troubling her.

" I'm afraid I haven't got a dress that will do," she said. " Only the white silk. That's high in the neck, you know, and dreadfully short. I'm really awful : I seem to grow out of everything."

" I've thought about that too," said Aunt Cathie, making her penance stage by stage with bitter satisfaction. " As a matter of fact we have a lot of your mother's things in the house. You're very much her figure. Fashions have changed, of course, but you can always do things with lace, and lace always looks good. Thirza and I will see what we can do about it. Now, my dear child, don't get excited about it like that ! There's plenty of time to spare. You can't even answer the invitation until you're sure that Mr. Wilburn will put up with you."

" But it *is* sweet of you, Auntie Cathie," said Clare.

She threw her arms round Aunt Cathie's neck and kissed her. Catherine Weir blushed and trembled as though her kisses had been those of a lover. She swallowed hard, to keep down the emotion which her penance, and, even more, Clare's generous acceptance of it, had given her. She was so embarrassed and disorganized that, without thinking, she put sugar into Clare's second cup of tea. And Clare, who hated sugar in anything, restored the balance of in-

debtedness by swallowing it without telling her what she
had done.

# VIII

## JUBILEE

A MORNING of sultry skies and moist, veiled sunshine ; a
torrid afternoon, dispelled, at evening, into a uniform haze
of gold. Queen's weather, they called it, as though the
empire of that august lady had mystically asserted itself
over the cyclonic systems of the North Atlantic. The
morning had been lazy as a Sunday, till, of a sudden, the
bells of Wychbury broke out into an orgy of clashing bob-
majors that made the air rock and eddy below the terrace of
Pen House.

As a rule the octave of Wychbury bells, beautiful as they
were in their faint discordance, had the power of filling
Clare with a vague unhappiness. On still Thursday
evenings, when Mr. Hemus, in his shirt-sleeves, led the
ringers' practices, the wavering peal enveloped Pen House
in a melancholy veil of sound from which she felt that she
could never escape. But that morning the bells spoke
with a gay and leaping exultation that made her heart
dance with them. Their voices made an airy maze, soaring
and wheeling dizzily above the steeple like swifts on a summer
evening, while beneath them, in the quivering heat-haze
that wrapped the Severn Plain, the bells of other villages
hummed, throbbed and trembled like a bourdon of bumble-
bees in the lime-blossom.

From her bedroom window Clare could see the red-striped
sail-cloth of the marquees that had been erected in the field
behind Mr. Pomfret's Vicarage ; and from this point, later
in the day, arose a babel of human voices no less exultant
than that of the bells, as the programme of sports and com-

petitions, athletic or merely ludicrous, which Mr. Pomfret had arranged for the occasion, developed itself.

For, after fox-hunting, the principal tenet of Mr. Pomfret's creed was Merrie England ; which meant that on certain chosen occasions, everybody in the parish, except himself and the landed gentry, should be induced to make themselves ridiculous in some way or other. " No shirkers, now ! " said Mr. Pomfret. On his face was the same grim smile with which he put his hunter at a " bullfinch."

Ellen, of course, was there, with her young sweetheart from the mill. Even Thirza Rudge had been induced to spend the day with Mrs. Harbord, who kept the sweetshop in the village. Thirza made a rule of never mentioning Mrs. Harbord's name. Almost as if there were something indecent about it, she invariably veiled Mrs. Harbord's identity under the title of " my friend " ; Jabez also had been released for the occasion ; and when Clare watched him hobble away down the drive with an old straw hat of his master's cocked on his head, she realized that she and Aunt Cathie and the doctor were to be left alone.

So evening came ; and still the waves of sound welled upward from the Vicarage field. Now dancing had begun ; the village band, in which Ellen's young man sweated beneath the weight of a euphonium, had jerked itself into the rhythm of *You should see me dance the Polka*. Clare and Aunt Cathie sat out on the terrace in a golden haze of midges, not so much because they wanted to hear as because they could not separate themselves wilfully from all the normal human activities of the festival.

The doctor insisted on joining them ; it was the first time that he had left the house that year. Between them they helped him out into the garden. Clare had never been allowed to do this before ; for he was fanciful, and always reserved the privilege for Aunt Cathie and Mrs. Rudge. It affected her strangely to feel the pressure of his skinny arm upon her hand ; for though she knew that he was thin she had always associated his thinness with a sort of steely strength, and now the arm which she supported seemed fragile and brittle, like that of a plaster cast. Its age and fragility awed her heart with mingled pity and reverence, making her guiltily conscious of her own youth. When they had settled him on the terrace in his chair he looked very grey and weary. Not even that warm evening sun could give his face the colour of life ; he couldn't even hear the blaring of the village band, and, after a little while, he settled down in his chair and nodded asleep.

Clare and Aunt Cathie sat by him for a long time in silence, and Clare, looking from one face to the other, saw, for the first time, how sinister in its admonitions of age and mortality a family likeness might be. Their presence made her youth seem an indecency of which she ought to be ashamed ; she wished that she could conceal the excitement that ran in her blood, the eagerness with which her thoughts kept racing toward her new frock and the Stourford party ; and though she kept on wondering if she ought'n really to go upstairs and begin dressing, the implied indelicacy kept her from asking Aunt Cathie what time it was : a foolish deference, as she told herself afterward ; for when she could stand it no longer and slipped quietly away, Aunt Cathie's eyes followed her with a smile of encouragement.

Now all the fields warmed to a golden hue, barred by the long, blue shadows of elms ; but in Clare's little bedroom the light had almost gone, for the casement was narrow and old-fashioned, and the dome of a pale, soft-breathing lime stood between it and the West. In this half-light the room took on a scented, shining mystery of its own ; for all its air was full of summer perfume, of lime flower, of roses, of lavender ; and the bright, dark surfaces of the mirror, the Sheraton mahogany dressing-table, the tall chest of drawers reflected a lucent richness in which all their imperfections of age were lost. The dusk which filled it was as profound and peaceful as that of a quiet sky at night, deeply, infinitely, mysteriously removed from all earthly turmoil ; and when Clare lighted the two Sheffield-plated candlesticks, one on either side of the mirror, their thin flames burned with the unwavering steadfastness of stars. The air was so still and sweet that when she took off her frock and stood with bare shoulders, its milky coolness made her shudder with such sensuous delight that she felt she could have surrendered herself for ever to its caresses.

On the blue coverlet of the bed lay the dress which Aunt Cathie had skilfully compounded from lace that had once belonged to Sylvia, ivory-white with age. Clare knew already that it was lovely ; but when she slipped it over her shoulders and saw, in the mirror, framed by sky, the delicate, insubstantial beauty with which it invested her own dark, glowing youth, she stood rapt in amazement. She could not believe that she, Clare Lydiatt, was really like this. Rather some ghostly visitant stood and mocked her from the mirror's shining oval.

She was standing rapt in this contemplation when she became aware of another face, dark, handsome, with black eyes, invading the corner of the picture behind her left shoulder. Aunt Cathie had stolen into the room, so quietly that she, too, seemed part of the same ghostly evocation. She looked, and spoke not a word, until Clare, suddenly awakened, and flushed, like a dark rose, with confusion.

" Oh, Aunt Cathie," she said, " how you startled me ! Will I do ? "

" Yes, Clare, I think you'll do very well." She spoke in her low, hard voice as usual. " Of course you can't go very far wrong with old lace like this. It's a little bit discoloured ; but that doesn't really matter. Anyone can see that it's good. Now do keep still a moment child. Don't wriggle like that ! I think the waist-line should be the very least bit higher. You see ? Just like that."

She stepped back and surveyed Clare with her cold, dark seriousness. " Of course the neck is rather low ; lower than you're used to. You must be careful not to sit in draughts after you've been dancing : I don't want to have two invalids in the house. Let's see . . . There's a Honiton lace scarf. That'll be most appropriate : the Queen always wears Honiton. You'd better have that as well."

She took a key from her silver chatelaine and unlocked the mysterious bottom drawer of Clare's chest, the one which was devoted to her mother's belongings. She threw the scarf over Clare's shoulders ; the fine net lay like gossamer on her white neck.

" Yes, that's much better," said Aunt Cathie in a measured voice. The two stood facing each other. Clare's lips trembled into a smile of pleasure and new excitement ; but as she smiled she saw Aunt Cathie's mouth stiffen curiously at the corners, saw her dark eyes go brighter. Suddenly she found herself in Aunt Cathie's arms, bound fast in a passionate embrace. Against her burning cheek lay Aunt Cathie's, downy and lax. She heard Aunt Cathie's softened, broken voice :

" Clare, my darling, my little Clare ! "

Aunt Cathie began to cry softly. She seemed so lonely, helpless, broken, with all the pride and hardness in her abased, that Clare, too, melted into tears. Against her own soft shoulder she felt the rigidity of Aunt Cathie's whalebone stays ; she gathered Aunt Cathie to her breast as though the sobbing woman were a child, and she, Clare, her natural protectress. There was no longer any reservation or doubt or grudging in her mind, no smallest resentment in her heart, not even pity : only love. . . .

But she could not speak. And fortunately there was no need for speaking. They heard a gentle tap at the door.

Aunt Cathie, swiftly, shamefully, released herself from Clare's embrace. She went to the door and opened it, and Ellen, her face as red as if it had been kissed all day, entered with the tray on which Clare's supper had been arranged. In her bunched white muslin she looked like some profuse bouquet of country flowers. Breathless with haste and excitement she burst into a spate of apologies.

"Oh, Miss Cathie, m'm, I'm that sorry I gave you the trouble to open the door. My hands were in such a tremble I didn't dare put down the tray. I've run all the way up from the field ; there's not a breath in my body. But I said I'd bring up Miss Clare's tray—didn't I, Miss ?—and I've done it !" She laughed nervously. "Shall I put it down on the bed, Miss Cathie, m'm ? Yes, m'm ? Oh, Miss Clare ! Oh, my, Miss ! Aren't you lovely ! Ain't she a sight, Miss Cathie, m'm ? Oh, ain't she a picture ? "

"That will do, Ellen," said Aunt Cathie, smiling, with the remains of emotion in her voice. "You'd better hurry back, or you'll miss the fire balloons. I think I'll bring a lamp up, Clare. You can't see to eat with candles in this light."

She took this opportunity of escaping from the room ; but Ellen, in spite of Jim Moseley and the fire balloons still lingered in a rapt ecstatic admiration of Clare.

"Oh, Miss Clare, if only you knew how sweet you looked. I've got to do it. I knew I'd got to do it when first I set eyes on you ; you properly took my breath away. You wouldn't make any objection, Miss, would you, if I made so bold as to kiss you ? "

Clare laughed. The evening was full of kisses. Ellen's moist, hot hands were on her arms as she kissed the shining peony of Ellen's face. Then they stood for a second smiling at each other and Ellen was gone.

## IX

### MUSIC AND MOONLIGHT

THE musty victoria jolted Clare and Dudley Wilburn through the lanes. On the box above them, a seedy, shrunken figure, old Jabez sat with more than his usual taciturnity, drowsy already, with the effects of Diamond Jubilee beer. The moon, in its last quarter, had not yet risen, but under the mild starlight, clouds of creamy hawthorn tufted the hedges, drenching the lanes with the perfume of their decadence, paving the ruts with a drift of rusty ivory. For half an hour and more these scented tunnels led them insensibly to the level of the plain, and through all that time Wilburn, seated at Clare's side, so close that her shoulder touched his arm, had neither stirred nor uttered a single syllable.

It puzzled her to find him so silent. She could not help remembering their last drive together up from the station when he had joked with her in his elderly privileged way, and made her thrill with a deeper emotion at her mother's name. It seemed that his mood had changed from the moment at which Aunt Cathie had waved good-bye to them at the end of the drive. " Now, mind you look after her ! " Aunt Cathie had called ; and Wilburn had laughed back at her : " Don't you trust me ? "

Since that moment never a single word. It was curious, but, as Clare quickly decided, rather nice of him. She had no great experience out of which to make comparisons ; Mr. Darnay was the only other man with whom she had known any intimacy, and her intimacy with Mr. Darnay, apart from the moments when his musical enthusiasms made his prominent pale eyes shine behind their spectacles, ruffled his red hair, and brought an irritating moisture to the corners of his mouth, had been limited to an earnest examination of religious tradition.

And yet, after a while, Wilburn's silence troubled her. The impulses of her own heart were so mercurial that this suspension of all physical activity made her feel as if she had been gagged and strapped in her seat. At last she could bear it no longer. Before she knew what she was saying she had spoken.

"Why don't you say something, Mr. Wilburn?" she said.

The words had no sooner left her mouth than she realized their childishness. For a moment he didn't answer; but, in the dark, she was aware of his smile. Then he spoke in his deep, rumbling voice, so low down in his chest that it always reminded her of a double bass:

"What do you want me to say, Clare?"

"I don't know. It seems so funny, saying nothing."

"I was thinking of a great many things," he said.

"I don't consider that you ought to think on a night like this," she told him.

"Of course you don't. And it's perfectly right that you shouldn't. Nobody has any right to think when they're eighteen. I'm sorry I'm such dull company, Clare. Still, you'll find plenty of young people at Stourford."

"I do wish you wouldn't always talk as if you were ninety," she said, "because you know, perfectly well, that you aren't."

"I know perfectly well that I am . . . very nearly. That's the whole trouble. I'm a very shy man, Clare. And when I find myself in the company of anyone so alarmingly young as yourself, I can't help feeling the enormous difference between us. You're rather rubbing it in, you know, by what you said just now. It would be much kinder to leave me alone."

"But I don't think it would be kinder," Clare protested. She was taking him very seriously. "Because . . . you see, I think it's rather silly of you. I don't think you ought to be encouraged. It isn't natural."

He laughed : " Do you want me to be natural ? No, no. It's much better that I shouldn't be, though I'm very glad that you are. And now, my child, you'd better pull yourself together. It's your last chance. By Jove, what a blaze of light they've got ! Sir Joseph must be wanting to show off his new electric installation. Think what it means to be a millionaire ! Now don't get excited before there's any need for it. Keep quiet and dignified. Just imagine for a moment that you're your Aunt Cathie ! " He laid a firm, restraining hand upon her knee. " Now, I suppose I'd better say good-bye to you. I shan't see you again. When you've had enough of it, you'll find me with the other chaperons in the library playing whist."

" But aren't you going to dance ? " Her voice was alarmed. " Oh, Mr. Wilburn, please, please don't leave me alone. Really and truly I shan't know anyone but the Hingstons and the Willises. I shall be simply lost if you leave me."

" You won't be anything of the sort. Lady Hingston will look after you, if you can't look after yourself. And of course you can."

" But I'm frightened to death of her ! " Clare gasped.

" So am I, my dear. But she can't hurt you. Then there's Vivien."

" Vivien's so dreadfully smart. She won't look at me."

" If she won't, her brother will. Let me get out first. Be careful of that lace scarf now ! Come along. You'd better take my arm."

" But, truly, Mr. Wilburn . . ."

It was too late. The door of the wide entrance hall stood open with a footman on either side of it. No sooner had Clare entered than she was swept into a long room on the left, where a tall, gaunt, elderly lady with grey hair and long yellow teeth stood in front of a pier glass, plunging hairpins viciously into her high coiffure, wincing at every thrust as if the points had entered her scalp. Her eyes glared fiercely at the figure of Clare reflected in the mirror. Then of a sudden, her mouth twitched into a smile, like that of a horse baring its teeth ; her hair began to nod like a tossing plume. Only after a moment did Clare realize that the smile and the ossing of the crest were made in recognition of herself, and that the lady was Mrs. Pomfret, the Vicar's wife, whom she had only seen before in the rigour of black satin on Sundays.

"So glad to see you ! Miss Lydiatt, isn't it ? My husband told me. A great pleasure to both of us. Dreadfully late, I'm afraid."

And with another bony smile she galloped out, leaving Clare to the empty magnificence of the dressing-room, strewn with rich cloaks and saturated by strange sophisticated perfumes. Never before had she felt so lonely and helpless. The rumour of laughter and voices that penetrated the closed door through which Mrs. Pomfret had boldly curvetted, sounded to her so easy, so masterful, so awfully confident, that she doubted if she could ever have courage to show her face. If only she could be sure that Mr. Wilburn was waiting for her ! She would never forgive him for the way in which, like a callous swimming-master, he had pushed her into this deep water and left her to gasp and splutter by herself.

But she could not stay in the dressing-room all the evening ; so, at last, pulling her courage together, she entered the hall. Wilburn, thank heaven, was there waiting for her, though, for the moment, she hardly recognized him, for she had not seen him in evening-dress before. His magnificence took her aback. Up to that time she had never realized what a handsome man he was. The tall starched collar, above his gleaming breastplate of shirt-front, emphasized, by the contrast of their smoothness, the strength of his dark, powerful face : straight mouth, firm jaw, and steady, confident eyes. Before this she had always conceived him as a rugged, cumbrous figure, rustic, almost, in the sturdiness of his demeanour. He now appeared to her strong as ever, or even stronger, but with a strength of polished elegance, like that of a supple, shining steel. And as for middle-age . . . What nonsense the man talked !

He gave her his arm, and they went forward together into the crowd that clustered round Lady Hingston at the foot of the stairs. In the company of such a cavalier Lady Hingston had no more terrors for her. Clare found her a neat, middle-aged woman, no taller than herself, with bright, bird-like eyes and a hooked nose that gave her a swift, falcon, brilliance which, in youth, must have made her dark wildness enthralling. Even now her eyes flashed, and her speech came with the quick, keen accuracy of a swooping bird of prey that made Clare feel her own mind soft and fuddled.

In Wilburn Lady Hingston found her match. It was evident that she recognized his quality for as she took his hand her eyes brightened and her swift wits acknowledged the challenge of his different strength in a wheeling display of virtuosity that left Clare abashed by the crudity of her own youth and inexperience. Then suddenly she came to earth and her eyes met Clare's with a naturalness that was as astonishing as her previous brilliance.

" So you're Clare Lydiatt," she said. " I know your grandfather well. There's nobody like him. I knew your mother too : I can see the likeness. Joe, do you remember Sylvia Weir ? This is her daughter."

Clare found herself shaking the lifeless fingers of Sir Joseph Hingston. She knew him well by sight ; but somehow the elegance of evening-dress, which had worked such a signal transformation in the case of Wilburn, had the effect of making the baronet less significant. He was a

short, plump little man, with a solemn, cunning face, pale
and pasty but for the bluish, semi-lunar pouches under his
neutral eyes. The livery of English civilization had the
effect of cheapening his whole appearance. His clothes, in
spite of their admirable cut, made him look like a small,
unprosperous shopkeeper, attired for a Masonic banquet.
Even when he smiled and welcomed Clare, his eyes had the
inward listless look of one whose mind was concentrated
on other things : as indeed it was, for by this ceaseless
brooding devotion he had made the fortunes of the great
firm that bore his name. Beneath this mask of inertness
it was evident that he, too, liked Wilburn and admired the
achievements of his lady in a sphere wherein he had no
desire to shine. Her brilliance and her social activities
belonged to a department of the business that he was prepared and proud to finance without prejudice to his own,
graver preoccupations. And as he held Clare's hand and
smiled, his eyes had slowly turned to her escort.

"Ah, Wilburn, I'm glad you've come. Furnival's here
already. If you can spare a moment we might have a chat
in the library."

He laid his hand dreamily on Wilburn's elbow and went
on speaking in an undertone as they drifted away.

"I know that Vivien is expecting you," said the clear,
crisp voice of Lady Hingston, "though goodness knows
where she's got to. There are lots of young people in the
drawing-room. I expect she's there. Come along with
me, Clare. Ah, here she is ! I'll leave you in her hands.
Vivien, darling, be sure that Clare has a good time. That's
right, dearest. Ah, Mrs. Pomfret ! How very delightful !
Now don't tell me that you've left the Vicar behind ! "

And there was Vivien with both her hands on Clare's
shoulders : a dark, flashing vision of electric blue, a skimming kingfisher, for she, too, had her mother's bird-like
swiftness, and in that brilliant flight Clare found herself

whirled away. Vivien spoke excitedly as they went together.

" Oh, Clare, I'm so glad you've come ! However did you get in without my seeing you ? Such fun, and the music's ripping ! You know Ralph told me that you'd come home. Months ago ! My dear, I'm dreadfully ashamed of myself. But just at that time it was the end of the season. I was out four days a week. Father was simply splendid : he boxed our horses all over the place. And now its nearly as bad ; we've just got bicycles ! You've no idea how exciting they are. You feel so helpless at first. Ridiculous, the way you want to run into everything ! But it's all right here, you know. Only the bullocks on the drive. Ralph taught me. George and Eleanor are far too middle-aged and sober. You must get Ralph to teach you. He's splendid. Oh, dear, that's the Blue Danube, and I believe I've lost my programme. Well, that's their lookout, isn't it ? Come along quickly, and I'll introduce some nice men to you. Oh, Edward, is it really yours ? I don't know my partners from Adam. I've lost my programme. I think I shall lose my head next. But do be a darling, Edward, and take Clare instead of me. Really and truly, I don't know where I am. You *do* know Edward Willis, don't you, Clare ? That's splendid, splendid ! "

And away she flashed, with her kindly, shining face, humming the tune of the Blue Danube as she went, leaving Clare in Edward Willis's awkward arms.

A queer, shy boy. He scarcely held her at all ; he kept so far away from her that their gyrations lacked a fulcrum. She might just as well have been dancing with a dummy. And yet Clare knew that he was nice, that his timidity might, with equal justice, have been called delicacy ; and though his dancing was ludicrous compared with that of the girls at St. Monica's, or, above all, that of the indefinitely receding Miss Boldmere; the music and the glassy floor of the Stourford drawing-room were inspiring beyond anything that Clare had ever known.

How could one dream of dancing to the music of a tinkling piano once having tasted the richness of these sensuous strings ? She thought of the dingy class-room at Alvaston, the rough, chalked floor, the forms piled against ink-stained walls under the dirty gas-jets, and compared them with this brilliant chamber of cream and gold, the lucent floor of teak, the chandeliers of sparkling Venetian glass on whose facets the white light of Sir Joseph's electric bulbs played with the fire of diamonds.

And from St. Monica's her mind, or some sombre part of it that lay brooding beneath these rich perceptions of colour, scent and sound, traversed the dark lanes of hawthorn that lay between her and Pen House, where Thirza had put her grandfather to bed, and Aunt Cathie sat with eyes strained above her embroidery frame. Poor, dear, Aunt Cathie ! And yet how sweet she had been. How sweet, how thrilling, how wildly intoxicating, was all this brightly-coloured tissue of life ! Her heart fluttered with the desire to live ; the life in her was swift and greedy as a flame. Nothing must escape her !

Too swift . . . too swift ! The music ceased. Together they passed over the slippery floor into the domed shadow of Sir Joseph's famous conservatory, into the cool smell of moss and dripping water and the faint, sickly perfume of gardenias. They sat down together. In the dusk she became aware of Edward Willis's earnest eyes, already pained with wrestling for some speech. It suddenly occurred to her that through all the transports of that waltz neither of them had spoken a word. Edward had been as dumb as Mr. Wilburn ; and yet his silence neither troubled nor irritated her. She smiled at him and at herself. She felt it her duty to help him out ; but by this time he had found speech and begun to talk about poetry. O'Shaughnessy !

Music and Moonlight. She had never heard of either; but even as he began a stammered exposition, Vivien pounced on them in one of her rapid kingfisher flights, and snatched her away.

"Thank you so much, Edward dear," she said. "I've kept the second extra for you as a compensation. I'm sure Clare's frightfully interested in what you're telling her, but it's my mission in life to get her programme filled. Here it is. I'm sure you're anxious to dance with her again, so you'd better book one at once. She dances beautifully. I watched you. Far better than you do."

And when the dance was booked, away they went. Within two minutes Clare found herself bewildered with an excess of partners; half a dozen immaculate young men from North Bromwich, two of Ralph Hingston's Oxford friends, and a number of Vivien's own hunting-field acquaintances.

"But where's that brother of mine?" she cried suddenly, when Clare's programme was nearly full. "He's spending the whole evening on the back stairs with Dorothy Powys. I shall have to look after both of them. He's no business to neglect his duty like this. Not duty, Clare dear," she added; "I don't mean that. I simply haven't time to choose my words. But I *do* so want you to have a good time. Ralph dances like an angel, and I know he's dying to dance with you. When he met you on Stourton station the other day . . . No, I won't tell you what he said. What lovely lace! It makes all our new frocks look positively common. Honiton, too. That's what the Queen wears. This must be number five. Clare, I must fly!"

So Clare's evening passed in a whirl of light and music. Her partners seemed, all of them, pleasant, clean young men of the type that might well be attracted by Vivien's own bright frankness. They all danced well, far better than Edward Willis, and by the middle of the evening she had become so accustomed to the variations of masculine steps that her mind was no longer concentrated on her feet, so that she had time to consider what her partners were really like through a series of waltzes, quadrilles and lancers.

In the last of these, a set complicated by the waywardness of Edward Willis, who could not keep the figures in his head, she suddenly found herself curtseying to corners with Ralph Hingston. Though she had often seen him dancing in the distance, this was the first time that they had been brought face to face, and the moment was awkward, for she couldn't help feeling that he had purposely avoided her. When the music struck up he bowed to her curtsey with a kind of mocking gravity that disturbed her. She was rather frightened of him, far more frightened than she had been on Stourton station. In his blue eyes there was a lurking wickedness that reminded her of Vivien's story of Dorothy Powys and the back stairs and compelled her to blush.

And yet, a moment later, when she had set to him and found herself whirling round with his arm about her waist, her shyness disappeared, and she felt that she had been dancing with him all her life ; as if he, with his honest eyes and smooth, fair face, were more powerful, more significant, more intimate, than any of the men with whom she had danced that evening. And as they met and parted throughout the changing figures of the dance, this intimacy was sealed by a series of quick whispers to which she found herself answering with an ease and a coldness that astonished her.

" Clare, I've been wanting to dance with you all night."

" You never asked me."

" That's Wilburn's fault. You came so late. When I saw you'd come, I felt quite mad about it."

" You seemed to be enjoying yourself, anyway."

" Don't talk rubbish. I've had a beastly time. I've been doing duty dances with the most awful old frumps."

" What about Miss Powys ? "

" Dorothy Powys ?  Lord Arthur's one of our directors.
I've got to take her in to supper.  Can't get out of it."

" Oh, do be quiet !  She'll hear you."

" I don't mind if she does.  Dorothy Powys is a sportsman.  She'll understand.  I say, Clare . . ."

" Do look !  We're holding up the set."

" Oh, damn the set ! "

And he was swept away from her on the vigorous tide of
the " Geisha " music.

But as they linked hands again and again in the weaving
of the Grand Chain, he caught her and contrived to finish
the sentence that the music had broken.

" After supper," he said.  " I shall look for you then.
On the steps."

" What about your duties ? " she whispered.

" Duties ?  I say . . . that's a promise ? "

> *Chon-kina, chon-kina, chon, chon, kina-kina,*
> *Nagasaki Yokohama Hakodate Hoy !*

The promise was never given.  At that moment, obeying
some strange communal instinct, all the dancers burst out
singing the nonsensical words of Sidney Jones's tune.  The
set ended in a fury of hand-clapping.  Clare found herself
breathless on Edward Willis's arm ;  Ralph was standing
with Dorothy Powys on his ;  but as the laughing dancers
streamed between them, he seemed to forget his partner.
His lips framed the word " promise " again, and Clare,
hardly knowing what she did, nodded and answered him
with her eyes.

# X

## THE BEACON

THEY ate their supper amid the ponderous oak of Sir
Joseph's dining-room, and as Clare sipped her borage-

scented claret cup, Edward Willis resumed the theme which Vivien had broken in the conservatory.

" He was an ichthyologist, you know. . . ."

Clare stared at him blankly. In the interval O'Shaughnessy and his works had been forgotten. She did not even know what an ichthyologist was.

" An ichthyologist. He spent all his life in the British Museum. Stuffed fishes, I suppose. Then he wrote *Music and Moonlight*, about thirteen years ago. Astonishingly good. There's one stanza. It's like nothing else."

He bent close above her, so that she might hear him among the clatter of plates and voices :

> *I think the sun's kiss will scarce fall*
> *Into one flower's cup :*
> *I think the bird will miss me,*
> *And give the summer up :*
> *O sweet place, desolate in tall*
> *Wild grass, have you forgot*
> *How her lips loved to kiss me,*
> *Now that they kiss me not ?*

She had begun to listen, smiling ; but as he recited, in his low, shy voice, the sensual loveliness of the words swept her mind away from her body's surroundings into that sweet place, desolate in tall wild grass, of which he spoke. Yes, it was beautiful. Strange, too, that on an evening dedicated to emotions so different from this, she should be able to respond to the appeal of such crepuscular words.

" Jolly, isn't it ? " said Edward Willis, apologetically, and brought her back to herself. Almost to herself ; for still there was a difference. Her heart warmed to this austere, shy young man who could achieve poetry in the Stourford dining-room and stir the secret deeps beneath that frothy surface. She looked at him again, with more respect than amusement ; and, in that moment, her mind made a swift comparison between him and Dudley Wilburn, standing solitary, erect and steady as a rock against the Corinthian pillars of the library door ; between him and Ralph Hingston, whose eyes caught hers with a smile above a lifted glass of champagne. It troubled her to realize the extraordinary variety of mankind ; she was astonished to confess that while Edward's whispered poetry had transported her momentarily to a sphere of experience whose very existence she had forgotten, and while Wilburn's presence inspired her, as usual, with respect for his power and stability, it was only Ralph Hingston's smile that brought a blush to her cheeks.

" He died in the same year as George Eliot," Edward was saying.

The words reached her like an echo, long after he had spoken ; and though she quickly apologized, and asked him to repeat them, a sudden access of shyness made him leave the subject in mid-air.

" I think they're going up the hill," he said. " Hadn't you better go into the dressing-room and get your wraps ? It may be cold."

She clutched eagerly at this opportunity to hide her confusion ; it even seemed to her that Edward Willis was relieved to lose her. When she emerged from the dressing-room, five minutes later, Ralph Hingston was standing outside. There, too, stood Wilburn with his hat in his hand. A panic seized her. The glance with which Wilburn greeted her was assuredly possessive, and, after all, Aunt Cathie had committed her to his charge. But she had given Ralph Hingston her promise ; and evidently he took its fulfilment for granted.

" Ready ? " he said, and as she smiled with embarrassment, he moved backward to let her pass, deliberately separating her from Wilburn. She hurried down the steps.

In a moment he was at her side. " I think Mr. Wilburn was waiting for me," she whispered.

Ralph laughed. " Let him wait ! " he said.

They crossed the drive and entered a grass alley within tall black hedges. The harsh odour of yews dropped, like a curtain, between them and the rose-gardens on either side. Sometimes it seemed as if the curtains swayed and a ravishing gust blew through, so that Clare was conscious, without seeing, of masses of June roses breathing out sweetness under the heavy night. They passed quickly down the dark alley, Ralph with his long, free strides, Clare fluttering silently at his side. Where the yews ended stood a fountain of grey stone and a circular Palladian belvedere. The spray of the fountain rose in a starlit mist ; its watery jets cracked in the air like whips ; and when they reached it, everyone, of a common impulse, paused for a moment and turned to look backward down the long yew vista to the fantastic bulk and blazing windows of the castle. In darkness, and at such a distance, the gatehouse tower and stucco battlements of Stourford lost their spurious air. On Clare, at least, they imposed an illusion of romance that recalled enchanted castles of the Morte d'Arthur and shed a knightly glamour on her companion.

In that stone circle, haunted by the fountain's sound, the steam of guests hung for a moment as in an eddy, then spilled and scattered beyond into the darkness of a broad, somnolent beechwood, its floor muffled with mast and roofed by motionless horizontal tapestries of leaf. All through that warm green crypt the path climbed continually ; and when they emerged from its shadows into an air that seemed, by contrast, cool and rarefied, they saw the hill's smooth shoulder rising close above them like a strung bow, blue-black against a tawny arc of sky that flared and paled with the leaping and subsidence of the hidden beacon's flame.

" Bad luck ! " Ralph cried. " I knew we should be late.

They've lighted it already. The wood's so dry it'll burn away in no time. Can you put on a sprint ? "

He grasped her arm ; together they strained panting up the hill's last and steepest contour by a path that twisted through vigorous bracken, until, on the plateau beside the standing stones, they saw the pyramidal beacon flaring in the midst of a huge, empty circle round whose circumference, like masses of curious insects, clustered the whole population of Stourford, fire-worshippers, rapt by the furious beauty of flame. And Clare, too, stood entranced, thrillingly conscious of the arm that he had now slipped about her, while the fire roared and crackled, drawing the breath out of her body with its draught, carrying her spirit upward, upward on its flying sheets of flame ; until, suddenly, Ralph's arm tightened and checked her !

" Look . . . look ! " he said. They turned together, and saw, beneath them, dragging over the furzy hillside, the straggling remnants of the Stourford party, their faces upturned and lit by the fiery reflex of the sky ; beyond these the void darkness of the Severn basin, and, further still, like the fires of slowly setting planets, the trail of beacons that ringed the March of Wales. From north to south they hung in a sinister crescent. Wrekin, Caer Caradoc, Radnor Forest, Brown Clee and Titterstone, Abberley, Malvern, with May Hill, a spent spark sinking into the Forest of Dean.

Clare caught her breath. The vision of this vast expanse of earth made manifest by the beacons' definition impressed her, but even more than its magnificence she felt the strangeness of her own position. She was no longer sure of herself. What power had whirled her out of the lights of Stourford on to this uplifted hillside. Who was this stranger whose arm encircled and possessed her ? What madness in herself allowed him to hold her like that ? The van of the Stourford party crawled upward and toward them. Half shy, half thrilled, she strained away from him ; but he had no intention of letting her escape.

" Come along," he said quickly, " let's get away from all this mob. We'll try the other side of the hill where it's quiet."

Indeed the whole hillside was scattered with pale summer frocks, flitting up, mothwise, from the villages of the plain. Amid the cries and laughter of this drifting flight, Ralph took Clare's arm and hurried her, through ankle-pricking acres of gorse, round the shoulder of the hill, where the crowd's tumult and the crackling of the fire were lost and only a gigantic reflex reddened the sky.

There, like a careless scarf, a fleece of firs trailed downward through the darkness of Uffdown Wood into the scorched basin of the Black Country, whose damped fires burned so low on that night of holiday that it might almost have reverted to its primal and pastoral greenness. On all that northern slope there was no sound but that of black pine-needles shuddering in uneasiness at the proximity of the fire, and, down in the June meadows, four hundred feet beneath them, the rasping of a single melancholy corn-crake. They sat down together on a tufted hedge-bank at the edge of the plantation where all the secrecy of night seemed to have been distilled into the mild and resinous air that enveloped them ; and Clare, with the excitement of the evening still throbbing in her brain, found that silence so sweet and reassuring that when he spoke she was filled with vague terror.

" Clare," he was saying, " Clare, I adore you. . . . You're far more lovely and wonderful than I ever imagined. I can't believe it's really you. You're so quiet, so cool. You're like a little ghost. For heaven's sake say something . . . anything . . . just to let me know that you're real ! "

He took her wrist in both his hands. His palms were hot on her cool skin. He held her so fast that she knew that he must feel the flutter of her pulses. She began to fear the pressure of his hands ; their strength was a symbol of something threatening ; they were closing not on her wrists but on her life ; an overpowering instinct of self-preservation called on her to escape them. It was too soon, too soon. She had been given no time to gather strength to meet him. Nothing but flight could save her from defeat, absorption, the annihilation of what she imagined to be herself. But though she strained away from him he would not let her go.

" Why don't you speak ? " he said. " You're not offended ? You're not frightened of me ? "

She was too frightened to speak. Not frightened, exactly, but unable to think ; for all the time, her brain was suffused with flushes and wanings of fire like the sheet of sky above the fringe of fir-tops.

Her silence troubled him. He was determined to break it. He drew her toward him by the wrists. She could feel the warmth of his breath as he whispered close to her face :

" Clare, Clare—I want to go on saying your name, over and over again. Clare, my sweet one, I love you. Why won't you look at me ? "

She dared not raise her eyes, for she knew that they were full of tears. The red light in her brain went on flushing and waning until, quite suddenly, there came a moment of suspension and quietude in which it seemed that she had found herself ; not the old self that she knew, for that could never be the same, but another : a hushed, calm consciousness, full of minute, delicious tremors like a countryside that shudders and holds breath in the night after a violence of summer rain.

In this new state she became aware once more of her surroundings. For a long while she had been lost in the palpitations of an emotion which was like light rather than thought ; but now she felt and saw the tufted hedgebank on which she was sitting, with Ralph so strangely kneeling at her feet ; she saw the velvety contours of tree-tops in Uff-down Wood, the vague vastness of the basin beyond. She smelt the dropping odour of pines and the thymy fragrance of turf. And, as her senses, one by one, awakened to a still poignancy of perception, her eyes rested with a curious, possessive boldness on Ralph's upturned face. Slowly, dreamily, uncontrolled, or, at most, controlled by some new spirit within her, they perused the features of this stranger and wondered at their strangeness ; the smooth, wide brow, the straight nose, the parted, eager lips, the blue eyes, black in darkness, whose burning eagerness she hadn't dared to face.

She wondered if it were possible that this was the boy with whom she had laughed and whispered under the sparkling chandeliers at Stourford an hour before, the creature whom she had accepted under the name of Ralph Hingston. No . . . he was different. It seemed that he, too, had changed as completely as herself. That Ralph had been a stranger ; but this new being, though far more strange, seemed as familiar as if she had created him out of her own dreams and desires. In this creation all past memory had been whirled backward into limbo. In this new birth they faced each other, coeval and coequal, transported and unashamed.

For a moment they gazed at each other in the revealing darkness without a word. Then, slowly, his hot fingers released her wrist ; his arms were folded round her, his lips burned against the coldness of her cheek. And gradu-ally it seemed to her that the strength with which his arms held her to him was not the violent and terrifying power which she had first imagined, that he was really no stronger than herself, perhaps, even, weaker ; so that her own arms, strangely potent and daring, embraced his body and held it, protectively, as though he were a child, in a grave, wise possession that she was eager to give and happy in giving.

Once more the visible, sensible world was lost. Only, above its sea-deep sounds and sights and odours, her brain was aware, as in sleep, of the corn-crake's monotonous sawing in the sunken meadows :

> *O sweet place, desolate in tall*
> *Wild grass, have you forgot*
> *How his lips loved to kiss me . . . ?*

The flare of the beacon faded from the sky beyond the wood ; the starry frame of Pegasus gaped above them, stealing slowly westward, marking the drift of moments that for them had no reality. Suddenly, without reasoning, the sense of time returned. Clare's fingers tightened. Her lips brushed his cheek. Then, with mysterious accord, they loosened their embrace. They rose to their feet and stood silently smiling at each other in the darkness that their eyes had learned to penetrate. Solemnly, lingeringly, they kissed again. Ralph took her without a word, and slowly, with his arm still about her, they passed along the dim edge of the pinewood and out on to the hilltop again.

By this time, as the sky warned them, the bonfire had flared itself away. Nothing now remained of it but a circle of lurid embers round whose circumference, like crippled, wing-singed insects, a few stragglers of the multitude that had fluttered up so gaily stood blinking at the ashes as though they were still too fascinated to move. For a little while they searched in vain for any remnants of the Stourford party. It seemed that they had been left behind, and so conspicuously that Clare began to feel an embarrassment that extinguished the last flickers of their secret fire.

" But they've all gone," she cried. " It will look too awful for us to come slinking in together. What will they say ? "

He laughed. He shouldn't have laughed. " They'll have to say it sooner or later. The sooner the better," he told her.

" But don't you see," she said, " how horrid it is for me ? I don't even know what the time is."

" Neither do I," he said. " I haven't the faintest idea. That's part of the fun of it."

" Fun ! Mr. Wilburn will be waiting for me."

" A little waiting won't hurt him. I'm not going to consider Dudley Wilburn's feelings . . . if he's got any."

" Oh, Ralph, *can't* you understand ? Everybody's bound to say . . . they can't help saying . . ."

" That I love you ? " He laughed again. " Well, so I do. I want to go on saying it so that you can hear : I love you, Clare, I love you, I love you. . . ."

However she protested, he would only tell her that he loved her ; and as they scrambled down the moonlit hillside together, hand in hand, like two excited children, the intoxication of swift, hazardous movement and of his words of adoration left her so dazed and breathless that she could protest no more. Among the pillars of the beechwood they went as silently as the brown owls that hunted in its shadow, recapturing, in another silent embrace, the ecstasy which she seemed to have lost.

" My darling, when am I going to see you again ? " he said. " To-morrow . . . somehow, somewhere ? We've only two or three minutes more, so we'd better settle that at once."

The question alarmed her. She had not even given a thought to their next meeting ; the moment of her un-spoken avowal had been self-sufficient, unrelated to space or time. She had a feeling that love such as this should continue, as it had begun, in miraculous independence of thought or provision.

" I can't live without seeing you," he said. " I suppose

I must talk to your grandfather about it. Why shouldn't I ride over to Wychbury to-morrow ? "

At the awful definiteness of this proposal her alarm increased. The vision of a formal visit : her grandfather glaring in his armchair, Aunt Cathie, grim and judicial, at his elbow, filled her with terror. At that moment her mind was so numbed and distracted that she couldn't even think of it. She could do nothing but throw herself on his mercy.

" Oh, please, please, don't think of anything like that," she said. " I couldn't bear it. You go so fast : I can't keep pace with you."

" Sooner or later . . ." he reminded her.

She shook her head. " No, no, I couldn't bear it. I couldn't."

" But it's so simple, Clare. I love you. You know that I love you. And you love me."

" Oh, Ralph, Ralph . . ."

" I shall speak to the guv'nor this evening . . . to-morrow morning . . . the first moment I can get him alone."

" No, no, you can't, you mustn't. If you go on like this I shall hate it. I don't want anyone to know, not even Vivien. Can't you see that if anyone knows but us two it'll all be spoilt ? "

He couldn't ; but though he would not admit her arguments, he allowed her to persuade him. These mysterious, incalculable reservations inflamed him the more by adding to the difficulties of his conquest.

" At any rate, there must be somewhere where we can meet," he said. " You can't tell me that you're shut up in a nunnery. Isn't there any other place where you can be found ? "

He was so insistent that, in the end, she told him of her early morning visits to St. Chad's.

" What on earth do you go there for ? " he asked her.

" I go to hear Mass." The word rang through her mind like the tolling of a bell.

" To hear Mass ? " he laughed uneasily. " What does that mean ? You're not a Catholic ? "

" Not a Roman Catholic," she told him. " Mr. Darnay says Mass there every morning."

" Good lord ! " he said ; and the tone of his voice was so awed and bewildered that a new sense of his strangeness and her own insecurity began to trouble her. Not that she loved him less. She still believed utterly, passionately, that she could love no other ; but beyond the blinding flame of this love she divined in him the existence of other mysterious qualities, virtues or deficiencies, integral parts of this overwhelming stranger which might be at variance with herself. She realized that she knew nothing about him : nothing at all except that she loved him. Was love enough ? For this enraptured instant, yes, and yes a thousand times. Yet, as they clung together in the darkness of the yew-shadowed fountain, with Stourford blazing like a great lantern at the end of the alley, her mind was clouded by an uneasiness which arose not only from the echoes of his perplexity, but from her consciousness of the matter that had perplexed him, the religion which, latterly, had dominated her life, and now, at the first breath of human passion, had faded from her mind. She knew this weakness, this betrayal, as a sin that could only be expiated by some signal penance ; the austere figure of Mr. Darnay loomed so pitilessly in her mind that she compelled herself to forget his spiritual imminence in the warm, consoling presence of the man she loved. " For God is Love," she told herself. " We know that God is Love . . ."

That night she and Ralph spoke no more together. Unnoticed they mingled with the crowd that hung about the steps of the moonlit gateway waiting for their carriages, and once more an instinct of self-protection took her to Vivien's side. There, too, a few moments later, Dudley Wilburn found her. In her eyes—perhaps it was fancy—he seemed more staid and self-contained than ever.

"So here you are, Clare," he said, smiling with compressed lips. "I think, for poor Jabez's sake, we'd better say good-bye. Are you ready? Very well, then, I'll wait here for you. Don't be too long."

Five minutes later they were ready to go. Almost to her relief Ralph had disappeared. But Lady Hingston, whom she now regarded in a new and interested light, swooped on her with a swift and brilliant gesture of farewell.

"Now that you've broken the ice," she said, "we shall expect to see more of you. You *do* play tennis, don't you? Vivien will love to have you. There seem to be so few young people about in these days. Ah, Mr. Wilburn! Good-bye, good-bye! It was so sweet of you to come. Vivien, I know you want to speak to Clare before she goes."

Then Vivien took her hand with an enigmatic smile.

"Well, Clare?" she said.

"Oh, Vivien, don't . . ."

Suddenly, with a quick, warm impulse, Vivien kissed her; and Clare, hotly blushing, returned her kiss. Vivien was wonderful. She had never known a girl so bright and generous. Wilburn's hand was on her arm; he drew her gently, firmly away.

And so, once more, they drove into the still, scented lanes. They had driven a long way before Wilburn spoke. In a hard, heavy voice, which seemed to emphasize his remoteness, she heard him asking if she had enjoyed herself. Softly she answered, "Yes." She could not trust herself to say more. But as she sat there beside him, so near and yet so distant, she was thankful for the shadows that hid her face from the waning moon's betrayal.

# BOOK TWO
## THE TIME OF ROSES

# I

## MIDSUMMER DAYS

EVERY morning Clare took her way over the fields to the Saxon chapel, and there, on the edge of the coppice, where his horse stood patiently, tied to the rusty hazels, Ralph would be waiting for her when Mass was over.

At first these morning devotions made him faintly jealous ; they represented a part of her life that he could neither possess nor understand ; for all that he knew of religion had come to him by way of routine in the chapel at Eton, and there was no shred of mysticism in all his mind. With the directness that was part of his principal appeal to her he dared to express a little of this jealousy. She received it gravely ; but he saw that she was pained by the mockery that had crept into his voice, and since nothing in the world could have distressed him more than to have pained her, he soon abandoned his enquiries and accepted her religion as something subtly feminine beyond his comprehension.

It was fortunate that Mr. Darnay's instruction had taught her to regard faith as a matter of Divine Revelation ; for if she had felt it her duty to proselytize she might have found Ralph a difficult subject. As it was, she appreciated the delicacy of his forbearance, and he, when once he realized how integral a part of her life these devotions were, was thankful, at least, that their regular observance brought her to his arms.

And indeed, if he had known it, they even made her more

113

beautiful. She came to him, on those mornings, with eyes full of a shining quietness, with the bloom and hue of a flower whose petals have opened secretly in the night, with an air so sweet and virginal that he almost feared to touch her.

Behind the hazel hedge rose a plantation of thinned larches, and down its alleys of rabbit-cropped turf they would walk together or stand lost in long embraces. The white sky hung low above them ; no birds sang ; the trees held breath. The place was so sequestered, so holy in its quietude that even the tumultuous beating of their hearts seemed impious. In such enraptured moments time passed with incredible speed. No sooner had they met than it was time for Ralph to hurry back to Stourford and join his father on their journey to the works at Wolverbury. Clare, in her sweet reluctance, stood by him while he untied his reins from the hazel boughs and fondled the velvet muzzle of Starlight, his big bay hunter. When he had mounted, Ralph would lean from the saddle and kiss her, while Starlight tossed his head with impatience; and all these kisses were flavoured with the harsh, pleasant odour of the horse's withers. Then he would ride away down the long slope and under the edge of the woods, till she saw nothing but his head rising and falling as he crossed the shoulder of Pen Beacon and dropped into the green cup where the Stourford chimney-smoke rose straight into the air.

Long after she had lost him Clare would stand there without moving. The world, for her, lay under an enchantment stiller and more intense than that of morning. She dreamed, and yet she was awake ; so wide awake, indeed, that all her senses were strained to an unusual acuteness. The hot scent of sweetbriar or trailing honeysuckle pierced her with a joy that she could scarcely bear ; for her heart was still full of her lover's image, his strength, his cleanliness, and the gentleness of his frank eyes.

June passed, and with it summer sank into the languors

of July : a season of thunderous skies, beneath whose pressure and the burden of their own leaves the woods were bowed ; a season of drifting scents ; for now the meadows along the base of the hills were being mowed ; the tall wild grass lay prostrate in swathes, and the crake of the landrails had given place to that of distant mowing-machines which stubbornly, pitilessly devoured their ripening covers. These sounds alone disturbed the silence of daytime. It was as if all the birds had fallen asleep. Sometimes the note of a cuckoo, languid and flattened, floated with bell-like melancholy out of the sky. Only at sunset, when the white dome deepened to a dim luminosity, did the thrushes in the garden at Pen House take heart to sing. But they sang out of thankfulness rather than joy, and soon, as though awed by the universal silence, faltered and were still. Evening fell, and in the hillside copses beyond the mill-pool, its one voice, a lonely night-churn, began his soft, intermittent reeling, spinning the threads of enchantment in which the new lovers were bound.

Already a month had passed ; and yet he could never be sure of her. Again and again he had begged her to let him visit Pen House and interview her grandfather ; she was as obstinate and perverse as she was lovely ; and so light-winged that when he thought he held her, she escaped his clumsy fingers like a butterfly and left him gaping. It was Clare herself who frustrated his well-laid plans ; she wouldn't even accept the invitations to tennis-parties at Stourford which Vivien sent her.

" I suppose you realize that you're making a fool of me," he complained. " One day you do that, and the next you pretend that you love me."

" If I didn't love you," she said, " I should want to go. It's the fact that I love you which makes me so awfully shy. Not shy, exactly. I can't explain it. Oh, Ralph, I wish you could understand ! "

" I can't," he told her flatly. " I'm sick to death of all this secrecy. You're not ashamed of me ? Then, why in God's name can't you be consistent and come to Stourford, where we can be together all the afternoon instead of meeting for a miserable half-hour ? "

" But don't you see," she said, " that's exactly my point ? We shouldn't be together. We shouldn't have a single moment without 'people staring at us. A lot of strange people that I've never seen in my life before. Your mother, too . . . and Vivien."

" Nobody at Stourford's going to eat you," he protested. " You needn't bother your head about mother. And Vivien's a ripper. I've always wanted you two to chum up."

" I know," she confessed, " and I like Vivien awfully. She was perfectly sweet to me that night. But that doesn't make any difference."

" You make me simply mad," he told her. " Do you really mean to say that you'll refuse again ? "

" I'm sorry," she said.

" Sorry ! I don't believe you're sorry in the least. If you refuse to come to Stourford I'm hanged if I'll come to St. Chad's."

She smiled. For though he rode off black with disappointment she knew that, next morning, he would return. She knew that their next meeting would be more ecstatic for the difference between them.

At first she could not accept these ecstasies without a sense of guilt. In former days, when Mass was over, she had sometimes waited in the disused graveyard of St. Chad's ; for the first part of her way homeward lay in the same direction as Mr. Darnay's, and more than once they had walked down the hillside together. But now, as soon as the last words of the office were spoken, she left the church at once, and hurried to their meeting-place with a heart that beat with more than religious emotion. She asked

herself how much of the eagerness with which she set out
every morning to St. Chad's was inspired by the Holy
Sacrament and how much by her desire to meet her lover.
It was a question that she dared not answer ; one that could
only be solved by Mr. Darnay's direction at the confessional.

And yet she could not bring herself to embody it in her
confessions. The rarest beauty of their love, she told
herself, had always consisted in its secrecy from all human
knowledge ; and even though she might think of Mr. Darnay
as priest rather than as man, her acute, instinctive shyness
told her that, if once he knew, something must be irrevocably lost. This was the one part of her life that she could
not surrender to his guidance. It was a secret between
God and herself, too fragile to bear the weight of human
intervention. To Him in prayer, she confessed the doubts
that troubled her, trying to believe that she had made
atonement for a dubious sin, convincing herself, at last,
that this confession was enough.

Ralph's passion seemed to gather strength from her
frustrations ; now he was no longer content with seeing
her once a day. Every evening, when Ellen had removed
the cloth from the dining-room table, when the doctor
nodded or snored in his chair, and Aunt Cathie brooded
over her embroidery frame, Clare would steal away into the
still, luminous night, and pass down the drive to the place
of their appointment. Usually, because of the enchantment of that quiet water, and because it had been the scene
of the first of these nocturnal meetings, she went towards
the mill-pond. She reached it through a breath of meadow
sweet, through fields where the ghost-swifts danced like
mayflies over the silvery swathes ; and Clare in her white
muslins, was like a ghost-moth herself, flitting among the
black alders whose twisted roots ran deep into holes where
chub were lying. At this hour the whole world was full of
white, phantasmal presences. The hedges were piled

with moony elder-flowers, pale campion, plumed cow-parsnip, whose blooms shone as with a phosphorescence fallen from the hot sky, where banks of floating cumulus carried the moonlight hidden in their convolutions.

At night a milky mist rose from the pool's surface. Clare and her lover would stand knee-deep in it, detached from earth, as though they were floating in a cloud. There they would cling together in long silences. It moved her to think that Ralph, a creature whom she judged so infinitely more material than herself, was contented with this silence, and realized, as she did, the impiety of words.

In that diffused moonlight she could better trust herself to meet his eyes, to allow her own to dwell on the modelling of his features. It was thus that she loved to think of them when he was away. And as they stood, she would wonder at her possession, while, through her mind, on another and distant plane of thought, the melody of Schumann's *Mondnacht* floated downward like starlight, filling her eyes with tears and her heart with an emotion that made her feel as if it surely must break.

Sometimes, on starry nights, they would leave the valley and climb high upon the lonely flank of Uffdown, where all the plain lay hidden in mist below them, and they lifted far above it into a sky of tremulous clarity. Sometimes she walked homeward with him through the lanes ; and when they had kissed good-bye, he could not leave her but must turn backward to the very drive-gate of Pen House. Then she would hurry upstairs with lips still tingling from his kisses, and she would undress in the dark, with closed eyes, trying to carry the memory of them with her over the bounds of sleep.

So summer fell away into autumn. And now their meetings were wrapped in an odour of dead leaves, their hot cheeks spattered with rain and swept by winds. In a little while they would no longer be able to see each other in the copse beside St. Chad's, nor could Clare find excuses for leaving Pen House at night. Beneath the pressure of these restrictions Ralph was growing restless; and Clare began to see for herself that their secrecy could not be maintained much longer. He pressed her, and she refused him so often that, in the end, it seemed as if they must quarrel again.

"I'm not going to put up with this much longer, Clare," he said. "You know jolly well that you're the only thing that matters to me. It isn't as if we didn't know our own minds, either. That's what makes it ridiculous. I'm quite ready to admit that I should be a nuisance at Pen House. With the doctor ill and all that I realize that they shouldn't be bothered with a pair of lunatics like us. But Stourford's different. I've told you, it's just like a big hotel. We all go our own ways, and nobody takes the least notice of anyone else. Even if any of them were critical, which they won't be, it needn't make any difference to us. I'm not a kid, Clare, though you treat me like one. I'm my own master. I've capital and income of my own—Aunt Gillian's money—and I've no need to be beholden to the guv'nor or anyone else. There's no reason on earth why we shouldn't be married to-morrow if we wished to."

"Oh, Ralph," she said, "but there *is*; there are a hundred reasons. I believe I know your mother better than you do."

"For heaven's sake, leave mother out of it."

"You can't leave your mother out of it, Ralph; you know you can't."

"Then, don't, my dear child, don't! That's what I've told you from the first. The sooner she's let into it the better."

"I wish you'd try to see what I mean," she said. "The whole point is that I'm just nobody."

"You're nothing of the sort. I love you, and I'm going to marry you. Isn't that enough?"

" And you're somebody," she persisted.   " Your father's
an important man ; he's a baronet."

" Baronet be hanged !  He gave thirty thousand to the
Wolverbury hospital ; that's all *that* means."

" But he *is*.  Your mother knows it, if you don't.  She'll
expect you to marry somebody like Dorothy Powys . . ."

" Dorothy Powys !  I'd see her damned first.  My dear
child, what rot you talk ! "

" It isn't rot.  If George died . . ."

" But George won't die, my dear.  And if he did, it
wouldn't make any difference.  George and Eleanor have
two twins already.  If you go on like this they'll have a
dozen by the time we're married."

She shook her head :  " That makes no difference to the
fact that none of them will think I'm good enough for you."

" Perverse little devil ! "

He was really angry, and yet, in her company, he could
not keep his anger for long.  He saw that it was no good
arguing with her ;  she was illogical ;  as soon as he had
cornered her by some reasonable argument she flew off at
a tangent or hurriedly completed the circle, arriving at the
precise point from which they had begun.  Sooner or later
he knew that he would have to force her hand.

# II

## THE BELFRY

DURING the last days of September, for the first time since
Clare's return, the health of Dr. Weir had been failing
steadily.  A bad patch, he called it, dismissing Aunt
Cathie's apprehensions with his usual brusqueness ;  but,
even so, he had consented, almost willingly, to another
consultation.  " It costs nothing, anyway," he had said,

as though that were the most important aspect of the business.

Next day Lloyd Moore came out again to Wychbury. " There's nothing fresh to report," he told Aunt Cathie. " Of course he's weaker than when I saw him two years ago ; but then, he's two years older. A wonderful man, Miss Weir, a wonderful man."

Aunt Cathie shook her head. She did not believe him. Experience had given her an insight, transcending science in all the minutest mechanisms of the old man's life. Watching him, she knew that he was changing under her eyes. Now, for hours at a time, he would sit without movement or volition. Not even the commercial pages of the *North Bromwich Courier* could hold his attention for long. The paper would slip from his hands on to the floor, and when she picked it up and gave it to him, he would not remember what he had been reading. Time after time, when she heard his bell's imperious jangle, she would hurry to the bedroom, expecting disaster, and he would only stare at her crossly, as if she were intruding, or had awakened him. And then, as likely as not, he'd grumble : " Well, Catherine, since you're here you may as well fetch me the black dispatch-box." The black dispatch-box contained his will. All afternoon he would lie there, fingering the stiff legal paper, as though it made him feel that the money to which it related was actually in his hands.

The sum of these disquieting symptoms cumulated in a burden which Aunt Cathie could no longer share with Thirza Rudge alone. One evening she took Clare into her confidence. Her red eyelids, her compressed mouth, the disjointed, awkward words in which she disclosed her fears, betrayed a degree of suffering which Clare was helpless to assuage. Aunt Cathie made that quite clear. " Of course *you* can't do anything," she said ; " but I thought I'd better tell you, so that you should be prepared . . . sup-

posing anything happens. Of course you won't mention
a word of this to Ellen," she added, " there's no reason why
the village people should be given something to talk about."

All through the next day Clare was troubled by a recurrent
vision of Aunt Cathie's anguished face and echoes of her
voice. They invaded her brain as she knelt in the dank and
stony air of St. Chad's, pleading for intercession ; they
shadowed the moments of her morning meeting with Ralph,
obstinately challenging her right to careless happiness amid
such suffering ; so that when he told her that evening that
he had arranged to take a week's holiday from Wolverbury,
Ralph found her unresponsive and could not understand.

" You sound as if you didn't care," he told her. " For
God's sake, tell me what I've done now ! "

She smiled. It was so like him to imagine that the fault
was his. She fondled his fair head as she began to tell him
what had happened ; and then, before she was half way
through with her story, she found that she was crying in
his arms ; not because she loved her grandfather and
feared to lose him, nor yet entirely out of sympathy for Aunt
Cathie, but rather because, poised between active poles of
joy and dread, of intense happiness and imminent sorrow, of
love and death, her mind became a field fit for fulmination,
and discharged its emotional content like an empty tropical
sky where nightlong lightning flickers. At last she was so
shaken by sobs that she was forced to abandon the story
altogether. She huddled close to Ralph's breast, allowing
her weakness to be lost in the comfort of his strength, which,
of itself, persuaded her to abandon the control for which she
had been fighting.

Ralph had never seen her cry before ; the steady impact
of her sobs filled him with unusual tenderness. They
revealed Clare, whose mettlesome spirit had already tantal-
ized him, as a creature capable of equally adorable weakness.
This revelation flattered his own strength : she was so

little, so pitiful ; it was his pride and privilege to protect
her. The physical surrender of her grief filled him with
an exquisite, intolerable mixture of emotions, with pain
and triumph, with gentleness and fierce desire.

" It's only," she said at last, " that I feel I can't leave
Aunt Cathie to face it all alone. Even if she doesn't want me.
You see, I'm so helpless. It was silly of me to cry like that.
I'm quite ashamed of myself."

" It was lovely of you," he declared. " Thank goodness
you didn't have to cry alone. That's what I'm for."

She gazed into his dim eyes. His gentleness and generosity had touched her. She felt that she had been cruel to
damp his enthusiasms with those weak tears.

" If everything's all right," she whispered, " I'll meet
you at the Sling Mill, immediately after lunch to-morrow.
But, darling, if you don't mind, I'd rather you didn't come
to St. Chad's in the morning."

And when the morrow came she was there before him,
in a muslin frock, with flounced skirt, puffed shoulders,
lace bertha, and a small sailor hat perched upon the top of
her high coiffure. The Sling Mill had been abandoned
many years before ; its windows were broken, the yard
overgrown with grass and weeds that had sprung between
abandoned mill-stones which lay there half embedded like
broken monuments of some prehistoric tribe. Against this
background of age and desolation Clare's vivid youth shone
like a flower. But still her eyes were serious.

" I think he's better," she told him. " But Aunt Cathie's
curious. She won't say another word, or tell me how I
can help her. It's almost as if she were jealous, though, of
course, it can't be that."

" But now you'll forget all about it," he said. " Clare,
do you realize that this is the first time we've ever been
properly alone ? You make me want to run away with you
and hide you somewhere. Now that I've got you I shan't

let you go in a hurry. Nobody but you and me, for six whole hours. And what a day for us ! "

It was an afternoon of blue and flying white, too clear, too brilliant to last. In the pit of the Sling Valley the air had been motionless ; but as they climbed the slope to eastward, a resinous wind came singing through the firs. Already the fronds of bracken were turning brittle, the foxglove spires were set with bulging seed-vessels ; only, on the tufted bank at the edge of the wood, hare-bells and sheep's-bit scabious danced in the bright air. Behind them they saw the dome of Uffdown ablaze with gorse, and Clare, to prove the proverb, must stop to take his breathless kisses.

On the top of Bromsley, by a broken gate, they halted for breath, and the west wind, blowing through Clare's muslin sleeves and tossing her dark hair, filled her whole body with a draught of life ; so clean it was, so cool, so swift, so stimulant, that it washed out of her mind all consciousness of her old narrow world. Around them, in every direction save where the shoulder of Uffdown crossed the sky, lay another, new and spacious, through which their spirits seemed free to expand down vistas of illimitable hope. The lightness of hill-air released imagination, the wideness of the land imposed no limits on its flight. They were alone, and joint possessors of a virgin earth in which even familiar places seemed too remote to have any claim on their uplifted hearts ; so that the grey clot of smoke that hid North Bromwich, and all that yellowish pall beneath which the Black Country stifled, were to them no more material than the shadows cast by slow-sailing clouds that mottled the dun green of the south.

In the field beyond their gate they found a point of vantage, a grassy knoll, that might well have been a barrow. On the slope of this Ralph lay, with his head in her muslin lap, a grass-stalk between his teeth, lazily recounting the names of distant hills over which the clouds came sailing.

" That's the Black Mountain," he told her : " the flat line which drops like the edge of a pit-bank. Then comes the Forest. The Powyses have some grouse-shooting there. Nothing to shout about, George says. And just beyond that there's a grey hog's-back—you'd think it was cloud, but it isn't—that's where the Welsh water they're making such a fuss about is coming from."

" I know," she said. " There's a river there . . ."

" Of course there's a river. That's how they get the water."

" And that's how I got my name," she told him. " There are three rivers. One's called the Claerwen."

" A jolly name," he said. " It's just right for you. I suppose you and the river are the only Claerwens in the world. But I love to call you Clare all the same."

For the moment she did not hear him. She was thinking of what Thirza Rudge had told her : how Lydiatt and her mother had hidden themselves in those mountains, in that low, blue cloud, immediately after their romantic elopement. How adventurously happy they must have been ! She wondered. . . . But by this time Ralph was asking her what the word Claerwen meant.

" It means clear-white," she said. " Do you think it's right for me ? " She bent over and kissed him.

" White is all wrong," he murmured, through her kisses ; " but clear . . . yes. That's the best part of you. One of them. You're as clear as spring-water. And I'm so thirsty, Clare."

So the hours passed in love-making, in quiet laughter, in long silences. Each moment, even their most trivial, seemed self-sufficient, lifted, by adoration above the ordinary computation of time. A heavier bank of cloud was blown between them and the sun ; the western face of the hill on which they were seated became too chilly for comfort ; so they left their barrow to go in search of tea. They found it in a cottage at the cross-road where the Halesby turnpike tumbles down into Bromsley hamlet, in a villainous little parlour which, even in that dry season, smelt of last winter's damp. When they had finished tea Ralph lit his pipe. Whenever she passed the door the cottage-woman looked in at them and smiled. Clare wondered if it would seem rude to close the door.

"You'd almost think she knew who we were," she whispered.

Ralph laughed at her alarm : "It's only that she knows how happy we are, and wants a little of it for herself, poor dear !"

Toward sunset they descended the slope once more. By this time the wind had fallen. The scents of fir and bracken lay low upon the hillside. It was so still that they could hear the rustle of the brake through which they moved and the clatter of pebbles that their feet dislodged. The squeal of a rabbit on which a stoat had sprung was echoed by the shrill call of a jay.

When Ralph told her the meaning of these sounds the wood became suddenly horrible to Clare. She took his hand as they hurried on together. The valley was cool and quiet as an empty well ; its silence intent, as though the mill's broken windows were watchful eyes. They spoke, as by consent, with voices subdued to defeat the ears of listeners. Under the trees, above the noiseless water, midges hung in clouds. There was something in the place and in the moment that filled Clare with inquietude.

"Do let us go," she said. "I've no idea what time it is."

He laughed. "Neither have I. I left my watch at home on purpose."

His innocent wickedness disarmed her. "I'm sure it's late," she said. "I hate this place too ; there's something wrong with it. Let's climb up over Uffdown and go home that way."

"I've something I want to show you first," he said mysteriously.

He wouldn't tell her what his secret was. Tempted by curiosity she allowed him to persuade her, to lead her down past the glassy fish-ponds toward the mouth of the valley.

"We're going miles out of our way," she reminded him.

"Miles," he agreed; "but it's still early, and we're nearly there."

"Nearly where?"

For answer he pointed to a white drive-gate, on the left of the road. He opened it for her, and they passed into a wood through which a wheel-track, brown with beech-mast, went winding like a brook in level fields. Behind them a yaffle gave its ringing laugh; before, a squirrel listened, with a beech-nut in his hands, then bounded off, trailing his feathery brush. The place had been secret enough indeed until they violated its sanctuary.

"But surely this must be the back-drive of Uffdown Manor?" Clare said.

He nodded silently.

"Then it's private: we're trespassing. I don't even know the Rentons. We'd better turn back."

"The Rentons left in June," he told her. "It's been empty for three months: nobody here but the gardener. You might trust me anyway."

The drive ended in a block of stables enclosing a square yard. The buildings were of red brick, with wrought iron window-grills and toothed string-courses. A solemn clock-face, in the gable above their arched entrance, dictated order to the whole. As they approached, it chimed five, with long pauses between the strokes, which seemed to reprove Clare's impatience and insist on the futility of hurry.

" You see, we're not so late after all," Ralph said, and then, with a more lively interest : " Fourteen loose boxes. Solid, well-ventilated place. These old fellows knew what they owed to their horses. It beats Stourford hollow. Come along ! "

They skirted the back of the house. " Don't look yet," he told her. " I want you to see it first of all from the front. Just shut your eyes and let me lead you."

He put his arm round her and she surrendered herself to his guidance. She guessed that they had crossed a gravel drive and thirty yards of turf. Then he stopped suddenly, kissed her eyes, and told her to open them.

Set against a background of tarnished elms and chestnuts she saw a miracle of sober loveliness : a Queen Anne manor, on whose bricks some hoar lichen had dusted a silvery bloom. For all the mass of its three stories, the gravity of its horizontal lines, it seemed graceful and fragile ; for the façade was lighted by rows of many-paned tall windows, with sashes and lattices painted white. To these, as also to the fluted pillars of the porch and the stone coping of the wide-angled central gable, the white sky gave an aspect of almost airy lightness. No cunning Georgian or Victorian had violated the design's virginity by the addition of wings or the planting of ivy or ampelopsis. The house stood there as it had been built, the creation of a wise and civilized taste ; and the trees that sheltered it, chestnut and elm, and sycamore- had kept their distance, as though respecting its integrity, leaving it to emerge alone and unsullied from lawns as smooth as water, so smooth that they might almost have reflected the walls that rose from them.

Clare drew her breath with surprise and with delight. From every line of it there breathed an air of peace, of benevolence, of wise and settled happiness that neutralized the sinister mood which had overtaken her by the mill. They stood with arms about each other, surveying it in silence. One wide-armed cedar reached benignantly above them.

" I want you to see the rest while the light lasts," he said. " It's like our luck to have lost the sun."

A garden of clipped yews and long box-edged borders ; within them Michaelmas daisies made a haze of amethyst. " I can smell lavender," said Clare. " And rosemary," he told her. He picked her a sprig of it, hued with the grey of evening ; its odours strangely permeated the still air. I shall always remember this scent, she told herself. Remembrance . . .

The straggling September borders spent their opulence of old gold against a hazel hedge with cobs in clusters. Beyond it an orchard, knee-deep with aftermath, in which moon-pale apples lay where they had fallen. The trees were haggard and twisted with age. It seemed as if the hoary lichen that made the house ethereal had spread its bloom on everything, so silvery, so unreal was the light. A brown owl whinnied in the coppice. They did not realize that the moon was in the sky.

" Well, what do you think of it ? " Ralph said at last. " Will it do ? " He spoke with a practical tone that broke her dream.

" I think it's the loveliest thing I've ever seen," she said. " Far better than Stourford."

" Oh, Stourford's a sham," he answered : " we all know that. And we're sham too ; that's why it suits us so well. But this is the real thing. I've had a good look at it : been over here half a dozen times during the last month. How do you think it would do for us ? "

" For us ? " Against her will she had taken fright immediately.

" It's for sale. I thought of buying it . . . if you like it."

" But it's huge," she said. " I couldn't dare to think

of it. And it's so beautiful. I should be afraid of spoiling it."

"*You* . . . spoil it?" He smiled at her. "And it isn't really big. I've been all over it. Of course it wants alterations, bathrooms and that. But the thing that took me most was the stabling : fourteen loose boxes, as I told you. And it's so handy for Wychbury—the station, I mean —when you want to box your horses anywhere." He changed his tone suddenly. "Clare, do you think we should be happy here?"

"You shouldn't ask me," she said.

"Then that's settled. I shall take it. I'll break the news to the guv'nor to-night."

"To-night?" Again her frightened instinct rose against him ; but this time he was determined to have his way.

"Just let me tell Aunt Cathie first," she pleaded.

He had had enough of her reservations and was merciless. "You can tell as many people as you like," he said. "If one knows, everybody knows. I feel that I've got you at last !"

As they tramped back to Wychbury, their minds aflame with visions of that unimaginable future, the sky grew dark ; for now that the wind had died the sailing clouds lost way and accumulated, obscuring the moon. By the time they reached the lights of the village the first drops fell. There followed a deluge of cold, hill-born rain that made Clare's flimsy sleeves cling to her shoulders. She grew alarmed, thinking not so much of the ruin of her frock as of the difficulty of concealing it from Aunt Cathie.

"I told you we were late," she said. "That clock must have been wrong."

"But you wouldn't have missed the Manor?"

"Of course not. This wretched muslin sticks so. I feel like a drowned rat."

He suggested that they should take shelter in the nearest cottage. At once her modesty was up in arms. " Everybody in Wychbury knows me," she said. He rallied her on her unreasonableness : " Even when we've got so far as choosing a house you still keep up these silly pretences."

" I know that I'm foolish," she said. " It's only that I can't get used to the idea all at once. You must be patient with me ! "

The rain beat so persistently that she could not see to pick her way between the puddles that swamped her boots. There was something triumphant and final about its savagery as though, in this sudden outburst, it had definitely accomplished the rout of summer and the ruin of the year. At that moment millions of leaves were being beaten to their death : by to-morrow they would lie sodden upon the mould of other years, to-morrow the trees would show their nakedness and the whole face of the land be changed. In her soaked wretchedness it seemed to Clare that the nature of their passion must change with the destruction of the beauty on which it had been nourished.

Raising her eyes for one moment she saw the sky blackened by the squat tower of Wychbury church. It offered her a chance of pulling her thoughts together.

" We could shelter in here. It's sure to be empty ; they never shut it till seven, and I don't think the rain can go on like this much longer."

The church door was unlocked. They entered together. As they advanced over the dry stone flags Ralph laid his hand on her arm. The wet sleeve clung so closely that through it his fingers could feel the softness and warmth of her skin. The sensation disturbed him. Out in that streaming twilight she had been no more than a presence ; this intimate warm contact restored her body to him ; but when he tried to take her in his arms she shivered and strained away from him.

"You're cold," he said; "you'd better take my coat."

"No, it's not that," she said, releasing herself.

She left him to find an explanation for himself. Dimly he saw her move to a pew on the south of the nave. She sank to her knees and crossed herself. Then, with bowed head, she knelt in silence.

He stared at her, full of wonder and a queer hostility. The jealousy with which her morning visits to St. Chad's had troubled him returned, in a more reasoned shape. He was ashamed of it. He told himself that he did not grudge her these religious emotions ; they were a feminine weakness from which not even the rational Vivien was exempt ; only he felt it a sacrilege—that was the word that occurred to him—that anything should take precedence of their love, and steal her from him. In that dim church, with its massive pillared nave, he found the stony strength of his enemy made visible. He wanted to pit his own strength against it.

And Clare, when she had finished her praying, knelt on, removed from him, torn in spirit, conscious of the hurt she had inflicted. She guessed the anger that was in his mind and longed to soften it ; and yet she saw that her love and her religion, each of which claimed a complete devotion, were, for the moment, incompatibles. It had been a mistake to let Ralph enter the church at her side. Alone in St. Chad's, the contest had not presented itself so forcibly ; now that she saw him baffled and glooming in the transept she knew that there was only one way in which the difference could be evaded : by keeping the two emotions in compartments rigidly separate. So she knelt on, desperately thinking, losing the consolation of either, while the rain hammered on the lead roof and thrashed the painted windows.

At last, mastered by sheer pity, she rose and joined him. She slipped her arm softly into his. He did not respond to this timid advance. He was afraid of her. There was a strangeness between them. He spoke in a hurt voice :

" It doesn't sound like stopping. If you're not too wet, I think we might as well sit down for a minute or two."

" Of course." She wanted to make it clear that there was no difference, to reassure him ; but as soon as she spoke the words sounded as if they had been addressed to an acquaintance, or at most, an ordinary friend. Once to admit this was to destroy the illusion of their love completely. She was silent, feeling that, for the present, nothing that she said could ring true. As they sat together she wondered what he was thinking. If their love had been all that she imagined she would have known. That was untrue. They loved each other as no two people had ever loved before. It wasn't her fault. Ever since that moment at the mill some sinister influence had overhung them. And now it was getting late. Late, and so cold.

In the porch she heard a footfall, a sound of coughing and a wiping of feet. A quick alarm seized her. This was worse than ever ; they were going to be locked in for the night. No, it couldn't be that : it was too early. But as she rose hurriedly the door creaked on its hinges. Somebody was coming in. An unreasoning panic took her ; she was like a child discovered in some mischief. The empty church offered only one place of concealment : the staircase that led to the belfry, which pierced the massive tower in front of them. Into this slit-like opening she passed, and Ralph, wondering what madness she was up to, followed quickly. The air within was stony and stifled.

" My precious child, what do you think you're doing ? " he whispered.

" Heaven knows, I don't," she whispered back. The ludicrousness of the whole situation overcame her. She began to laugh helplessly. " I ran in like a rabbit," she said. " It's too ridiculous ! " And with that laughter they were themselves again, or entered once more the plane of their illusion. He knew it as well as she did. Standing on the step below, he put his arms about her, kissing her cool neck. With lips together they listened to the ping of the intruder's hobnails crossing the nave. A moment later she freed herself from his arms and vanished, ghostlike, up the spiral above him. He followed, wondering what new game of coquetry she was playing, and found her awaiting him, breathless, in the belfry. Above their heads the mouths of eight great bells yawned cavernously.

" I've never seen them before," she said. " How huge they are ! "

Ralph struck a vesta and held it up to examine the gaping cups of bronze : the largest seemed at least four feet in diameter. Each was inscribed with elegant eighteenth century lettering. By matchlight he read the inscriptions and spoke them softly for Clare to hear.

" I . AM . THE . FIRST . ALTHOUGH . BUT . SMALL.
I . WILL . BE . HEARD . ABOVE . YOU . ALL.

I . SEND . TO . BED . THE . SICKE . REPENT.
IN . HOPE . OF . LIFE .. WHEN . BREATH . IS . SPENT.

I . TO . THE . CHURCH . THE . LIVING . CALL.
AND . TO . THE . GRAVE . DOTH . SUMMON . ALL."

" Rather grisly, aren't they ? " he said. " Some of them have initials at the end ; but on this big chap there's something else." He struck another match. " Yes, I've got it : *Aaron Hackett fecit.* 1765. I wonder if that's an ancestor of Edward Willis ? Hackett is their family name. Willis, Hackett and Willis. Hello . . ." He started suddenly. " What the deuce are they up to now ? "

A rope tautened and scraped the hole in the oak floor through which it passed, communicating its movement to the mountings of the great bass bell whose inscription he had read last. There followed a groan of old wood in distress as the giant began to swing in its oak hanging, and then, as the clapper smote its concave bronze, a volume of sound so monstrous that it seemed as though their eardrums must give way. In that small chamber there was no room for anything but these cruel vibrations. They broke forth angrily, then swooped, swerved, hovered, searching each corner of the belfry for some living thing whose senses they might overpower.

Clare and Ralph stood deafened among these stormy waves of sound. A ringing-practice, she thought at first. She pictured Mr. Hemus and his ringers below, each man standing to his woolly rope. If one bell were so monstrous, a practice would be hell let loose in that restricted space. But when the last pulsation had died down to a meditative hum, like that of a great tuning-fork, there was silence for a moment. Then, suddenly the rasping and creaking began again. The bass bell swung. Once more the belfry was filled with a torment of sound.

"I can't stand this," Ralph shouted. "Come along." She saw his lips shape the words and followed him. The echoes pursued them malignantly down the spiral steps. He had been speaking and laughing all the time. Now, of a sudden, his voice became audible :

"It's a passing-bell," he was saying. "I suppose some poor devil's dead. It must be someone of importance, or they wouldn't do it at this time. I wonder who it is."

Again the great bell boomed. Clare felt once more the unaccountable dread that had crept over her by the deserted mill. But this time she knew the meaning of it. Her heart stood still.

"It's my grandfather," she said. "Oh, Ralph . . ."

He answered almost angrily : "Why do you imagine such things ? I can't think what's wrong with you to-day."

"It's true," she said. "It's true. I know it. It's

George Vigors, the sexton. He worshipped grandpapa. I know when it happened, too," she went on, as if she were speaking to herself. " Up at the mill : I felt there was something wrong. Oh, poor, poor Aunt Cathie ! " She put her hands to her eyes and began to cry quietly. It was for Aunt Cathie that she cried ; for pity, not for grief. For the second time that day he had to comfort her.

Emerging from the staircase door they saw the sandstone pillars of the nave illumined with a pale bloom of moonlight. The storm had passed. They left the church together. All through the village he took her arm, and now she made no protest. Soon they were climbing the steep lane to Pen House. Beneath them, in the mist that lay on Wychbury, the big bell went on booming, slowly, heavily, as befitted the death of an aged man.

## III

### SHADOWS

In the middle of the afternoon, just before the falling of the breeze, Dr. Weir died. He died as he had lived : alone. On the tick of five, Mrs. Rudge, entering his room with a pot of tea and four fingers of dry toast, found him propped up in bed, with fallen jaw and eyes staring full into the empty orbits of the articulated skeleton which hung on the opposite wall and which his spare frame now so closely resembled. In the last moments his fingers had closed on the pages of his will, as though he had done his best to take it with him.

One look was enough for Thirza Rudge. She knew : for, in her time, she had buried a husband and five children. She put down the tea-tray, crossed the room on tiptoe, carefully closed his eyes, removed the will from his stiffening fingers, and folded the lean hands decently upon his chest. It would never 'a' done, she thought, for Miss Cathie to have seen him like that. Next she pulled down the blinds, as though she were dutifully concealing some indecency, and lit a candle, by the light of which she patted his nightshirt and bedclothes as if she were preparing him for some momentous interview. Then, the preliminaries of her office completed, she took a long draught of the unwanted tea, to steady herself, closed the door quietly behind her, as though the old wolf might still snap at her for her clumsiness, and waddled away down the hall passage to find his daughter. As she went, she picked up her bunchy apron and mopped her eyes with it. " Poor dear lamb, too ! " she sighed.

Aunt Cathie was " resting " in the drawing-room. She always rested in the afternoon when Mrs. Rudge was on duty. She was sitting in the low, waisted chair that she fancied ; a little cylindrical cushion behind her neck ; beneath her feet a bead-work stool with clawed feet. On her lap lay the antimacassar that the cushion had displaced and the embroidery frame over which her hands were folded. Her mouth was open. She slept so quietly that she scarcely seemed to breathe at all. But her eyes were closed. That was the difference. Otherwise, as Thirza confided later in the day to Mrs. Harbord, there wasn't a button to choose between the two of them. It was as if sleep and death had conspired to split the difference in years, to reduce the features of father and daughter, of middle age and senility, to one sinister mean. The likeness gave Mrs. Rudge a turn. She touched Aunt Cathie's shoulder. Aunt Cathie woke and fumbled for consciousness.

" Why, Thirza," she said, with a spurious air of briskness, " you came in so quietly that I never heard you ! I was just wondering if you'd dropped off to sleep. It must be nearly five."

Thirza averted her eyes from the yawn that Aunt Cathie could not quite suppress.

" I've just taken in his tea, Miss Cathie," she said solemnly. " He's gone. Poor soul, too ! "

" Thirza . . . What do you mean ? "

She knew well enough what Thirza meant. The words were a protest springing instinctively from that part of her consciousness which, for five years and more, had disowned reality. Now this same instinct mustered all its strength to fight for time, to soften the blow by denying comprehension.

" He must have 'a' passed away a good half-hour since," said Thirza. " And now he's at peace, Miss Cathie, poor old body." Feeling her words inadequate, she added : " He's a lovely sight, Miss. I shouldn't be surprised if it wasn't in his sleep."

Aunt Cathie rose unsteadily to her feet. The embroidery frame fell to the carpet. Thirza, breathing heavily, picked it up. In the mind of Aunt Cathie the dread word echoed emptily. Gone . . . gone ! She could not hold it. In her brain there opened a core of central emptiness that spread its boundaries till it possessed the whole. She could not think ; she could not speak ; her mind was as blank as if she had died herself. This state was neither grief nor pity ; it was annihilation. She stood there childishly, stupidly helpless. Thirza took her arm.

" Now, do 'ee set down," she cooed, " and I'll bring you a nice strong pot of tea. Thy will, not mine, O God," she added, with apparent irrelevance.

The text meant nothing to Aunt Cathie. For years on end she had been stiffening her courage with props and stays of conscious effort, reinforcing the pride of her martyrdom with that iron sense of duty which was her substitute for religion. Within this formidable structure she had felt herself fit to face calamity with confidence, even though its grimness isolated her from the rest of her kind. And now, bewildered and only half awake, she saw this creation of wasted strength and sacrifice crashing to earth above her head. Her mind, adapted and fixed to the ideal of independence, continued its vain struggles, like the tail of a lizard that goes on twitching when it has been severed from the trunk but her body, swayed by some deeper, physical source of energy, impelled her to seek refuge in Mrs. Rudge.

" Oh, Thirza, Thirza . . ." she cried.

And Thirza gathered into her arms this angular woman whose soft and childish limbs she had once fondled. Tears flowed over Thirza's old, puckered cheeks ; her face was like a fondant melting in the sun ; her lax mouth worked spasmodically.

" Don't 'ee, don't 'ee now," she cooed, relapsing into the idiom of Aunt Cathie's babyhood. " Don't 'ee, my handsome ! "

For her the broken creature whose moods and asperities she had supported for years was now the child whom she had nursed in infancy : for Aunt Cathie Thirza's arms were once again a refuge and a protection. They clung together in the darkening drawing-room, comforted by that communion ; two creatures, one of whom could hardly hope to live for many years, and one whose life was more than half spent, reduced to equality by the presence of death. Neither of them gave a thought to Clare. She belonged to another generation, immune from these sombre admonitions.

" He looks a rare treat," Mrs. Rudge moistly murmured at last. " I've seen a' many corpses in my time, Miss Cathie, but never a one that looked more lovely than the doctor. Innocent as a babe unborn : that's what he do look ! " She took Aunt Cathie's arm. " Now do 'ee come along of me, Miss, and have a peep at him."

Aunt Cathie shuddered : " Not, now, Thirza, not yet,"

she said desperately. She pulled her wits together. "We must do something at once."

Even to the macabre mind of Thirza this proposal was a relief. She became at once a counsellor of experience who knew the moves of the game.

"I'll send that Ellen down along to my friend," she said. Even in this emergency the taboo of Mrs. Harbord's anonymity must be respected. "She makes a regular business of laying them out. She's a knowledgeable woman, and clean as paint. Many's the time she's said to me, Miss Cathie: 'Night or day, Mrs. Rudge, it's all the same, I'll come for the doctor.' Then old Jabez had better run off for Mr. Wilkins. I mind the doctor saying that Wilkins had 'a' got his measure—he'd always have his joke, poor soul, too !— but I reckon Mr. Wilkins 'ld like to have a squint at him just the same . . . and, my dear life ! if I wasn't forgetting the mourning and the gloves."

"Ellen had better call at the post-office too," Aunt Cathie murmured dreamily. "I must let Mr. Wilburn know at once."

Mrs. Rudge did not hear her. She had just discovered that the blinds were not pulled down. She waddled to the window and lowered them scrupulously. Aunt Cathie, suppressing a movement of irritation, scribbled her wire to Wilburn in the dark. Thirza took it from her and disappeared.

For a long while Aunt Cathie stood aimlessly in the middle of the room. Outside, rain had begun to fall. The sound of it, pattering on the ivy and lashing, in sudden gusts, the blinded window-panes, evoked a memory of all the years of fortitude and repression that she had suffered there. Now all that central portion of her life was blank confusion, a waste from which the purpose had gone. She could not focus the details of a monotony so vast; only its general greyness and triviality survived. For half her life she had been bound to their barren futile routine. Now she was free, and her freedom promised an equal sterility. Too late, too late . . . Awed and disconcerted by the future, her mind clutched backward at past happiness. She saw herself sitting at the piano with Lydiatt bending over her, his hands on hers, his face pressed against her cheek. She shivered at the remembrance. There, in the doorway, Sylvia smiled and mocked her. Sylvia or Clare. Poor little Clare! Clare too, in the end, must come to this. Everyone—everyone. . . . The darkness was full of ghosts, and life as ghostly as death. Ruthlessly undoing Thirza's pious labour she pulled up the blind. And still the rain fell drearily in the twilight.

An instinct more deeply rooted than these reflections reminded her that the antimacassar that she had folded on her knees before she slept lay rumpled on the floor. She picked it up, and smoothed it, and replaced it. She punched the indented cushion into shape and put it on the sofa to which it rightly belonged. She placed the chairs in proper order, and closed her writing-desk. The tea-tray? How stupid of her! Thirza had not brought it.

When the mechanical workings of her brain were satisfied that all was in order, she passed out into the dim hall and surveyed it with the scrupulous care of ordinary days, remembering Ellen's perverse habit of leaving the carriage umbrella on the wrong side of the entrance and stowing her goloshes under a chair instead of in the cupboard. And all the time her ordered progress was bringing her nearer to the doctor's door which she always entered at this hour. Each afternoon of late she had opened it with an awed uncertainty. Now the uncertainty had vanished, but the awe was more terrible than anything she had known or imagined. Sooner or later the dreadful moment must be faced. She could not face it alone, like this. Why had she rejected Thirza's wise and kindly offer to escort her? She could not bring herself to go and find Thirza in the kitchen ; for, if she did so, she knew that she would cry. She stood there for a moment helpless, paralysed. Then, with a supreme effort of courage, she composed her trembling lips and passed inside.

## IV

### BLINDS DOWN

As Clare turned the corner of the drive, the two black Wellingtonias, wakeful in moonlight, gave a sudden shudder and rained upon her head drops that were like heavy tears. The long house lay silent and placid as ever ; a light was burning, as usual, behind the blinds of the doctor's room. It seemed to her that if he were really dead that light would have been extinguished. And yet she knew. She knew with an increasing certainty as she hurried through the empty hall and crept upstairs to change her sopping clothes ; but even into that sanctuary the unusual quality of the silence penetrated, so that when once she had reached it she was loth to leave it, for fear of encountering someone who would tell her the dreadful truth. The thought of such a meeting and the agony of finding words to deal with it were enough to bring her to the verge of tears ; and that seemed strange, for she was honest enough to remember that she had never really loved her grandfather nor thought of him as anything but an alien and neutral figure, a presence rather than a man.

It struck her suddenly that, at least, she ought to pray. She knelt beside her bed and besought God for the rest of his soul. As she prayed she thought how he would have hated it ; she could almost hear his short, destructive laugh ; and yet the action mysteriously steadied her. When she rose from her knees she knew that it was her plain duty to go and find Aunt Cathie and share as much of the burden as she might be allowed to bear. Fortified in this resolution she made a tour of the desolate house in search of her. She visited the dining-room, the drawing-room, even Aunt Cathie's bedroom in vain. As she stood hesitating at the doctor's door, it opened quietly, as though moved by some spiritual mechanism, and Aunt Cathie herself appeared.

This was the critical moment, in which, it had seemed to Clare, both of them must be involved in some unbearable tenderness. They stood in the dusk of the narrow passage, each blocking the other's way.

" Aunt Cathie, dearest," Clare began, then stopped ; she could say no more.

" Is that you, Clare ? "

Aunt Cathie's voice was firm and unemotional.

She could only answer : " Yes." The syllable sounded feeble and pathetic. She had come to this encounter with an open heart, prepared to prove herself, to fulfil the utmost demands that could be made upon her affection ; she had not doubted that Aunt Cathie would receive her with an equal frankness and generosity. Evidently she was mistaken. The silence that followed made her feel not so much hurt as foolish.

But Aunt Cathie's moment of weakness had passed. During the half-hour that she had spent in that terrible room she had compassed the spiritual evolution of half a lifetime. At first she had sounded depths of desolation and despair, sobbing her heart out, like a lonely child, beside her father's bed. Even as she knelt there she had seemed to hear his voice in its strong, half-bitter kindliness : " Now, Catherine, no nonsense ! " It was almost as if he had spoken the words aloud ; and so potent, even in death, was the habit of discipline and submission, that she had controlled herself, stiffening her lips and putting her grief behind her with a fortitude that she knew the old man would have approved. Grimly the dead mouth smiled its approbation. She left him, proud and determined to see the bitter business through, in a composure that neither Clare nor any other should be permitted to undermine.

" I didn't know that you had come in, Clare," she said. " I suppose Thirza has told you ? "

" I heard the bell tolling, dearest. I guessed," said Clare softly.

" The bell ? Ah, that must have been old George Vigors. He was devoted to him. The doctor saved his life." Aunt Cathie paused for a moment ; then her hand dropped to the door-handle again. " Would you like to go in and see him, Clare ? " she said. " He looks so calm and peaceful. You needn't be frightened. If you like I'll come with you."

She was compelling herself, by a definite test of courage, to enter the room again.

" Aunt Cathie, darling," Clare stammered. " I think I'd rather not."

Before the words had left her lips she was afraid that Aunt Cathie would be offended, that she was transgressing some unwritten law. She was prepared to do anything that Aunt Cathie wished.

" If you think I ought to," she hastily continued.

" No, no. If you don't want to there's no reason why you should," she answered, with a harshness that made Clare certain that she had committed an indiscretion.

" Aunt Cathie," Clare began again, " I'm so sorry I was out. If I could have . . ."

" You couldn't have done anything. Nobody was with him. He must have gone quite quietly in his sleep."

Even against this baffling negativity Clare's sense of piti-fulness and duty drove her to another effort. Timidly she reached out for Aunt Cathie's hand. It felt unresponsive and cold as ice.

" Dearest," she said, " please tell me if there is anything
I can do . . . anything at all."

Above their heads the front door bell startled them with
an agitated jangle. For one second Aunt Cathie's cold
fingers gripped Clare's hand ; whether in surprise or in
a shy, painful recognition of her offer she could never tell ;
then she left Clare and hurried to the door. Outside in the
moonlight, dumb with knowledge of her importance, the
daughter of the Wychbury postmaster stood waiting with
a wire. Aunt Cathie tore it open and read it rapidly.
" Thank you, Jinny, no answer," she said. The girl still
hesitated. " Father told me to tell you, Miss, that if there
was anything . . ."

Aunt Cathie smiled bleakly, crumpling the telegram in
her fingers.

" There's nothing, thank you, Jinny," she said. " Please
tell your father that there's nothing at present."

She closed the door. " It was kind of Mr. Martin," she
said ; " you can see how they all respected him. Mr.
Wilburn is coming down by the seven-forty. Please tell
Thirza that we'll have supper at half-past eight. And ask
her to tell Jabez to meet the train. If you don't mind," she
added, with an unusual, inexplicable courtesy that made
Clare feel like a stranger without obligations.

Bewildered by the suddenness of her dismissal she took
her message to the kitchen. She found Thirza Rudge
sitting on a high-backed chair at the side of the range. The
light of an oil lamp which she had for once neglected to
trim illuminated her solemn, sagging features. For all
her comfortable plumpness she looked broken and dreadfully
old. Her reading-glasses lay in their case on the table beside
her. On her apron reposed the open Bible over which she
invariably went to sleep on Sunday afternoons. She sat
there in state, waiting for the arrival of Mrs. Harbord. It
was just so that her friend would expect to find her. The

appearance of Clare with her messages disturbed this setting. Thirza sighed, and rose heavily from her chair.

" Well, that's a comfort, my dear," she said. " At a time like this you do need one man in the house, and the doctor, poor lamb, he can't help hisself. My dear life, it's a marvel how quick these telegrams do go. I reckon Postmaster Martin must have put it through with his own hands. But then, you can't do less than oblige at these times, and that's a fact ! Everyone, no matter who, must put their shoulder to the wheel."

" Oh, Thirza, I wish I could do something," Clare cried. " Something for poor Aunt Cathie, I mean."

Thirza Ridge shook her head. " Miss Cathie's her father's daughter, my dear," she said. " I do know them, as I'd ought to. The best thing you can do is to keep out of their way, like any mouse. Now where can that slow coach Ellen have got to ? Running round from house to house like a flipperty-gibbet, I reckon. I shouldn't wonder if the little toad hasn't gone to Wilkins's first, instead of my friend's, like I told her. The mourning can wait, sure enough, but you can't put off the laying-out. Well, he was a fine man, the doctor. There's not a many of our sort left, my dear. I'm seventy-two, next January that comes. Seventy-two, my dear ! Now what was that you were saying about supper ? "

She put the Bible handy for emergencies and faced the practical aspects of the situation.

" Half-past eight. Well, I don't suppose Miss Cathie'll have much of an appetite ; but Mr. Wilburn, he's always hearty, and I reckon the train journey'll have made him peckish. Now be a good girl, Miss Clare, and save my legs by telling old Jabez."

There he sat in the leathery smell of the harness-room, polishing the hames of the horse's collar. He had always seemed to her old and shrunken, but the weight of this calamity seemed to have compressed him to a drier gnomish-ness. How old they all were, these people of Pen House ! So old that on them the presence of death must fall with a heaviness that she could not appreciate. Often as a child she had been rather frightened of Jabez with his crusty tongue and the air of importance that he assumed in the province that was under his command. Often he had made her feel as guilty as a marauding bullfinch. Now she could only see him as he was : a little, bent old man, polishing his hames in a pitiful attempt to forget the shadow that lay already on the house, and, with each hour, advanced in his direction. He was so absorbed that he did not notice Clare's approach. When he saw her he rose quickly and touched his cap. It was as if the doctor's death had invested her with a new importance in his eyes.

" Yes, Miss," he said. " Certainly, Miss. The seven-forty. Time and enough to spare."

He hurried to reach down the harness. She saw him stretching up his frail, bent back. He went on muttering : " Yes, yes . . . seven-forty," to himself. Then, suddenly, his crushed brain took courage. " Miss Clare, Miss," he wheezed, " I wouldn't have had this happen for anything. He was a good man, the doctor. A proper gentleman. There bain't many of his sort left nowadays. Seven-forty. Very good, Miss."

With her sense of helplessness unabated Clare shut herself up in her room. By this time the sky had cleared to a mellow, moonlit loveliness. The rain had ceased its dropping from the shrubbery trees : the wind had died. It seemed as if all the animate green things that the old man had planted for his pleasure were holding themselves in attitudes of mute and reverent grief or wonder. Their stillness, their silence, was sentient and a little eerie. She could not bear to look for long at these humanised, intimate things ; their attitude was too near, for her comfort, to that of the poor old man whom she had just left in the stable.

Beyond the moon-frosted branches of the orchard she saw the vast, soft outline of Pen Beacon. Here, at last stood something big enough to be impervious to mortality. The great hill rose and dreamed above the plain, even as it had stood since the Arenig glaciers had moulded it and bared its contours to the stars. There was the unchanging skeleton of earth made manifest. Clare gazed and held her breath. *I will lift mine eyes unto the hills*. . . .

Gazing thus idly, and gathering from her dreamy contemplation some measure of the hill's impressive calm, she marked the fleece of fir that spilled itself downward from the summit into the Stourford valley. Ever since the first strokes of George Vigors' passing-bell, even in the moment of his kisses at parting, the thought of Ralph and the day's adventures had vanished from her mind. Now, in seeing the very shoulder of hill that met the Stourford chimneys, it suddenly and overpoweringly returned.

That day, from start to finish, had marked a momentous period in their love. Ralph's stratagem of the visit to Uffdown Manor had transported their ideal love-making to a practical plane. The cool definiteness of his proposals had shown her that their marriage, an event that she had been content to regard as distant and visionary, was near and practicable. On their way back to Wychbury her reason had compelled her to accept his new conditions. One spasm, indeed, of the old panic had disgraced her in the church · but when, in the belfry, she recovered herself, she had realized her folly and determined to struggle no more. Though the step was logical and inevitable, her submission filled her with an excitement in which the prospect of a new liberty and the romantic possibilities of Uffdown Manor were mingled. Her mind glowed and expanded in a new dignity. She could not help thinking how childish and ineffective her previous reservations had been.

For a moment she surrendered herself to the intoxication of this mood ; it seemed at first to gather strength and lustre from the sombreness of her surroundings ; but, in a little while, the brightness began to fade. Her conscience told her that her exultation was selfish and sinful : that she had no right to be so happy ; that her attitude should have been one not of triumph but of humility. Slowly, inexorably the contrast bore down upon her, compelling her to compare her lot with that of the human beings who surrounded her : her youth with their age, her vivid life with their mortal admonitions, her new-born ecstasy with the grimness of their distress. It was unbearable ; she could have cried to think of it ; and yet, perversely, she was happy.

The subdued summons of the supper-gong reached her from below. At that moment any distraction of movemen⁺ was welcome to her. She tidied herself and went down. Now, more than ever, the house seemed stricken by a consciousness of death. At the foot of the stairs the old clock ticked solemnly. She remembered that last Sunday her grandfather had wound it. His hand had generated the strength that the rocking pendulum slowly released. There in the tension of coiled springs a part of the dead man's energy still survived. The swift thought made her shudder. It was sinister, unnatural. She hurried away from it, frightened in the dark.

Aunt Cathie and Wilburn were already seated at table in their accustomed places on either side of the doctor's chair. Wilburn rose to salute her with a suppressed cheerfulness. Aunt Cathie seemed infinitely more at ease. A trifle pale, but marvellously composed, she spoke in a quiet voice of ordinary things. Sometimes she even smiled, but with a queer self-consciousness and pride, as if she realized that the doctor would have approved of her smiling. All through the meal the three of them were as conscious of that empty chair as if the old man had been sitting in it. One after another they glanced toward it and lowered their eyes.

Neither Clare nor Wilburn could help admiring the virtuosity of Aunt Cathie's courage. It was the mark of a proud, superior spirit, schooled and self-contained. How different, Clare thought, from that of the unfortunate Ellen, who, breathless still from scouring the village on her tremendous errands, had lost her head completely and waited on them with a dazed stupidity that, on any other occasion, would have driven Aunt Cathie frantic.

After supper they gathered round the fireless grate ; and there, again, the doctor's chair surveyed them with a quiet, cynical interest. Aunt Cathie persisted in discussing business details ; the proving of the will, the funeral arrangements. Clare sat and listened in silence. There was no reason why she should have stayed in the room. She hated it. And yet she felt it would be cowardly to leave them. All through the evening the brutal, realistic words that fell from Aunt Cathie's lips wounded her ; but whenever she winced at them it seemed to her as if her grandfather smiled. She wondered, mysteriously, if now he was able to read their unspoken thoughts. How it must satisfy his grim sense of humour to see them playing up to his ghostly presence like this !

Wilburn was admirable. Never before had Clare realized the power and clarity of his well-ordered brain. He spoke little, and yet his skill, his tact, his kindliness, were ready, on the instant, to deal with every problem that Aunt Cathie presented to him. He was so different, in every way, from Ralph, that his attractiveness was all the more remarkable. How jolly, Clare thought, it would be to have a man like that for a brother ! It was curious that neither she nor Aunt Cathie had ever known that relationship. With her, of course, it was unnecessary : in Ralph she had found completeness of adoration and companionship. But poor Aunt Cathie . . .

Once more Aunt Cathie's desolation saddened her. Her courage failed ; she felt that, after all, she would be driven to retreat ; but at that moment when she had resolved to do so Thirza Rudge tapped at the door to tell them that Jabez was waiting, and she was saved. The firm handclasp of Wilburn steadied her, it was as though his straight eyes said to her : " Be brave, be brave ! "

Confirmed in this vicarious strength she forced herself to wait at the foot of the stairs for Aunt Cathie's return. Aunt Cathie came back, grey and haggard, but as composed as ever. Clare threw her arms round her neck and hugged her. It was only by this instinctive gesture that she could relieve the conflicting stresses that distorted her heart. Aunt Cathie yielded passively to this hot embrace. Then, gently releasing herself, she kissed Clare's forehead.

" Good-night, my child," she said.

And that was all.

## V

### EPITAPH

THEY buried him, the proud old infidel, in the Nonconformist cemetery at Stourton. Not that Mr. Pomfret would have denied him the last hospitality of consecrated ground. On the contrary, the Vicar resented this deliberate post-mortem discourtesy. Whether he liked it or no, the old man had been one of his parishioners. He could prove it, geographically, by maps. After all, Dr. Weir and he were both gentlemen, and it was understood that, after death, the differences of gentleman ceased. He could only deprecate, in a dignified way, the behaviour of one who persisted in maintaining his feud beyond the grave. Without the least thought of a burial fee he was hurt by the perversity and ill manners of a social equal who could instruct his executor to have him buried among the dissenters. To have chosen a Parsee tower of silence would have shown a greater sense of decency. And Mrs. Pomfret, naturally, agreed with him. He begged her particularly not to mention their feelings to any outsider. Their conduct in the matter, at least, must be beyond reproach.

Dudley Wilburn had been appointed sole executor. On his way back from Wychbury he had glanced at the will which Mrs. Rudge had taken from the dead man's hands. He himself had planned the first draft ; but, since that time, the document had been so mutilated by erasions and codicils that it had lost its shape and intention, leaving little of the original but the clause which insisted on the absence of religious ceremony—" mummery " had been the doctor's own suggestion—and that which appointed him to the executor's office. From these two paragraphs the old man's spirit flared its last protest against the ignorance of superstition and the capacity of women to manage their own affairs.

The funeral party drove down from Pen House in two hired carriages. Aunt Cathie, Wilburn and Clare occupied the first, Thirza, Ellen and old Jabez followed. Ellen, from start to finish, dissolved behind a black-bordered handkerchief which her mother had saved from some forgotten obsequies ; Jabez, confused by his black clothes and his sudden transference from the box to a cushioned seat inside, held himself upright and intense, as though he were still responsible for the guidance of the horses. Thirza, in the glory of as much crape as would festoon a catafalque, her pink face glowing with appreciation of a well-run affair in which her experience entitled her to be considered the principal performer, sat forward, alert as a dog, noting with interest and satisfaction the avenue of drawn blinds through which they passed down the length of Wychbury village. As they came abreast of one of the last windows a corner of the blind was lifted, and she gave a sigh of content, for she knew that her friend had seen her stately passage.

Even in the first of the funeral carriages there was no community of feeling. To the mind of Aunt Cathie, now numbed by reaction from the strain which she had borne so bravely, this drive seemed futile and purposeless. If they had taken her, not to Stourton, but to the ends of the earth, she would not have protested. Only at Wychbury cross-roads, where a little group of the doctor's club-patients stood waiting in the drizzle with bared heads, did she become, for one moment, capable of feeling ; and even then her emotion was not so much one of grief as of pride in her father's virtues, in the probity, the generosity, the ruthless kindliness which they remembered and she remembered too. They didn't realize that the man to whom they paid this final tribute of respect had died eight years ago, on the day of his first stroke. Nobody but she and Wilburn, her confidant, realized that. She wondered if Wilburn knew what she was thinking.

Whatever he may have thought, the face of Wilburn showed no signs of feeling. His full-skirted frock-coat, buttoned high on the chest, his dead black Ascot tie, his tall hat, dulled by a three-inch band of crape, seemed to contribute to the impersonal, professional grimness of his figure. He was no longer a friend but a uniformed legal functionary, playing his part in the sombre ceremony with a propriety and an efficiency which equalled that of Mr. Wilkins, the undertaker, seated on the box in front of them.

Wilburn's mouth was set with more than its accustomed firmness ; the solemnity of black clothes was reflected in his rigid features, in the concentrated steadiness of his eyes. Clare had never before been so deeply impressed by him.

He looked so handsome too, in his funeral magnificence, that she was almost afraid of him. It seemed impossible that this was the jolly companion who, in Aunt Cathie's absence, had joked and laughed with her on equal terms. Perhaps she had only imagined this relation. It were better so; for it would be shameful to think of poor Aunt Cathie having been deceived. Clare's heart went out to this mute, unknowable creature.

She dared not look at Aunt Cathie for fear of crying, nor at Wilburn, lest her glances should betray their guilty intimacy. She sat with lowered eyes as the procession paced slowly through the village and, as they left it, broke into a cheerful trot. And as they jogged through the rich hues and scents of the autumnal lanes, she was conscious, all the time, of the letter from Ralph which she had received that morning, just before they left Pen House. She could feel its uneven pressure within her black bodice, where she had hurriedly stowed it, and, in her brain, its phrases kept on forming themselves, as if they had been burnt upon it to the exclusion of all other thoughts.

*My own darling* (he had written),

*Until I heard the news this morning I couldn't believe that you were right. I went up to the chapel just the same, but you weren't there. Clare, I can't put down a thousandth part of what I think. I never knew him as you did, but everyone seems agreed what a fine man he was. Anyway, he was your grandfather, and that's enough for me. Now I must ask you to forgive me. You will, my sweetest, I know you will. The thought of you all alone in that miserable place was too much for me. I couldn't bear it any longer, so I went into the library to the guv'nor after dinner, and told him all about us, as we arranged. Don't be alarmed. He was quite reasonable about it, agreed that I was my own master, etc., etc. Of course he doesn't know you, or he'd have been delighted. Vivien was,*

*in her funny, off-hand way. She said it wasn't any news to her.
I left it for the guv'nor to tell mother. I suppose they'll have
a family council over it.*

*Oh, my sweetheart, I can't bear you to be alone. I rode
half way to Worcester this afternoon, but it's no good. I can't
be happy till I take you in my arms like I did yesterday when
you were frightened. That's the only thing that matters,
Clare, for us two to be together. I don't want to disturb you,
darling, at a time like this, but I must see you. I want to
take you away right out of it, Clare. Oh, my love, my love,
how I do love you.*                                   *Ralph.*

*PS.—I can't bear it much longer, Clare. I shall come to
Pen House to-morrow evening, and then, my darling, oh,
then . . .*                                              *R.*

And then, oh then. . . . The lyric words went singing
through Clare's mind, so clearly, so triumphantly, that it
seemed as if her mute companions must hear them. She
glanced at them timidly ; both faces were blankly set in the
same sombre mould. Aunt Cathie's head was swaying
from side to side with the movement of the carriage as if
it didn't belong to her ; and as Clare watched it, absorbed
and fascinated, she began to realize that all the raptures of
which Ralph's letter had persuaded her to dream were
conditioned by her duty toward Aunt Cathie's loneliness.
However easy their marriage might seem to Ralph this new
factor must be considered. Aunt Cathie, she told herself,
had devoted to her the best part of a life. It would be
selfish and cruel to desert her, as Ralph so lightly proposed,
at a moment when the world had fallen in ruins about her.
Monstrous and impossible. So, out of her dream, the
thought of Aunt Cathie's desolation snatched her ruthlessly
backward. " She has been patient for years," Clare told

herself, " now I must show her that I can be patient too."
But Ralph ? The preaching of patience to the author of
that ardent letter was another matter.

Little by little the pressure of these sobering facts reduced
her spirits to the general level. By this time they had skirted
the prim suburbs of Stourton. They passed the red
sandstone church in which she had been confirmed. The
sight of it awakened in Clare no ecstasy of reminiscence.
The sky above them was shrouded in yellow fog, thin edge
of the monstrous coverlet that the fires of the Black Country
are always brewing. They penetrated a zone of brickyards,
glass-works, and clay-pits. A smell of burning earth and
cinders embittered the air. On the edge of the clay-pits
Clare saw an open field in which were ranged on end, row
after row, the china baths by whose exploitation that little
market town had been debauched. They stood there like
uniform tombstones in a cemetery, reminding her of their
grim errand, which she had almost forgotten. The hillside
beyond them had broken out into an angry rash of uniform
red-brick cottages. Through these they passed at a trot,
the carriage wheels jolting and grating over unrolled clinkers.
Slatternly women came to their doors in aprons, shouting
for their neighbours not to miss the spectacle. The place
was bleak and sterile as the grave itself.

At last the carriages pulled up before an ugly iron gate
slung upon massive pillars faced with terra-cotta. Clare
rose hastily to descend ; but Mr. Wilkins called on her to
wait. This was the moment of his apotheosis ; he was
the mystagogue ; they sat and waited on his instructions.
They saw him run forward to the closed coupé attached
to the hearse. From it four satellites emerged. They wore
long frock-coats, like Mr. Wilkins, and small black skull-
caps. Wilburn rose and gave his hand to Aunt Cathie.
She dismounted, and Clare followed her. As she stood
there beside them Catherine knew that it was no use fighting

any longer. Bereft of thought, bereft of everything but feeling, she collapsed into desolate tears.

## VI

### CONFIDENCES

WHEN they returned to Pen House they found a bright fire burning and tea already laid on the dining-room table. No ordinary tea either ; for Mrs. Harbord, once having witnessed her friend's triumphal passage, had trudged up through the rain and taken possession of Thirza's kitchen. There she had baked hot scones for the occasion, and set the table out with all the best of the silver, cakestands and salvers, and the Queen Anne tea-set that Thirza cleaned weekly, on Fridays, but had never presumed to use in all her forty years of service. This she had placed at the head of the table, opposite the doctor's chair, which, since his death, had been left vacant as by consent ; and round it, gleaming in a comfortable lustre of blue and gold, she had ranged the Crown Derby tea-things that were the pride and anxiety of Aunt Cathie's life. At the other end of the table, plump, crisp and golden, stood the ham on which Thirza's respect for local custom had insisted.

Obedient to Mrs. Harbord's knowledge of tradition, Aunt Cathie took the place that was assigned to her. Her eyes were still red with crying, and yet, as she poured out, she began to talk with a challenging sprightliness that was half bravado and half the dissembled symbol of a genuine relief. Wilburn accepted her challenge clumsily ; he began to make little jokes with Clare, teasing her, as though she were still a schoolgirl. He had not treated her in that way for months, and yet, on this occasion, his lame humour had the effect of putting them all at ease. Aunt Cathie smiled at him as he teased. They talked like people who have come home from a dance in the small hours and are tempted to easy laughter by consciousness of others sleeping above their heads. They were all of them hungry, too, and this running-fire of conversation enabled them to conceal the shame of their natural appetites.

When they had finished tea, Aunt Cathie turned to Clare and said in a significant whisper : " Clare dear, if you'd like to, there's no reason why you shouldn't go upstairs and change " ; which meant that from Aunt Cathie's point of view there were urgent reasons why she should. She went obediently ; evening was falling ; and then, oh then . . . It was almost as if Aunt Cathie had guessed that she did not want to meet Ralph in her mourning.

Wilburn and Aunt Cathie sat solemnly on either side of the fire while Ellen cleared the table. Then Wilburn asked if he might smoke. And Cathie assented hurriedly. It was the first time she ever remembered anyone smoking at Pen House ; the doctor, having no taste for tobacco, had always preached against it as a poison. What would he think of this easy desecration of his favourite room ? And wha would Thirza think ? Aunt Cathie was becoming a little cautious of Thirza as a tyrant of the old regime ; but she liked to see Wilburn sit there lighting his pipe in that homely way ; it gave her a thrill of emancipation and daring to have permitted it.

" I don't want to bother you with business," he began.

" It won't bother me," she assured him, " I'm not the least bit tired. If there is anything special . . ."

" It's usual, on these occasions," he said, " to read the will. Of course, in this case, there's no need for that. I expect you know what's in it ? "

" I've not the least idea. He was always very mysterious about it, particularly just lately. He never spoke of its contents ; so, naturally, I didn't ask him. He wouldn't have liked it. ..1e didn't even tell me that he had appointed you his executor. Perhaps you'll be good enough . . . not to read it . . . just to explain."

"There's nothing much to explain," said Wilburn, turning the pages. "His first intentions were simple enough. Latterly he seems to have become less sure of what he wanted. During the last year he's added no less than five codicils. They're all quite properly attested by Mrs. Rudge and Jabez. Only one of them is really important."

"He was always getting them in to sign something or other," Aunt Cathie smiled. "He used to frighten them out of their lives."

"Well, I'll just give you the gist of it," said Wilburn. He put aside his pipe and leaned forward in the doctor's chair. "First of all, comes the clause we've already acted on ; his objection to being buried with any religious ceremony. It's a curious thing, isn't it, that a man so reasonable as he was should have taken the trouble to express all these prejudices of his in his will ? "

"He felt very strongly."

"I know. And yet he must have been aware that nobody was likely to read all this—there's a whole page of it—but you and me. Perhaps it gave him a sort of satisfaction to think that even after his death his opinions would survive on paper."

"He felt very strongly," Aunt Cathie repeated. She thought it her duty to take the old man's part against this posthumous criticism.

"That shows itself later," said Wilburn. "Do you want me to read that clause ? "

"No. There's no need. I know exactly what he thought. Suppose you just give me an idea of what follows."

"Very well," said Wilburn. "He was not a wealthy man."

" I know that."

" Not nearly as wealthy as he gave us all to understand. Of course he showed great wisdom in his investments."

" You advised him."

" Yes. But he didn't always take my advice. Sometimes he was wiser, much wiser than me. First of all there's the house. That will have to be valued for probate. I suppose you will want to go on living in it ? "

" Here ? Oh, of course." The idea of an uprooting made Aunt Cathie shudder. " I couldn't dream of leaving it."

" Still, you have to count it as part of your income. Then here is a complete schedule of his investments. He lost a good deal of money last year. Perhaps he didn't tell you ? There remains a number of securities, mostly industrial shares, representing a capital of, roughly, nine thousand pounds. The bulk of them are Sedgebury Main Preference. You remember we came to a decision about those the other day. They'll produce an income, at present, of just under four hundred pounds."

Aunt Cathie shook her head. " You'll think me stupid," she said, " but that means nothing to me. I've never had anything to do with money. He handled all the bills himself. I suppose it'll be enough to live on ? "

" At your present rate of living it's ample. If the Colliery shares develop, as I think they will, you'll have money to spare."

" Well, let's be thankful for that," Aunt Cathie sighed. " It's been very good of you."

" But wait a moment ; I haven't finished," said Wilburn, with a smile. " I haven't told you yet how the money is left."

" I'm sorry." She blushed. In that moment of timidity he could almost have declared that she was pretty. " You see," she went on hurriedly, " I thought you were executor and had to do all that. You know I trust you so absolutely . . . just like he did. . . ."

She stopped, and he, to cover her embarrassment, made haste to continue :

" To begin with, there are a number of small legacies to servants. His clothes to Jabez and three years' wages ; the same sum of money to ' my devoted servant, Thirza Rudge ' ; a year's wages to Ellen Higgins. Medical books and instruments to Mr. Lloyd Moore. That's curious ; I don't suppose their value can be anything but sentimental. No bequests to charity. He says : ' I consider that my work through forty years of practice in Wychbury represents the whole of my obligation to humanity.' "

" That's true," Aunt Cathie murmured. " He gave up his whole life to that."

" Then comes the curious part. Originally he had divided the residue of his estate in equal portions between ' My daughter, Catherine Weir, and my granddaughter. Claerwen Lydiatt, absolutely.' Then, in a codicil dated - let me see—the seventeenth of June, 1897—that is this year —he revokes the whole of his bequest to Clare." Wilburn paused.

" I don't quite understand," said Aunt Cathie quickly. " You mean that Clare gets nothing ? "

" Nothing. Not a penny. The codicil gave me a shock. He must have changed his mind three months ago. It seems so unlike him."

Again Aunt Cathie blushed. " It *is* unlike him," she cried. " You've no idea how just, how generous he was. But you remember, don't you ?—I told you that he'd changed . . . after that last attack. He wasn't himself any longer, poor darling. We can't, we mustn't consider him responsible for this. Of course it can be altered."

" It can't be altered," Wilburn explained. " The will is perfectly valid and must be proved as it stands. What puzzles me is why his feeling toward Clare should have changed. I'm sure poor little Clare can't have done anything to deserve it. Do you think that in these last months he began to brood on that old business: Sylvia and Lydiatt ? "

It was the first time that Lydiatt's name had ever passed between them. The sound of it threw Aunt Cathie's heart into a panic. With Wilburn, of all men, this was a subject that she could not bear to discuss.

" No, no," she said, " it wasn't that. I think I know what it means. When she was at St. Monica's, Clare got into the hands of some High Church woman or other who worried her into being confirmed. You know, it's quite common with schoolgirls, that emotional religious phase. Mr. Pomfret, the vicar, you know, passed her on to that man Darnay, the very type that the doctor hated most. She used to go every morning to early service at St. Chad's. You know how strongly he felt about all that sort of thing. Somebody must have influenced him." She hesitated.

" Poor kid ! " said Wilburn, with a little laugh.

But as he laughed Aunt Cathie met his eyes, firm and judicial, staring straight into her own, and the meanness of her prevarication stood naked in their steady flame. The shame of having lied to him, the one man living in whose eyes she wished to appear at her best and truest, was insupportable. A wave of redness swept upward ; the blood beat in her temples ; she was inspired, heroic in her need for absolute frankness in the humiliation of herself and the vindication of her father. Wilburn watched the emotion rising in her with alarm ; her face was distorted with passion.

" No, that's not true," she said, " I'm not going to tell you a lie about it. It was I who told him. I couldn't help it. I know it was mean and horrible of me. I think I must have been mad. Now you know the very worst of my meanness. How you must hate me for it ! "

There was no hatred in Wilburn's mind. He was only shocked and embarrassed by this sudden access of passion in a woman whose calmness and restraint he had always admired. There was something grotesque in Aunt Cathie's vehemence. At the end of her outburst she had fallen to her knees and clasped his hand in utter abandonment of weeping. He pitied her ; he thought that this nervous collapse was nothing but the logical outcome of the intolerable degree of fortitude which she had shown him during the last three days. Sooner or later something must have given way. Now her resistance had flown asunder like a taut cable and left her a mass of bruised and lacerated nerves. For the moment he didn't even take her violent self-accusation seriously. Judged by the standards of his profession her offence was trifling, no more than the natural impulse of a woman sorely tried, who showed, by the very torture of her shame, her essential goodness. He took the hand with which she had clasped his and clumsily caressed it.

"My dear Cathie," he said, "you simply mustn't take it as hardly as this. You're overwrought. It's perfectly natural. To-morrow, when you've had a good sleep, you'll see that it's not half as terrible as you imagine. Just now you can't possibly look at anything in its proper proportion." She went on weeping bitterly. His hands were wet with her tears. A feeling of utter helplessness seized him. "Would you rather I left you and sent in Mrs. Rudge ? " he said.

She only clung to him more tightly.

"No, no," she cried. "Don't leave me ! Don't leave me ! " Her tears had ceased, but her body continued to be shaken by hard, hollow sobs ; her voice made a piteous whining noise like that which a dog makes in its dreams. "Can you ever forgive me ? " she gasped. "Can you ever forgive me ? "

"Of course, of course," he assured her. "There's nothing to forgive."

"But Clare; she won't," Aunt Cathie sobbed. "She'll hate me for ever. And I do love her so!"

Gradually, with a patient, kindly insistence, Wilburn constrained her to raise herself from the ground. She lay back, trembling, shrunken, exhausted, in the doctor's chair. Gradually her raw features regained their composure.

Timidly glancing at him she began to speak.

"Of course I shall put things right," she said, "just as if the—what do you call it?—the codicil had never been made, that will be easy, won't it? There's nothing to prevent me giving her her share? Isn't there such a thing —I seem to remember—as a Deed of Gift? And if I do that, you see, there's no real reason—is there—why Clare should know about it. Nobody need ever know a word about it but you and me? Isn't that so?"

"Of course it's quite easy," he told her, "the important thing for the present is that you shouldn't worry your head about it. You've had more than enough trouble to go on with."

"And Clare needn't know?" she persisted.

"You can leave it all to me."

"If I thought that Clare was going to suffer . . ."

"She shan't. I'll promise you that."

"You're a good friend, Dudley," she murmured with a wan smile; it was the first time that she had used that name to him since the blow had fallen. It came to her lips quite naturally; but when she had spoken it, she was half afraid that her familiarity might have offended him. Evidently it hadn't. He bent over her and took her arm in a gesture more intimate than any of those which she had treasured. His voice was low and thrillingly gentle as he spoke.

"You need think no more about it," he said. "Now promise me that you won't."

Warmed and strengthened by the pressure of his hand, she gave her promise. This act of submission filled her with a rich, peculiar content. Wilburn pulled up a chair and sat down beside her. His fingers settled on her arm. From their contact a shiver of pleasure ran through all her body. The downward directed rays of the lamp were concentrated on the table ; the shadow of Wilburn lay between so that she could not see his face.

"Now, that we're making confidences," he said quietly, "I want you to listen to some of mine. You say I'm a good friend to you. I hope and believe it's true. We ought to be friends, you know. After all, we've known each other, you and I, for more than twenty years. Looking backward, upon my soul, it seems like half a century ! We're neither of us as young as we were, Cathie. A day like this reminds me that we belong to the older generation, and we've both seen ups and downs to show us what life is like. Still, I won't complain. I've had my share of happiness too. I don't think you ever knew my wife ? "

"No," Aunt Cathie murmured. "I never even saw her. There was a sort of big gap at that time, wasn't there ? "

He did not answer. "She was very young and sweet," he went on softly. "Quite different from Sylvia. You remember, when I was a boy I was mad on Sylvia ? Well, Edith was quite her opposite ; fair and soft, extraordinarily gentle. . . . We'd been married four years when I lost her. It was cruel. I thought I should never get over it. Such hope, such happiness ; and then such desolation ! Of course, Joyce and Evelyn were too tiny to realize. They don't even remember her. Perhaps it's a good thing. . . .

"And then they began to grow up. When they were quite little it didn't matter much. We had Edith's nurse, you know, an old body something like your Thirza : absolutely devoted and trustworthy. And I, of course, was so absorbed in my work that I scarcely ever saw them. I'm never quite at my ease with children. But now it's becoming more difficult." He hesitated.

"You see, if the children had been boys," he went on, "it would have been more plain-sailing. The sooner small boys get their angles rubbed off them at school the better for everybody. A man has his own experience to fall back on and knows what he's about in dealing with his sons. But with girls it's different. The old woman's failing— you know just what that means—and sooner or later I shall have to pension her off. In any case, I don't think the society of very old people is good for young children. Particularly servants ; even the best of them. What they want now is the influence and attention of somebody like their mother ; a cultured woman of our own class. And that's not as easy as it sounds. It's a great embarrassment for a man of my age to have a governess in the house. Rather risky, too. I've no sister of my own, and my brother's a bachelor. You see the fix I'm in ? "

Aunt Cathie assented breathlessly.

"Well, there you are ! " he continued. " These children of mine are getting beyond me. They're quite delightful ; I adore them ; but all the time I realize that it's impossible for me to do my duty by them. I've spoken to one or two people about it. Yes, you're the third. They all say that my obvious course is to marry again. That's all very well, Cathie. I can't just take it as easily as that. It's more than five years since Edith died—the kids are six and nine—and in the meantime I've settled down into a regular old bachelor. I'm cautious, too. That's the penalty of being a lawyer. And in spite of my cautiousness, although you'd never believe it, I'm a romantic person. When I talk about my age, I know that it's really nonsense. I'm much younger than I pretend to myself. And so are you, too. You don't mind my talking on like this ? "

" No, no," she said. " I take it as a compliment, an honour."

Aunt Cathie's hand reached out to find his. He moved his arm, and she withdrew it timidly.

" So, during the last twelve months," he went on, " I've been turning this over and over in my mind, and trying to persuade myself that I'm not such a staid old man as I've imagined. Then, latterly, your father's business began to bring me frequently over here. I was glad to come. I admired the old man tremendously ; I liked him for trusting me, and it made me feel younger to come right away from North Bromwich to a place where I'd often been when I was a boy. But that wasn't the only reason why I began to look forward to my visits here. . . . Cathie, can you imagine what I'm driving at ? "

She held her breath. She could hardly trust herself to speak. The strained sweetness of the moment was intolerable.

" Tell me," she said at last.

Wilburn laughed and rose to his feet. He moved away from her. Her heart yearned after him.

" My dear, I thought you'd have been clever enough to guess."

She shook her head. She dared not look at him.

" It's Clare," he said.

Aunt Cathie drew her breath in a deep gasp. The blood left her head. Her mind was a whirlpool through which Wilburn's figure and the shapes of the familiar room swam monstrously. She put out her hands in front of her, as though to ward off a blow. Then they fell limp in her lap. The blood beat back into her brain with a rhythm of galloping hoofs. Her heart raced like a runaway horse, and she was whirled away with it. It was from a distance as remote as death that she heard Wilburn's voice clearing itself in the middle of a sentence.

" . . . that night when she came back from school," he was saying. " I wonder if you remember it ? I'd always thought of her as a child before that. After all, that's what she was. We drove up from the station together in the dark. I noticed how fresh and eager she was ; but so composed too. You remember how she came down to supper that night ? Of course. . . . You were a bit upset. She took my breath away ; it wasn't only the likeness to poor Sylvia. And ever since then I've been thinking about her, and telling myself not to be a fool. A man of my age and a girl of eighteen ! She's nearly nineteen, isn't she ? Well, that's not quite so bad. And in some ways, too, she's old for her years. There's a kind of quiet strength about Clare. It must have taken some courage to break away from you all over this religious business : that's what I thought when you told me. And now I don't try to deceive myself any more. I'm in love with her, and I want to marry her."

He stopped, as if he were aware of something unusual in her silence.

" You don't say anything," he began.

" I can't," she answered. " I don't know what to say. Such a thing has never entered my mind."

Her voice was as cold and sepulchral as if it came from the other side of the grave. It chilled him. He supposed that his passion had carried him beyond the limits of propriety.

" I'm sorry," he said. " I shouldn't have spoken about it to-day. I'd no right to give you a shock. As a matter of fact I thought you'd be pleased. Remember, you're partly responsible. It's my enormous respect for you that assures me she's been well brought up. And it seemed a good opportunity for me to speak of it : I mean the fact that the doctor had left her out of his will. You see, you needn't worry about money matters as far as she's concerned. I thought it might relieve your mind."

She did not answer. Her silence forced him to continue in his own defence.

" Of course you needn't suppose that I'm in any inordinate hurry. I don't want to dislocate your life again. Even if I have to wait a year or two—say till she's twenty-one— there's plenty of time to spare. I'm not going to steal her from you, Cathie, don't think that. I wanted—well, I suppose I wanted to tell you as the nearest person to her and an old friend. I wanted the encouragement of your good wishes. Now tell me, if you like, that I'm a romantic fool. What do you think of it ? "

He faced her with such commanding confidence that her task was harder. With another effort she mastered her whirling brain.

" I think Clare's very lucky," she heard herself saying.

The compliment dazzled him so that he could not see what struggle lay behind it. " So you'll give me your blessing ? " he said. " For the present we'll leave it at that. All I can ask you to do is to hold a sort of watching brief on my behalf. I can't tell you what a relief it is to feel that you're behind me."

Aunt Cathie rose mechanically to her feet in obedience to a blind instinct that compelled her to escape. She knew that he expected her to speak, and speech was impossible. When Wilburn saw her rise he interpreted her movement as a signal of dismissal. No doubt she was too exhausted and overwrought to deal with a stranger's presence any longer. He supposed that he was partly to blame. As she came toward him on her way to the door with the automatic concentration of a somnambulist, he was overwhelmed with pity and respect for her devotion, with amazement at the age and weariness that showed themselves in her face. He was impelled to take her arm as she passed and hold her for a moment.

" Good-bye," he said. " Don't think of seeing me off. I'll look after myself. I think you're the bravest woman I've ever known."

He bent and kissed her forehead. Then he opened the door and she passed out.

## VII

### LOVE AND DEATH

Blow after blow. Out of the wreckage of her shattered world Aunt Cathie's misery drove her aimlessly. There was no refuge for her. That house, which had sheltered her whole life was empty and haunted. Outside, the rain beat down as if it would never cease. Within the room from which she had fled, Wilburn cleared his throat. She heard a rustle of stiff paper. No doubt he was reconsidering the details of the doctor's will in the interval before the carriage came for him. Then, once again, the hall was possessed by an unusual silence. She could not account for it until she realized, of a sudden, that the grandfather clock had stopped ticking. For the first time in all her life. She stood and peered up into its blank face. It was too dark to read the letters engraved on it. She knew them by heart. *Arthur Tunstall, Kidderminster*. 1824. This was death indeed.

Ten minutes later, stretched on her bed, cold and inanimate, she heard the wheels of the victoria squelching on the sodden drive, and the voice of Thirza Rudge cooing appropriate good-byes to Wilburn in the hall. Then silence again ; or only the sound of rain.

At last she could stand this loneliness no longer. It

frightened her. She dared not relax lest something new and monstrous should take her unawares. Aimlessly, for all she knew, she rose from her bed and passed along the landing to the door of Clare's room. Why she should have gone to Clare she could not imagine. It would have been wiser to avoid her. It was Clare whose reincarnation of Sylvia's beauty had dealt her this last, most stunning blow. She denied it ; Clare was not responsible ; rather those supernal powers, which the doctor had always taught her to despise and discredit, had made a cynical adjustment in the balance of their account.

Before such mysterious dispensations it was useless to struggle or protest. By fighting against them she could assure her own defeat. Her only hope of salvation lay not in passive surrender, but in an eager acceptance of her loss. To save her life she must lose it ; to restore her dignity she must court extreme humiliation. This paradox offered a mystical solution of her difficulty, and yet it had a primitive logic of its own which satisfied her reason. She was not the first pagan who has found comfort in the Christian doctrine of self-sacrifice. Armed and elevated by its assumption, she entered Clare's room, determined not only to confess her fault, but also to discharge faithfully the hateful embassy with which Wilburn had entrusted her.

Yet when she found herself in Clare's presence, she was as incapable of speech as she had been with Wilburn. Clare had discarded the black frock with sombre trimmings of crape which she had worn at Stourton. She had put on another, her best, without a hint of mourning in it and stood with her back to the door by which Aunt Cathie had entered, looking through the window over the wet orchard, thinking of Ralph, and wondering if he were on his way.

Aunt Cathie drifted into the dark room like a ghost. Like a ghost suspended in some eddy of air, she halted midway. But Clare neither heard nor saw her ; for her heart was full of sweet, warm tremors and flutterings of expectation.

" It's like a dream," Aunt Cathie thought, " she doesn't even heed me." She compelled her ghostly lips to speak :
" Clare . . ."

The child gave a start and turned to meet her with a quick eagerness.

" Aunt Cathie, dearest, how you startled me ! I never heard you come."

Aunt Cathie's lips spoke again. " The clock in the hall . . . it's stopped," they said, " and there's no one who understands how to wind it." It wasn't a bit what she wanted to say.

" I'm sure Mr. Wilburn could show us, dearest," said Clare.

" No, no, he's gone. He went half an hour ago."

Wasn't it significant that Clare should straightway mention his name ? A reminder ? They needn't be afraid. She was going through with it. Only give her time :

" He went half an hour ago," she repeated. It seemed that her strength was returning. " I want to talk to you about him, Clare. You know the doctor always trusted him ? And through these awful days . . . well, really, I don't know what we should have done without him. We owe him a great debt of gratitude, Clare. He's such a strong, upright man. I don't think I've ever known anyone so sane, so dependable, so good."

She broke off suddenly in the midst of her eulogy. She had to speak as she was driven : " Clare, there's been a dreadful mistake about the will, my darling, and I'm to blame for it. You must forgive me. Clare. No . . . don't let's talk of that. He says that it can be put right. I want to talk to you about him. He admired your mother, you know. Years and years ago. You do like him, don't you, Clare ? "

" Of course I like him, Aunt Cathie. We've always been good friends." The sudden change of direction bewildered her.

" Good friends . . . of course." Aunt Cathie drove herself steadily onward. " He's always treated you as a little girl, hasn't he ? But that's all over, Clare. You aren't a little girl any longer. You're a woman. I want you to think of him as if you were a woman, darling. I want you to think most seriously. . . . What's that ? "

She started. A bell had jangled in the passage below. Its sound broke the spell of puzzled wonder in which Clare had been listening. She knew what it meant.

" It's the front-door bell," she said.

" I wonder who it can be. Ellen will answer it."

" I'll go myself, dearest. I'd rather Ellen didn't. I must."

She hurried to the door, her face was all aflame.

" Clare ! Don't be foolish ! Listen. . . ."

" I can't, Aunt Cathie. I know who it is. It's Ralph."

" Ralph ? Who do you mean ? "

" Ralph Hingston. He wrote last night to say that he would come this evening."

" Clare . . . I don't understand."

" Of course you don't. Oh, dearest, I'm so happy. I know it's wrong. I wish you could be happy with me." She hugged Aunt Cathie suddenly to her breast. " Dearest," she whispered, " Ralph loves me, and I love him. And it's so wonderful. Oh, don't be angry with me ! "

The bell gave another impatient jangle. She was gone.

## VIII

### HER LADYSHIP

LADY HINGSTON sat before a lacquer writing-table in the high window of her boudoir. When first the family had moved to Stourford they had called it " the boudoir " in joke, for their sudden translation out of the smoke of Wolverbury into these stucco battlements had made them all a little self-conscious ; but now the name had been adopted as a serious and habitual description of her private room by servants and family alike. Boudoirs were fashionable. Even the unpretentious Mrs. Willis had one at Mawne Hall. It was part of the new nomenclature, comparable to the " music-room," where Ralph and Vivien practised Badminton, and the " library," where Sir Joseph stored his cedar-wood cabinets of cigars.

It was a pleasant room, facing the hills and the south-east. Even on this autumnal morning, when the wind drove before it a drooping, tattered sky and ploughed through the sere beechwoods with a roar like that of the sea, it was warm and grateful to the senses. On the wide sweep of the drive, forty feet below her, gardeners, with big besoms, were sweeping the dead leaves into heaps that the wind, of sheer malice, whisked about their ears ; and all the time a drift of other fugitives, hurrying perpetually westward like migrant hordes, escaped them, travelling over the gritty surface with a soft, sibilant whisper.

Lady Hingston watched them idly. Within the double windows she could not hear the roaring of the wood nor the whisper of dead leaves. Wrapped in her ermine dressing-jacket she contemplated the boisterous commotion as from another world. She dipped her pen in the silver inkstand meditatively. She frowned, and began to write in the large rounded hand that the amplitude of the note-paper suggested.

*My dear Miss Weir,*

*I have been meaning to write to you for several days to say how deeply we all of us sympathize with you in your great loss. Although it is some years since we have seen anything of your dear father, we cannot help realizing what a noble and striking figure has passed away from us.*

" Passed away from us," her mind repeated. There was a certain consoling richness in the phrase which use had consecrated to save people the personal expression of emotions too real, or too unreal, to be written without discomfort. " Passed away from us . . ."

" Mother, dear."

Behind her, in the doorway, stood Vivien. Lady Hingston looked round with a smile that inadequately disguised her irritation.

" Yes, darling ? "

" I'm so sorry to disturb you. I promised Ralph that I'd remind you to write that letter."

" That's just what I'm doing. I shall have finished in a few minutes."

" Passed away from us . . ."

*Naturally,* she continued, *we all feel it all the more at a moment when our two families——*

" Naturally " was all very well. As a matter of fact it made no difference to their feelings. However . . .

*——are going to be so intimately connected. We are all of us very fond of Clare. She is a sweet child ; so unaffected and well brought-up. We know that she must have been a great comfort to you in your great sorrow . . .*

With evident satisfaction she underlined the last three words.

*You must pardon my boy if he is a little impatient. Though I know it seems cruel to steal Clare from you at a period like this, I am wondering if you could spare her to stay with us for a short time. The young people have so many important things to discuss! Supposing we send over for her to-morrow (Saturday) afternoon?*

That was the important part of the letter, tactfully accomplished. Her pen leaped forward to the triumph of a generous ending :

*Of course, if you would care to come over with her and have tea with us, we should all be too delighted to see you. But, perhaps, you'd rather not?*
> *Believe me,*
> > *Yours most sincerely,*
> > > *Margaret Hingston.*

She sighed and laid down her pen. Vivien, who had been hovering over her like a kestrel, descended with a swoop.

" Had it better go into the bag, mother, or shall we send it over ? "

" I think the post is better. It looks rather peremptory to send it by hand."

" But it *is* peremptory really," said the candid Vivien. " We must get Clare somehow out of that awful house. Ralph says it's too dreadful. Yesterday morning they had the mattresses out to air on the drive. *His* mattresses, you know. As for Miss Weir, she's like a funeral."

" Miss Weir's an unhappy, lonely woman, Vivien. You should be sorry for her."

" I am, dearest. But Clare's so young, and it's such a shame. Mother, I don't believe you realize what a darling Clare is."

Lady Hingston smiled. In a swift, half-mocking glance her eyes appraised and accepted the young, frank eagerness of Vivien's face. A wave of maternal pride warmed her heart. She answered quickly :

" It's not for the want of your telling me, anyway. I believe you're more in love with her than Ralph is. I've never known you quite so enthusiastic about a man."

" Oh, mother, how like you to say that ! " Vivien flamed. " But even you can't deny that she's lovely."

" Yes. No. I'll admit she's a nice little thing. And she's a lady. Of course she's very young. I'd always imagined. . . . But that's beside the point. Your father and I are far too up-to-date to make any objection to our children's fancies. Ralph's in love with her, and I suppose he knows his own mind."

" He always does, mother. We all of us do. That's your fault, and dad's."

" You needn't throw it in my face. Still, I'm getting over it by degrees. I hope you haven't any more shocks up your sleeve for me just yet, Vivien."

" *Me ?* " Vivien laughed outright. " My dear mother, don't worry your head about me ! I'm perfectly contented as I am, thank you. May I have the letter ? I promised Ralph I'd be responsible for it."

Lady Hingston surrendered the document ; then repented.

" No, wait one moment," she said. " I'd better address it myself. It looks more courteous. What do they call the place ? Pen House, isn't it ? And now I suppose I shall have to make myself presentable."

She rang the bell for Marguerite, her maid. Vivien, her purpose accomplished, bent over and kissed her hurriedly. It was pleasant to feel the firm, soft coolness of her daughter's cheek. As she gathered her dressing jacket about her, Lady Hingston shrugged herself inside it like a cat that has been stroked and is on the verge of purring and rather like some small and glossy animal she looked, nestling in the snowy pelt with her clear skin and her eyes so darkly shining under the powdery whiteness of her hair. That hair and the brilliance of those black eyes gave her an air of sharp, concentrated clarity, which she was always at pains to augment by dressing in white and black, wearing no jewels but a string of pearls, her wedding ring, and a single diamond whose white rays matched the crystalline brilliance of her eyes. Her hair had been white for many years ; thanks to her pride in it and the devotion of Marguerite its unchanging whiteness above her delicate cheeks gave to her rareness the permanence of a piece of porcelain, an air of perpetual youth, which, reinforced by the activity of her swift and passionate intelligence, were invariably fatal to men of middle age, to men, in short, of the generation most useful to her ambitions.

The consciousness of this power, so sedulously nursed, had made her the terror of the neighbourhood, particularly of the women of her own station. Even her generosity, which was lavish and unbounded, had become suspect. You never knew where you were with her, people said ; the point at which the flame of her scathing intelligence might leap out and sear ; the moment when her kindliness might give place to an insolence, unpremeditated, but none the less intolerable. By the imminence of this terror she ruled her household, hovering over them like a hawk above a pen of chickens. With her children she was usually complacent, recognizing, perhaps, beneath their various exteriors, and particularly in the case of Vivien, some germ of her own ardent nature.

To her husband, the principal victim, as people supposed, of her humours, her attitude was curiously complicated. There was no doubt that she had put him through the mill ; Marguerite and Parker, the butler, could testify to that ;

and yet this solemn, pasty little man, with his pouched and neutral eyes, was the only creature on earth whom she respected. He was her masterpiece. The baronetcy, the splendour and ease of Stourford, the vast impressiveness of the works at Wolverbury, all these she had created; and, now that they were firmly established, her whole life was consumed in care and respect for her creation and for him, its inadequate symbol. In private she still bullied him; on occasions she still bullied him in public; but the pursuit of her cult had crystallized into a conviction that, in the end, her creation could do no wrong, so that, in later years, she had found herself deferring, quite astonishingly, to his judgment.

Sir Joseph, whose cunning had developed beneath her tutelage, was quick to recognize his advantage. On a different plane he was as intelligent as his wife. By nice experience he knew the exact point at which he might assert himself. He had done so in the moment of exhaustion that followed the tempest aroused by the announcement of Ralph's engagement to Clare. He liked Ralph. The boy's placid nature was nearer to his own than those of George or Vivien; and when once he had carried his point, like a savage who imagines that he can extract virtue from the skin of a monster that he has killed, he had wrapped himself in the spoils of his triumph and flaunted them before the whole household, insisting not only on Clare's recognition, but on her invitation to Stourford.

The principal sufferer from the struggle was Marguerite. A big-boned, middle-aged Italian-Swiss, with a high-coloured complexion, creaking corsets and large, insensitive brown eyes, she had submitted for five years to the embarrassments of the Anglo-French dialect which Lady Hingston, in her more tranquil moods, had invented as a means of communication between them. By perseverance she had mastered the grammar and pronunciation of this original tongue so that, when she wasn't flurried, she could speak it with reasonable fluency ; but when Lady Hingston lost her temper Marguerite lost her head, and relapsed pitifully into French as it is spoken in Lugano. " Don't gabble like that ! *Comment est-ce-que vous osez parler avec cet accent abominable ?* " her mistress would cry. And Marguerite, abashed by the inadequacy of her native tongue and too frightened to recollect the syntax of that which Lady Hingston had invented, would clutch feebly at the language that she spoke in the servant's hall, muttering : " Pardon, my lady, I have not understand." With the result that the bulk of their conversations were bilingual : the commands of Lady Hingston being issued in execrable French and Marguerite's replies in equally execrable English. Since the news of Ralph's engagement the bilingual phase had lasted for four days ; and although Lady Hingston was " getting over it by degrees," Marguerite feared from a certain birdlike fierceness in her glance that there was more to come.

" *Bon jour*, Marguerite," she sniffed, without looking at her.

" Good morning, my lady." The worst was to be feared. Marguerite went red in preparation.

" *Je suis beaucoup en retard ce matin. Je dois m'habiller tout-de-suite.* This petticoat is *trop longue. Je le connais bien. Portez des epingles ! Àl'instant !* Are you asleep ? "

" *Non, madame.* . . . No, my lady. . . ."

Creaking like a hamper Marguerite dropped to her knees, her wide mouth, like a Chinese monster's, bristling with pins.

" *C'est ici,*" said Lady Hingston. " *Plus qu'un* inch. On the left. *Mon dieu ! Etes vous folle ? J'ai dit* left, *pas* right ! "

Marguerite swayed from one knee to the other, painfully straddled. sticking pins with a devoted desperation into the petticoat's hem that swirled in her eyes as Lady Hingston wriggled with impatience. Then suddenly, as if she had forgotten all about her, her mistress darted to the writing-table and closed the lid of the inkpot. Marguerite followed ludicrously on her knees, shedding pins as she went.

" One moment, my lady," she gasped.

" *Quoi?* " said Lady Hingston. " *Ca ne fait riens Trouvez moi un autre. Le vert. Et rammassez les epingle.* Marguerite ! *Vous êtes sourd?* "

" Yes, madame. . . . No, my lady. . . ."

" *Ecoutez. La fiancée de Monsieur Ralph vient ici aujourd'hui. Il faut que vous êtes sa* maid, *n'est-ce-pas? Comprenez? Elle est une fille de bonne famille, mais d'un type un peu bourgeois.* Kindly keep that to yourself. No gossip in the kitchen. *Eh bien, peutêtre elle n'a pas des confections convenables. Voyez si ce n'est pas quelque chose de noir dans les tiroirs de Mademoiselle Vivien, n'est-ce-pas?* "

" Yes, my lady," spluttered Marguerite, her mouth full of the scattered pins. She creaked on to her feet again. " But the petticoat : I shorten ? "

Lady Hingston tossed her head. Already she had stepped out of the pin-puckered garment. She darted towards the door of her dressing-room, a slight but militant figure in her ermine jacket. She turned.

" *Le vert. N'ai-je-pas dit? Où est votre tête?* Remember, *je vous confie pour la faire presentable. Allez, allez !* "

She closed the door in the face of the disconcerted Marguerite. Marguerite, with tears in her big eyes, stood staring at the door like a cow, making piteous movements up and down with her joined hands.

## IX

### STOURFORD

So Clare came to Stourford. Alone : for behind the gracious phrases of Lady Hingston's letter Aunt Cathie was quick to perceive that she wasn't wanted. The doctor had never liked the Hingstons, she told herself, and that was enough for her ; her conduct had so long conformed to the standard of the old man's prejudices that even now they continued to direct her.

" They might have realized," she complained, " that I am still in deep mourning. It's quite out of the question that I should go gadding out to tea-parties. Particularly to strangers," she added.

She insisted, however, that Clare should be driven over by Jabez in the victoria.

" It isn't as if we hadn't a carriage of our own," she said. " As a matter of fact, we were carriage-folk long before the Hingstons. I do hope, Clare darling, you won't allow yourself to be patronized."

" They're not a bit like that, Aunt Cathie," Clare told her.

Aunt Cathie shook her head : " Of course I don't presume to interfere in your affairs. You're old enough to look after yourself ; but Lady Hingston has the reputation of being a very difficult woman. You must be careful to hold your own."

She busied herself with the preparation of Clare's wardrobe as though she were arming her for a battle. An inadequate armament, she was bound to confess. " Still, you're in mourning," she repeated with a macabre satisfaction, " and they'll have sense enough, I hope, to realize it That excuses everything. Besides, black is always good and ladylike."

As they stood on the doorstep waiting for Jabez to stagger out with the luggage the postman arrived with the afternoon letters. Aunt Cathie possessed herself of them greedily. One was addressed to Clare in Wilburn's formal hand. Aunt Cathie's eyes followed it so eagerly that Clare was forced to let her see its contents. They were brief, and to the point :

*My dear Clare,*
*Your aunt has written to me, announcing the news of your engagement. I hasten to send you my congratulations, and every good wish for your future happiness.*
                    *Believe me,*
                         *Always yours sincerely,*
                              *Dudley Wilburn.*

It was not an exciting letter ; but Clare's mind was so flushed with the prospect of her adventure that everything seemed new and roseate. " It was sweet of him to write so quickly, wasn't it ? " she said, with dancing eyes. " He *is* a dear ! "

" Yes," said Aunt Cathie. " Here is another for you."

The writing was that of Mr. Darnay. Clare took it hurriedly and put it in her pocket. But Aunt Cathie's eyes were no longer curious ; she was staring at the half-sheet of Wilburn's letter, reading into its stiff phrases the force of a concealed emotion. For the moment her self-interest had vanished ; she was suffering with Wilburn, admiring the fortitude, the graciousness with which he had taken his blow, remembering the frank honesty of his confession, protesting, with all her soul, against the criminal lightness of this chit of a girl who could throw herself into the arms of a boy like Ralph Hingston when she might have had this paragon of sobriety and strength. If only I had been younger, she thought, I could have shown him what true devotion means !

" All ready, Miss," old Jabez panted. " Jump in, Miss Clare."

The little victoria creaked as she stepped into it ; the brake-handle grated on its ratchet ; they moved off slowly, the old horse whisking its tail, and Clare sitting bolt upright in her black silk frock and the hat which she had worn at the funeral.

They had almost reached Stourford before she realized how formidable this adventure was. As they passed beneath the unfinished freestone gateway her heart began to founder. The victoria, old Jabez and herself seemed curiously shabby and out of date, reduced to insignificance by the lavish expanses of park through which the drive wound upward. The boisterous wind, sweeping over open ground, had blown her hat awry. She wished that she had not submitted to Aunt Cathie in the choice of clothes. Her black frock made her feel like a new housemaid driving up from the station in a fly with her tin box behind, and all the stucco battlements of Stourford regarded her with contempt. But as they pulled up at the foot of the steps Vivien came flying down to meet her, Vivien, with her dark hair streaming and all the kindness of her soul in her ardent face.

" Clare, darling," she gasped, " I've been watching the drive for hours. How sweet and demure you look in that black foulard ! No, never mind about your luggage ; the footman will see to that. Come along in at once. Ralph's over at Wolverbury doing his duty, so I shall have you all to myself. And tea's ready. Mother's waiting in the hall."

If only Lady Hingston had not been waiting it would have been easier. There she stood, small, but incredibly potent, in black satin and an osprey toque pinned with a flying arrow of diamonds. Her skin was so pink and clear beneath her silvery hair, her nose so delicately curved, her lips so red, that Clare was dazzled. I shall never be able to look like that, she thought, as long as I live.

With a curious mixture of graciousness and frigidity she took Clare in her arms and kissed her. In the contact of this clear, cool skin of Lady Hingston's cheek she was conscious of a delicate, faint perfume of ambar which seemed to her the physical emanation of the elder woman's refinement.

They sat down to tea at a folding table fitted with a silver tray. The cups were Worcester, thin lipped, with scrolled gilt handles—Lady Hingston, as a member of the new aristocracy, believed in patronizing the county's industries —but the tea inside them was thin and tasteless : very different from that of Thirza, who liked some body in hers. As Clare sipped it those clear black eyes were on her. She felt that she was gulping like a child at a school treat. Her appetite deserted her. She could not help despairing at the delicate relish with which the pretty, brilliant teeth of Lady Hingston devoured the curls of bread and butter as if they were her natural food. She sat amazed before such virtuosity.

" I hope you will be comfortable, Clare," Lady Hingston said at last. " Vivien will show you your room, won't you, darling ? And my maid, Marguerite, will look after you. You'll find her very clever. Of course you *do* speak French ? "

" A little," Clare confessed. She had a vision of the class-room at St. Monica's, herself mumbling a paragraph of Erckmann-Chatrian.

" She'll understand you better if you do," Lady Hingston's voice was melodiously persuasive, each syllable slipped through her lips complete, as though those pretty teeth had applied themselves to its perfection. She rose and touched Clare's shoulder in a little, friendly gesture. Then she held her at arm's length and looked into her face with an amused and quizzical air. Clare felt herself going shy and red beneath this scrutiny. She smiled nervously with trembling lips, and as she did so Lady Hingston smiled too, in a sudden comprehension of the child's youth and innocence. " I want to see what you are like," she said. " Yes . . ." On the long-drawn sibilant she stopped. Then she took Clare's face in her two hands and kissed her. " I hope you'll be happy, my child," she said.

" I do love him so," Clare whispered.

Lady Hingston gave a little laugh. " I have such a heap of letters to write," she said. In any embarrassment her correspondence always overwhelmed her. " This Primrose League will be the death of me. Now, Vivien, don't for goodness sake forget that dinner's early this evening : half-past seven. And see that Clare has everything she wants. Run along, children ! "

And Clare still smiled ; her heart was bursting with gratitude for the other's generosity.

" She's so pretty," she said, as they ascended to Vivien's bedroom.

" Who's pretty ? " Vivien asked.

" Your mother. Don't you think so ? "

" Oh, mother's all right," said Vivien carelessly. " Of course, you know, we're all a little mad ; all except George. But then, we're really rather nice with it. Mother's a chameleon. One day she looks about twenty-five, and the next she's ninety. It just depends how the fancy takes her, how she wants to look. It's funny, you know ; she puzzles everyone except me. I know her inside out. There's one thing certain, and that is that she likes you. I don't think she particularly wanted to ; but she does. Of course she couldn't help it."

" Vivien, you make me shy when you talk like that."

" Well, you are *rather* nice, you know. Several people have noticed it. Including Ralph."

They sat on the bed talking. The relation was new to Clare, but curiously happy and reassuring. There was an

air of bright spaciousness in this room of Vivien's that
seemed strange to her after the low-ceilinged bedrooms at
Pen House with their ivy-shadowed lattices and ponderous
furniture.  Here everything was clean and shining as a new
needle ; from the gay print curtains to the polished floor
the room was full of air and light ; a faint, hygienic scent
of beeswax pervaded it.  It was not beautiful, and yet its
lack of beauty was atoned for by its freshness, its clarity,
its freedom.  Like Vivien herself, Clare decided ; for when
you examined her in detail Vivien was not beautiful, though
her features, like those of the room, suggested a happiness
unhampered by memories of the past, serenely confident
of the future, a pleasant, uncomplicated tenor of life, so
completely detached from care that in it one could be contented with the mere joy of being alive.

They talked for a long while about this life of Stourford,
so different from anything that Clare had known before,
so free from the domestic preoccupations that enveloped
Aunt Cathie's, so innocent of meditation or the subtle pains
of art, so clean, so empty.  Talking of it and inhaling its
atmosphere, Clare felt as if she had been transported into
a high, rarefied air, sparkling as wine, but a little intoxicating.
It was difficult to reconcile her black silk frock and the
crape on her hat, those sombre reminders of Pen House,
with this stimulating altitude.  She felt happy, and yet
a trifle giddy and unreal.

A knock at the door.  In answer to Vivien's cheery
" Come in ! " Marguerite entered.  Her keys !  Immediately Clare's rapture faded.  She saw her poor little trunk
exposed in pitiless light, contemptuously rifled by the hands
of this tall foreigner.  Vivien would not allow her to escape
exposure.  The keys were produced and surrendered.
Clare felt like a convict entering a jail, like a vanquished
defender delivering the keys of a fortress into enemy hands.

Later, in her own room, a sumptuous, bow-windowed

chamber of blue and gold, with a four-poster sheltered by the wings of golden eagles, she found that she had no need to dread the discreet Marguerite. Her baggage had disappeared ; its lamentable contents had been disposed in drawers of modern Chippendale that smelt of lavender. Her bath stood waiting for her, its temperature precisely regulated ; and when she returned from it, glowing and exhilarated, she saw her white party-frock from St. Monica's laid reverently on the brocaded counterpane. How easy a life, she thought, in which one didn't have to think what one should wear !

Marguerite creaked into the room in tight-fitting bodice of black sateen and a lawn apron.

" Your hair, Ma'm'selle ? Perhaps you speak French ? "

A little. Marguerite sighed in relief ; for Clare's schoolgirl French was simplicity itself compared with the dialect invented by Lady Hingston. Marguerite let herself go. As Clare sat before the gilt mirror with closed eyes, hypnotized by the swishing of the brush and the light touch of the maid's skilful hands, she found herself listening to a spate of rapid speech on whose surface she clutched at floating straws of intelligibility.

She had lovely hair—*mais ravissants !*—and so much of it. What a pity that she should dress it with such unbecoming simplicity. Simplicity was one thing. A natural wave. Let her wait and she should see. Like this ! Marguerite's fingers flickered and darted like spindles, twining the dark strands into whorls and spools and curled shells. The hairpins grazed her scalp so lightly that she ceased to dread their thrusting. How fortunate a young lady ! M. Ralph was the best of the whole family : so calm, so handsome, so veritably English. They were all kind, the family Ingson. Ladyship was a little nervous sometimes ; she made her lose her head till it was empty as a balloon. But then, so generous ! One could not have all the qualities. Mr.

Parker too. A brave man, with dignity, and respectful
So different from the people in the village. The young men
in Stourford, knowing she was a foreigner, took it for granted
that she was a person of loose morals. She, a married
woman, or at least a widow, with a daughter of seventeen !
Her husband had been an Italian, one of the first chefs in
Lugano. He had died of *poumonite*, suddenly. A fine
man : more than ninety-five kilos. A hot kitchen, and
cold winds from the Alps. His relatives were farmers on
Lac Majeur : her daughter was still with them. " And
I am here," she ended. " *Regardez, Mademoiselle ! Enfin !* "
Marguerite stepped backward with clasped hands and surveyed her art in triumph. Now the white dress. A little
out of fashion : the neck too high, the sleeves not full
enough ; but when one had youth these things were nothing.
A little string of pearls—not big ones, like the ladyship's—
*tout, tout petites ?* No ? But, perhaps, it was better.
A young lady had no need of jewels : the eyes, the lips, the
teeth ! Like that. . . .

Her dark eyes widened with an admiration as naive as if,
in Clare's adornment, she had achieved a vicarious sensation
of youth : a youth innocent of black sateen and white lawn
aprons, in which the young girls, with combs in their dark
hair, strolled arm-in-arm along the quays under the shadows
of plane-trees, glancing sideways at youths in their Sunday
clothes, seeing the placid shapes of wooded mountains,
and the reflections of cypresses that pierced the still lake-
water like the points of spears. She turned to go, half
reluctantly. My lady would be wanting her. Would
Mademoiselle wait here till Miss Vivien came to fetch her ?
Miss Vivien had sent that message.

Clare was alone, rapt in the contemplation of her transformed self. A knock startled her, as though her vanity
had been discovered. She hurried to the door.

" Good evening." It was Ralph's voice, soft and modulated by respect for the modesty of her bedroom. "How are you?" he said. "Everything all right? I suppose I can't see you?"

She didn't really know, but before she could answer he had continued:

"Open the door a little bit and put your hand through. No, not that hand, you silly child, the other one!"

Standing behind the door she felt his fingers close on her wrist, his warm lips kissing her palm. Then something cold encircled her third finger.

"Look at it," he said, "and see if it's all right. I got it this afternoon in North Bromwich. That's why I'm late."

She withdrew her hand. She saw a gold circlet set with a single diamond whose facets flashed blue and green and orange and blood-red.

"Oh, Ralph, it's lovely," she whispered back. "You darling!"

He laughed softly. "Clear-white," he said. "Can't I see more of you?"

She opened the door. To the danger of Marguerite's coiffure he took her and crushed her in his arms.

"My love, my love," he whispered.

# X

## DINNER AT STOURFORD

IT was unfortunate that her first evening had coincided with a dinner-party. Sir Joseph always entertained on Saturdays, when the week's work at Wolverbury was over, usually as an excuse for carrying his business with him to Stourford. That evening he had invited one of his directors, Lord Arthur Powys, whom he always called his "bowideel " of an aristocrat, to spend the week-end with him and meet the guiding genius of the Sedgebury Main Colliery, that Mr. Furnival of whom Clare had heard so much from Wilburn at Pen House.

At dinner she had sat between them. She liked Lord Arthur, a long-legged, rather shabby creature with a silky, straw-coloured beard, through which he mumbled as though he were always talking to himself, and kind, blue, meditative eyes ; but Furnival she hated. There was too much of the animal in his turbulent, fiery hair, his unkempt beard, his greedy mouth and eyes. For one moment those eyes had swept her with a devouring intensity that made her skin burn. His glance was like the breath of an unopened furnace. It was as if it had appraised and rejected her. When it had passed she felt that she no longer existed, except for one embarrassing moment, when she had felt against her thigh the warm, disquieting pressure of his knee and had withdrawn herself into a constricted space. After the soup Furnival had talked across her, projecting his vivid personality into the dull eyes of Sir Joseph, or Lord Arthur's languid body, so that she felt herself feeble, isolated, out of place, and appallingly remote from Ralph.

At the other end of the table Lady Hingston, in white satin, gleamed and flashed her plumage like a bird of paradise. On her right hand Mr. Pomfret, in a silk waistcoat, followed the giddy gyrations of her flight. Next to Sir Joseph rose the bare and bony shoulders of the Vicar's wife. She sat there with a fixed smile of satisfaction in her surroundings, pretending to listen to her neighbour, George Hingston, a tall, spare, sallow version of his father, but actually straining her ears to catch the enormities that Lady Hingston's lips were launching at the Vicar. She hated Lady Hingston with a deep and bitter grudging. They were excellent friends. But that evening she had set out with the intention of seeing that the Vicar was not bullied,

Dead opposite to Clare sat her future sister-in-law,
Eleanor, George's wife, a matt and rather lifeless beauty,
with magnificent diamonds and a compressed, unhappy
smile. Ralph had habitually spoken rather scornfully of
Eleanor ; Vivien had never mentioned her name ; and this
made Clare anxious to see what she was like. It was difficult ; for whenever she stole a quiet glance in her direction,
Eleanor was regarding her fixedly with her dead, grey,
beautiful eyes. Once only Clare caught them glancing at
her husband ; and then she was aware of an enormous
spiritual separation. There was a barrier more absolute
than Vivien's body between Eleanor and George. The
stony serenity of Eleanor's unhappiness chilled Clare's
heart. She thought : " This woman, far more refined
and beautiful than me, has married Ralph's brother, and
see how unhappy she is ! Supposing . . ." But even as
the idea disquieted her she caught Ralph's eye ; he smiled
and secretly lifted his glass, and all her confidence returned.
He was so different from George, so different from all of
them. It only troubled her to know that Eleanor's cold eyes
had intercepted the gay confidence that passed between
them.

By this time the circulation of Clicquot had stimulated
Sir Joseph's end of the table to a loud discussion on the
finances of Willis, Hackett and Willis, the great steelworks
at Mawne. Suddenly the penetrating voice of Mrs.
Pomfret rang above it like a clarion. Her quick ears,
pendulous beneath her crow's nest of grey hair, had caught
the echo of her hostess's last phrase.

" And what has the poor church done *now*, Lady Hingston ? "

A sudden silence fell on the whole table. Beneath it
could be heard the sombre voice of Parker attaining the
discretion that Marguerite admired : " Ice-pudding or
meringue, madam ? . . . Meringue or ice-pudding, sir ? "

Lady Hingston smiled wickedly, her head thrown back like a white peacock's when it spreads its tail. She did not answer. Sir Joseph blinked; Lord Arthur thrust out a bony hand for salted almonds; only Mr. Furnival smiled with the satisfaction of a collier at a dog-fight.

"And, pray, what has the poor church done now?" the militant voice of Mrs. Pomfret repeated. Her husband gave a beseeching smile at Lady Hingston. "Meringue or ice-pudding, sir?" Parker murmured confidentially. Lady Hingston, like an actress waiting for her cue, allowed time for Parker to finish his question, and the Vicar to mask his confusion by a slice of pudding. Her voice was innocent and persuasive.

"It's what the poor church *hasn't* done, Mrs. Pomfret," she said.

Furnival's lips twitched upward in a shrill cackle of laughter. Lord Arthur leant forward and smiled behind his beard. The Vicar's face was contorted with the cold of an immoderate mouthful of ice, and Mrs. Pomfret, red to the ears, relapsed into Sir Joseph's tactful protection.

"Ice-pudding or meringue, Miss?" said Parker, solemnly.

A moment later, sparkling with triumph and generosity, Lady Hingston rose and shepherded her opponent to the drawing-room. Clare followed them with Vivien, who soon dutifully deserted her for Mrs. Furnival, a tiny woman in a shapeless Liberty djibbeh, who had spoken in monosyllables throughout the evening. Clare found herself alone in a corner with Mrs. George, who continued to examine her critically with her lovely cold grey eyes. Her shoulders were white and smoothly moulded, with a faint silky lustre, like that of a soapstone carving, they seemed too perfect to be alive; her voice was low, her pronunciation delicate and precise; but when she was not speaking her lips relaxed, by habit, into a smile that suggested nothing but unhappiness. She spoke with a curiously distant manner of Clare's engagement.

" I hear you are going to live at Uffdown Manor," she said.

" Oh, it's hardly as definite as that," Clare told her, " Ralph had some wild idea . . ."

" I should keep him to it," said Eleanor. " George and I are forced to live at Wolverbury. The smoke is simply dreadful ; it soils lace curtains in less than a week. George doesn't know the difference. He spends every moment of his day at the works. They might just as well rivet him in a bed of concrete like one of the rolling mills for all I see of him."

" But you have your children," Clare suggested.

" Yes."

" I've never seen them."

" No. You'll have to come over one day with Ralph. Is that your engagement ring ? "

Clare held out her finger. All through dinner she had been stealing shy glances at it to see if it were really there. Eleanor surveyed it calmly. In the light of her own diamonds it looked a little insignificant.

" Yes," she said, with the first gleam of keenness in her magnificent eyes. " I don't see any reason why you shouldn't be happy. The family are a queer lot. Don't be put upon by George's mother, that's the great thing. You've seen how rude she can be. I had it out with her six years ago, and now we get on quite well. I mean we simply don't exist for each other. All she worries about is that I should look nice. I'm part of the window-dressing for Wolverbury. Admiralty inspectors and so on. We have to give them lunch."

" I think you're simply lovely," said Clare in a timid burst of admiration.

" Yes, I know," said Eleanor, lifelessly. " So are the

children. And now I suppose I'm going to have another."

Clare blushed. The only thing she could think of saying was, " Are you ? " and that seemed inadequate.

" Well, Ralph's the best of them," Eleanor added suddenly. " Here he comes. I suppose I shall have to surrender you."

She didn't look as if she minded. Clare watched her calm eyes following the movements of George. Ralph whispered in Clare's ear : " Let's get away out of this," and a moment later they were alone in the empty morning-room. Nobody seemed to notice their going. The wide, warm house was as impersonal as an hotel ; it was only when they were alone that she could rid herself of the feeling that even its most intimate luxuries were designed for the entertainment of strangers, that Lady Hingston herself was rather a beautiful and efficient ornament than a real person, filling, at Stourford, the place which Eleanor was forced to occupy at Wolverbury. Ralph was real enough, thank heaven ; so was Vivien, and so, indubitably, was Marguerite. But Mr. Parker . . .

It was nearly midnight when Ralph took her along the wide, soft-carpeted corridor to the bedroom door. Their good-night kisses had a new and curious quality in these luxurious surroundings. It seemed to her that Marguerite's sophisticated fingers had changed more than the shape of her hair. Her whole personality was changed. And Ralph, too, seemed different in the sleekness of his evening-dress, his carefully-smoothed hair, his face, that looked more sanguine than ever above the high starched collar. Of course he was more handsome and she more elegant ; and yet, in their unusual brilliance, something had been lost. As he kissed her she closed her eyes to shut out Sir Joseph's electric light and tried to wish herself backward into the atmosphere that she knew, of darkness and soft air and whispering leaves. It was useless. Haunted by a vague dissatisfaction she closed the door behind her.

Nor could she sleep. Under the spread wings of those gilt eagles she lay and stared into the dark canopy. Since the day of her grandfather's death life had moved too swiftly for her. She wanted a breathing space in which to collect her thoughts. Hitherto her life had been compact of dreams and meditations. At Stourford there was not room for this quietist existence. By day and night the place was flooded with strong light that allowed no relaxation or privacy. It was like living in the midst of a moving crowd out of which, perpetually, as she lay awake, she could hear the butler's sepulchral voice demanding, " Ice-pudding or meringue, sir ? Meringue or ice-pudding, madam ? " With so many sounds and visions and shadows of strange personality racing through her mind, it was useless to think of sleep. It suddenly struck her that in her excitement she had forgotten to read her appointed text from *The More Excellent Way*. Miss Boldmere would not have forgotten. By now, no doubt, Miss Boldmere was asleep in that little room at St. Monica's, faintly scented with incense. How unsubstantial, how utterly remote Miss Boldmere seemed ! Clare switched on her bedside lamp and read the passage listlessly. It had no meaning for her, and yet, by association, it reminded her of the letter from Mr. Darnay which she had left unopened. She took it from the drawer in which Marguerite had discreetly concealed it.

> *Bellevue Villas,*
> *Wychbury, Worcs.*

*My dear daughter,*

*Since last I saw you your life has been very crowded and exciting. I was distressed for you when I heard of your dear grandfather's death, and, above all, for your poor aunt, on whom the blow must have fallen even more heavily. I have been thinking a great deal about your grandfather, for even though he was not by profession a Christian, and, therefore, cannot have passed to the next world in a state of Grace, his works were full of the spirit of Christ, and we, of the Church Militant, may hope that we do rightly in invoking the intercessory prayers of the Blessed Saints on his behalf. I know that you are doing this daily. Remember that such invocations are always most effective during the Eucharistic Sacrifice.*

*Then, as a still greater surprise, I hear from the Vicar the news of your engagement and approaching marriage to Mr. Hingston. It astonished me all the more because I do not remember your having mentioned his name to me at any time. Perhaps it has slipped my memory. You know, I feel sure, how deeply I feel for and with you in this solemn moment, and how ardently I pray for your true happiness. I think you have been thoroughly instructed in the attitude of the Church toward the Sacrament of Holy Matrimony and realize its solemnity. I hope you will not let the natural excitement of the occasion divert your mind from this aspect of the matter. At Stourford you will meet many strangers who will flatter you with the importance of your engagement. Remember that this is a season for humility and prayer rather than for elation. I think it would be a good thing for you to go into retreat for a few days. It would calm your thoughts, and give you a chance to meditate. It has alarmed me a little not to have seen you at Mass for nearly a week.*

*Believe me, my dear daughter,*

*Yours, in Christ,*

*Cyril Darnay.*

*Day of the Holy Guardian Angels, 1897.*

This letter, kindly and gentle as it seemed, was full of veiled reproaches. Clare knew that she deserved them, every one. It was true that she had not mentioned Ralph's name to Mr. Darnay in her confessions ; true that she had absented herself from St. Chad's ; true that she had failed in her duty of pleading for intercession on the doctor's behalf ; that she had not thought of her engagement in the terms that Mr. Darnay suggested. Lying there under the gilt canopy and staring at the dainty meticulous hand of Mr. Darnay's letter, she realized that she should have felt guilty and repentant. Honestly she felt nothing of the kind : only very sleepy and rather irritated. It was not that she questioned Mr. Darnay's right to instruct and direct her, but that these directions and instructions seemed to come to her from a distance only less remote than that of Miss Boldmere's ; they were unreal and fugitive, like the remembered perfume of stale incense. Her mind was so full of new experience, her life so crowded with urgent practical necessities and enthralling dreams, that there was no room in either for Miss Boldmere or Mr. Darnay. She did not reject religion as an integral part of her life ; but she began to realize that it had previously engrossed her because her emotions had no other means of expression. On this new plane of existence it began to assume proportions more modest in relation to the rest of her life. " After all," she told herself, " I'm not going to become a nun."

She saw herself, in retrospect, as an inhuman little prig, and wondered at the forbearance with which Ralph, dear thing, had treated her. " To-morrow," she thought, " is Sunday. I'll get him to walk over with me to St. Chad's." To-morrow ? It was Sunday already. She folded the letter under her pillow and switched off the light. As she fell asleep she was conscious not of the folded paper, but of the unaccustomed pressure of Ralph's ring upon her finger.

# XI

## BROADSIDES

FROM that night forward she found herself caught up in the machinery of Lady Hingston's unceasing activities. They gave her no respite. Only at night, when she lay down tired on her canopied four-poster, or in those short, sweet evenings which she spent alone with Ralph, had she time to project her thoughts in any direction but that of the engrossing moment.

On the following Wednesday Ralph snatched an afternoon to make a second pilgrimage to Uffdown Manor. This time they rode over on the new bicycles, armed with keys and measuring tapes. Vivien accompanied them; and somehow the atmosphere of that enchanted house seemed subtly changed. It was not that the silvery façade of brick was less sedately lovely; over the tangled borders an October sky hung low and grey, impressing the suspended calm of autumn on the slow-winged fluttering of late Vanessae; peacocks and red admirals, which spread their eyes and bars of velvety gloom as listlessly as if they knew that the season of flight and gaiety was over. Greedily they sucked the fermented juices of fallen fruit whose skins the wasps had wounded with their powerful jaws. They were so drunk and sluggish that no human shadow could disturb them.

Within the house the air was warm and full of a faint flavour of old oak floors. The rooms were small, but beautifully proportioned, the walls made lovely in themselves by oblong panels with conventional Adam designs. The place was not nearly as big as Clare had imagined; but the skilful handling of its dimensions made each room seem gracious and calm and self-possessed, in vivid contrast to the pretentious restlessness of Stourford.

While Ralph and Vivien laughed and grew hot in the tangles of their tapes, Clare wandered away from them into a private dream in which she found herself imagining the life that she would live there, so different in every way from the repression of Pen House and Stourford's glaring publicity. She began to feel that it was already her own. Here, where the tall windows faced westward, she would make her music-room. A black Bechstein, over whose shining cover, innocent of the ornaments which infested Aunt Cathie's silk-pleated Broadwood, she could gaze outward, downward, past the rounded heads of elm trees, into the rosy air that bathed the unseen plain. There she would sit, at sunset in springtime, waiting for Ralph to come home from Wolverbury, playing all old and formal music, the stately movement of minuet and sarabande and pavane, and her playing would carry her back into the century when that gracious room was planned, so that the kindly spirits of those who had built it would wake and smile on her.

" Why, there you are ! " the voice of Vivien exclaimed. " Poor old Ralph's been scouring the whole house in search of you. Ralph, Ralph, darling, I've found her ! " she cried. " No, honestly, Clare, I call that shirking. Look here. We've got the measurements of nearly everything except this. Catch hold of the end of the tape, my child, and do your duty. Seventeen feet exactly ; remember that until Ralph brings the book. Seventeen feet wide. . . . I say, what a jolly floor for dancing ; you could slide on it. Clare, I should have a window-seat there ; no, not a window-seat, you know what I mean, a settee, to catch the view out of this window. It gets the evening light."

" No. The piano goes there," Clare murmured.

" Oh, does it ? " Vivien laughed. " So you've not been dreaming after all. Well, if you want to dance of course you must have one."

Not Vivien's sort of dancing, Clare thought ; and yet how sweet she was with her ardent eyes, her clean, flushed cheeks, and that faint dusky down on her upper lip above the good-natured mouth. They heard Ralph's voice :

" So here you are," he echoed. " Clare, I simply must have a look at those stables before I go. They're the most attractive thing about the place. I had a long yarn about drainage and ventilation with Barwise, the vet. the other day. Give me that big key, Vivien, there's a love. Then you can lock up here and catch us up."

Vivien laughed softly : " Huh . . . _I_ know what that means."

And so did Clare. It was the first time they had managed to slip her all afternoon. Now they were really engaged Vivien wasn't half so tactful as in the days before ; and even Ralph seemed to forget his opportunities when he had swung the big door of the stable yard upon its rusty hinges. Clare viewed his enthusiasms indulgently ; he was so definite in knowing what he wanted, and this exaggerated love of horses seemed so integral a part of him. It would be awful, she thought, if he were to feel that she was unsympathetic. She must qualify herself to share it with him ; she must make herself understand and see and feel as he did.

How much a part of him this passion was she realized a week later when hounds met at Stourford. She awakened early to a sound of cracking whips and whimpers and a stamping of iron-shod hoofs on the drive, for the huntsman and his whips had clattered over from the kennels with the dog-pack. She ran to her window. The dew-frosted lawn was scattered with hounds who waved their feathery tails and sprawled and sniffed and gambolled in a restless morris of white and tan, or sat upon their sterns, staring at nothing, with their handsome, solemn faces.

By the time that Clare descended the hall was full of clinking spurs, and of the odour of leather and buckskin and melton coats that smelt of clean horseflesh. Since Sir Joseph, who preferred the smell of steel, had set off as usual for Wolverbury, Ralph did the honours of the house. Very handsome he looked with his close-shaven sanguine face above a high white stock, fastened with a gold pin shaped like a hunting-horn. He wore a black, full-skirted coat, white breeches and black riding-boots. His eyes shone, his physical completeness gave him an air of gallantry and daring. Clare could see how popular he was with this unfamiliar breed of clean, wire-sinewed men with steady eyes, high complexions and hands made callous by habitual contact with leather, who looked like grooms and spoke like gentlemen. Ralph knew them all, he passed among them smiling, playing the good fellow to perfection, while Lady Hingston, herself smooth and dainty as a thoroughbred, sparkled among the crowd.

Now the expansion of the drive began to fill. Strangers, whom Clare only knew by name, came rolling up in jingles, pony-carts and high wagonettes. Their faces were all fresh and healthy as that crisp morning with its nip of frost in the air and its warm hues and odours of dead leaves ; their eyes shone like the dew on blackberry clusters. In every face she could see an eagerness ; it was as though the restless waiting pack had infected their blood.

The master gave his word. There was a sudden tumult of horses backing and turning, of stampings and curses and quick encouragement. The pack streaked away down the drive with three black velvet caps bobbing above scarlet. The word was passed from mouth to mouth : " Hell Wood . . . He's drawing Hell Wood first. With this wind he'll run into the osiers at Stourhead." Vivien waved her crop gaily. She looked unusually slim and elegant, her silk hat was no more glossy than her dark hair. She was as graceful and sleek as the chestnut mare of which she seemed a part. Ralph came up to Clare ; he slipped his arm about her and drew her into the cloakroom to kiss her good-bye. His breath smelt of whisky. She didn't like it ; and yet somehow it seemed in keeping with his flushed, full-blooded face.

" What a pity you don't ride," he said. " We must begin to-morrow. I'd love to pilot you over the Stourhead country : by Jove, that'd be worth living for. And such a ripping day ! Good-bye, my darling."

He kissed her again. From the top of the steps she watched him leap on to Starlight's back and make a short cut over the dewy grass of the park. He flew like a skimming swallow. It was heartening, splendid, heroic, this sure, swift co-ordination of movement.

" Thank God that's over," sighed Lady Hingston.

By this time Clare was no longer shocked by these frequent invocations of the Almighty ; they were one of Lady Hingston's little mannerisms. What was more, she knew that, even if the relief were genuine, her future mother-in-law had enjoyed the meet as a social occasion on which she could shine to perfection. It was part of the function of Stourford to do this sort of thing as well as, or better than, the other great houses in the neighbourhood. Even if Mawne Hall had possessed the covers—which it didn't— she knew quite well that the Willises couldn't have carried it off like this. The middle-classes might scoff ; but the county would soon realize that when the Hingstons had bought Stourford they had come to stay. The excitement of the breakfast had left her with such an overflow of energy and activity that she must needs whirl Clare off upon a shopping expedition to North Bromwich.

" It's far too lovely a day to go in by train. We'll drive, and get back for tea. Are you ready ? "

Clare assented, but by the time that she had spoken Lady Hingston was gone. Indeed, there was no question of refusal ; for, once having accepted her presence, Lady Hingston seemed loth to let her go. Wherever she went, in Ralph's absence, she expected Clare to go with her. It was as if she had deliberately set herself to impress her personality on Clare, to mould her to a satisfactory type in the shortest possible time. And Clare, in her new and all-embracing generosity and goodwill, could not reject this interest and kindness nor question its motives. She had begun to like Lady Hingston for herself, to appreciate the diamond-like incisiveness of the little woman's mind, to condone her violence in virtue of its honesty. By comparison with Lady Hingston all her former friends, from Miss Boldmere to Aunt Cathie, seemed blurred and soft in outline, like amateurish water-colours set against a steel engraving. Sometimes, in the back of her mind, she remembered Eleanor's warning and Lady Hingston's general reputation, but when once they were together her heart was innocent of any misgivings, completely subjected to the spell of her new protector's brilliance and power.

From the Stourford gates to North Bromwich was a ten-mile drive. The pair of big greys did it in an hour and twenty minutes ; on such an enchanting morning as this the distance seemed too short. Lady Hingston sat back in the rubber-tyred landau like a queen, silent in the concentration of her own ardent thoughts, an elegant, potent figure in sleek sealskin. Only once or twice she spoke in her crisp, incisive way, pointing a deprecative finger at the hollow in which the hanging woods of Mawne Hall drooped above the Stour, and the smoke-pall of the Mawne furnaces, suspended behind them. They bowled softly through Halesby, that bewildering mixture of beauty and squalor, and climbed the hill on whose slopes the beeches of Shenstone burned with a flame that the poet's verses have lost for ever. They passed through the high hamlet of Tilton ; where the chill air of the plateau made Clare shiver, and entered the suburb of Alvaston by the Halesby Road, a wide, smooth highway, with the dwellings of the North Bromwich plutocracy on either side : houses too exalted for publicity, yet too self-conscious entirely to forgo it. Suddenly Lady Hingston touched Clare's sleeve.

" That's Dudley Wilburn's new house," she said. " He must be doing well."

A tall block of red-brick Gothic, ornamented with string-courses of freestone, and a pretentious porch, with mullioned stained-glass windows. At least it looked expensive.

" How foolish to build it so close to the road," said Lady Hingston. " I believe there's plenty of land. He told me that there's a delightful garden at the back."

Clare nodded. She was thinking less of Wilburn's prosperity than of his loneliness. It seemed strange to think of that handsome, competent figure living with his children in that impressive house. It was to this porch that he returned when he had left them at Wychbury. She could see him entering it, alone, and looking for no welcome ; the two children asleep upstairs, and Wilburn coming in tired to so much bitter comfort. It was pitiful. It seemed to her more pitiful as she recalled the terms of his con-gratulatory letter, so staid, so formal, so rigidly repressed. " If only he could bring himself to marry Aunt Cathie," she thought. " I'm sure they'd be happy, and she'd simply worship the children."

It was almost as if her companion had divined her thoughts.

" Dudley Wilburn ought to marry," she said emphatic-ally. " I've told him so a dozen times. It's perverse of him. A man with an income like his ought to have the pleasure of spending it. My husband respects him, and so do I, but the truth of the matter is he's a selfish bachelor. So is his brother ; but Ernest, at any rate, knows how to enjoy life. Dudley's a queer, cold fish."

They lunched daintily at Battie's, and, after coffee, plunged into a whirlpool of shopping. Very different, this, from shopping with Aunt Cathie. Aunt Cathie was always a little deferential to the magnificence of the North Bromwich shops. Lady Hingston was equally, brilliantly, polite ; but beneath her condescending courtesy lay a determination to get exactly what she wanted in the shortest possible time. Aunt Cathie fumbled with her purse and spelt out her address as if she were ashamed of it ; Lady Hingston had actually left her purse behind, and called on Clare to pay the bill for lunch. The words Hingston and Stourford were sufficient to send any shop into a fury of anxiety to please. She ordered without asking the price of anything, and with a lavishness from which her prepotent spirit seemed to derive a reinforcement.

Before Clare knew what had happened she found herself glowing inside a fur-coat as luxurious as Lady Hingston's own. " You can't drive twenty miles on a day like this,' she was told, " in a thin merino costume."

" But I've got a coat," she protested. " It's my own fault leaving it behind."

" I've seen it," Lady Hingston sniffed. " I saw it on the night of the dance, and I don't want to see it again."

" But I can't let you give me a thing like this," Clare protested.

" I haven't given it to Claerwen Lydiatt," said Lady Hingston brusquely. " I want you to remember that you're engaged to Ralph."

" But really," Clare persisted, " really I'd rather. . . ."

" Don't be a little fool," said Lady Hingston shortly.

It was late in the afternoon when they returned to Stourford. In spite of all her activity—or, perhaps, because of it—Lady Hingston was by this time jaded and irritable. Time after time her black eyes flashed on Clare, appraising her handiwork. She smiled when Clare caught them, but their glance was guarded and wary, daring her to utter any further words of thanks or protest.

As they passed up the steps at Stourford Parker threw wide the door. He bent and spoke to Lady Hingston in a confidential voice.

" Why can't you speak up ? " she snapped. " Who did you say ? "

" Miss Catherine Weir, my lady."

" Miss Weir ? " She swept a look of offended majesty on Clare, accusing her of complicity in this unwelcome intrusion. Poor, poor Aunt Cathie !

" I'll go and see her at once," Clare suggested.

Lady Hingston's eyes blazed at her in a way that made Clare feel guilty of an impertinence. She stripped off her white veil and tossed it behind her. It fell at the feet of Parker, who bowed his head as if in honour of it. " How horribly hot it is here," she said. " Parker, will you kindly see that all the windows are opened ? " Then she turned to Clare. " I suppose you'd better come with me," she said. She swam to the drawing-room door like a three-decker going into action.

In the centre of that vast chamber the small black figure of Aunt Cathie was seated on an Empire chair. As Lady Hingston entered she rose and faced her. Could it be possible, Clare thought, that this shrunken, dowdy creature was actually Aunt Cathie ? Or was it the detachment of life at Stourford that enabled her to see Aunt Cathie as she really was ? From the first glance Clare realized that Aunt Cathie was on, or over, the brink of one of her " heads." She was wearing a small toque swathed in crape, whose blackness emphasized the dyspeptic flush of her complexion. Her folded hands looked monstrous and misshapen in black cotton gloves. Her bodice was constricted at the waist, and ended behind in a short, rhomboid appendage, like the tail of a duck. She wore, as usual, elastic-sided boots. In comparison with Lady Hingston she seemed incredibly mean and pitiable. Perhaps it was a sudden appreciation of the contrast that took the wind out of Lady Hingston's sails; her guns were worthy of a more considerable victim.

"Miss Weir?" she said. "How do you do? It is too delightful to know you; I was so sorry you couldn't come over the other day when we invited you. Of course I quite understood."

In spite of herself Aunt Cathie flushed with pleasure.

"I'm so glad not to have missed you, Lady Hingston," she said.

"I'm only afraid that we've kept you waiting?" Lady Hingston conceded.

"Oh, not at all," said Aunt Cathie. "I've been here just over an hour."

"I do hope they gave you some tea?"

"Really, Lady Hingston, it wasn't necessary; not in the least."

"These wretched servants have no discrimination!" It was only too obvious that they had. "You must join us in a cup at once. Clare, dearest, will you kindly ring? You must be tired," she added, with exaggerated sweetness, "after your long walk."

"Oh, not in the least, I assure you," said Aunt Cathie. "I drove over in the victoria." She spoke as if she selected it from an embarrassing superfluity of vehicles.

"Then if you'll excuse me," said Lady Hingston with the wickedest of smiles, "I must really go and make myself fit to receive you. We've been shopping all day in North Bromwich. It gets dirtier every day. Clare, will you entertain your aunt until I'm ready?"

They were alone; and at once Clare's compassion was turned to discomfort. Aunt Cathie regarded her so fixedly, so critically. "Well, Clare," she said at last, "have you nothing to say to me!"

"Of course I have . . . lots! But I was so surprised to see you."

" Surprised ?  No doubt.  I didn't want to come.  I only considered it my duty to drive over and see how you were getting on.  You appear to be very well satisfied with yourself."  Her voice was harsh and emotional.

" Who ?  I, Aunt Cathie ? "  Clare cried.

" Yes, you.  Come here, Clare, let me have a look at you. Where did you get that coat ?  Did Lady Hingston lend it to you ? "

" No, dearest, it's a present.  She brought it for me in North Bromwich this afternoon."

" A present ?  Indeed.  We're not so poor that we aren't in a position to buy our own clothes, my dear.  H'm, seal-skin.  I hope you won't bring it back to Wychbury with you. Possibly you've forgotten that we're supposed to be in mourning ? "

" But sealskin, dearest. . . . It couldn't be blacker."

" The lining isn't black," said Aunt Cathie.  " Besides, it's the spirit that matters.  People in mourning are not supposed to go dashing about the country dolled-up in expensive furs."  She surveyed her own garments with complacency.  " And what's that dress underneath it ? Let me see.  Upon my word, Clare, I can't think what you've come to !  If only the poor doctor could see you ! "

" But Aunt Cathie, dearest," Clare protested, " don't you understand. . . ."

" Most certainly I don't, and you needn't raise your voice like that in a house that's full of prying servants."

" You see," Clare explained in a whisper, " they entertain so much.  So many people come here that I simply have to . . ."

" To accept their charity," Aunt Cathie interrupted. " Oh, well, if you've no more dignity than that !  That woman's condescension !  Of course everybody knows who she was.  It nearly made me sick."

" I thought she was sweet to you," Clare protested.  As

she spoke she remembered the calculated insolence of Lady Hingston's smile.

" Sweet. Yes. Exactly " Aunt Cathie bitterly repeated. " How vulgar and ostentatious this room is. There's not a stick in it that doesn't look as if it had come from Maple's last week. Haven't you any eyes in your head, Clare ? " Her voice rose plaintively. " I've been sitting here looking at it for an hour and a half."

" If only you'd written to say that you were coming," Clare suggested, " we could have stayed at home."

" We. Yes, I like that word. You mean that in spite of the bore, you'd have condescended to wait for me."

It was no use trying to modify this perversity.

" My dearest, you must be reasonable," Clare cried. " I'm dreadfully sorry. I might have known. I'm afraid this waiting has brought on a headache."

" A headache ? " The mere suggestion was enough to release all Aunt Cathie's pent indignation. " Nonsense ! I'm perfectly well. Never better in my life. But I think you might realize that to come over here and be stared at by a lot of insolent flunkeys, just as if I were a gipsy selling clothes-pegs. . . . And then to be smiled at in that patronizing way. . . . You're smiling yourself, Clare. You've . . ."

" Tea is served in the hall, Miss," said the voice of Parker in the tones of a dentist's assistant summoning a victim to operation.

" I don't want any. I don't want it," said Aunt Cathie in an agonized whisper.

Lady Hingston was wearing the black satin and pearls that had devastated Clare on her arrival. Beneath her silver nimbus her clear, pink face looked innocent as a child's. Only her eyes were wicked.

" Now, come along," she said. " You must both of you be dying for your tea. I'm sure I am. Sugar and cream, Miss Weir ? What, neither ? "

Clare knew quite well that Aunt Cathie habitually took both. Only just in time her tact rescued her from the uncomfortable revelation. Aunt Cathie would not eat; and when she lifted the teacup to her lips her hand trembled. Lady Hingston, with a devilish innocence in her black eyes, continued to make the politest conversation. She talked of the Pomfrets, the only Wychbury people with whom she was on calling terms. It was disastrous. Clare could see that Aunt Cathie imagined she had mentioned the hated name on purpose. And Cathie was sitting gingerly on the edge of her chair, with her black duck's tail poking out ludicrously behind. She spoke in clipped and huffy monosyllables. At last, with one friendly, bewildered glance at Clare, Lady Hingston gave it up.

" I expect," she said, " you have a lot of private things you want to talk about. Please don't take any notice of me. I have an enormous number of letters to write. Wouldn't you like to take Miss Weir up to your bedroom, Clare dear ? Or, perhaps, the drawing-room . . ."

The drawing-room had hardly been a success.

" We'll go upstairs," Clare decided. " Come along, Aunt Cathie."

" And if I don't see you again, Miss Weir . . ."

Lady Hingston held out her delicate hand. Aunt Cathie took it in a grip of damp, black cotton.

As they entered the bedroom Marguerite was in the act of spreading a dust-cloth over one of Vivien's dinner dresses that she had adapted for Clare's use. She bowed discreetly to Aunt Cathie.

" *Bon soir, madame*," she said, and hurried from the room

" Who is that woman ? " said Aunt Cathie indignantly. " And why can't she speak English ? "

" She's Lady Hingston's maid," Clare told her. " She's Swiss. Wouldn't you like to lie down for a moment dearest ? "

" Why should I lie down, Clare ? " Aunt Cathie was still smarting from the affront of Marguerite's nationality. " Swiss, indeed ! I've told you already that I'm perfectly well. It must be extremely unhealthy sleeping under a canopy like this. I drove over on purpose to talk to you Clare," she went on. " No, thank you, I prefer to stand. I feel it my duty to speak seriously. People at Wychbury are beginning to talk. Of course I know that in a small place that can't be avoided ; we've always kept ourselves above that sort of thing ; but then, we've also been careful not to give them material for gossip. I don't suggest, my dear, that you have given them the opportunity deliberately —I shouldn't like to think that—but I *do* think you've been thoughtless and foolish and easily led away."

" I, Aunt Cathie ? " Clare cried. " I don't understand you."

" That only shows how thoughtless you have been. Thirza has told me that her friend has seen you three times in Wychbury on a bicycle. Three times. No, Clare, it's no good protesting. Even a tricycle is hardly ladylike. But a bicycle ! Such horrid, vulgar things. And at a time when you're supposed to be in mourning. Mrs. Harbord was terribly shocked. You must remember that people of our station in life are supposed to set an example."

" But dear Aunt Cathie," Clare begun, " we had to go over to Uffdown to prepare the rooms. You must see . . ."

" No, Clare, I won't. Three times have you ridden through Wychbury without once coming to see me. You must have passed within two hundred yards of the house. Do you imagine that everyone in the village doesn't know about that, and realize that you've completely lost your head ? It's a matter of common talk, and very humiliating, I can tell you, to me. As I've said already, I don't entirely blame you. You're young and inexperienced, and easily led away. Please don't interrupt me. I haven't finished yet.

" In *my* day," Aunt Cathie continued, " it was not considered proper for young engaged people to stay for long periods under the same roof. Please don't think that I'm distrustful of you or Mr. Hingston, I'm only stating a straightforward fact. When I allowed you to come over here, at Lady Hingston's request, I understood that you were only going for a few days—those were her very words —to make the acquaintance of your fiancé's family. That seemed to me perfectly right and proper. But now—I don't suppose you even realize it—now you have been here more than a fortnight. No doubt you have become so accustomed to luxurious surroundings and late dinners and Swiss maids that Pen House seems too humble for you. Of course things like that wouldn't appeal to me ; but I'm prepared to make allowances. What I'm not prepared to do, Clare, is to neglect my duty. As long as you remain unmarried I consider that you are under my protection ; I consider that I'm responsible for you, and any thoughtless, selfish thing you may do reflects on me. It's me that the people will laugh at, Clare, don't forget that. Time after time, during the last week, I've thanked heaven that your grandfather was not alive to see it. I've talked it over seriously with Mr. Wilburn."

" Mr. Wilburn ? " said Clare suddenly. " But what on earth has Mr. Wilburn got to do with *me* ? "

Aunt Cathie flushed darkly.

" Mr. Wilburn is your grandfather's sole executor. He's our best and oldest friend. The doctor respected his judgment in everything, and so do I, and so ought you to do, if you haven't taken leave of your senses. Mr. Wilburn's a man in a million, as you'd see for yourself if your whole nature hadn't been changed and ruined—yes, ruined—by contact with these odious people. If only you'd eyes to see, Clare, Mr. Wilburn . . ."

But Clare could stand it no longer. She spoke quickly

and with a white intensity : " Aunt Cathie, you needn't say any more. What do you want me to do ? "

" To do ? " The directness of the question had checked her flow of rhetoric. She began to hedge. " Why do you ask me that ? " she said, with an uncomfortable laugh. " Ask your own conscience, Clare, not me ! If you have any sense of duty left . . ."

" It isn't a matter of conscience, Aunt Cathie," Clare replied. " I suppose you mean that you want me to come back to Wychbury at once ? "

Aunt Cathie shook her head piteously ; once more the name of Wilburn formed itself on her lips.

" If you really wish it, Aunt Cathie, I'll come back to-morrow."

The unexpectedness of Clare's submission overwhelmed her. It was so sudden that the cup of triumph went bitter on her lips.

" I knew that you'd be reasonable, my darling," was all that she could mumble.

" I'm not reasonable—not what you call reasonable," said Clare quickly. " If you want me to come, I'll come, and there's an end of it. To-morrow morning. I'll be back for lunch."

" For dinner," Aunt Cathie obstinately corrected. " In that case, Clare, I think I'd better be going. No, please don't tell Lady Hingston : I've said good-bye already, and I'm sure she doesn't want to see me." She had become almost pitiable in her timidity. " Perhaps you could get one of the servants to send a message to the stables and let Jabez know that I am ready ? I think I'd rather stay here until the carriage is at the door."

She went, like a thief, leaving Clare face to face with the difficulties created by her surrender. With Ralph they resolved themselves more easily than she had imagined ; for she found him lazily complacent, drugged with his day's hunting. She was tactful enough to suppress the details of Aunt Cathie's argument and to suggest—with perfect truth, as she told herself—that nothing but her own feelings compelled her to return to Pen House.

" The poor thing is so lonely," she told him, " that it nearly made me cry to see her. You can imagine how perfectly awful that house must be."

" Can't I ? " he said ruefully, " that's the very reason why I mean to keep you out of it."

She shook her head : " No, my darling, that's the very reason why I must go."

" Why should you sacrifice your life to *her* ? " he exclaimed.

" I'm not going to do anything of the sort ; but even if I were, we mustn't forget how much of hers she's sacrificed to me. Besides, the time's so short. She knows that we've got to separate for ever sooner or later, and naturally . . . *don't* you think it's quite natural ? "

" Of course it's natural, my child, but it's damned unpleasant. I think it's splendid of you to consider her. I know jolly well that I shouldn't. But where do I come in ? "

" You ? " she said. " Of course you are always first. You see it needn't really make any difference to us. It'll be just like those wonderful first days when you used to walk over in the evening. You see, darling, you're always at Wolverbury during the day ; even when I'm here, I don't see much of you, and when you come home there are always people about. At Pen House there'll be nobody, only just ourselves. Don't you see ? "

" She'll sit and stare at us. I know the sort of thing."

" Of course she'll do nothing of the sort," Clare laughed.

" I don't know how mother will take it," he said.

Neither did Clare ; but after dinner that evening, when Sir Joseph had scuttled away like a rabbit to his burrow, and she and Vivien and Ralph were left alone with Lady Hingston in the drawing-room that Aunt Cathie had found so offensive, the matter did not remain for long in doubt. It was Ralph who broached it, heroically.

" This is Clare's last night," he told her. " She's going back to Wychbury to-morrow morning."

Lady Hingston's body stiffened.

" Oh," she said. " This is the first I've heard about it. You didn't tell me that you were going, Clare."

" I couldn't very well," said Clare. " I only made up my mind this evening after Aunt Cathie's visit."

" And what has Miss Weir to do with it ? " The words were cold and crystalline as icicles, as cold as Lady Hingston's eyes.

" But couldn't you see for yourself," Clare said, " how dreadfully pathetic she was ? Of course you didn't know her before, so you couldn't realize the change, but it was quite a shock to me. Surely you must have noticed ? "

" I only noticed," said Lady Hingston, " that she was evidently determined to make herself awkward and offensive."

" No, no, it wasn't that," Clare eagerly protested. " You don't understand. It's her shyness. Always having lived alone. She's usually strained and difficult like that. I don't know how to put it."

" I do," said Lady Hingston venomously, " and if you like, I'll tell you : I thought her whole attitude was abominably rude. And if she's always like that, I can't for the life of me imagine why you should want to go back to Wychbury. As a matter of fact . . ."

" Mother," the slow, dark voice of Vivien interrupted. She was lying curled up on the sofa like a cat.

" As a matter of fact . . ." Lady Hingston continued, then stopped. It seemed that she had lost her thread. The black flame turned on Vivien.

" Well, Vivien, what is it ? " she asked irritably.

" A few days ago," Vivien drawled, " you were saying that Miss Weir ought to be pitied."

" Was I ? " Lady Hingston laughed shortly. " Well, then, I hadn't seen her. Now I reserve my pity for Clare, or anyone else that has to do with her."

" You needn't," said Clare quickly. " You see, I understand her ; I know how awfully good she is. When she came over this afternoon . . ."

" To fetch you," Lady Hingston interrupted.

" She didn't come to fetch me. She only wondered when I was coming back. You see, I was only supposed to be staying here a few days, just to get to know you. And now it's more than a fortnight. It's my own fault. I ought to have gone and seen her when we rode over to Uffdown. After all she's the only relative I have in the world. She's looked after me just like a mother all my life. Don't you think it's my duty to consider her a little ? "

Lady Hingston was silent. After her first and grudging acceptance of Clare she had regarded her as a fit and promising subject for education. She had set about breaking her to Stourford as puppies are broken to the gun. To this end she had kept her jealously at her side, imprinting on her, by the very persistence of her presence, and her generosity, the mark of her potent personality. The result had flattered her sense of power. Already she and Marguerite between them had achieved a physical transformation ; there seemed no reason why, in another few months, Clare should not become a credit to the firm, more plastic, if less signally decorative than Eleanor. And now her pupil was showing signs of the basest and most primitive instincts. She stood above her as a keeper might stand above a trained retriever with a bloody and mangled carcase in its mouth. There were whips in her eyes.

" You actually mean me to understand that you are going back to Wychbury to-morrow ? "

The shade of Eleanor stood at Clare's elbow : *Don't be put upon by George's mother, that's the great thing.* She answered : " Yes."

" Even if I wish you to stay ? "

" I'm sorry," Clare said. " Of course I'd love to stay here. You've all been sweet to me, you and Sir Joseph, Vivien, everybody. But I've made up my mind to go, so there's an end of it. I shall see Ralph just the same. And don't, for heaven's sake, think I'm ungrateful for all your kindness. Don't think . . ."

She hesitated, and Lady Hingston swooped swiftly into the breach :

" You needn't suggest what I'm to think or not to think. I think you're a stiff-necked little fool, if you want to know."

Now Ralph was on his feet, his wide face flushed and angry, his blue eyes burning.

" Look here, mother, I'm not going to allow you to speak to Clare like that ! "

She smiled at him, as though she knew that he was no match for her. The blue flames and the black crossed in the air between them like swords. Clare clutched his hand : " Don't, Ralph," she whispered, " don't ! "

Then Lady Hingston gave a quick laugh. She hated Clare's restraining influence ; now that the battle was joined she needed the sting of some answering violence to justify and augment her own. She threw another challenging invitation at Vivien, who surveyed them from the sofa with a lazy disinterest. Vivien would not help her ; and so, pushing herself to an artificial access of fury, she let go on Ralph.

" Yes, that's very pretty," she said. " You needn't waste your time in defending her, Ralph. Clare can look after herself. And don't talk to me about gratitude. *Gratitude!* "

Before he could speak she had swept her skirts like a whirling tornado out of the room.

" I'm so sorry," Clare began.

" There's nothing to be sorry about," Ralph answered angrily. " Mother's impossible." She could feel the stiffened muscles of his arm. " I shouldn't blame you if you never set foot in this house again."

" Gently, Ralph," said Vivien's level voice. She uncurled herself from the sofa and yawned. " Don't take any notice of either of them, Clare, darling," she said. " We're like that. I've told you before that the whole family's mad, except old George and father. It's our principal charm. When Ralph's as old as I am, he'll have learnt to see the joke of mother's little tantrums. Clare sees it already, don't you, Clare ? "

Vivien closed her eyes, sleepy with the intoxication of the run from Stourhead Withies, and stretched her arms. Then the lids puckered, and she began to chuckle to herself.

" What the devil are you laughing at now ? " Ralph burst out angrily.

" It's no laughing matter, really," said Vivien. " I was thinking of poor Marguerite. Good night, darlings. I'm nearly dead. Behave yourselves. Oh, dear, dear, dear ! " In the doorway she spoke again : " At what time do you want the carriage to-morrow morning, Clare ? I'll tell Parker." Clare looked at Ralph enquiringly.

" At half-past ten," he said. " I shan't go to Wolverbury. I'd better drive over with her. I can see I shall have to draw the line somewhere."

" Brave little fellow ! " Vivien mocked from the doorway.

## XII

## THE RETURN

FROM that day, life at Pen House went ticking on as quietly as the old clock in the hall, which Wilburn had restarted. It seemed strange to Clare that the shock of the doctor's death should not have modified its rhythm, until she reflected that this calamity had fallen on its occupants with the quietness in which an aged tree sheds a decayed branch that drops from the trunk of its own weight in the stillness of night. They were too old, too deeply rooted to see catastrophe in one of the ordinary processes of nature. There was something in this vegetative calm, this perpetual and half-conscious hibernation, that made Clare long to assert her difference by some act of wilful violence, if only to convince herself that she had not fallen victim to the house's enchantment, that she was still alive. It was clear that they regarded her, if not as a returned prodigal, at least as one who had been tainted by contact with an alien world. In everything that related to the routine of Pen House they seemed assertive, and were, in fact, apologetic; which showed her that what she had lost in innocence she had gained in worldly prestige.

" Well, Clare," Aunt Cathie proclaimed, with satisfaction, " you'll find us jogging along here just as usual. We've been like this as long as Thirza can remember, and I suppose we shall go on in the same way till the end of our days. The doctor never countenanced social entertainment; he thought it was simply a sign of having no resources of your own; and so do I. No doubt it's a necessity for empty-headed people. Nowadays folk who live in the country seem to do their best to imitate town-life; but heaven knows that even as it is, what with one thing and another, keeping the dust down and looking after Ellen, who's got a mind like a sieve, and Thirza, poor dear, whose memory is failing, my time seems as full as ever it was when the doctor was alive. From eight o'clock in the morning until the supper's cleared they keep me on my legs. Really, I don't know how other people find time for driving about the country. Every night when supper's over, I'm almost too tired to work or read, as it is. I simply fall asleep in my chair until bedtime, and then there's another day gone."

Clare offered to relieve her of some of this burden of furious superintendence.

" My dear child," said Aunt Cathie, " what could *you* do ? A house like this has to be run on certain fixed lines, or else the whole thing is thrown into hopeless disorder. I couldn't trust it to Thirza, even after all these years. No, I've lived long enough to learn that if you want things properly done you must do them yourself, Clare, and the sooner you learn that the better for you too. Otherwise you'll only find yourself at the mercy of a lot of ignorant, slovenly, servants."

The veiled allusions to Marguerite and Mr. Parker did not escape Clare. And yet, even while she proclaimed her martyrdom on the domestic altar, Aunt Cathie's general attitude was curiously kind, and, on occasions, respectful. She allowed Clare's clothes to pass without any comment on their shameful origin, and in the matter of Ralph's daily visits to Pen House she played the game so scrupulously that Ralph himself was prejudiced in her favour.

" You'd have thought to hear mother talk," he said, " that this Aunt Cathie of yours was a dragon. She isn't a bit. The poor thing looks as if she wouldn't hurt a fly. But that's mother all over ; when once she gets an idea into her head she can't help working it to death ; and then one day she realizes she's overdoing it, and swings round to the other extreme. There's one good thing about her ; she's never ashamed to change her opinion. As a matter of fact she's never ashamed of anything; she's more nerve than all the rest of the family put together. Do you know," he went on, clumsily, " there are times when your Aunt Cathie looks almost pretty? There's something about her eyes—not always; just now and then—that reminds me of you. If she knew how to dress, like mother does . . . if she could condescend to move with the times."

But that, of course, was quite out of the question. Aunt Cathie could not move with the times; in her life all time was stationary. It was only with the greatest difficulty that she could persuade herself that it was proper for her to leave the lovers alone when Ralph came to Wychbury in the evening. The concession hurt her more than she would confess. She would never have made it, but for the sudden, unaccountable liking that she had taken to Ralph, to his frankness, his courtesy, his astonishing lack of all the pretentiousness that she associated with the Hingstons. Perhaps there was more than this in her surrender; perhaps she smiled on their love because, with her, the season of love was now irrevocably past, because from their ardours, she recaptured, vicariously, a little of the ecstasy that time denied her.

And Clare was grateful. For her, at least, this new period in their love-making had a quality of calm freedom which she had never known at Stourford. There she had always been forced to adapt herself to new conditions, there, even in her relations with the kindly Marguerite, she had been unnatural and conscious of Lady Hingston's critical eyes. At Pen House, however, shabby it might seem, she was living in surroundings that were natural to her and imposed no strain on her behaviour; she was her own mistress, and her lover, isolated from the claims and customs of his family, was more surely hers.

The face of the dying year seemed appropriate to this placid state; it was a season of subdued light that gave no violence to the eyes; the land had sunk into a dun and russet resignation against which the brightness of their hope shone as vividly as the hips and hawthorn berries lighting bare hedgerows, or the golden death of elms that streaked the sombre plain. Often, when their busy house-making at the manor was over, they would break away up the valley, where the fishponds lay dark as Roman mirrors of steel, and the water of the brook that fed them ran brown, turbulent and unapproachable; and from there they would pass the mill, no longer sinister, and climb the bank to their old point of vantage on the barrow. But now the southern plain lay drowned, as though its ancient waters had reclaimed it: a waste of leaden fen and stagnant gleaming channels among which the elms and spires of villages rose like lost islands against the stormy sunset.

The chill of winter ran like wine in their blood, lending an ecstasy to all things warm and human, so that the ruddy windows of Pen House beckoned them with a new zest, and when they reached the drawing-room, where the fire glowed, or crackled into shadow-casting flame, they would sit for long hours of silence and repletion before the hearth, listening to the tick of the old clock in the hall and to the unhurried beating of each other's hearts. For them, as for Aunt Cathie and old Thirza, those ceaseless measurers of time were vain and meaningless.

In some such moments of drugged content Clare's senses would suddenly return to her, and the familiar shapes of the little room, which had been lost in a warm, dreamy consciousness of her lover's presence, would regain their definition. Obedient to some secret suasion, she would raise her cheek from his, and free herself from his embrace, passing in silence to the old Broadwood, where she would sit and play in the dark. Ralph never made any comment on her playing. It was better so; for, by this time, she had discovered that music meant little to him. For him it was enough to watch her lazily in the fire-lit dusk, contented with his possession ; but for her these moments meant much more. Sitting at the piano, and always conscious of his presence, it seemed as if, in giving new birth to the passion of lovers long since dead, she were enabled to free her soul of a rapture and a tenderness that her body could not express, even in its moments of completest physical abandonment, even in those long kisses that left her blind and shaken. When she had finished, and her hands dropped to her knees, she would turn and gaze into the dark eyes that watched her, and her heart would cry to him : " That is all that I can give ; this is the emptying of my soul. My love, my love, do you understand ? "

After they had taken supper with Aunt Cathie, Ellen would bring a lighted lamp into the drawing-room, and it was never the same ; for then, even though they were still alone, their talk would be of everyday things ; of the progress of the builders and painters at Uffdown Manor, of Lady Hingston's latest vagaries, of the riding lessons which had never material-ized. But though Clare lent herself eagerly to these dis-cussions, she knew that they did not really matter ; that even their reluctant parting on the wintry drive and under the high Pleiades was bereft of one particular magic. The great moment had passed.

When she returned to the dining-room where Aunt Cathie sat over her embroidery on the accustomed chair, just as though the doctor were still glowering in his on the other side of the fire and she were waiting to perform some sudden imperious service, Clare felt that she had brought in with her some appreciable aura of passion that subtly offended Aunt Cathie's virginal niceness. She knew it was her duty to obtain a kind of moral pratique before she entered this uninfected port.

" Ralph's gone, Aunt Cathie," she would say.

Then Aunt Cathie would lay down her work and take off

the steel spectacles whose bridge left a red furrow at the root of her nose.

" We're very late to-night, Clare," she would say, glancing at the clock. " You know the doctor never approved of such late hours ; but I suppose we have to make allowances for young people in these days. I hope you have not forgotten to put out the drawing-room light and take the coals off the fire ? "

Every night, with the regularity of an evening prayer, this formula was repeated, and when she had spoken it Aunt Cathie would sigh and push back the doctor's chair from the hearth, patting the cushions as if, out of sheer habit, they still retained the imprint of his lean haunches. Then, with a smile, excruciating in its kindness, she would say goodnight, and offer her cold cheek to Clare, and Clare would kiss it, not as she kissed Ralph's lips, but with a kind of devotional pity and gratitude, which her full heart was powerless, and forbidden to express.

It was enough to suffer the accusations of self-sacrifice in Aunt Cathie's eyes ; Mr. Darnay's were more difficult to face. From the moment in which Clare had read his studied letter of congratulation at Stourford, she had felt that the nature of their relation was changed. When next she met Mr. Darnay she was conscious of a gulf between them that revealed itself, not so much in the words that either spoke, as in the awkwardness of Mr. Darnay's manner. She had always made allowances for a certain shyness that he usually showed in her company ; but now he was not shy. He looked her through and through with eyes that she did not know, eyes that were not less kindly or anxious for her spiritual welfare, but veiled and lacking the transparent candour to which she was accustomed. They scrutinized her on the sly, as though they were searching her face and figure for token of the physical adventures that his celibate brain abhorred. They made her so conscious of

Ralph's kisses that she felt as though the traces of them were discernible on her lips. No glance of his had ever discomforted her so acutely.

Even in the confessions, which she had now resumed, she was conscious of a certain silent eagerness on Mr. Darnay's part, as though he were waiting anxiously for the moment in which Ralph's name would pass her lips. That moment never came. Now more than ever she clung to the reservation that her early shyness had imposed upon her. She remembered the way in which he had hinted at this in his letter. Looking backward it seemed to her that he had no right to do so. Confession was a matter that lay between her and her conscience, and, as regards Ralph, her conscience suggested nothing that it was her duty to confess. In all her love there was nothing that did not seem to her inviolably sacred. She knew that Mr. Darnay could not believe this ; that he was suspicious and dissatisfied ; that he regarded her nature as changed ; and this made her shrink from further contact with him in a widening vicious circle of discomfort and distrust.

She could not believe that she was entirely to blame. If she were changed it was only because she had adapted herself to changing circumstances. It was natural enough that she should look at everything, religion included, from a different angle as time went on. Most of her schoolgirl enthusiasms now seemed to her extravagant in kind and in degree. She couldn't, for instance, now imagine herself fainting with delight to hear the rustle of Miss Boldmere's reseda Shantung.

At the time when she left St. Monica's her heart had been empty and eager for love ; Miss Boldmere had satisfied this half-spiritual, half-sensual need by the warmth of a personal intimacy and the teaching of a mystical creed. But now the love of Ralph had filled Clare's heart to overflowing ; the image of Miss Boldmere grew fainter and fainter, and it seemed to her as if the love of Christ were strangely inter-mingled with her human passion, informing it, inspiring it with light and beauty until she could not longer separate one from the other. And so confident was she in the rightness of this fusion, that Darnay's grudging eyes, which lamented that she had ceased to be a schoolgirl, seemed to her increasingly inhuman and threw her into a mood of opposition.

Gradually she freed herself from the tutelage of this dark figure, and was happier for it. She ceased to number herself among the devout band of spinsters who went shiver-ing in the early morning to St. Chad's. It was enough for her to hear Mass on Sundays and on the greater feasts. Aunt Cathie, in her way, and Ralph, in his, regarded the change with relief and satisfaction.

One weekday afternoon, just after lunch, she heard the ping of Ralph's bicycle-bell on the drive. It was thus that he often announced his arrival, in order to escape a meeting with Aunt Cathie. That day there was no need for such precaution, for Aunt Cathie had already gone to rest and had passed beyond the reach of voices.

" But what are you doing here ? I thought you'd gone to Wolverbury," Clare said.

He leaned his bicycle against the porch ; there was a look of triumph and excitement in his eyes.

" Anyone 'ld think that you weren't pleased to see me," he said. " Let's go into the drawing-room. I've got some news to tell you."

" Aunt Cathie's resting," she told him. " Don't talk so loudly."

" So much the better," he said ; " let's go to Uff-down."

They set off together, his arm about her waist. His happiness was gay and boisterous, never had he seemed to her so radiantly handsome.

" I've got it off my chest at last," he said. " I've done it ! "

He laughed at her failure to understand him.

" How slow you are ! This Wolverbury business. I had the whole matter out with the guv'nor this morning in the train. I think he must have been prepared for it, he took it so jolly well. Of course he knows already that my heart isn't in the job—you know where my heart is, don't you ?—and that I should never make a success of it, like George or Edward Willis. Our family have always been farmers, and I suppose I'm a sort of throw-back. I loathe Wolverbury and everything connected with it ; anyone with two eyes can see that. What's more, there's no necessity for me to stick there. He had to admit that. Of course he began to preach to me about an idle life being no good to a young man and all that sort of thing. He's said that so often that he probably goes on saying it in his sleep. But I'm not idle ; I never have been ; I'm so busy that life simply isn't long enough for all the things I want to do. It'll take me all my time for ten years to get Uffdown into decent order after the mess the Rentons left it in ; and it's just about as much as one man can manage to look after you ! Anyway, it's settled. I'm leaving Wolverbury ; I hope I shall never set eyes on the damned place again. I keep my holdings in the company ; I told the guv'nor that if he wished it, I'd increase them out of Aunt Gillian's money ; he can do what he jolly well likes with it as long as they don't worry me. But why on earth don't you say something ? You *are* a queer kid, you know. If I didn't realize what a quiet mouse you are, I should think that you were disappointed. Can't you see what it means ? I'm free . . . *free ! "*

There, in the open roadway, he caught her in his arms and kissed her ; but Clare was too deeply troubled to match him in enthusiasm.

" I can't quite take it in," she said. " You've done it all so suddenly. Don't you feel you ought to have thought it over a little longer ? "

" Oh, I'm no good at thinking," he told her. " I'm sick of thinking and thinking and doing nothing. But now it's done, and you don't seem to realize what it means."

" I know one thing that it means," said Clare. " Your mother will say that I've made you do it. She'll put it down to me."

" And what the deuce does it matter if she does," he laughed.

" She'll say that I've unsettled you."

" And so you have ! But that's beside the point. You don't know mother as well as I do. Ever since that row she's been as mild as milk. She's like that. If you'd knuckled under, when she went for you, your life wouldn't have been worth living, like poor old Marguerite's ; but now that you've shown your spirit, she respects you. Honestly she does. And anyone can see from the way she speaks of you since you left that she's really fond of you too."

" She talked about ingratitude," said Clare. " That's what I couldn't stand. I'm not ungrateful, Ralph. Really, I'm not."

" Oh, gratitude ! My sweet child, that word's the biggest bee in her bonnet, she's always talking about gratitude. When the guv'nor tells her about our new arrangement, she'll say that I'm ungrateful. She'll come over the whole house like a tidal wave, and Marguerite'll get the backwash."

" Poor Marguerite ! "

" Don't you believe it. If poor Marguerite didn't think the game was worth the candle she'd have left mother years ago. Marguerite's a hard-headed Swiss, and she has the whole situation balanced to a centime. Don't go breaking your soft little heart over Marguerite, or mother either; both of them know how to look after themselves a sight better than you do."

"She'll hate me," Clare persisted.

"Yes. For five minutes or five days. The guv'nor's going to face the brunt of it. Then she'll get over it and come up purring like a nice white cat. Whatever she thinks or doesn't think needn't make any difference to you and me. You're out of reach; and with me she knows better. But don't let's talk about her. Even now, you don't see what it means."

She shook her head.

"Why, what it means is this: it means that as soon as we can get Uffdown made habitable, you and I have got to be married. To-day's the twenty-fifth of November. That leaves a month to Christmas. We ought to be married early in the New Year. Now tell me, seriously, if you know of any just cause or impediment!"

"But, dearest, it's only three months. . . . Aunt Cathie's still in deep mourning."

"Aunt Cathie?" he cried impatiently: "'For this cause shall a man leave his father and mother and cleave to his wife.' You see I'm not such a heathen as you think. And as for mourning. . . . After all he was only your grandfather. Good Lord, how I detest this tyranny of dead people! We're living, Clare, we're living. For God's sake, let's take as much of life as we can. You never know . . ."

"Oh, darling, don't speak of it," she whispered. The shade of his last words had fallen on her heart like night. She knew that he didn't mean them, that the idea of separation had no serious existence in his mind, yet even when they were spoken in a conventional phrase they filled her with terror. "I'll speak to Aunt Cathie this evening," she said. "It's only her that I'm thinking of."

That evening as soon as Ralph had left Pen House, she fulfilled her promise. Aunt Cathie blinked behind her spectacles and went pale as Clare spoke. Her lips trembled; at first she could not trust herself to answer, and in her eyes Clare saw a shadow of approaching loneliness which made her feel that her marriage was a betrayal. First the doctor, next herself, then Thirza; she saw Aunt Cathie's solitary life stretching onward so bleakly that she could almost have taken back her words. Gradually Aunt Cathie controlled her uncertain lips. She spoke in a voice of complete dispassionateness.

" It seems to me extremely precipitate and hardly wise," she said. " However, I will ask Mr. Wilburn. I hope you haven't forgotten to take the coals off the fire ? "

## XIII

### BOTTOM DRAWER

THE date of the wedding was fixed for January the fifteenth. " Mr. Wilburn," Aunt Cathie gravely announced, " sees no objection."

Clare smiled to herself. What difference could it have made if he had seen a hundred ? And yet, in spite of her solemn anxiety to do the right thing, Aunt Cathie now showed herself so reasonable that Clare felt it her duty to humour her.

" That leaves us very little time," Aunt Cathie said. " It means that I shall have to put everything else on one side to get you ready." She spoke as if Clare would have to be subjected to one of her heroic spring-cleanings. " I'm not going to have the Hingstons saying that you came to them without a proper trousseau, although, no doubt, they'd like nothing better than the chance."

" They're not a bit like that really, Aunt Cathie," Clare protested.

" I don't think Ralph is," Aunt Cathie admitted. " I must say that I've found him extremely natural and good-hearted, from the little I've seen of him. I confess that I don't know what the daughter's like ; but if she resembles her mother . . ."

" She doesn't," Clare assured her ; " not in the very least."

" Let's hope that is so . . . for her own sake as well as yours," said Aunt Cathie. " The most important thing, as I always say, is not what's on the top, but what's underneath."

" Well, Vivien's all right in any case," said Clare. " She's awfully attractive to look at, and her heart's like gold."

Aunt Cathie smiled wanly :

" You've mistaken my meaning, Clare, and you needn't fly into a passion anyway. I was speaking of underclothes, not of Miss Hingston. In my day there used to be a rule. Half a dozen of everything. But I'm afraid we shall have to exceed that in your case. Being married in the middle of winter like this, you'll need an unusual number of warm things. The doctor always used to insist on wool next the skin."

" But we're going to Italy, dearest," Clare told her, "and by the time we get back the winter will be over."

" I know nothing of Italy," said Aunt Cathie, as if she were proud of it, " but friends have told me that winter on the Riviera is most treacherous. The doctor had a patient who died there, of pneumonia, if you please, and in February."

So, gradually, the half-dozens of everything took shape ; a rather dubious shape, Clare thought ; for when it came to making them the matronly wisdom of Mrs. Rudge intervened with careful and sinister provisions for the contingencies of matrimony that made Clare wince. She had never thought of marriage in these terms ; but Thirza, it seemed, had never thought of it in any others, and gloated over her cunning contrivances with looks of unutterable sagacity and side whispers to Aunt Cathie that seemed, to Clare, obscene.

Three or four times they went into North Bromwich for shopping ; not in a spanking brougham, but by rail, third-class. Aunt Cathie knew that railway journeys always gave her a headache ; she embarked on them with a glazed look of martyrdom in her eyes, and carried with her in her leather bag a little phial of bromide and antipyrin, the doctor's prescription. Half of it she swallowed as she entered the compartment ; half she preserved, as a kind of nauseous liqueur, for her lunch at Battie's, where she persisted in eating pastries that she knew were fatal to her. " I may as well be hanged for a sheep as a lamb," she said. " It's got to come in spite of the antipyrin ; so I think I've a right to enjoy myself."

She did so : at Clare's expense. All afternoon they dragged Aunt Cathie's headache from counter to counter in an air stifled by the chemical odour of Manchester goods. Aunt Cathie would not be hurried ; whenever Clare tried to hasten her choice she became haughty and irritable, persisting in ridiculous questions, fingering bale after bale of flannel and longcloth and nainsook, as if she distrusted and hated the whole race of shopkeepers. Later when Clare was fainting with desire for a cup of tea, and staggering under the weight of parcels that Aunt Cathie would not trust the tradesmen to deliver, she would throw the remains of her energy into a mad rush for the station. " Tea ? " she would say. " For Heaven's sake don't mention it ; the very idea of swallowing anything makes me feel ill. You might have known it ! "

Once, having missed their train, they sat for an hour under the station's dome of echoing glass, where the clanking of goods-wagons and the whistles of engines made Aunt Cathie hold her ears in agony. And when they reached the halt at Mawne Road she was sick.  It was bad enough for Clare to see the disgust in their fellow-passengers' eyes without Aunt Cathie's looks and murmurs, which suggested that she, with her inordinate haste in getting married, had been responsible for the tragedy.

But next morning Aunt Cathie appeared as if nothing had happened, gulping down her breakfast in a hurry to unpack the parcels and get the sewing-machine to work, a process that involved the suspension of all the house's other activities ;  Thirza Rudge peering over the materials with her cutting-out scissors and her obscene asides, and Ellen, made stupid by excitement, standing in attendance with her mouth open.  To Ellen, as she herself confessed, the whole business was as good as a play.  It was a Chinese play, whose performance spread itself over a week at a time, during which the wheels of the sewing machine hummed and flickered like a chorus of bees in barberry blossom.

It was part of the penance that Aunt Cathie imposed on her that Clare should watch each moment of her trousseau's manufacture.  " You may as well learn as much as you can, Clare," she said triumphantly, " for when you're married, you'll have to do all this sort of thing for yourself."  It never seemed to occur to Aunt Cathie that underclothing, or clothing of any kind could be bought ready-made, or that Clare would ever be able to afford to buy it.  Clare often smiled to herself when she thought of Lady Hingston or Vivien wrestling with rods, poles or perches of calico.

" You'll have to get a machine for yourself, too," Aunt Cathie warned her.  In her vocabulary only one kind of machine existed.  " In these days," she confessed, with an unusual concession to modernity, " it's waste of time to sew the servants' linen by hand.  Of course you'll have quite enough to begin with, if you're careful ;  but I can't for the life of me understand what young people like you are doing with a house of that size.  I suppose you never stop to calculate the expense. The amount of soap you'll use on lace curtains alone !" The buzzing of the machine rose into a scream of protest. "Why, what's the matter ? Where are you dashing off to now ? "

For Clare had heard the shrilling of a bicycle-bell on the drive.

" It's Ralph," she said. " I promised to go over to Uff-down with him before lunch. Before dinner," she corrected herself hastily. " A whole load of furniture has arrived, and the men won't know where to put it. I'll bring him in here."

" What are you *dreaming* of ? " Aunt Cathie gasped. " For Heaven's sake give me time to put those under-clothes away ! " As Clare ran to meet him she heard Aunt Cathie's voice complaining in the distance behind her : " As soon as you hear a sound you lose your head com-pletely . . . no balance . . . no sense of dignity."

Unfortunately Aunt Cathie could never realize that her part in the preparations was not the whole of them. To Ralph she was always indulgent ; he was a stranger, and, even more significantly, a man ; the doctor had trained her to defer to male opinion. But whenever Clare went with him to Uffdown, her going was treated as a frivolous defec-tion for which it was her duty to apologize, and this unreason-able demand became wearisome ; for now the interior of the Manor was taking shape, and the proceeds of Sir Joseph's generous wedding-present to Ralph were arriving. Ralph was untiring ; he never knew the moment at which Clare's strength was exhausted, so that when they came to the end of their labours in the evening she was too weary even to make love. He could not understand it ; he expected her strength to match his own, and whenever she wilted or was silent he threw himself into a fever of anxiety, imagining that he had offended her or that she was ill.

" There must be something wrong with you," he said.

" You're not yourself. Do you think I can't see that ? For God's sake tell me what it is."

She tried to soothe him : " I'm only tired," she said, " and goodness know, that's natural enough. I'm not a great, big, powerful thing like you. You don't realize how little I am."

Her words melted him into passionate tenderness and reproaches.

" Then why on earth didn't you tell me I was tiring you ? " he said. " Surely you weren't afraid to speak to me ? "

" Oh, don't worry, my darling," she begged him. " I've told you I'm just a bit fagged, that's all."

But this would not satisfy him.

" I believe you're ill," he said, " and you're keeping it from me." He grew alarmed and insisted that she should see a doctor. " You're so precious," he said. " Supposing you were really ill and didn't know it. Supposing . . ."

She was forced to laugh at him. " I think you might take my word for it," she said. " The truth is that you know nothing about women. You can't always expect them to be at their best. Ask Vivien. Besides, I've told you already. I'm a bit tired."

" And no wonder," he said, " considering the way in which this business is dragging itself out. It's another six weeks before the fifteenth, and every week seems like a year to me. We made a mistake not to fix it a month earlier."

She smiled at his impatience. Once it had troubled her ; but now she was getting used to it. She was so tired that when he left her she could have fallen asleep in the drawing-room chair. It was strange to think that for him time dragged in its passage ; for her it went whirling past at a speed that bewildered ; the day had no sooner begun than it was ended and weeks went by like days, passing so quickly that she felt like a swimmer fighting against a current with the roar of dangerous rapids deafening her ears. How dangerous they were she had not time to think ; the hints and whispers of Mrs. Rudge suggested mysterious horrors. Aunt Cathie had never been married ; but the portly Thirza had shot them on three courageous occasions, and should know. She and Mrs. Harbord, who now relieved her in the kitchen, had knowledge enough between them to face Niagara. Why were they so secretive with their knowledge ? Why should they speak in lowered voices and with mysterious signs ?

She told herself that she was being frightened needlessly ; that marriage, and even the greater mystery of child-bearing, was, after all, the common lot of womankind. She thought of her own mother, boldly embarking on a far more dangerous adventure. She wondered if she had lain awake and held her breath before the same uncertainties ; and it seemed to her the cruellest fate of all that she was not alive to hold her hand and whisper in her ear. Through all those wakeful hours that delicate figure, whose shade she had invested with such love and graciousness, seemed tantaliz-ingly near to her. At times her presence was so real that Clare could almost persuade herself into listening for the voice that she had never heard. But no voice came ; and so she comforted her loneliness with the memory of Ralph, of his strength, his honesty, his gentleness.

" Perhaps he is just as puzzled and anxious as I am," she thought, " and I'm behaving like a selfish little brute. What is the use of pretending that I trust him in everything if I don't trust him in this ? Oh, my darling, my darling, if only you know how silly and unworthy of you I am ! "

At Christmas time the fierce rhythm of this too-rapid life was broken by a visit to Stourford. Aunt Cathie also was invited, but refused the benefit of any concession on " that woman's " part. She could never forgive the Stourford drawing-room for being what it was. As a protest against it she intensified the deepness of her mourning, appearing, on the day of Clare's departure, in a hot aura of crape.

Clare gathered that Mr. Wilburn had approved her attitude ; for though his visits to Pen House had ceased at the time of her engagement, Aunt Cathie continued to write to him enormous letters, marked " confidential," which she formally sealed in Clare's presence, as though she thought that they would be steamed open in the kitchen.

" There's no reason why you shouldn't leave me for Christmas, Clare," she said. " I am used to being alone. The doctor always despised women who were without resources. I shall read *Romola*—that will be most appropriate, since you are going to Italy so soon—and I shall finish all those cambric chemises. I've told Thirza to buy a chicken. The very thought of cold turkey makes me ill. They're such immense birds."

" I shall be back again in three days, dearest," Clare assured her.

" No doubt you will have a gay time," said Aunt Cathie dolefully. " A quiet person like myself would be totally out of place. Besides, I suppose I must get used to being without you. I don't suppose I shall see much of Thirza. I've allowed her to invite her friend to dine with her, and Ellen, of course, will go home to her parents on Christmas Day."

By this time Clare had deliberately steeled herself against these harrowing resignations. She knew that Aunt Cathie would be much happier in the company of George Eliot than in that of George Hingston. She kissed her good-bye with an untroubled face, and the embrace which Aunt Cathie returned was surprising in its warmth and tenderness.

Even on this occasion the approach to Stourford seemed formidable ; there was no knowing with what new brilliant variation of the offensive Lady Hingston might not confound her ; for since the day of the wedding had been fixed they had only met among the crowds which ebbed and flowed through the hall at Stourford like people at a railway station.

Then Lady Hingston had treated her with a sort of gracious contempt, acknowledging her presence as a harmless, necessary evil ; now she might make a final protest against the evil's necessity.

She did not. The Hingstons were people who, apart from its religious significance, took Christmas seriously. The festival had feudal aspects that they were anxious to preserve. It gave them a chance of showing their tenants the benignity of the old regime—new style—at its best ; and the process was so exacting that Lady Hingston's energies were absorbed in it. She was too busy to think of quarrelling with anybody, and the addition of a new helper, even in the questionable shape of Clare, was welcome to her.

On Christmas Eve they made a feast for servants and tenants in the long music-room. After dinner the room was cleared for dancing, and Clare found herself revolving solemnly in the arms of Mr. Parker. Mr. Parker breathed noisily through his nose, for, in ordinary life, such rapid movements were not compatible with his dignity. His eyes were busy all the time watching for any signs of impropriety in the behaviour of his staff. He bore Clare round the room as carefully as if she had been an entrée. From first to last his lips uttered no word ; and Clare was almost thankful that they didn't, so convinced was she that, if words came, they must take the shape of, " Ice pudding or meringue, Miss ? "

Marguerite did not dance. Not even with Ralph. No doubt she felt that knowledge of her dissolute nationality might tempt the footmen to unseemly advances. She sat upright and superb, an emblem of invitation and discouragement, unconscious of the sprig of mistletoe that hung above her head. Vivien and Lady Hingston were everywhere, like bright birds thridding the constrained and sombre company. The sullen loveliness of Eleanor's eyes followed them wherever they went. She was more lifelessly beautiful that night, Clare thought, than ever before. Her two children, little Harold and Enid, came romping to her knee, but not even they could bring a breath of life into her face. It seemed incredible that anything so vital as they could have been born of Eleanor's coldness. And like a soul strayed out of some distant circle of purgatory into another, Sir Joseph Hingston moved shyly round the room's outer edge, always wavering toward the door by which he might have escaped, always recalled to his melancholy duty by his wife's black eyes.

Suddenly, when she least expected it, he threw himself upon the mercy of Clare. It was embarrassing, for she had never been alone with him before, and on her former visit he had not seemed to be aware of her existence. He sat with one leg awkwardly cocked above the other, his bald head sunken between his shoulders, and began to talk in a low monotone about her grandfather. The subject carried him back to the days before the overwhelming prosperity of Wolverbury. He spoke of them almost with regret.

" We had a neat little works in those days," he said, " and if it hadn't been for the boom that followed the Franco-Prussian war I expect we should be there still. That war was a marvellous thing for the Midlands. It made our friend Walter Willis, as well as me. War's a grand thing for iron. But Walter Willis "—he shook his head—" there's something wrong with him. He's a clever fellow in his way, is Willis ; but his head's not steady enough ; he can't stand oats, as our Ralph would put it. I don't say that Mawne isn't a fine concern to look at. It's all right on paper, my dear. But when the slump comes, as it's bound to, folk like Walter Willis'll have to put on their thinking-caps."

He lowered his voice to a whisper, almost as if he were making confidences to a fellow iron-master. Clare listened intently, though she could not understand half of what he was saying. He began to talk of the new Sedgebury Main Colliery, the masterpiece of the red-bearded Furnival whom Clare had met at Stourford two months before.

" Walter Willis has gone into that like a mad bull," he said, " and our George is every bit as wild about it as he is. I'm chairman of the company. I couldn't get out of it. You see they wanted my name. Well, well, they can have it. But when it comes to money . . . I'm not a geologist, my dear. Fortunately, we're in a position to pay for the best brains in that line, the same as any other. Kneeworth —he's the professor at Astill's College in North Bromwich, you know—Kneeworth says Furnival's right. Well, maybe ; I don't know. But one thing I do know, and that is that my old grandfather worked down that pit hewing coal for thirty years, and I can recollect sitting by him, just as it might be you, my dear, and hearing him say : ' You mind my words ; I can smell water in that pit,' and whenever I hear Furnival speechifying these words come back. George says I've got water on the brain. Maybe he's right, but I've got summat else as well, as we used to say."

He stopped and stared in front of him into the glazed eyes of Parker leading a quadrille. Then, clumsily, he patted Clare's hand.

" I'm glad to have had this bit of a chat with you," he said. " I can see that you've got a heart, Clare, and our Ralph's a lucky chap. He's right to have cut himself out of Wolverbury too. He's not built for it any more than young Willis is, though his dad won't see it. That's what I meant just now. D'you see ? No, we've no room for passengers in concerns like ours. What's more, you've helped me to make up my mind about this business of Furnival's. It's extraordinary how a quiet talk puts your ideas in order."

His hand went fumbling to his waistcoat pocket, as though his mind concentrated on Wolverbury, grudged the energy necessary to direct his fingers. He pulled out a folded piece of paper and slipped it into her palm.

" I made this out for you this morning," he said, " and you may as well have it before twelve as after. It's just a trifle to buy a bit of hair-ribbon with, as they say. Don't lose it, there's a good girl ! And now I think you might give your father-in-law a kiss under the mistletoe."

Clare did so willingly. Before that evening she had always thought of Sir Joseph as remote, and possibly unfriendly, so detached from all humanity had he seemed. Now she realised that the Sir Joseph of Stourford and the Sir Joseph of Wolverbury were different beings, and that when he was torn away from his works he left the greater part of his personality behind. In all the long meanderings of their talk the smaller fragment had been straining away from the music-room in the direction of its complement. Thanks to her silence it had almost succeeded in its quest. He kissed her ; even his kiss was curiously impersonal ; and then, fired with unusual courage, he hurried from the room. Vivien pounced upon Clare and dragged her into a set of lancers. Later, when she had time to look at the paper which he had put into her hand, she found that it was a cheque for a thousand pounds.

Nor was this astounding document the only one that excited her during her stay at Stourford. Ever since the announcement of the wedding, presents had been pouring in ; for trade, in the North Bromwich district was booming, and most of its wealthier manufacturers were eager to stand well with the Hingstons. Ralph took their generosity for granted. He had been brought up in a house where luxurious possessions counted for little ; but to Clare the accumulations of presents that blew into the library like a snowdrift from every quarter of the compass were almost terrifying ; they seemed to turn her wedding, which hitherto she had considered as an affair that concerned nobody but themselves, into a public event. It made her thank Heaven that the actual ceremony, which was to take place at Wychbury and from Pen House, would be more in keeping with her modesty.

On Christmas Day the family dined in state. They played the game of peace and goodwill so effectively that if Parker had not been in their service for years he might easily have imagined that they were as united as they appeared to be. They all drank Clare's health and Ralph's in a magnum of Pommery : a dangerous experiment ; for Lady Hingston was already reacting from the democratic good-humours of the night before, and alcohol, in any form, was apt to make her irritable. At once she began to lay down her own law on the subject of Eleanor's nurse and the conduct of Eleanor's children ; her black eyes flashed ; her accusations became more and more outrageous ; it was as though she were giving Clare an exhibition of the kind of thing that she would have to put up with when she and Ralph were married. But an instrument keener than Lady Hingston's tongue was needed to pierce the apathy of Eleanor ; for lack of fuel her violence blazed away as harmlessly as a fuse that stops short of detonation ; and Vivien, dashing in gallantly to the rescue with some calculated stupidity, saved her mother's face.

It was a dull evening ; for though they pretended that they were enjoying themselves, they were all too familiar and too individual to find amusement in each others' company. No doubt it was partly this lack of communal interest that had compelled them to make Stourford the open house which it was. When the children had been packed off to bed, and the effects of the champagne had evaporated, long periods of silence fell upon them. Little by little the artificial bonds were loosened and the company began to split up into its natural grouping. Lady Hingston took out a pack of patience cards. George and Sir Joseph edged away towards the library, where the cigars were kept. Vivien and Eleanor sat talking with voices lowered for fear of disturbing Lady Hingston's concentration on her cards. Ralph leaned over Clare's shoulder from behind and whispered her away into the morning-room. As they stole out together Clare felt as furtive as if she had pilfered the drawing-room silver; but when they passed the card-table Lady Hingston looked up with a smile so charming that she was compelled, by a sudden impulse, to stoop and kiss her.

"Why did you do that?" Ralph asked her afterwards, a little jealously, as if all her kisses belonged by right to him.

"I don't know. I wanted to. I'm like that," she told him.

"Yes, it's like you," he agreed, "but awfully unlike the rest of us here. Imagine Eleanor!"

"Poor Eleanor," she said. "It's tragic that anyone so beautiful should be unhappy."

"Don't waste your sympathies on Eleanor, my child," he laughed. "Eleanor's as hard and sharp as a piece of high-speed tool-steel. We're a hard lot, if you only knew it."

By the time they left the morning-room everybody but Mr. Parker had gone to bed. Ralph switched off the light at the end of the corridor and took her to her bedroom door. For a long while he would not let her go.

"You were right to fly back to Wychbury," he said. "It's simply unbearable to have you in the house here, so near, all the time, with only this damned door between us. Why should we be separated in this stupid fashion? Why should I leave you like this, just when I want you most? You're mine, Clare, and I'm yours. Why, in the name of reason, should I let you go? You can't honestly say there's any sense in it."

"Three weeks, my darling," she said. "Only three weeks."

" Oh, Clare, what a cold-blooded little thing you are ! "
he cried. " Are you pretending ? Don't you understand ? "

" Yes, but you're so impatient," she whispered. " Now
let me go, my darling."

He released her unwillingly. " Three weeks," he said.
" It's like three hundred years."


XIV

PROTHALAMION

THREE weeks, two weeks, then one.

One evening, to Clare's surprise, Aunt Cathie announced
that Wilburn was coming by his usual train and staying to
supper. Luckily for her the Hingstons had accepted an
invitation to dine with the Willises at Mawne that night,
and, in Ralph's absence, Clare was free. It was the first
time that they had met since her engagement ; and she was
fluttered to receive him, for in spite of the authority with
which Aunt Cathie now persisted in investing him, she could
not forget how much his friendship had meant to her in
earlier days.

When she heard the grating of Jabez's wheels upon the
drive she ran to open the front-door. Wilburn entered,
massive in his dark overcoat, and met her eagerness with
a formal handshake. He looked to her worn, worried, and,
somehow, older. His heaviness damped her enthusiasm
and made her shrink into herself again. He did not mention
her engagement, nor even the Hingstons' name; and this
seemed strange to her, for she knew that he was always in
touch with Wolverbury. No effort of hers could bring
a hint of lightness to the supper-table, and when the meal
was finished, he produced a roll of legal documents, which

he handed to Aunt Cathie without speaking. This was no business of hers, Clare thought, and so prepared to go.

Aunt Cathie looked up sharply. "Where are you off to, Clare?" she said. "You'd better stay here. This is a matter that concerns you."

She went on reading seriously without another word. Wilburn leaned over to Clare and explained. "Your wedding settlement," he said.

The phrase meant nothing to her. She did not know that such a thing as a wedding settlement existed. She and Ralph were going to be married, and it seemed grotesque to her that so simple and intimate a matter should be complicated by protocols like a treaty between two hostile powers.

Aunt Cathie finished the document and handed it on to her.

"This seems very satisfactory," she said. "Clare had better read it for herself."

"I don't want to in the least," said Clare. "For one thing, I shan't understand it. Besides, I'm sure there's no necessity for anything of this kind."

"That," said Aunt Cathie, "is a matter for your lawyer to judge. Of course it is necessary. Dudley, I wish you would explain to Clare what it is all about."

This was the first time that Clare had ever heard Aunt Cathie make use of Wilburn's Christian name. The shock was so great and the implication so perplexing that she could scarcely listen while Wilburn explained.

"It's just the usual thing, Clare," he told her. "Experience shows that marriage is a rather uncertain state. A number of things might happen. Your husband might go bankrupt; in which case you'd be destitute. At some time you might have differences that compelled you to separate from him . . ."

"But that's ridiculous," Clare broke in. "It's absurd

to think of such a thing. We're not that kind of people, Mr. Wilburn."

He paused and looked at her with a slow smile in which were mingled admiration and pity for her generous resentment.

"Or supposing," he went on steadily, "your husband were to die suddenly with an ambiguous will, or, perhaps, no will at all."

Clare shuddered : "I can't even think of it."

"My dear child," said Aunt Cathie, almost kindly, "you mustn't take up an emotional attitude. You know the facts of human life as well as we do. It's our duty to face them in a rational manner, as the doctor always said. Ralph has signed the paper that Mr. Wilburn's explaining. You're simply being sentimental."

"I'm not sentimental, Aunt Cathie," she answered hotly. "It's only . . . it's only that I can't bear to admit that it's even possible."

Aunt Cathie went on muttering something about facing facts ; Wilburn turned over his papers uneasily.

"We'll say no more about it if it hurts you, Clare," he said. "I'll only explain the provisions that have been made for you. Mr. Hingston is settling a thousand a year on you, together with the use of Uffdown Manor during your lifetime, or until your eldest son attains his majority. As a matter of fact, he's also executed a will that's quite in order. I have it in my office, and I can assure you, as far as that goes, that you need have no anxiety. I shall keep this settlement as well, so you needn't give another thought to it. Incidentally, he's done me the compliment of making me trustee. I'm sorry it's upset you. I didn't imagine for one moment . . ."

"It hasn't really upset me," Clare assured him, "only that one part of it. I'm sorry I behaved so stupidly. It was just . . ."

Wilburn helped her out of her difficulty. He rose and patted her shoulder. It was the first sign of humanity she had seen in him that evening, and the surprise of it almost unnerved her.

" I want to wish you every happiness, Clare," he said, " from the bottom of my heart. Ralph Hingston's a lucky fellow, and a good one too, I think."

" Oh, Mr. Wilburn," she said, " you don't know how good he is."

" Oh yes, I do," he laughed. " I know all about it. I've been in love myself. But don't forget your old friends altogether."

" I shall never forget that you are my friend," she said.

And yet, later, when he had gone and she was alone, the memory of the night-black shadow troubled her. The idea of disagreement or separation was one at which she could afford to smile out of her faith and security ; but the other she could not dismiss so easily from her mind ; for she had been accustomed to take it for granted that their love had sprung from an eternal seed, immune from time or mortality. Yet here, on the very verge of its fulfilment, were sober-minded and not ill-natured people making assurance against the shears of fate. Their care seemed impious and hateful, and vain in its materialism ; for if she should lose her love she knew that the possession of all the world would mean nothing to her. For love such as theirs, she thought, there could be only one proper end : a common and instantaneous annihilation. The suggestion that she might have children could not change her mind. Children were lovely playthings. So she had thought when she romped with Eleanor's twins at Stourford ; but the idea of having children of her own was nothing to her but a distant and delicate dream. Even if she had no children, she told herself, she would be contented ; for her heart had no room in it for any but Ralph's imperious image. He was husband and child in one ; in himself the completion of all desire. She saw him now, in the closed brougham, driving home from Mawne ; and as she closed her eyes she seemed to feel the firmness of his lips against her own and the soft hollow of his eyes and his crisp, fair hair. In the security of this possession she fell asleep.

On the afternoon of her last day at Pen House and of her maiden life, Clare was kept busy packing her new initialled trunk for Italy and stowing in others the remainder of Aunt Cathie's half-dozens, which Jabez, in her absence, would drive over to Uffdown to await her. Now, once again, the pace of time had quickened, since the things that had been left till the last moment were too many to be contained by it. All through the day she had been unable to count on Thirza's or Aunt Cathie's help ; for Aunt Cathie, in spite of mourning, had decided that the doctor would have wished his granddaughter to be married decently, and both of them were busy, in kitchen and dining-room, preparing refreshments—not a wedding-breakfast, she insisted—which should prove to the Stourford party that, without the least pretensiousness, the Weirs were as good as they.

The lower storey of the house was full of movements and whisperings and savoury smells. Of course Mrs. Harbord was there, exalted from her traffic in sticks of liquorice and bottles of herbal beer to Thirza's lieutenancy ; for Thirza would not allow that Ellen to poke her clumsy fingers in anything, and wanted company. Nor could Aunt Cathie dream of letting Ellen, with her special talent for dissolving china in her hands, set touch upon the antique services of Spode, blue Worcester and Crown Derby which left the shelter of their accustomed cupboards. She washed them, every piece, with her own hands, fingering their fine glaze with a reverence which was the deepest that she knew ;

and Ellen, unwanted in kitchen or in dining-room, was sent upstairs to help Clare with her packing.

An Ellen speechless and abashed, who handled Clare's fine tissues as reverently as Aunt Cathie handled her old china, an Ellen that Clare did not know, with pale, awed face, and big eyes that seemed to be upon the point of crying. So strangely, mutely emotional did she seem that Clare was at some pains to joke her into the naturalness and confidence that were usual with her. In vain ; for Ellen was in no laughing humour. They worked away until nothing was left except the clothes that Clare was wearing and those in which she was to be married and travel on the morrow. Then came a fearful wrestling with the straps of her Italian luggage. The heavy domed trunk refused to close beneath their double strength.

" Don't worry, Ellen dear," Clare said at last. " You'd better call Jabez."

" Old Jabez ? " Ellen cried indignantly. " Why, Miss, I'm stronger than what he is."

She threw herself, in a final effort, upon the recalcitrant lid and closed it.

" There now ! " she said, and at that moment collapsed into loud tears. It was difficult for Clare to deal with this unreasonable outburst. In the ordinary way Ellen was not emotional. She could not imagine what accumulation of feeling had found this ungainly outlet. Ellen had sunk to the floor like a sack, and clasped her knees so desperately that the impact of her weeping nearly upset Clare's balance. She did her best to comfort and restrain her.

" Why, Ellen," she said, " you mustn't cry like that. What is the matter with you ? Don't cry. Just tell me what it is."

It flattered and half amused her to think that her going should have affected Ellen so deeply. Her hands, caressing the bowed and agitated head, encountered the tight mass.

shaped like a teapot handle into which Ellen's hair was twisted.

"Surely you're not crying because I'm going away?" she said. "You shouldn't in any case, because I'm so awfully happy, and I want everyone else to be happy with me. I'm not going away for ever, you know. We shall be back in a couple of months, and then you'll come over to Uffdown and see me on your afternoon out."

"No, Miss, it isn't that," Ellen gulped between her sobs. "At least it is and it isn't. It's seeing you so happy, Miss, and going off like this on your honeymoon into foreign parts, just like it might be a dream, when I'm that down and werrited, Miss, I could make a hole in the canal. It was seeing them shimeezes that started it, and the drawers. I run up three pairs myself, leastways mother did for me. Lovely things they were ; but I reckon I might as well chuck them in the ash-pit for all the pleasure I'll ever get out of them. Or give them to *her*. She'll have more use for them nor me. Twenty-seven pounds, too, I got saved in the Post Office for the furnishing. And Jim knows it, Miss ; he's seen the bank-book with his own eyes. They always say they're changeable, Miss ; but Jim Moseley—well, you'd never have thought it of him, not if you'd known him particular, like I have."

"But what's the matter with Jim Moseley?" Clare enquired. "I don't quite understand. Surely you and he have been walking out for the last two years. You don't mean to tell me . . ."

"Not walking-out, Miss," Ellen corrected her. "Far beyond that, Miss. That was a year ago. Ever since the Jubilee we've been courting. And all the public knows it. The young lady at the Post Office made a remark when I put the last sovereign in. 'I suppose you'll be married before long, Ellen,' she says. 'Yes, miss,' I says, 'as soon as we've got enough for the furniture.' 'Well, Ellen, you're getting on,' she says, ' judging by the book and barring accidents,' she says. ' Don't speak of it, miss,' says I. And the very next Sunday, Miss, last Sunday that is, when you was over at your young gentleman's, I saw my Jim stroddling along arm in crook with that chitty-face that's housemaid at the Vicarage. He seen me too, did Jim : I know him that well ; I can look through the back of his head. He told her I was coming up behind ; I know he did. They both started laughing, Miss, and went on up the lane as peart as peacocks. I knew where he was taking her, too, I wonder he had the heart. We always used to go that way."

By this time Ellen's indignation had got the better of her distress. She stood up, panting, with tears flashing in her neutral eyes and two big patches of red upon her cheeks, so warm and human and tremulous that she seemed almost beautiful.

" Well, that's all over, Miss," she said, with a twisted smile. " You must excuse me for telling you. I know I oughtn't ; but the sight of them underthings all laid out ready got the better of me, and I feel more myself, like, now that I've spoken out. It was like a worm, Miss, gnawing and gnawing in here." She clutched the breast of her print dress as though the pain were still inside it.

" Someone had better speak to Jim Moseley," said Clare, " and show him how badly he's behaving. Perhaps Aunt Cathie . . ."

" Oh no, Miss. That wouldn't do. I shouldn't like Miss Cathie or Thirza to know about it ; and I couldn't demean myself by letting anyone speak of it to Jim. You've no idea what a good boy he is, Miss, really. He may get over it. There's naught to be done that way. There's only one thing, if I might make so bold as to mention it."

" Don't be foolish, Ellen," said Clare, " you know you can tell me anything."

" I do, indeed, Miss Clare. Now that Jim's gone, you're the only one I can speak to. How I wish you wasn't going away ! No, Miss, I can't say that. That's downright wicked of me. But it's like this : I can't for shame to stay on here in Wychbury, where all the public knows how it was with me and Jim. I've got to go away, Miss, somewhere where I bain't known ; leastways, until my Jim gets his senses back. I was wondering if you could find room for me at Uffdown. It's more out of the way like, and you know, Miss, how fond I am of you. I reckon I've finished with men for good and all. I'd like to stay along of you to my dying day, like Thirza, if so be that you'd have me."

She seized Clare's hand and kissed it clumsily. The moment was so affecting that tears came into Clare's eyes. She compelled herself to be reasonable.

" You know, Ellen," she said, " that I couldn't possibly steal you from Aunt Cathie. You're very happy here."

" Not when you're gone," said Ellen. " Miss Cathie's all right, but old Thirza, she gets more fussy every day. It's ' Ellen this,' and ' Ellen that,' till my head's all moithered. No, Miss, I've got to leave here in any case ; and I don't want to go into service in North Bromwich ; I'm not like other girls. If only you could say you'll have me if I'm free. And I'm that fond of children ! "

Clare laughed. Ellen's naive imagination went so fast. And yet she gave her promise. When Ellen had left her the poignancy of this minor tragedy, so heightened by its contrast with her own content, dwelt in her thoughts and subdued them until the bell summoned her to supper below.

The greater part of the dining-room was now occupied by the table, extended with two leaves, on which Aunt Cathie had displayed her answer to the vulgar splendours of Stourford. She had reason to be proud of it. Everything that fine linen and bright silver and the rich hues of old china could accomplish had been done. Clare found her, pale, but calmly triumphant, at a small tea-table which Thirza had laid immediately in front of the fire. Their supper was cosy and intimate. The fire drew so brightly under the frosty sky that when Thirza had cleared away, Aunt Cathie, who was too tired for needlework, told her to put out the lamp. For a long while they sat on in silence. Clare knew that this was no time in which to tell her of Ellen's troubles ; and, indeed, they were soon forgotten, so heavily did the significance of this last evening together press upon them both.

Out of that quiet firelight a new, strange vision of Aunt Cathie was created in Clare's mind, a vision sweetened and humanized by the memory of all the years they had spent together. For the first time in all her life Clare seemed to see her, not as a conventional figure vested with painful authority, capable of sudden, bewildering kindness, but as a woman, like herself. It was this human relationship that she had never appreciated. From earliest childhood she had taken Aunt Cathie for granted. Now, peering backward into those dim recesses, she began to question the meaning of little things that she remembered, and all the incidents that obstinately and illogically rose and challenged her out of the darkness, clamoured for interpretation.

They appeared from the most unlikely levels of her past life, kindnesses and small injustices commingled. She remembered, for instance, one summer day—she could not say how many years ago—when Aunt Cathie had slapped her for a lie that she had not told. She remembered another evening, earlier still, when Aunt Cathie had suddenly caught her in her arms and hugged her till it hurt. That must have been in summer too ; a moth was fluttering round the chimney of the lamp and dashing itself against the opal globe. That globe had passed away into the limbo over which Jabez presided, the ashpit by the second appletree. Again she remembered Aunt Cathie, chill and judicial, standing above her box on the eve of her first term at St. Monica's ; herself a lanky little girl in short skirts and black, ribbed stockings. She remembered the alarms which Aunt Cathie had soothed and explained. There was no end to this smoke of arbitrary memories ; and in all of them Aunt Cathie appeared, always the same, a presence, not a person.

Yet, as they cleared and faded, she began to realize more and more the deepness of her debt. She saw that through all these nineteen years of dim half-consciousness Aunt Cathie's care had shielded and her wisdom directed her. There, as she sat, Clare knew that it was this sombre, fading woman who had made her what she was, for better or for worse. Without her she might not even have been alive, and if she were living . . . thought could not carry her further ; but a wave of love and gratitude, unquestioning, all-forgiving, rose in her heart, engulfed her, and threw her, she could not say how, at Aunt Cathie's knees. She found herself sobbing there, her head buried in Aunt Cathie's lap; she heard Aunt Cathie's voice, strangely distant, and most strangely soft.

" Clare, my little Clare," she was saying. " It's better that you should cry if you want to. Don't take any notice of me, my darling, I understand. There, there now . . ." Aunt Cathie's own voice wavered curiously.

" I only wanted to tell you how I love you, dearest," Clare sobbed.

" Yes, yes, I know. And I love you too, my darling. I don't always show it, I'm afraid. But that's how I'm made. The doctor was just the same. Now that he's gone . . ." She swallowed pathetically and stopped. " You see, Clare darling, I'm getting on in years. No, I'm not really old. I know that. But when old people die and young ones go away from you, there's a sort of emptiness.

I'm not exactly frightened of being alone, Clare ; it isn't that. I'm used to it, in a sort of way. The doctor wasn't what you'd call a companion. And yet when he was sitting there night after night I felt—it's difficult to say—I felt that somehow things were all right. But after to-morrow . . ."

" I know, dearest, I know," Clare said. " That's what makes me so unhappy."

" But you mustn't be unhappy, my child. And you aren't unhappy really. You must be happier than you've ever been before. I don't grudge you your happiness. It's far the most important thing I have left in my life. You see, Clare, it's a kind of happiness that I shall never know, and yours is the nearest I can get to it. You mustn't pity me, darling : I'm quite . . . resigned isn't exactly what I mean . . . contented, that's the word."

She paused for a moment, then went on dreamily :

" I suppose that's partly why you're so precious to me, Clare. I've always thought of you, right deep down in my heart, I mean, as if you were really my own baby. There was another reason. I don't believe I can bear to tell you . . . Yes, I will . . . Clare, darling, this is a thing that I've never told to anyone, not even to the doctor. I don't think your mother even knew about it. I was in love with your father. He gave me to understand that he was in love with me and let me go on loving him. It was a lie. It was cruel and horrible of him. Even when your mother went away with him, up to the very hour, I thought he loved me. It nearly killed me, Clare. It did kill part of me. Part of me's been dead ever since that day. I expect that explains why I can't say all the things that I want to ; there's something that won't answer, just as if some nerve had been cut. For quite a long time I couldn't bear anyone to look at me or to look at anyone. I hated everything, everything in the world until I began to love you ; and even then I hated myself for loving you. Of course that was a long, long time ago. Twenty years. Now I never think of it. If I did, I couldn't have told you. It's passed out of all reality. Why, if he came into the room at this moment, I don't think it would disturb me. I could forgive him if there was anything to forgive."

There followed a long silence. Clare felt that to speak would be a sacrilege. Yet during this long confession she knew that Aunt Cathie and she had attained an understanding that they had not known before. A sense of loyalty, confirmed in complete knowledge, made her heart glow with a good will more satisfying than her impulsive love. She was so confident in their unity that, at last, she dared to ask if Aunt Cathie knew where her father was, or if he were still alive.

" I don't know," she answered calmly. " I don't think I want to know. He must still be a man in the prime of life, well under fifty. Possibly he is still in Canada. He married again, you know, that was why you came here. He didn't want to take you with him, or, perhaps, it was his wife. I'm sure it was better for all of us."

Better indeed, Clare thought, for if he had taken me with him I should never have met Ralph, and Ralph would have married someone else, which would have been monstrous and intolerable.

" I think you had better go to bed early, Clare, darling," Aunt Cathie was saying. " You have a big day in front of you to-morrow. If you feel restless you can come into my bed. You must do just as you feel."

" I think I shall sleep quite well alone, dearest," Clare told her.

" Then I'll come in and kiss you good-night," said Aunt Cathie, smiling, " just like I used to when you were a little girl."

These final interviews were all distressing. In each of

them Clare had to bear the shock of the various emotions that her conditions aroused. At the foot of the stairs Ellen was waiting with the excuse of some improbable duty. She did not speak but, as Clare passed, she clutched her hand and stole a long, moist kiss. Laughing, Clare hurried upstairs. In the door of her bedroom Thirza Rudge was standing.

" Why, Thirza, what are you doing here ? " Clare cried.

" Just seeing that Ellen's put everything ready for 'ee, my love," said Mrs. Rudge. " Well, well, my handsome, God grant that this is the last night in your life as you'll sleep alone." Her soft eyes gloated over the prospect. " Marriage be a queer old game, Miss Clare, and needs some understanding. There's some maids takes to it like a duck to water, and some as can't never put up with it. There was my Alice now, as I said to my friend this mornin' . . . but that's not here nor there. You never know until it comes to you, and there's no call to get scared beforehand. There's happy marriages and unhappy, as I always say. But one thing I'll tell you, my love, and if you're a wise maid you'll never forget it." Her voice sank to a mysterious whisper : " Always oblige your husband in the bedroom," said Thirza Rudge.

# BOOK THREE
## CLARE HINGSTON

# TRANSIT OF VENUS

DURING the next week the fate of that friend of Aunt Cathie's who had died of pneumonia on the Riviera in February was often in Clare's mind. The lights of Paris resigned themselves to a watery death ; between them a funeral cortège of huge-caped coachmen dragged slowly over the stone setts of the boulevards. They crossed the Alps in the thick of a mist of snow, so still, so listlessly suspended, that it seemed as if the rarefied air were slowly crystallizing about them ; through this white silence the train thundered down into Italy, like a thing that had taken fright at the spectral mountain-shapes which thrust their bleak and monstrous summits through the crystalline veil. At Turin the snow had ceased, but through its wide streets and endless colonnades an icy wind blew downward from the Alpine barrier.

" If this is Italy," Ralph said, " why, give me Wolverbury. The next honeymoon I have I shall try Iceland."

He grumbled all the time, half earnestly and half in jest ; for already they had made the discovery that they were not the responsible married people that they had imagined themselves to be. In this new, engrossing pretence Ralph was a little boy, in whom the most outrageous speech and behaviour were smiled at and forgiven by Clare, his indulgent mother ; while Clare, in the shameless innocence of an affected childhood, shed all the modesties which she had gathered round her since the days of St. Monica's. Sometimes she stopped to ask herself if this abandoned stranger were really herself, and wondered what Aunt Cathie would think if she saw or heard her ; but these questionings filled her with amusement rather than shame ; she found it a whimsical paradox that she and the shy girl who had knelt on the chancel steps at Wychbury were really one and the same. Smiling to herself, she took a new and proper pride in the completeness of her abandonment. All reticence seemed cowardly and half-hearted. In the complete fusion of body and soul that she desired there was no intimacy that love could not hallow, no modesty that was not shameful and unworthy. It was her privilege to give not part of herself, but all, and more than she knew. She gave passionately with open heart and hands ; there was no end to her happiness in giving ; and though the wind drove down from ice-bound Alp and Appenine their hearts were warm ; their love was a glowing crucible in which all baseness melted away and only gold remained.

Each day Clare seemed more beautiful to herself and in Ralph's eyes, with a loveliness confident and serene. All through the wintry cities of Italy they passed southward, surrounded by their own enchantment, carrying Spring captive in their train ; and beauty rose to meet them as though she were glad of their possession. For their ecstasy was not that of hope but fulfilment. Beyond the passing moment or before it they could see nothing, nor wished to see ; within it, life surrendered its ultimate essence. There was nothing more that they could ask of it. The universe was theirs. *My beloved is mine and I am his.* So, through the death of winter, Clare sang her Song of Songs.

On the hallucinated Campanian shore the footstep of a real Spring surprised them. When they left the train at Naples a tramontana was blowing the smoke of Vesuvius seaward from his snow-streaked cone, and petulant dust-storms whirled about the dark and frozen streets ; but as they woke next morning to a lazy consciousness of life and of each other, Clare saw that the louvres of the Persian blind were barred with a gold that set her heart on fire. She raised herself on her elbow and looked at Ralph. He lay beside her, his fair face flushed with sleepiness. He smiled and surveyed her with lazy satisfaction through his half-closed eyes.

" The sun in shining," she told him. " I must get up. The bell's on your side. I wish you'd ring for *colazione*."

" Do it yourself, you little nuisance," he murmured sleepily. " I was just dreaming. I dreamt hounds were drawing the Stourhead osiers. A ripping morning for scent. So you see what a mess you've made of it."

" You're just like a dog yourself," she told him. " You're always growling and hunting in your sleep."

" Oh, Clare," he yawned, " I wish to heaven you wouldn't call them dogs. A hound's a hound, you little silly. I've told you that before. And you haven't said good morning to your husband properly either."

She laughed and slid above him, so that her lips were on his. Then she released herself from his arms. She rang the bell for breakfast, and ran to the window where the golden light barred her white feet. She dragged the blinds sideways ; sunlight dazzled her. Then she flung wide the windows and held her breath.

Immediately beneath her the green-black crown of a stone-pine leapt out above the clustered roofs of Naples. Beyond, from Ischia to Punta Campanella, the gulf spread its floor of shimmering sea, bright as the skimming body of a kingfisher, but paler, with the satiny lustre of an Adonis butterfly's wing. The dark, volcanic coast of the Sorrentine peninsula, and high St. Angelo stood clear, blue, opaline, like a frozen cloud, or a cloud given substance by some magic warmer and softer than that of frost ; and like blue cloud becalmed in shapes of precision that no cloud ever attained, the crags of Capri swam above the horizon's gentle bow, islanded in air like the lands of Brendan's vision. And all the space in which this peerless intaglio was set was so enriched and interfused by light that it acquired a shining texture of its own. The air itself seemed one vast scintillating diamond.

Down in the well-like streets below her, life was already stirring, as into a flight of sun-hatched ephemerids. It teemed with movement and colour. It rose, in a bright babel of speech and song. It passed through the open windows, this pullulating flood, buoyant and radiant on the crystalline air. It permeated Clare's flesh and ran through her limbs, bidding them dance. It burst from her lips in unbidden laughter.

" Oh, Ralph, get up, get up ! " she cried. " My darling, you don't know what you are missing. Do, do come quickly."

He rolled out of bed and came clumsily to her side at the open window. He passed his arm about her waist. Her flimsy nightdress slipped smoothly over her polished skin. He frowned at the sunlight, and stood in silence ; for it was Clare's beauty, not that of the gulf that engrossed him. She was so smooth, so slender and so soft. There was no end to her white body's loveliness. The waiter knocked at the door and called " *Permesso ?* " She started away from him.

But all through that day, and others that followed, Naples infected and inspired her. For Naples is not Europe, but rather some isolated fragment of the sunken Tyrrhenian land whose life resents its new climatic epoch, and only reveals itself when the sun is shining. Daily the sun shone, in a windless, halcyon blue ; and beneath it the sordid alleys festooned with multi-coloured washing hung out to dry, the scabrous piazzas with house-fronts of painted plaster, the bright-tiled cupolas of neglected churches, shone like the flower-market stairways of the Chiaia. And Clare herself was like a flower, a daffodil that has freed itself from frozen earth, dancing and glancing in the sun. She was

lithe and palpitant, like the lizards that stole out to sun themselves and lay with quick-beating hearts under the tarnished
palm-trees of the park. Like them she was swift and darting,
as though her inherited darkness had taken fire from some
lost spark that smouldered in her northern blood.

She was so swift that Ralph could never keep pace with
her. This full light seemed a cruelty to his misty Saxon
eyes, more fit for wide fields of green and cloudy woodlands.
The sun that inspired her filled his long limbs with languor.
Like a tired Goth he stalked beside her, magnificent in his
fairness, slow-moving, slow-spoken, aloof, and a little
contemptuous of this vivid, vivacious race.

In the north Clare had dragged him like a captive through
miles of picture galleries and museums. He had submitted
to this penance because he could not bear to be separated
from her, and because he understood that this was the right
thing to do. He realized that all her eager cultural aspirations, the seed of which had fallen on her from Miss Boldmere's albums of foreign travel, were foreign to his nature.
He could not guess their meaning and was distrustful of
their value ; and yet he was so jealous that no part of her
should escape him that he followed her, and even underlined
his Baedeker over his pipe at night. But in Naples, to his
relief, Clare's passion for the fine arts seemed to forsake her,
and his head was no longer troubled with the barbarous names
of *cinque-cento* painters. She was engrossed in life rather
than art ; her quick eyes sought its varieties with an unin-
telligible eagerness; she could not have enough of it ; and
so they sat for hours on the terrace of a cafe commanding
the tangled central knot of the city's activity ; Clare with
her eager brain delighted by the coloured pageant that
passed before them, he, with a half-litre of pallid beer to
sip, appraising the quality of Neapolitan horses, roused to
proprietary resentment by the bold glances of dapper
cavalry officers that Clare's alien beauty attracted. The

horses were not so bad, if only these fellows wouldn't hammer their hoofs to perdition on the stone setts ; the beer lacked body ; Italian tobacco was unsmokable. He wondered if he could get a parcel of civilized honey-dew sent to him from Oxford by post.

The chilly mornings, for all their sunshine, brought back to his thoughts the miry lanes, the smell of leaf-mould along the covert-side, the whimper of hounds breaking silence, the thudding of hoofs on turf, and, at the end of glowing days, a hot bath with a sprinkle of ammonia in it. The bathroom at their hotel was like the temple of a forgotten cult, and he himself the sole and stubborn worshipper. By the time they reached Uffdown the Woodland Stourton's season would be nearly over. Naples was a city ; and he was country bred. But the wine of Gragnano, of which he drank a bottle every evening at dinner, made him see the charms of Parthenope and Clare in another light.

He felt thankful when Clare had exhausted its possibilities of excitement, and decided to move on. Ralph would have been more happy if they had turned their faces homeward ; but, every morning when she opened their windows, the shape of Capri had beckoned her. They still had a fortnight left, the first in March, and nothing would satisfy her but that they should spend it in peace upon that dreamy island. As well there as elsewhere, he thought ; for in spite of an occasional twinge of northern nostalgia, he knew that he could be happy anywhere with Clare ; the spell of her magic still lay so heavily upon him that he was grudging of anything that distracted her from absorption in himself. On Capri they would be alone. So much the better.

The winds conspired to make their segregation more complete. On the day they left Naples the alchemy of scirocco turned the golden gulf to lead ; a white-capped swell drove inward from the spray-shrouded island, and brought Ralph's Midland heart into his mouth. The little steamer rode it like a dancing cork ; she was tossed skyward, then wallowed in sickening glaucous troughs. He watched Clare greenly as she climbed into the bows. The warm, grey, wind rushed through her hair ; the salt spattered her face and whipped the blood into her cheeks ; she knew the exultation of man that rides the waves ; she found herself singing down the singing wind, secure in its boisterousness that nobody could hear her voice.

When she returned to him she was ashamed of her rapture ; his face was blanched and pitiful, and his smile so wry. So she settled down beside him and held his hand as though he were a child ; her maternity embraced this limp and sea-defeated creature who had always seemed to her so strong. It amazed her to think that his strength should need the protection of her, who was like a baby in his arms ; but she would not let him know what she was thinking for the world, so she subdued her storm-excited spirits and was very tactful.

That night the south wind veered to westward. The unprotected anchorage of the island was swept by seas so savage that for two days no steamer could disembark. Once on dry land, Ralph could afford to laugh at waves. The roar of the sea encompassed them ; the mountain-tops were stripped by a gale that seemed an extension of the loud sea's savagery, carrying in its talons sheets of salt rain that might well have been snatched upward from torn coamers. Lizard-like the inhabitants of the island kept closed doors ; the wet pavement of the little piazza was empty and bright as steel, and yet, between the wind-harried bursts of rain, an obstinate sun shone whitely, and the air was as warm as that of a wet English May.

This more familiar weather put new life into Ralph ; the moist air loosened his sinews and stimulated them to an answering violence. All the lassitude of their sedentary town life disappeared. The sight of the forlorn stree

inspired him to assert himself and show these soft South-
erners that English people were not afraid of rain. Clare
was not loth to share this sudden birth of energy. Storm
sent her blood tingling no less than crystalline calm. They
set off together scrambling over the island paths which the
rain had converted into so many singing torrents. They
hung, like brown wind-buffeted kestrels under the crags,
while the sea boiled a thousand feet beneath, or the wind
blew the waves of tortured olives below them into flaws of
streaking whiteness that simulated foam.

The wind was soft, for all its violence, and laden with the
scent of the last narcissus, still lingering in sheltered crannies
of rock, and sudden wafts of single, purple-flowered stock,
self-sown on grassy ledges that even Ralph's hardihood
could not reach. Clare went hatless in the wind ; her hair
was decked with crimson strawberries of arbutus that Ralph
had stolen from the *macchia*. Never in all their wanderings
had they known such a gay carelessness, such youth, such
nice adjustment of physical well-being as in that strenuous
week of storm ; never had the country food seemed so
enticing, nor wine more generous, nor sleep so dreamless in
its satisfaction.

The wild wind backed. Once more it blew from the
north ; first keenly, with the thrust of an icy blade, from
the serrated snows of the Appenine, and then more gently,
till the sky cleared and the sea subsided into the shimmering
halcyon calm that they had already known. But now the
easy island life had permeated Ralph's blood. Their little
room, with its wide windows facing the vertical cliffs of
Monte Solaro where they shot into the southern sea, had
become homely, familiar, a shrine of remembered delights.
The sun reflected from the green banks of the olive groves
was no longer the enemy that had blinded him in the white
streets of Naples. He still remembered the sea-passage
with discomfort ; but life went so well with him that he

began to count the dwindling days with regret. Indeed, there seemed no reason why they should not prolong their stay in Eden.

"It isn't as if there were any real necessity for us to hurry back," he said.

"Except the end of the hunting-season," she told him, mischievously. "You'd never forgive me if I brought you home too late for that."

"I don't know," he said, reluctantly. "I think one might amuse oneself here all right. I'm always seeing fellows going about with odd-looking muzzle-loaders on their shoulders. Yesterday, down below Anacapri, I put up three woodcock, and that porter chap told me that the place'll soon be stiff with quails."

She smiled at his earnestness. Often her smiles puzzled him.

"Besides," he went on hastily, "you know perfectly well, my sweet, that I should be happy anywhere with you."

He held out his arms to her ; she laughed and eluded him.

"No love-making on the edge of precipices ! I've told you already there ought to be a close-season for that sort of thing. Oh, Ralph, you're perfectly dreadful ! " she said, though her lips encouraged him. "Are you never, never going to get over it ? "

"Never, my sweet one, never, as long as I live."

And so the last day dawned in a still radiance that seemed to mock the foolish haste of their departure ; the pale sea lay smooth as polished marble with pools and veinings of indigo and malachite ; the land seemed to be lifted above it, swimming in opaline air, an island of mirage, as Clare had seen it first from her Naples window. But when the sun began to climb no strand of mist clung to it. The craggy contours of Solaro shone above them in chiselled clarity, cut like a gem ; the *macchia* of the foothills, rain-refreshed, sparkled like one gigantic emerald. They knew it would be a crime to miss one moment of this brilliant air, so they made the hotel-keeper cut them sandwiches of anchovy and mottled *salame*, and set out up the mountain together.

At the corner where the rock road narrows to a giddy ledge an oak-wood lifted dry branches, ochre yellow, against the deep blue sky. They stopped to take breath and to gaze at them.

" You see what a fraud this island is," Ralph said, " it isn't really Spring. The oak-buds at Stourford must be as far advanced as these."

She laughed at him. He was always ready to find an incongruity that showed how much better ordered everything in England was.

" How you will label things," she told him. " Of course, it isn't Spring. It isn't any season. It's just living. But if that isn't Spring, it's awfully like it. Look . . . look ! "

The lower slopes of the mountain up which they climbed were dusted with peach-blossom of so ethereal a pink that it seemed to hang among the dark foliage of orange-trees and loquats like a suspended flight of butterflies. As they climbed higher among the brushwood, the blossom beneath resolved itself into a pale mist ; above them the limestone crags impended in clear, hard shadows and gleaming pinnacles of white. Women were crouching among the *macchia* in ungainly postures, reaping the wiry growth with short-handled sickles, cutting and tearing by turns ; from the bruised and lacerated stems there rose to meet them a savour, hot, pungent, aromatic, issuing from the oily sap of myrtle, lentisk, rush and creeping rosemary ; and as she breathed it Clare's thoughts fled back to Uffdown, to the grey garden with its bushes of rosemary from which, on their first visit, Ralph had plucked her a sprig.

" Whenever we walk in the garden at home," she told him, " and smell the rosemary hedge we shall be able to think of this day. That's for remembrance, my darling. And then—you know what funny things scents are—we shall be able to recall all these other smells. We shall have to close our eyes and think of nothing. I know how it's done. I've often taken a school book and recalled St. Monica's. Attar of Capri : that's the name I shall give to it."

Now they had climbed right under the pinnacles of sun-bleached rock. A little cleft, like the gap in a stone wall, admitted them to an unsuspected plateau, hidden in the mountain's crown. Here the banks were mossed with moisture ; bramble and bracken straggled down them ; the whole air tasted moist and sweet and English ; the turf was dappled with gardens of a sturdy orchis, with blood-red uprights and velvety purple falls, that Clare had never seen. Another world, they said, but this was not the world for which they were seeking.

They found it, their desire, on the cliff-side westward of the hermitage of Cetrella, a high and stony eyrie, under cascades of lithospermum, bluer than Ralph's eyes. From it their imagination could swoop in swift and easy flight through blue air downward upon the coloured cubes of Capri, spilled beneath them like a child's box of bricks, or, sailing further afield, rise to the purple crags that crown the Sorrentine peninsula, the wolf-haunted chestnut forests of Sant' Angelo, the dim recesses of the Gulf of Salerno, and sea that stretched to Sicily. " . . . up into a high mountain," Clare thought, " and showed him all the kingdoms of the world." Yet all the kingdoms that she desired were in Ralph's heart and her own.

They ate their lunch and talked in their new language of those little things out of which they had made their own world. The wine that Ralph had insisted on bringing with him made them somnolent, as did the murmur of the sea, and the resinous air that whispered through the Aleppo pines behind them. Ralph spread his long limbs and was soon fast asleep. His gentle breathing was only another soothing sound, and Clare soon followed him, her dark head rising and falling on his breast.

How long they slept she could not imagine. She was wakened by a swift rush of air above her eyes, the dark passage of something incredibly keen and rapid, like the swish of a scimitar. She wakened with a start, and saw, a hundred feet below her, the spread wings and rock-blue body of a peregrine falcon whose flight had skimmed her eyes. They had lain so still that the bird had taken them for stones.

She roused Ralph, who was still sleeping heavily, and told him what had happened. The sun was sinking. He yawned, confessed that he was chilly ; but the brisk walk upward to the pass soon brought the blood back to their limbs. At the gap in the wall they faced the red sun setting southward of Ischia. They watched it founder in a white and glassy sea. Below them the village of Anacapri lay darkening with long shadows ; through the lanes that converged upon it they saw slow figures, bowed beneath enormous burdens, winding wearily homeward from their work beneath the olives. From all the chimneys of the village smoke rose into the air and drifted slowly along the base of the mountain like mist. Through one great cleft that seemed to lose itself in sea the olives, too, were like a downward-curling smoke. Suddenly from the belfry in the little piazza the agitated clamour of the Angelus rose above the hushed, clear rumour of the disappearing village. If they hung upon the mountain longer they might stumble on the stones. They hurried down. It seemed to Clare that something with a mystical significance had come to an end. She did not regret it.

" There has never been a day like this," she told him.

" Never a day like this," he repeated.

And never, they thought, would there be such another night. When they went upstairs after dinner the full moon had risen and filled their little bedroom with enchantment. The light was so silvery and strange that Clare protested against the sacrilege of candles ; so they did without them, undressing in the fantastic shadow. For a long time they would not sleep. It was too beautiful for sleep. They lay, almost silently in each other's arms, and each seemed strange to the other, when their eyes met, yet no less wonderful. For Clare knew that this mysterious visitant was a god among men ; and to Ralph her moony whiteness was of an immortal texture.

## II

## UFFDOWN

At Uffdown Manor, Ralph had decided, they would run to earth. There nothing should disturb the continuity of their absorption into the secret and enthralling manner of life which they had discovered in Italy. This beatified state was to be maintained jealously and indefinitely. United they were self-sufficient. All intrusions would be discouraged. If people insisted on visiting them they must be prepared to take the risk of being embarrassed by a pair of unconventional lovers. They called themselves unconventional ; the word had a sound that pleased Ralph's arrogance. But Mrs. Rudge would have known better.

They arrived at Wychbury in a flurry of April snow. The station platform looked more forlorn than usual. Mr. Hemus, the porter told them, was in bed with influenza. They drove up to Uffdown in the shining brougham, with the new coachman, Bissel, whom Ralph had engaged, on the box. The village street was empty ; it allowed them to pass without disturbing itself, though Clare, half-bold, half-shy, peered out of the carriage windows to look for familiar faces. She saw no soul that she knew, save Mr. Wilkins, the undertaker, trudging along with his collar turned up and an elm plank over his shoulder. She would have waved to him, out of her excitement, but wasn't quite sure if the occasion on which they had met was sufficient to constitute an introduction.

Ralph appeared a little conscious of his dignity as Lord of Uffdown returning to his Manor.

"You're like a jack-in-the-box, Clare," he told her. "It's no good trying to recognize anybody. Nobody with any sense 'ld be out of doors on an evening like this. I wish we'd put in another day in London. It's a pity we missed seeing Finney dive at the Westminster Aquarium."

There was no moon ; the one that they had left serenely sailing above the crags of Capri was now obscured by the earth's shadow ; but the brand new carriage-lamps swept a moving beam along snow-sprinkled hedgerows, and showed Clare that their life was still asleep. And yet the smell of them ! As she drew the familiar humid air into her lungs, the memory of Italy faded from her like an escaping dream. It was here, here, in the heart of a moist, Atlantic country that she belonged. The poignance of this emotion made her clasp Ralph's gloved hand. He smiled and returned her pressure.

"Who, but a couple of fools," he mumbled, "would think of coming home on the first of April ? "

Beech-mast deadened the whisper of the carriage wheels ; the roof of the columned lane was blacker than any night. Bissel touched up his horses ; the beam of the carriage lamps shone on the lucent leaves of laurel bushes. The front of the house glowed like a lantern ; every window ablaze, casting out light on to the lawn's snow-powdered surface, on to the pancakes of snow that clung to the horizontal cedar branches, on the congealed and half thawed borders that marked the junction of grass and flower-bed, undercut, like ice that hangs on the edge of a stream. Out of the black earth within them rose spikes and budded heads of the daffodils that Clare and Ralph had planted in September.

The brake grated in its ratchet, the horses stamped, and Vivien was on them, jumping into the interior of the brougham like an untrained puppy, grasping Clare's hand and Ralph's, kissing their snow-chilled faces with her eager lips. So warm and welcoming was she that she seemed a bodily emanation of all the house's light and comfort.

"You dears," she cried, as she dragged them in. "I want to look at you. Take off your coats so that I can see you properly. No, you've not changed a bit. Only Ralph's fatter—exercise is what you want, my boy!—and Clare has got more colour. Where did you get that frock, Clare? Paris, I'll be bound. Of course, I haven't seen it before! Oh, I do hope you dear people'll be comfortable. I've lighted fires everywhere—simply tons of coal—but you're sure to feel the cold after all that sun. We scarcely notice it. I wish you'd stop me talking. You must both of you be longing to change out of your travelling clothes. Do come along upstairs."

She laughed. They all three laughed together. From the dark panels of the hall, Sargent's portrait of Ralph, brilliant in hunting pink, surveyed them with a good-humoured smile, as though he were pleased with his double's return.

"How awful I am," Vivien burst in again. "I'm talking just as if the house were mine instead of yours. It really feels like mine, Clare. I've been here in full possession for three days. How funny it looks to see you and Ralph going into the same bedroom, I can't believe you're really married. Dear, dear, and I'm forgetting all my messages! Mother, Ralph, darling. She sent her love to you both and asked me to say how sorry she was. She's laid up with this influenza. We've all had frightful colds. Poor Parker's actually been in bed for a week. And Clare, dear, your aunt was over here the day before yesterday. She said something about some maid of hers that's leaving. Ellen, was it? Oh, my poor memory! I do hope you'll find everything as you like it. The water hasn't got cold, has it? Clare, you darling, I simply must kiss you again. You look splendid. Evidently it suits you. Oh, did I tell you? Eleanor's had her baby, another girl. Mother is furious, and says it's Eleanor's fault; but Eleanor, apparently, doesn't see the joke."

She left them. The room was as quiet as if a thunder-shower had passed. How soft and cosy and homelike it seemed after the impersonal bedrooms of hotels! Ralph had vanished; Clare heard him whistling in the adjoining dressing-room. This room was theirs; not for a night or a fortnight, but for always. It had a snug, close-fitting, luxurious quality, like a well-made glove. Clare's eyes saw with delight small things that she had carefully chosen for herself, strange, yet familiar and subtly comforting; she had chosen them so long ago, in another life, that they seemed like benignant ghosts gathered round her. Everything looked somehow more complete than she had imagined it would be, all ready waiting for her in its appointed place. The whole room seemed part of her, as the shell is part of the snail.

Ralph came back out of the dressing-room in his shirt-sleeves and caught her bare arms.

"Well, my sweet, what does it feel like?" he asked.

"Like us," she answered, as though the one word represented an all-embracing criterion.

She was so happy. And yet, as she took her place at the foot of the oval mahogany table in the dining-room, she knew that she was no longer the self that she knew. The

richness of her new possessions did not embarrass hei ,
she accepted without question the fiery scintillations of cut
glass, the gleaming napery and chased silver, the silent
ministrations of the well-trained strangers who were her
servants. She listened, smiling through the long meal, to
Vivien's ceaseless, eager chatter about people and things
at Stourford ; and yet she knew that her attitude towards
the room in which they sat and life in general was different
from Vivien's, or her own, as she remembered it. Her mind
was sober and contained. She knew that she was the
responsible owner of all this strangeness, its controller and
director. In the very carriage of her body she felt that
the pliancy and amorphousness of irresponsible youth had
disappeared ; its fibre had stiffened, not with pride, but with
seriousness and the desire to do justice to the possessions by
which she was now possessed.

And, as the first weeks went by, it seemed to her as if
the spirit of the house had actually taken her in hand, and
set about moulding her to the shape of its sober dignity.
She had thought of it, at first, as her creation. In a little
while she began to wonder if her new self were not created
by it, so gracious and well-proportioned, so foreign to all
her old ideas, was the influence that it shed on her. At
times she would actually see it as a personality, setting its
spiritual seal upon the living things that had grown up
about it, the cedars, the beeches, the humble lawns and
flower-beds, no less than on its inhabitants. In this anthro-
pomorphic reverence she would treat its unspoken judgments
as oracles, anxiously waiting on its mute approvals and
disapprovals, applying them as a touchstone to matters of
everyday life. It was a curious game that she played with
herself, and one to which Ralph and Vivien, for obvious
reasons, were not admitted ; but, in the end, it became so
intimate a part of her ordinary mental processes that she
would speak to herself in terms of it, and accept its visionary

standard as part of a new religion, applying them, unconsciously, to the visitors who now began to call on her.

They were many; and that, again, was partly the fault of Uffdown Manor. Uffdown was known as a calling house. Its inhabitants had always been included in the invitation lists of the northern corner of the county; the horses of the country gentlepeople stopped at its doors as automatically as, in the days of coaches, coaching teams would stop at stages.

Uffdown was the extreme northerly limit to which the "county" reached. Immediately beyond it there began a zone of dubious gentility; houses that once had been respectable, such as Stourford, Mawne Hall and Cold Harbour, now regrettably fallen into the hands of new North Bromwich people. The Hingstons were new; far worse, Lady Hingston was known to be clever; the county shivered at stories of her tongue's corrosions. The Weirs, on the other hand, had a record of several hundred years of minor gentility, and Ralph, having finally dissociated himself from traffic in base metals, of which iron was the basest, had sent a handsome subscription to the Worcestershire hounds, with whom he now proposed to hunt, and backed it up by showing himself a sportsman over Worcestershire hedges. Mrs. Pomfret, whose husband was a late survival of one of the big families dispossessed, had certified that Clare was neither vulgar nor clever, and the county decided with relief that the advanced station of Uffdown had not fallen again into the enemy's hands, and that they might continue to call there without risk of offence or infection.

One after another a strange variety of vehicles rolled up the Uffdown drive, discharging a series of supporters of the old order; the Misses Abberley (barony extinct), two hunched little things in black lace dolmans that looked like performing shrews; Squire Tardebigge, who drove a seedy tandem in irreproachable style, and spent the regulation fifteen minutes in putting on and off his dog-skin gloves, while Mrs. Tardebigge, in claret velvet and a bustle, deplored the irreverence of Miss Marie Corelli—" Say what you will, Mrs. Hingston, the woman has power ! "—the Dowager Lady Lovell, of Moreton Starkes, a thin, grey woman who once had been a beauty, and, saving her title, something rather worse, accompanied by a lady-companion, excessively genteel, in a jet toque that bobbed and twinkled in time to her continual twitching smiles at Lady Lovell's witticisms on the subject of the poor Miss Abberleys ; a horde of Ombersleys and Powyses, all rather shabby, horsey, doggy, all marvellously self-composed, and most contriving to be acutely critical beneath a mask of quite admirable manners.

The type was new to Clare. Intrinsically they did not interest her ; and yet she liked them, because in their kind they seemed a natural product of the land that lay upon the edge of the black-country's advancing desolation, a fauna gradually growing rarer, with whom she sympathized in their approaching extinction. But what endeared them to her more than anything else was their attitude toward Uffdown.

The house, she learned, had once belonged to the Ombersleys, and though the Ombersleys had been forced to sell it, had remained dear not only to the remnants of its owners' family, but to other members of the same caste. Uffdown was not a great house, but, for all that, it was respectable. It was part of a tradition, and, as such, they revered it. When they drove up to call on Clare their eyes moved eagerly in search of alteration or innovation. They were jealous, not of Uffdown's beauty, but of its integrity as a landmark. Clare saw the most unlikely people clinging to it like ghosts unwilling to leave the scenes of their first life ; all the county society of that corner of Worcestershire was a little ghostly ; there seemed to be no people of her own age among them, and most of them were so con-

versant with the house's history that she had only to lead
them on to learn things that were valuable to her cult.

Many of them referred to an old Miss Betty Ombersley
as the principal authority. Miss Ombersley was older than
the Queen, and remembered Uffdown in the early thirties.
She lived alone in a black and white house on the skirts of
the village to which her family had given its name, and everybody assured Clare that she was far too old to leave it.
Mrs. Pomfret achieved the impossible, and drove her over
in triumph, a tiny creature in a bonnet like the Queen's,
with jutting, inquisitive features and a voice that seemed
an echo from her own girlhood.

It was a great excitement for Clare to receive her, and also
a great responsibility, for Miss Ombersley looked so fragile
that she seemed likely to die on her hands if she were
questioned too closely. Luckily contact with Uffdown
filled her with a mystical transfusion of life. She passed
from room to room, leaning on her ebony stick, her long
skirts trailing behind her. She moved as quietly as a cat,
sniffing the air as if to test its authenticity. There was no
need for questions. All the time she kept up a running,
distant commentary to herself, to which Clare listened spell-
bound, and Mrs. Pomfret nodded approval, like a keeper
rejoicing in the sagacity of his ferrets.

She sniffed at a wainscot: " Here there used to be
panels." She pointed to the ceiling: " This one was painted
by a Neapolitan gentleman, a political exile in the Emperor
Napoleon's time. Roger Ombersley *protected* him. No
doubt the colours faded with damp and the Arkwrights
had it replastered. In Ferdinand Ombersley's day these
two rooms were one. The Arkwrights had them divided
and put in the sliding-doors. I imagine it would be enormously costly to restore them."

She looked anxiously up the oak staircase, mounting it in
imagination, for her poor little legs would not permit her

to ascend. Mrs. Pomfret, who treated her throughout as a small performing animal and her exclusive property, announced the exact moment at which she should be fortified with tea. She took it in Clare's drawing-room, now beautified by the gleaming ebony of the Bechstein grand that George and Eleanor had given her.

"This," she said, "is the room that is haunted by the ghost of Annabel."

"It's my favourite room of all," Clare told her. "I can't say that I've ever felt anything ghostly about it."

Miss Ombersley shook her head. She was too polite to say that no person so unlike the Ombersleys as Clare was likely to be capable of such refined perceptions.

"Poor Annabel died in seventeen sixty-three," she said. "She is supposed to have been in love with the author of *The Schoolmistress*, the poet Shenstone. She was a great wit and musician. The Ombersleys were always a cultivated family. Mr. Pope wrote some verses for Annabel's seat in the Dutch garden when he was on a visit to the Lytteltons. The Arkwrights destroyed it. Uffdown is not what it was."

Clare was so conscious of her possible share in the Arkwrights' black guilt that she implored Miss Ombersley's approval of what she had done ; but the old lady would not commit herself further. "The less you do the better, my dear," she said, and left Clare with the feeling that it would be a vandalism to remove a grain of dust from anything that was subject to Annabel's ghostly scrutiny.

On a bookshelf at Pen House she found a complete edition of Shenstone in two volumes that the doctor had picked up at some sale, and these, out of respect for the vaporous Annabel, she would read, on sad Spring evenings, in Annabel's own room, finding in their artificial elegiac mood something in keeping with the formal graciousness of the age to which Uffdown still belonged ; for, to her, the house seemed always to be looking backward on peaceful, ancient things, and she was now so full of life and hope that the contrast gave her a sense of rest and stability.

Ralph viewed these new devotions with the patient but charitable misunderstanding that he had shown toward her religious phase. That, strangely enough, had fallen into a decline ever since the day of her marriage. Strangely, too, she did not regret it. She accepted the change as one of life's mysterious growth-adjustments, as unquestioningly as a young tree might regard the modifications forced upon it by conditions of weather or soil. The days of her first enthusiasm seemed to her to have belonged to another life. She smiled when she remembered how once she had imagined Ralph and herself kneeling together at their bed-side in prayer. Never in all the time since their marriage had she seen Ralph pray in private ; and though the omission had once mildly shocked her, she now knew that he was none the worse for it.

On Sundays, with respectable regularity, they drove to Wychbury church, and listened to Mr. Pomfret's eight-minute sermons ; but St. Chad's knew her no more, for, while they were away in Italy, Mr. Darnay's passion for incense had removed him to a more fragrant cure in the East End of London. Ralph welcomed the distraction of these formal religious observances, for on Sundays the men did not work, and his fury of farming improvements was such that he could not bear to see a morning of inactivity.

On Sunday afternoons they usually paid their weekly visit to Stourford, and this was the only occasion on which Clare met her mother-in-law ; for Uffdown, as Ralph had cunningly calculated, was well out of the track of Lady Hingston's carriage-wheels. Her life was orientated in the direction of Wolverbury and North Bromwich, so that she had no time to spare for anything south of the hills. She had no use for the society of the Ombersleys, Abberleys or

Tardebigges. She despised them as a vanquished and disintegrating race who would never re-establish themselves, and the fact that they were equally supercilious of her husband's wealth aggravated her scorn. She knew that she and her kind would laugh last and longest. Often she would talk of Clare's new visitors as though she pitied her and Ralph for the surroundings that they had chosen. She would even bring herself to speak well of her hereditary rivals, the Willises at Mawne, to show her derision of Clare's " county " callers.

Aunt Cathie was more impressionable. The fact that Ralph and Clare had cut themselves off from Stourford, and that she could visit Uffdown without the risk of encountering Lady Hingston, encouraged her to come there more often than she had expected. Two or three times a week the old victoria drew up before the steps, Aunt Cathie peering anxiously round the box to see if any other vehicle were there. It pleased and excited her to meet the county in Annabel Ombersley's drawing-room ; theirs was the kind of society in which, but for the doctor's seclusion, she would always have been competent to mix. She resumed the habit of dropping her " g's," on which the doctor had always corrected her, and when she returned to the solitude of Pen House at night she would fall asleep with the fat volume of Burke's *Landed Gentry* on her knees. In it she would trace the intricate threads of the Misses Abberley's collateral relationships, naively communicating her discoveries to Clare on her next visit, as if she had had them at her fingertips all the time.

She approved of Clare, and showed her approval by a lively and careful interest in all the domestic problems of Uffdown. Little by little she was tumbling to the realities of their financial situation, realizing that Ralph's inherited wealth entitled them to a standard of living that she had not imagined. This added to Clare's dignity in her eyes ;

her only anxiety was that this dignity should not be vitiated by the Stourford influence. It was proper, she admitted, that Clare should be surrounded by costly possessions, as long as their costliness was carefully concealed and deprecated in the eyes of people who had more right to them than herself.

" Yes, Clare, it's good," she would say, regarding some new purchase or present of Ralph's, " but don't you think it would be wiser to put it somewhere in the shade."

Clare always smiled and followed her advice. Since the night of Aunt Cathie's astonishing confession, her whole attitude toward the elder woman had changed. She had vowed to herself that never again would she be guilty of any lapse from the tenderness which she owed to her ; and Aunt Cathie, too, by this one moment of completest candour, seemed to have freed herself of all the grudging repressions that had complicated her relation with Clare.

In these new days she seemed definitely older and softer, as though some irritant had been excised from her soul and left her weak and gentle like a surgical convalescent, bereft of all power of malice, charitable, and easily amused.

The change had its pathetic side. Now, for the first time in her life, Aunt Cathie had time on her hands. Since Ellen had gone to Uffdown she and Mrs. Rudge were left alone in Pen House, and her domestic duties, in spite of her passion for order and cleanliness, were not enough to keep her occupied. In the long years of devotion to the doctor's declining strength, she had lost the habit of reading; even George Eliot still remained unread ; and though she had forced herself to break the old inhibition that kept her from the piano, life offered nothing but a vista of increasing loneliness in which, though she still regarded herself as a woman with the resources that the doctor approved, the only vital interest was Clare. Gallantly she set herself to conceal her desolation from Clare and from herself ; but Clare was less easily deceived than she, and when, in the evening of her Uffdown visits, she saw Aunt Cathie leave the fireside with a sigh, and ask her to ring for Jabez, her conscience pricked her with so violent a pity that she stifled an impulse not only to beg Aunt Cathie to stay the night, but even to ask her to make her home at Uffdown.

She smiled at herself, when Aunt Cathie had driven off into the dusk, thinking how horrified Ralph would be at such a proposal. And yet, in spite of the attentions which Uffdown always demanded, Clare herself was sometimes a little lonely too. It was not that Ralph's passion for her or her devotion to him had declined ; rather it had reached a new phase of understanding more stable and secure than any of their Italian raptures. No shadow of disagreement had ever troubled them. Ralph was always the same, half-child, half-lover ; and yet it seemed to her sometimes that he took their love for granted. A compliment, maybe ; for it showed how firmly established, how unquestionable it was. But when he left her after breakfast, spurred and booted, and kissed her on the steps, he seemed to move away right out of her life. As soon as the hunting-season ended in a foam of hawthorn blossom he began to throw his restless energies into the rehabilitation of the Uffdown land. He was always, as he had protested, a farmer at heart ; and though, when he returned to her with his farmer's appetite, she would try to enter into his world of crops and stock and markets and fertilizers, she knew that her interest was artificial and guessed that he saw through it.

The exacting strain of this purely physical life seemed to exhaust his energies, so that the attentions for which she still looked to him became a little perfunctory, as though her demands, if still adorable, were a nuisance. When he had finished his story he always asked her what she had been doing with herself ; but when she told him, her tale seemed hardly worth the telling, and it was no surprise to her when he scarcely listened.

After dinner he would sit nodding in front of the drawing-room fire, and she would play to him on Eleanor's Bechstein as she had played on the little silk-pleated Broadwood at Pen House. When she paused between the pieces he would collect himself and thank her.

" That's a jolly thing," he would say. " I wish you would play it again."

But she knew that, in point of fact, he didn't know one thing from another ; and though she repeated it dutifully, and tried to persuade herself that she was playing to him with all the concentration of which her soul was capable, the music, as it left her fingers, seemed to lose itself in an unreceptive emptiness. Never, in all those evenings, could she recapture the mystical jubilation of a final act of self-expression which had overwhelmed her so often when he lay and listened to her at Pen House. The walls of Annabel Ombersley's room regarded her innocence with gentle, half-critical amusement. And so she would close the piano finally and go to seek the missing ecstasy in Ralph's arms.

He gathered her to him sleepily ; this, so it seemed was an expression of love more easily comprehensible ; his hands passed drowsily over her shoulders, her breast, her body, as though of themselves they were verifying and appraising the shapes of beauty that they knew. With her face pressed close to his she could hear his heart-beats quickening beneath the calm, contented rhythm of his breath. She loved him so dearly that she was angry for herself for wondering what she had lost.

## III

## DR. BOYD

The new doctor drove up from Wychbury in a gig with bright yellow wheels. He was flattered to call at Uffdown, and adjusted his tie as the trap swung round the curve of the drive; for the Rentons had not been patients of his, and this was a substantial house to be added to his list. Aunt Cathie, who had been present at the discussion of which this visit was the result, had been horrified at the idea of calling him; for he had succeeded her father as the principal practitioner in Wychbury, and everybody knew, so she said, that since the doctor's retirement the poor people had perished like flies. But Ralph had met Dr. Boyd in the hunting-field; he had seen that he rode straight, though ill-mounted; he had watched him put up a fractured thigh with a gate-bar, and though he knew nothing about surgery, he had liked the fellow's style and the clean way he set about it. He over-ruled Aunt Cathie and scribbled a note to Boyd, asking him to make a point of calling at the Manor on his round next day.

Ralph hung about the house all morning, waiting to receive him. Clare, as Aunt Cathie had instructed, stayed in bed. It seemed rather ridiculous to her to lie in like this on a soft May morning, the first that had smelt of summer, when she had never felt better in her life; but Aunt Cathie's decision was adamantine, and Ralph, who had been bothering her to consult a doctor for weeks, had determined to see the matter through.

At last Dr. Boyd entered the bedroom. He was a little man, with thin sandy hair, a neat figure, and very keen, blue eyes under his bushy eyebrows. Even though they were keen his eyes were always smiling. Clare liked them for the humorous challenge that they flung at lay indefiniteness. He sat beside the bed, and began to question her shrewdly. His speech had a faint, persuasive Irish brogue that did away with her shyness and put them on easy terms. She noticed his hands, which were small, broad, firm, and of the shiny redness which constant antiseptic scrubbings gives. Aunt Cathie, who had made the journey on purpose, stood staring out of the window in disapproval, ready to protect her niece from any modern enormity. The interview was more embarrassing to her in her spinsterhood than to Clare ; but she had determined to behave in a manner worthy of Dr. Weir's memory.

" Well, well, that's all very excellent," said Dr. Boyd at last. " Everything's just as right and normal as it can be. I don't expect you'll want to see me again for a long time ; but just in a friendly way, I'll give you a look up now and then. I'm leaving you in good hands. Miss Weir will look after you."

Aunt Cathie, who wasn't quite certain how to take the compliment, led him seriously downstairs. Ralph, a little pale and agitated, stood waiting for them in the hall.

" You've not been long," he said, as though he were not sure that so short a consultation could be effective.

The doctor laughed. " Let's hope the whole affair will be as speedy. Don't worry yourself, Hingston. Everything's going on first-rate. Couldn't be better."

" When will it be ? "

" We'll say the first week in November. No need to think about it yet."

Aunt Cathie was thirsting for a definite regimen and a six-ounce bottle of medicine.

" For Heaven's sake, don't turn your niece into an invalid," the doctor told her. " This is a normal physiological process. What she wants is an ordinary life. Plenty of exercise. Not violent, naturally. As I've said before, think no more about it, and when the time comes leave her to me. She's a splendidly healthy young woman, and in these matters youth is everything."

He hurried away. By this time Ralph was in the best of spirits ; but to Aunt Cathie the world was full of indefinite threats of danger. From that day forward she watched Clare with uneasy eyes. She was so used to anxiety that this new one filled something of a gap in her life ; but at times Clare found it hard to bear with her seriousness.

" My dear Aunt Cathie," she said. " Anyone 'ld think that you were going to have this baby, not me."

And then she was sorry that she had spoken ; she knew the meaning of that quick flush on Aunt Cathie's cheeks.

But she would not let them make an invalid of her. In this, at least, she stood firmly on Dr. Boyd's advice in spite of Aunt Cathie's gloomy assertion that these modern doctors left everything to chance. It was easy enough to persuade Ralph to her way of thinking. Aunt Cathie could not shake his faith in so excellent a sportsman as Dr. Boyd, and when once he had overcome his first vague dread of this experience so unimaginable to a man he was eager to expel it from his thoughts, and impatient that a lot of old women—that was how he described Aunt Cathie and the inevitable Mrs. Rudge, who had never missed any opportunity of being in at a death or birth—should shadow the happy prospect with boding faces. He was so pleased and proud. A little too naively pleased, Clare sometimes thought, for he seemed to give himself credit for the whole affair, which may have been natural, but was hardly just, seeing that she had to bear its inconvenience.

And yet she could not grudge him his triumph ; for one effect of her condition had been to bring about a passionate renewal of his delight in her that was almost comparable to the raptures of their early days in Italy. Now, when he parted from her in the morning, she no longer felt that he was passing away into another world. She knew that his interest was centred in her and her precious burden. When he came in tired from the fields, his eyes no longer disregarded her, but watched her with solicitude. He could not be happy unless she were in his sight; he was always eager to save her exertion or disturbance, anxious to show, by small considerations and tendernesses, how dear she was to him. And this new kindness of his aroused in her an answering emotion of gratitude so different from any that she had felt toward him before, an emotion so warm, serene and satisfying that, even if their passion faded, as someday it might fade, she believed she could be content.

At least she had no lack of counsellors. Aunt Cathie had been first in the field; but as soon as the news reached Stourford, Lady Hingston swooped upon the scene. Her interest was very much to the point; for though Eleanor had already done her duty and was now doing it again, the succession to Sir Joseph's baronetcy must be assured at least three deep before she could be satisfied. She made it clear that the responsibility was entirely Clare's; but that the fruits of it were her own exclusive property. She even attempted to sweep Clare back to Stourford in order that everything might be accomplished under her eyes. Uffdown, she declared, was damp and abominably isolated; this Irish doctor, whom Ralph had picked up in the hunting-field, was a dangerous, unknown quantity; the Uffdown servants, and particularly the awkward Ellen who had gaped at her on the doorstep, were barbarous and untrained; no woman entrusted with the privilege of producing a possible heir to the Hingston title should be left to the chances of such haphazard surroundings; and, worst of all, in the shadowy gardens of Uffdown, she had caught a glimpse of Aunt Cathie.

"If you allow that woman to hang round you, Clare," she said, "something is positively certain to go wrong. I warn you."

Clare smiled. The thought of the innocent Aunt Cathie being invested with such sinister powers was amusing.

"You don't know her," she said, "and you've no idea what a help she's been to me. After all, you mustn't forget that she's looked after me nearly all my life."

Lady Hingston snorted. As if that had anything to do with the birth of her grandchild.

"She's an old maid," she said, "and that's quite enough to condemn her. They know nothing about these matters, and pretend that they know everything. Do you realize that you haven't a single married woman in the house, or even within reach? Don't tell me I don't know her. I know them all ; and I can tell you beforehand that she'll fuss you to death when the time comes. If you came over to Stourford, where we've every possible convenience, you could be certain of being properly looked after by experienced people. Here there's no knowing what mad foolishness you mayn't . . ."

The sentence stopped for want of a word. Not even French could help her out of her difficulty. At that moment Aunt Cathie wandered into the room. Lady Hingston's eyes blazed with instinctive anger. They recoiled from each other sideways like two unfriendly cats. Aunt Cathie was the first to recover herself. Had not she taken tea in that very room with the Miss Abberleys? And who might Lady Hingston be?

"Good afternoon," she said, thereby committing her first offence ; for Lady Hingston was fond of the sound of her own name, particularly the first half of it. "We don't often have the pleasure of seeing you. How do you think Clare's looking."

That "we" incensed Lady Hingston with its proprietary assumption. Clare lay between them like a disputed bone.

"I think Clare's looking as well as can be expected," she said ; "but I'm just telling her that Uffdown is no place for her at the present moment. I'm telling her that she has no experienced person in the house in case of an emergency."

Aunt Cathie smiled. "Clare's very near to Wychbury, after all," she said, "and I am able to give her a good deal of my time."

"Well, that is very nice for her, no doubt," said Lady Hingston, controlling her natural impulse to say: "Oh, *you !* " In spite of the slight she managed to put into her answer she felt that Aunt Cathie had forced her into an awkward position, and hurriedly retreated to her second line.

"But even so," she went on, persuasively, "you must admit, Miss Weir, that Uffdown isn't a convenient place."

"The Ombersleys," said Aunt Cathie, "apparently found it satisfactory for nearly two hundred years. Miss Betty Ombersley assures me that it has always had a healthy reputation."

She knew that she shouldn't have mentioned the Ombersley's name, but the consciousness of her recent social triumphs was too strong for her. Lady Hingston swooped upon it quickly.

"The Ombersleys," she sniffed. "Is that tiresome old woman still alive ? She must be the only one of the family left, if that says anything for the healthiness of Uffdown. The Rentons, I know, declared that it was damp. That's why they left it."

"The Rentons ?" Aunt Cathie repeated. "Oh, yes, those brass manufacturers from North Bromwich. I didn't call on them." She was still smarting from Lady Hingston's reflections on her august acquaintance. "But really I've never known Clare better," she went on hurriedly, to evade the possibility of another swoop. "You must remember that I've had every opportunity of understanding her constitution, having reared her from a child."

Again Lady Hingston retired, but only for a moment.

" Clare tells me," she said, " that you have called in this new doctor from Wychbury. I confess that I know nothing of him." It was equivalent to saying that, in that case, he couldn't be any good ; and this new assault was awkward for Aunt Cathie, since she herself had been doubtful of Dr. Boyd, as Clare, whose eyes were fixed on her in amused suspension, knew.

" We've been told," she said, " that Dr. Boyd is very clever in these cases. As a matter of fact, *I* didn't send for him ; he was Ralph's choice. Of course, he was Dr. Weir's successor in Wychbury."

She spoke as if that, in itself, were a sufficient ground for the confidence that she didn't feel. Lady Hingston was quick to seize her advantage and throw Ralph to the winds.

" I think," she said, " that my son was most precipitate in acting without advice in a matter of this kind. Ralph is only a boy. No responsible person should have allowed him to do so. That is my point, Miss Weir. If Ralph is permitted to do perfectly wild things like that at this stage, Heaven only knows how we shall finish. Do you see what I mean ? "

" Perfectly," Aunt Cathie replied. " But, after all, Ralph is Clare's husband, and the baby, when it comes, will be his."

" No it won't, it's mine, it's mine, it's Wolverbury's ! " Lady Hingston's mind screamed. She said :

" We have to remember, in this case, that the baby may be a very important person."

" Naturally," Aunt Cathie smiled smoothly, disregarding all that she knew Lady Hingston implied, " a first baby always is, isn't it ? Particularly, in our case, when the baby is dear Clare's. I always think of myself just as if I were her mother, you know. Clare darling, don't you think I'd better ring for some tea ? "

" Thank you, I don't want any," Lady Hingston snapped.

But Aunt Cathie rang all the same ; the act was equivalent to throwing up new entrenchments under her enemy's eyes. It showed the visitor how very much at home she was, and revenged in one blow the humiliations that Stourford had inflicted on her.

Lady Hingston would not retreat without a final demonstration.

" Before I go," she said, " I should like to have this matter settled. In my opinion Uffdown is unsuitable. If Ralph were here, I'm sure he'd agree with every word I say."

" What a pity ! " said Aunt Cathie, " he never comes in till it's dark. If you could wait another hour . . ."

" I can't wait," said Lady Hingston, irritably. " We have a dinner-party this evening. You'd better tell him when he comes in, Clare, that I want to talk to him about this. He keeps away from Stourford for months at a time ; I can never get hold of him in these days. Now, don't forget ! "

" I'll tell him, mother," said Clare. The word gave a stab to Aunt Cathie's heart. " But I know quite well," she continued, " that he won't want me to go to Stourford, and even if he did, you know, I shouldn't go."

" Really, Clare," Lady Hingston began.

" I wish you could understand, dear," Clare went on quickly, " that I'm absolutely happy where I am. It's my home, you see, and Stourford . . . Well, Stourford isn't. And please don't worry yourself about Dr. Boyd either. I like him most awfully ; he's such a reassuring, friendly person."

" You know nothing about him, absolutely nothing," said Lady Hingston. " Except," she added, " that he was Dr. Weir's successor."

" That was extremely rude of her," Aunt Cathie said, when Lady Hingston had gone, " to drag in the doctor's name."

" You asked for it, my dearest," Clare told her, laughing, " you really did."

" I found it difficult to defend Dr. Boyd," Aunt Cathie admitted, " but when that woman attacked him it seemed the least I could do."

" You're each of you as bad as the other," Clare said.

" I hope, at least," Aunt Cathie murmured anxiously, " that I did not say anything as unladylike as that."

Clare laughed again. She knew that it was impossible to make Aunt Cathie see the joke. That was the worst of them all, their solemn intensity. To taste the humour of the situation was a prerogative of youth. She often regretted that Ralph was a little heavy on the hand at times. Luckily his mother's proposal to transfer her to Stourford threw him into furious opposition.

" When I do see mother, I'll damnèd well tell her what I think of her," he said.

" You won't do anything of the sort, my darling," Clare assured him. " It'd be waste of time. She's quite clever enough to know what you think of her already. She can't help acting on violent impulses, but all the bees in her bonnet go buzzing away sooner or later. I believe I understand her far better than you do. She'll have forgotten all about it by this time. Oh, Ralph, I wish to goodness all of you wouldn't treat me with this ghastly seriousness. It makes me think about myself all the time, and I don't want to ! "

## IV

### TEMESIDE

SHE was determined not to think about herself, and yet, as May days lengthened into June and midsummer passed, there were too many reminders to let her forget. Ralph was getting more impatient as the time went on ; he was always in a hurry about everything ; his anxiety made him stand about so helplessly that Clare, out of sheer charity, was forced to urge him to leave her, to play tennis at Stourford or cricket at Wychbury ; and though he protested that he didn't want to, he was really glad of the excuse, for his fine muscles grew lax by keeping pace with her limited activity ; there was no hunting to shake his liver into order or black thoughts out of his mind.

Only when the haymaking began at the beginning of July, for the year was late, did he find a real justification for his existence. Through those long days he laboured early and late, and slouched in at night, dog-tired, the fair skin of arms and neck and face burned to a fierce brick-red ; and, though she did not like to admit it, Clare was glad of his absence, for it gave her a chance to abandon the game of pretending to be her old self.

Those summer days at Uffdown were very sweet to her. She would sit for hours with her work under the shade of the last cedar, within range of the rosemary hedge that smelt of Capri, listening to the clatter of Ralph's mowing machine away in the fields, letting the peace of that old house and garden, to which the high light of summer gave a golden bloom, sink into her body through every sensual channel. There she would sit and sew, breathing the scent of hay, listening to the hushed voices of thrushes somnolent as her thoughts, to the unceasing bourdon of bees in the flowered borders. She herself was so drugged with summer pollens that she was content to dream in her warm garden like a bee in the heart of a flower.

At tea-time Ellen would bring her a plate of Uffdown strawberries that were an essence of summer's fragrance ; then she would sew again, till the rooks came flapping home, and midges, turning the low sunlight into a golden haze, compelled her to take shelter in the house.

Sometimes, when she was sitting out in the garden alone, the fear that she had determined to banish from her mind seized her suddenly ; it carried with it a moment of silence, in which the muted birdsong, the multitudinous murmurs of the summer day, were blankly suspended, as though the whole world had caught its breath with hers ; and so she would pick her work up hurriedly and fly to the refuge of Annabel's drawing-room, where Eleanor's piano stood by the window facing west. There she would sit and play for an hour at a time ; it did not matter what she played so long as music filled her ears, and so, for the most part, she chose the tempestuous sonatas of Beethoven, and Fugues of Bach in whose sonorous intricacies she might lose herself.

She could not always lose herself ; but even when her thoughts moved against music like a toneless counterpoint, she was comforted, and happier, somehow, than when she was playing to Ralph. For when Ralph listened to her, or pretended to listen, her mind was always divided between the music and him. She always hoped that Steven—the baby must be a boy, and Steven was his name—would share this intimate part of her, so that from the music that she had given to him she would be able to extract the particular sympathy that she lacked in Ralph. She had a fancy that when she played to herself like this she was making sure of the desired inheritance. He shall have music wherever he goes, she told herself ; all his life should be surrounded by things that to her were beautiful, and not least the beauty of Uffdown, which absorbed her every day more intimately, as though it had finally made up its mind about her and accepted her ; the beauty from which Lady Hingston, in her misguided enthusiasm, would have snatched her away.

Ralph disapproved of these long piano recitals. More than once he had found her sitting at the piano with a white face and eyes that burned with a light that he took for tiredness.

" That's what you do when I leave you," he would say. " The trouble with you is that when once you get stuck at this blessed piano you don't know when to stop. You'd be better at Stourford, where they keep it locked. Beethoven, too. You know, you've no business to play that gloomy stuff. It's enough to give anyone the blues."

He scolded her, and yet he was kind, so kind. Ardently as she adored him, she could never have believed him capable of the angelic patience and unselfishness that he showed her in those days. Aunt Cathie was kind enough and patient in her way, but, when she came to compare them, her gentleness was nothing beside that of Ralph. In Aunt Cathie's company she was never wholly immune from fear ; in Ralph's the word had no meaning for her.

As summer passed, her hunger for Ralph's presence grew more acute. She dreaded the first cubbing days that would take him further afield. Now she no longer sent him away from her. She could not bear to be separated from him. She was most happy at night, when she could snuggle up to him and feel the physical support of his robust body against her own. Wherever he went, if it were not too far for her, she insisted on going with him. It was as though she felt it necessary that he should take his part in their joint adventure.

One evening he came back to Uffdown from a director's meeting at the Wolverbury works. Even though he was no longer active in the business, Sir Joseph had insisted on keeping him on the directorate.

" I met Lord Arthur Powys," he told her. " The poor chap was as bored as I was. He's a keen fisherman, you know, and the grayling are rising like mad in his water on the Teme. He wanted me to go over for a day "—Clare's heart sank suddenly—"but of course I told him that I couldn't."

"Oh, Ralph darling," she said, "I think it's simply beastly, the way you have to give up everything for me."

"Only another month," he told her, "and then we'll kick out again like anything. By the way, I've heard from Harley of a mare that'll suit you. You've got to hunt next season, don't forget that."

She snuggled up to him like a kitten.

"I want to do everything that you do," she said. "About this fishing. The Teme isn't so very far away, is it? Why shouldn't I go with you and sit on the bank and watch?"

He laughed. "You talk as if you thought I was going to fish for roach in a canal, with half a gallon of beer in a basket. Fly-fishing, my child, is a strenuous business; there's over a mile of water to cover."

"Still, even if I didn't see you, I could sit on the bank," she said. "I should hate myself if you missed going, Ralph."

"No risks at the last moment, my dear."

"But if Dr. Boyd said I could go?" she persisted.

And in the end he allowed her to persuade him into sending a note to Wychbury. "Certainly," the doctor wrote, "as long as you take it gently, and don't play tricks. I've told you before she's not an invalid."

Aunt Cathie heard the news with horror. It confirmed her deepest distrust of Dr. Boyd's competence; the very idea was monstrous and unthinkable. But Clare was determined that all Ralph's opportunities should not be spoiled. "Then let him go alone," said Aunt Cathie. "You needn't feel lonely; I'll come and spend the day with you." "I want to go with him," Clare told her. "I'm tired of being in one place. I want to see something new and think of something different." She was so obdurate that Aunt Cathie, for one moment, thought of calling her enemy, Lady Hingston, to her aid. She saw that even this sacrifice of pride would not avail her, and Ralph was useless. " It's better," he said, " to let her have her way. You can trust me. I'll take good care of her."

Aunt Cathie retired to Pen House in a huff, washing her hands of Dr. Boyd and the pair of them.

The day dawned, peerless and sparkling with such a brilliance as only September can show. Ralph was out at the window early. The sight of the dew-frosted lawn filled him with excitement. " It couldn't be better," he told her. " This nip in the air is just what grayling like. If the sky keeps clear and the sun warms the shallows, they'll come up like anything."

Clare smiled at him out of her cosiness as he moved about the room collecting the casts that he had put in to soak overnight. In any matter of sport the gay keenness of his anticipation was like that of a pointer released on a shooting morning ; like a pointer he sniffed the favourable air, and darted here and there with restless movements.

They drove down gently to Wychbury station. The sun had risen ; the little platform smelt clean and dewy. Mr. Hemus was there in his shirtsleeves and begged her to accept one of his prize chrysanthemums ; the great flower was a ridiculous encumbrance, but Clare knew that he could not have paid her a higher compliment. It pleased her to think how all these railway people deferred to Ralph. In a compartment permeated by the chrysanthemum's autumnal odour they travelled to Stourton junction and changed. From her seat on the long platform Clare could see the long lines of china baths, set up on end like gravestones, which had impressed her on the day of the doctor's funeral, a hundred years ago.

Her thoughts were all her own ; for Ralph was intent on his fly-book, picking out the delicate " green insects," and " red " and " orange tags " that he was going to fish with.

They crossed the Severn at Bewdley. The stream ran low and clear after a fortnight of drought. " Better and better," Ralph told her.

Once beyond the Severn the character of the country changed. Now they ran northward through the fringe of the Wyre Forest, an immense wood of stunted oak-trees already tarnished by autumn, and hugged the knees of Clee. Clare had never been so far west of Severn before ; she had only seen this mysterious Marchland from Uffdown, as a jumble of blue hills melting into the mountains of Wales ; and now she found them curiously familiar, like the landscape of a recurrent dream, familiar and vaguely exciting, as though they had existed already in her consciousness. Their rediscovery made her tremulously happy. She could not say why, until she reflected that with every moment the train was carrying her nearer to those hills and that white river from which her life had sprung, the mountains of Radnor and the impetuous Claerwen.

Ralph, having finished fiddling with his flies, grew more impatient than ever. He caught her in the midst of her dreams and wondered why she was silent.

" You're not feeling seedy ? " he asked her anxiously. " This branch-line goes so slowly. That's Tenbury Church, the tower in the trees beyond the river. In another five minutes we'll be there."

They dismounted alone at an empty wayside platform, and when Ralph had hoisted their luggage on to his back they set off slowly in the direction of the Teme. Too slowly for Ralph ; he was so eager now that in spite of all restraint he continually outpaced her. The air hung heavy in the river valley ; for although the sky was as clear as Ralph had prophesied, a bank of mist ebbing slowly southward, still obscured the sun, and in it a layer of imprisoned land-scents surrounded them ; the odour of trellised hop-yards, from which the sleepy clusters had been stripped, of field-fires, trailing blue smoke over the misty levels, of pungent, minty savours, rising from ditches and depressions that flood-water had fertilized. The cowls of red-brick oast-houses all pointed southward down the river ; but there was no wind to fill them with its draught.

On the edge of the hop-yards they flushed a covey of partridges from the plough. Ralph's arms twitched upward automatically, as though he were carrying not a rod but a gun. The covey disappeared, low-flying, over a spinney of alders, lining the river bank and standing still and black against red cliffs beyond the stream. Their sharpened senses sniffed the smoke of a stick-fire and an appetizing odour of frizzling bacon that rose from an encampment of Lancashire cloggers who had knocked off work for breakfast ; a little group of stunted, weather-beaten men, who called to them in flat North-country accents and wished them good luck as they passed.

" Good luck be hanged ! " Ralph grumbled. " Those fellows are double-dyed poachers, every one of them. I don't mind betting they've been worming for trout already this morning and made a mess of the water. I'd better start half a mile lower down, and fish up-stream to you. You needn't fag yourself by walking down with me. I don't suppose they'll interfere with you, and if you should want me, you could send a message by one of them."

He knelt on the grass and began to assemble his rod, taking the lengths of polished greenheart out of their case. The snug stoppers came from the suction-joints like corks from a well-fitting pop-gun. All Ralph's fishing-gear seemed as clean and springily efficient as himself ; Clare liked the texture of his shining casts, the smooth, greased, silken line, the rod, that was so delicate that it trembled with life as he raised it to his shoulder. He kissed her and left her sitting on the green bank. The cloggers, their breakfast over, moved past without a word.

She was alone, and very happy. She sat there thinking of untroubled things, glad of the inspiration that had taken her away from Uffdown. Possibly this was the last day on which she would be able to leave home for many months. It would have been a pity to have missed this opportunity of rearranging her thoughts, which too familiar surroundings had accustomed to one groove ; above all in a solitude so sweet as this.

For it was strangely quiet. The impacts of the cloggers' axes, splitting wood, only seemed to emphasize its quietude. The stillness of the riverside was like that of night, but far more kindly. It was only when it had sunk into her mind and calmed it that she became aware of the fact that this silence floated, detached above Teme's ceaseless watery murmur, and that the stillness, in fact, was made up of innumerable shy movements ; of leaves that were shed upon the stream's hurrying surface ; of dippers that bobbed their white breasts upon rocky ledges and flew like shadows up-stream ; of anxious moorhens that clucked among the roots of alder and watched their chickens swimming in black procession at the water's edge. Sometimes a blackbird left the humid hawthorns and shot across the river with a stutter of alarm ; and once Clare's eyes were dazzled by a travelling flame of blue that was the body of a kingfisher burning through his flutter of dark wings.

Lulled by the influence of sounds as smooth as silence and movements so gentle that they suggested immobility, she must have fallen asleep ; for when her senses returned Ralph was standing over her, his face flushed with the exertion of walking in waders, and, in his eyes, a light of happiness that she had not often seen of late. His bag bulged with the capture of three grayling. He turned them out proudly on the grass beside her, and showed her their silver-mottled bodies and the great dorsal fins.

" Smell them," he said. " They're supposed to smell like

thyme ; but I think cucumber is nearer to it. I'd have had some more, but the beggars are rising short. Lord Arthur said the same. There's a splendid hatch of fly out on the water, and I'm dying for lunch."

Clare, too, was hungry. They ate their sandwiches greedily ; for Ralph had been so intent on his short-rises that it was already afternoon. Never had they made such a jolly careless meal together since the days of their mountain picnics under the crags of Capri ; but when they had finished not even his after-lunch pipe could keep Ralph longer from the water.

" I want to fish the slides below the weir," he told her. " The water shallows to a ford, under these cliffs, and if I don't get a basket there I shall be surprised. I shan't move much, so you had better come and watch me."

He lifted her gently from the grass and carried her water-proofs to the edge of a high bank, where sandstone cliffs and a hanger of beeches shadowed a pool into which white water came roaring over the glassy rim of the weir. The water drummed and thundered so loudly that they could scarcely hear each other speak.

" The river's risen a good three inches in the last hour," he told her. " It must have been raining in earnest some-where up in Wales. That's the worst of this stream, always subject to flood. '

He scrambled down the bank and waded through the tail of the shallows. She watched his skill happily. The rod was a tapered extension of his strong hands ; it switched in the air ; the line slid out straight before him on the water's swiftly sliding surface, the fly fell like thistledown above the dimple of a fish. She saw a swirl of silver. His lips framed the words : " They're rising short again " ; but though he was shouting, the weir deadened his voice.

As she watched him the fascination of his frustrated skill began to engross her ; partly that, and partly the predatory instinct of a human animal fired by the zest of hunting ; for now he had become an incarnation of her own will and his quarry was hers. Slowly he waded against the current, casting always as he went. In the black pool a big fish rose, head and tail ; she saw it stretched in a silver bow, but Ralph, intent on his fly, could see nothing but the widening circle of its fall. She trembled with excitement, and cried, and pointed. He nodded back to her, and moved cautiously forward. All her desire was concentrated on the capture of that leaping, gleaming crescent. The emotion was savage and sweet.

So he crept forward ; the cast was still too long for him. He felt the bottom cautiously with his nailed brogues, now rising, now sinking thigh-deep, as he followed the uncertainties of the rocky ledges. Once, stepping forward warily, he drew back and changed his direction. She marvelled at his restraint in that exciting moment ; it showed her the alertness of his well-poised brain. At last he reached a point where he could go no further. He cast again and again, letting out line, and with every cast the fly that he switched backward would have fallen nearer to the spot from which the agitation of the rise had disappeared. At last he let it drop. Clare held her breath. It could not have been neater. The glassy surface dimpled ; the reel screamed ; the upright rod stretched to a lovely curve. He smiled and shouted back to her : " I'm in him : a big one ; I think it's a trout."

She watched the contest breathlessly. Thrice his rod-point dipped as the fish left the water, then rose again as the singing reel measured a furious downward rush into the depths of the pool. Gradually the tension of the rod began to tell. She saw Ralph warily reaching for the clip that held his landing-net. He drew his prey gently towards him, the net outstretched. He moved his feet a little to be surer of balance ; and the movement filled Clare with such

fear of the depths beneath him that a cry came to her lips:
" Be careful, darling, be careful ! " she cried. Her voice
seemed thin and feeble. He did not hear her, her alarm
increased to a panic that compelled her to get on to her feet
and scramble down the bank. Somehow or other she must
make him hear.

" Ralph, Ralph, be careful. It's deep ! " she called again
and again.

Suddenly, through the roaring of the weir and his own
preoccupation, he heard her voice. He turned his head
and saw her shouting to him, and all thought of the hooked
fish suddenly left his brain ; for he imagined that she must
be in trouble. He turned and hurried to reach her, and in
that moment his caution forsook him. Agonized, she
watched him make the false step that she had dreaded. He
went in backward, with hands stretched behind him. His
waders, swollen with water, pulled him down into a twelve-
foot channel cleft between the rocks. The current seized
him and dragged him down. Clare saw his smashed rod
and tweed hat swirled away ; but Ralph himself had disappeared beneath a glassy blackness. Paralyzed with terror
she stared at the unbroken, rapid surface ; then, as the power
of thought swiftly returned, she found that she herself was
wading out into cold water, driven by some mad, uncertain
aim. It wouldn't matter if she, too, were carried away ;
she had lost him, lost him, and, with him, everything.
Still, she was crying aloud, and still the roaring weir deadened
her cries.

Then, twenty yards below her, a black arm emerged,
clutching at an unseen ledge. It clutched and disappeared.
She followed, downstream, blindly. The current contemptuously caught her legs from under her and tossed her
headlong into a gravelled shallow. The chill of the water
made her gasp for breath. This was the end, she thought.
But even as she surrendered hope, she saw the bulk of

Ralph's body lifting and clinging to the lower edge of the shoal that had received her, and a moment later he was stooping over her and helping her to her feet. For the moment there was nothing but frustration in his mind; his face was white and ugly.

" What is the matter ? " he spluttered. " Nothing ? Then why, in God's name, did you put me off like that ? You might have done for both of us. This river's full of dangers."

" I know, I know," she sobbed. " I took fright. I was shouting to you to be careful."

" Careful ! " he panted. " Careful ! " Then suddenly he burst out laughing and gathered her in his wet arms. " You poor darling, you poor darling ! " he said. " But even if I'd been drowned, you needn't have drenched yourself like this. What can I do with you ? "

" Oh, don't, Ralph, don't ! " she cried. She did not know what she was saying. In that extreme of thankfulness and reaction from fear she might just as well have been drowned herself, she had simply ceased to exist.

He supported her to the bank. His own balance was still uncertain, his movements elephantine, for his waders were full to the brim of leaden water. He made her settle down on the bank while he stripped them from his legs. She lay there quiet as a child, sobbing softly to herself. He came and lay beside her and kissed her ; she had never seemed to him so helpless and pitiful as then, with the wet skirt clinging to her body.

" It's all right for me," he said, " it's you I'm thinking of. What a hopeless pair of fools. That rod's gone to glory all right. Clare, my sweet, you're shivering. We mustn't stay here any longer in the open. There's a hotel at Tenbury, but that's too far for you to walk. I think we'd better make for the stationmaster's cottage and keep warm there till the next train."

The sun was already sinking behind the beeches that hung to the red cliffs above the pool ; once more the mist, which had dissolved at midday, invested the ploughland, and trailed among the trellises of the hopyard. They trudged heavily back to the station. Ralph knocked at the cottage door, and the stationmaster's wife, a spare and acid woman, surveyed Clare's soaked, ungainly figure with suspicion.

"We've had an accident," Ralph told her, and the name of Lord Arthur worked such wonders that in half an hour they were drinking a hot sweet infusion of tannin in front of a crackling fire. By this time Clare had recovered from her fright. Clad in the Sunday garments of the stationmaster and his wife, they huddled close to the fire, waiting for their own clothes to dry and for the evening train to come puffing down from Woofferton, laughing at the strangeness of their adventure and the cold douche with which it had ended.

The train was cold, comfortless and appallingly slow ; it seemed to Clare as if the journey would never end ; her limbs were chilled and heavy, as if they did not belong to her. On the platform at Stourford they had to run to catch the Wychbury connection, and as Clare dragged behind, she was seized by a sudden gasping pain, different from any that she had felt before. She told herself that it was nothing, that the ducking had given her a cold ; but as soon as they had settled, panting, into their compartment, it came again, catching her breath so sharply that she was forced to cry out.

"What's that ? " Ralph asked in quick alarm. "What's that ? "

"Nothing," she assured him, " just a stitch in my side ; we had to run so."

But now he was alarmed, and when the pain came again ɪe saw her features shrunken and contorted, so that she was bound to confess what she feared ; what, in her heart, she knew.

" Good Lord," he said, " our luck's out completely. As soon as we get to Wychbury, we'll drive straight to Dr. Boyd's."

" I'd rather go straight home," she told him. She was now so cold and frightened that she felt she could not control herself away from the friendliness of Uffdown. She was like a stricken rat hurrying to its hole ; but Ralph was so persistent that she allowed him to drive her to the doctor's house.

A fool of a maid opened to them ; the doctor was out on a country call ; she could not say when he would be in. Clare heard the announcement pitifully from the interior of the brougham. It seemed to rob her of her last hope ; for ever since they had left Stourton her mind had been concentrating itself on Dr. Boyd as the solution of all her distress. Ralph came back to her rattled and distracted ; she was thankful that it was too dark for him to see her face ; she tried to modulate her voice in such a way that he would imagine that she was at ease.

" I'm going to leave you," he said. " Bissell will drive you home as quickly as possible. I shall send up a trap from the Royal Oak to fetch Aunt Cathie. Then I shall set off as fast as I can to intercept Boyd. He's gone to one of the farms below Bromsley. You won't mind my leaving you, my darling ? "

She told him that she would not mind. She was thankful, in fact, that he would no longer be able to see or hear her. She wanted to be alone, and, above all, to reach her home at Uffdown. When Bissell had touched up his horses and the darkness of night received her, she felt an extraordinary sense of relief.

It was more than two hours later when Ralph returned to Uffdown in Dr. Boyd's gig. He had found Boyd just as he was leaving the farmyard at Lower Bromsley, and implored him to come at once. The doctor took his summons as if it were the most ordinary thing in the world, and listened without surprise or emotion to Ralph's story of their riverside disaster.

" A bit of rough luck," he called it.

" We'd better drive along at once," he said, " and see if there's anything doing. Just jump up here beside me. That's the style ! "

But when Ralph had mounted the gig he went on talking to the farmer about his patient as though Uffdown and Clare were minor interests in his practice.

" For God's sake hurry up ! " Ralph begged him ; but the pace at which Boyd drove was as leisurely as one of the ponderous processes of nature. He smiled at Ralph's impetuousness, evaded his eager questions, and let the tired horse go as it would over the hilly road that led them towards Uffdown. In the intervals between his cases he refused to let people treat him as a medical man. He talked of the Woodland Stourton's last day in Brimsley Bottom.

" You're far too grand for us in these days, Hingston," he said. " Personally I much prefer this country to the Worcestershire's. If I were as well-mounted as you are I might change my mind. As a matter of fact, I like a hunt that's run by farmers ; there's a naturalness and goodfellowship about it that you never get with the big packs. What's more, the truth of the matter is I can't afford capping. Let's see, now, which road's the better ? "

" Keep to the right," Ralph answered grimly. " I can't stand this much longer."

" You won't have to, my boy," the doctor told him. " As a matter of fact, we've been going like the devil. I'm looking forward to seeing your wife out with us this winter. What about that mare of Bostock's that you were speaking of ? She's a neat little thing ; his daughter rode her last week, and I liked the look of her. Steady now, you brute! Don't get excited!"

The words, which were addressed to his horse, were equally applicable to Ralph, for as the doctor spoke them they had swung into the Uffdown drive. Ralph jumped down before the trap had stopped. Ellen had opened the door to receive him, her face all white and pulpy with emotion. She burst into a torrent of speech:

"Oh, sir, thank Heaven, you've come, sir. Yes, sir, the mistress is upstairs. Miss Cathie and Thirza Rudge and Mrs. Harbord are along with her; they come about an hour ago, and told me to wait down here and let you in, sir, and take the doctor's coat, sir."

But Dr. Boyd had already performed this office for himself and had passed to the foot of the stairs.

"Now, Hingston, keep your pecker up!" he smiled as he disappeared.

Ralph was alone with Ellen in the firelit hall. The pallor of Ellen's amorphous face was treacherous to his nerves. He could not look at her; nor could he trust himself to tell her to go, although she showed no signs of leaving him. He picked up a paper and stared at it in the firelight. The same old story: South Africa. What did he care for South Africa? Ellen stood mute in the background. He stole a glance in her direction, hoping that she would take the hint and leave him. It had the opposite effect, emboldening her to address him, for the first time in her life, as another human being:

"Don't you take on, sir," she blurted out. "Miss Clare's a real brick, she is; she's got a good heart in her body. She'll be all right, sir, with Thirza and Mrs. Harbord. Everyone in the village says that that there Mrs. Harbord's a wonder. Oh, hark at me now! If I bain't forgetting the doctor's there too! And Miss Clare—the mistress, I ought to say . . . 'You see that the master gets his dinner,

Ellen '; those was the last words she spoke to me. So, if you don't mind, sir, I think she'd feel more satisfied like if you took a bite."

Dinner . . . The very word was an outrage to him. It was unbearably pitiful to think that Clare, in this extremity, should have given thought to such a trivial thing ; but Ellen's voice was so tremulous and persuasive that he could not treat her roughly.

" No, Ellen, I couldn't touch anything," he told her. " Bring me the whisky bottle and a syphon of soda-water."

He felt unspeakably kindly toward Ellen, this creature whom a common love and anxiety had endowed with a quality of sisterhood, and kindlier still when, having placed the tray at his elbow, she silently retired. He poured out a stiff peg of whisky, but could not drink. The old house was so subdued and silent, so callous in its accumulated knowledge of human birth and death. If he could have heard a sound he would have been contented. If he could have heard a sound, fear would have killed him. His Clare . . . his clear-white darling . . .

There was no sound ; only the comfortable whisper of the fire and embers settling easily downward. He could not contain himself much longer like this. Longer . . . Why, sometimes this double torture lasted a night, a day and a night ! " Never again," he told himself, " never again ! "

Suddenly the figure of Dr. Boyd appeared at the head of the stairs. Ralph rushed to meet him. He was leisurely and smiling ; he rubbed his shiny red hands.

" Is she all right ? " Ralph gasped. He could not trust these smiles.

" Yes, she's all right." The doctor laughed at him. " They're both all right. It's a boy."

" My God, Boyd. My God . . . My God ! "

He was laughing himself, with a high, breathless laughter.

" My God . . . I can't believe it ! "

" Try a spot of whisky, Hingston. Thanks, I don't mind one myself."

Ralph poured it with shaking hands ; the doctor settled down with a sigh into an arm-chair. Beneath the swirl of his thoughts Ralph heard him speaking :

" You know it's an eight month's baby ? Don't worry yourself ; it'll live all right. Strong as a lion. Of course that made it easier. Your wife was splendid, Hingston. Between you and me—for Heaven's sake, don't tell Miss Weir—she's had a first-rate time. Youth and health, you know. Well, well, that's over. I'll just ave another look at her before I go. We'll get the nurse out first thing to-morrow morning ; too late to-night. Oh, and there's one thing more : I'm trusting you to get those two old women out of the house, particularly Mrs. Harbord, as soon as you can. That old ghoul is a family curse in Wychbury, and yet I can't get the village people to see it." He rose from his chair. " Pack them off, Hingston, pack them off ; they're like a couple of damned vultures," he repeated as he moved again to the stairs.

Ralph watched him go with his leisurely indolent satisfaction. He gulped down whisky from the glass that he carried untasted in his hand. He knew that his mouth was smiling foolishly, triumphantly ; but still his mind was incapable of consecutive thought, and still, out of its exultant emptiness, the same words kept on forming :

" My God . . . My God . . . My God ! "

Oh, brave, brave world, oh, world of unimaginably sweet miracles ! Oh, Clare, Clare, Clare . . .

## V

## STEVEN

HIS name was Steven. From the moment when first his existence was dreamed of that had been his name. He was dreadfully tiny, Clare found ; his face of a dark, carnal red that resembled the colour of the terra-cotta bricks of which the new North Bromwich law-courts were built. Out of this brick-red amorphous piece of flesh, crinkled and puckered like the petals of a field-poppy that has newly burst its hispid calyx, two slits of eyes disclosed pupils of a bluish blackness. Not even Clare could have proclaimed him beautiful, and Ralph, used as he was to the sight of new-born sucklings of other species on the farm, surveyed his son with mingled awe and misgiving ; for, strapped in the linen binder that Mrs. Rudge had applied, the girth of the creature's chest was hardly as great as that of his own fore-arm. Ralph's face, indeed, was so bewildered, yet so tact-fully composed to conceal his doubts on the normality of their joint production for fear of distressing her, that Clare was forced to encourage him with a wan smile.

" He won't always look like that," she assured him. " He'll grow out of it. Look at his nails ; they haven't reach ed the tips of his fingers yet, poor darling. That's how they know his real age, Thirza tells me."

" As long as you're all right," he told her, " nothing else matters. Boyd says he's strong enough in any case."

" Of course he's strong, and I'm as right as can be. You should hear him cry," said Clare ; and Steven, already sensitive enough to resent the rhythmical agitations which Thirza Rudge thought essential to the nursing of babies, proclaimed it in the mewling of a famished kitten. This feeble and rather disagreeable sound filled Clare with a tenderness that differed from anything which she had experienced before; it caught at her heart and filled it with a soft warmth that overflowed from there into every corner of her lacerated body and her weak, dizzy brain; and when she had persuaded Thirza to place the baby near to her, and felt the overplus of this strangely generated heat steal through her skin into the creature's grotesque body, the act of transmission filled her with a drowsy content which her numbed senses refused to accept as real. Again and again she wakened from a doze to reassure herself that the time for which she had been waiting for so many months was really over; that the baby, whom Thirza had taken from her when she fell asleep, was no dream's figment but a creature of flesh and blood; her flesh; her blood; her son; Steven. The dreaded event had been too swift and preceded by excitements too strenuous for dread. It was over; she was tired; she wanted to sleep.

Youth, as Dr. Boyd assured them, was everything. Next day, when the nurse arrived from North Bromwich, it seemed to Clare ridiculous to be treated as an invalid. She wanted to laugh at the woman's mysterious precautions and prohibitions, at the awkwardness of Ralph's stealthy approaches, his anxious face, his hushed voice. Within half a week her natural resilience rebelled against further imprisonment. The nurse looked shocked: " Even the working classes take ten days, my dear," she said. " Ladies *always* a fortnight." Dr. Boyd chaffed her for her impatience, but was firm, and Ralph, taking courage from her smiles, abandoned the religious seriousness with which he had approached her bedside; for the state of maternity, which he had half dreaded as one that would separate her from him and change or age her in some undivinable way, seemed actually to have made her younger and more desirable—so tenderly, inexplicably young that, with her dark hair braided, she looked like the schoolgirl that she had been before he fell in love with her.

For hours on end, under Nurse Wilson's supervision, they played together like a pair of furtive children. In the relief of that one shadow's withdrawal they had no age; but while Ralph could think of nothing but Clare's adorableness, Clare's eyes and ears were anxious for the least sound or movement on the part of the baby, who still seemed to Ralph a grotesque and unexplained phenomenon.

Dr. Boyd, in the wisdom that lay behind his puckered, smiling eyes, had declared that Clare must nurse the baby herself, and as Steven's mealtimes came round, Ralph found that Nurse Wilson displaced him in favour of his son. They made a joke of this, as of everything else; and yet, when he saw the baby's round head nuzzled against Clare's white breast, and Clare's eyes softened to a look which she had never given to him, Ralph often felt a pang of something that was near to jealousy. It was an emotion for which he hated and despised himself; he was at pains to conceal it; but he need not have troubled himself, for at those times Clare seemed to be rapt in a kind of physical ecstasy, commingled with subtle satisfactions of soul, protective and generous, that made her almost unaware of his presence. Sometimes he felt this estrangement so acutely that he would find some excuse to go away from her; but though Clare smiled at him, she was so absorbed that she scarcely noticed his going.

He began to grow restless and eager for the day when this absorption in the duties of maternity would be over, and he could have her to himself. He found consolation in making plans for a renewal of their life together; a life that she would be able to share with him more completely than that which the coming of the baby had complicated. Uffdown, as Lady Hingston had declared, was a remote, unfriendly spot. Unless he could be sure of Clare's companionship the life he led there must be lonely compared with that to which he had been accustomed at Stourford.

She had promised that she would keep him company in the hunting-field. Already that mare of Bostock's, about which he had spoken to Dr. Boyd, was installed with Starlight and the big grey in the Uffdown stables. Maternity was all very well ; but neither Clare nor anyone else need think that it was going to deprive him of his wife.

He had not long to wait ; for when, at the end of the month Nurse Wilson departed, there was no lack of competition for the possession of Steven. By this time, as even Ralph was forced to admit, his son had developed into a presentable baby. He was still exceedingly tiny ; but now the slit-like eyes had opened to the promise of a blue as vivid as Ralph's ; the red skin had cooled to a creamy whiteness, and the unshaped features had defined themselves in a mould that Ralph was flattered into considering a copy of his own. All the world seemed as bent on establishing these tenuous likenesses as if they were essential evidences of legitimacy.

" A Hingston," his mother told him. " The child's as Hingston as he can be ! He's the living image of what you were at his age. Of course you were much bigger and stronger. *All* my children were as healthy as they possibly could be. I never took any risks, and we always lived in dry, healthy houses, not in a damp, decayed place like this. No doubt you realize now that if Clare had taken my advice and come over to Stourford the baby would have had a better chance."

" A Hingston ? " said Aunt Cathie indignantly. " Really, my dear Clare, I don't know how they have the face to say such a thing ; they'll be claiming you as a Hingston next ! Why, anyone with eyes in their head can see that he's the very image of the doctor. He has the doctor's nose. He's an entirely different type from you or Ralph either. Thirza noticed it the very moment he was born."

Clare smiled. It seemed cruel to her to associate this

little creature, so frail, so alarmingly young, with the harsh old figure who had tyrannized Pen House, to compare the small pink dab of Steven's nose with the aquiline beak that used to thrust itself forward above Dr. Weir's blue lips. She knew, in fact, that Steven was the image of Ralph. Whether that were enough to establish Lady Hingston's claim was another matter ; for Ralph, as she had always told herself, resembled neither of his parents, and her baby, however they might try to bind him to the past, was really neither Weir nor Hingston, but her son, a new, miraculous creation, endowed by her with body and soul alike.

It pleased her none the less to see the way in which these other eager claimants bowed before him ; for though Lady Hingston was as overbearing in her proprietary assertions as ever, always ready to be scandalized at Clare's methods of upbringing and Dr. Boyd's modernity, Clare found her betrayed into such unimaginable tenderness in the baby's presence that she began to wonder if she had not always misjudged her. Aunt Cathie, too, was entirely transformed. She haunted Uffdown persistently. It seemed as if Pen House had given place, as the centre of her life, to Steven's nursery, a gay, white-panelled chamber on the first floor, facing south. There she would sit, hour after hour, silent in an anxious adoration, more sedulous than Clare's, reluctant, even, to surrender Steven to his mother's arms. There Clare would sometimes find her sitting with the baby hugged to her breast, and, in her eyes, the rapt, holy placidness of this vicarious maternity which made Clare's heart glow with thankfulness that such a rapture had been vouchsafed to her, with regret that she would never know another.

" I believe you're a better mother than I am," Clare told her.

" My dear child," said Aunt Cathie airily, " you talk as if I weren't used to babies. Kindly remember that I took charge of you when you were very little older than Steven, and looked after you with my own hands, which is more than Lady Hingston can say for any of her children, in spite of all her pretensions. You needn't trouble yourself about Steven when I'm here, need she, my sweetest ? " And as she spoke she would press the baby's rounded face to her own lax cheeks as if, by some physical miracle, she could make the fragile body blend with her own.

Even when she was not at Uffdown Steven occupied Aunt Cathie's mind to the exclusion of her new studies in genealogy. She and Thirza Rudge would hang over the fire of an evening discussing all that had taken place in the Uffdown nursery during the day ; and Thirza, still a little huffed by her unjust exclusion, would open the stores of her traditional experience, which Aunt Cathie smiled at, but greedily absorbed. In every spare moment her fingers were busy with the knitting of minutely ridiculous garments that anticipated the baby's growth, while the hoarding instinct which had disfigured the later stages of the doctor's life began to assert itself in small economies, to Thirza inexplicable and distressing, from the proceeds of which she determined to accumulate a nest-egg, as she called it, for her baby's future. Even at this date she seemed unable to measure the degree of Ralph Hingston's affluence.

Between these forces that competed in their various ways for the possession of Steven, Ellen, more surely than all the others, made him her own. It was in this hope that she had left Pen House for Uffdown ; and as soon as the professional nurse departed, Ellen came into her own. This office made her radiantly happy. It mattered nothing to her that Jim Mosely had now deserted his smart housemaid for another and more exalted quarry ; no less, this time, than Miss Wilkins, the undertaker's daughter. Steven, whatever others might call him, was her boy, her pet, her handsome. Hers was the sacramental function of the bath ;

by her he slept in the lace-hooded bassinet at night; in every essential, menial office she was his keeper and protector. She had no other object or devotion in life.

So, in an incense of adulation, and in a faint, half-sickly odour of soap and milk and Fuller's earth, the baby grew and throve, staring at the moulded Queen Anne ceiling with wide blue eyes, kicking, with pink legs, the fleecy blanket with which Ellen tried to cover him in vain, laughing, without reason, at Spring suns, that fringed the beeches with a light that was subdued and tender as the songs of willow-wrens, and fired the aged brick of Uffdown to a silvery warmth.

# VI

## WOODLAND STOURTON

For Clare, also, the new year brought swift, ecstatic days. Never in all her life had she felt so well; it was as if this first adventure of maternity, in subjecting her body to the last natural function unperformed, had brought it to a maturity that represented the highest point of normal physical fitness. When once she was freed from the restrictions which Steven's early delicateness imposed, the tide of life, at its spring, carried her buoyantly, exhilaratingly forward into the open sea. Before Christmas her riding lessons had begun; and since she was strong, fearless, and dowered with a nice muscular poise, it was not long before she was out with Ralph in the hunting-field, recapturing the sense of adventurous companionship that had seemed in danger of being lost in the months before Steven was born.

The first days of the new year were consumed in this excitement. Now that Clare was with him Ralph no longer boxed his horses far afield for days with the fashionable hunts in the southern part of the county. The Woodland

Stourton country lay at the doors of Uffdown and sufficed them. Leaving Steven in the devoted hands of Ellen and Aunt Cathie, they hunted regularly four days a week. Ralph rode with the predatory keenness of the born sportsman ; for him hunting was a passion in itself ; but for Clare these days in the mired woodland and over the dun fields were full of delights that he could never guess. On them she attained a new and intimate knowledge of all the country that lay hidden in the hills' gigantic folds ; each day revealed some new secret of its beauty, inspired her with some new love for strange green alleys, trailing wind-breaks, and tawny-sanded brooks.

Never until that Spring had she realized how deeply, how inextricably the spirit of the country from which her stock had sprung was incorporated in her own. Other loves might entrance her momentarily—she still remembered Capri and the light that burned out of its lilac crags—but this subdued and dreamy landscape of the Clents, its black rain-beaten spinneys, its grassy uplands falling into the plain, were the background against which her figure found its natural setting. It was her country, and Ralph's, and Steven's ; for even when she was most absorbed in it or in the breathless enchantment of a galloping field with hounds streaking out ahead, Steven was never far from her thoughts. When Steven was older she would have so many secrets to show him : that pinewood where the squirrels sprang from swaying branch to branch ; that lost lane where, even in February, white violets and primroses were to be found. Even if Ralph could not share these ecstasies, which he regarded with a tolerant amusement as something alien but inherent in her adorable complexity, Steven would understand them some day. For Steven was not a beloved stranger, but part of her own body and mind.

Sometimes, indeed, Ralph found it difficult to sympathize with her discoveries. Hunting, with him, was a serious business. As a breeder of pheasants he diverted into the pursuit of the fox the frank enmity which, in a ruder age, he might have directed against his neighbours ; and most of the people who hunted with the Woodland Stourton were cut to the same pattern as himself. That Clare was fearless as a rider was a matter for personal pride ; but the fact that, even when hounds were running, other things could engross her, puzzled him, and made him self-conscious on her behalf ; for now that he had become a country gentleman with a stake in the county, the least deviation from the conventional seemed to him perverse and disintegrating, and all eccentricity discreditable.

He wished, in short—and there was nothing behind this wish that failed to recognize Clare's essential goodness or qualified his devotion—he wished, in some ways, that she was more like Mrs. Elvery, the comet whose apparition had lately dazzled the Woodland Stourton's field. Nobody knew exactly where Mrs. Elvery had come from ; but the admirable way in which she was mounted implied that she was well-to-do. She had hunted in the Shires—so much he knew from Charlie Burnett—and carried with her into the Stourton meets an atmosphere of elegance that would have done credit to Kirby Gate or Wymondham Roughs. She was a slim, dark, childlike woman, older and shorter than Clare ; but when she was mounted the trailing habit concealed her deficiency in height. The colour of her cheeks was a thought too high, her mouth a little hard ; but when she spoke to men she had a trick of blinking her eyes that called attention to their dark brilliance and made them think of nothing else. She was used to men's society ; she liked it, and evidently understood it ; for wherever she went they clustered round her, laughing, and listening for the drawl of a smart tongue that was more than a match for the kind of intelligence it attracted.

One morning Charlie Burnett had sidled up to Ralph and

told him that Mrs. Elvery wished to know him. She hadn't said that she wanted to know Clare, but Ralph was flattered by her evident approval of himself, so obviously her physical complement in his big blondeness. Often, in later days, they found themselves together ; for Ralph was by nature a thruster, and Clare, whom he had forbidden to take risks, could be considered safe in the company of Dr. Boyd. He liked Mrs. Elvery. She didn't flirt with him as with the other men. Generally his presence seemed to make her shy ; she veiled her eyes persistently, and when she flashed a look at him it was usually to speak of Clare. She told him that she thought Clare lovely, and him a lucky man, so happily placed with a house of distinction, a young wife, and an heir in the nursery. She flattered him ; yet, when she spoke of Clare, a sidelong criticism was implied, as though the gentleness, the innocence, the beauty that she praised were pathetic rather than admirable in the eyes of a woman of the world. In her presence Ralph was excited by the dangerous suggestions of her personality ; afterwards, in Clare's, he was annoyed to think that a woman so obviously inferior should be able to wipe Clare's eye in style, in horsemanship, in all the indefinite things that contributed to Mrs. Elvery's brilliance.

He felt it so necessary to his new dignity that Clare should shine with an identical brilliance that he slowly detached her from most of her new acquaintances, the Abberleys and Ombersleys and Tardebigges who had frequented Uffdown during her year of inactivity, replacing them by the smarter and more rackety society of the hunting set ; and since it was part of his programme to make Uffdown a place of liberal entertainment such as he had been used to at Stourford, Clare found herself committed to an endless series of dinner-parties crowded with guests with whom she had little in common and whose presence seemed, in some subtle way, an affront to the sober dignity of the house. Uffdown was still, with her, a touchstone for the judgment of human society, and on these gatherings its mute commentary was severe.

She suffered them because, in all such matters, she thought it her duty to submit to Ralph's authority. He enjoyed them frankly. To him they represented a continuation of the life to which he devoted himself during the hunting-season, but in Clare the false intimacy of nicknames, the masculine indelicacies of speech, the poverty of a conversation that concentrated on personalities and horses and food and drink, aroused nothing but regret for the quiet evenings which she and Ralph had spent together, and, above all, for the silent piano, which seemed to contemplate their noisy vulgarity with dumb distaste. She could not bear to think that Steven's future would be surrounded by an atmosphere of this kind ; for then, she told herself, he would not be like her at all.

Something of this misgiving must have shown itself in her manner toward her guests, for, one evening, when the last of them had gone, Ralph scolded her about it and gave the matter air.

" You're a queer sort of hostess," he said bitterly. " You sat through the whole evening like a funeral. Everyone must have noticed it. You looked as if you hated the lot of them."

His face was flushed and scowling ; he stumbled over his words ; in the irritable violence of his movements as he undressed and the bitterness of his tone she could see that he had drunk more than was good for him. She felt that it was her duty to herself to be honest with him now or never.

" I did dislike them, Ralph," she said. " They're not our sort of people."

" Not our sort of people ? My dear Clare, I don't know what the devil you think you're talking about ! They're my friends. That ought to be good enough for you."

" It isn't, Ralph," she said. " There's not one of them that's good enough for *you*, and you ought to know it. They're people without a single idea in their heads. I don't like the way they talk with women in the room. That story of Captain Burnett's. . . . Possibly Mrs. Elvery did. And I don't like their familiarity. I object to Mrs. Elvery using my Christian name. I don't know her. I don't want to know her. All they come here for is just to drink your wine, and they drink far too much of it. I'm not sorry if I showed what I felt."

He stared at her in astonishment. This was not the complacent Clare that he knew.

" Burnett ? " he said. " I'd no idea you'd object to a thing like that. It's only his fun. Charlie Burnett's as innocent as a lamb, and a damned good sportsman. And Kate Elvery's the best woman to hounds in the county. You'd be none the worse for taking a leaf out of her book in several things. She's as smart as paint, Kate Elvery, and a jolly attractive woman too. . . ."

" So it seems," Clare heard herself saying. " You had no eyes for anyone else all evening."

It was out, this grudge that had lain hidden so deeply and for so long. As she spoke she was appalled by the vulgarity of her own words, and the thought that she could have been capable of uttering them to Ralph. But he was too surprised to think of them in this light. The sense of an injured, technical innocence threw him into a rage.

" My God, Clare," he cried, " how dare you speak to me like that ? It's a piece of the most damnable insolence ! I won't have it ! "

She knew that he was innocent ; but the way in which he had risen to her taunts and the violence of his words gave her the justification for which she was longing.

" You needn't shout like that," she said. " The servants will hear you. You forget that Ellen's in the next room."

" Ellen be damned ! " he cried, more loudly than ever. " What does that matter ? "

" Oh, don't, don't ! " she entreated ; but now his indignation, like that of Lady Hingston, had fed upon itself and could not be stayed, and his raw and fuddled mind insisted on a retraction.

" Look here, Clare," he said. " I know you're a little prig ; but I'm not going to have you accusing me and my friends like that. You've got to tell me what you mean by it."

She couldn't. By this time her accusations had no meaning to her ; but he stood there glowering at her so uglily that she knew that there could be no evasion. She began to speak passionately.

" I mean," she said, " that your precious Captain Burnett is just a parasite. As for Mrs. Elvery . . . Well, I won't tell you what I think of her, since you're so sensitive about her, and if you're such a fool that you can't.see for yourself. You needn't think I'm jealous either. I'm not. Only it makes me sick to see anyone . . . anyone that I care for like you . . . being so stupidly taken in. And when I think of what we used to be. . . . And Steven . . ."

The word was too much for her ; her voice broke in the middle of it and all the fight went out of her ; she collapsed into tears. She could have kicked herself for breaking down like this. It was weak and shameful of her to do so at a time when she was fighting for her own inalienable rights. She knew that she wouldn't have done so if she hadn't loved him so dreadfully. But when Ralph, harrowed and disconcerted by this sudden, pathetic revelation of her frailty, regained his senses and tried to take her in his arms, her spirit stiffened against him, denying him the satisfaction of such an easy victory. He caught her by the arm so strongly that it hurt.

" Don't, don't ! " she cried. " I can't bear you to touch me. You're hurting me. You smell of whisky. I hate it. . . . I hate it ! "

And when he persisted, hoping by the sheer force of their habitual intimacy to woo her back to normal happiness, she relapsed into a sullen bruised silence, which was the only state of which her lacerated nerves were capable. He could not make her speak ; she lay stiff and frigid and alien in his arms, suffering his kisses without a tremor of recognition ; and in the end he abandoned his coaxing and left her, passing into the dressing-room with the feeling of a man who has suddenly lost all touch with the reality of life, reduced by each new wave of pity or resentment to a more desolate impotence.

As soon as he had gone Clare hurriedly undressed and crept into bed with the pins still in her hair. She closed her eyes. Her heart was beating with an aimless precipitance, driving the blood into a brain that could not think, or, indeed, do anything but suffer. Ralph, by this time sobered and as miserable as herself, put out the light and lay down heavily beside her. He knew better, he thought, than to renew his attempts at endearment. She was a creature beyond all understanding, and if it gave her any satisfaction to feel that she had made him suffer, let her take it.

They lay there in the dark together, silent and wakeful. Clare's eyes were wide open, staring at the ceiling on which a screened fire illuminated the conventional plaster scrolls with which some Georgian Ombersley had carefully embellished it. The house was deadly quiet ; not a creak in the stairs, no sigh of wind in the frost-enchanted air. It listened, curiously, she thought, for sound or movement from these divided lovers. It was so old, so old, so spiritually remote from such soul-harrowing trivialities as theirs ; too old even to smile at them ; carrying, in the indelible records of its ether, memories of so many bitter words and passionate reproaches, spoken, repented, and merged at last in the undistinguished lives that had flowered and withered within its walls. In this contemptible difference it could not or would not help her, even though her sense of justice reaffirmed, again and again, the rightness of her indignation.

She was more lonely than she had ever been before. Between her and Ralph, who had absorbed a half of her existence into his own, lay the physical symbol of their spiritual separation, a foot of icy linen sheet. It was not for her, the injured, to bridge that interval. He, who divided her soul, had insulted her with incredible violence; and it was only just that he should pay for it. Even so, she told herself, it was not in his power to abate her loneliness. If only she could have her baby ; if only she could take Steven in her arms all would be well and this ugly episode, so dreadfully unworthy of their love, forgotten.

And once again the thought of Steven, innocently sleeping in the adjoining room, betrayed her courage, so that, in spite of all her will to prevent it, her body was shaken again by sobs. She felt the broken rhythm of their impact agitating the bed beneath her. Surely Ralph must feel it. But Ralph did not care. If he did not care it was her own fault, for she had repulsed him. If only, when he had tried his forcible wooing, he had said that he was sorry for having wounded her, she could have borne it better ; but that essential thing, it seemed, had never entered his mind. Ralph was stupid and obtuse in matters like that ; he had no apprehension of the little delicacies that meant so much to her. And yet, beyond his obtuseness, how good and patient he was : how sweet he had been to her in the days before Steven came ! In his simplicity he was almost as much of a baby as Steven. She had been foolish not to treat him as the child that he was. Perhaps, even now, he wasn't lonely ; with him you could never tell ; but surely, out of these ruthless sobs which she tried so hard to stifle, he could imagine the depth of her desolation ? She held her breath. He was speaking in a strained, unnatural voice :

" Clare, my sweet, I can't bear this much longer."

So he, too, had been suffering in silence. Her own heart was full of pity for him. For a moment her sobbing ceased. But when he stretched out his arm and touched her hot and throbbing side, she could not speak. She lay as quiet as a vixen feigning death until the outstretched arm enveloped her and drew her burning body close to his. She felt a shudder run through her as he clasped her ; his fingers encountered the hairpins in her abandoned hair.

" Be careful," she whispered, " you're hurting my head."

His voice made a tender, inarticulate sound ; his lips brushed her wet cheek as they came in search of hers ; his hands, with their old cunning, verified the shapes of the body that he adored. With no word spoken, with eyes closed against the flicker of the dying fire, they sought and found each other, and later fell asleep in each other's arms.

# VII

## DOLLY GRAY

THEY were so young ; and since this was the first difference that had ever separated them, Clare emerged from it ashamed and anxious to prove to herself that the episode wasn't as serious as she had imagined. At first she was a little shy and conscious of it as an ugly background to the renewal of their love , but their eager timidities, their forced affectation of a simplicity, like that of children in disgrace, made this renewal very sweet and different from the love that had gone before. Each was so tender, so thoughtful, so assiduous to prove that nothing of moment had occurred, so anxious to make amends.

And, as it happened, the cause of the quarrel was soon to be automatically removed; since the hunting season was now nearing its end : an ironical provision of fate, for Ralph, by this time, had come to see that Clare's estimate of his new friends was a sound one, and Clare, her jealous crisis once resolved, realized that she had nothing to fear from Mrs. Elvery ; that Mrs. Elvery, for all her dashing smartness and dangerous guise, was really a lonely, pathetic figure, making a game fight against the passage of time, reduced, for lack of love, to these equivocal comradeships, and more to be pitied than feared.

Moved by these scruples of conscience, Clare made an effort to repair the wrong she had done her by shy friendly overtures ; but the dark eyes of Mrs. Elvery remained suspicious—evidently she was unused to frankness on the part of women—and her hard voice assured Clare that she might have saved herself the trouble of her advances. With the end of the season Mrs. Elvery's lease expired, and Uffdown saw no more of her.

Perhaps it was better so. Now that the hunting was over and summer coming in, Uffdown was at its best. All life was at its best ; for now Steven had begun to find his tongue and his feet, and Ellen, who had bound his infancy in her cares as in a chrysalis, must now surrender him to Clare. Ralph, too, was forced to see his son's capacity for entertainment, and though he never quite abandoned his male detachment, they would spend long hours of idleness together, watching the child's bold, inco-ordinate movements, amused by his comical perversions of speech.

To Clare the fascination of this pursuit was endless , she could never tell what new, astonishing phrase Steven might not produce from Ellen's provincial glossary, nor with what exquisite inappropriateness her ears might not be ravished. Now Steven's brain was like a maze in whose intricacies she was content to lose herself all day ; and his small body, in the soft mould of which she watched Ralph's beloved lineaments gradually forming, was so young, so sweet, so white, that when, enraptured by some new, fantastic revelation of his little soul, she caught him in her arms, she sometimes felt that she could eat him. " You're a pair of savages, the two of you," Ralph told her. What did it matter, if Eden were as sweet as this ?

Midsummer came, and with it the season of haymaking ; soft dawns, in which the folded valleys echoed to the drowsy clatter of many mowing-machines. Ralph watched his crops and the barometer anxiously ; each day the whispering acres of grass grew more burnished, like tropic seas, ripening to a rare and perfect harvest ; each day full sunlight embalmed the Uffdown valley, turning the scarlet garden roses purple and hedgerow roses white.

Ralph held his hand until the glass began to fall. Then there was work for all of them ; Ralph and Clare and Ellen and Bissell and all the other servants tossing the sweet swathes of hay from dawn to the transfiguration of sunset. They laughed and worked together, bright faces and bronzed arms, until the mounded haycocks stood in rows, and a great wain, red and blue, came swaying down the alley between them, to carry the aromatic harvest to the ricks. And Clare, when she was tired, would leave the silvery green of the mown fields to look for Steven, who crawled upon a rug spread in the shade of the hedge under the tutelage of the gardener's youngest boy. And Steven, as she called to him, would smile and stretch out his arms, as though he believed it in his power to reach her from a distance. Then, happy in luxurious fatigue, she would tell the gardener's boy to run away. and lie down beside Steven, who crawled above her, suffocating her with the pressure of his sticky hands ; and the nearness of the living child was the richest of all the physical pleasures on which that summer smiled. Even when his fingers tried to open her sun-dazed eyes the discomfort was a pleasure to her, she laughed and laughed, like a vixen at play with her rolling cubs in the shade.

But Steven's bedtime was early ; and when Ralph saw that she had risen, he would leave the other haymakers and come over to her with the long strides into which labour had loosened his limbs. He would pick Steven up and perch him on his shoulder, and Steven would chuckle with joy as he swayed at that safe and giddy height, while they walked over the sharp stubbles to the house, so old, so mellow, so kindly ; Ralph in his white rolled shirt-sleeves, the down bleached golden on his brown arms ; Clare, walking in silence beside him, absorbed in a serenity as hopeful and complete as that of the immaculate sky.

A great hay-harvest, as Ralph triumphantly had prophesied. It seemed no sooner to have been gathered than autumn was on them, for time had flowed so smoothly that, gazing on their mirrored happiness, they had not noticed its flow. By the middle of September frost lay on the lawns.

" In six weeks," Ralph told her, " cubbing will have begun."

She was thinking less of foxes than of Steven's birthday. It was incredible to realize that a whole year had passed since that terrific day which Ralph, in his lordly acceptance of life, seemed to have forgotten. If time were always to pass as swiftly as this she would be old before she knew it.

Yet, as the day approached, she found that he had prepared a little surprise for her. Once more the date of the board meeting at Wolverbury had come round ; once more

Lord Arthur had lured him with the prospect of Teme grayling.

"What do you say," he said, "if we make another day of it ? No nonsense this time, mind. If I'm to drown, I drown. That's understood ? "

They laughed together over his persistent fatalism, by which she always pretended to be shocked.

"It's Steven's birthday," she told him. "We oughtn't really to leave him."

"Steven won't know the difference, you silly child," he scoffed ; and in the end she was forced to admit that he was right.

All the way westward in the train he found her strangely silent. "A penny for your thoughts," he said. She blushed, and it was only when he had taken her in his arms that she could bear to whisper to him what she was thinking.

"I was trying to go through all the year," she said, "thinking of everything that has happened. I love to do that. I used to do it years ago at the end of every term at school. Things seem so funny when you look back at them."

"Well, what do you make of it ? " he said.

"I don't think I shall tell you."

He knew that tantalizing game of hers so well that he followed the rules of it and would not rest till she had made her confession.

"It's just this," she said at last. "If you look at me so seriously I can't say it. It's just that I think I love you a million times more to-day than I did then."

As they reached the junction on their return the Wychbury train was steaming out of the station. "At any rate, we shan't have to run for it this time," they said. But this time there was no hurry. They spent the half-hour that they had to wait walking up and down the empty platform, warm arm-to-arm, talking of Ralph's fine basket of grayling and laughing at the gossip of the stationmaster's wife who had given them tea in her parlour. The air at Stourton was still and frosty ; through it the furnace flares of the black country and the twinkling pit-bank fires above Mawne Road shone like the lights of a vast army in bivouac. The down express for Worcester came thundering in, disgorging a handful of passengers, among whom they recognized the insignificant shape of Sir Joseph Hingston. Ralph called to him as he was hurrying out. He turned and moved towards them. He was carrying a copy of the *Evening Courier*, which he waved as he advanced. A gesture so positive on his part was extraordinary, but when he reached them they saw that his pasty face was lively with excitement.

" Have you seen the news ? " he said.

" No. We've been fishing at Little Hereford. What news ? " Ralph answered.

Sir Joseph unfolded his paper excitedly.

" It's war," he said. " You saw Chamberlain's last note ? Kruger has answered with an ultimatum. Withdraw all British troops. You see ? Evidently the Boers want to fight. Madness ? Of course it's madness. Unless there's more behind it. Germany, I suppose. It's that business of Delagoa Bay. Still, this means war : a nation like ours can't take an ultimatum lying down. You can have the paper if you want it : I've no time to spare. I must get on to London and keep the wire open if I can. George went to Sheffield as soon as the news came through. Good-bye then. I telephoned your mother at once. She'll be waiting for me."

" What does it mean ? " Clare asked, as soon as he had hurried away.

" Not much to us," Ralph told her, " but a devil of a lot to Wolverbury. It was the Franco-Prussian war that made us. War means shells and rifles, and shells and rifles mean steel. That's where Wolverbury comes in. But though the old man's excited, it won't be much of a flare, unless, as he thinks, there's more beneath the surface. It hasn't half wakened him up though."

" But what is it all about ? " Clare asked. " You know I never read the papers, and I don't understand."

" It's these Boers," he told her. " They've been getting uppish for a long time. Ever since the Jameson raid. You remember that, don't you ? The Uitlanders . . . eh, it's a deuce of a long story. The fact is that this fellow Kruger, an ignorant old devil by the look of him, has been making things uncomfortable for British subjects, and naturally we aren't going to stand it. We've got to teach him a lesson. All these savage peoples have to be taught manners, just the same as you train a dog."

" But war . . ." Clare persisted. " It seems to me perfectly horrible to think of. You can't teach people by killing them. · I should have thought that in these days they'd have found some other way."

" That's rubbish, my child," he told her. " War's the only argument that counts in the long run. An Empire like ours is always at war somewhere or other. We have to assert our prestige."

" It seems dreadful to me," she said, " that Wolverbury should make money out of it. That means that we shall get more money too ? "

" Of course it does," he laughed.

" I hate the idea."

" Well, that's merely silly of you. Still, I don't imagine it means much. The guv'nor's exciting himself over nothing. If they don't climb down it'll all be over in a month. You needn't worry your head about the British Army. I suppose Burnett'll be called up. He's on the reserve."

" I'm glad you're not a soldier," she told him.

But, even though he pretended to take the Boer ultimatum

so coolly, it had stirred Ralph's imagination, and was so much in his thoughts that when they reached Wychbury he told Bissell the news.

" Old Kruger has sent us an ultimatum, Bissell," he said, as he stepped into the carriage.

" Is that so, sir ? " Bissell replied politely. " Well, sir, I reckon it served him right."

Already Stourford and Wolverbury were in the grip of an immense activity. Sir Joseph was soon in touch with Admiralty and War Office, darting backward and forward between London and Wolverbury like a shuttle. Stourford became a house of passage for Government inspectors and officials whose eyes were dazzled by Lady Hingston's sparkling flights. The stables buzzed with perpetual comings and goings. Night-shifts at Wolverbury and Mawne filled the sky with a blood-red reflex, like that of a roused volcano. All through the dark hours hammers thudded unceasingly, the opened furnaces disgorged their pillars of flame, the sound of suffering metal in the rolling-mills shrieked on the night, and died against the wooded bases of the hills that protected Uffdown.

The house itself received all these alarms with a contemptuous calm. It had seen wars before ; the repercussions of Ramillies and Waterloo, of Alma and Sedan, had left it standing, superior to small human destinies. In the long orchard grass apples fell, as before. That was the only sound that disturbed its placid nights ; and when day came, in its dank, autumnal peace, the garden was as quiet, save for the angry flight of wasps that settled greedily on the night-fallen fruit. All the rare sunshine must be caught for Steven. Steven knew nothing of wars, and Steven's life was Clare's.

It was natural that Ralph, whose thoughts were less absorbed than hers and subject to the excitement that filtered through from Stourford, should be infected by the general commotion. At breakfast he sat so deeply submerged in the morning papers that Clare could not get a word out of him, and in the evening Bissell was despatched to Wychbury to fetch the *Courier*. This war was a bigger thing than any of them, except Sir Joseph, had imagined. The black country rejoiced in it. A war for gold was what the cranks and visionaries called it. The people of the black country knew better. Their god, the god of iron, had decreed it, and his earthly representative, their own Joe Chamberlain, had made it possible, directing into their swollen coffers the golden stream. They followed the fortunes of good old Buller's army as once they had followed those of their football favourites, cheering and howling derision as the game swayed to and fro and booing the celestial referee when things went wrong. A game that paid better than football, and was just as exciting and safe for the spectator. The papers published small-scale maps. Ralph pinned one to the panels of the hall at Uffdown, and Steven, in Clare's arms, stretched out his hands and cried for the coloured flags.

It was only in the hunting-field—for, with November, cubbing had begun as usual—that any difference could be detected in their ordinary life. Mrs. Elvery had not renewed her lease of Woodcote. Charlie Burnett had sold his horses—horses were selling well for remounts—and rejoined his regiment of hussars. The fields were thin ; for many of the leisured members of the hunt were on the reserve. Now only the farmers hunted. It wouldn't do to let the stock of foxes decrease. In the black days of December the master volunteered. He took Ralph aside during the meet at Stourhead Osiers and gave him his confidence.

" I feel I can't stand aside any longer, Hingston," he said. " I'm not as young as I was ; but, after all, I'm a bachelor with no responsibilities except the blessed hounds—hey,

Music, damn you, stop that !—nothing to keep me, as I was saying. Now, you're a married man, with a wife and kid of your own. You've every reason to sit tight. As a matter of fact, I'm probably making a fool of myself ; the whole thing'll be over before I get to Capetown. Still, it's a cavalry war . . . mounted infantry, anyway ; and that's the one job on earth I'm cut out for. Now what do you say to taking on the hounds ? I hope you will. I don't mind telling you there's no one else I'd sooner see handling them."

Ralph flushed with pleasure. It seemed as if his good luck had reached its zenith.

" There's no immediate hurry," said the master. " Think it over for a day or two, and let me know how you feel about it. Then I'll put it up to the committee."

He shouted to the huntsman, and the hounds moved on.

Clare was not out that morning. The fox ran up the wind toward the gorse on Uffdown, a desperate line, five fields of plough on end. As Ralph and Starlight sweated over them he was thinking all the time of the chance that luck had given him to test his theories. And then he began to think of that morning's miserable meet ; for by now volunteers were being enlisted, the war had ceased to be a professional affair, and half the farmers' sons who had ridden to hounds were already flaunting the romantic slouch hats of the Imperial Yeomanry, that corps of gentlemen riders who were to sweep like a grass-fire over the veld of the Transvaal. Even now there seemed to be very few men of his own age left. Nobody really knew how long this damned war would last. At first they had said that a month would finish it. Good old Buller ! But good old Buller lay like a stranded hulk on the Tugela. Now it was Roberts. Little Bobs would do the trick. And Fighting Mac and Backacher Gatacre. There seemed to be a certain virtue in these nicknames ; and naturally, in the long run, the British Empire must win and Wolverbury grow fat, however long it lasted.  Trust the " absent-minded beggar " for that.

And yet, when he thought of the slaughter and frustration of Modder River and Magersfontein and Colenso, blows that had fallen one after the other during the past fortnight he couldn't help feeling that his position at Uffdown was a little ignominious.  In the last of these engagements Charlie Burnett had been killed.  Only six weeks ago he and Charlie Burnett had been galloping together over that line of country.  A good fellow, whatever Clare might say.  One of the best.  That sinewy, laughing comrade, lying crumpled with a bullet in his brain.  He grew angry as he thought of Charlie's extinction.  He would like to have a whack himself at the dirty Boer sharpshooter who got him.  Hunting the fox was a poor game in comparison.

Of course, as the master said, it was no business of his.  He was a married man, and had a right to sit tight if he wanted to.  But now that he came to think of it, hounds or no hounds, he didn't want to sit tight.  He couldn't hunt the Woodland Stourton with a clear conscience when older men had gone to South Africa.  It was a question of pride rather than of conviction.  He decided to refuse, and felt more virtuous for the renunciation.

As he rode home that evening in the dank December dusk he was puzzling his brain as to how he should break the news of his decision to Clare.  Never had the warm and steadfast lights of Stourton seemed to him so homely.  As he stalked into the hall in his plough-spattered hunting-kit Clare was sitting in front of a wood fire, with Steven sprawling in the red glare at her feet.  She looked up to greet him, smiling, with bright eyes and cheeks.  He could not face her yet.  Evading her questions, he discarded his boots in the gun-room and went upstairs to his bath.  Its warm consolations, and the feeling of clean, physical spruceness and efficiency with which he dressed for dinner, together with a whole bottle of *Chateau Larose*, put new courage into him.

After dinner, when they were alone, he found himself as tongue-tied as ever, and Clare, who interpreted his silence as a sign of tiredness, passed quietly to the piano and began to play. In the ordinary way her music had no power to move him, but that night the fibres of his mind were strung so tautly that they vibrated in sympathy with her playing ; stirred by its plangency, his imagination pictured the moment of parting, her loneliness, and the high-coloured scenes of his own adventure. Her playing seemed to reinforce the poignancy of his picture. It made him see himself and Clare and Steven, objectively, removed, like the romantic figures in an opera It affected him so deeply that he dragged her off to bed before their usual time.

There, in the kindly darkness which concealed his harassed face, he took her in his arms and began his confession.

" Sir Gilbert is going to South Africa," he told her. " He's offered me the deputy mastership."

" Oh, Ralph, how splendid," he said, and " how jolly of him ! "

" Of course it's a compliment. I realize that. But I've refused."

" Why on earth did you do that ? " she said. " Would it be too expensive ? "

" No. We could afford it quite easily. The works are full of War-Office orders. It isn't that."

" There couldn't be any other reason, my dear boy."

He was silent for a long while.

" Look here, Clare," he said at last. " I know I'm going to hurt you, my darling ; but I've got to get it off my mind."

He clasped her closely, as if in this way he might fortify

her. Clare held her breath ; she had never known him so serious before.

" It's like this," he said. " Ever since we heard about poor Charlie Burnett the other day I've had it on my mind. That business knocked me more than I can say ; and now that a middle-aged man like Cashel is going, I don't see how I can possibly stand out. All the fellows of my own age in the district have joined the Yeomanry. Cashel was awfully nice about it—couldn't have been nicer—but when he put it to me like that I felt such a rotten shirker. . . . I don't know . . . that I couldn't stick it any longer. I've got to go, Clare. There's nothing else for it. I've simply got to go."

She listened in a silence of annihilation. Instead of thoughts there came into her mind the words and tune of a vulgar song that the butcher's boy whistled in the drive when he came trotting up to Uffdown :

> Good-bye, Dolly, I must leave you,
> Though it breaks my heart to go,
> Something tells me I am needed
> At the front to fight the foe.
> See the soldier boys are marching
> And I can no longer stay . . .

In a moment a stronger emotion of dread and something akin to anger at this monstrous perversion had torn the tissue of the arbitrary song to shreds. Against its persistent echoes her lips were speaking with a chilled voice :

" You're going to leave me. . . . And Steven . . . Oh Ralph . . ."

" Clare, my sweet, I can't help it. I've got to. Of course it breaks my heart. (Again that accursed song !) As a matter of fact it's only a . . . a matter of form. Everybody says it will be over in a few weeks. They can't keep it up much longer, and now that Roberts is taking it on . . ."

" Oh, Ralph, Ralph, darling . . ."

" As Cashel says, the odds are that we shan't even be wanted. Even if we get as far as Capetown, we shall probably be sent home on the next boat. In any case, this is the regular army's job ; they'll only use us on railways and block-houses and so on. There's no danger to speak of ; only the separation, and that only for a short time, though God knows it's bad enough ! Still, Clare, I couldn't look my own servants in the face if I didn't go; and I don't believe you could."

She was silent while he continued his persuasions ; she did not even listen to them, for she knew the quality of his obstinate mind. Little by little the thing that had seemed an enormity bore down her protests with the weight of accomplished fact ; and out of her acceptance emerged a new emotion : a feeling of spurious pride in his heroism, and, another, more genuine in its origin, of pride in her own capacity for courage and self-control. She was not alone in this trial. All over England other women were courageously facing a like emergency and putting a brave face on it. How could she show less courage than thousands of other Dolly Grays ?

" You must do what you think right, my darling," she said at last.

She had her reward. It was almost worth the sacrifice and the suffering that she had endured to hear him call her his own, brave girl, his splendid, his wonderful, wife ; to be told that not one woman in a million would have shown her sense of honour, her courage, her steadfastness. She lay in his arms and listened, with a sick, elated heart ; and that elation, so bright and false and hectic, sustained her, at least in Ralph's brave presence, until the day that followed the sinister tidings of Spion Kop, the twenty-first of January, when the sound of cheering died away upon the quay at Southampton, and she found herself alone and staring at the harbour filth that lapped the landing-stage where, half an hour before, he had thrown her kisses from the transport's deck.

## VIII

### TRANSIT OF MARS

FOR what they were worth Clare had no lack of comforters. The Stourford people rallied at once to her loneliness. In Sir Joseph this sympathy took the obvious form of cheques, which was the only one in which he could express himself ; while Lady Hingston, delighted to find that Ralph, for once in a way, had contributed to the prestige of Wolverbury by volunteering, proceeded to exploit her as a walking advertisement of Stourford's patriotism. All of them, even Vivien, seemed to take the credit of Ralph's adventure to themselves, as a gallant, romantic gesture, in keeping with the family character, with nothing but the very slightest spice of danger in it. None of them, except, perhaps, Marguerite, who unnerved Clare with the pitiful glances of her melting eyes, seemed to realize the desolation in which Ralph's departure had left her.

Once more she found herself falling back on the society of Aunt Cathie and her first Uffdown friends. Aunt Cathie knew that war, even this romantic South African picnic which was always going to be over within a month, was a desperate business. As a little girl she remembered tearing up sheets to make bandages for the wounded of eighteen-seventy, and though she couldn't, like the Abberleys and Ombersleys and Tardebigges, isolate from the daily lists of casualties the names of family connections who had fallen, and share in the proud sufferings of the military caste, she behaved, in every respect, as though the Weirs were a family of soldiers, whose ramifications permeated the army list from cover to cover, and she herself a typical representative of the old stock into whose hands the military destinies of England were committed ; so that when the Miss Abberleys lost a nephew, or the Tardebigges a second-cousin, infinitely removed, she would persuade herself that her own family was involved in the casualty and bring the virtue of heroic patience to bear on it.

" You must never forget, Clare," she said, " that one of your own great-uncles was a lieutenant in the Marines and retired with the rank of captain in the senior service ; and the doctor himself was one of the very first to join the volunteer movement in eighteen-fifty-nine. Riflemen, they used to call them. We still have his helmet and his sword —I don't suppose you ever noticed it hanging up in the hall ? I'd almost forgotten them myself until the other day. The plume on the helmet was dreadfully moth-eaten ; but Jabez has polished up the sword with pumice-stone, and now it looks quite deadly."

Aunt Cathie had become an assiduous reader of the new *Daily Mail*. It was she who kept the movements of Ralph's flags on the map of South Africa up to date. Clare could not even bear to look at them ; but with Aunt Cathie the ceremony was a sacramental duty ; her heart thrilled with joy and thankfulness when she pinned the Union Jack into the spots marked Ladysmith and Kimberley, as though the relief of the beleaguered *dorps* were a personal triumph in which her enthusiasm had played a vicarious part. At Pen House she had a map and flags of her own ; but she could not bear to think that the one at Uffdown was ever out of date, and so, whenever there was any signal movement to record, she hurried over and forsook her task of visiting reservists' and yeomen's wives to drive pins into Dutch-named towns with something of the belief in sympathetic magic that impels a black magician to pierce the waxen effigy of his enemy.

Clare smiled at her, and yet the fact that Aunt Cathie's interest in the war was not, like that of the Stourford people, primarily commercial ; that she was " in it " heart and soul, regarding it as an ordeal and a penance rather than as a brilliant smile of fortune, made her glad of her company. Beneath Aunt Cathie's brisk enthusiasms she knew that she could count on a genuine and serious sympathy ; there was no other who realized the strain of hope and fortitude that lay beneath her own serenity. It came as a surprise to her one day when she found Ellen, with Steven in her arms, silently weeping in front of the flag-spangled map. Her own voice trembled when she asked what was the matter ; for Ellen's father and brother, as she knew well enough, were still hammering ploughshares in Wychbury.

" It all come over me of a sudden, ma'am," said Ellen. " It's Jim Moseley I was thinking of."

Clare smiled. " Jim Moseley ? Why, Ellen, I thought you'd finished with Jim a year ago and more. Didn't you tell me that he was walking out with Miss Wilkins ? "

" He was, ma'am," said Ellen, " but now he's gone and joined those yeomanry. Last Sunday that ever was, I seed that chitty-face of his laughing in the horse-road as bold as if he'd never gone. I felt that mad I could have scratched her, behaving herself like that when my poor Jim's out along with them dirty Boers. She hasn't got a heart as big as my little finger, ma'am, and my poor Jim's that simple ; supposing they was to shoot him, he'd never know." She began to cry again, and Steven, overwhelmed by the proximity of her emotion and shaken uncomfortably by her sobs, thought fit to imitate her.

" Why, Ellen, you mustn't cry like that," Clare told her. " I'd no idea that you were still thinking of Jim."

" I bain't, ma'am ; I bain't," Ellen helplessly protested. " It only just come over me."

" But if you feel like that," said Clare, " you can't have

forgotten him. I'll tell you what we'll do. We'll get Miss Weir to find out his address and you shall send him a card, just to show him that someone is thinking of him."

"Oh no, ma'am, I couldn't do that," said Ellen, flushing magenta. "I couldn't so demean myself; indeed I couldn't!"

Yet, now that she knew how Ellen was sharing in secret a little of her own preoccupation and dread, Clare felt less isolated in her loneliness. Shyly she found herself, on small pretences, seeking Ellen's society and speaking to her of Ralph, as though the equality in kind of their anxiety had made the nursemaid her most fitting confidant. She saw that Ellen, like herself, found her most effective diversion in Steven, and sometimes hesitated, as in honour, to deprive her of that solitary consolation at moments when she seemed most happy and courageous. And Ellen, just as in the old days at Pen House, would talk to her about Jim Moseley's love-making, and show her what a splendid fellow Jim was if only he hadn't lost his head. A strange sisterhood, she told herself, but one that made her respectful of Ellen's steadfastness and glad that she had taken her to Uffdown where she was understood.

She felt, indeed, so tenderly for Ellen, that when Ralph's first letter arrived from the Cape she took pains to conceal her elation. That precious document coloured her life for many days on end. She read it over and over again, even when she knew every word of it by heart, trying to extract from the smudged pencil-lines and Ralph's characteristic, awkward phrasing the essence of a personality that he was powerless consciously to express.

*My own sweet darling* (it ran),

*This is just a line to let you know that we've arrived in Cape-town. My squadron are a good lot of chaps, the squadron-leader hunts with the Croome, and most of the troopers are young farmers. The food was pretty bad, especially when we crossed the line, but Capetown was all right, apart from the wind. It's a bit like Italy, that coast we used to look at from Capri. I forget the name of it. Now I hear that Roberts is expected to enter Bloemfontein any day, which means, I suppose, that our lot won't see any of the fun. We're in a place called Stellenbosch, not so bad on the whole. Oak trees in the streets that the Dutch planted. They make you a bit homesick. The place is full of remounts and poor devils that have been sent back here by Kitchener, who seems to be a thruster. There's a river that looks as if it ought to hold trout, but as it's autumn here the water's low and gin-clear. I forgot to tell you that our staff-captain, a fellow named Hart, a regular, was a pal of poor Charlie Burnett. No other news. Kiss Steven for me, and all the kisses in the world for yourself, my sweet.*

*Your loving husband,*
*Ralph.*

*PS.—The news has just come through that Bobs is in Bloemfontein, and we shall go up the line for garrison duty. They say the whole show will be over in a fortnight, so you can expect me soon. I hope the men are behaving decently. I've written Bissell separately about jobs I want doing.*

It was so like him ; simple, unimaginative, confident, brave—perhaps, even, a little ordinary ; but, at this distance, all these qualities, the last included, had power to enrapture her, just because they were his. That letter had been written more than three weeks ago. Now the occupation of Bloemfontein, of which he spoke as a rumour, was an old accomplished fact. Each day Clare watched Aunt Cathie's flags moving relentlessly northward, the symbols of a physical barrier that shielded her love from harm ; for now, but for the protracted siege of Mafeking, the fighting seemed to be as good as over.

Ralph wrote as baldly and cheerfully from Bloemfontein. There seemed to be no chance of moving from that accursed spot. A rotten hole, he called it, full of dust and corrugated iron ; the nights, under canvas, were growing bitterly cold. They were killing time, he said, until French had mopped up the remainder of the Boer forces further north. Always, in his letters, the end of the war was a matter of weeks ; the phrase became so monotonous in its repetitions that she counted on it no longer. " *As soon as there's any sign of moving*," he wrote, " *I'll send you a cable. It can't be very much longer.*"

Early one afternoon the two Miss Abberleys came to call in mourning deep enough to represent the sum total of the family's losses. Their nephew, a gunner, and one of Kitchener's Stellenbosch victims, had written to them, a little jealously, about the scandals of Capetown.

" I suppose *that sort of thing*," said the elder, " is inseparable from the idea of war ; but it does seem monstrous, as Rupert says, that while we are bearing the brunt of the struggle at home and praying for our dear ones night and day, a lot of frivolous society women should have the power to pull strings—that's how it's done, my dear—and get out there, where there are no restrictions, simply to prey upon the husbands of women who are doing their duty in England."

Clare had never heard so much as a whisper of these harpies.

" My dear," said the younger Miss Abberley solemnly, " they're flooding the whole country. They stop at nothing, I'm told. Of course, they wear a Red Cross uniform. It makes me grow white with anger when I remember Florence Nightingale. They follow our poor men like the *vivandieres* that are attached to the French army—perhaps you have never seen *The Daughter of the Regiment ?*—and I'm sorry to say that several ladies from these parts are among them. I wonder if you remember a Mrs. Elvery, who took Woodcote for the hunting season two years ago ? Well, she's in Bloemfontein. She sent a postcard from there to Mrs. Merriman, an old servant of ours, who used to keep house for her."

" In Bloemfontein ? " Clare gasped.

" If I had any influence," Miss Abberley continued, " I should make a point of writing to the authorities and warning them myself. I understand that General Kitchener is a confirmed bachelor, and naturally can't be expected to notice things of that kind."

In Bloemfontein ! From the moment that she had heard the word Clare lost her head completely. Beneath the conventional politeness with which she bade the Miss Abberleys farewell her heart was beating with a renewal of wild fear ; for now the simplicity, which she had adored in Ralph, seemed to threaten all their happiness. Suppose he were " killing time " with Mrs. Elvery ?

Suddenly the atmosphere of Uffdown became stifling. She felt that she must escape from it, and from herself. Bundling her precious letters together she set off wildly up the Sling valley and into the high air of that hill top, by Brimsley, which had become one of the sacred places of their love. There, on the grassy mound of the old barrow, she sat under the sullen April sky and read her letters over and over again. She read of the dreariness of Bloemfontein, the dusty streets, the frozen nights. In all his letters, as she knew already, there was no mention of Mrs. Elvery. Bloemfontein was a small town ; it couldn't be possible that he didn't know that Mrs. Elvery was there. Why had he never mentioned her ? The answer was easy enough : to spare her feelings. But, oh, how foolish of him ! Mightn't he have known that it would have been easier for her to hear it from him than from these prurient, cackling old maids ?

M

Her doubts—she would not admit that they were doubts —all crystallized into a furious, sick hatred of the unfortunate Abberleys, who had merely performed their usual function of propagating scandalous small-talk. She wondered if they knew more ; if they had actually introduced the subject and Mrs. Elvery's name to put her on her guard, to break the sudden impact of her fall. The hill-top was sullen and desolate. Northward the smoke of Mawne and Wolverbury rose like a symbol of the war's brooding energy ; southward the dun plains fell away over the earth's curve into the seas and continents that rolled between her and Ralph. Her doubt, her desolation, came to her lips in a lonely cry, as feeble as the bleat of a lost lamb :

" Oh, Ralph, my love, my darling ! "

But, though she had almost expected a reply, nothing answered her. She knew that she had no right to an answer. This blind, unreasoning panic of hers was beneath contempt. " *Why are ye fearful, O ye of little faith ?* " she asked herself. Ashamed, humiliated and miserable beyond words, she made her way homeward ; but even when she had reached the protective shadow of Uffdown her fear was not healed, for there every shape of stone or tree accused her faithlessness, calling to mind a hundred rapturous moments that should have assured her.

Craving the support of these she crossed the lawn, where now only the black cedars were in leaf, to the grey hedge of rosemary and the orchard beyond. It was there that she and Ralph had stood and kissed on their first visit to Uffdown ; surely some influence of that sacramental occasion must cling to its air. The twisted apple-trees stood shagged with a silvery blight ; beneath them the grass of last year's aftermath straggled above the new green of spring. Clare stood there in the fading light, and gradually the inertia of that unchanging silence weighed upon her spirits and calmed them. There was no movement anywhere, save on the lawn, where Waldron, the gardener, was moving about like a hedgehog in the dusk, on some unimaginable business. Suddenly her suspended senses came to life. She called to Waldron, who answered, and began to hobble over to her. He touched his cap, and waited for her commands.

"I've just been looking at the orchard, Waldron," she said. "It seems to me most awfully untidy, with all the grass growing high like that. I shouldn't like your master to come home and find it such a perfect wilderness. You know he may come home any day now and take us by surprise. Don't you think you could scythe it or something, and make it look a bit more tidy?"

"Well, yes, m'm," said the gardener, scratching his head. "I don't see as something couldn't be done; though, rightly speaking, if you can take my meaning. . . . You see, it's like this, m'm : this here eddish, as they call it . . ."

She did not listen to him. Ellen was hurrying over the lawn with Steven in her arms. She shouldn't have carried him out like that in the damp evening air. She hurried straight up to Clare and held out a telegram.

"It's just come, ma'am. The boy's waiting for an answer. I just caught sight of you and thought it might save time."

Clare took it and opened it. Waldron paused, out of politeness, in the middle of his apologies. "You shouldn't have brought Steven out into the damp like this, Ellen," she said. And all the time she was thinking : "At last ! He's coming home. What a fool I've been ! It must have been this that made me speak to Waldron about the orchard."

"I'm sorry, ma'am, I didn't think of it," Ellen murmured humbly. "I thought, being a telegram, it must be something urgent." Her reply dwindled away to nothing ; for Clare was still straining her eyes to read :

"*Regret to inform you*," she read. "*Lieut. Hingston . . . enteric . . . Bloemfontein.*"

She was speaking:

" It doesn't matter about the orchard, Waldron. Your master died yesterday. In Bloemfontein."

She turned her back on them and moved desperately into the orchard. They looked at her bewildered, then constrained by an instinctive delicacy, went away together. Clare passed blindly into the dusk of the apple-orchard, neither knowing nor caring where her feet might carry her. Her heart was so broken that she could not feel the wet grasses that waylaid her shuddering limbs. She had no words or thoughts of her own. Only through the white-hot vacuum of her brain a single phrase went singing, madly, madly : *O sweet place, desolate in tall, wild grass. O sweet place, desolate, desolate, desolate . . .*

There, in a stupor that seemed more terrible than death, Aunt Cathie, whom Ellen had discovered glued to the evening paper, found her. Aunt Cathie could do nothing with her. Clare only wanted to be left alone.

" But you'll catch your death of cold, my darling. Do come with me," Aunt Cathie persuaded her.

She allowed herself to be led back to the house, where she lay curled up on the sofa, before the hall fire, like a sick animal. Aunt Cathie sat and watched her, with dry and dreadful eyes, far into the night.

" I want Steven," she said at last.

Aunt Cathie passed on tiptoe upstairs and took the sleep-flushed child from Ellen's arms. Poor Ellen could not sleep. She wanted Steven too. Aunt Cathie put the baby into Clare's arms. Clare hugged him and hugged him desperately, but still she could not cry. It was harrowing to see this dry and ice-bound grief. Steven was so drugged with sleep that he never opened his eyes. At last in the middle of the night, Clare spoke again :

" I can't stay here," she said. " Do you think we could go over to Pen House ? "

" Of course we could, my darling. I think you'd be happier there."

" Happy ? " Clare echoed in a strangled voice. " How can you say such a word ? It's the end of everything . . . everything."

Aunt Cathie shook her head in pitiful silence. For her also, many years ago, the world had come to an end. And yet she was still alive, its last and obstinate survivor.

# BOOK FOUR
## FATHERLESS BAIRN

# I

## BO-PEEP

ON Steven's tenth birthday his grandmother, Lady Hingston, gave him a Shetland pony. It was only two feet seven inches high, and its name was Bo-peep. From the moment on that crisp September morning, when **Auntie** Vivien rode smiling up the Uffdown drive with Bo-peep on a leading rein, the pony entered and possessed all **Steven's heart.** If he could have taken her to bed with him he would have done so; but since this privilege had been denied him in the case of Sly, the rough-haired terrier, who was much smaller than Bo-peep, he had to surrender that ambition, and Bo-peep slept, with infinitely more comfort, in a corner of the one occupied box in the empty quadrangle of stables, along with Angus, the last of the great Clydesdales, which Bissell, the coachman, and Steven's father had bred in the days before the Boer war. Angus and Bo-peep had taken to each other immediately; Steven's mother told him that this was because they were both of Scots descent.

But even if he couldn't take Bo-peep to bed with him, Steven could be present at her morning toilet. So he used to bolt his breakfast and scandalize Miss Pidgeon, his governess, in order not to miss a moment of it; and Bissell, who, in this diminished Uffdown, had time on his hands by which the pony's coat profited, would prolong the ceremony well into the hour of the Scripture lesson by an endless flood of secular information and reminiscence about the good old times when the Uffdown stables were " something like."

" In those days, Master Steven," he'd say, " the master had as pretty a string of 'unters and 'acks as you'd wish to set eyes on. Every one of them but poor old Starlight, what we 'ad to shoot, went out to Africa. Horseflesh didn't count for nothing there. And them Clydesdales of ourn ! Folks'd come from all over the country to see them . . . get over, Angus, yer durned old fool ! No, Master Steven, the times is changed, and no mistake, what with this here Lloyd George—a pro-Boer I hear he was : 'e wouldn't 'ave been pro-Boer if they'd copped 'im as they copped me ! —and them stinking motor-cars, bost them ! Now then, Bo-peep. Now then, little girl ! "

Then Bissell's voice would subside into the soft hiss of a burst hose-pipe—all the stable hose-pipes at Uffdown were tied up in rags—and Steven, watching, would surrender himself to a hypnotic mixture of sensual sedatives compounded of Bissell's homely drawl, his hissing, the stable-odours of hay, old wood and horses, and the pungent golden dust from the curry-comb, under which his heart gloated lazily on its new possession, that toy horse with the shaggy, pleasant-smelling neck, the obstinate forefeet, the muzzle of living velvet, and the big dark eyes, mysteriously blinking at him out of a head three sizes too large.

Over and over again, in these slow-spoken memories, Bissell would hark back to Steven's father, the master, as he called him ; his mother did the same ; and to each of them Steven listened with a polite distraction, his true mind being set on matters of more personal moment, such as Bo-peep, the pink-nosed ferrets in the keeper's bag, or the rat, trapped overnight in the cobwebbed loft, whose beady eyes, full of fearful hatred, stared at Sly out of the corner of its wire cage. This father, of whom everybody whispered to him so reverently, had no real existence in his mind. Unrealizable by any feat of memory, the figure took its place beside other vague mythological abstractions with which his elders bewildered him : such as God and Jesus Christ, to whom his mother had taught him to say his prayers ; Mr. Arthur Balfour, the only man (she said) that Miss Pidgeon could ever have married ; the Doctor, whose image dominated the admonitions of Aunt Cathie, or the bogey-man, who made terrible the stories of Aunt Cathie's Thirza Rudge ; shapes that inhabited a world outside his own, which was already sufficiently full to keep him busy.

That world of his, though bounded, in fact, by the narrow limits of Uffdown, Pen House, Stourford, and the hills that sheltered them, was so crowded with interests living and inanimate that, even if he had been aware of others beyond it, Steven's mind could scarcely have expanded to embrace them. As yet those parts of it which lay beyond the beech-shadowed drive were still foreign and adventurous ; but within the gates of Uffdown, the limits—saving Miss Pidgeon—of legitimate freedom, there was no person over whom he couldn't—and didn't, on occasion, assert his prerogative.

That Steven should have been spoilt was the inevitable result of the pathetic circumstances of Clare's young widow-hood, and the unusual legacy of strength and beauty which he had inherited from his father ; but with this dangerous endowment was blended the Hingston strain of wilfulness, so marked in his paternal grandmother, which people, according to the nature of their relations with her, described alternately as genius or insanity.

From the very first Steven had shown himself a passionate child. Even in babyhood, the least opposition to his wishes had thrown him into a red tempest of inarticulate rage, so ludicrous in its futility that Clare, knowing herself unable to subdue it, would stand and smile at him until the tea-cup storm was over. But, as the years went by, these passionate disturbances had become no matter for smiling. Behind them, with the growth of an intelligence precociously acute

—and, for the lack of other children's influences, mature—there lurked a stubborn and calculating will, a ruthless concentration on the attainment of his own ends that was almost frightening in so young, and withal so beautiful a creature.

On Clare herself the violence of these miniature thunderstorms rarely fell. Perhaps she was blind to them ; perhaps the unconscious workings of her love for Steven were cunning to foresee and to avoid them ; perhaps the child's own passionate affection, and the knowledge that, in the end, she was incapable of denying him anything, spared her. But the servants, from Ellen, Styles, the butler, and the admirable Bissell downward, knew all about them ; and, more than anybody, the governess, who had come to Uffdown when Steven was seven, through the recommendations of the Vicar, Mr. Pomfret.

Miss Pidgeon, familiarly known as " poor " Miss Pidgeon, was a middle-aged young woman with a record of employment in superior families, whom circumstances had reduced to an unfamiliar but never undistinguished level in the social scale. Other people might sometimes forget that Miss Pidgeon was a lady ; Miss Pidgeon never forgot. On Steven's half-holidays, when she took tea in her own room, she made it in her own silver teapot and served it on a silver tray ; and Ellen, who washed the teaspoons in the still-room afterwards and was corroborated by Mr. Styles, the butler, reported that each of them was embellished by a crest—an unquestionable pigeon—with a scroll and the motto, *Harmless as Doves*, beneath it.

When first she came to Uffdown Miss Pidgeon assured Mr. Pomfret that Steven was a sweet child though sadly undisciplined. " But we shall soon alter that," she added confidently. " The thing that disturbs me most," she added, " is the fact that, apart from the usual childish prayers, his mother appears to have given him absolutely no religious instruction. You know, Mr. Pomfret, I'm not a bigoted woman ; but when a bright child of seven has never even *heard* the story of Samuel and Eli . . ."

Mr. Pomfret checked her with an understanding smile. " It's a sad business," he assured her cheerfully. " Mrs. Hingston lost her husband early and tragically in the Boer war, and I don't think she has ever quite recovered the—er —faith which this blow shattered. Before her marriage she was—I might almost say—morbidly religious. She is still very young ; no doubt with the swing of the pendulum, or, rather, in God's good time, she will return to the—er— golden mean ; and as for Steven, you, I'm sure, Miss Pidgeon, will more than supply the deficiency."

" I'm sure I hope so," said Miss Pidgeon, glowing beneath the compliment. " I must confess," she added, " that I am rather distressed to feel the general lack of discipline at Uffdown. One might almost describe it as a disorderly house."

Mr. Pomfret flushed suddenly. " I hope, Miss Pidgeon, you will never do that," he said. " The word ' disorderly,' in that connection, has a technical significance."

What that significance might be Miss Pidgeon's respect for the cloth prevented her from enquiring. She returned to Uffdown encouraged by his approval, and conscious of a new mission in life, which was very nice for her ; and, for a little while, Steven, impressed by her tall thinness, her gold spectacles, and, above all, by the shining silver belt that fortified her solar plexus, was as sweet and mild as any dove engraved upon her teaspoons.

His sharpness amazed her ; within a few months he was as pat with Old Testament genealogies as herself. It was only when his acuteness realized that the silver belt concealed extremely vulnerable emotions that the wisdom of the serpent declared itself. From that moment, as Bissell vulgarly and perhaps maliciously put it, he had Miss Pidgeon on toast. For three years he had kept her there, tempering the fire of his mischievous tortures with periodical bastings of an emollient, an utterly disarming sweetness which softened the heart that she had hardened against him.

From the first poor Miss Pidgeon had realized that in matters of discipline she could not rely on anything but a formal support from Steven's mother. In Clare's eyes the child could do no wrong that could not be expiated by a few mild words of reproof and an orgy of forgiving kisses. Miss Pidgeon was far too proud to enlist the sympathies of servants ; and Mr. Pomfret, for all the reverence due to him, was not as serious as she would have wished a rural dean to be. She knew that her duty towards her own self-respect required that she should own herself beaten and retire in good order from Uffdown ; but making tea with a silver tea-pot in a cheap bed-sitting-room was an experience that she had known already and could not face again. At times she thought of appealing to Steven's grandmother ; but, when the moment came, the presence of Lady Hingston was so overpowering, the challenge in her black eyes so scornful that all Miss Pidgeon's fine determinations shrank into a little frozen lump beneath the centre buckle of her waistband. In any case, she consoled herself afterwards, whatever else she might be, Lady Hingston wasn't a lady, and wouldn't have understood her.

As a last resort, with proud and shameful tears, she confided her troubles to Aunt Cathie. Miss Weir, as she had anticipated, listened to them in a sympathetic and ladylike way.

" I'd no idea it was as bad as that, Miss Pidgeon," she said.

" It's worse," Miss Pidgeon declared passionately. " Sometimes I can hardly restrain myself from saying that he's a devil—and then, at others, he's so sweet. I'm really very fond of him, Miss Weir. Only I can't . . . I simply can't go on like this."

" You've spoken to his mother . . . seriously ? "

" Oh, dear, yes—a thousand times.  Excuse me ; perhaps I'm exaggerating a little.  But you know yourself, Miss Weir, what Mrs. Hingston is.  Compared with you and me, she's nothing but a child herself."

" The fact of the matter is," said Aunt Cathie, " that Steven has an abnormally strong character like his grand-father, the doctor.  I'm sure there's no real evil in him . . ."

" Oh no, no real evil ! " Miss Pidgeon agreed.

" And it's equally clear that he needs the influence of *men*.  He ought to go to school."

A vision of that bed-sitting-room chilled Miss Pidgeon's heart.

" Perhaps I've been exaggerating ; I'm sure it will all come right," she ventured.  " I'm afraid it's that dreadful pony that's turned his head."

"You can leave the matter in my hands," said Aunt Cathie, decidedly, flushed with a sense of triumph that, for once, it wasn't in Lady Hingston's.  Miss Pidgeon's final attribution of the whole mischief to the demoralizing influence of Bo-peep provided her with a cause of righteous indignation with which to start her campaign.

## II

### AUNT CATHIE'S SPOKE

Two days later, Aunt Cathie, who, since the death of her old coachman Jabez, had so far compromised with the spirit of progress as to purchase a bicycle, came whizzing over from Pen House to Uffdown and launched her attack.  In the interval her mind had brooded constantly on the Shet-land pony's iniquity.  The fact that Lady Hingston had given Bo-peep to Steven would have been sufficient to damn the beast and everything connected with it in her eyes; but since these feelings were hardly a valid basis for argument, she had to find others.

"My dear Clare," she began, "I don't like to think that Steven is spending so much of his time in the stables. Of course I know that this wretched pony is a novelty and that he's bewitched by it for the moment; but we have to think of the future. The child's at an impressionable age, and the company of grooms is not a refining influence."

Clare shook her head. "My dear Aunt Cathie, Bissell's such a safe man; I don't know what I should have done without him. And he's absolutely devoted to Steven. Honestly I don't think he can come to any harm."

"I'm not thinking," Aunt Cathie maintained, "of his *physical* safety. I'm quite sure Bissell has sense enough to look after that. But you forget, my dear child, that Bissell, with all his virtues, is a coarse man who began life as a stud-groom. Their standards are very different from ours. I don't mean that Bissell would consciously set out to corrupt the child; but Steven is inquisitive; he may ask questions on unpleasant subjects, and Bissell, in all good faith, may answer them." Aunt Cathie lowered her voice: "I've been told," she said, "that more children lose their innocence through coachmen than in any other way; and I quite believe it."

She spoke so solemnly that a little wave of anxiousness ruffled Clare's serenity before she could reassure herself.

"No, no," she said at last. "You mustn't be too serious. I've every confidence in Bissell, and Steven would be devastated if he were separated from Bo-peep. It's in his blood. Steven's a manly child. The Hingstons are mad on horses. You remember Ralph."

Aunt Cathie bridled: "It passes my comprehension, Clare, how you can persist in saying that Steven's a Hingston. There's nothing Hingston about him. He grows more

like the doctor every day. All father's little tricks . . .
Thirza was only pointing out last week the way he puts his
little head on one side. It's the doctor to the life ! He's
a Weir from the top of his head to the soles of his feet.
Why," she added triumphantly, " he even has my headaches ! "

Aunt Cathie proclaimed the mournful fact as if it had the
virtue of a hall-mark ; and Clare, although she knew it only
too well, forbore to suggest that the bilious attacks that
prostrated the child descending suddenly as a thunderstorm, condemning her to sit for hours beside him in the
darkened dressing-room which had once been Ralph's, were
usually sequels to his visits to Pen House or Stourford,
where Aunt Cathie and his grandmother, in brief assertions
of their proprietary rights, each contrived to steal a march
on the other in the small animal's affections by loading his
stomach with rich and poisonous delicacies. Nobody, at
any rate, could accuse Aunt Cathie of not practising what she
preached ; and Clare, remembering her orgies of cream-
horns at Battie's, was silent.

" I know, Clare," Aunt Cathie persisted, " it's no good
my telling you all over again how I feel about Stourford.
You realize what I think, and I'm not in the habit of changing my opinions, thank heaven ! But, all the same, the
older people in the district "—the shadow of the surviving
Miss Abberley tinged her voice with offended propriety—
" do feel that Stourford is getting more vulgar every day.
What with the hundreds of thousands they made out of the
war, and the Prime Minister's staying there, and then, these
motor-cars ! I heard they had got another, bigger than
ever ; but fortunately I hadn't seen it till the other day.
I was riding quietly along the lane on my way to pay a call
on Susan Abberley when the horrid thing came hooting
and smelling round the corner in a cloud of dust, so violently
that I nearly wobbled into the ditch. I rang my bell, but

it made no difference. The *chauffeur*, or whatever they call him, gave me the most withering stare, and Lady Hingston, lolling in the *tonneau*—everything about the wretched thing is foreign !—never as much as looked at me. I suppose they expect us all to lie down flat like natives in front of a Juggernaut. Now do admit it, Clare : isn't it enough to make the poor doctor shudder in his grave ? "

" Even worse than horses, Aunt Cathie," Clare murmured.

" Now you're laughing at me ! But haven't we any more law or order in the country ? Can't we respectable, inoffensive cyclists protest against it ? Really, I don't know. I must ask Dudley Wilburn what my legal position is. Personally I always make a point of dismounting and putting my handkerchief to my nose to remind them, supposing they have any feelings of the smell and dust they're making. But that, my child, is only a symptom, as the doctor used to say, of the kind of life into which Steven will be dragged if you're not careful. A fast life, Clare ! "

" Oh, Aunt Cathie ! "

" No, no, I love you, and you're a dear good child ; but I know that that's the line of least resistance, and I don't believe you're strong enough to fight against it yourself. If only poor dear Ralph had been alive to strengthen your hand ! "

" By this time, dear Aunt Cathie, he'd have been as mad on motoring as Vivien."

" Of course you think you know more about it than I do ; but the fact remains that the Stourford people do spoil him."

" We all spoil him, my darling. You and I and Lady Hingston and Vivien and Miss Pidgeon and Thirza and everybody. You can't help spoiling him ; and I don't believe he's any the worse for it ! "

Aunt Cathie made a gracious exception :

" Not if the spoiling is your kind or mine. But as things

are, with so many influences at work, the poor child will never get any sense of direction. He's ten years old, Clare." Aunt Cathie took Clare's hand in hers. " I know you'll hate me for saying it, but you and Miss Pidgeon can't educate him between you : he needs the influence of a man, and not the influence of a man like Bissell. Poor Miss Pidgeon, I'm sure, is far too well-bred to leave you in the lurch ; but the woman's nerves are worn to shreds. Steven is too old and strong for her. She'll have to give in."

" Why ? " Clare suddenly warmed. " Has Miss Pidgeon been complaining to you ? "

" Of course she hasn't. What an idea ! " said Aunt Cathie, lying briskly.

" When did she tell you that ? " Clare persisted.

" I really don't know. Some time ago. The day before yesterday," Aunt Cathie confessed in stages, quailing before her conscience and Clare's eyes.

" Why on earth didn't she tell *me* ? "

" Because, my dear child, she knew it would be waste of time. She doesn't want to go : anyone can see that. But really it's Steven, not poor Miss Pidgeon, who must be considered . . ."

" How cruel these old maids are," Clare thought.

" . . . and, in any case," Aunt Cathie continued, " her feelings are one of the disguises of Providence. It's really time that Steven went to school."

Once she had shuddered at it ; but the word had an ominous sound in Clare's ears. Of late she had heard it so often that, like any terror endlessly repeated, it had lost some of its power to frighten her.

" I know that you're right," she said. " Sooner or later it's got to come. Lady Hingston was only talking about it last week."

" Oh, *was* she ? " Aunt Cathie answered hastily. " No doubt she has some new, big, fashionable ideas on the subject. Don't think for a moment I mean *her* kind of school, Clare. Now, Dudley Wilburn . . ."

" Thank you for reminding me ; he's dining here to-night on his way back from Worcester Assizes. I'd quite forgotten. But you mustn't be unjust to her, Aunt Cathie. They want me to send him to Cheam . . . preparatory for Eton, you know."

" I know nothing of the sort." Aunt Cathie hastened to disown acquaintanceship with anything that was common knowledge at Stourford. " The doctor," she continued, " was at Rugby under the father of Mr. Matthew Arnold. By all accounts that's a much more manly school. A healthier situation, too, and so much nearer home," she added persuasively. " That afternoon when Lady Hingston nearly ran me down Miss Abberley was telling me that in these days all kinds of rich and vulgar people send their sons to Eton ; in fact, it hasn't anything like the distinction it had at the time when the Duke of Wellington spoke so nicely about the playing-fields, which everybody says are generally under water. Clare, you're too gentle, you let these people come over you. Now Dudley Wilburn . . ."

Her voice died away and was lost in a confidential under-tone.

Yes, Dudley Wilburn ! Clare thought. Whenever it wasn't the doctor, it was Dudley Wilburn : in her private pantheon Aunt Cathie must always erect some male idol to whose oracle all the problems of life should be submitted ; and though the monitory cult of " the doctor " still formed the basis of her religion, the new revelation of his successor was now more often quoted. Whenever she expounded the gospel according to Dudley, Aunt Cathie glowed with a fierce and righteous conviction. As Clare saw her now, the autumnal firelight playing on her weathered cheeks, illuminating the furrow that the agony of innumerable headaches had graved, like a scar, between her brows, and the undeniable moustache that had replaced the shadow that once bloomed her upper lip, she couldn't suppress a vague wonder at the transformation which twelve years had wrought in the appearance of the Aunt Cathie whom she remembered in her childhood. That sanguine, prepotent figure had somehow reached another stage in the process of desiccation which finally must convert her into a little withered, tiresome old woman. Perhaps it was the tweed "cycling costume," with its bunched Norfolk jacket and mannish collar and tie, which Aunt Cathie had adopted, together with the surviving Miss Abberley, that made her look as if she had shrunk. Certainly, except in those moments when the thought of Lady Hingston stiffened her, she was softer and kinder now than she had ever been. And her devotion to Steven, dear thing, was strangely touching.

"So that," Aunt Cathie ended triumphantly, "is the considered opinion of a sane, impartial mind."

Silence. "You see, Aunt Cathie, Ralph was at Eton," Clare heard herself reply. "So, somehow, it seems natural . . ."

"My darling Clare," she answered, with disarming tenderness, "Steven is your own child; but sometimes I can't help feeling he's a little mine as well. I think I ought to tell you that I've altered my will. Dudley Wilburn very kindly helped me to do so the other day; a codicil, I think they call it. Of course I realize that both of you are quite well provided for; but that makes no difference to the sentiment, and so I've left everything to Steven."

"Oh, dear, dear Aunt Cathie, that's very sweet of you."

"Well, we can't expect to live for ever, my darling, and you and Steven are all I have in the world. Poor old Thirza's failing very fast." She pursed the shadowed lip determinedly, distrustful of emotion. "Of course there won't be very much," she went on: "Just Pen House and my little income and all the doctor's things—I couldn't bear to feel that those might fall into the hands of strangers; he was so particular about them."

" I wish you wouldn't think of such things, my dear; I'm sure you needn't," Clare told her.

Aunt Cathie smiled courageously and shook her head, for she knew better. " Now I must be trotting," she said. " No, no, of course, you mustn't. I'm still quite capable of looking after myself. No, Clare, I won't allow it. Kiss Steven for me. I do hope I shan't meet any more of those dreadful motor-cars."

## III

### SIMPLICES SICUT COLUMBÆ

SHE went. From the drawing-room window Clare watched the red eye of Aunt Cathie's lamp turn the corner of the drive. In the outer stillness she heard the bicycle bell tinkle; for although the drive was certainly, and the lanes most probably, empty, she knew that Aunt Cathie would go on ringing it all the way back to Wychbury.

As she left the window, and sat down gazing at the fire a restlessness stole over her. Such moods were rare, but this one was of a kind that she could not easily overcome, though she despised herself for giving way to it. She turned on the light; but even the familiar aspect of Annabel Ombersley's room could not restore her. There was something unquiet and threatening in the air that evening which had crept into it with her sudden realization of the physical change in Aunt Cathie and the ominous mention of Aunt Cathie's will. As she sat before the fire, with her hands to her eyes, she felt suddenly, unreasonably, desperately lonely; and to this unaccountable mood was added the prospect of the more definite loneliness which must fall on her when Steven went away to school. Perhaps that was the real explanation of all her discomfort ; the central problem which she had shirked but must now face.

" It isn't the first time I've been lonely," she told herself, " and yet, so far, I've always been able to get over it."

Seeking for consoling precedents she remembered the days when first she had come back from Pen House to Uffdown after Ralph's death. Those, surely, had been of a deeper loneliness than any other she was likely to encounter in life, and yet she had survived them. She remembered the determination—at this distance rather pathetic—with which she had set her life in order. " He loved Uffdown," she had told herself, " so now it is my duty to keep everything just as he would have wished it when he was alive until the day when Steven is old enough to take his place." And in this piety she had found a vocation that had filled her mind and absorbed her body's activities.

At first she had been transported by the idea of keeping the land and the stables running exactly as Ralph had planned them ; his desk in the gun-room was full of notes and account-books in which the last entries of his boyish hand seemed to have been blotted only yesterday ; but as she came to deal with them, even when the admirable Bissell returned from the war, she found that she was losing money heavily for the sake of a sentiment. The figures in her bank-book frightened her ; for Ralph had always laughed at her bad business head and excluded her from this part of their life.

One day, in a panic, she had called in Sir Joseph Hingston, who showed her, in a few moments, her own incapacity.

" You see, my dear," he explained, " you've been trying to do what even a man can only accomplish with special aptitude and training. Bissell may very well be an excellent stud-groom and Watkins an admirable bailiff ; but you can't run dairies and stud farms without the management being in the hands of the man who foots the bill. As it happens there's no harm done ; there's no reason why you shouldn't pay for this expensive hobby if you want to ; but if you imagine you can make a success of it, you're mistaken ; and the anxiety of making a failure of it will turn you grey in no time, which is the very last thing we want."

" I know you're right ; but I must *do* something," she pleaded.

" If you did properly half what you've been doing now you'd have your hands full," he assured her. He glanced at her, charitably amused. " There's the house and the garden. . . . Bless my soul, they're both big enough ! What about making a rockery ? I'll send you over some alpines from Stourford."

Then, for his thoughts were already back in the smoke of Wolverbury, he put his hand in his breast-pocket absent-mindedly and wrote her a cheque, this action being his habitual panacea for all human ills.

From that moment, her career as the complete landowner frustrated, she had concentrated her energies into a narrower sphere. The alpines duly arrived from Stourford ; the garden was planned and replanned ; between the sandstone boulders of the rockery in spring poured her cascades of aubretia and sweet alyssum ; in sheltered crevices gentian, starch-hyacinth and chinodoxa mocked with their living blue the surly Midland winter ; within the box-edged borders, beyond the rosemary hedge of such sweet memory, new generations of roses bloomed and fell in June ; and Ernest, Dudley Wilburn's bachelor brother, infected her with the passion for carnations which had given him his nickname in the North Bromwich clubs.

A sweet, a leisurely, an engrossing duty ; for no garden that was ever planted has yet been brought to the gardener's ideas of perfection. In every season of the year the birth of some shy, new, lovely creature claimed her care and repaid it a hundredfold. There was something in the gentleness of these new charges, their dependence, their rewarding gratitude, that softened the passage of seasons and of years by a promise always to be fulfilled. As Clare knelt beside them, the trowel grasped in the clumsy fingers of her coarse gardening-gloves, listening to the laughter of Steven that echoed, as he played, from those old walls, or guessing by some maternal seventh sense that he was standing with held breath beside her, she sometimes lost all consciousness of time, and only knew that she was alive and happy. These green things grew as Steven himself was growing, continually, imperceptibly. Sufficient for each day was its own miracle.

It was not that she had forgotten Ralph : only that his memory, as it grew more indefinite, had diffused itself into a faded yet mellower benevolence ; so that often when she returned to the house, with Steven hanging and chattering on her arm, the gallant Sargent portrait seemed to smile down upon them both with the friendly gaiety of that eternal youth in which its features had been fixed, and Clare, meeting that frank and boyish gaze, could smile back with her pride in Steven, and without tears.

No, no, she told herself as she sat and gazed into the fire that evening ; in all those years, except the very first, most dreadful ones, she'd never been really lonely. She mustn't allow herself to give way ; Ralph would be ashamed of her. To-morrow she must plant those new bulbs—babianas, were they ?—that Sir Joseph had sent her ; a present from one of his engineering friends in Johannesburg. South Africa . . . Strange how this evening, wherever she turned her thoughts by way of escape, they should run up against these reminders of time and of mortality ! No, never lonely, she affirmed, and now the worst was over, long ago.

" It's right and necessary that he should go to school," she told herself. A manly school, as Aunt Cathie said. Manly : the word was just ; yet it spelt the beginning of the end. From the first moment of his going Steven would be lost to her. Ten years. They had passed like a short dream ; already the eleventh was hurrying on its way. In another ten, another space of dreaming, he would be a man, a lover, married perhaps. And that was a woman's life, she told herself. So short ! Was there nothing more ?

The clock in the hall, the Wolverbury work-people's wedding-present, rehearsed the Westminster chimes, then paused, and solemnly tolled six. It seemed to her that this lifeless piece of machinery was signalling a definite stage in her life : a halting place—alas, there was no halting !— rather the beginning of a new phase. Six o'clock. In another two minutes at most Steven would be with her demanding the attentions of that precious hour before bedtime to which he looked forward all day. Sometimes she must read to him, sometimes tell him stories, with the growing weight of his body pressed on hers, of which it never more surely seemed a part. Sometimes he would command her to play to him : all through his life she had hoped to make her music part of him as well, the best of all music blended into the fibre of his mind. She knew that his ear was good, for often they would sing the Scott-Gatty nursery-songs together, herself with lowered voice listening for the clear, thin notes of his. Like a little lamb, a baby thrush, she thought ; and when he took his breaths in the wrong places she could have eaten him all up. Her lips smiled as she thought of it.

*Found in the garden, dead in . . . his beauty.*
   *Ah, that a lin . . . net should die in the . . . Spring !*

Children shouldn't be taught to sing about death !

*Come out, dear Dolly, and . . . make a snow . . . man !*

That was better. Ten years . . . " I'm actually twenty-nine," she thought : " much, much older than Ralph was when he left me, and yet, in spirit, I'm not so very much older than Steven—certainly very little older than when I left St. Monica's." Was it possible that human beings never realized when they grew old ? Did that account for Aunt Cathie's pathetic sprightliness. " In another ten years." she thought, " I shall be as old as Aunt Cathie used to be, and in a few more, probably, I shall have a moustache like hers. Vivien has one already, and Vivien's not much older than me. I hardly ever see dear Vivien now. Vivien's like Ralph was ; she has this passion for breeding things— Clydesdales or retrievers, it's all the same. If only she'd married, as she could have done a dozen times, all that precious energy wouldn't be wasted on those foolish puppies, even though they are darlings at first."

That school business. . . . However far it might wander, her mind returned to it. " I'm not going to be bullied," she told herself, " by Mother Hingston or Aunt Cathie or anyone else. I shall decide by myself ; or if I ask anyone's advice, it shall be Dudley Wilburn's. Yes, that is better. I think I'll get it over and speak to him to-night after dinner."

The idea of submitting her problem to Wilburn, even though it couldn't mitigate the ache inherent in it, was consoling and enabled her to dismiss it, for a moment, from her mind. As one of the trustees under her husband's will he usually made a point of calling in at Uffdown to see her whenever business took him to Wychbury. All through the years of her widowhood, his tact, his understanding, his keen but wholly unobtrusive interest in her affairs had established him, almost without her knowing it, in a position only a little less oracular than that which he occupied in Aunt Cathie's eyes ; and even though she smiled at Aunt Cathie's paroxysms of hero-worship their steady persistence had an effect of suggestion on her mind. Whenever she found herself in danger of being torn to pieces between the opposing forces of Stourford and Pen House, the way of least resistance and satisfaction seemed to lead her in the direction of this benevolent neutral of whom both sides approved. Little by little she had come to rely, far more than she suspected, upon his judgment, not only because he offered her a way of escape, but because the solid but kindly impassivity of his professional manner, which, in the old days at Pen House, had been sufficient to impress her grandfather, had now settled into a composure so judicial that it seemed natural to accept his judgments with complete confidence in their wisdom and impartiality.

That Clare, in her lonely dependence, should have found Wilburn impressive was not surprising; for time, and the nature of his profession, which carried with it the constant obligation of prudence, level-headedness, and secrecy, had confirmed and emphasized the physical characteristics which had made his early reputation.

The appearance of Dudley Wilburn, at forty-six, was everything which that of a prominent family lawyer should be. His tall and sturdy figure had thickened into middle-age; with no less strength, it had gained a certain solidity which made his movements more calculated. His face, always clean-shaven, had scarcely aged at all, though the furrows of slow, deliberate concentration added a new square-ness to a mouth which had always seemed determined, and a powerful chin. His hair, which had receded slightly to the brow's advantage, was still coarse and vigorous, but of an iron-grey that made more striking, by contrast, the steady light in his eyes. An Atlas, who carried on his shoulders half the cares of the North Bromwich business community, yet bore them so easily and with such reserves of strength that fear and solicitude both gave way to admiration.

It was the consciousness of these matters, weighty beyond all comparison with the small domestic problems that troubled her, that made Clare shy and diffident of consulting Wilburn when he came to Uffdown. The memory of his predominant position at Pen House had made her always a little afraid of him ; yet, as soon as the ice of his formal arrival was broken and she had grown used to the measured scrutiny of Wilburn's eyes, she invariably took courage, only to find him more simple, more interested, more sympathetic than any of her other advisers. Over and over again she marvelled at his patience, his gentleness. Indeed, but for the gratuitous sense of triumph the admission would have given to Aunt Cathie, who, on the strength of it, would have ridden over her as ruthlessly as Lady Hingston's Juggernaut, Clare would have been ready to confess her belief in the oracle's validity as implicitly as Aunt Cathie herself.

The idea of submitting the problem of Steven to Wilburn's judgment was so reassuring that she had almost forgotten Steven himself. She bent down and looked at her watch in the firelight. It was ten past six. Whatever excitements detained him Steven was never late for this one, precious hour. Her old discomfort took a new and sinister shape. Where was he ? What had happened to him ? Monstrous ideas of accidents filled her mind. As she approached the door the turning of the handle brought a reflux of blood to her fluttered heart.

" Why, there you are ! " she cried. " My darling, wherever have you been ? "

## IV

### PRUDENTES UT SERPENTES

THE door opened. It was not Steven.

" Oh, Miss Pidgeon," Clare said, " you quite startled me ! Haven't you finished tea ? It's nearly a quarter-past six."

" We have had no tea : I have put Steven in his bedroom,"

Miss Pidgeon answered with a tremulous voice. " I have locked him in his bedroom, Mrs. Hingston. Here is the key. I think you had better take it and deal with him. I can do no more . . ." She thrust the bedroom key into Clare's hand.

Her voice was so strained that Clare herself was genuinely distressed by it. She took Miss Pidgeon's arm and closed the door gently behind her.

" Do come in and sit down," she said, " and tell me all about it. I'd no idea that you'd been so unhappy. If I'd known, I shouldn't have allowed it. Why, your hand's quite cold ! Come nearer to the fire."

Miss Pidgeon obeyed her in silence. She sat down, upright, in an easy chair, her cold hands clasped before her ; the silver plates of her belt expanded and closed like the armour of a rhinoceros with her shallow, rapid breathing ; behind her spectacles tears glimmered in the firelight.

" I think," she said, " that Steven has completely lost his head."

" What do you mean, Miss Pidgeon ? "

" I mean," said Miss Pidgeon, marking each adjective with a nervous movement of her clasped hands, " I mean that he is naughty, disobedient, wilful, wicked, and profane."

" Profane ? "

" Oh dear, Mrs. Hingston, don't let us go into details. I don't think I can bear to do so. My nerves have been so on edge that if I talk about it I'm sure I shall break down. You've been awfully sweet to me ; nobody could have been sweeter ; but, after this evening, I don't feel I can stay here another day. If you can find some other lady to look after him I shall be much obliged."

Her lips quivered like a guinea-pig's ; she put her hands to her eyes.

" My dear Miss Pidgeon," Clare said, " you mustn't upset yourself. Try to be calm, and tell me exactly what happened. I must confess that I hadn't noticed anything wrong myself."

"Oh no, you wouldn't," said Miss Pidgeon passionately. "He's too clever. He takes good care of that. If you scold him now, he'll be as sweet as honey. You'll find him more innocent than a baby, with those blue eyes ; and yet I can tell you, all the time, his thoughts are the thoughts of a grown man."

"Yes ? " Clare encouraged her, softly.

"I can't possibly keep pace with him," Miss Pidgeon went on. "The moment my eyes leave him he disappears and I have to spend hours and hours in hunting for him. It's so humiliating for a woman in my position to go round asking the servants ten times a day if they've seen him. Usually he finds his way to the stables—I think the men encourage him. This evening, when tea had been spoiling on the schoolroom table for half an hour, I went to search for him and found him hiding in the loft. I knew he was there because the dog barked. And when I called to him to come down . . ." Miss Pidgeon stopped, speechless with agitation, then, gulping, recovered herself: "I've been called a fool before, Mrs. Hingston, not only by him ; and perhaps, in some people's eyes, I am one. If I weren't, I shouldn't have put up with this so long. I've swallowed many insults of one kind and another in my life. But never, never, *never* before, Mrs. Hingston, have I been called a silly old bitch ! "

Miss Pidgeon shivered as she pronounced the awful word, and Clare, for all her genuine concern, found it difficult to suppress a smile. Obviously there was very little to be said. She rose, and patted Miss Pidgeon's shoulder.

"Of course that was very wrong of him," she said. "You'd better stay here quietly and get warm while I go and deal with him."

She left Miss Pidgeon sitting as stiffly as though she had

been frozen, and went slowly upstairs. The Sargent portrait surveyed her with humorous, quizzical eyes, as though it knew that she had no clear idea of what she was going to say to Steven. One thing, at least, was clear : the little monkey, by this last outrage, had unconsciously forced her hand. Providentially, too, in a way ; for, as Aunt Cathie had cunningly suggested, Miss Pidgeon's voluntary retirement would save her from the evasive awkwardness of a dismissal. " What cowards we are ! " she thought ; and then : " Of course I shall have to give her a handsome present when she goes." Stourford : Sir Joseph's cheque-book panacea !

She made her way through her own bedroom to Steven's door. The monkey had bolted it on his own side.

" Steven," she called. " Open the door at once."

No answer.

" Steven ! Open the door ! Obey me ! "

Strange that the resistance of so small a creature should flutter her like this ! A moment before she had been smiling patronizingly at Miss Pidgeon's agitation. She heard his small bare feet patter over the wooden floor. He opened the door, in his ridiculous striped pyjamas, and stood his ground like a Highland bull-calf, the fair hair tousled over his determined eyes. He was so small, so stubborn, that the position was almost comical. She had to force herself to see no humour in it.

He was obstinately silent. She had seen that look in Ralph's eyes when Starlight refused a jump.

" Miss Pidgeon tells me that you've been wickedly rude to her," she said.

" Then Miss Pidgeon's a sneak," said Steven.

" She's nothing of the sort, Steven. She's your governess, and it's your duty to obey her and behave properly. What were you doing in the stables at tea-time."

" I was watching Bo-peep have her tea first. Everybody ought to be kind to animals "

"You weren't kind to Miss Pidgeon, were you? And you weren't in the stable either. You were up in the loft. I've told you a hundred times that those stairs aren't safe."

"As a matter of fact," he explained, "there was a rat there. Sly heard it and went up first; so I *had* to go and protect her."

"Oh no, you didn't. You know quite well that Sly can look after herself. You were hiding from Miss Pidgeon. I can't allow you to do things like that, Steven. It's very naughty of you. I'm very glad that Miss Pidgeon sent you to bed without your tea. You deserved it."

"I wasn't hungry, thank you, mummy, so it was all right. May I come down now?"

"Most certainly not. I haven't finished talking to you yet. When Miss Pidgeon found you in the loft you refused to come down and called her a most dreadful name."

"I'm *sure* she's mistaken, mummy." A bland, angelic innocence filled Steven's eyes. "I can't think what you mean."

"Now, Steven, it's no good gazing at me like that. You know quite well that you're not telling the truth, which makes it worse than ever. You'd better think again, before I get more angry with you. Think carefully. You called her a silly old . . ."

"Oh, *that*, mummy. Of course I remember. I was speaking to Sly, not to Miss Pidgeon."

"Steven, Steven, you musn't tell lies like this, or I can't possibly love you."

"You see, dearest," he explained, "she had her nose in a little hole in the boards and was scratching away like mad. It *was* silly of her, mum, and she *is* an old bitch."

"No, Steven, I don't believe you."

"She is, mum, truly. You ask Bissell if she isn't."

"You know quite well that I don't mean that, Steven. In any case, ' bitch ' is a horrible, disgraceful word."

" Why, mum ?  It sounds all right."

" And in any case, you're only making excuses.  You must apologize to Miss Pidgeon, and if ever I hear of you using that word again I shall punish you most severely.  Do you understand ? "

" I suppose I do, mum," he answered sullenly.  Then he pounced on her like a small whirlwind and clung to her. " Now I may kiss you, mayn't I ? " he whispered.

In a flush of emotion that masked her sense of cowardice she picked him up and kissed him.  He snuggled his soft cheek against hers.

" And now, mum," he whispered again, in conscious, babyish tones, " mayn't I come down into the drawing-room, just as I am ?  Only for ten minutes, mummy darling ? "

The thought of poor Miss Pidgeon, whom her conscience showed her still sitting in anguish before the drawing-room fire, made Clare refuse when she would gladly have yielded.

" No, no, it's far too late," she said, " and, besides, you're still in disgrace, until you've apologized to Miss Pidgeon."

" You might ring for her," he suggested, lordily.  " Then I could get it over."

Clare hid a smile.  " You'd better get back to bed," she said.  " I've no more time to waste on you ; I've got to dress for dinner."

" In that case I'd better watch you dress," he said.

" I oughtn't really to let you ; but if you'll promise to be good . . ."

" Of course I will, darling."

He quickly established himself at the foot of her bed, and as she wrapped the golden eiderdown about his shoulders she thought how little and precious his body was, nestled, like that of a small, warm-blooded animal, inside the billowy silk, and had to hug him and kiss him again, unasked ; and Steven, knowing that he had got round her and was forgiven, became all sweetness and gentleness incarnate, watching her in silence as she stood, like a little girl, in her chemise, and swept the swishing comb through her dark hair.

That evening, out of compliment to Wilburn and her own beauty, which in this moment of reconciliation, seemed more pleasing than usual to her eyes, she had chosen a flounced dinner-frock of primrose taffetas with a band of cherry-coloured velvet narrowing the waist. It gave her joy to wear it ; for at Uffdown, of late years, her pretty clothes had been wasted on the eyes of servants. The end of the skirmish with Steven and Miss Pidgeon had left her in a state of relieved excitement, in which she was glad to see her slim shape flash across the surface of the oval Chippendale mirror ; an old perfume of youth seemed to envelop her. When she had given the last bloom to her toilet and turned to put Steven to bed, she found him staring at her with wide blue eyes.

" Oh, mum, how lovely you are ! " he said.

The spontaneity of the compliment made her laugh.

" You never say pretty things like that to poor Miss Pidgeon."

" But then she *isn't*," he answered, with irrefutable logic.

" Come along then and kiss me good-night," she said, " because mother won't be able to come up after dinner to-night."

" Why won't you, mum ? " he asked reluctantly.

" Because somebody's coming to dinner."

" Who's coming ? " he persisted.

" Mr. Wilburn. Now hurry up, darling."

" Mr. Wilburn ? Oh, mummy ! "

" Why, what's the matter ? "

" I don't like him, mum, really."

" Oh, Steven, don't be silly. Come along."

" He *looks* at me so."

" Well, there's no reason why he shouldn't look at you if he wants to."

" No "—doubtfully—" I suppose there isn't. But I *don't* like him."

She smiled : " I suppose you're shy. That's not like you, Steven."

" When he comes to dinner, mum, you're all different."

" Ridiculous child ! Of course I'm not."

" And you don't kiss me good-night."

" You don't deserve it this evening, after being so naughty. I suppose I shall have to carry you to bed. Be quick."

" No. I don't want you to carry me. I'm too old. Oh, I *do* wish he wasn't coming."

" Steven, Steven, I do believe you're jealous ! "

She put her arm round him and shepherded him to bed. He was silent ; a puzzled unhappiness clouded his eyes. Her heart was between laughing and crying at his quaint unreasonableness ; all her emotions were very near to the surface that evening.

" Now turn over and go to sleep at once," she whispered with her lips on his, " and promise me that when you wake up to-morrow you'll be mother's good boy. Promise ? "

And she gave him a kiss that was longer than any lover's.

## V

### *DEUS EX MACHINA*

WILBURN awaited her in the chair where she had left Miss Pidgeon freezing an hour before. Clare came into the room so lightly that he didn't hear her ; but the downward tilted mirror over the mantelpiece showed her his face, so lined, so heavily serious in the flicker of firelight that the sight of it checked the flood of her happiness, brimmed to overflowing with Steven's kiss. In a moment her gay mood faltered, the joy of her elegance lost its brightness ; her high spirits fluttered earthward like a newly-hatched butterfly whose blooms are dashed by rain. That mirrored face showed such anxiety that her own elation seemed a selfish impertinence. She wondered what had distressed him and wished that she might share his trouble. Yet, when he rose to greet her, it seemed as if the firelight had played a trick on his eyes ; his hand-clasp was as firm, his slow smile as kindly and serene as ever ; his serious eyes were quick to notice her brilliant dress.

" Why, Clare," he said, " I needn't ask you how you are. You're very beautiful to-night. Am I to flatter myself that all this magnificence is in honour of me ? If it is, I'm afraid I can't live up to it. Turn round, and let me look at you."

She obeyed him, like a little girl displaying her party-frock, smiling over her shoulder into his judicial eyes. Even now she couldn't be quite sure of him ; a little, timid doubt underlay her innocent coquetry, and begged for his approval.

" Quite overwhelming." He gave her a mocking bow. " What is the matter with you this evening ? I've never seen you look better in my life."

" What is the matter with *you*, Dudley ? " she answered. " I saw you before you caught sight of me. There's something wrong. It's very sweet and brave of you to pretend there isn't ; but between old friends like ourselves . . ."

He stopped her with a laugh. " My dear Clare, you're far too clever. Also, I'm far too fond of you, and far too tactful by habit, to dream of asking you to give me your professional opinion on all the briefs that I've prepared for the assizes. Of course I know that you're an authority on Company Law. Perhaps, after dinner, you'll spare me five minutes of serious . . ."

" Ah, now you're laughing at me," she broke in. " I don't feel like being teased to-night. I want five serious minutes with you as well. But that can wait till after dinner too. Don't let's be serious just yet. So I *was* mistaken ? Do tell me, Dudley, your face quite worried me."

" My dear child," he smiled, " if you only knew what a fag these blessed assizes are, with a crotchety judge and the Shirehall full of the smell of hops ! "

" So it wasn't anything special after all ? " She laid her hand on his arm.

The butler's announcement that dinner was served absolved him from the duty of answering. He stepped aside to give her passage to the door, and by the time they were seated in the red-lighted isolation of the dinner-table the question was forgotten and Clare found herself talking of matters less intense. Under the comforting influence of his whisky-and-soda Wilburn's detachment resumed its usual benevolence and the shadow that had fallen between them lifted. Consoling herself for the remains of her concern Clare remembered that he was always what Ralph would have called a slow starter ; that, however often or rarely they met, Wilburn's reserve made him seem like a stranger at first—an obstacle that made it all the more delightful when time discovered him to be unchanged.

For half an hour they talked of happy, unimportant things ; old memories and present gossips of Clare's narrow world. She told him Aunt Cathie's story of the new Hingston juggernaut. He laughed, but behind his laughter a look of pain or concentration showed itself in his eyes at the mention of Aunt Cathie's name, so that when she went babbling on he seemed no longer to be listening to her. Then, suddenly, he changed the subject.

" We wanted to ask each other something, Clare." he said. " Five minutes, wasn't it ? Time's getting on, so, as a lady, I think you'd better have first go."

He pushed back his chair and sat looking at her as though he were behind his office desk at North Bromwich, and Clare's own face grew serious.

" It's Steven," she said. " You know we've never talked of this before ; but now, I think, something will have to be done with him. Aunt Cathie and his grandmother, for once, are in agreement. They both say that he ought to go to school. Of course I can't bear the thought of it ; but I suppose they're right. I know I spoil him ; I simply can't help it. But I mustn't go on spoiling him for ever : it wouldn't be fair."

Wilburn nodded slowly. " Let me see. . . . How old is he ? "

" Ten . . . and two months. Time passes so quickly."

" Terribly quickly. Nobody realizes that, Clare, more than I do. Of course he's been doing lessons of some kind with Miss What-d'you-call-her ? "

' Miss Pidgeon. But Steven carries far too many guns for her. He's dreadfully precocious and clever. That's part of the trouble. This evening Miss Pidgeon gave me notice : the poor thing wouldn't have done that unless she felt pretty strongly."

" Why did she give notice ? "

Clare laughed softly as the vision of Miss Pidgeon's indignation rose before her eyes. " Steven was quite disgraceful : he called her a bitch."

And Wilburn's serious mouth was switched into a smile : " Of all the epithets I might have thought of for Miss Pidgeon I think that's one of the last I should have chosen."

" I'm afraid it's Bissell. Lady Hingston gave him a pony. Aunt Cathie says it's all her fault."

" Of course she does. But I think they're both right about the other matter : school, I mean."

" I knew you would," Clare told him. " I wonder if you would make some enquiries for me."

" I'll begin them to-morrow."

" You see, Dudley," she went on, " as usual I'm between two fires, and you're so beautifully neutral. If I sent Steven to some place preparatory for Rugby, where the doctor went, his grandmother would be indignant. And if I sent him to Cheam, I should never hear the last of it from poor Aunt Cathie. You see she thinks Steven is absolutely her property. She was telling me only this afternoon about the will that you'd made for her."

" Yes." Once again that painful look came into Wilburn's eyes. He sat staring in front of him for a moment of distressful silence in which all the comfort that Clare had gathered from him vanished.

" I suppose I'd better tell you what's happened, Clare,' he said.

He paused, as though seeking for words in which to put his announcement, and Clare, hanging uncomfortably on his silence, wondered what was coming. Among these fantastic speculations one outbid all others : Wilburn was going to marry Aunt Cathie ! Strange, after all these years ; strange, and for some inexplicable reason disquieting. Yet, why should he hesitate to tell her ? His voice, with a queer, emotional hardness, interrupted her surmises :

" The truth of the matter is that Aunt Cathie has nothing to leave him. I only heard of it this evening : it must have happened about the time when she was with you. All your Aunt Cathie's money is in the Sedgebury Main. The old man put it there on my advice. And the Sedgebury Main's under water, done for."

Clare gasped : " The Sedgebury Main ? I can't believe it. We were always told that nothing could be safer. You mean it's failed ? I don't think I understand."

" I mean what I say," he answered impatiently. " Water. Suddenly. It came like a flood. It's the biggest mining disaster we've had in the district for years. God knows how many lives and half a million of money swamped in an hour. Of course we don't know the worst or the best of it yet. The evening paper in Worcester had the first report."

" They can't do anything ? "

" Not with water on this scale. It's up to the higher levels already ; billions of tons of it. It isn't easy to realize at first. I'm hard hit myself, and so are most of my friends ; but it's the little people like your Aunt Cathie who'll suffer most. At this moment, apart from her balance in the bank and Pen House, the poor soul hasn't a farthing in the world. Do you know, Clare, when I heard the news in Worcester, she was the first person I thought of ? I feel that I'm responsible. It was I who persuaded the old man to go into Sedgebury Main. He fought against it. I can remember him as if it was yesterday. ' I like to see my money on the top of the earth ' : that's what he said. Well, he was right. We put our money on Furnival. Furnival's a big man ; I still believe in him ; but Furnival can't fight against the waters that are under the earth."

For a moment they gazed at each other in silence. No wonder he looked worried, Clare thought. What a light-headed little fool he must have thought her in her primrose frock ! And poor Aunt Cathie . . . More pathetic than any vision of piteous drowned bodies floating in grimy abysses or widows wailing at the pit-head was that of Aunt Cathie pedalling back to Wychbury through the dark lanes with her bicycle-bell tingling all the time for company, and, in her heart, the triumph of having left her little fortune to Steven. For Clare that was the intimate, the representative tragedy in which the vaster implications of the unknown were concentrated and made real.

" Oh, the poor darling," she cried. " It was so little, Dudley, and she thought so much of it ; she was so proud of having been able to leave her money to Steven. Dudley, can't we keep it from her ? "

" No, no, my dear. She reads the papers. She'll find it in the evening edition of the *Courier*—probably much exaggerated. I'm afraid she'll have seen it by now. That's why I want to leave you early, Clare. I should like to call at Pen House and make the best of it on my way home."

" Yes, yes. Of course you must do that. But, Dudley, do you think she'll realize at once what it means ? Is there any real reason why she should know about her losses ? Couldn't we . . ."

He shook his head. In her urgency Clare laid her hand upon his arm. " Of course, it's easy ! " she cried. " Why didn't I think of it before ? I know dreadfully little about these things, but I have money, haven't I ? All the money that's paid into the bank every quarter : I'm sure I don't spend half of it. All Aunt Cathie's business is in your hands, isn't it ? " He nodded. " Then, of course, it's as easy as can be. Listen : I'll tell you what happened. Last month, or the month before—you'll have to be careful about dates—you sold out all Aunt Cathie's Sedgebury Main. You sold them to me at the market price ; although, of course, Aunt Cathie must never know who bought them. If I haven't enough money in the bank to pay for them, you must lend me some—you will trust me, won't you ?—and the beauty of it is, you see, that nobody will be any the worse for it. All my money is for Steven, and anything that I pay to Aunt Cathie will come back to him. Isn't that splendid ? Doesn't it work out wonderfully ? "

He stood, smiling gravely at her passionate illogicality, and, all the time, his mind was haunted by memories of another scene : the evening when he had read the doctor's will at Pen House ; the face of Aunt Cathie, shrunken and shattered, in the doctor's chair ; the suffering voice pleading for Clare as Clare now pleaded for her.

" Nobody need know a word about it but you and me. Isn't that so ? "

The voice was Clare's ; but the words were Aunt Cathie's, reshaping themselves like phantoms that can only take form in ether charged by present human emotion. As ghosts his own words returned to answer hers, forming themselves automatically on his lips like those of an actor which come, without thought, to answer the cue in a part which he has played and forgotten many years before :

" Of course it's quite possible."

" And so easy," she persisted.

He laughed. " Well, hardly that. You speak as if altering dates and cooking accounts were part of my ordinary routine of business. You don't appear to realize that I'm a respectable lawyer."

" But nobody need know except ourselves. That is the beauty of it."

" That's always the beauty of compounding felonies until they're found out. Then people think they're ugly. Of course the whole disgraceful business must be thought out. It's just as well to remember I'm your trustee. I'm not an expert in criminal methods ; but if you're determined to finance the crime . . ." He stopped.

" Dudley, if she's not to suffer dreadfully something ought to be done at once, oughtn't it ? "

" You can leave it to me, Clare."

" My dear, you're a good friend," she whispered, clasping his hand.

" Ah, Clare, don't say so. It's you who are good, my child." His hand tightened on hers.

This sudden emanation of feeling from a voice in which she had never heard such tones before, aroused, in Clare's tense mind, vibrations of an answering emotion, adding to the trust and admiration with which she had always regarded Wilburn a tenderness that made these clamour for expression. In this wave of sympathy she realized, with shame, how much she owed him already, how unworthy of the generosity to which she pretended had been her return. Now with the impulse to give at its richest and strongest, she felt it an almost physical necessity to express what she felt.

"You put me to shame," she told him, "because what you say isn't really true. Good? I'm not good at all. I'm not good for anything. It's only when things happen like this that I begin to realize how useless I really am."

"No, no," he told her, "you're wrong; you've been brave, you've been splendid."

She disregarded him: "All through these years since Ralph left me I've had everything done for me by you and poor Aunt Cathie and Lady Hingston. I can't even deal with Miss Pidgeon without bothering you. I've made no return whatever; just sponged on you. You're all so good to me that I've taken it for granted; I've never even thanked you. Ungrateful little beast! But I do thank you now, Dudley; heaven knows I'm not as ungrateful as I seem."

"Clare, Clare," he begged her, "you mustn't talk like this."

"I've got to. Somehow, to-day, so many things have happened. It feels as if the world were less solid than usual. I've been so happy and so miserable. What's going to happen next? I don't know where I am; I'm almost frightened." She paused. "I don't know why I'm telling you all this, Dudley, making myself a nuisance again. I suppose it's really the thought of losing Steven. Of course I've known, all the time, that it had to come sooner or later. I've gone on pretending to myself that it wasn't true; but now that it has come I'm just a coward; I want to take back everything I've said to you. It makes me shiver when I think of this great big empty house and me all alone in it. It's the loneliness that frightens me; and nobody can help me in that."

He answered her slowly: "My dear child, there's no

reason why you should be lonely. There's no reason why you should stay here at Uffdown."

She laughed bitterly : "What can I do ? D'you want me to go to Stourford to be bullied and patronized by Lady Hingston ? There wouldn't be a soul in the place with whom I had anything in common but Vivien and poor Marguerite, who have their own lives to live. Or Pen House ? I love Aunt Cathie ; but that's not the same as living with her. It's all very well to talk of moving. Where could I go ? "

" To North Bromwich, Clare. With me."

" North Bromwich ? " For a moment she could not grasp his meaning, and even when it came to her she couldn't believe it."

" If you would marry me, Clare. Heaven knows I love you."

She gazed at him in silence ; and Wilburn, taking advantage of her stupefaction, continued rapidly : " My dear, don't think I've taken advantage of this disturbance to speak to you or that I've thought of it on the spur of the moment. I've been in love with you and nobody else but you for more than eleven years. I can tell you the moment it began : a night that you can't possibly remember, when we met on the station platform at Wychbury and drove up to Pen House together. You were too young for me to tell you then. I kept it all to myself until the day of your grandfather's funeral ; and then I found I was too late—too late to think of marrying you, I mean ; for I've gone on loving you from that day to this."

He stopped. Out of the tumult of her amazement Clare was recalled and harrowed by the anxiety in his face.

" Oh, Dudley," she said, " don't think I'm callous because I can't say anything. The idea's too strange . . . too big for me to grasp. If you'll be patient with me . . . For the moment I can't even think."

" My dearest," he smiled, " I've been patient for eleven

years and can easily keep it up a little longer. I don't want to frighten you or hurry you in any way. I know I'm not the ideal of a romantic lover ; but neither are you a child, although you look one. We've both of us known what it means to be bruised by life; we've both of us known the meaning of loneliness. I shouldn't have dared to speak to you like this—though God knows how much I want you !—if I hadn't felt that things were getting a little too complicated for you to deal with by yourself. And then there was Steven. I know how much he means to you : I don't imagine for one moment, Clare, that I can fill his place when he's separated from you ; but I see—I've seen for long enough —that no woman, and least of all a mother, can be expected to deal with the kind of problem he's bound to offer you. If he's to be a man, he needs the influence of a man to make him one. And that's what I want to give you as well as the love you've always had. I want you to be happy and untroubled, my dearest. I'm speaking the literal truth when ꞁ say that that's the only thing I desire in life ; and if you feel that I can't give you this peace and happiness "—he hesitated—" well, well, my dear, so much the worse for me, though that, of course, won't make any difference to my loving you as long as there's a breath in my body."

He turned away. She put out her hands to him :

" Dudley, will you forgive me if I can't say anything yet ? "

" Forgive you, Clare ? I love you."

" All that I owe you . . ."

" You owe me nothing at all. Twelve years ago I was a broken man. It's the thought of you and nothing else that has made life possible. I've come here as often as I dared, just because the joy of seeing you meant so much to me. I've come here with my heart beating like a boy's, and gone away telling myself that I'm a maudlin middle-aged fool for my pains. Even if you feel that the exchange is too unequal—as it is, of course—I shall go on worshipping you for the rest of my days. Whatever happens, you'll always be able to count on me. I won't say any more. There's nothing more to say. Let's talk of something else," he continued in a voice devoid of emotion. " Do you think if I rang for Styles he could get Bissell to drive me over to Wychbury ? This business of Aunt Cathie's will have to be dealt with."

For the moment she could not bring her brain to deal with matters so ordinary. Taking her permission for granted he rang the bell and sent his orders to the stable. Once more he stood before her in a silence that compelled her to speak. She tried, but failed, to imitate his naturalness.

" May I write to you to-morrow ? " she asked, almost timidly.

" To-morrow, the day after, whenever you like."

She held out her hand ; he bent and pressed it with his lips. At that moment his strength, his goodness seemed so rare to her that she could have given him more.

" Good-bye," he said, and was gone.

# VI

## GHOSTLY LOVES

SHE waited until she heard the front-door close behind him ; then, like a cat that has been watching for the moment to escape, took refuge in the drawing-room. Her face, she knew, was burning with a stunned excitement. Nobody, not even the faithful Ellen, must see it to-night.

While they were dining, the butler had made up the fire with fir-logs from the coppice ; it talked and chuckled to itself, shooting out resinous tongues of flame that licked the curved flanks of the Bechstein with spurts of light and flying shadows. Clare stood motionless in the middle of the room, a small and lonely figure. Her heart was fluttering and flaring like the fir-wood fire ; like soft, enormous bats the shadows flickered over her.

" I am ridiculous," she told herself, " to feel so nervy. If I sit down quietly and play to myself I shall soon feel easier. I mustn't think about anything yet. I can't. There's plenty of time to-morrow."

Methodically, yet always dividedly conscious of her own movements and of her tremulous fingers, she lit two slender candles, one on either side of the music-rest. The thin flames dipped, and then burned steadily ; they and their Georgian silver candlesticks shone deep into the lucid ebony, as though suspended upside-down in a peaty pool. She sat down at the piano, in her rustling taffetas. Her fingers lay upon the keyboard, pallid as the ivory keys. Wilburn had kissed her fingers. Not knowing how or why they shaped the first phrase of the *Frauenliebe und Leben*. The last note died away into silence.

" No, I can't play," she thought. " Why can't I play ? "

In all those years, whenever she felt most lonely or out of tune with the world, it had been her solace to sit there at the piano and think of Ralph. This room, above all others, was sacred to those quiet thoughts, the piano itself a consolation, a refuge. To-night the place refused its consolations. Why ?

Sitting there, powerless to answer this question, there came into her mind a memory of the day on which she had seen it first. Twelve years ago . . . They had bicycled over from Stourford, she and Ralph and Vivien, to take measurements for carpets and curtains in the empty house. Vivien had left them, laughingly dismissed on some ridiculous errand, and Ralph, as soon as Vivien's back was turned, had taken her in his arms and kissed her till she pleaded ror breath. It was in this very corner, by the window, on the spot where she was sitting now.

She closed her eyes, half fearful, half wishing to remember; then quickly repented. It was too late: the gates were open; she could not close them. The memory of that kiss invaded her; it made her shiver, as though a cold wind had blown out of the darkness into her heart. Behind it there came an endless drift of kisses: the first, on that night of flame, when the beacon had flared up in her heart and blinded her; innumerable secret kisses of their magic Spring; those wild, sweet, storm-snatched kisses of Italy; long lovers' kisses in the moon-drenched Capri night. Wherever she turned these treacherous memories haunted and pursued her, as though the dark, malignant wind were driving them into her brain. She started up in panic; she could bear it no longer.

"I can't stay here," she thought. "I shall go mad if I stay here."

She left the candles burning and fled incontinently upstairs to her bedroom.

"Steven is sleeping in Ralph's dressing-room," she thought. "I must be careful not to wake him, poor darling. If I had Steven in my arms I think I could feel happier. No, no, I mustn't give way."

She undressed hurriedly. The primrose frock lay stiffly on the sofa. Out of her mirror a frightened, frightening face surveyed her. She turned away quickly; she hated it; it was not her own. She switched off the light and huddled into the bedclothes.

"If only I could sleep," she thought.

But she could not sleep. Out of the darkened bedroom those memories of her old love returned to her; dead moments, marching in procession like the ghosts of armies broken in battle.

"Oh, Ralph, my darling," she whispered, "why do you

torture me like this ? What have I done to you . . . What have I done ? "

In the first years of loneliness she had dreamed of him constantly, night after night ; of late such dreams had visited her rarely, evanescently, as though the original strength of his spirit were fading away, so that he could no longer find his way with certainty into her sleeping brain. Now, when he seemed to have found his way again, the image that came to her was strangely lifeless and blurred, less clear than anything in the scenes which it carried with it. In all this driven cloud-race of memory his was the only form that lacked distinctness. There was nothing real in it but Steven's eyes and the pink hunting-coat of the Sargent picture. To this painted shape, rather than to any form of her own imagining, she found herself pleading in the darkness ; desperately, like some peasant woman who kneels before a plaster saint.

" What have I done ? " she sobbed. " Oh, what are you thinking of me to-night ? "

Vain question. The gallant portrait only smiled.

" Oh, Ralph, my darling, I shall never, never love anyone but you. But I am so lonely, Ralph, and you can't help me, my dearest. You mustn't ever think that I'm disloyal."

That she could even dream of marrying Dudley was a hateful disloyalty. Disloyalty to what ? However she pleaded, the painted lips could only smile at her. Disloyalty to his memory ? And what could he remember ? To Steven, his perpetuation in the flesh ? But it was in Steven's interest, above all others, that she must be disloyal. Steven disliked him. That was a childish whim, to be smiled at rather than taken seriously. Steven was determined. Ah, but he would outgrow it. A new disloyalty : to Uffdown, to Ralph's beloved Uffdown, the place that had been invented by and for their love ? The panelled walls of the dark bedroom returned no answer; the lives and loves of passing mortals could not trouble them.

"No, there is nothing to bind me," she told herself; "these loyalties that I've invented are unreal; they're ghosts, and I mustn't let them frighten me."

In all the world there was only one predominant reality, and that was Dudley Wilburn himself. Out of her shadowy uncertainties his figure emerged substantial as a welcome landfall. It was to him that she stretched her arms for salvation from the stormy night, and was comforted.

Now, thinking of what had passed between them, she began to wonder if she had not treated him badly. It seemed to her unfair to have sent him away without an answer, to have kept him waiting on her caprice as if he were an impetuous boy. Hadn't he waited long enough already, and didn't she already know enough about him to decide? Their friendship was of too long standing, her respect for him, her admiration too deep for such casual treatment. This man was no sudden and alarming stranger; the heart which he had opened to her by his avowal showed nothing with which she wasn't acquainted but this amazing love. Its steadfastness, its patience, its nobility; she knew them all—she had not been Aunt Cathie's pupil for nothing—and now, by asking her to marry him, this paragon of all the virtues, had shown her the greatest honour that it was in his power to offer. How many women of his acquaintance would give their eyes for the chance of taking it?

"But I don't love him," the obstinate thought returned. "No woman has a right to marry a man she doesn't love. What would he think if I began by telling him that? Would he be wounded, affronted?" No: he was too strong, too reasonable, too wise for that. Surely he would understand. Love was a thing apart, a miracle. And miracles were rare; once, perhaps, in a lifetime, if one were fortunate; but never again.

"And even in this we are equal," she told herself. "We are not children. Both of us have known what love means, and what it means to be treated roughly by life. We have our lives to live and must make the best of them. And I am tired of fighting; I've fought so long."

It seemed to her that she had always been fighting with one thing or another; with money, with Lady Hingston, with Aunt Cathie; with Steven, the servants, even poor Miss Pidgeon.

"I can't keep it up for ever," she thought, "and Dudley is so strong. Things that seem monstrous to me are just nothing to him. He can resolve everything for me; his mind's so clear and well-ordered, and now I shan't have to keep things worrying me until he comes to see me. He'll be there always, and life will be so simple. What he can give me is rest; I need it so badly; and if I'm not able to give him love in exchange . . . Who knows?"

The question was unanswerable.

"I must think no more about it," she told herself. "I must go to sleep, like a sensible woman. To-morrow . . . to-morrow morning early . . . I will write to him."

But, as she closed her eyes and put all thought behind her, Clare knew that she would marry Dudley Wilburn.

# VII

## SEDGEBURY MAIN

*Yes, Dudley, I will marry you,* she wrote to him next morning, *but don't let us tell people anything about it until everything is settled; at any rate, until Steven has gone away to school.* . . . How cautious, how cowardly I am! she thought, remembering how she had pleaded for secrecy long ago, in the days of Ralph's courtship. Then, perhaps, a maidenly modesty might have justified her shyness; but that a widow of several years' standing and the mother of a boy of ten should insist on these virginal reticences needed explanation. *People will make such a dreadful fuss about it*—she explained it as she wrote—*and say such disturbing things that I'm sure it's healthier for them to wake up one morning and find it's all over. Then they can talk as much as they like, and I shan't mind. Don't you agree with me?* "

Of course Wilburn agreed with her; he was too thankful for his good fortune, too elated by the long success of his careful tactics, to question anything. As long as he had won her, it mattered nothing to him what people said or didn't say; but as for gossip or interference, Clare might easily have set her fears at rest; for the moment one theme absorbed the thoughts and feelings of everyone inhabiting their small world—the disaster at the Sedgebury Main.

The morning paper, which Clare had left on one side to write her letter, was full of it. Even the *North Bromwich Mail*, that last rampart of Midland hard-headedness, cynicism and common-sense, conceded leaded headlines. Not only in the city itself but in every village and hamlet of the district the savings of small investors were involved; wild rumours, distorted and reinforced by every mouth through which they passed, fluttered hither and thither over the countryside. The disaster was not so much a catastrophe as a crime; experienced miners had warned the management that they were on dangerous ground; the villain of the piece, among a dozen others which included Sir Joseph Hingston, was the consulting engineer, that callous megalomaniac Furnival, a man who gambled with lives as his victims gambled with pence; the magnitude of the disaster had been exaggerated by the directors who were already secretly buying up the depreciated shares; the magnitude of the disaster had been concealed by those same directors for fear of arousing the righteous indignation that they deserved; the roll of casualties reached fantastic figures that swung upwards and downwards like a barometer in a typhoon; each hour hatched out a swarm of harrowing circumstantial horrors spontaneously generated in hundreds of excited minds, rumours that buzzed like flies above a rotting carcase.

Yet nobody—not even the gaunt Furnival, stalking about with the light of battle in his eyes and his red mane flying like a banner, not even the rescue-gangs of volunteers, shivering on the hill-top like soldiers waiting for a barrage to lift; not even Sir Joseph Hingston, that plump little man, all pinched and pasty in his fur-lined coat, nor the haggard groups of women who hung together outside the barbed-wire fence with check shawls tightened round their suffering faces and children tugging at their bedraggled skirts—not one of them knew, with any certainty, the truth of what lay hidden in the sooty flood three hundred feet beneath them.

Nothing but time, that slow-footed monster, could reveal which men were dead, which ruined; which women widowed, which children orphaned. But down in the basin of the black-country, from under the sooty haze that rose continually in smoke from furnace and factory and pit-head, then hung in the acrid air and settled on their denizens like a blight, men moving about their business and women standing slatternly at the doors of mine-cracked tenements would see, above the western skyline, the twin, gaunt head-gear of the Sedgebury Main, now, and forever afterwards, known as Fatherless Bairn, and shudder, and turn again to their sordid tasks, hoping, by this distraction, to escape the thought of what new mischief the coal-black Moloch might have in store for them. Through all those days of waiting, when the wind whirled smoke and grit into the upper regions of the sky, the sunsets over the ridge of Sedgebury, were of a red and lurid magnificence, as though the motion less head-gear of Fatherless Bairn were a signpost pointing the way into the mouth of hell.

At Uffdown, sheltered under the Southern slope of the hills, these sinister signs could not be seen ; and Clare in the confused emotions of her new orientation, was too absorbed to heed the reminders of the general excitement that the servants brought her. It was only in the late afternoon, when Aunt Cathie's bicycle came skimming over the drive like a solitary Mother Cary's chicken, and Aunt Cathie herself, most ludicrously flustered with her hat blown on one side, had kissed her with wind-cold lips, that she realized the significance of what Wilburn had told her the night before.

" What, Clare—do you mean to say you haven't heard ? But didn't Dudley *tell* you, and haven't you read the papers ? My dear, it seems to me you go through life like a parcel through the post. It's a tremendous thing—yes, yes, I'm dying for tea ; I've been dashing all over the country ; I *had* to tell Susan Abberley the news, the poor old thing's so out of it—what was I saying ? The most tremendous thing—and now I've scalded my tongue ! More than two hundred lives to begin with. Mr. Hemus assures me it can't possibly be less. Too ghastly to think of ! I'm sure the majority were married ; those colliers always are, and have the most enormous families. If you think of two hundred widows and five children apiece "—she paused to multiply—" that makes two thousand, doesn't it ? "

" Not quite." Clare smiled at the macabre wish that fathered Aunt Cathie's calculation.

" Well, anyway," Aunt Cathie declared, " that's near enough. It *shows* you, doesn't it ? And then there's the money. I don't know what the capital was : somebody, I forget who it was, mentioned two million. So widely distributed too ! There's scarcely anyone who hasn't a finger in it. People like Mr. Hemus at the station and

poor Miss Pidgeon, poor souls! Gone, every penny of
it! It's too tragic, isn't it? Of course," she went on
cheerfully, " *I'm* one of the lucky ones—I suppose Dudley
told you last night? It was so sweet of him to come over
specially and set my mind at rest !—but when I think of the
position that other people are left in and what I might have
had to face, it leaves me quite breathless. I feel "—she
paused, but immediately the current obsession supplied
a parallel—" I feel as if I'd just escaped by the skin of my
teeth from being run down by a motor-car." And that,
at the moment, was exactly how she looked, Clare
thought.

" But there are two things," Aunt Cathie continued
solemnly, " that this dreadful business proves, and every
moment makes them seem more remarkable. The first is
what a marvellous brain the doctor had. You know, Clare,
from the very first moment that the Sedgebury Main was
floated, he foresaw *exactly* what would happen! I can't
positively say that he mentioned the word water ; but he
*knew*, in that wonderful way of his, that the business wasn't
sound. Naturally he was always suspicious of anything
that the Hingstons had to do with. And then, of course,
there's Dudley's cleverness. Upon my soul, it's almost
uncanny! To think that more than a fortnight ago, at
the very top of the boom, he put my Sedgebury Mains into
Astill's Breweries ! If he'd consulted me about it, I believe
I should have been frightened by the change, though of
course he knows what confidence I have in him. But
doesn't that show what insight, what wisdom he has ? I
know that you always laugh at me in secret when I rave
about him, Clare, but you've no excuse for doing that in
future. No doubt, I could have managed to look after
myself if the worst had happened ; but it's Steven who
would have suffered, bless his heart ! "

So Dudley had pulled it off without arousing the innocent

Aunt Cathie's suspicions. How splendid of him, Clare
thought ; how magnificently reliable he was !

" I don't think you're sufficiently impressed," Aunt
Cathie persisted. She wouldn't be satisfied till Clare had
subscribed to every article of her Wilburn cult ; and Clare,
who found a relief for her own feelings of admiration in
confessing her orthodoxy, was so infected by Aunt Cathie's
enthusiasm that she was almost ready to believe that the
miracle by which Aunt Cathie had been saved was really
and entirely due to Dudley's inspired foresight, and not
in the least to the pious fraud that her own pity had contrived.
It was a passionate luxury with her to outdo Aunt Cathie's
raptures for the paragon of virtue and wisdom who had
chosen her for his wife ; and, as she spoke, the reticence
which her queer modesty had imposed on her, was driven
to the winds, so that her mind became a battlefield in which
prudence and the instinct of self-preservation fought stiffly
against the desire to proclaim her conquest ; " This king
among men," her heart cried ; " he is mine, mine ! I am
going to marry him."

" I am glad," said Aunt Cathie, " to see that you agree
with me at last. I hope you'll realize now what kind of
people you ought to rely on for advice. I don't want to be
spiteful, Clare, or to appear to take pleasure in anyone else's
misfortunes ; but I have it on the very best authority, the
postmaster's to be exact, that the Hingstons are ruined.
Sir Joseph, I know, was managing director, and that makes
it probable. I'm only thankful to think that your money
and Steven's happens to be in Dudley's hands. You have
to thank *me* for that. I made a point of it at the time when
your settlement was made. Think of it ! But for that lucky
chance you might be in the same boat as Lady
Hingston ! "

The look of disgust on Aunt Cathie's face and her pursed
lips implied that under no possible contingency of marine

disaster would she submit to sharing Lady Hingston's company.

"And, after all, my dear Clare," she reasoned, "nobody with any perceptions of rightness and decency can deny that it's a case of poetical justice. When you think of nice unpretentious people like Mrs. Willis of Mawne—I'm afraid they're in it too—who has just as much right to be ostentatious as the Hingstons, and would never *dream* of flaunting her furs in motor-cars all over this part of the country where people know her origins, like that woman, you realize the difference between natural gentility and . . . the other thing. You don't suppose, do you, that they imagine they're respected ? All the country people—everyone who has any feeling for horses—despises them. I was only talking the other day to Ellen's father, the blacksmith. He was just as disgusted as any of us. 'They won't last, Miss Weir,'—that's what he said. And he's right, Clare ; simple though he be, the man has commonsense. Clogs to clogs : three generations, as the doctor always used to say."

## VIII

### MOBILIZATION OF STOURFORD

HOWEVER sound in theory Aunt Cathie's prognostications of the decline and fall of Stourford may have been, for the present that hostile power showed no signs of crumbling. It was true that the Hingston fortune, and, even more, the prestige attached to the Hingston tradition of good-luck, had been hard hit by the Sedgebury inundation ; but other names—and notably that of Walter Willis of Mawne—had taken the blow more hardly, and Sir Joseph's determined conduct of the meeting at which his directors decided to cut their shareholders' losses, to abandon Furnival, and to close the pit, showed a courage that commanded confidence of itself.

During the month that followed Wilburn's proposal, which included such stirring incidents as the despatching of poor Miss Pidgeon and all her silver to a sister in Somerset, the harrowing farewells of Steven to Bo-peep and her darling's departure to the preparatory school at Weston-in-Arden that Clare and Wilburn had chosen, and culminated in the announcement of their approaching marriage, Stourford possessed itself in an ominous immobility, like a volcano that sulks beneath the cloud of its last eruption ; but early on the morning after Clare had posted the letter that revealed her plans, the new Lanchester, with the French chauffeur clutching the tiller in front, and Lady Hingston, erect as Boadicea, behind, came whizzing up the Uffdown drive like a chariot going into action, and, in another moment, as Mr. Styles told Ellen afterwards, " the fur was flying, and no mistake ! "

Time had dealt as kindly with Lady Hingston as if, like everyone else, it were afraid of her. Now, in her fifty-seventh year, her spare, efficient figure seemed as potent, her eyes as keen, the delicate, almost childish texture of her admirable skin as clearly exquisite beneath the snowy toupet, as on the evening when Clare had first encountered her at Stourford, eleven years before. Only the network of wrinkles that radiated from the corners of her eyes, the fine, vertical puckers that marked her upper lip in repose, betrayed the loss of elasticity appropriate to her years. And now, as whenever she saw her, Clare's first thought was : " How young, how pretty, she is ! " But there was nothing pretty in the peregrine sweep with which her black eyes skimmed the breakfast-table.

" What, you've not finished yet ? " she said. " At Stourford everybody has been up and working an hour ago."

" It's only—" Clare began. She stopped. The habitual

excuse died on her lips. She knew that Lady Hingston hadn't risen with the lark—and with poor Sir Joseph—to comment on her domestic arrangements; she knew that she was in for a fight.

This morning, for the first time in her life, her blood rose to meet it. Although her heart was plugging like a steam-hammer, she felt that she was no longer afraid of Lady Hingston. The sensation was encouraging and frightening at once. In the old days, when Ralph was alive, she had kept the peace for his sake, acquiescing in the Stourford tradition of letting storms blow over; later, during the years of her widowhood, she had felt the disadvantage of her loneliness; but now, with the miraculous strength of Wilburn behind her, now that Steven, her precious hostage, was well out of range, now that Uffdown and all the impedi-menta of the old life to which she clung no longer em-barrassed her, she had a curious, brave feeling of being stripped for action, an inclination to test her own, incal-culable strength. Flushed and made reckless by this access of courage, she faced Lady Hingston and waited for the attack. Lady Hingston also was waiting—for the butler to clear the pitch; she harried and embarrassed poor Styles until he fumblingly disappeared. Before the door had closed behind him she opened fire.

" I've read your letter, Clare," she began, then stopped, as if, at the mere mention of this enormity, defences must collapse, " And I can only say," she continued, " that words fail me."

If words failed Lady Hingston, Clare thought, the battle was half won; unfortunately they did nothing of the sort.

" I think you must have taken leave of your senses," she went on, " even to dream of a marriage of this kind without consulting my husband and myself. I shall be glad if you'll tell me what you mean by it."

" I mean what I wrote, dear Lady Hingston. I'm going to marry Dudley Wilburn on Thursday week."

" On Thursday week ? Ten days ! You never mentioned anything of the sort. It seems you have committed yourself further than you told us."

" We shall be married very quietly by special licence. I didn't think, and I don't think now, that the date concerns you. Still, now I've told you, so you mustn't complain."

" Complain ? I consider your conduct is monstrous, Clare ; there's no other word for it. If you had breathed a word of this to me . . ."

" That's why I didn't, Lady Hingston ; if I'd done that . . ."

" If you'd done that, we should soon have put a stop to this nonsense."

" Oh no, you wouldn't," Clare told her. " You couldn't, you know."

" That depends entirely on whether you have any feelings of decency left in you. I suppose you still consider yourself a member of our family ? "

" Why should I do so, Lady Hingston ? You never come here except at times like this, when you want to manage me. We have very little in common except our name ; and after Thursday week, we shan't even have that."

" I see you're making a joke of it. Of course, you're in a position, thanks to the money that Ralph left you in that iniquitous settlement that Dudley Wilburn was sharp enough to make him sign, to do without the name that he gave you. But let me tell you this : without that name you wouldn't be lounging here in comfort over your breakfast at ten o'clock. Not a bit of it ! You'd be earning your living in some third-rate girls' school, or starving over at Wychbury with that impertinent aunt of yours Our name, indeed ! I think it's time you realized what you owe to it and to us."

" To you, Lady Hingston ? No, don't say that. To

Ralph, if you like. If you had had your way he wouldn't have married me."

" I'm glad you admit it. In your sly way you're clever. If you want the truth, he married you because he was a fool and knew no better ; and you married him, let me tell you, because you'd caught him and his money and knew better than to let him go. Don't think I didn't see through you and your blessed aunt. . . ."

" That's a lie, Lady Hingston, and you know it. I married Ralph because I loved him."

Lady Hingston laughed out loud : " Loved him ! And now you show your love and respect for his memory by making another of these romantic love-matches ! Of course it never occurred to you that Ralph was wealthy ? Oh, no, not for a moment ! And it's never occurred to you now that Dudley Wilburn is trustee to the estate, and that all Ralph's property will be in your hands and out of ours. Oh no, of course, it didn't ! You're lucky, Clare, to find romance so extraordinarily convenient."

With the first mention of Ralph's name Clare's lip had trembled ; her declaration of her love for him had brought her to the verge of tears ; but the tears that now filled her eyes were tears of anger. She clasped her hands and wrung them, as if, by this gesture, she could master some part of her will that was slipping away from her. As she gazed at Lady Hingston, speechless, Lady Hingston smiled, and, like the stimulus of a galvanic shock to a hysteric, that smile restored Clare to herself. She spoke calmly :

" You can say what you like about me ; your lies don't affect me , but, Lady Hingston, if you are not content to leave Ralph's name out of this and to say no more of Dudley Wilburn, I shall have to ask you to leave this room. You can say what you like at Stourford, but I'm not going to listen to your abominable insinuations in my own house. I think you had better go. If you don't go, I shall."

She moved toward the door; Lady Hingston, seeing that she was determined, caught her as she passed. For the first time in their twelve years' acquaintance, possibly for the first time in history, she apologized.

"No, Clare, don't go," she pleaded. "My feelings got the better of me. I'm like that, you know. I'm sorry. Please forgive me."

Clare turned and looked at her. A fine dew of perspiration was showing itself on the drawn white skin beneath Lady Hingston's eyelids and on the lips that nervously smiled at her. The black eyes faltered for an instant as they met hers; they were angry and puzzled, like those of a cat that clings to a wounded bird and will not let go.

"No, you're not sorry," Clare answered coldly; "that's not true either; you're not sorry a bit. What do you want to talk about? It's no use talking now. I suppose you want me to tell you something."

"How can I ask you, if you glare at me like that?" said Lady Hingston pitifully.

"Well, I won't look at you," Clare sighed. "If you're not going, I wish you'd sit down."

Lady Hingston gratefully collapsed into a chair. They sat down in silence for a moment. Then lightly, tactfully, as though she were merely changing the subject, she began:

"Where's Steven?"

"Steven? He went away to school a week ago."

"To school?" Lady Hingston gasped.

"Haven't you been worrying me to send him to school for the last six months? Well, Dudley and I went into the matter very seriously, and I think we've found the best place in the district. He's at Weston-in-Arden. I think he'll be happy there."

For a moment Lady Hingston wrestled with the impulse to be violent again and mastered it.

" Don't you think, Clare, that was a matter on which we might have been consulted ? " she asked quietly.

" No, I'm afraid I don't. It had to be dealt with, and, candidly, I thought it would be better to get it over without outside interference. I'm tired of it."

" Interference is a strong word," said Lady Hingston, softly. " I see you're determined to cut yourselves off from us. I must say, considering Mr. Wilburn's very profitable connection with Wolverbury, that this strikes me as hardly politic on his part."

" You mean you'll get back on him ? I expect he's thought of that. However, that's what we decided."

" You're very arrogant all of a sudden, Clare." The flush of anger came back into Lady Hingston's delicate cheeks ; another outburst gathered and was dissipated. She spoke again, calmly ; but the diamonds on her fingers glittered as she twined them.

" It hasn't struck you that Steven may be the loser by this . . . obstinacy ? "

" Not in the long run. It's no good threatening me."

" I wasn't threatening you, Clare. I'm merely suggesting what I've a right to suggest. Steven's our grandson ; the only persons between him and the title are George and little Harold. Harold is delicate. If anything happened to him . . . You see ? In a case of this kind we have to think ahead." She left the subject suddenly : " Where are you going to live ? "

" In Alvaston, naturally."

" Then what will happen to Uffdown ? "

" For the present we intend to let it."

" We ? We ? It seems to me that everything is ' we,' " Lady Hingston repeated impatiently.

" Why not ? The house will eventually be Steven's. I am his mother, and Dudley's his trustee. . . ."

" And Sir Joseph is his grandfather," Lady Hingston

interrupted energetically, " and Stourford, now that you've decided to throw in your lot with Mr. Wilburn's, is his natural nome. Your new life will be very different from the old one, Clare. Obviously, it's your duty to live where your husband lives," she continued with studied moderation, " but it seems to me unfair that Steven, a growing boy, should be handicapped by the fact that his stepfather lives in a town. Steven's birth, his position entitled him to more spacious surroundings. To be brought up in a suburb is a misfortune for any child—you must admit it—and, really, with all the new interests and friends you're bound to find in Alvaston, I shouldn't be at all surprised if you found it more convenient in every way to let him think of Stourford as his real home. In the holidays . . ." she hurried on precipitately, as though she knew that she would be interrupted, but before she could find another word Clare had risen and faced her with blazing eyes :

" So that's what you've been driving at, is it ? " she cried. " That's the real reason why you came here to-day ? You want to steal Steven from me, and make him your own ? " She paused ; all her fury was concentrated in a deadly deliberateness. " Listen, Lady Hingston. I'll tell you something. If I were starving in the gutter and Steven crying with hunger, I'd die before I let you have him. And that's the answer that Ralph would have given you."

She turned her back on Lady Hingston, fearing that she could control her feelings no longer.

" I think you'd better go now," she said. " I've nothing more to say, so it's no good your staying."

Her voice wavered treacherously as she spoke. In the silence that followed she heard Lady Hingston's petticoats rustle with the sound of an offended turkey spreading its tail. Once, in the doorway, she turned, as though she were pulling herself together for a final salvo. Apparently, unless breath failed her, she thought better of it, for a moment later, the roar of the Lanchester's engine announced her retreat.

More shaken by this signal victory than by any of her previous reverses Clare took her fluttering heart into the solitude of Annabel Ombersley's drawing-room and cried until her emotion was exhausted. Half-an-hour later, when she stole up to her bedroom and bathed her eyes, she felt her spirit lightened as that of a bird that has escaped from a cage. The sense of freedom and relief was so embarrassing that she didn't know what to do with it; her body craved for space and movement in which to express this spiritual amplitude; so she put on her hat, determined to walk over the hills to Wychbury for lunch, and tell Aunt Cathie of her brave adventure. Aunt Cathie, too, would have read her news this morning.

As she reached the foot of the stairs, Sly, Steven's terrier, came bounding to meet her, scenting the prospect of a conducted rabbit-tour, leaping and sniffing and laughing in her face.

" Do you want to come with me, Sly, darling ? " she said. She picked the trembling warm body up and cuddled it, for it was part of Steven. " Do you know what's happened, Sly ? " she laughed; and the creature snuffled its answer in her face. " Good dog, then, come along ! Sly ! Where's your master ? "

But as soon as the door was open, Sly was off like a whirlwind, skimming in widening circles over the dewy turf, barking and rolling and laughing back at Clare's own laughter. A soft, autumnal wind rustled the tree-tops; the fallen splendour of beech-leaves glowed along the vista of the drive. Behind her, sunlight mellowed and ripened the red brick of Uffdown, and, as she turned to gaze on it, the old house smiled.

" Don't be afraid to leave me," it seemed to whisper; " I am old, I'm used to waiting; you are mine, I am yours, and some day, when you come back again, you'll find me here and just the same."

A thin tinkle swelled in her ears.  Aunt Cathie's bicycle. Aunt Cathie herself, more flushed and breathless than ever, dismounting with a rush and folding her in her arms, while the bicycle fell with a crash on to the gravel.

" My dearest, I was coming over to lunch with you," Clare laughed through a blizzard of cold kisses.

" Lunch ?  I don't care if I never have lunch again," Aunt Cathie cried.  " This is the proudest, the happiest, the most wonderful moment in my life, Clare darling."

With tears of joy streaking her wind-reddened cheeks, Aunt Cathie's heart sang its *Nunc Dimittis* to the golden sky, while Sly sniffed curiously at the tyres of the prostrate bicycle.  " If only the doctor had lived to see this ! " said Aunt Cathie.

And three days later, in a business envelope that bore the stamp of Wolverbury, Sir Joseph Hingston sent Clare a cheque. . . .

# BOOK FIVE
## CLARE WILBURN

## TUDOR HOUSE

ONE hundred and ninety-seven, Halesby Road, Alvaston, North Bromwich.

Although two months had passed since the evening of sleety misery on which she and Dudley had returned from their short honeymoon in Bournemouth, chilled to the soul by the long cross-country railway journey through Didcot and over wintry Cotswold, Clare's waking consciousness had never yet accepted the change of scene. Now, in the early morning, when her eyes were still closed and her brain but half awake, she lazily envisaged the shape of the room, the outline of the windows from which the first light came, imagining the windows of her room at Uffdown, those Queen Anne windows, so peerlessly proportioned, and, beyond them, over dim lengths of dreamy lawn and coppice and kindly elm-tops, sweet, sleepy meadows, sloping gently southward into the mists of the Severn Plain. Then suddenly out of the silence her ears perceived an unfamiliar sound : the hoofs of plodding horses, the rumble of laden cart-wheels on macadam, that made her think she must be back at St. Monica's, a school-girl again : an explanation too fantastic even for her drowsiness to accept. So, puzzled, but still too lazy to think, she opened a chink of her eyelids and saw against the smoky grey of dawn and the yellow beam of the street-lamp which some civic providence had planted opposite the front-garden gate, an outline of Victorian Gothic mullions, tall, leaded casements, the frayed edge of a blind, and the Nottingham lace curtains, looped up like a charwoman's skirts, which had already become a torment and a despair. " Yes, they're still there," she thought, " of course. . . ."

Those curtains whose hideousness, with a persistence that things of beauty can rarely achieve, had already survived twenty-two years of ill-treatment at the hands of Alvaston laundries since Clare's predecessor, Edith Wilburn, had matched them with their kind in the windows of one hundred and ninety-six neighbours, had troubled Clare's æsthetic sensibilities from the first. There seemed no reason why their life should not be prolonged indefinitely ; for when she had suggested their removal to her husband, he had merely answered : " Why ? I don't think they're worn out yet." And Clare had not persisted nor attempted to explain. An explanation of this particular dislike would have implied so many others, and the other dislikes were so delicately intimate that she couldn't, for the world, have mentioned them. Besides, in these early days, she was walking tactfully ; and though she couldn't admit that Nottingham lace curtains were necessary to social salvation —as indeed, they had been in the Halesby Road in eighteen hundred and eighty-eight—her mind was so deliberately subjected to Dudley's that she couldn't help feeling, for some inexplicable reason, that his answer to her objections was complete.

And so the curtains stayed, and Tudor House—that was one hundred and ninety-seven's other name—remained, in its window decorations, true to type. At any rate, on this iron morning, they would conceal her toilet operations from the curious eyes of passengers, bored and freezing, on the top of the Tilton 'bus, which went by every hour like a stage-coach, with the harness of its four horses jingling ; and also, if one took the trouble not to peer through them, they did conceal the more depressing features of the houses opposite ; their weedy privet hedges, bald lawns and monkey puzzles ; their blue slate roofs, on which the morning rime left blotches of unevaporated moisture ; and, hideous behind them, in a mist that was nearly fog, the sanitary plumbing of other houses that backed them, facing the more doleful and less fashionable thoroughfare of Astill Road.

Those curtains—her drowsy mind persistently returned to them—were, after all, no more than representative of a hundred other inanimate reminders of Dudley's former life which she would have been happy to remove. For instance, there on the whorled supports of the yellow mahogany mirror, whose oval now began to show against the grey, hung a faded hair-tidy ; an obviously respectable hair-tidy, but one that, equally obviously, had been used by someone else. Time after time, with a rising spiritual nausea, she had contemplated this accessory of the toilet and been tempted to throw it in the fire. And yet, she had thought, supposing Dudley should miss it ; supposing he viewed the wretched thing with sentimental attachment ? You never could tell ; he was so silent, so engrossed in his work, so seemingly severe. Hardly severe ; to call him that were an injustice. . . . Say rather so ordered, so standardized, so fixed in his habits and his surroundings, that if you dared to penetrate toward the centre of his steadily revolving life you'd find yourself thrown outward to its periphere by sheer momentum, like a straw in a centrifuge. And if, by some unspeakable rashness, you should endeavour to check the established rhythm of revolution, heaven knew what disaster might happen ! " It would be like stopping the revolutions of the globe," she thought ; " we should simply fall off into space or something of that kind, and Joyce and Evelyn would say it was all my fault ! "

The travelling alarm clock, that stood on the cabinet at Dudley's side of the bed, discharged itself with a whirr and a tinkle that put an end to her reflections. Although she had heard the thing go off on more than fifty mornings in succession, its explosion always had the effect of startling her. At any rate, now there was no risk of mistaking where she was. Wilburn rolled over on to his back and stretched his arms. He put his clenched fists in his eyes and spoke : " Are you awake, Clare darling ? "

The word of tenderness always moved her. " Yes, Dudley," she said. She was always awake, or half awake, long, long before him. Even if her mind were full to bursting with questions, she kept them to herself ; when a man went to bed every night dog-tired, as he did, he had a right to have his sleep out ; and when he was once awake, except on Sundays, it was too late.

He yawned, then kissed her. " Well, I suppose I shall have to get up," he said.

Breakfast at eight. In this new life, at any rate, no Lady Hingston could reproach her for the lateness of her uprising. Of course she could have stayed in bed another hour if she'd wanted to, especially on these raw winter mornings, when the air of the front bedroom was bleak enough to bite your nose off ; but Dudley had to be at his office and Joyce at her hospital by nine, and, even though she knew that they could get their breakfast perfectly well without her, Clare would have felt that she was failing in her duty if she had'nt been down with them.

On the landing she could hear her husband harrying Joyce out of the bathroom. His bath and his shave took him twelve minutes to the tick ; so, if she didn't want to be in his way she'd better hurry up. She slipped her feet out of bed and shivered as she regarded the fireplace. At present it was filled by a fringed and sooty fan of coloured paper which Mrs. Marple would replace by another at the season of spring-cleaning. From mid-October till May, as Dudley had told her with satisfaction, the house consumed exactly thirty hundredweight of coal a month. Never, except in case of serious illness, was that allowance exceeded. What

Spartans these North Bromwich people were! At Uff-down . . .

But it was no use thinking about Uffdown. " It would be nice," she thought, " if he'd allow me to pay for more coal myself." But of course he wouldn't. In matters of this kind, as Aunt Cathie agreed with satisfaction, his sense of fairness was extremely delicate ; and since he had insisted on sharing the expense of housekeeping a special arrangement would put him in an awkward position. " And, anyway," she thought, " if I go on sitting on the edge of the bed like this, he'll find me frozen when he comes back." How lucky it was for him, and for Joyce too, that both of them seemed to be at their very best first thing in the morning. " I can't possibly see to dress in this light," she thought, " and if I turn on the gas it may warm the room a little."

Of course Dudley was quite right to be careful about the bedroom gas ; gas was so easily wasted ; that was what he said when she had asked him why they didn't have a gas-stove in the kitchen ; but on these gloomy December mornings you simply had to light it in the dining-room for breakfast ; and dressing, for a woman at least, was just as important as eating, although you didn't have to read the paper while you did your hair.

By the time she reached the breakfast table Dudley and Joyce were already in their places. When Clare entered, he dropped his *Courier*, and rose to pull back her chair for her. It was a little, ordinary gallantry that always gave her pleasure, if only as a contrast to the curt nod that was Joyce's salutation. Then Dudley lifted the cover of the Sheffield-plated entrée-dish in which the breakfast congealed. At a hundred and ninety-seven it wasn't usual to help oneself. He raised it, always, with an air of hearty expectation. " Now, what have we here ? " he'd say ; " Clare, may I give you . . ." Eggs and bacon. He needn't have hesitated. If it had been anything else in that house the roof would have fallen in ; but this affectation—she oughtn't really to call it that—of novelty and surprise was only part of the morning air of briskness by which he showed how wide awake he was.

" Joyce, my child . . . ? "

" Please, dad."

Clare poured out coffee. She sat with her back to the wintry window, opposite her husband, while Joyce's back received the radiation of the newly-lighted fire. She was a slim, dry girl, three inches taller than Clare, a medical student at the North Bromwich University, already more than half way through her training. She wore a dark blue tailor-made, a college tie, and a white starched collar that made her thin neck look like a spindle on which the pinched face with its ruthlessly-knotted hair was balanced precariously. At this meal she rarely spoke to Clare unless she could help it, aping, perhaps, the reticence of her father, who had the excuse of the *Courier's* financial pages for his silence ; but what her curt and cynical tongue refrained from saying was all too evident in the sidelong, critical glances of her greenish eyes. She carved her bacon as she cut through life, with the cold precision of a surgical instrument, with the regularity of a piece of machinery that is neither subject to moods nor influenced by physical conditions. When, having dealt with her eggs and bacon, she cut across Clare's reflections with : " Pass the marmalade, please," the word " please " had a contemptuous flavour which implied : " Of course you, with your woolly intelligence, wouldn't see that I had finished." She despised Clare ; she despised everyone in the house except her father, whom she apparently acknowledged as an organism equally efficient with herself, and even loved—as one might say—" in vitro."

You would have said that Joyce despised—although, where Clare was concerned, she admitted her as an ally—

her younger sister Evelyn, who now came lounging into the room with an air of pretended astonishment at her own lateness and an apology for it which took the form of a question that nobody troubled to answer. She kissed her father, ostentatiously, and subsided into the warm chair next to Joyce's with a contented sigh, greedily watching the bottom of the dish whose lid Dudley had momentarily lifted to supply her.

" Oh, thank you, dad, that's plenty ! " she protested ; but held her plate until the last morsel was scraped on to it, then settled down to eat with a fat smile. " She is rather like a pig," Clare thought ; and then, as if to do Evelyn justice : " a nice, clean pig. . . ."

For Evelyn's face, which still, at seventeen, retained an adolescent plumpness ; her hair, which was silky and abundant and of an almost flaxen fairness ; her voice, her clothes, her brain, the whole of her body, mind and personality were of a soft and indeterminate texture which made her the very opposite of Joyce. Yet when they were together, as now, there arose between these opposites a conspiracy of sympathy, from which Clare, the intruder, was carefully excluded. They spoke in lowered voices, apparently for fear of disturbing their father, but actually, Clare felt, to make herself uncomfortable ; they answered each other in monosyllables, full of implications, with covert smiles and sniggers and sudden, tactful silences, deliberately left for her imagination to fill.

Behind and above them, on the left-hand side of the mantelpiece, an enlarged photograph of their mother, Edith Wilburn, gazed down on them with a fixed, impartial, unintelligent smile. Evelyn, people said, was like her mother, that white-skinned, blue-eyed, bland, insipid beauty ; but in Evelyn's soft and almost aggressively innocent face there were reservations that Clare could not find in Edith's. Behind the good-humour, the easy indolence of Evelyn's too-blue eyes there lay a core of selfish obstinacy as hard as, or even harder, than Joyce's ; for Joyce's mind, in spite of its central hardness, was radically just, while Evelyn's, for all its superficial softness, was mobile and treacherous as a quicksand.

" Well, children, what are you doing with yourselves to-day ? "

Wilburn laid down his *Courier*, folded it methodically, and put it in his pocket. This was the usual signal for his departure.

" Work, as usual," said Joyce, severely.

" I imagine I shall go out calling with Clare, she's going to the Miss Isit's and Lady Astill's," said Evelyn.

" You needn't, if you don't want to, Evelyn," Clare replied.

" Oh, but I'd love to," said Evelyn effusively, satisfied that she had already indicated her willing sacrifice.

" Calling ? Well, I suppose you'll all amuse yourselves." Already Wilburn's mind was miles away from them. " I must be off in any case." He crossed the room to Clare and kissed her.

" I'll come to the door with you, Dudley," she said, glad of the opportunity of escaping from the blank, bewildered gaze with which Joyce and Evelyn had watched the conventional embrace, as if they were thinking : " However can he do it ? "

She watched him go with his despatch case down the garden path. " A fine-looking man," she told herself, " a splendid man : there's no one to compare with him. It's wonderful to be so consistent, so strong, so self-contained. I ought to be proud of him."

What heretic had ever so much as suggested that she wasn't ? A jingling bus pulled up at the gateway, almost as though it belonged to him. The conductor smiled and touched his cap. The frozen outside passengers looked down and smiled at his farewell. These people knew his worth and respected him, she thought. Then Joyce came scuttling down the path like a rabbit and boarded the bus's footboard with a leap.

It was gone. Slowly Clare turned back along the frosty path and re-entered the house. " And now," she thought, " my day begins."

## II

### DRAWING-ROOM

It began, as usual, with Mrs. Marple, the cook-housekeeper whom Clare had taken over with the other Victorian furniture of the house ; a prepotent, flat-chested Cheshire woman with a North-country accent that made her least pronouncement seem brusque and dogmatic, a bird's nest of greying hair, large, knotted hands, and a wide face that dyspepsia and the glare of the kitchen range had inflamed to a redness which simulated perpetual anger.

There was nothing intrinsically wrong with Mrs. Marple. On a visit to Alvaston, during their short engagement, Clare had made her acquaintance, and heard, from Dudley, with faint misgivings, the impressive story of her honesty, her efficiency, her wisdom, loyalty, economy, her unfortunate matrimonial history and her varicose veins—in short, the catalogue of incredible virtues which made her indispensable.

" I hope we shall get on well together, Mrs. Marple," Clare told her.

" If we don't madam," Mrs. Marple declared, " it won't be *my* fault."

Indeed, there was nothing in Mrs. Marple's behaviour then or since that Clare could describe as lacking in respect or propriety. Her virtues were only too evident. It might even have been admitted—at least in the beginning—that she was as indispensable as Dudley had suggested; for without her the reliable clockwork of Tudor House, which had gone on ticking comfortably for twenty years with no more lubricant than Mrs. Marple's monthly wages, would have stopped dead, as if its mainspring were broken.

But what Clare couldn't accept quite so comfortably was that Mrs. Marple knew she was indispensable, and had determined to remain so for the rest of her life. On the first of these morning interviews—so different, alas, from her leisurely consultations with the housekeeper at Uffdown —Mrs. Marple had brought her the keys of the house, of the linen-room, the wine cellar, the stores, of all the mysteries in which, for the last twenty years she had held undisputed possession, and to emphasize this act of surrender had thrown them, figuratively, in her new mistress's face, then stood, with flushed cheeks and folded arms, to see what kind of mess she'd make of them.

Clare knew that the challenge had to be accepted; but Mrs. Marple's obstructions were so nicely calculated, her honesty so transparent, her ignorance so carefully simulated that, within a few weeks, Clare found herself faced with the alternatives of conciliating Mrs. Marple or confessing herself a domestic failure. And she would rather have failed than conciliated Mrs. Marple; for, all the time, in the back of her mind, she knew that Joyce, or, at any rate Evelyn, invisibly sustained Mrs. Marple's bony arms; and Mrs. Marple, like many women with limited horizons, was never happy unless she was taking sides, and knew, or thought she knew, on which side her bread had been buttered for the last twenty years. Which was short-sighted of her, since, with a little intelligence, she might have guessed that Clare was as stubborn as herself, and that the third, and most obvious alternative of resolving the stale-mate into which her game seemed to be drifting, was for Clare to take the law into her own hands and give her notice.

That morning, as if some inkling of this truth had penetrated her brain, Mrs. Marple was as soft as rather rancid butter. As was her custom on Saturday she brought with her a sheaf of grubby tradesmen's books and bills. Since Clare's arrival Joyce had resigned to her the keeping of household accounts, the very sight of which, as Mrs. Marple knew, was enough to " keep the mistress quiet." As for food, there was practically nothing to order, for the custom of the house, as emphasized by those bills, demanded that Saturday should be a day of penance, on which the remains of the week's food should be consumed to clear the way for Sunday's monstrous joint. It seemed, in fact, that Mrs. Marple, for once, was at a loose end, and Clare decided to take advantage of her leisure by putting into action a plan that had been seething in her head for weeks : That dreadful drawing-room. . . .

After the light and spacious dryness of Annabel Ombersley's room at Uffdown she found it more than she could bear. For though, at night, with a crackle of fire and the gas-jets of the chandelier lit, its discomforts seemed more tolerable, by day, when the dank north light filtered past straggling ivy and green repp curtains over the filaments of an overgrown asparagus-fern which blocked the remaining window-space like a tuft of seaweed, motionless in subaqueous gloom, this room, with its dim wreckage of late-Victorian furniture, seemed fitter for the habitation of aquarium specimens than of human beings. During his widowerhood, Dudley told her, it had never been used except for callers. Now, since the idea of sitting in the odour of a finished meal was repugnant to her, she had determined to make a job of it.

" This morning," she said, " I want you to turn out the drawing-room."

Mrs. Marple's face grew redder than an angry turkey's comb.

"The day for the drawing-room's Monday, ma'am," she said.

"Yes, yes, I know." Clare told her. "But I don't like the present arrangement of the furniture, and I want to see if I can make it lighter, more . . . comfortable. I know you'll help me."

She spoke kindly, persuasively. With equal propriety an infidel might have taken upon herself to reform the ritual of the Church of Rome, or a new member of the Athenaeum suggested the rearrangement of the club library.

"The drawing-room's been like that, ma'am," said Mrs. Marple, "for the last twenty years to *my* knowledge. There's not a stick been changed in it all those years."

As she spoke she went—as far as she was ever capable of going—pale.

"Well, yes," said Clare, "and that's exactly what it feels like. As things are now, there seems to be a lot of unnecessary work in it."

"*I* have never found it so, ma'am," said Mrs. Marple, with her back to the wall, "and I'm quite sure Mary hasn't."

"Lunch is cold to-day, isn't it ? " Clare continued, with conscious sweetness. "So when you have put the kitchen in order, you can come and give me a hand."

"I'm sorry, ma'am," said Mrs. Marple, escaping from her corner, "but I'd arranged to take the opportunity of speaking to Mr. Walsh about that sirloin he sent us and ordering the coal."

"That sirloin," as Clare knew, had been hanging, literally and figuratively, on the air for the last four days ; she was glad to be free of it.

"In that case," she said, " I can get Mary to help me."

"Mary," said Mrs. Marple triumphantly, " is doing Miss Joyce's bedroom."

"She can do that to-morrow just as well."

"To-morrow, ma'am?" The enemy had played into her hands. "To-morrow is Sunday; and if she don't do it to-day, if I may say so, I don't know when it'll get done. In a house like this you have to take things in their order."

"Don't worry then, Mrs. Marple. In that case I shall have to do it myself."

This breach of all precedent filled Mrs. Marple with horror.

"That's hardly a lady's work, ma'am," she suggested, going exactly as far as she dared; and Clare, concealing her irritation, said no more.

It pleased her to think that, apart from the submissive Mary, who was now engaged in Joyce's bedroom, reading, by stealth and in trepidation, a treatise on the Diseases of Women, with edifying coloured illustrations, she was, for once, alone in the house. She put on an apron, and, with the fervour of an iconoclast, entered the drawing-room. Something of the vague religious awe which may have assailed the heart of a servant of Akhnaton scattering destruction with his chisel in the Theban temples of Amen, overtook her as she began the deadly work; for all the abominable ornaments and pieces of bric-a-brac that her fervour displaced—and half of them, reluctantly, she spared—had been objects of reverence, or, at least, affection, in the eyes of Edith Wilburn.

The soil in which these parasitic knick-knacks throve most persistently, like mussels and limpets on a discarded hulk, and for the same reason, was the top of the piano. Not Clare's beloved Bechstein. That had been left at Uffdown for the desecration of alien fingers. "Don't let's encumber ourselves," Dudley had insisted, "with anything that isn't useful. The idea of having two pianos, and one a grand, in a house of this size is ludicrous, and none of us, except my brother Ernest, is the least bit musical. Of course, he added, " I realize that that is our loss." Which was modest, but untrue : the loss, alas, was Clare's.

This Tudor House piano, acquired, in payment for a debt, from the stock of a bankrupt client, a North Bromwich musical instrument manufacturer, had the peculiar insensitiveness of pianos that are never played on except by casual visitors who strum the C Minor Prélude of Chopin, to " try their tone." " And yet," Clare thought, " if all this rubbish were cleared away, the poor thing might almost come to life again." She stripped it, ruthlessly, hesitating only when she came to the last of the useless objects that infested it : a plush-framed photograph of Edith Wilburn, one of the many that, like the oleographs of a patron saint in a convent, littered the house.

At this she stopped, instinctively abashed by the gaze of those mild eyes, so curiously half-closed like Evelyn's, which regarded her from the level of her own with a melancholy innocence. " Spare me," they seemed to say ; " do not be harsh with me," they pleaded : " for you are young and strong and full of life, while I am nothing but a poor shadow. Life has its obligations ; be generous ! "

And, as she gazed, the yellowed photograph went misty before Clare's eyes, so that for a moment she almost regretted what she had done already. The vague sense of sacrilege now defined itself ; she knew that the thing which she hated and had destroyed was all that remained of the personality of Edith Wilburn, clinging pathetically to the mean objects on which its living affections had been set like those of a child devoted to some maimed and hideous toy.

" But I am not really ungenerous," Clare told her. " When I am dead, as you are, I shall have to accept the change ; but now I'm alive, and have my own life to make the best of, and if I thought of you . . ."

Did Dudley think of her ? she wondered, stifling the faint

jealousy with which the thought troubled her heart; did Joyce, did Evelyn think of her? Of course they didn't; for Edith Wilburn had died when Evelyn was born and Joyce was only four. "They are like me," she thought, "and yet, though I had no mother, I had Aunt Cathie, and they have no one." It seemed to her that she had already failed in her duty toward them, that the wan appeal in Edith Wilburn's eyes had taught her a lesson. "I must try again," she thought, "I mustn't expect too much; I must be more patient, and, if they'll let me, I must try to love them."

As a superstitious act of penance and piety she left the plush-framed photograph on the top of the piano. This symbol satisfied her conscience; for the rest, as token of her right to live and express herself, she went on with her reorganization of that melancholy chamber as she pleased. The luncheon gong surprised her dusty but triumphant. Strong in the virtue of her resolution to be more patient and understanding she prepared to put it into practice with Evelyn in the dining-room. But Evelyn, who with her cat-like love of downy cushions combined the cat's mysterious intentness of movement, and also feared, perhaps, the penultimate incarnation of "that sirloin," was nowhere to be found. Nor could Mrs. Marple, the only representative of the established order, now darkly impressive in her shopping get-up, imagine where she had gone.

"I've been out of the house all morning, as *you* know, ma'am," she said resentfully. "Miss Evelyn doesn't tell *me* where she's going."

Miss Evelyn, as Clare suspected, told her most things.

"Then I won't wait for her, Mrs. Marple," she said.

"That's as you wish, ma'am," Mrs. Marple replied in tones that made Clare feel she had driven home another nail in the coffin of her reputation.

And yet, when the sombre lunch, which tasted, like everything else at Tudor House—and even in Mrs. Marple's absence—of Mrs. Marple, was over, Clare felt, in spite of all her kindly resolutions, a wicked relief that Evelyn had decided not to go out " calling " with her. The ordeal of facing all these strange Alvaston people whom Dudley's profession compelled her to know was sufficiently embarrassing without the added consciousness that Evelyn's pig-eyes were holding a watching brief for the established interests. Wherever she went in these strongholds of North Bromwich respectability, in the drawing-rooms of the " older people " which so closely resembled that of Tudor House, she felt the drag of Evelyn's fat inertia on her shoulders, and knew, like a suspect under arrest, that anything which she said might be used against her.

Even now, as she dressed, she could imagine the poisoned honey of Evelyn's flattery. " Oh, Clare, how awfully smart you are to-day ! " she would say, suggesting a hard and selfish magnificence deliberately planned by Clare to put their home-made clothes in the shade.

" But if," Clare meditated before the mahogany mirror, " I as much as suggested giving either of them any of my own clothes, they'd talk it over with Mrs. Marple and decide it was an insult. However, Christmas is coming, thank goodness, and then I shall be able to buy them some pretty things without being sniffed at."

She smiled as she came downstairs ; for Christmas suggested not only the possibility of proving her benevolence toward Joyce and Evelyn without offence, but also the radiant happiness of recovering Steven. How wonderful that would be ! she thought. Already her mind was full of rapturous plans for that amazing moment.

" Evelyn . . . Evelyn ! " she called ; but no voice answered her : only the low rumour of Mrs. Marple laying down the law, in her shopping finery, to Mary at the kitchen dinner-table. " It isn't my place, nor yours," Mrs. Marple was saying, " to give an answer when you're not called by

name. Let her shout till she's hoarse. Give her a long
enough rope, my girl, and mark my words, she'll 'ang
'erself."

For Mrs. Marple had seen the drawing-room.

## III

## BATTLE OF MARPLE

" I'm glad I didn't wait for her," Clare was thinking, as
she stepped out into the Halesby Road; but before the
thought had ended, Evelyn was forgotten in the sudden and
joyous revelation that greeted her.

The iron-coloured mist, whose particles of suspended
carbon choked the pores of the atmosphere like a film of
bacteria on a porcelain filter, was vanishing before her eyes.
The sun was beating downward through newly-clarified air
with the golden warmth of a premature spring. And
suddenly, as though their vibrations had been freed and
amplified, all sounds and colours attained a new and startling
vigour. The front-gate swung behind her with a pleasant
click, as though it approved the cunning mechanism of its
own latch; a robin hopped and sang in a shining holly-
bush; the privet hedges were alive with light; the blue
slates of the opposite houses shone like happy skies, and
down the slope from the fountain the Tilton 'bus came
swinging with the crack of a whip and all the gay abandonment of a stage-coach in a Christmas number.

" What a bright day," she thought, " and how happy
I feel! I'd no idea that Alvaston could be so beautiful."

Even in the faces of the people whom she met, the red-
cheeked nursemaids, wheeling woolly babies, the timid old
ladies and elderly gentlemen with mufflers round their necks
who issued from their orderly retirements to take the air,

she caught the radiation of an unconscious pleasure akın to her own. They smiled at her, a stranger, and Clare smiled back at them, for no other reason than the lightness of her heart.

And as she walked briskly over those clean, spacious thoroughfares and under the high sky she was thinking all the time of Steven whom she hadn't seen—so Dudley had decreed it—since their return from Bournemouth. It was now less than three weeks till the beginning of the Christmas holidays, and during those three weeks she would be able to think all the time of the hundreds of little things that would make him happy at Tudor House ; the children's parties to which he would be invited ; the pantomimes ; the Christmas tree, with all its crackers and coloured candles and mica frost ; the little room which was to be his own, and which she would try to make as nearly as possible like the dressing-room at Uffdown ; the absorbing mysteries and surprises of his stocking. Even when she tried to fit Joyce and Evelyn into the picture she was confident ; for nobody, she thought, however difficult their natures, could help loving Steven—not even the settled gloom of Tudor House could resist his youth, his brightness. She smiled as she thought how happy they would all be together ; she was still smiling as she reached the object of her first call : The Cedars, Enville Road, the habitation of two ladies who had left their cards on her.

*Miss Isit. Miss Ellen Isit :* so the cards proclaimed them. As she stood on the doorstep and heard a cracked bell tinkle feebly behind panes of coloured glass, she continued to smile, wondering how she should ask for them : " *Is this the Miss Isits' ? Are the Misses Isit in ? This is the Misses Isits', isn't it ? ''* Whatever else she did, she mustn't make fun of Dudley's clients.

The Misses Isit kept her waiting for a long time in a draw-ing-room which, but for its faint odour of breath-cachous, might have been transported bodily from Tudor House ; the same north light, the same subaqueous gloom ; the same green chenille tablecloth and asparagus fern ; the same dead, upright-piano, draped in an embroidered catafalque and infested with trinkets and photograph frames. Alarmingly the same : for when she came to look more closely, there was the face of Edith Wilburn framed, not in plush, but chip-carving. And suddenly, as she met those half-closed eyes, all the unconscious gaiety that she had carried with her faded away. The past, it seemed, was following fast on her heels ; she could not escape from it.

Miss Agnes Isit, the elder, who swam into the room with sea-green draperies trailing and a string of glaucous beads hanging like pale, submerged corals from her skinny neck, succeeded in making her feel even more oppressively at home. She held Clare's hand in clammy, fish-like fingers, then examined her closely in the melancholy light. Her teeth were looser than they should have been, and, when she smiled or spoke, passed out of her control, so that her thin lips were always in a state of unstable equilibrium that she corrected by rapid gushes of speech which also happily concealed an unfortunate impediment.

" I'm sorry, so sorry that my sister's out," she said. " We'd been so looking thorward to making the acquaintance of dear Mr. Wilburn's bride. You see we consider ourselves among the oldest thriends of the thamily. We both knew dear Edith when she was quite a tiny tot. You see we always keep her thotograth on the piano. Of course we realise how thrighthully risky these second marriages are. But then, dear Mrs. Wilburn, this isn't your thirst either, is it ? Besides, you won't theel lonely. The girls are so nearly your own age and will make everything easy for you. Joyce, as we always say, is a thascinating child. And little Evelyn . . . we're so *thond* of her." Words failed Miss Isit ; but she smiled until it was just too late.

" And now that we've seen you," she gushed, speaking for her absent sister as well as for herself, " we realise that dear Mr. Wilburn is as thortunate as you are. It's quite a romance, isn't it ? You lucky, lucky girl! He's such a remarkable man ; so thirm—without thear or thavour, as we always say. And then you have that adorable Mrs. Worple ! Of course you've lived in the country—we know all about you, you see—and probably have no conception what a trial these town servants are. You see how they keep one waiting when it's only a matter of serving a cup of tea."

She agitated a woollen bell-pull ; wires grated ; a bell tinkled in some cavernous kitchen. Clare begged her not to worry ; she had other calls to make.

" What ? Do you think I could let you go without a cup of tea ? " Miss Isit cackled. " That would be too inhospitable. Now what was I saying ? Servants . . . ah, servants ! "

They talked of servants. It seemed to Clare that these ladies of Alvaston never talked of anything else ; in all these houses, except those of the wealthy, who subsidized housekeepers, as fat nations subsidize mercenaries, to act as buffers between them and reality, the " servant question," as it was beginning to be called, displaced all other topics of thought or conversation. She didn't understand it. At Uffdown, at Stourford, at Pen House, the " servant question " had never presented itself. Now it was beginning to loom on her horizon in the shape of Mrs. Marple.

It was a relief when, having left the Miss Isits' drawing-room and come to the surface again, she reached the gilt gates of Old Alvaston Hall, the abode of the brewer, Sir Joseph Astill. For Lady Astill, even if she were vulgar and festooned in her husband's rich *ex votis* like the image of some miracle-working Madonna, was a comfortable soul who accepted Clare not as a substitute for the lamented

Edith Wilburn but as the daughter-in-law of her friend
Lady 'Ingston. Indeed, in the days when Edith's pale
charms had flourished, Lady Astill had been working a beer-
machine behind her husband's bar in Lower Sparkdale ;
for the Astill reputation, which now flourished on quassia
and molasses, had been founded on honest malt and hops,
which the baronet still brewed, on Sunday afternoons, for
his own consumption.

" Now you must let them run you home, my love," said
Lady Astill, as Clare rose to leave her. " There's two big
Deemlers eating their 'eads off in the garage, and Joe would
never forgive me if I let you walk. Mr. Wilburn doesn't
' run ' a car ? Well, I don't blame him. In our position
you simply 'ave to keep abreast of the times, but my 'eart
often 'ankers after a carriage and pair. It's difficult to drop
the things you've been brought up on ! "

Lady Astill, apparently, had not been brought up on
aitches. . . .

In spite of her persuasions Clare decided to walk. The
evening was clear and frosty, with street-lamps already
shining on a thin bloom of rime. In the still starlight the
stark trees of the Alvaston gardens emitted a woodland
scent that conjured away the shadows of the houses that
they sheltered, and caught her mind backward to the nights
of Uffdown. How lovely Uffdown must be on a night like
this ! She dared not even dream of it. Over the wide and
glittering macadam of the Halesby Road the light in the
dining-room window of Tudor House beckoned, commanded her to face the present. She hoped that she would
be able to slip up to her bedroom and change for dinner
unnoticed ; but, as she stood on the doorstep, she discovered
to her annoyance that she had left her latchkey behind.
She rang, and the funereal figure of Mrs. Marple opened
to her.

" Is Mr. Wilburn in ? " she asked.

" The master's been back an hour or more," said Mrs.
Marple.

" You've put a fire in the drawing-room ? "

" I told Mary to light it, ma'am ? " said Mrs. Marple,
disclaiming any contact with the desecrated place. And yet,
beneath her vindictiveness, it seemed to Clare that Mrs.
Marple smiled.

She dressed hurriedly and descended to the dining-room.
Evelyn lay curled up on the hearthrug ; Joyce and Dudley,
with his spectacles on, were reading in two arm-chairs on
either side of the fire. The air of the room seemed colder
than that of the night outside ; the hand that Dudley
reached out to her as he smiled his welcome was cold as ice.

" Why, you're all frozen here ! " she said quickly. " I'd
better put some coal on."

Dudley hesitated. " I think it's hardly worth it, Clare,"
he said. " We shall be moving into the other room in less
than an hour." And Joyce, with a silent, upward lifted
glance, approved, as though it pleased her to see Clare put
in her place.

" I know where my place is," Clare's thoughts swiftly
answered her ; and she took it, perching herself on the arm
of Dudley's chair, with her elbow on his shoulder and her
fingers in his hair. The gesture was one of bravado, in
assertion of her rights ; and while she pretended to read
the evening paper that he was holding, her mind was so
troubled by the look of insolent scorn in Evelyn's eyes that
all her generous resolutions of charity were swept away.

" They are intolerable," she thought ; " they never as
much as raised a finger to make room for me ; but he's my
husband, he's mine, he's mine ! "

All through the meal the sisters maintained their attitude
of obstinate silence, irritating Clare into a show of unusual
vivacity that she was far from feeling ; a vivacity so successful that she excelled herself in mimicking the gushes of the

elder Miss Isit and poor Lady Astill's struggles with the letter aitch. She felt forced to joke for fear that she should forget that such things as jokes existed ; but Dudley, as she had long ago discovered, had little sense of humour. Or rather, his sense of humour was not hers. The jokes that he laughed at, after a long period of reaction, rarely seemed funny to her ; and now that she was really on the top of her form, he smiled slowly, in spite of himself, as if he weren't quite sure of her humour's propriety.

" Ah, yes ; I see—I'm sorry," he said with a short laugh. " I'm afraid I was taking you seriously."

And Evelyn, who had pretended not to hear, looked up and stared discouragingly with her pig-eyes, while Joyce, who had seen the joke and resented it, looked up from her plate with the expression of annoyance that she might have given to a tiresome puppy.

" You're very excited to-night," Wilburn said to her as they rose from the table. " Whatever's the matter with you ? "

She laughed and kissed him so that Joyce, who was looking down her nose contemptuously, must see. She whispered as she kissed him : " I've a surprise for you, in the drawing-room. You'll see in a moment."

They passed through together, his arm about her waist ; but when the drawing-room door was opened, the surprise was hers. The room was complete in every detail as she had found it that morning. Everything that she had moved in her reforming fervour had been studiously, exactly re-placed. Not a chair, not an ornament, not a knick-knack out of position.

" Well, Clare, and what's the surprise ? " he rallied her.

" I'll tell you later," she gasped.

' You curious child ! Whatever's the matter with you ? "

How could she sit through the whole evening in face of her defeat ? Of course she would tell him later ; she would tell him everything. Why later? Why not now, before these smug creatures whose muteness showed their satisfaction; before Mrs. Marple—Mrs. Marple was in it —who carried in the washy coffee as though its very beastliness symbolized the triumph of the established order. Dudley was tired with work; all through that brilliant Saturday afternoon he had been stewing in his office: it would be cruel, at the end of such a day, to involve him in a full-stage row.

"But if I take this lying down," she told herself, "I shall have lost more ground than I can ever recover. I'm bringing in pity to explain my cowardice. Two children and a dour old woman! If I'm afraid of them I might as well throw up the sponge at once. What would Aunt Cathie think of me?"

She smiled in spite of herself; she could hear Aunt Cathie passionately invoking the doctor's memory. Aunt Cathie would stand no nonsense! But Aunt Cathie was far away, over the starlit countryside where owls were squealing in the Pen House orchard.

"And if I get it over now," she thought, "heaven knows what will happen; I may spoil Steven's Christmas. It would be dreadful for Steven to come here for the first time in the middle of a fight of that kind."

So she possessed her soul in a bitter patience, while Wilburn left her side and lit his cigar. Remote and secret, isolated by the thin, coiling smoke, he sat and meditated on the labyrinth in which the Sedgebury Main's finances resembled its drowned galleries. The old weight pressed upon her, subdued and separated her. What intimacy was possible under the stony glare of Edith Wilburn's photographs of her Victorian friends? What joy, what lightness could flower beneath the disapproval of that sombre, hideous furniture, in a scene which seemed to be set for macabre events, such as funeral reunions and the reading of wills?

What life, what spontaneity, what gaiety were possible where Joyce's spectacled eyes were chained to the " Pathology of Hepatic Sclerosis," and Evelyn, dazed with hockey, sat sucking caramels and sixpenny magazines among her cushions ? What human tenderness, of the kind for which she longed, could penetrate this atmosphere of smouldering hatreds ? Then why did she hesitate ? Why didn't she boldly fan it to a blaze, even if it meant that she would be scorched and charred by it ? Let her, for once, be splendidly outrageous, taking her lesson from Lady Hingston !

It was all very well to think of Lady Hingston. She knew she couldn't do it. Not just yet : that was the way she comforted herself. She couldn't even beat a retreat and leave the field to them ; for all that house seemed bleak and hostile to her ; no fire was allowed in any other room but Mrs. Marple's kitchen ; and the thought of the smile of victory which her exit would bring to Joyce's lips restrained her. All through the evening they sat there, like hostile animals forced by a menagerie keeper into one cage. Their minds were like walled and jealous Spanish cities whose gates are barred at sundown ; nothing entered and nothing left them, and Clare was alone and shivering outside in the empty plain.

At ten o'clock the sisters yawned and filled hot-water bottles. They snapped good-night at Clare ; kissed Wilburn, and went to bed.

" Now I can tell him," she thought ; but no sooner were they gone than Mrs. Marple crawled in to take her orders for the morning. Was it mere force of habit that made her address herself entirely to Dudley, and await her instructions from him ? Wilburn, apparently, took the attitude for granted and noticed no intentional slight in it. When Mrs. Marple had gone, Clare came close to him. He fondled her hand as she knelt beside him. But though he did this he wasn't really thinking of her, for, when he spoke, it was only to say : " Clare, darling, do you realize it's Saturday night ? What about those accounts ? "

Accounts : they were the bane and terror of her life. At Uffdown, starting her married life under Aunt Cathie's direction, she had kept accounts of sorts ; but that accountancy had been a romantic diversion—at the most a matter of form—and, after a little while the test to which she submitted it had been simplicity itself. At the end of each quarter the bank sent in her pass-book ; if the pass-book showed a balance, she closed it with a smile of relief ; if, on the other hand, the word " charges " appeared, she guessed, without any precise knowledge of its significance, that something was amiss, and began to practice economies in the hope that, by next quarter, it would have disappeared.

But Dudley, and the custom of Tudor House, demanded that all accounts should be balanced weekly, and balanced to a halfpenny. In the old days Joyce had kept them ; and Joyce, she knew, would have helped her with them now if she had asked her ; for Joyce was not above being helpful on occasions when her efficiency could make other and lesser intelligences look small. But Clare's pride would not allow her to accept this help that took the form of a humiliation, and preferred to struggle with them by herself. However much they bothered her, she knew that Dudley had a right to insist on accuracy, since, with Aunt Cathie's fervent approval, he shared the expenses of housekeeping. It would have been easy, she often thought, so easy to put things right with her own money when figures were obstinate ; but Dudley's brain was too scrupulous and exact to accept these jugglings.

So, now that they were alone together, they sat—for an infinity it seemed, over the greasy tradesmen's books, the blood-stained butcher's bills, casting and recasting the figures that she had so painfully transcribed and that wouldn't, simply wouldn't come right.

" But, Dudley dearest," she begged him, " it's only threepence. What *does* a penny matter here or there ? "

" In terms of money, nothing," he agreed ; " as a matter of principle, just as much as a thousand pounds."

" Well, anyway, they *won't* come right," she told him, " and it seems to me ridiculous that a man with a brain like yours should waste this valuable time and energy over stupid details. I can see you're tired already. For heaven's sake leave them, and I'll have another try to-morrow."

But no : in these things there seemed no end to his patience, no trifle too small to escape him. He looked as if he really enjoyed it, sitting with his arm about her waist in the drawing-room that grew colder every moment as the embers deadened ; treating her protests gently, half-humorously, like an affectionate teacher with a backward child. Like a quick water-spider his pen-point skated over the page ; his lips moved silently as they shaped the figures.

" Ah, now I've got it," he cried, recapturing the missing pence. " You foolish child . . . d'you see what you've done there ? "

And she forced herself to echo his enthusiasm, though she was stiff with cold, because it evidently meant so much to him ; but no sooner were the figures adjusted than she found herself caught in another snare.

This time the milk. . . . For the two Jersey cows at Uff-down, unlike her Bechstein and Bo-peep, had been brought over to Alvaston and pastured in the little blackened paddock at the bottom of the garden. They were Clare's business, Dudley had decided ; it was her duty to pay for their winter keep and provide the wages of the gardener who fed and milked them, to supply the household and sell the surplus. In her anxiety to be exact, Clare had debited the household accounts with payments for milk and cream.

" I see we're paying your dairy," he said ; " but there's

no mention, on the credit side, of the money that Hadley receives for the milk he sells."

" I thought we agreed," she told him, " that the cows were my affair."

" Exactly, my child ; but you can't have it both ways. You see," he continued gently, " as things stand I'm paying for half of it. That's obvious, isn't it ? And that was never intended."

Clare pondered. " But, Dudley, so am I," she said. " And if Hadley's profits are included as well it seems to me I lose in every direction."

He laughed. " Why, Clare, your business sense is developing ! "

It wasn't. Her brain was in an absolute muddle. With puzzled eyes she tried to straighten it. " The cows are mine," she thought. " I'm paying for their food, and Hadley's wages ; I'm already paying for half the milk I've already paid for ; but if I put in the money that Hadley gets, surely I shall be paying for everything twice over ; it's heads I win, and tails you lose, but Dudley . . ." The problem was too stiff for her.

" I suppose you must be right, darling," sh said.

He sat with pen uplifted : " Which way will you have it ? "

" Perhaps you'd better cut it out altogether."

" Very well." With a business-like stroke he crossed out the disputed item, and shut the account-book. He seemed in better spirits than usual, slipping his arm round her waist and kissing her as he turned off the drawing-room gas. Yet, even so, she was not satisfied. Could it possibly be that he was mean ?

Beneath such a distressing speculation the incident of Mrs. Marple and the drawing-room sank into relative unimportance. That night she could not speak of it. Next night she knew it was too late.

## IV

## ESCAPES

EVEN now, when things seemed at their ugliest, it never entered her head to criticise Wilburn, much less to blame him, for the difficulties of her position. The hero-worship with which Aunt Cathie had infected her over a long period of years had exalted her ideas of him to a plane above these everyday troubles ; and even if she couldn't share his magnificent isolation from their pettiness, she was proud to feel that, whatever happened, she was his wife. She knew that if the struggle became too hard for her she had only to say a word and he would come to her help. Someday, in the near future, she might be forced to appeal to him ; but as long as she could manage to hold her own, she felt it beneath her dignity to do so.

At times, she was forced to confess, she found him puzzling. Their married life was different, somehow, from what she had imagined it would be. From the first she had never admitted the illusion that it would offer her the raptures of her first, her only love. At the most she had expected to enjoy a sane and settled comradeship, a sense of stable security and protection. In the superfluity of his strength he could give her this without effort ; and she, in return, could give him, if not love, a boundless admiration and devotion.

Now, slowly, she was beginning to realize that the intimacy, the comradeship which she had expected were confined to one small portion of their married life. And this, if it flattered her, did not content her. His established bachelorhood and the habitual, forbidding reticence of his profession denied her the confidences, the sharing of everyday experience, which she had expected him to give her, and froze her own confidences on her lips ; and though she spent long hours in his company, eagerly waiting for the chance to sympathize, the greater part of his life was closed against her as completely as if she had been a stranger. There seemed no reason to suppose that their relationship would ever be different ; he was no nearer to her now than he had been at any time during the last ten years except in those surprising moments when he suddenly and passionately revealed himself as lover or husband.

The idea of marriage as such an unequal compact, the way in which his life was divided into watertight compartments, puzzled her. It was natural enough for her to regard him as a superior being ; but hardly right, she felt, for a husband to acquiesce so complacently in her attitude. She couldn't happily go on for the rest of her life—the fantastic phrase leapt suddenly into her mind—living in sin with a distinguished stranger. However satisfied he might be with the arrangement it wouldn't combine with her sense of personal dignity ; however mysteriously he might veil himself from her she determined to penetrate his disguises, to discover the person behind the oracle's admirable shape.

And when she set herself, through that white night, seriously to investigate, she shuddered to find not merely that she knew nothing of the man she had married, but to doubt whether, beyond the mystery of his impressive exterior, his honesty, his unforgettable kindness, and the admitted acuteness of his legal mind, there was very much to know. Except in the discovery of a faintly incongruous passion, the figure of Wilburn, after two months of married life, remained, in essentials, precisely what it had appeared to her ever since she had known him. And when, in the absence of Aunt Cathie with her rose-coloured spectacles, she began to examine this figure in detail, it seemed to her that Dudley Wilburn, as she had known and admired him at Wychbury or Uffdown, differed from the Dudley Wilburn of Alvaston in much the same way as a flower in a specimen vase differs from the same flower growing in a tangled bed, or as the pearl in the pin that fastened, every morning, his professional Ascot tie, might differ from the same pearl in its original oyster.

Every evening, when he came back from the city, she hoped to recognize the Wilburn of her—or Aunt Cathie's— dreams. Every evening as they sat together before the drawing-room fire, the magic qualities with which her renewed enthusiasm had gifted him dissolved and vanished like September hoar frost.

" The fault must be mine," she told herself. " I'm making a horrid mess of the whole business. Dudley is different from other people. I haven't taken enough trouble to understand him. If I had any sense I should have managed to penetrate his thoughts by this time. He's so used to living alone that it surprises him when I want to share them. I'm growing stupid, that's what's the matter with me. This house is like a prison ; I'm suffocating ; all that I'm really suffering from is lack of movement and fresh air. If only there were a garden for me to work in and forget everything ! "

There was a garden ; a big garden by Alvaston standards : a long rectilinear patch with a tennis-court in the middle surrounded by a gravel path and attenuated beds which Hadley converted yearly into tricoloured ribbons of geraniums, lobelias and calceolarias. It thrilled her to think that, if the new tenants permitted it, she might diversify this formal wilderness by rock-plants brought over from Uffdown. But when, a few days later, she announced her intention, the proposal aroused a tempest of disapproval from Joyce and Evelyn.

" But don't you see, Clare," they protested, " that it would ruin the tennis-court. We lose enough balls as it is without planting jungles of rock-plants everywhere."

And Dudley was equally discouraging. " You see," he

said dubiously, " we have to think of Hadley. He's been with me fifteen years, and I doubt if I could get another man to do the work at his wage. You can't spoil the tennis-court, as Joyce says, and if you interfere with his vegetables there'll be the devil to pay. I think, on the whole, you'd better leave things as they are. After all, there's not much point in keeping a gardener and doing all the work yourself."

She submitted to his verdict. " And yet," she thought, " I must have space ; I must have liberty to expand in some direction."

Liberty ? She was as free as the wind, if only she had sense to leave her prison. There at her door lay this elegant suburb of Alvaston to begin with ; and beyond, where the watershed dipped towards the valley of Trent, the thirty-odd square miles of the City of Iron invited the attention of anyone who chose to realize the aggregate of human will and aspiration which, in a hundred years, had turned it from a sleepy market town into a city renowned or at least notorious, through all the civilized world.

If Alvaston had little to give her but the invigorating cleanliness of its upland air in road after road of an irre-proachable trimness, bordered by replicas of one hundred and ninety seven to the nineteen thousand and seventieth, which each reflected, according to the degree of its owner's prosperity, the identical spirit that had frozen her imagina-tion within the walls of Tudor House, the older and less respectable districts of North Bromwich, from the sober Georgian facades of Easy Row to the impenetrable bricky jungle of Lower Sparkdale, offered her curiosity a spectacle of human activity as various as any at which tourists gape in the bazaars of Cairo or the warrens of Canton.

Up to this point she had taken North Bromwich for granted. Now she set out, with all the curiosity of an explorer, to discover it anew, recognizing, behind its uniform and devastating mask of soot-blackened brick, the unceasing, ant-like human activity whose accumulated effect had made the city the industrial portent that it was.

Now, as she tramped, with curious eyes and aching feet, over the blue-brick pavements, through mazes of mean streets which opened, here and there, on empty squares whose churches of crumbling stucco and grass-grown graveyards mournfully perpetuated the spiritual aspirations of mid-Victorian dead ; through deep-cut channels, where iron-laden wagons came trailing in a slow tide between the tall blear-windowed factory-backs toward canal wharves, dead and beautiful, after their fashion, as those of Bruges ; through livelier but no less sordid thoroughfares, where the steam-trams, like antediluvian reptiles, went snorting fire and flying sparks toward the eastern suburbs, she began to realize, dimly, what this city was.

In the first years of her married life Ralph had taken her over to Wolverbury ; she had seen and wondered at the Hingston Steelworks, unique, as Sir Joseph had modestly told her, of their kind. But here, in the black heart of North Bromwich, a dozen Wolverburys could have been hidden and forgotten in two square miles. This city, whose confines pressed upon the mild amenities of Alvaston, was full of Wolverburys in gross or miniature, from the blank-walled factories of the great engineering works and brass-foundries, whose hot draught made the sky quiver above them in the depth of winter, whose black mud grimed the streets and made the close air heavy with oily odours, to the clinking domestic forges of nailers, and the dim twelve-foot square chambers of working jewellers, where stretched sacking caught the falling ruby and the flame of bunsen gas-jets and purring blow-pipes dried the throat.

Wherever she went the air was acrid and volcanic with the smell of fire ; noisy with the whirring of lathes, the shriek of high-speed tool-cutting steel, the steady grating of saws, the thunder of sheet-iron, the sighs of furnaces, the thudding of hammers. From dawn to sunset, in every lost purlieu of the town, those sounds of tense mechanical labour never ceased ; the fingers of pallid stunted men by thousands were cutting, filing, twisting, hammering, moulding, stamping, some stubborn matrix of metal into shapes minute or monstrous for the adornment, the fancy, or the use of half the world.

In face of these enormous and persistent labours, absorbing the brains and hands of half a million people, it seemed to her that her own vague discontents were mean and futile, that she had not even begun to grasp the scope or perspective of human life. Of her own state she had used the words " slavery " and " imprisonment " ; she had not known the meaning of either, and even now she could only guess at them. Yet, as she stood and listened to the hard, the brave, the good-humoured North Bromwich speech issuing from the mouths of scabrous " courts," where ragged children shouted themselves hoarse and pregnant women dragged themselves about with last year's babies in their arms and smiled at her, or when she mingled in the crowd that tainted the entrance to Joyce's hospital with odours of dirt and iodoform, she realized that these people took their slavery, their duress, more bravely than she did. They had no time to think about themselves ; or, if they had it, knew better than to waste it.

One morning, in the middle of some such voyage of exploration, she found herself in a street which, though it resembled a hundred others, seemed strangely, particularly familiar.

" I have been here before," she thought, instantly referring her knowledge to one of those submerged dream-landscapes which suddenly, mysteriously are lifted like volcanic islands above the seas of normal consciousness. The very pavement was familiar to her. Before she knew what had happened she found herself on the steps of the

church of St. Jude, which, thirteen years before, she had
visited with the adored Miss Boldmere.

In a spirit of curiosity rather than of piety she entered the
mean brick building that once had been transfigured in her
eyes. She made her way up the nave to the chairs which she
and Miss Boldmere had occupied. She sat down ; for her
feet were tired, and the silence, impregnated with incense,
was grateful after the cries and clangour of the street. The
little church was empty, save for one small, hunched figure,
prostrated rather than kneeling in front of the tabernacle on
the altar in which the Sacrament was reserved.

Sitting there silently she opened her heart and mind to
receive the consolations that religion had given her in the
days before Ralph's paganism had weakened its appeal and
his death killed it. But no angel troubled the waters of
her still mind ; it lay, like a sombre pool, reflecting not
opened heavens but the material meanness of that poor
church. The woman kneeling at the steps of the altar
inspired her not with sympathy but with a vague and pitiful
wonder, not only for that hunched figure but for her own
departed youth. How thin, how ghostly, all those old raptures seemed ! How little they meant to her now ! Those
ardours, those emotions, she could no more recapture them
than turn herself into the pigtailed child who had knelt and
wept at Miss Boldmere's side. The incense made her head
ache, and after a little while she was thankful to escape into
the noisy street.

" That is all over now," she told herself. " It only hurts
me to think about it. It's silly to imagine that one can ever
go back. I'm a different person. I'm not only older, I'm
harder. Hard and bitter and sceptical. But I can't help
it. That is only what happens. . . ."

However bitter she may have believed herself to be, the
excitements and flurry of her Christmas shopping and the
thrills that seized her heart whenever she thought of Steven's

return were sufficient to keep it younger than she imagined. The Christmas celebrations of Uffdown had always been lavish, following the tradition which Ralph had transplanted from Stourford, where, with the business instinct that had made Wolverbury famous, Sir Joseph had realized the convenience of concentrating the year's performance of his duty towards God and his duty toward his neighbour into forty-eight hours. During that period the Stourford generosity was boundless, and Clare, at Uffdown, had allowed her benevolence to flow with an equal profusion.

The fact that she was now living in Alvaston made no difference to these obligations ; even if her new tenants at Uffdown relieved her of some of them, she couldn't forget that she was Lady of the Manor, and that Steven, some day, would return like an exiled prince, to enjoy his own again. And now the repressions of Tudor House, the memory of those miserable pence over which she had been forced to puzzle her brain, found relief and reaction in a veritable orgy of spending, a generosity that was exciting in itself but doubly exciting as a protest against the meagreness to which she had been condemned.

The weather was chill and gloomy ; but the shop-windows of North Bromwich, habitually provincial and self-contained, had given themselves over to a metropolitan splendour ; their bright lights, gleaming through the fog, invited its inhabitants, for once, to let themselves go, and proclaim the Iron City's wealth and magnificence ; and Clare, with her long list of benefactions due, went hither and thither among the lights and the holly-berries and the frosted festoons thrilled by the daring of her own munificence and never stopping to count the cost of it. The Uffdown list was the longest and most lavish ; but Tudor House should share in Uffdown's astonishment ; Aunt Cathie, Thirza, the Pomfrets, Bissell, Ellen, cottagers by the dozen—even Mrs. Marple should be forced to admit that her new mistress was generous and forgiving ; even Joyce and Evelyn should confess that, however obstinately they resented her, she bore them no ill-will.

At the end of her third morning's shopping she found herself, hungry and elated, in the neighbourhood of Sackville Row. It was a mild, dry day ; pale sunlight tingeing the gracious cupola of St. Clement's Cathedral with wintry gold. The wide flagged pavements of the churchyard, where hawkers spread their toys and one old woman fingered her Braille Bible, seemed clean and wholesome after the clammy streets. At this hour they were full of the holiday faces and mistletoe buttonholes of prosperous business-men hurrying away to lunch from the high blocks of offices whose grey facades surrounded this square of opulence and ease. Its light and airiness, so different from the vitiated atmospheres in which she had been shopping ; the air of freedom, kindliness and good-humour that pervaded it enchanted her and made her unwilling to return to the solitude of Tudor House. She had so many enthralling things to talk about, and no one to tell them to.

Suddenly it struck her that there, on the far side of the square, was Dudley's office. Aunt Cathie had often pointed to its wide stone steps, yet, since their marriage, she had never entered it. She wondered if Dudley had gone out to lunch ; for, if he hadn't, it would be jolly to make him take her with him and tell him all the excitements with which her heart was bursting ; so wonderful, for once in a way, to have him to herself.

She hurried across the square and entered the block of offices, a building as sober and impressive as Dudley himself, its pillared doorway thick with brass-plates carrying familiar names : *Metalfolds Ltd. ; The Great Mawne Colliery ; Elphinstone Bros. ;* and, finally, on a surface so worn by polishing that the words were scarcely decipherable, *Wilburn, Wilburn and Wilburn.* She climbed two flights of stone steps, clean-swept, but worn in the middle. A glazed door, of conscious unimportance, directed her to *Wilburn Bros. Solicitors*. Flushed, and a little breathless with her climb and the weight of her parcels, she knocked on the pane. Nobody answered.

"He has gone," she thought. "Oh, what a pity! I shan't be able to tell him." But surely in an office of such importance somebody must be left behind?

She opened the door, and found herself in a plainly-furnished ante-room. On a high stool behind an antiquated desk sat a fantastic figure : a man of indeterminable age in a seedy frock-coat, whose solemn, moon-like face was bowed above an open book. As soon as he perceived her he thrust the book away from him guiltily, and stared at her with eyes that seemed to consider her from some unimaginable distance.

"I beg your pardon," she said. "Is Mr. Wilburn in ? "

"Which Mr. Wilburn ? " he asked her, gradually returning within range.

"Mr. Dudley Wilburn."

"I'll see."

He climbed down from his stool and slouched away. "Really he might have offered me a chair," she thought. "I wonder if Dudley's clerks treat all his clients like this."

From some inner chamber she heard Dudley's voice. "Why the deuce didn't you ask her what her name was," he was saying. The voice was harsh and irritable. She smiled to think how pleased he would be when he heard it. The clerk mooned back again :

"Your name, please, Madam."

"Mrs. Wilburn, Mrs. Dudley Wilburn," she answered smiling.

Impervious to the humour of the situation the clerk disappeared.

"Mrs. Dudley Wilburn," she heard him repeat.

" Show her in, Grosmont," the voice of Dudley answered with a grunt.

" Please step this way."

" One would imagine," she thought, " that he wasn't pleased to see me." Her high heart fell. " But surely, at this time, he can't be working ; there's nobody there ; and he hasn't even come to meet me." She wondered if she had committed some dreadful breach of etiquette ; she felt like a criminal climbing the dock as she entered the room ; and when he spoke to her it was as though he were addressing a client.

" My dear Clare, whatever are you doing here ? "

His tone put her on the defensive, but pride would not allow her to show it. She kissed him lightly as though the equivocal welcome had not been spoken and nestled up against him with the seductions of a purring cat, so that he had to stroke her.

" Do you want me to go away ? " she whispered.

" Ridiculous child ! I was thinking ; and you were the last person in the world I expected to see. What on earth induced you to come here ? "

" I found myself near by," she said. " This shopping is so tiring, and I thought, if I were awfully good, you'd give me lunch somewhere. You will, won't you ? "

" Lunch ? My dear child, I never go out to lunch now-adays. Grosmont runs round to the Dairy and brings me a snack of some kind. If you're too late to get home you'd better go to Battie's."

" So that's how you live when you're away from me ! " she said. " No wonder you're fagged out when you come home at night ! Put on your coat and take me somewhere. I've such heaps to tell you."

He shook his head. " No, I'm afraid it's too late already," he said. " I have an enormous list of appointments in front of me." He ran his fingers down the page of the open diary.

" Mr. Aggs, Mr. Baggs, Mr. Caggs, Mr. Daggs, Mr. Boffin," Clare murmured.

He stared at her for a second, as though he weren't quite sure that she hadn't taken leave of her senses. Her smile enlightened him ; his stare dissolved in a short, uncomfortable laugh. " Ah, yes, of course . . . Dickens . . . For the moment. . . ."

" Oh, Dudley, *why* are you so serious ? " she cried.

He felt it incumbent on him to show her that he wasn't, for her physical nearness moved him to see that she was beautiful. He put his arm round her and drew her to his knee—a thought perfunctorily, as though he realized that the time and place were not exactly suitable ; and yet, as he took her, she warmed to him : she was meek and gentle, being thirsty, at that moment, for even so little love. And Wilburn, though the consciousness of that page of appointments never quite left his mind, was forced to humour her, because she was so young, so soft, so lovely in her excitement.

" My sweet one, if you could always be with me," he murmured.

" Oh, Dudley, why don't you say things like that to me more often ? " she said.

" I always love you, Clare."

" But you hardly ever say so."

" You know it, my darling. Can't you take it for granted ? "

" No, no, I can't. I don't think anybody could. Unless you keep on telling me again and again, I begin to feel I'm just a . . . a nuisance."

She hid her face against his : " Because I've nobody but you," she whispered. " And Steven . . ."

" Clare, Clare . . ." he said ; and his voice was broken so that the strings of her heart were strained in sympathy with its vibrations. Unless she did something to relieve the tension she felt that she must dissolve into shameful childish tears. If she did that she would become a nuisance indeed; so she broke away from him and let her emotion flow into a laughing, triumphant recitation of her lavish purchases; the lordly Uffdown presents, Steven's bicycle, Aunt Cathie's cafétière. "And, oh," she said, "I've found the sweetest frock you can imagine for Evelyn at Kendrick's. It nearly broke my heart not to keep it for myself. It's the new colour—fuchsia. Really I must show it you !"

She unwrapped one of her parcels; out of a foam of rustling tissue-paper she lifted the flimsy, shimmering thing, stood back, and held it in front of her. Never in her life had she seemed to him so desirable as in this moment when cheeks and lips and eyes were transfigured by the joy of giving. And yet, as he watched her, and smiled to see her smiling, a hard look of reservation came into his eyes.

"At Kendrick's, did you say ?" he asked her. "Isn't Kendrick's very expensive ? What did you pay for it ? "

"Oh, let me think . . . Twelve guineas. It's from Paris. Isn't it sweet ? "

"Twelve guineas ! My dear, that's half Evelyn's allowance for the whole year."

"I know, poor child ! That's why I thought it would be such a treat for her to have just one thing that wasn't home-made. I'm sure she's been worrying her head off what to wear at all these dances."

"How many yards of this—what did you call it ?—fuchsia-coloured material are there in it ? Four, at the most. I don't suppose it costs more than ten shillings a yard. . . ."

"But it's the *model*, Dudley. It's from Paris. There's the label inside it look, *Rue de la Paix !* Why, that'll thrill her to death to begin with; she'll only wish she could wear it outside . . . I know," she went on, "that clothes would be wasted on Joyce ; she's so awfully self-contained that it's difficult to give her anything that'll please her. Then I had an inspiration. I've got her a typewriter."

" A typewriter ? Why should she want a typewriter ? "

" Oh, for her notes and things. . . ."

" If she wants her notes typed she can do them here in the office . . . after hours."

" But this is the sweetest thing. It's portable ; all aluminium. I'm sure she'll love it. You don't sound very enthusiastic, Dudley. . . ."

" I wonder if you've any idea," he said, " what you've been spending."

She laughed. " Not in the very least. One never does at Christmas ; it wouldn't seem right."

" You've paid for them, I hope ? " His tone was ominous.

" Oh, Dudley, of course I've paid for them ; I had my cheque-book."

" We have no right," he said, " to go flinging money about like that. It gives a bad impression ; it makes other people envious and discontented."

" It makes other people happy, too. And, Dudley, it's my own money. It *is* my own money, isn't it ? "

" You have your settlement. Yes. But most of it is supposed to be devoted to Steven's education during his minority. You can't go through life thinking nothing of the future. Nothing's infallible : not even Wolverbury. Supposing Wolverbury got into difficulties, like Willis's concern at Mawne, and you had nothing in reserve : where would you and Steven be then ? "

" But even," she began . . . " But even if I had nothing, darling . . . Oh, Dudley, you wouldn't want me to be mean ? "

" You're talking childishly," he told her. " Money isn't just figures in a pass-book. It's a symbol of work and forethought and skill. It isn't meant for spending . . . as you spend it, without a definite purpose."

"Then what is it meant for? I'm not disputing you. It's only that I don't understand you, and want to know."

"I'm afraid I can't make you understand, Clare. We'd better say no more about it. There's nothing more to be said."

There was much more to be said, but the turbulence of her emotions would not let her say it. To conceal them she began to fold the discredited fuchsia frock into its shallow box. For the moment nothing was heard in the room but the rustle of tissue-paper. Then, of a sudden, wild words came out of her brain; she faced him with flushed cheeks and tears in her eyes.

"Money," she said. "I hate it! If you keep it in your hands it soils them; if you let it stay in your mind it poisons you. Not to be spent . . . why, Dudley, it's only when you're spending it, using it, trying to make people happier with it, that it's the slightest bit of use to anyone; and if I thought that Steven were going to think as you do . . ."

She stopped; she was afraid of wounding him, and heaven knew what enormity her passion might compel her to say next. But Wilburn, firm as a rock in his office chair, was only smiling, with an amused, superior tolerance in his steady eyes that made her feel foolish and extravagant. He laughed shortly:

"You'd better tell Sir Joseph Hingston that when next you see him."

A tap at the door. The moon-faced clerk, solemnly carrying a tray on which were four sandwiches and a pot of tea. Wilburn thanked him and looked at his watch.

"Well, Clare," he said, "are you going to join me? Come along. Two sandwiches apiece, and there's plenty of tea in the pot. We can share the same cup." He spoke with a challenging good-humour. "I see I have just five minutes before my interview with "—he hesitated—" Mr Boffin."

She laughed. She adored him for having adopted her little joke. If only he were always like that it would be so easy to reinstate in her imagination the picture of kindly strength which she had always cherished. She hurried once more to his arms, fond and repentant. " Oh, Dudley," she pleaded, " am I so awfully silly ? You see I was so excited and happy with what I'd done, and . . . well . . . you simply froze me. Of course I'm sure you're right, and I'm quite wrong. I know I'm extravagant, dearest, dreadfully. . . ."

" Yes, you're extravagant," he seriously agreed, " but that's part of yourself, and I love you. I think I've told you that before. Four minutes. You'll have to hurry up if you're to get those sandwiches."

" I couldn't dream of it," she told him. " I'm shocked already to see you starving yourself like this. It's very naughty of you, Dudley. I shall have to speak to Grosmont about it."

He laughed. " I warn you you won't get much change out of Grosmont. Grosmont's a Welshman. Three minutes. If I were you I should go along to Battie's and choose a really expensive lunch : say caviare and lobster mayonnaise. Two and a half. He kissed her. " Goodbye, my darling. Be happy ! "

# V

## GRAND MIDLAND

SHE went. Not even his last words could give her happiness. Under the clear sky, the square sparkled in a dry brilliance ; an icy, alpine clarity that made the cupola of St. Clement's seem delicate and brittle as though it were fashioned of frozen vapour rather than stone. She stepped out, faint with hunger, on to the heedless pavement, and stood there, wondering where on earth she should go. Suddenly, behind her, she heard a voice so like Dudley's that she almost wondered if he had played a trick on her :

" Hello, Clare ! Whatever are you doing here ? "

A hand grasped her arm ; it was that of Ernest Wilburn, who had taken her on the flank as he issued from Rogers' music-shop.

" Oh, Ernest," she smiled, " you quite frightened me ; I thought you were Dudley."

" What ? Are you frightened of Dudley . . . already ? That will never do ! "

He laughed as he took her arm and walked along with her. Indeed it was difficult to imagine how Dudley's voice could inhabit a person so radically different from him as his elder brother, this debonair bachelor with the prize carnation in his buttonhole, urbane and shining from his patent-leather boots and creased cashmere trousers to his gaily tilted top-hat and polished finger-nails. A trim and elegant figure, less powerful yet more closely knit than Dudley, he walked beside her, his sharply humorous eyes acknowledging the salutations that his popularity compelled, completely master, as it seemed, not only of himself, but of all the wintry brilliance of Sackville Row ; alive to everything, and pleasantly conscious of the pretty woman on his arm. " Of course you've lunched ? " he was saying. " I haven't ; but now I've found you, if you've nothing better to do, you might give your hard-worked brother-in-law the pleasure of your company for half an hour."

" I haven't lunched," she confessed. " I was just thinking of going to Battie's."

" To Battie's ? " His red face wrinkled into a smile. " Battie's in Christmas week, when all the old ladies are shopping ? No, no, you must lunch with me like a Christian woman. I never throw away my chances ; they come so seldom."

The mixture of familiar gallantry and deference with which he took possession of her was flattering, if only because she was so unused to it. He seemed to imply that though they hardly knew each other they were already friends ; and when, a moment later, they were sucked through the revolving doors of the Grand Midland into a serene and tepid air, Clare felt that the softness of the warm-toned Turkey carpets, the luxurious silence, the courteous recognition of the porter, who bent his stiff back in a maroon and golden bow as Ernest Wilburn entered, were tokens of an easier, more generous life, of whose existence in North Bromwich she hadn't even been aware. The reflected brilliance that emanated from Ernest Wilburn's popularity enveloped her in its warmth. All the hotel servants knew him, and hastened to serve him with an eagerness that, contrasted with the more formal respect which Dudley's name or presence aroused, seemed personal and human.

In the high-vaulted dining-room he was equally at home. The *maitre d'hôtel* in person hurried to find them a table and stood waiting to take their order, with the wine-waiter behind him. Ernest addressed him in French—not Lady Hingston's French, but a fluent and confident speech that compelled her admiration.

" I'm ordering the lunch myself," he told her, " because the chef's a particular friend of mine and will take trouble over it. You don't mind waiting ? You're not in a dreadful hurry ? But I believe you're famished. Can you bear oysters ? "

And when the ordering was finished he looked her up and down with an approving eye, complimenting her on her frock. Dudley had never noticed it ; but Ernest, among his other graces, soon showed her that he understood the mean-

ing of women's dress and considered it a subject of importance. "These North Bromwich women haven't the least
idea about it," he assured her.

"But you are a bachelor," she said. "You oughtn't to
be so expert."

He laughed: "Yes, I'm a bachelor . . . by force of
circumstance; but that doesn't prevent me from being
interested on purely aesthetic grounds. And if a woman
gives me aesthetic pleasure, as you do . . ." He stopped,
as though he didn't wish to pursue the subject, and pass
on lightly to another: the tickets which he had just been
buying when he met her. "It seems," he said, "that we
are going to get some good orchestral music at last. Oldham, the critic of the *Mail*, is responsible for it. It's not
that North Bromwich is musical; but Oldham has been
pushing Leeds and Manchester down their throats, and
North Bromwich people can't bear to think that anyone else
is ahead of God's Own City, so they're buying a new
orchestra, just as they'd buy a new sewage-farm or fire-
brigade or a new Velasquez, to show the others what their
money can do. And humble people like myself and Oldham
get the benefit of their stupid competitiveness, so we mustn't
complain, even if they, poor souls, are bored. Sir Joseph
and Lady Astill will go to every concert. Sir Joseph will
make a speech and talk about 'Aydn. I wonder if music
means anything to you, Clare?"

"I can't tell you how much it means. For years it meant
nearly everything."

He looked at her quizzically: a little doubtful. "What
kind of music?"

"My music is all haphazard. I'm very ignorant. I pick
up things here and there," she hesitated, "but I think Bach
means more to me than anyone."

"Do you really mean that?" he said, fixing her like
a witness under cross-examination. "Are you quite sure?"

" Yes, I'm quite sure," she answered seriously. " Am I so awfully old-fashioned ? "

" Old-fashioned ? No, my child." He took her hand in his and spoke as fervently as a martyr making his last profession of faith :

" Bach is my God ; Bach means to me the highest expression of human beauty and grandeur. But this is astounding ! I'd no idea that we had so much in common. I never suspected it. You've never breathed a word ! "

" We scarcely know each other."

" But we must know each other, Clare. Let's make a beginning. You play, of course ? "

" A little. It's ages since I played."

" There's no piano at Tudor House ? "

" You can scarcely call it one. My own piano, my darling Bechstein, was left at Uffdown."

" But that was criminal ! It's quite easy to bring it over."

" I know. But Dudley didn't wish it. He didn't want me to bring over anything that wasn't useful. You see he isn't musical."

" No, Dudley isn't musical. I understand. Dudley has all the virtues . . ." And none of the graces, his hesitation implied. " But Joyce, I think, is musical after a fashion ? She ought to encourage you."

" Joyce is not . . . encouraging," was all she could say ; and then, as his intent silence invited confidences : " You see, my music is quite different from Joyce's. I feel it, while she analyses it ; and if she listened to me—which she'd hate to do, really and truly—my fingers would simply go numb. I should feel so uncomfortable that . . . oh, I can't explain."

" Yes, yes, I know what you mean," he reassured her. " Joyce is a queer girl. I never quite get to the bottom of her myself. I think she's capable of feeling, if she weren't too proud to confess it ; but all her admirations and enthusiasms

seem to be born "—he laughed, as though excusing himself
—" by a process of parthenogenesis ; they're like laboratory
experiments. You know what I mean ? "

" Indeed I do." Her heart clutched at his sympathy and
understanding, and yet a feeling of disloyalty checked the
emotion ; for, in criticizing Joyce, she knew that they were
also criticizing Dudley, and that would never do. She
determined to retreat at once from this dangerous ground ;
but Ernest, as her ill-luck would have it, seemed unaware of
her panic.

" The extraordinary thing," he said, " is that Dudley,
who knows my weakness, has never told me."

She was silent : " And yet, she asked herself, why
shouldn't I be frank ? He's Dudley's brother ; he's known
him for nearly fifty years ; there's nothing that I could
say that he isn't perfectly aware of already."

Uncannily he echoed her own thought :

" I hope I shan't offend you," he went on, " if I say that
I understand Dudley better than you do ? Of course it's
an impertinence, but also it's probably true. And if I talk
about Dudley—if *we* talk, I mean—it's on the understanding
that we're both tremendously fond of him. You are his
wife, and wouldn't have married him if you weren't ; and
I, as his brother, am devoted to him. That's understood ? "

She nodded ; she was afraid of any words.

" But what you've been saying," he continued, " or rather
what you haven't said, makes me feel that—oh, well, let's get
it over !—that I may be of some little help to you ; first of
all because I'm fond of Dudley, and then because I'm a
susceptible bachelor and you are a beautiful woman and
a charming woman, and naturally I want to make the most of
the privilege that my age and my relationship give me.
You see I'd give anything in the world for you to be happy.
And you're not happy, you know. And it's your own fault."

He looked at her so kindly that she couldn't meet his

eyes. " If he says another word," she thought, " I shall simply cry and make an exhibition of both of us." In the middle distance she caught the eye of Edward Willis, of Mawne, who was lunching with his father and a small party of ironmasters. He smiled across at her; she bowed spasmodically, and the momentary distraction saved her, so that when Ernest Wilburn spoke again his tone seemed less dangerously sympathetic.

" First of all, Clare," he was saying, " you've got to be yourself. Dudley will always be himself; he always has been, ever since I can remember. He's a good husband, although I say it : a much better husband than I should ever have been. He's more single-minded, more honest than I am ; you can count absolutely on his sense of justice, his loyalty. As you see him, so he is : there's nothing in him that isn't evident to the whole world. Even his faults—I won't pretend that anybody's perfect—are as evident as his virtues. You don't resent me talking of him like this ? "

" No, not a bit. I wish I had a friend as loyal as you are."

" But Dudley," he went on, " has lived to himself for forty-eight years. Even when he was married to Edith— you don't mind my mentioning her ? Of course you don't ; you're sensible—even in those days he lived to himself. And you can't change him. It's no good trying to do so. He lives his own life, and neither you nor I nor anyone else can get an eighth of an inch inside it. So, if you're lonely—you *are* lonely, you know—you mustn't imagine it's his fault. And all the others : Joyce, and that nice plump creature Evelyn, are just as individualistic as he is. They're like the walls of Jericho ; it needs a miracle to get inside them. and even if you did get inside you'd only be as disappointed as if you found yourself living in Jericho itself to-morrow. Old mother Marple's another ; an honest, irritating old body ; but then, of course, you treat ter as a joke. They're all a joke, my dear, if you only knew it."

Clare shook her head : " I'm afraid you're right. The trouble is that I'm losing my sense of humour."

" You mustn't," he insisted. " Take it from me, who am old enough to be your father—though God knows age and wisdom aren't synonymous—that humour's the most important thing in life. If you lose that you might just as well throw up the sponge at once. You see you have a life of your own : music's a life in itself to begin with. You've got to live that life ; and don't, for the love of heaven, let Tudor House get on the top of you. If you do, it'll crush you—not because it wants to, but because you get in the way and it can't help doing so. You have to live your own life, make your own interests, find your own friends ; and if you can't do that in a city with three quarters of a million of inhabitants there must be something wrong with you— which there isn't, my dear : there's nothing wrong with you at all."

" That is the trouble," she told him, " I haven't any friends."

" Oh, yes you have. There's one sitting opposite you at this moment, if you'll be kind enough to accept him. If you want to play Bach, you can go to his music-room and worry his Steinway. If you want to let go, you can give him the honour of asking you to lunch with him. If you can tear yourself away from Mrs. Marple you can come on Tuesday evenings and help him to listen to Beethoven symphonies. Here is the season's programme : he's going to send you the serial ticket this evening—that is, of course, if you're prepared to put up with him. And now," he said, " let's talk of something else."

" Ernest," she said, " you know this is awfully sweet of you."

" No. no it isn't," he laughed ; " it's nothing of the sort.

Mine is a very complicated life, Clare, and I have to find out my own selfish ways of making the best of it. You're one of them—at least I think you are. Dudley's, on the other hand, is amazingly simple; it's all black and white; while yours and mine are as multicoloured as a solar spectrum. And now, my child," he said, " I'm afraid I must leave you. I see Walter Willis over there and must have a word with him before he goes back to Mawne . . . No, no, of course not. I'll see you to the door. My cab will be waiting outside."

Once more she found herself outside the swinging doorway of the Grand Midland. At the kerb stood the private rubber-tyred hansom with its driver in bottle-green livery which Ernest characteristically affected. He apologized for its flavour of antiquity.

" I hate motor-cars," he said. " I am a real Victorian. With the last of the hansoms England is losing all its distinction. This is the true aristocracy of bachelor locomotion; there's only room for two."

She told him the story of Lady Astill's " Deemlers " that were eating their heads off. They laughed together on the pavement. Once more he evaded her thanks.

" Nonsense," he said; " you're making too much of it. I love pretty women, and if Dudley, lucky devil, has married one I can't afford to miss my opportunities. Now jump in quickly and make yourself comfortable. One moment . . . I'm going to assert the last of my privileges—I'm going to kiss you. You don't mind, do you ? "

He did so, and was gone ; but as the rubber-tyred hansom went bowling smoothly along Sackville Row, past the pillars of the Council House, the Italian Gothic campanile, the Corinthian Town Hall, the University, the tented statue of Sir Joseph Astill with his furled umbrella, and on to the new wood-pavement of the lower Halesby Road, her heart was fluttered not by Ernest Wilburn's perfunctory kiss, but by the discovery of a personality that she had not suspected. It was strange, she thought, that Dudley had hardly ever spoken to her about his brother, had never suggested that they might be friends ; and, stranger still, that Ernest and he were brothers at all.

Why had he never spoken to her of Ernest, with whom, in the office, he passed the greater part of his day ? The fact that they were so different could hardly explain his reticence. Puzzling her brain for an explanation she remembered some chance words of Lady Hingston's, hints that her brother-in-law's bachelorhood was not as ascetic as it might be. " He has a bad name with women " ; she seemed to remember the words. Of course he liked women ; he had admitted it, half humorously, in his explanation of his attraction to herself. Then why on earth, if this were so had he never married ? " He ought to be married," she thought. " It's not only that he's fond of women. He understands them. Nothing could have been more understanding than the way in which he spoke to me to-day. He's so good-humoured, so sensitive, so generous, so beautifully polite ; and when he says he wouldn't make as good a husband as Dudley, it's only his modesty. If he could have married a girl like Vivien . . ."

The unconscious match-making instinct, which had already declared itself so strongly in Aunt Cathie, launched her into extensive plans for Ernest Wilburn's future. Perhaps he couldn't marry. Hadn't he hinted that his life was full of complications ? Was it because of these complications that Dudley had kept her away from him ? Perhaps ; for in Dudley, as she had often noticed, there was a queer strain of prudishness. " A compliment to my innocence," she thought. " And yet I believe that in matters of that kind women are far more charitable than men. Whatever he told me I don't believe I should be shocked ; I'm not so much of a child as he always pretends. I really think he might have confided in me."

That evening, when Dudley came home, he seemed more happy than usual. It appeared that he had survived the shock of her Christmas extravagances ; he even teased her about her lunch at Battie's.

" I lunched at the Grand Midland," she told him.

" At the Midland ? Well, you are going it, and no mistake ! "

" Ernest took me there."

He flushed slightly. " Oh, Ernest. Yes, that is one of his haunts," he said, and then was obstinately silent. She could not leave it at that.

" You never told me, Dudley, that he was musical."

" I can't say it ever occurred to me. Ernest and I haven't very much in common."

" His voice is exactly like yours. It's quite ludicrous."

" Yes, that's about the sum of our likeness."

Again she tried : " He's asked me to go with him to the new series of orchestral concerts."

" Well, are you going ? "

" Of course I want to go. It's an opportunity I've never had before. But if you've any objection . . ."

" *I've* no objection, Clare, as long as he pays for you."

" Oh, *why* do you put it like that ? " she cried, for the words wounded her.

" You silly child, I was only joking," he said.

But beneath his reticence she knew there was no joke.

# VI

## COMPENSATIONS

FROM end to end of the platform a fog, that was coloured like sulphur and smelt of it, welled steadily out of the black tunnel-mouths into the glass-domed cavity of the Midland Station. It was as though some superhuman chemist were generating noxious gases and passing them into a sealed retort, in which, like imprisoned vermin, the crowd of which Clare formed part, ran hither and thither in a sort of dazed and doomed automatism, coughing and gasping as they hurried about their inconceivable business, harassed by the shrieks of engines, the melancholy echoes of shunters' horns, the detonations of distant fog-signals, the rumbling bourdon made by thousands of other human feet crossing the wooden bridge that spanned the station. In the midst of this turmoil, deafened and half suffocated, Clare stood with icy feet and tried to compose herself to meet the moment for which she had been living.

She had come to the station—much too early, of course ; though Dudley had warned her that every train would be late—in a curiously uneasy frame of mind. She was tremulous, transported by the anticipated ecstasy of finding Steven in her arms again ; and yet, between the imagining and the realization, there rose a barrier that once had seemed trivial, but which now, as the moment of fulfilment approached, grew monstrous and threatened the very foundations of her happiness. Between her and that part of herself that was Steven there lay the shadow of a secret unshared. For Dudley, as soon as the child had been packed off to Kingston, had dissuaded her from telling him anything of the new marriage.

" He's only a baby after all," he had said. " Even if you explain it to him he won't understand all that it means. Words have so little weight with children beside their practical illustration ; and when he comes back to you at Christmas and finds the accomplished fact, the situation will explain itself without your finding words for it. Like all small animals he'll soon adjust himself. New scenes, new interests . . . And of course nothing will really matter as long as you are there. You'll begin to spoil him again as soon as you set eyes on him."

She wondered. " But Steven isn't like other children," she said.

" Ah, that's your maternal heresy," he laughed. " Of course he's like all other children. If you feel that you've got to make excuses, really there's nothing more to be said. But don't you think your whole attitude is a little ridiculous ? As soon as he's with you and you've got him to yourself, you'll be able to do what you like with him, and he'll be perfectly happy. At any rate he ought to be."

" Yes, that's what really matters," she thought, as she turned and saw the minute hand of the great clock on the bridge jerk forward clumsily to three-forty-six. " And yet I wish to goodness it were over," she told herself ; " this endless waiting makes everything seem more difficult. I suppose there's nothing wrong."

The local train from Kingston had been due at three-thirty. Only that morning, in the *Courier*, she had read of a railway accident near Coventry. She caught a harassed porter and questioned him.

" The local ? " he said, good-humouredly. " Why, lady, don't you know it's Christmas-time ? I reckon the line's got blocked with turkeys or summat. The Scotch express was fifty late at Durby, and they've got to get her clear before they think of locals. Ay, here she comes. Stand clear there, please ! " he bellowed.

Out of the black tunnel-mouth in a cloud of her own steam she came, impelled, Clare thought, by the thunder of her coupled engines to overshoot the platform. The crowd surged toward her, as though sucked inward by the vacuum she created, clinging to the door-handles of the carriages, dragged along with her ; and Clare and the friendly porter were sucked in with them, to be thrown backward by the weaker but equally determined wave that issued, like a back-wash, from the opened doorways. *Glasgow—Carlisle— North Bromwich—St. Pancras :* the wayboards proclaimed.

There was snow on the carriage roofs; snow drifted into the angles of the fog-bleared windows; and Clare watched the doorway of the carriages opposite her, intently, illogically, as though, from any one of them, she might suddenly see Steven emerge, although she knew that the local was safely side-tracked in some lonely siding out in the fog-bound Midland plateau.

The long train emptied and refilled itself; the engine snorted like an over-driven monster; rapt faces peered at her from the moving carriage-windows as the express gathered speed and slid away, leaving its passengers marooned among their piles of luggage. The porter gave her a friendly wink as he passed: " She's signalled, lady, now we shan't be long ! "

And a moment later, like a spent runner who finishes the course half-humorously as a matter of form, the little local came puffing in. " If I stand here," Clare thought, " he's bound to see me." It was difficult to stand still; her heart was beating so rapturously, her eyes so eager; she stood and trembled like a young girl in love. Then, as her eyes caught the red and black of a parti-coloured cap, her resolution to stand still went by the board; she was running, breathless and smiling, beside the moving train.

But the school cap was not his. It belonged, in fact, to a boy with a sallow, pimply face, a year or two older than Steven, who stared at her emotion with stolid contempt until the arms of a red-faced, blowsy mother, who had shared Clare's vigil, received him. Then, as she turned back disappointed, she heard Steven's voice, and a moment later—oh, sweet wonder !—his fog-cold face was pressed to hers.

" My darling," she laughed, " I didn't see you. I caught sight of a cap and ran after that other boy."

" Yes, that's Barlow Major," he answered—in the respectful tones with which, in North Bromwich, one might say ।

" Yes, that's Joseph Chamberlain "—" and I suppose that lady's his mother," the blowsy woman having gained prestige by Barlow Major's distinction. " I suppose," he went on, " that as he's with his people I'd better not say good-bye to him ; he mightn't like it."

" If you want to, you'd better," said Clare, faintly amused by this unusual etiquette.

" No, I don't think I will," said Steven, seriously. " And anyway, she's not half as pretty as you, mum."

She laughed. This baby of hers, so sturdy in his grey knickerbocker suit and school cap, was quite the man of the world, so different from the wild little monkey who had left Uffdown three months before—so different, yet so adorable in his new seriousness that she had to pick him up and kiss him. It seemed, however, that her demonstrativeness embarrassed him, and though he was too well-mannered to tell her that kissing in public was " bad form," the decided way in which he changed the subject was a reproof to her tactlessness.

" I've no luggage, mum, only this bag," he said. " If we're going over to the other station we'd better hurry up ; the fog is simply beastly."

" We're not going to the other station, darling," she said.

" Are we going to drive all the way out to Uffdown ? That will be fun ! "

" No, we're not going to Uffdown this afternoon. We're going to Alvaston."

" To Alvaston ? That's where Barlow Major lives. Lots of our men live in Alvaston. Why ever are we going there, mum ? "

The evil moment had come. She temporized.

" Wait till we get this luggage on the cab, darling, and then I'll tell you." She caught her friendly porter, who picked up Steven's baggage with a will.

" Ah, now I understand what you were waiting for," he

said. " I've got a couple of nippers of my own. Look out, George," he cried, as he hoisted the boxes on to the top of a cab. " A merry Christmas, lady," he said, pocketing the unexpected florin that Clare gave him.

Steven surveyed the shabby four-wheeler with disapproval.

" This isn't ours," he said. " What's happened to Bissell ? "

" Bissell's at Uffdown. Hurry up, darling ; jump in ! "

" But where are we *really* going ? " he persisted as the growler rumbled over the station cobbles.

" To Alvaston," she smiled. " I've told you."

" Yes, but whose house ? "

" Mr. Wilburn's."

" How rotten ! I don't much like *him*, mum."

" Oh, Steven, Steven," she cried, " you mustn't say that. That's stupid and naughty of you. If you knew him you would. I want you to know him and like him, darling, because . . ." And again her courage failed her. Why should she be frightened, abashed before this child ? She took him in her arms and hugged him. " Listen to me, darling. When you had gone away to school mummy was dreadfully lonely, right out in the country, you know, at Uffdown with nobody to talk to except poor Sly. She couldn't stay at Uffdown and go on being unhappy without you, darling, could she ? And then an old friend, a very dear friend, Steven, whom she loved very much, wanted her to come and live with him in Alvaston. And so she came to live with him, and that's where we're going."

" But we shan't *stay* there, mummy, shall we ? We shall go on to Uffdown this evening, shan't we ? "

" No, not this evening, darling . . . not just yet. I can't leave anyone who's been so good to me, can I ? "

He looked at her blankly for a moment. His face changed.

" Oh, Steven, Steven darling, don't look at me like that ! "

" I hate him . . . yes, I hate him ! Oh, mummy," he wailed. " Why did you go and do that ? You might have told me. You might have asked me first."

" Darling, darling "—she hid his scowling face with hers —" you're too little, my sweetheart, too little to understand. It wasn't a thing that mummy could easily explain."

" You might have told me," he repeated ; he took her kisses stubbornly like a cat that lies flattened by the hand that strokes it yet thinks only of escape, and his blue eyes were as cold and hard as Wolverbury steel : Ralph's eyes, despising, accusing her out of this baby face. She went on fondling him desperately, went on explaining the thing that could not be explained ; but she knew by his sullen mouth that he wasn't listening ; for the first time in her life she felt that she was excluded, frozen out of everything that was passing through his mind. " I've lost him," she thought. " I've lost him : he'll never be mine again." Aware of her own futility she went on persuading, painting for him the novel delights of the Alvaston world : the railway cutting at the bottom of the paddock where the trains of the Marbourne branch line came grinding up the gradient ; the Christmas pantomimes ; the circus at Dingley Hall ; the Halesby Road 'buses.

" Just think," she said, " they run right past the door ! You've always been wanting to go for rides on the top ; now you'll be able to do it as often as you want to."

" I don't want to ride on the top of 'buses any longer," he answered tragically ; and then, as though he had reached at last the bottom of his thoughts : " Is it a big house, mum ? " he said.

" Yes, it's a big house, darling . . . fairly big," she told him, bewildered by the sudden change of subject.

" Is it as big as Uffdown ? "

" Well, hardly that, sweetheart."

" Are there sixteen bedrooms ? "

" Not quite as many as that." There were six.

" Well, there you are ! " he cried, for the first time really passionate. " That's done it, mummy. Oh, it is beastly mean of you ! "

She couldn't understand. " Listen, my darling. You've a lovely little bedroom of your own, bigger than the one at Uffdown, and it looks out at the back, right over the railway. I know you'll simply love it."

" Oh, it isn't *that*," he declared. " I don't know *what* I shall say. You see I told the other men that we had sixteen bedrooms. They wouldn't believe me ; they said I was coxy about it. And now Barlow Major will see for himself—I'm sure he lives quite near—and he won't believe I was speaking the truth."

It was unanswerable : Barlow Major wouldn't.

" Well, well, my darling, you'll have to explain that you were talking of Uffdown."

" You can't explain a thing like that," he replied angrily. " It's awful. And anyway he wouldn't believe me now." He paused, as though he were searching his mind for anything else that might seriously injure his prestige with Barlow Major. " I hope," he went on dismally, " Miss Pidgeon's not there."

" No, no, Miss Pidgeon went away long ago."

" Well, that's one comfort," he sighed. " Where's Bo-peep ? "

" Bo-peep's at Uffdown. She's quite happy. Bissell's looking after her."

" Isn't she here ? Oh mum, mum, mum, I'd so looked forward to her ! "

And with this heart-wrung cry he broke into desolate tears and was a baby indeed. . . . In this abandonment, she thanked heaven, he was easier to deal with, for now he lay, without resistance or question, in her arms, so that she felt, for the first time he was her very own again. As the slow cab approached the level of Tudor House she made him sit up, and wiped his eyes. For her own sake even more than for his she was anxious that their arrival should not be spectacular, and, as luck would have it, the door was opened to them not by Mrs. Marple, who had swept off like a black knight to break a lance with the baker, but by Mary, the housemaid, who, freed from Mrs. Marple's intimidations, was inclined to be friendly.

" Miss Evelyn's gone out too, ma'am," Mary informed her ; " she said as she wouldn't be back to tea. I expect the young gentleman's hungry ; I shouldn't wonder if he'd fancy some hot buttered toast on a day like this."

So they had tea together and alone in the drawing-room, and the melted butter with which Steven greased his fingers and lips had the effect that tradition ascribes to the same emollient when it is smeared on a kitten's paws ; for, by the time they had finished, he was beginning to take an interest in the contents of Edith Wilburn's room, finding the things that Clare detested enchanting, simply because they were new to him. For the first time in her life she had reason to bless her predecessor's lack of taste ; for among the jetsam of bric-a-brac in which Steven rummaged like an urchin playing on the tide-line, the tragedy of Bo-peep was temporarily forgotten.

Later, as he wandered with her, sniffing everywhere, over the empty house, from the attics, where a dyspeptic cistern gurgled, to the dank cellars, where Hadley's potatoes sprouted wanly and a well that drained the foundations reflected their two faces haloed in candle-light, she was forced to acknowledge, not ungratefully, the wisdom of Dudley's prophecies. For the very sordidness of Tudor House, the mean restrictions of imagination that made it so different from Uffdown, were full of romantic novelty for Steven. He even seemed a little disappointed by the pains which she had taken to make his bedroom resemble the one in which he had slept at Uffdown, regretting the black japanned bedstead with brass knobs which they had glimpsed, with some temerity, in Mrs. Marple's; and, above all things, he was impressed by the curtains of Nottingham lace.

" I don't suppose that Barlow Major has curtains like that, mum," he said. " They're lovely, aren't they ? "

At that moment, to please him, she would have been willing to admit the superiority of any horror imaginable, to share, with all her heart and soul, his anxiety to submit everything to Barlow Major's exalted standards of taste.

" But where do *you* sleep, mummy darling ? " he asked her suddenly.

" In here, sweetheart. You see," she added, " it isn't very far away from you."

" Oh, I wasn't thinking of that," he assured her hurriedly. " I'm not afraid of sleeping alone now."

He surveyed the bedroom critically. " Of course," he admitted, " those curtains are beauties, aren't they. But what an enormous bed, mum ! Where does Mr. Wilburn sleep ? "

" In here with me, darling," she told him, as shamefully as if she were confessing some monstrous immorality.

" With you ? Oh, mum ! "

" You see, sweetheart," she explained, " when people live in the same house like this they have to be married. Mr. Wilburn is mummy's husband now, and he'll be your father too. . . . You're very lucky, Steven, to have a father like him."

Once more his puzzled eyes darkened.

" But I don't *want* him. I don't want any father at all. I'd much rather have you. Besides, I always thought you were married to daddy. I've never heard of anybody having two. You can't really have two fathers, can you ? "

" Not really, sweetheart ; but he'll love you just the same, for mummy's sake. . . ."

This side of the question failed entirely to move him. He disregarded it. He stood and stared at her with the eyes of the stubborn bullock that she knew so well. Then, solemnly, ridiculously, he answered her :

" Well, I don't know," he said, " but it seems to me you've made a big mistake."

The words awoke a devastating echo in her own consciousness. *Out of the mouths of babes and sucklings.* . . . But even to admit the possibility of their being true would undermine the foundations of her existence. So, rather than run the risk of the theme's development on his lips or in her heart, she hurried him away from these perilous soundings into smoother water, and, clutching eagerly at the nearest means of diverting his too-curious attention, abruptly and rashly jettisoned the most exciting of all his Christmas presents, the miniature bicycle which she had bought, and concealed from Dudley, on the day of her disastrous visit to Sackville Row. Even as she did so she was conscious of the indignity of purchasing a love that should have come to her unbought ; but the end, in this case, seemed to justify the humiliating means ; for at the sight of the glittering machine, the last signs of preoccupation left Steven's eyes, and, seeing his delight, her own heart leapt with joy and gratitude.

" Oh, mum," he cried, " how spiffing ; it's an Austin ! "

" That will make up for Bo-peep," she told him.

" I should think it just would ! " he agreed.

" And when you've learnt to ride it, sweetheart, we'll go out together on wonderful expeditions, won't we ? Someday we might even ride over to see Aunt Cathie."

This prospect seemed to meet with less approval. " I think I'd better begin to learn at once," he said, " if you could come down the garden and hold me on a bit."

" You'd better leave it where it is for this evening," she told him. " To-morrow morning I'll ask Hadley to help you. It's getting dark, now."

But though, reluctantly, he allowed her to drag him away from this new and precious possession, his tongue went on babbling excitedly about its charms and possibilities. " I must learn to ride really well in the garden first," he explained ; " because it'ld be awful, wouldn't it, if I came a smeller in the road and Barlow Major saw me ? You see he has a bicycle, mum ; he's always bucking about it, but I don't suppose it's an Austin, and someone told me secretly that his father bought it second-hand, and, really and truly, it isn't his very own, because his brother, who's at the Grammar School, has half of it."

That evening he talked of bicycles and nothing but bicycles until it was time to go to bed. She gave him his supper and followed him to the scabrous bathroom, where Evelyn's and Joyce's toothbrushes and Dudley's shaving tackle littered the window-sill. From the days of his babyhood she had always taken a pleasure in bathing him herself ; she loved to see his clean little body naked, to kiss him as he sat on her knees with his bare arms round her neck, for at these times he seemed more near to her than at any other, reawakening in her the subtle physical satisfaction that she had felt when she had nursed him as a baby at her breast. But this evening, as he stood in his Jaeger dressing-gown, he seemed almost to resent her presence.

" You needn't help me, mummy darling," he said with a deliberate endearment; " you see I'm quite used to bathing myself now."

" But I love to watch you, Steven," she told him. " I can see for myself what a big boy you're growing."

" Oh, well," he admitted reluctantly, " I suppose it's all right. But I shouldn't like the other men to know that you bathed me. They'd think it awfully funny."

She saw that in yielding to her he was straining a point to be kind, and loved him for it, feeding her hungry eyes with the sight of his milky skin, the straight little back, slim hips, the well-arched feet and small, straight toes that she had played with when he was a baby. And when, at last, all pink and steamy, he jumped up on her knees and through the folds of towel she felt the warmth of his small body and his heart beating like a captured kitten's under her hands, it seemed to her that he was really her own Steven with all the accretions of schoolboy importance washed clean away from him, and that the shyness which had set her wondering whether the age of innocence had not yielded to teachers more gross and less tactful than Bissell (whose influence Aunt Cathie had feared) was no more than a token of his anxiety to assure himself that he wasn't a baby any longer. But he was a baby, just the same ; for Clare he would never be anything else as long as he lived ; and when, regardless of the dignities that his consciousness of Barlow Major imposed on him, she picked him up in a bundle and carried him to his new bed, her heart was rich with an elation so tender that the alien insensitiveness of Tudor House had no more power to wound her ; she was as young, as happy, as untroubled as when, in that sweet summer before the war, she had taken her baby from Ralph's arms and carried him to the night nursery at Uffdown.

" Now you will sleep like a top, my darling," she told him when he had said his prayers ; " and if you wake up and are frightened, you can ring this little bell and mother will hear you."

" Of course I shan't be frightened, mum," he said, indignantly. " What an idea ! But you will come and kiss me, won't you, when you go to bed ? I'm sure I shan't wake ; but I should like to know you're there just the same."

She turned the gas down and left him quietly. When

she descended she found the family already assembled in the dining-room. Dudley looked up and smiled : " Well, have you got him ? "

" Yes, he's in bed. The train was frightfully late. He's grown—you'd never imagine ! His grown-up way of talking is quite comical. Of course he's off his head with delight about the bicycle."

" You mean you've shown it him already ? "

" I simply couldn't resist it. Was it so weak of me ? "

" Spartan mother ! " He laughed at her ; and yet his amusement was more kindly than usual, as if he realized that in this one direction the impulsiveness that he deprecated must be forgiven. But Joyce, who was listening to them while she pretended to read the evening paper, confirmed the contempt of her silence by a glance of withering disdain for Clare's weakness and his condonation, to which, for once, Clare was impervious, not only because she felt that Dudley was on her side, but because her spirit had drawn strength and generosity from her contact with Steven in such abundance that no words or looks of grudging could distress her. Before, she had been divided ; but now she was complete, and this completion must have shown itself not merely in the new freedom and courage of her inner self, but outwardly in her brightened cheeks and eyes and in the smile of happiness that came so readily to her lips in spite of all discouragements.

Dudley, at least, did not discourage her. All through that evening his eyes never left her face. They watched her with the expectant eagerness of a lover, taking advantage of the emotion, fruit of an older love, that made her more beautiful for himself ; and when the girls had gone to bed he made her come to him and drew her into his arms with the intense, tremulous passion that she remembered on their wedding night.

" Clare, you are lovely this evening," he whispered.

" What has happened to you ? You're not my wife. You're like a girl of seventeen."

She laughed : " Am I really ? It's only because I'm happy, dearest."

" Why shouldn't you always be happy ? I love you, Clare."

She kissed him solemnly, then lay like a child in his arms. She was glad that he loved her. That night her heart was so full that she had love to spare, not only for him, her husband, but for all the world ; and Wilburn, in his turn, felt the warmth of her radiance and was shaken by it, feeling that, whatever its origin might be, it was himself, the living man, who would profit by it and enjoy it.

Swept by an emotion too strong for speech he clung to her in the dark hall and passed upstairs with her. On the landing she freed herself from his arms and hesitated.

" What is the matter ? Where are you going ? " he whispered.

" To Steven. Only for a moment, dearest. I promised him."

" What nonsense ! The child's asleep. You'll only disturb him."

" No, no, I shan't wake him. If I didn't keep my promise he'd never forgive me."

" My child, he'll never know whether you've kept it or not. Don't be so silly. It's nearly midnight."

But though he drew her away she was gently persistent : " I want to see him anyway. He looks so sweet, Dudley."

" All right," he grumbled, " but don't be an hour about it."

She could not bear his brusqueness ; she was so anxious to be kind. She took his arm : " Dearest, won't you come with me ? I wish you would."

A little awkwardly he consented. They went together on tiptoe along the landing and entered Steven's room ; but as soon as they were within it, although she grasped his arm more firmly, as though by intention, he saw that on a plane of consciousness far deeper than that in which words were formed or muscles bidden to contract, here, on the verge of possession, she was more remote, more unattainable—though more desirable—than he had ever known her. The love that filled her eyes with tears and lent to her living body the motionless mould of some compassionate madonna in a carved *pietà*, was such as neither his passion nor his entreaties could ever command ; and when, still smiling and transfigured, she turned to him, and, out of her redundance of feeling, pressed her cheek to his, his spirit violently rejected the contact for which his body was on fire. In the wide-set, closed eyes of the sleeping child, in the fair head of tumbled hair, the beautiful, petulant mouth, he could see nothing of Clare ; only the features of Ralph Hingston, whom he had envied and despised, reborn to mock his advancing years with shining, invulnerable youth, and to reawaken a jealousy of which he believed he had magnanimously purged himself when death had entered the lists upon his side.

"Oh, Dudley," Clare was saying, "if only you could realize how dear he is to me. If we could share this too, dearest ; if you could love him as I do ! That's what would make me happier than anything else on earth."

Controlling himself he became, once more, serene, masterful, diplomatic :

"My darling, the mere fact that he was yours would make me fee . . . differently."

Impulsively she drew closer to him. "Oh, Dudley," she said, "can you feel what joy that gives me ? "

But that was not the joy he wanted to give ; and when she bent cautiously above the child to pay him the debt of her promised kiss, the sense of being made an object of charity, of being flattered into complaisance rasped him.

"Now come along Clare," he said, "we can't spend the night here."

"I'm coming," she smiled, "I was only . . ."

"And for goodness' sake," he went on irritably, "don't leave that gas burning. He's not a baby."

She obeyed him like a child ; her mind was too generously exalted to feel his irritation or question his carefulness ; and when, a little later, he took possession of her almost fiercely, as though he were determined to stamp his own image on her body and soul to the exclusion of all others, dead or living, there was no shadow of reservation in her ; he could almost have believed, against belief, that she loved him.

# VII

## HOLIDAY

THE four short weeks of the Christmas holiday passed smoothly. It was enough for Clare that Steven should be happy. And happy he seemed to be, for his young nature adapted itself to change more easily than hers. As yet he was nothing more than a little animal ; and, animal delights being as accessible on the macadam of Alvaston as in the Uffdown woods, Steven pursued them with little regard to her. By Boxing-Day he had tracked down not only Barlow Major but two other school-friends, and having asserted his social qualifications to this and other distinguished company by the possession of a football—the proceeds of Aunt Cathie's new half-sovereign—and the very latest thing in bicycles, was off at once, like a wild thing, playing scratch matcnes in the public parks, sliding on the precariously frozen reservoir, exploring, under Barlow Major's auspices, a romantic Alvaston whose enchantments were invisible to Clare's eyes.

At times she felt a little doubtful of these new friends of his, and wondered if their " influence " were good. She urged him to bring Barlow Major in to tea, and much to Steven's embarrassment—for the thought of those non-existent sixteen bedrooms still troubled him—Barlow Major came : a stolid, pimply figure with nothing in the world to distinguish him but an incredible appetite for dough-cakes that reduced him to dumbness during the whole of his visit. She even determined to set her mind at rest, or learn the worst, by calling formally on Barlow Major's unprepossessing mother ; but when she announced her intention to Dudley he only laughed at her.

" There's nothing to be gained by it," he declared. " You'll merely land yourself with the acquaintance of a woman who'll bore you."

" I should like to know what kind of people they are."

" I can tell you that at once," he said. " I know the father by sight. He's a doctor, a general practitioner, and an extremely dull fellow ; but if it's respectability you're after, about as respectable as they make 'em. In any case," he went on, " you can't keep Steven under a glass case. He's had to associate with the Barlow boy at school for three months on end, and if any harm's to come from it you may be sure it's been done already. You can't modify the laws of nature, Clare. Even if you never let Steven go out of your sight you can't stop him growing. He's got to develop by himself like all the rest of us. All over the world at this moment there are women fighting against the idea of losing their babies. And it's no good. Sooner or later they lose them just the same."

" Oh, Dudley, you put it so brutally," she complained.

" Well, it's the brutal truth, my child," he told her.

Wherever Steven was concerned, he seemed to take a delight in making the truth as brutal as possible ; so brutal that now she shrank from discussing Steven with him.

For the present, at least, she could persuade herself that the evil day of his prophecy was reasonably remote. The bleak Midland evenings closed in early, and with them, punctual as a roosting pigeon, Steven flew home to her on his bicycle, flushed and exultant with fresh air and exercise, but so beatifically tired that he allowed her to do what she liked with him.

And those long, fireside evenings were very precious to her, for then he would sit on her knee while she read to him the books with whose images she wished to fill his mind. Sometimes they sang together the nursery songs which she had taught him at Uffdown. Sometimes—for she was still determined to make the music that she loved a part of him, accustoming his ears to sweet and noble sounds—she would sit down at the piano and play to him the simpler melodies of Grieg and Schumann and Mendelssohn, until Joyce sent down a message by Mrs. Marple to ask the mistress if she couldn't play a little softer, please, because it disturbed her reading. A little unwillingly; for though Mrs. Marple was still not averse from giving pin-pricks to Clare, some vestige of a maternal instinct had made her "take to" Steven, who wandered into the cockatrice's den with a disarming innocence, and was regaled there with the fiery peppermints by which Mrs. Marple sought to cure, and actually aggravated, the "windy spasms."

And, though these delicacies made the drawing-room smell like the gallery of a theatre, Clare was thankful that Mrs. Marple—and indeed the whole household—had accepted Steven more readily than they had received herself; for Joyce, who, during the vacation, was reading pathology in a bedroom pickled with lysol and cigarette-smoke, contented herself with giving him, at meal-times, the kind of scrutiny which she might have devoted to a bacillus under the microscope; while Evelyn, mollified by the fuchsia evening-frock, was so kindly disposed to all creatures of the opposite sex that even one of Steven's tender age might, *faute de mieux*, provide material for a minor conquest. And Steven, delighted by the tomboy in her, flattered her by a ready submission to her charms.

Yet Clare would willingly have dispensed with the friendliness of Joyce and Evelyn toward Steven if only he and Dudley could have been friends. In one emotional moment, when Dudley and herself had stood together, hand in hand, above the sleeping child, she had prayed and believed that this might be possible. But Steven sleeping was very different from Steven wide awake. Whenever they faced each other that deep, instinctive dislike of his for Dudley declared itself in the dumb irreconcilable obstinacy which Clare remembered so well in Ralph Hingston's eyes. Steven would never speak to Dudley if he could help it ; even in the gay familiarity of Christmas Day he had shrunk from contact with him. However bright or lively he might be, the appearance of Wilburn was sufficient to reduce him to silence, and send him straight to Clare's arms, where he clung to her, like a dog in a manger, defying the other to approach his possession, while Wilburn, who, at the best of times, was awkward with children, regarded him with the puzzled tolerance that a Newfoundland might have given to the yapping challenge of a Pekingese.

" Oh, Steven, Steven," she implored him when they were alone together. " Why *do* you behave like that ? You make me shy for you. You ought to be ashamed of yourself."

But Steven was not ashamed. " I'm awfully sorry, mummy," he told her. " I'm afraid I can't help it. You can't *compel* yourself to like people, can you ? "

" But it hurts me, darling. For my sake you might be nicer. You've no idea how kind he's been to you, how much he's helped me to do things for you, sweetheart."

" I never asked him to, mummy darling. I'd so much rather you'd do things for me yourself."

" But, Steven darling, you don't understand. There are lots of things that mummy couldn't do by herself—like sending you to school. And when two people whom mummy loves very dearly . . ."

" You loved me first, didn't you ? " he broke in. " You love me a thousand thousand times more than you do him. You're only pretending to love him. I don't believe you love him at all, mummy ! "

" Oh, Steven, Steven, how wicked of you to talk like that ! If you say dreadful things of that kind I shan't love you any longer. No, I won't let you kiss me. I'm very angry with you." She closed the book that she had opened. " If you're like that I don't think I want to read to you to-night. You're not my boy."

He gazed at her with his determined eyes, and, as he gazed, the wilfulness faded from his face ; the hardness melted away from it ; his lips parted in a soft, a beautiful, a cunning smile.

" In that case, mummy," he said, " I should love you to play the piano. You *will* play to me, darling, won't you ? I'll be ever so quiet."

She smiled in spite of herself, divining the guile that underlay his simplicity yet quite unable to resist it ; and he, realizing his victory almost before Clare herself was aware of it, flung himself into her arms and covered her face with warm kisses whether she would or no. Even when he pained her most she could not resist him, as Steven knew far better than she did, and when their peace was made her eyes were full of tears of gratitude for this soul-consuming love, so that when she yielded to him and played, while he sat like a little mouse beside her, her fingers seemed inspired and her soul overleapt the music as it had done in the early days of her love in the twilit drawing-room of Pen House.

Even when she was forced to scold him they played like children together, two children playing in a lonely house, in a world to which they neither of them really belonged—a world in which, ultimately, however hard she might try to be detached and judicial, the only thing that mattered was their love for each other.

Yet, though she surrendered herself to the seductions of this idyl, Clare knew, as Dudley had warned her, that it could not last for ever ; and later, when Steven had gone back to school, even more than during those holidays when the problem was imminent and pressing, its seriousness troubled her. For when she came to think it out alone she realized that no spiritual geometry could square the triangle of incompatibility or reconcile the divergent lines of force that composed it : her own desire for peace, divided between love and loyalty ; her husband's awkwardness, resultant of a high sense of justice and jealousies unconfessed, and, in Steven, a feeling less complicated yet more potent than either : the instinctive, inexplicable dislike which Wilburn had always aroused in him.

" In time he will grow out of it," she told herself ; for had not time already softened the angles of Joyce's and Evelyn's hostility and changed the malignant Marple from a militant harridan into a troublesome but still tolerable servant ? Yet when she considered Dudley's inflexibility and that flinty Hingston obstinacy, which she had known so well in Ralph, and recognized again in Steven, she knew that she had reason to dread the moment when these two clouds no bigger than a man's hand might meet and all her sky be shattered by thunder or jagged with lightning.

She was thankful, indeed, and had reason to be thankful, when these, the first, and many other holidays went by without provoking the threatened cataclysm. In the meantime life at Tudor House had become far more simple and its human relationships less alarming. Perhaps it was Clare who had adapted herself to them, mainly as the result of her growing friendship with Ernest Wilburn, whose kindly advice she followed with an increasing confidence and whose company supplied an interest that had been miserably lacking before.

It seemed as if nobody approved of this new intimacy. Dudley, whose standards of loyalty were too exacting to allow him to criticize his brother, received it with a dispiriting neutrality. Aunt Cathie, on the other hand, who, since the motor-buses began to displace the Tilton four-in-hand and ran right through from Wychbury, occasionally descended on Tudor House, reluctantly admitting the usefulness of petrol, was characteristically downright in her disapproval.

" That man ! " she said. " Why really, Clare, I don't see how you can afford to be seen about with him."

" I like him," said Clare, " and after all he's my brother-in-law. I wish you'd tell me what you have against him."

" He visits London far too much. He has been *seen* there," Aunt Cathie added cryptically.

" My dear Aunt Cathie, that's hardly enough to condemn him."

Aunt Cathie shook her head. . . . " Susan Abberley," she continued, " has a cousin in London. Ernest Wilburn frequents places that are not suitable for a man in his position."

" Then how has Susan Abberley's cousin seen him ? "

" That is entirely beside the point," Aunt Cathie declared. " I have it on the very best authority that Ernest Wilburn is intimate with . . . actresses." Aunt Cathie hesitated, as though she could scarcely bring herself to pronounce the word.

" Well, everybody knows, my dear, that Ernest is a great ladies'-man. He'd be the first to admit it himself."

" Clare, I don't like to hear you treat the matter so lightly. I'm thankful the doctor isn't here to hear you."

" But Aunt Cathie, you're not imagining that Ernest could make love to *me* ? We're far too good friends for that."

" I can see at any rate," said Aunt Cathie, " that you're very greatly changed ; and I must say I think it's Dudley's duty to protect you. In a Hingston this attitude might be quite in character ; in a Wilburn, no. However . . ."

With this " however " she resigned Clare to her fate : a very pleasant fate as far as Ernest Wilburn was concerned. He sent her, every week, great bundles of the prize carnations for which his garden was famous. They lunched, they dined, they went to concerts and theatres together. Often, in his solitary music-room in the Alvaston house, she played his Steinway. Sometimes they played duets, piano arrangements of orchestral scores. Though his technique was faulty, he understood the anatomy of music more clearly than she did, and would give her the leads and explain the orchestration as he played. In this way she came to know the Ring and Meistersinger and Tristan almost by heart. Sometimes he sang, and she accompanied him in Oldham's new discovery : the incomparable songs of Hugo Wolf. He made her the confidant of all the new artistic enthusiasms that were replacing his old pre-Raphaelite devotion : the painting of Steer and Sickert, the etchings of Cameron and Muirhead Bone. He lent her books of every variety : Jean Christophe, Sudermann, Henry James. And always, alone or in a crowd, she found him smiling and courteous, sensitive and urbane : the voice of Dudley, which she had always loved, tuned to a subtlety, a sensibility, a delicate humour that Dudley lacked.

## VIII

### THUNDER IN THE DISTANCE

WITHOUT Ernest Wilburn her life at Alvaston during the next few years would have been a singularly drab affair in which the poor little aspirations to culture that she had brought with her from Uffdown must have shrivelled to nothing in a brazen wilderness of Astills or lain submerged and forgotten beneath an ocean of Isits. For to Dudley the whole social duty of woman consisted in politeness to clients, and the narrow, if eminently respectable, circle of his firm's clientèle at no point intersected that other circle, whose centre lay in the University and the great Unitarian families who had made it, within which Clare might have found the soul of North Bromwich expressing itself through mediums more gracious than the heavy metals.

It was fortunate indeed that her widowhood had accustomed her to loneliness; for the distance of Alvaston from her old home, and her natural repugnance from visiting the desecrated Uffdown had deprived her of the few friendships which she had ever made. Aunt Cathie, having sung her *Nunc Dimittis*, was quite content to leave her in Dudley's hands, the more so since old Thirza had given her a new interest in life by beginning to " break up," and demanding an exercise of the nursing skill that she had acquired during the doctor's decline.

Since the morning of Clare's victory at Uffdown Lady Hingston had finally washed her hands of her. Vivien, whom Clare had always liked, was far too busy breeding animals of one kind or another, or hunting, or tinkering with motor-cars, to give a thought to her. Indeed she might well have imagined that Stourford had ceased to exist but for Sir Joseph's cheques, which still continued to arrive, impersonally and automatically, at Christmas and on the date of Steven's birthday.

Even the monotony of Tudor House itself had been deepened by the passage of time; for Joyce had qualified and now wasted her brilliance in an Oriental zenana mission, and Evelyn, that great huntress, had led her ultimate victim to the altar of St. George's, radiantly plump amid the whispers of all the Miss Isits in Alvaston.

Yet time was exacting, in return for these kind offices, a toll the heaviness of which Clare realized when, on the evening after Evelyn's wedding, Dudley and herself sat down to the solitary anticlimax of their evening meal. Their solitude, the stiff magnificence of their wedding garments, the mingled atmosphere of constraint and relief, of uneasy gaiety and of fatigue, reminded her, against all reason, of the last domestic ceremony of the kind at which they had both assisted : the supper at Pen House on the evening after the doctor's funeral. But now, alas, there was no Aunt Cathie to enliven them with her forced and pathological vivacity. They sat and ate, at opposite ends of the dining-room table ; for Mrs. Marple, being a creature of habit, and having established ideas as to the proper places of master and mistress at table, had left them still separated by the chair that Evelyn had occupied.

In this remoteness, over the empty waste of damask, Clare found herself considering her husband with an unusual detachment. For most of her life, it seemed, she had taken him for granted ; their intimacy had kept her at too close quarters for her to be able to realize him as a whole. Now that the foreground of white table-cloth posed him like a portrait on an easel in the middle of an empty studio the details of his physical conformation leapt out at her with a brutal, a stereoscopic clearness.

And, as she gazed at him with a secret curiosity, she knew that this was not the man whom she had taken for granted, most certainly not the man whom she had married four years before. Within the unusual constriction of his wedding clothes Dudley appeared to have undergone some internal process of shrinking, of desiccation, in which the skin, deprived of its proper support, save where the craggy orbits and the circular muscles of the lips sustained it or the skull stretched it into an oval of shiny baldness beneath the sparse grey hair, fell into flaccid folds and wrinkles like a dry and punctured bladder. Indeed, as the yellow gaslight descended on him, its ink-blue shadows defined and threw into relief the cavities and protuberances not of the face she knew, or imagined that she knew, but of the bones beneath. It was the face of an old man, with admonitions of that which lies beyond age. It shocked, it troubled her.

" He isn't much more than fifty," she told herself, " and fifty is nothing in these days. Why, grandpapa . . ." She seemed to hear the voice of the doctor snarling : " A man is as old as his arteries, Catherine." And Dudley's arteries— if they were arteries ?—stood out upon his temples like branches of coral. " Yes, he is old, he is old," she told herself, " far older than Ernest. I suppose, if only we knew it, we are all growing old together." She was overwhelmed by a sudden gust of pity, for herself, for all the ageing world, but particularly for Dudley. " He works so hard ; he wears himself out ; and yet's he's so obstinate, poor darling, so confident in his own strength that he won't allow me, who am so much younger, to take a share."

For he shared nothing with her. " We go on year after year," she thought, " quite near to each other, parallel, like railway lines, with just the width of this table between us ; and so we shall go on until we're both of us too old to think any more about it."

She saw herself reaching a point at which this strength of his that she had always reverenced might end by becoming dependent on her weakness. . . . Then Dudley himself became aware of her scrutiny. He raised his head, by the movement of an inch escaping from the spell in which this cruel trick of lighting had entangled him ; his lips moved in a smile ; his face became alive.

" What is the matter, Clare ? " he said. " You're staring at me as if you didn't know me. Is my tie crooked ? " He laughed. " These wedding dissipations ! "

" No, darling," she answered hastily ; " I was only thinking. It seems so strange to be here alone, without Evelyn or anybody."

He rallied her : " You've always complained, my child, that we never got a chance of being by ourselves, and now you'll be hoisted by your own petard, whatever that means."

He came and took her face between two cold hands, kissing her brow with an attempt at gallantry that was pathetic, for now he rarely appeared to her in the guise of a lover.

But as Clare lay beside him, sleepless, that night, she was tormented by memories of the gaslight's distortion. " For I shall never see him now in any other light," she thought. The burden of time lay heavy on her brain, forbidding it to sleep, telling her that what she had seen that night in Dudley another would see to-morrow in herself ; that, whether she fought against it or submitted, the end toward which the spinning world now bore her was identical with that of the stricken leaves which the night wind drove with a dry rattle over the asphalt footpath of the Halesby Road. " And once you realize that," she thought, " what is the use of life ? What am I lying here for, at Dudley's side ? Why am I living at all ? '

" For Steven, of course," was the answer, and that, to a certain extent, contented her, though even in this most precious of relations, the fingers of time, the healer and the destroyer, were closing on her joy.

Steven was now fourteen. A year ago he had left Kingston-in-Arden and Barlow Major behind him, and in defiance of Stourford's distant thunder had entered the School House at Rugby, where that old soldier his great-grandfather had been hardened in Arnold's time. And now, however hard she tried, Clare could not treat him as a baby any longer. During the last three years his body and mind had developed with an alarming rapidity. Physically he had shed—as a growing lion-cub sheds the vestigial markings that show its relation to other feline species—all those childish shades of character by which Aunt Cathie had been able to claim him as a Weir. Now, shooting up as straight as a young poplar, already overtopping Clare by several inches, the conformation of all his fair-haired, loose-limbed body proclaimed him not only Hingston but, literally, the living image of Ralph. A little tightening of the ligaments, a little hardening of muscle, and Clare, as she met him in his blue and white colours on the Midland platform, might easily have imagined that it was Ralph himself who took her to his strong arms. And spiritually, too, the Hingston strain asserted itself; not only, as always, in the Hingston obstinacy, but in the love of all field sports that had been the obsession of Ralph's and Vivien's lives, and in a passion for everything mechanical, in which his mind reflected that of the founder of Wolverbury.

She was so proud of him, yet, even in her pride a little puzzled, a little alarmed. He was growing away from her, this boy of hers; a child not so much of her own body as of a generation which seemed, in comparison with hers, less kind, less soft, more ruthless in all its reactions; and the differences between them which her love and his dependence on her had once been sufficiently powerful to reconcile were becoming magnified in this period of violent growth to a degree that frightened her. Once she had fondly thought that she could mould his nature to the shape of hers, that she could instil into him enthusiasms and tastes which later they could share: such as the music which had always meant so much to her.

But Steven, when once the age of nursery rhymes was over-past and his cracked voice refused to obey him, revealed himself as utterly unmusical as Dudley. Of all these intimate interests which had affected her early life the only one that Steven appeared to share was, paradoxically, that which she had earliest abandoned: the religious fervour that had invaded and possessed her at St. Monica's. It took, in

Steven's mind, the shape of a passionate curiosity about Church history and forms of ritual, subjects in which she could no longer simulate enthusiasm now that the images of Miss Boldmere and Mr. Darnay had died away from her mind. But Steven, fired by the influence of the priest who had prepared him for confirmation, was as earnestly concerned with the findings of the Council of Trent as with the rules of the Rugby Union : a combination of interests so incongruous to Clare's mind that she abandoned all hope of understanding it.

Indeed, the one and only characteristic of his childhood that remained unmodified was that which she would most gladly have seen the end of : his deeply-rooted dislike and distrust of Dudley Wilburn. It seemed as if this ancient threat to her peace of mind would never be removed. As time went by, and Steven's individuality grew harder and more assertive, her position midway between these high potentials became more precarious. In this, as in everything else, she made Ernest Wilburn her confidant.

"When those two are together," she told him, "the room is like the sky before a thunderstorm. You can feel its heaviness, Ernest ; it's suffocating. When Joyce and Evelyn were about it didn't feel so dangerous. I could look on them as—how shall I put it ?—lightning conductors. But now, with just those two, there's an awful emptiness in which anything might happen. I feel as if I were on the top of a mountain with the clouds close to my head. I'm frightened, Ernest dear."

"Nothing has ever happened yet ? I mean nothing dreadful. . . ."

"No, nothing dreadful. No lightning. Only an occasional growl."

"Dudley is very level-headed, you know. I've only seen Dudley lose his temper once in my life ; though then, I must admit, it was rather magnificent than pleasant."

" Ah, Dudley is wonderful," she admitted. " Dudley's an angel. It isn't Dudley I'm frightened of."

" I suppose," he went on after a moment's reflection, " you're right about their being at too close quarters. The place isn't big enough for both of them, and obviously you can't move Dudley. Next holidays, I think you'd better send Steven to stay with his Aunt Cathie. In the country he'll have more room to amuse himself."

" And leave me alone ? " she cried. " Oh, Ernest ! But can't you understand that Steven's holidays are all that I live for."

" Yes, yes, I understand, my dear. But, you see, you can't have it both ways."

She was determined to have it both ways ; yet, every day the painful dichotomy was declaiming itself more plainly.

She knew that Ernest Wilburn was speaking the truth.

" I can't let him go away from me. If once he goes, I feel I shall lose him for ever."

" God bless my soul, it's not as bad as that ! Why shouldn't you go there too ? "

" Away from Dudley ? He'd never let me. Ernest you've no idea how fidgety he's getting just lately."

" Haven't I ? My dear, I happen to be his partner. As a matter of fact we are going through a rather difficult patch. Business conditions aren't what they might be in the Midlands just now, and Dudley takes everything to heart. You never better things by worrying over them, Clare. I think you must have caught the trick of meeting trouble half-way from Dudley."

" I haven't to go half-way to meet it, Ernest," she told him. " I feel that it's coming, and wish to heaven I knew which way to run from it."

It came, in fact, a few months later from the quarter where she least expected it, and so disguised that, in the beginning, she didn't recognize the danger. It was Dudley who brought her the news in which it lay hidden.

" I've had a telephone message from Stourford," he told her. " Bad news, I'm sorry to say. That boy of George's has had appendicitis at Eton. They operated—apparently just too late. He died last night."

" Oh, Dudley, poor, poor Eleanor ! "

She remembered that Christmas at Stourford, three weeks before her wedding, when the twins had danced and romped about them ; she remembered the stony loveliness of Eleanor Hingston's face, so null, so perfect ; she saw the face of Niobe wet with tears ; but below the words of compassion that her lips shaped there rose a wave of awed thankfulness that this haphazard blow of fate had fallen on Harold and not on Steven.

" It was Sir Joseph who rang me up," Dudley was saying. " He asked me to let you know that the funeral will be at Wolverbury on Friday."

" Do you mean that I shall have to go to it ? " Clare asked anxiously. The only funeral she had ever been to was the doctor's at Stourton ; but these sombre ceremonies were the commonplaces of Dudley's life, as she sometimes realized when she saw him come home in his crape-bound hat. " Do you think that they'll resent it if I don't ? I'm sure they can't really want to see me, Dudley. I've heard nothing of George or Eleanor for four years."

" I don't think you can avoid it this time," he said. " I feel we must regard this message as a kind of overture. You realize, of course, what Harold's death implies ? "

She hadn't realised anything, for the moment, but poor, cold Eleanor's sorrow and her own thankfulness for Steven. Wilburn explained to her with a voice in which he could not entirely conceal a subdued triumph :

" Harold, after George, was heir to the Hingston baronetcy. Now that he's gone that place is taken by

Steven. Of course he mayn't keep it for long : you understand that Eleanor may produce another heir. But that,
I think, is unlikely. From rumours that I've heard I don't
think things are going too smoothly at Wolverbury : it's
said they haven't lived together for several years. Not that
a baronetcy's anything to scream about in these days—this
cursed Liberal Government's created them by the score ; but
Stourford, as I happen to know, is entailed, and Steven's
not only the heir but, fortunately for himself, the only male
Hingston living—apart from George ; which means, as I see
it, that not only Stourford but most of the Hingston property
will come to him. Hence the *rapprochement* on this very
mournful occasion. I think you'll have to accept it, as they
say, in the spirit in which it's obviously intended, just for
Steven's sake. You see this sad business has turned you
into a person of importance for them."

" But Dudley," she protested, " I'd rather die than go
running after them on that account."

" You needn't go running after them. They've asked
for you—which, for the old lady, is a pretty considerable
climb-down—and you, out of the kindness of your heart,
will consent to go. It's no good being intense and proud
about it, Clare. You're Steven's mother, and in these new
circumstances they have a right to be interested in him."

" They haven't any right to take him away from me,
Dudley. That's what she'll try to do. Oh, don't I know
her ! "

He smiled at the primitive mother in her. " You speak,"
he said, " as if it were a question of kidnapping a baby
Steven's nearly fifteen. In six years' time he'll be of age.
He has a decided will of his own already. You can't
separate him from Stourford for the rest of his life. He'll
go there anyway, sooner or later, and, if I know anything
about it, he'll find it very much to his taste. If you're not
there you'll lose your influence. So, don't you see, if you

persist in being unfriendly you stand to lose a good deal more than you'll gain ? Why not anticipate the inevitable by a charming and magnanimous gesture."

" Oh, but it isn't that ; you don't understand," she told him. " It's not that I find it difficult to forgive her. If that's all she wants, heaven knows she's welcome to it. But if it implies admitting their claims on Steven . . . Oh, how I loathe their money and their wretched title, Dudley ! "

" It's merely silly to talk like that," he told her. " Someday you may be very glad of both. In any case, all sentimentality apart, you can't avoid them. And you can't," he insisted, " with any respect for decency or politeness, refuse to go to Wolverbury."

" Then you'll come with me, dearest ? " she entreated.

" Yes, I'll come with you," he agreed.

## IX

### STOURFORD INTERVENES

THEY stood together in the graveyard at Wolverbury beneath the shadow of the terra-cotta church that Sir Joseph had built to teach his workmen to turn the other cheek and submit themselves to their lords, their masters and the spiritual pastor he chose for them. Six foremen from the steelworks carried the pitiful coffin. A mean crowd of children and women with shawls pulled tight round their cheeks clung to the churchyard railings and peered inside. Within the church the air had been sickly with the scent of arums and chrysanthemums. Outside, a bitter wind was blowing from the East, in which the towering smoke-stacks shook out funereal pennons. Its biting air contracted and made yellow the faces of the family group at the grave-side ; and Clare, who had met none of them for several years, was shocked to see how time had dealt with them all, pinching and drying up their bodies as did the East wind, so that they all seemed worn and shrunken within their black clothes, their features a series of tragic masks in parchment.

She looked at Sir Joseph. He was mopping his pouched cheeks. Vivien was crying unaffectedly; she didn't mop her tears; but her lips quivered and her nose sniffed. The head of George was bent so that all his face was hidden; but Eleanor, who stood beside him, her face as pale and motionless as alabaster, had no tears in her eyes. Fixed in an apathy more terrible than any movement of grief she stood. Her eyes were raised. Above the rest, beyond them, they seemed to stare unseeing into the low sky, past the black pennons of the smoke-stacks into heaven knew what distances of blank space, like the eyes of forgotten statues, stonily staring, for ever changeless and beautiful, over the sands of deserts where no men come. " She must be all stone," Clare thought, " if she cannot feel this." For Clare herself was crying as miserably as any of them.

The last words were spoken, and, in the silence that followed, she heard the shriek of tortured iron that issued from the rolling-mills. On every side the sounds of monstrous labour that, during the intense moments of the funeral service seemed to have tactfully submerged themselves, broke out into a new fury, as though they were hurrying to make up for time that they had lost and grudged. The foremen shambled awkwardly away, anxious, without an appearance of indelicate haste, to return to their working coats and neck-cloths. The crowd swayed from the railings and stood sheepishly gaping on either side of the churchyard gates about an alley already marked by the mud-trampled confetti of an earlier ceremony. A scornful electric tram advanced and scattered them, jangling its bell impatiently along the kerb. There was a roar of starting motor-car engines. Dudley clutched Clare's arm.

" I think you'd better speak to Lady Hingston," he whispered.

" Need I ? "

" You'd better. She'll expect it."

There were no more tears in Lady Hingston's eyes than in Eleanor's. Hard and bright as yet beneath the dainty, powdered whiteness of her hair, they boldly proclaimed her confidence that even if George's son had failed to maintain the Hingston tradition of fitness to survive—which was doubtless Eleanor's fault—the name which that enormous background of black-plumed smoke-stacks symbolized was still secure and, indeed, imperishable.

" Well, Clare," she said, " it's you, is it ? You look extremely well. Black suits you. So, apparently, does Alvaston."

Yet Clare knew that this approval was not intended for herself, but for the mother of Steven.

" We never seem to meet nowadays," Lady Hingston went on with exquisite insolence, " and it's no good trying to talk in this icy wind and with all these rude people gaping at us. I can't imagine where the police have gone to. Why don't you ever come over to Stourford, Clare ? If you can spare us an afternoon I'll send the car for you. To-morrow ? Now don't for heaven's sake make difficulties," she continued, before Clare had spoken. " Surely, at a time like this, you're not going to quarrel with me again ? That would be too boring ! Of course you needn't come if you don't wish to. We've known each other long enough to be candid. What my husband wanted to ask you was this : Will you let Steven honour us with part of his next holidays ? If you like to come with him, I needn't tell you that you'll be welcome. You know what we're like, and you'll take us as you find us. Yes, yes, Joe dear, I'm coming. I was asking Clare about Steven. I gave her your message. Perhaps she'll believe me if you speak to her yourself."

Sir Joseph smiled wanly. He took Clare's hand in limp, black-gloved fingers and pressed it. He looked crushed, shrunken, pitiful, uncertain of himself. Clare's heart went out to him. Evidently he at least had suffered.

" Well, Clare," he said, with a shy glance, that seemed to apologize for his clandestine cheques and his wife's behaviour, and almost begged her to be merciful : " On a day like this . . ." He stopped. His hand wandered to his breast pocket as though he were feeling for a cheque-book. " You see," he almost pleaded, " Steven's my only grandson. Let bygones, be bygones my dear. For poor old George's sake. . . ."

As if poor old George had anything to do with it ! He and Eleanor had already disappeared ; the crowd was melting away ; only those four stood on the windy pavement.

"When you get on in years, my dear," Sir Joseph murmured, " you feel the need of having young people around you. I suppose that's only natural. I hope you'll let him come to us. We'll try to make him happy ; we won't spoil him ; and if you come you know you'll be welcome too."

Clare knew exactly what that welcome would be ; yet, when she talked it over with Dudley that evening, she saw that it would be perverse and unreasonable to keep Steven away from Stourford. She was only too thankful that Dudley didn't insist on her going there too. Indeed, he almost seemed to encourage her in her aversion ; and such was her sense of uncertainty and suspicion in those difficult days that she found herself brooding over his motives, wondering if his apparent concern for her comfort were no more than a disguise for his desire to separate her from Steven. And even the approval of Ernest Wilburn, on whose counsels she relied so implicitly, was powerless to fortify her against Aunt Cathie's disgust at her decision.

"Upon my soul, Clare," Aunt Cathie declared, " I

thought you had more nous. Why, anyone as blind as
a bat could see it's a trap! You've fallen into it, right up
to the neck, my dear. I can't conceive why you didn't let
me know what was happening, even if you didn't see fit to
ask my advice. You may be quite sure that *I* shouldn't
have minced my words. Really, I can't imagine what
Dudley was thinking of. Honestly I should have given
him credit for more sense. However, thank heaven, it's
never too late to mend. The sooner you write and get out
of it the better."

" No, no, my dear," Clare told her, " I can't get out of it
now. It's all settled. He'll go there straight from Rugby
at Easter."

" Then you'll have to go with him," Aunt Cathie decided.

" How *can* I go with him? She's just the same as ever.
It'd only be asking for trouble, as Steven would say."

" You'll get your trouble whether you ask for it or not,"
said Aunt Cathie gloomily. " If you don't go to Stourford,
you'd better come and stay with me at Pen House. Then
you'll be handy, so to speak, in case of emergency."

Aunt Cathie didn't explain what kind of emergency she
meant, or how she expected Clare to deal with it if one
arose ; but the fact that Clare declined to sit waiting for it
at Pen House offended her, and when she went off in a huff,
Clare felt more doubtful, more apprehensive, more powerless
to cope with the gloomy prognostications which she shared
than ever.

At Easter Steven went to Stourford and entered, like
prince, into his inheritance. Not even a schoolboy of
fifteen could fail to realize the difference between that new
spaciousness and the constriction of Tudor House. All
Stourford was his to command, and Lady Hingston, than
whom nobody could be more charming when she wished it,
displayed a malicious delight in accentuating the contrast,
making herself a devoted and omnipotent slave for the

R

gratification of all his desires, enveloping him in flatteries that would have turned a stronger head than Steven's, cramming his short ten days of holiday with more excitements than he had known in all the rest of his life.

With Vivien he rode to the last meets of the Woodland Stourton season on a mount whose magnificence would easily have eclipsed—if that had been necessary—all memories of poor Bo-peep. With Henri, the chauffeur, he explored the mysteries of Vivien's runabout, and learned to drive it over the gravelled stretches of the park, and through the lanes round Uffdown. Wherever he went, tenants and servants smiled on him : he was " the young master," and they let him know it. Finally, with a cleverness that recognised his mechanical bent, his grandmother took pains to send him to Wolverbury with Sir Joseph, where, in a rapture of self-realization, his mind took fire from contact with the greatest machine of all.

For three days on end he wandered over that city of steel-works, ravished by opening vistas of mechanical efficiency and power, watching the puddlers at work in the haze of heat that trembled above beds of molten metal, deafened and fascinated by the thunder of the rolling mills, the sighs of super-heated blasts, the hum of dynamos, the screeching of monstrous lathes, and the hissing of forged steel. In a high crow's nest among the blackened girders of the forge roof, he pressed an electric button that bade the smooth arm of a hydraulic press descend, and saw the shaft of an Atlantic liner squeezed and moulded like butter forty feet below him. He was the iron-master, the master of iron, with the power of many thousand horses in his fingertip ; and, as he hung there, like a divinity enskied, iron, and the romance of iron, entered into his soul.

Something of the exaltation of this new passion still clung to him when, with a mechanical punctuality, the Stourford Lanchester delivered him ten days later into Clare's eager arms. Her eyes devoured him in search of all the changes that she feared. Changes indeed there were ; for, during the last term he had grown taller and more manly than ever. His voice had definitely broken ; there was down on the lips that she kissed ; his whole body and mind had attained a balance, a precision which seemed to show that he had left his childhood behind ; but while she glowed with pride in his transformation, her heart sank at the thought of what he, and she, had lost.

The way in which he settled down to the rest of his holiday showed her, quite definitely, that he regarded Alvaston and herself as in the nature of an anticlimax. Of course he decided to make the best of both of them ; but however honestly he tried to identify himself with the milder interests with which she entertained him, she could see that his point of view was changed. Something of the arrogance of Stourford clung to his manner ; even in his speech the Hingston inflections that she knew so well betrayed themselves ; and always, beneath their greatest intimacy, she detected reservations that took the form of an unnatural disinclination to talk about his adventures at Stourford : a secrecy more deeply wounding than any spoken word.

Before this time he had always been frank with her ; lured by her passionate sympathy he had made her the confidante of secrets in his school-life which he would not have breathed to any other living soul. This novel reticence haunted and distressed her. She felt that she could not live unless she broke through it.

" Why do you never tell me anything about Stourford, darling ? " she asked him.

His brow clouded. " I don't know, mum," he said. " I suppose it's because I feel you wouldn't want to listen."

" But, Steven, Steven, what a silly idea ! You know quite well that I'm interested in everything about you. Who on earth has put such a ridiculous idea into your head ? "

He wouldn't answer this question, but cunningly relapsed into vagueness.

" I don't know," he repeated, " it's just a general idea. After all, you never let me go to Stourford before, mum."

" Oh, Steven, that's not quite true. As a matter of fact, they never asked you."

" Didn't they ? " He eyed her narrowly, as if he were questioning the truth of her defence. " Well, mum, I'm sure it can't be my fault anyway. You must have done something to stop them."

" No, no. That isn't true, my darling. I haven't done anything."

" Well, I don't understand," he declared. " Evidently there was something wrong. And it isn't my fault. Grand-mama's rather funny when she talks about you. She doesn't say much ; but it sounds as if you'd quarrelled."

" No, not exactly quarrelled," she told him. " It's true that we haven't agreed in everything."

" Well then "—he became emphatic—" all I can say is I think it's very silly of you, mum."

" No, Steven, don't think that. It's a very old story, and would take a lot of explaining. If you knew every-thing . . ."

" I *don't* know everything. Of course I don't. You've never said a word about it. But I do think it's a bit shabby of all of you to have kept me from going there. I haven't quarrelled with anybody. And it's much nicer at Stourford than it is here."

" Oh, Steven, just when we're together . . ."

" Oh, mother, mother, you know what I mean. Of course I love being with you. It isn't that. I suppose it's so long since you've been there that you've forgotten. Everything's different at Stourford. If you'd come with me it would have been perfect. But all the same . . ." He paused, and then, encouraged by her silence, went blundering on ;

" After all, they are *my* people, even if they aren't yours ; and I don't see why I should be mixed up in your quarrels ; really I don't."

He stopped abruptly, as though he were sorry that he had spoken the truth ; and still Clare was silent. He kissed her, offering immediate amends.

" You see, darling," he said, " there really isn't an awful lot for me to do here. North Bromwich is rather a rotten hole compared with the country, isn't it ? Even if we had horses, there's nowhere much to ride. And we haven't, anyway. Nor cars either . . ."

He began to lose his awkwardness in telling her how he had helped the chauffeur to take down the engine of Vivien's single-cylinder Rover. He spoke of carburettors, magnetos, cam-shafts, timing, big-ends—things that meant nothing to her, with an almost passionate joy.

" You see," he explained, " I knew all about it on paper, so to speak, but I'd never seen the inside of anything bigger than a motor-bike ; and now I know that I could take the whole engine to pieces and put it up again. You've no idea, mum, how I love machinery ; I'd rather be an engineer than anything else in the world ; I seem to understand that sort of thing without having to think about it ; the chauffeur told me so. If we had a car, mum, I'm sure you'd never need a mechanic. I can't think why we haven't got one ; everyone seems to have a car in these days except us. I do think we might keep a little one, like Auntie Vivien's. Why can't we get one ? "

She shook her head, telling him that Dudley wouldn't hear of it.

" But why ? " he persisted. " That's stupid and old-fashioned. You've got to move with the times."

" It's a matter of expense, my darling. You've no idea how much a motor-car costs ; and that's only the beginning."

" Oh yes I have, mum," he assured her. " I know exactly

what they cost and what it costs to run them. It's nothing to make a noise about. Surely we aren't as poor as all that ? "

" We're not exactly poor, Steven darling ; but we have to be careful. Mr. Wilburn knows exactly what we can afford to spend. We have to think of the future."

" The future ? But that's rot ! The future's all right. I didn't realize that until the other day ; but now that I know I'm going to have a pot of money when grandpapa dies, it's different."

" Steven, you mustn't lose your head over ideas like that. It's horrible to hear you talk about people dying. Besides, anything might happen between now and then."

" Oh yes, I know," he answered impatiently ; " but all the same it's perfectly true. Grandmama told me so."

" She shouldn't have told you. You've no business at your age to be thinking about such things. I can see she's been unsettling you."

" No, mother, that's not fair to her. She's not done anything of the sort. That's just the worst of you : you always treat me as if I were a kid."

" Well, so you are, my darling," she smiled, drawing him towards her, trying to change the subject. But Steven's obstinacy would not be satisfied by caresses. The idea of injustice rankled in his mind, and nothing now would turn him from expressing it ; the lion cub had licked blood.

" And even if we cut out the future," he continued with ruthless logic, " we have money of our own, mum. There's Uffdown to begin with. If we could afford to live at Uffdown before we came here, I'm sure we can afford to keep a car now. Father must have had lots of money ; he couldn't have hunted if he hadn't. He didn't take it away with him when he died, so I think I ought to know what's happened to it. Didn't he leave it all to you and me ? "

" Yes, darling, of course he did. You see it's very compli-cated. You wouldn't understand."

"But I *want* to understand," he persisted, "and I think I've a right to, mother. If all that money is ours I've a right to know where it is, and I think we've a right to use it instead of going on like this. Where is it, mum? I think you ought to tell me," he ended defiantly.

"I'll tell you all I can," she answered gently. "Before your dear father died he knew that it would be difficult for me to manage everything, and so he appointed a trustee, a man in whom he had confidence, to look after the estate until you came of age. I've never told you this before, Steven, because . . . because I think you ought to make your own life without relying on what comes to you from other people—I think that every man ought to be capable of earning his own living, however rich he's going to be. So all this money of yours is accumulating in a safe place until you're twenty-one."

"Well, that's all right, I suppose," he admitted solemnly. "I'm going to be an engineer anyway. But surely it can't all be accumulating like that : we must have something else to live on?"

"Of course, my darling. I have an allowance on which we have to live in the meantime. It provides for your education during your minority. It pays for your clothes and your fees at Rugby and things of that kind."

"But if we *have* money of our own, mum"—he returned to the original theme—"surely we can spend it in any way we like? And there's no reason why we shouldn't have a car."

"Oh, Steven, Steven, how persistent you are! I can't just go and spend whatever I want to."

"But . . ." Steven's store of "buts" was inexhaustible. "But if this money was left for us to live on, we have a right to spend it, haven't we? I'm sure we can't spend all of it the way we're living here. Who pays it to you, mum?"

" The trustee. Really, my darling, I don't see why I should tell you."

" Who's the trustee ? You didn't mention his name."

For the best of reasons ; and yet she couldn't keep it from him any longer. " The man whom your father trusted more than anybody, Steven. Mr. Wilburn."

He flushed. " Oh, him ! I might have known as much. That explains everything. That's what they meant when they said he was living on you."

" Steven . . ." Her face was white ; her indignation would scarcely allow her to speak. " Steven, what do you mean ? It's a lie ! It's monstrous ! You must tell me at once who said a thing like that ! "

He hedged ; he was acute enough to realize the danger of her intensity.

" Oh, nobody said it. It was just my own idea."

" And now you're lying, Steven. That makes it worse than ever. Tell me at once . . . I insist . . . who it was that suggested such a thing ? "

But no. He evaded her with a deliberate, smiling sullenness, repeating, however she persisted, that the accusation was his own idea.

" But I tell you, Steven, it's wicked ; it's monstrous ; there's not a shadow of truth in it. There's not a better or more honourable man in the world than he is. That you could even dream of such a thing makes me ashamed of you."

He took her vehemence calmly. " Oh, well, if it isn't true I'm wrong. But you know how I loathe him, mum. I can't change that. If I pretended that I didn't, I should be really lying. You know what I think. I think he's mean and detestable. I always have done. I hate him ! "

As he spoke, his emotion strangely overpowered him. Tears started into his eyes ; he fell to his knees, he buried his head in her lap, and harsh sobs shook him as he cried

to her : " Oh, mother, mother, why did you ever marry
him ? We should have been so happy, mum, if we'd stayed
at Uffdown."

She tried to console him ; but she was crying too. " Oh,
Steven, you hurt me so, you're so cruel ! " She gathered
him in her arms, their tears were mingled, and in this misery
she was far happier than she had been for many days. Yet
in that exquisite mingling of pain and delight she was
haunted by the inadmissible truth which he had spoken : if
they had stayed at Uffdown, they would have been happy ;
with him, at Uffdown, she could be happy still. And
though her loyalties to the imagined figure of Wilburn could
not be abandoned without knocking the bottom out of her
life, she knew that Steven, fortified by the whispers of
Stourford, was too strong for her. She couldn't oppose
him without the risk of precipitating a larger disaster. Instead, she began to temporize and placate him. It was too
late in the holidays, she said, to think of things like motor-
cars, but while he was away at Rugby she'd consider it, and
talk the matter over with Dudley. His wry face showed
how little confidence he felt in that.

And from this moment, the joy of the holiday on which
she had counted so eagerly faded away from her. Beneath
all their intimacy, even beneath his demonstrations of affection, lay sullen depths of reservation that she could neither
disregard nor penetrate ; behind his eyes, even when they
smiled, she felt the presence of a spirit detached and critical ;
the steely spirit of Stourford, piercing the tissue of fable in
which she had wrapped herself, denuding her heart of all its
careful pretences, revealing, whether she wished it or no, the
uncomfortable truth.

For now, in spite of her quick indignation against them,
she feared that the suggestions breathed against Dudley
by someone unknown at Stourford were not unfounded.
When Steven, with ill-concealed relief, went back to Rugby,

she had time to investigate them more closely. She remembered the gesture of confidence and generosity with which Dudley, when first they were married, had proposed the opening of a joint bank-account. At that time she had taken it as a compliment, a confirmation of the trust he had in her. Into this joint account the quarterly instalments of her jointure were paid. Against it she drew the cheques which met not only Steven's school-fees but her half-share of the housekeeping. And now examining the pass-book with haste and the sense of guilt with which she might have read his private letters, she discovered that Dudley's contribution to the household expenses appeared there beside her own. Once more she found herself involved in the coils of mathematical calculations; once more her perplexed brain insisted that she was paying for everything twice over; once more the consciousness of her incapacity for dealing with figures reminded her that, probably, she was doing Dudley a gross injustice. It was the story of the milk account all over again.

But this time, she dared not question him; for if, as was probable, he proved her to be wrong, she felt that he would never forgive the baseness of her suspicions. By consulting Ernest she might have set her mind at rest; but Ernest, after all, was Dudley's brother, and her intimacy with him was far too precious to be hazarded by confessing doubts so unworthy. She could not even take the risk of laying her difficulties before Aunt Cathie; in Aunt Cathie's eyes Dudley was hedged with divinity. Apart from these two she had no other confidants. Left to itself, the yeast of suspicion grew and fermented until it poisoned her whole life.

# X

## THE STORM BREAKS

INCREDIBLY, Clare was almost thankful when the summer holidays swept Steven off again to Stourford. She comforted her loneliness with the thought that he, at least, was enjoying himself. Aunt Cathie had seen him dashing through the lanes in Vivien's runabout.

" I'm glad to say he waved to me," she said, " but I do think, being so near, he might have spared an afternoon to come and see me. I suppose the explanation is that that woman won't let him. You may not realize it now, Clare, but some day you'll have to pay heavily for the mistake of ever letting him go there. You can't touch pitch, as the doctor used to say. Of course I *never* gossip—you know that as well as anybody—but quite a number of people in the village who mix with the Stourford servants say he's very wild. The Pomfrets appear to be quite mad on him, if that's any recommendation. Susan Abberley has seen him three times at early service or whatever they call it. He seems to be taking after you in that unfortunate respect. Really, it's most disappointing. I always understood that Rugby was such a manly school. However . . ."

In early September, when Steven returned to Alvaston, as to an unwilling penance, Clare realized that the remainder of these holidays was going to be more embarrassing than the last. In Steven's mind, as in hers, the poison had been working ; she could not guess by how many new suggestions the original dose might have been reinforced. His manner was full of a secret impatience. It seemed as if the physical limitations of Tudor House cramped limbs that had grown used to the spaciousness of Stourford ; as if its very quietude were irksome. Out of her single devotion Clare could not supply the flattery with which the attentions of everyone at

Stourford, including Lady Hingston, had smothered him. He seemed to her alarmingly sure of himself. Before, he had treated Dudley with a sort of sullen deference. Now, in his wide blue eyes, there flashed a challenge; on his petulant lips she read a determination to hold his own.

" You promised me," he reminded her, " that you would see about that car."

" My child," she parried, " if you only knew how busy I've been ! I haven't even had time to think of it."

He smiled. It was plain that he knew she was evading him. His directness humiliated her.

" Well, mum, it's not too late. We'd better see about it at once."

" I'll ask him this evening."

But she didn't ask Dudley that evening. All through the summer she had found him growing more gloomy, more preoccupied, more fussy than ever about expenditure. The only matters over which he showed any enthusiasm now were the weekly accounts. Last month he had kicked at Hadley's demand for a new lawn-mower. Sometimes, unusually, he hinted at business worries that warned her to go gently with him. And as for motor-cars . . .

" Well, have you asked him ? " Steven persisted next morning.

" No, he's too worried just at present, darling; I must choose my time."

" Why should you choose your time to ask him about spending your own money, mum ? If you're as frightened as all that I'll ask him myself."

" For goodness' sake don't think of such a thing ! I'm *not* frightened, Steven. You've no right to suggest it."

" Then why not go ahead, mum ? I've only three weeks left."

" Steven," she said, " I'm not going to let you bully me."

But even Mrs. Marple's lessons in the science of obstructionism could not help her to resist him for ever. She knew that Steven saw through her secret stratagems as she had seen through Mrs. Marple's, and that this knowledge unshared, was falsifying, disintegrating, the most precious relation in her life. That Steven loved her she never doubted; but she wasn't quite sure that he didn't, also, despise her. His attitude toward her was cynical and patronizing, as though, by Stourford standards, she was a poor and weakly amiable creature with whom, in spite of a traditional affection, he was losing patience. With this new Steven all her old allurements—her books, her music, her kisses, were unavailing. It seemed as if nothing that she was able to give him could satisfy his central discontent. He was bored and sullen; obviously at a loose end; full of a vague resentment against North Bromwich in general and Dudley in particular.

"I'm sick of this hole, mum," he told her. "There's absolutely nothing to do here; it gives me the blues. I think I'd better go over to Wolverbury to-morrow; they're putting in a new hydraulic press."

She was so anxious for his happiness that, even though it would take him away from her, she encouraged him. They looked up trains together in the local time-table.

"You see it takes years," he complained. "With a motor-bike I should be over there in twenty minutes. It's all ridiculous, mum. I could get a good single-cylinder for sixty pounds."

"I'll see what we can do about it, darling," she told him.

"I know what that means, mother," he answered bitterly. "Can't you do anything without asking him about it?"

"If you talk like that, Steven, I shall do nothing at all."

That evening he kept watch over her, like a cat beside a mouse-hole, waiting for her to speak to Wilburn. His manner was reckless and scornful of her lack of courage; he laughed, he spoke more loudly, more emphatically than usual, as though he wanted to convince her that he, at least, wasn't afraid of anyone.  From time to time he gave her a taunting glance that " dared " her, more clearly than words, to keep her promise ; and at last, seeing that she wouldn't accept the challenge, he forced her hand.

" Are you going to ask Mr. Wilburn about that bike, mother ? " he enquired, with a too-conscious sweetness.

She turned her answer timidly in the direction of Wilburn :

" Steven wants a motor-bicycle to go over to Wolverbury with, Dudley."

" A motor-bicycle ?  H'm . . . what's wrong with the train ? "

" Why, everything," said Steven, blandly.  " To begin with, it takes about an hour to travel seven miles."

" A motor-bicycle," said Wilburn, " costs a lot of money."

" Oh, not so much as all that," said Steven.  " Some-where about sixty pounds."

" Not much ?  If you had to earn it, young man," Wilburn grunted, " you'd realize it's more than you think."

" But I don't have to earn it, do I ? " said Steven calmly.

" You'd better get your grandfather to give you one," said Wilburn, apparently unconscious of the insolence that underlay the question.

Clare felt the situation slipping out of her grasp.  Beneath an unbroken surface the flood was sweeping them, all three, toward the lip of some incalculable Niagara.  The others seemed unconscious of their danger or else determined to defy it.  She made one last attempt to check the current.

" Dudley, if we could afford it," she began.  But neither of them heard her.  Already the thunder of the cataract was in their ears.  Her sentence was broken half-way by Steven's reply.

" I don't see why I should do that," he was saying, " when I have money of my own "

"Money of your own? You don't know what you're talking about. You have no money of your own," Wilburn replied.

"There you are, mum! What did I tell you?" Steven cried excitedly.

He rose from his chair and faced them with burning eyes. She took his arm, trying to calm him: "Steven, don't shout like that; everyone will hear you!" Wilburn was sitting with folded arms, as solid, as motionless as a block of granite. His steady eyes surveyed them without a flicker. With an impatient gesture Steven freed himself from her hands.

"Leave me alone, mum, I don't care a damn who hears me!"

"Leave him alone, Clare," Wilburn echoed grimly. "I'll deal with him."

"You? Who the devil are you, I'd like to know?" Steven cried.

Wilburn smiled slowly. He, too, rose from his chair. Towering above them he spoke with more than his usual calmness.

"Steven, you're distressing your mother. I'll not allow it. Go to your bedroom at once."

"I'll go when I want to, Mr. Wilburn. I don't take my orders from you. I know what mother would say if she weren't afraid of you, don't I, mother?"

"Oh, Steven," she entreated, "you know nothing about it. Do as you're told at once, darling. Quickly," she whispered. "I'll come to you later."

Steven stood glaring from one to the other as though he hated them equally.

"So you're against me too, mother? That's pretty rotten."

Wilburn approached them, with a heavy determination.

"Go to your room," he repeated. "I shan't ask you again."

" You can ask me till you're blue in the face," Steven cried. " You can bully mother, but you can't bully me. I'm not going anywhere till I've said what I want to. You can pocket all the money that father left us all right, but you can't stop me knowing about it or telling other people if I want to."

" Oh, Steven, Steven," Clare cried. " How can you be so wicked ? "

She took his head in her hands and pulled him toward her as though she could stop his mouth. He wrenched himself free ; her gentleness could not hold him. Wilburn was near them, breathing heavily.

" Now, for the last time," he said. " Are you going ? "

" No, I'm not going for you. I'm damned if I am."

Clare flung herself between them. " Leave him to me, Dudley," she entreated. " He'll go with me. I know he will. Come along, darling."

He was too hot to be moved by persuasions. " Why mum, you're as bad as he is ! I tell you, I'm not going anywhere unless I want to." And when she tried to draw him away with her he snarled at her : " Don't be a silly fool ! "

Above his collar Clare saw Wilburn's neck go suddenly brick-red.

" If you speak like that to your mother," he said, " I'll thrash you."

His big hands closed like vices on Steven's shoulders.

" No, Dudley, leave him to me," she cried, " leave him to me. Don't, Dudley," she cried, " you'll hurt him Dudley . . . don't ! "

But Wilburn did not hear her ; and Steven, though she still clung to him, was torn away from her, struggling like a wild animal in Wilburn's arms. The man's muscles were too strong for him ; little by little his strength was over powered. A chair went over with a crash, the portière was ripped from its hanging. Slowly, at first by inches, then more quickly, the struggle passed away from her. She heard them panting in the hall outside. A disgraceful, a humiliating scene. Suffering, perhaps more deeply than ever before in her life, she stood among the wreckage of their struggle, blinded by heart-broken tears.

At last, after an endless, cruel silence, disturbed by nothing but the gasping of her sobs, Wilburn returned to her. He stumbled and cursed the portière in which his feet had become entangled. He was flushed and out of breath. His collar was torn from its stud-hole ; his Ascot tie undone. The wheal of a nail-scratch had risen on his cheek. He smiled, with twitching lips, as he took her in his arms and kissed her. This contact made her sob more uncontrolledly than ever. His awkward consolation had no effect on her.

" I wish you'd shut the door," she gasped at last.

He closed it, ponderously, and returned to her.

" What have you done with him ? " she asked, tragically.

' I took him to his room, and locked him in."

" Dudley, you haven't hurt him ? "

" Hurt him ? No more than he deserved for speaking to you like that. He needed a lesson, and he's had it." He took her hand and pressed it. " My child, it's damnable that you should be made to suffer like this. It's nothing to me, Clare ; but you, my poor darling . . ."

She allowed him to lead her to a chair. She sat upon his knee, not knowing where she sat. He fondled her, caressed her. The contact of his hands was distasteful to her. They seemed swollen with violence. Their strength was brutal ; it offended her. He went on talking and fondling her as in a dream, but her heart was not with him. It had flown away out of her body to Steven ; and though the big hands thought they held her, they closed on nothing but the shell of her. Straining her ears to catch other sounds that mattered she heard Wilburn talking to her as from a distance in time and space :

" This is pure Stourford," he was saying. " The old lady may live to be ninety, but nothing will ever cure her tongue. She's a genius and a madwoman. Sir Joseph realizes that and makes a good job of it simply by imagining she isn't there whenever she breaks out. And she's vindictive, Clare ; particularly toward people whom she's flattered because they were useful to her and dropped because the devil that's in her compels her to insult them. When once she's behaved outrageously she has to go on hating them to justify herself ; and then there's no stone that isn't good enough to throw at them. Not even Steven. If she couldn't keep him at Stourford, she could make sure that he'd give us trouble here. I don't often lose my temper, Clare ; but that was too much. Something had to be done. You realize that ? "

" Yes, Dudley, yes," she said. But she realised nothing : only that Steven had been hurt, and that she, in her own heart, must feel the pain of it.

" I think," he went on, " that it would have been better if he'd stayed there. You can't have it both ways, you know. That was the mistake."

" The mistake ? ' The word aroused her. " Dudley, what do you mean ? "

But before he could answer there came a discreet tap on the door.

Mrs. Marple, who had heard the sound of the scuffle in the passage, had sent the housemaid to investigate the Olympian situation. The practical exigency brought Clare quickly to herself.

" Your collar's torn, Dudley. They musn't come in."

She hurried to the door. " Is that you, Mary ? You'd better go on with your supper. I'll ring for you to clear the table when we're ready."

When she returned to Wilburn there was only one thought in her mind.

" I must go to him now, Dudley," she said.

" I think you'd much better leave him alone, Clare. Give him time to come to his senses."

" No, I can't leave him," she said.

" Don't go up just yet," he entreated her. " It's wiser. I'm sure. Stay here with me a little while. I want to talk to you. Come here, my child."

She obeyed mechanically. It didn't seem to matter. They sat down together in silence.

" You heard what he said about money ? " Wilburn began at last. " You realize that for the last four years we've been living well within your income. I've taken care of that. You see I am naturally prudent, and you . . . well, Clare, you're not, exactly. There's been a balance of several thousand pounds that we haven't touched. It's all been reinvested in your name. If ever you need it, you can do what you like with it. I could sell the securities for you to-morrow. You didn't believe what Steven was saying just now ? "

" No. I know nothing about it. I don't know what to believe."

" Then you mean ' Yes.' Good God, Clare, I thought you knew me better."

" Dudley, I don't understand." She hesitated. " I think your passion for economy is rather dreadful. It hurts me sometimes. It chills me ; it freezes me ; it takes all the joy out of life."

" You'll never understand money matters, Clare."

" No, I suppose I shan't," she admitted. " Oh, Dudley, I wish there were no such things in the world."

He shook his head. " You're a queer child, Clare," he said.

And then, out of the silence that followed, the desire that

had been rushing to her lips again and again with the blind persistence of a wild animal newly caged found speech.

" May I go now ? " she said.

The very childishness of her persistence softened him. He couldn't refuse her.

" I suppose you had better get it over," he admitted. " But don't, for heaven's sake, be too gentle with him, or all this trouble will have been wasted."

He kissed her hand, at arm's length, as she broke away from him ; his fingers parted unwillingly with hers ; but this unusual tenderness, that once she would have welcomed, meant nothing to her and even embarrassed her now . . . Like the wild creature that was her desire, her body escaped from him ; out of the littered dining-room, through the dark hall, up the mean staircase to which her feet were accustomed. Breathless and trembling, like a young girl in love, she fumbled for the keyhole of Steven's door. " It's only me, darling," she whispered, eager to reassure him that Wilburn had not returned. " Steven, it's mother. Why don't you answer me ? "

But nothing answered her. " Oh, Steven ! " she said, as she groped her way through the darkness toward the bed. She bent above it and stretched out her arms to envelop him in all the warmth of her love and her forgiveness. The bed was empty. She couldn't believe that he was hiding from her. " Where are you, darling ? " she said. Her voice was thin and tremulous in the silence. Standing with the pitiful resonance of her own words in her ears, she became aware of a dank autumnal air that chilled not only her skin but the heart within her. She moved quickly toward the window, and found it wide open. In the darkness outside she could see nothing but the fog-bloomed street-lamps of the City Road, endless, stretching northward in the direction of Wolverbury.

" Steven ! " she cried again, but did not hope for an answer, for she knew already that he was not there.

She hurried back to the landing and called for Wilburn. He came heavily into the hall and stood staring up at her, with a pipe in his mouth.

" What is it ? " he asked her quietly. " What's the matter now ? "

" Dudley, he's not there. He's gone ! "

" Gone ? " he repeated. " What do you mean ? I locked the door."

" The window's open. He's not there. What can we do ? "

He came upstairs to her with long strides. " Are you sure he's not foxing ? You'd better look again. It's only more of his nonsense."

He lit a candle and went before her into the empty room. His slowness, his steadiness, they made her hate him.

" By Jove, I believe you're right. He's gone through the window. Over the roof of the outhouse."

" But where . . . where ? " she cried. " Oh, why did you do it ? Where has he gone to ? We must find him at once ! "

She broke into a torrent of utterly futile tears ; she clung to him entreating, questioning. Her passion only irritated him.

" Clare, Clare, for heaven's sake control yourself ! You don't mend matters by behaving like a lunatic. He's not a baby. He's able to look after himself."

" I know, I know," she said ; " but that makes no difference. Look in the garden, Dudley. He may be there."

She tugged at his arm to draw him away from the window. He resented her urgency ; he liked to do things in his own way, in his own time. As if the wretched boy hadn't bothered him enough already, without these hysterics ! He didn't like the sound of her voice. There was a disturbing shrillness in it ; the anguish of an overstretched string. He must put a stop to that.

"Yes, yes, I'll look," he answered irritably. "All in good time. It's no use losing your head."

"It's you who have driven him away," she replied illogically.

"Don't be ridiculous, Clare. You're becoming dramatic."

She didn't mind if she was. His hardness drove her further.

"Dudley, I shall never forgive you. If anything happens . . . You don't understand him. . . ."

"If anything happens !" The words were not worth answering. "For God's sake calm yourself and try to be a little more reasonable. If you shout like that the servants will think that we're quarrelling."

He hadn't considered the servants before ! The words came to her lips, but she checked them. "Oh dear," she thought, "how vulgar we're becoming ! "

"Now, if you're quiet," he said, "I'll have a look in the garden."

She watched him clump downstairs. There was something stiff, unelastic about his descent that made her see him as an elderly, undistinguished man with whom she had nothing in common. His age, his clumsiness, the obstinacy of his bald neck repelled her physically. Over the widening distance she saw and hated him without a shadow of shame. He knocked at the kitchen door and asked Mrs. Marple for a light. He spoke, and Mrs. Marple answered, with an exaggerated politeness. Servants, indeed ! As if they hadn't already listened greedily to every word of it ! He went out into the garden carrying the handlamp in front of him, and Clare, like a ghost, slipped down behind him.

"Steven !" he called, sternly, as if he hated the name.

How could he expect him to respond to that ? " Steven . . . Steven, darling ! " she echoed from the cold path ; and, hearing her, he looked back over his shoulder as though he were incensed by her following him. A fine, cold drizzle made a circle of mist about his moving lamp. Finally, he looked into the outhouse ; slammed the door and locked it.

" How many times have I told them to lock that door at night ? " he grumbled. " Well, now I hope you're satisfied. He's gone. No doubt he's off to Stourford. You needn't worry. I wish them joy of him."

" To Stourford ? Then we must telephone at once," she said.

He turned, in the doorway of the dining-room. " Do, for heaven's sake, be reasonable, Clare," he answered with annoyance. " Kindly remember that it's ten miles to Stourford. He can't have got there yet. The walk won't hurt him, and the rain may cool his temper. Try to be sensible for a moment. Come and sit down and wait."

" I can't sit down," she told him. But, all the same, she did so. Wilburn sank back tiredly into his accustomed chair ; and she sat opposite him, with set lips and unseeing eyes ; for though her body was there in the hateful room, her soul was scouring the dark, rolling countryside between them and Halesby. Seeing her aloofness and feeling that it would be waste of time to coax her, Wilburn relapsed with a sigh into his evening routine. He relit his pipe, with a sort of leisurely automatism, and opened the sheets of the *Courier*, which lay folded, as usual, at his right hand. . . . Then, as though vaguely conscious that something was missing, he put down the paper and grunted as he bent to exchange his boots for slippers.

" He is like a machine," Clare thought. " He goes on doing the same thing over and over again for ever and ever." She saw his big hands fumble with the laces. " A clumsy, blundering machine ! "

But this sight, which once might have stirred her to pity, or to that protective emotion which she had acclaimed as a substitute for love, no longer had power to move her. Now she saw nothing but his insensitiveness, the quality that she had misnamed strength, stability—that string of high-sounding words which she had adopted so easily from Aunt Cathie's enthusiasms. And all the time, within her, her heart was bruised, aching, resentful, as if it had been herself, not Steven, who had been beaten by those clumsy hands. At last she compelled herself to speak.

" Now we can telephone ? " she asked.

He lowered his newspaper and took out his watch, flicked back the cover, then closed it. He shook his head. " Not yet," he answered with a smile that was teasing but not unkind.

" I think you might try," she said.

" My dear child, he can't fly there. Why waste money ? Stourford's a trunk call. It costs sixpence."

He laid down the paper and sat gazing at her, quizzically, through the smoke-wreaths of his pipe. He went on puffing steadily, automatically, like a slow engine. She wanted to snatch the pipe out of his mouth ; he was so distant, so contained. And suddenly she realized that there was more in her heart than an indefinite resentment. This slow automatism had crystallized the saturation of four years. She knew that she hated Wilburn ; and the realization, which swept through the recesses of her mind like a flash of white fire, blinded her with a deeper sense of shame than any she had ever known. Trying to escape from herself, most vainly, she rose to her feet ; and Wilburn's eyes followed her with a lazy curiosity as to what she would do next. If he had asked her she couldn't have told him, and, as she stood, lost and indeterminate, a tap on the door recalled her to her surroundings.

Wilburn called sharply : " Come in ! " and Mrs. Marple

entered. Her face was grey and funereal. It was obvious that she knew what had happened. Her eyes accused Clare. "*You* are responsible for this," they said ; "these sort of games didn't happen in *my* time ! " And Clare, her heart still hot with the realization of her hatred for Wilburn and its shame, suddenly found that her lips, which no longer belonged to her, were set in the habitual smile with which she now received these evening visitations ; her limbs moved her, unbidden, to Wilburn's side ; her hand lay on his shoulder as she answered Mrs. Marple's valediction.

"No, nothing else, thank you, Mrs. Marple," she was saying. "Breakfast at eight as usual."

"Very well, ma'am. Good night sir . . . good night ma'am," Mrs. Marple cheerfully replied.

She went, closing the door behind her with exaggerated care ; and still Clare stood, as though petrified, in the attitude which she had unconsciously assumed ; a smile on her lips, her hand on Wilburn's shoulder. And he, out of an amazing, crass obtuseness, imagined that it was her will that had brought her thus to his side. He put down his pipe and taking the hand that lay on his shoulder began to fondle it, so that the shame in her heart was changed to a blank wonder that he, of all men living, should be unaware of the hatred in her heart. But she could not raise her hand any more than she could move her lips.

"Clare, Clare, my little one," he was saying—and his voice was broken—"I can't tell you how sorry I am that this should have happened." His fingers caressed the dead hand that didn't belong to her. "But sooner or later, you know," he went on, "something of this kind was bound to come. You knew that ? Of course you must have fore-seen it as clearly as I did. I'm afraid, my child, there's no way out of it. It's obvious, isn't it, that we can't allow a child to dictate to us ? Well, well, we are growing old, my dear. We must take things as they come and make the best of them." He drew her toward him gently : " Clare, aren't you going to kiss me ? "

The idea of kissing him filled her with horror. Was it possible that he could be so stupid as that ? She saved herself, in a panic, by asking :

" Don't you think we might telephone now ? "

He laughed. With the air of humouring her he pulled himself up in his chair and went straight to the telephone.

" Now that it's gone ten," he said, " we shall get six minutes for the same money." He began to telephone. " Trunks . . . Yes, trunks. Give me Stourford . . . Stourford double-two."

He waited, scratching his moustache between the thumb and index finger of his right hand.

" Hello. Is that Stourford Castle ? Who is that speaking ? Oh, Vivien, is that you ? This is Dudley Wilburn. I'm speaking for Clare. She wants to know if you have Steven with you. Steven. Yes, *Steven* . . ."

Clare waited, breathless. Distantly, over the singing wires, she heard the bleating of Vivien's voice, whose vibrations made the mica diaphragm crackle like a staccato of Morse.

" No ? Really ? Nothing at all ? " Wilburn was saying, in the rich, rolling bass that his voice assumed when he wished to be polite. " Then please excuse me. I'm sorry I troubled you. Yes . . . he is out ; and Clare was getting anxious. I hope I haven't pulled you out of bed or anything ? " Clare heard the ghost of Vivien's voice crackle into rapid reassurances. " How nice of you ! " Dudley continued with a dreamy and level resonance. " We only just wanted to know. Good night . . . good night . . ."

" Please let me speak," Clare interrupted. She would have snatched the receiver from his hand, but he had rung off already.

" Why did you do that ? " she asked him angrily.

"My dear child, you heard what I said. Was there anything else to say? He isn't there, and that's the end of it."

"They might have sent the car to meet him, Dudley."

"The car? That's fêting the prodigal with a vengeance! A little bit of discomfort will do him good. Besides, we don't even know for certain that he's gone to Stourford. He may have changed his mind by now; it's beginning to rain pretty sharply." He laughed, a bit uneasily.

"You ought to have told Vivien what happened. All you'll have done is to make them curious."

"Well, let them be curious," he yawned. "I don't want to wash all our dirty linen for the amusement of Stourford. I think after all these alarums and excursions we might go to bed. Come along, now, Clare. Be sensible. It's no good looking tragic. This sort of thing will happen in the best regulated families."

He tried to draw her along with him. Even now he couldn't understand her.

She was thousands of miles away from him and as cold as ice.

"No, I shall wait here till he comes back," she told him—not because she thought for one moment that Steven would come, but because, since that moment of revelation, the company of Wilburn had become physically and spiritually intolerable to her. And now he was clever enough to realize the obstinacy, if not the reason, of her determination. Left alone, she might come to her senses, like an ill-tempered child.

"Very well," he said. "If you choose to make a fool of yourself I won't stop you." He moved determinedly to the doorway. "Only, when you've tired yourself out," he continued, "you'll oblige me by turning the gas off."

"I'll turn it off now," she said.

He went, with some grumbled answer that she could not distinguish. She heard the bedroom floor above her creak with the ponderous, leisurely movements of his undressing ; she knew his routine so well that she could follow every one of them. At last they ceased, and she knew that he was in bed. Within five minutes he would be snoring, mercifully unheard—for if she had heard him to-night she would have felt like murdering him. Released by silence from the consciousness of his being near her she surrendered herself to the stupor of expectant bewilderment into which the miserable scene had plunged her. Even if she had wished to consider what had happened she could not have done so. Her mind was as chill and numb as her exhausted limbs, incapable of thought, incapable of any feeling but one cruel, indefinite pain. It was as though the blows which had fallen on Steven's body had bruised her soul.

Suddenly—in the middle of the night she supposed, for she had lost all sense of time—she was stabbed into consciousness of a world that existed outside the clot of chilly darkness which enveloped her by the brisk trilling of the telephone bell. She rose to it like a creature newly created or miraculously awakened out of timeless sleep. Uncannily clear, through the night's silence, Vivien's voice was speaking to her :

" Is that you, Clare ? How lucky ! I thought it was long odds against anyone hearing the 'phone. I rang up on chance to tell you that Steven has just arrived. He's here, beside me. He'll speak to you himself. Hold on a moment."

There followed a tingling silence, through which she could hear her own heart fluttering like a captured bird. Then Steven's voice, clear, heartless, unemotional :

" Is that you, mum ? I'm here."

" Steven . . . my darling ! " How should the vibrations of her love declare themselves over these inanimate wires ? " Are you all right, my sweet ? " So lame it sounded !

" Yes, I'm all right, thanks. Of course I'm drenched. The walk was rather fun if the rain hadn't been so beastly."

His tone was casual, fearfully self-assured ; he sounded as though he resented her emotional enquiries as though they were conventional and he a stranger. Ten miles ? He was a hundred miles away from her.

" Oh, Steven," she said, " how could you frighten me like this ? If only you knew what pain you've given me ! "

" I'm very sorry, mum," he answered awkwardly. " But surely you couldn't expect me to stay in the house after that ? "

" If only you'd told me, my darling ! "

" I couldn't tell you, mum. The brute locked me in. I had to shin down over the roof of the outhouse. But I'm all right, you know. Only wet."

Her instinct bade her reprove him for the term in which he had spoken of Wilburn ; but, at that distance, the idea seemed curiously futile.

" You'll come back to-morrow morning, darling ? " she suggested tremulously.

" Come back ? Not I ! Whatever do you take me for, mother ? "

" Steven, you kill me when you talk like that."

Silence. And then : " I'm sorry," he repeated, lamely. " I'm sorry, mum, but really I've had enough of it. I think I shall stay here till the end of the hols. If you don't mind," he added doubtfully.

" But Steven, darling, that's quite impossible."

" I'm sorry," he said again. She knew there was no more to be said. She could only wonder if it were true that he was sorry. It seemed utterly useless, in any case, to continue her persuasions with ten miles of empty country-side between them. If she could have taken him by the hand and gathered him in her arms ! But there, in the cloakroom at Stourford—how well she knew it !—his heart

was entirely insulated from the warm current of her love;
her voice, no doubt, would sound to him just as cold, as
dispassionate, as his to her. Disarmed by distance and
by the dehumanizing influence of that cold mechanism her
arguments must seem as impersonal as those of a problem
in Euclid. With a feeling of utter impotence and frustration she gave up the struggle.

" Good night, my darling, God bless you," was all she
could say.

" Good night, mum." As if out of spitefulness the
telephone permitted her to recognize in his voice his relief
that the interview was over. She waited anxiously for
another word ; but no word came. As she put back the
receiver the bell gave a trill that sounded like mocking
laughter.

She was alone once more. Nothing but the discomfort
of that dark and sordid room could have compelled her to
leave it. In all the world, apart from Steven's presence,
there was no solace for her. Upstairs, beside the sleeping
Wilburn, there awaited her, at least, warmth for her aching
body. It did not seem to matter much where she
went ; and so, as habit asserted its power, she groped her
way upstairs and began to undress in the dark ; quietly, in
the hope that Wilburn would not be awakened by her
movements. As she crept into bed, as miserably as a dying
rat that crawls into its hole, the creak of the mattress aroused
him. She felt him stirring uneasily in the dark and shrank
away from him.

" Is that you, Clare ? " he murmured at last. " What
time is it ? "

" I don't know," she answered. She knew nothing.
She hoped that he would turn over and fall asleep ; she
hoped he would not touch her.

" I thought," he went on, " that I heard the telephone."

" Yes. Vivien rang me up," she told him.

" He's got to Stourford ? "

" Yes."

" Well, I wish them joy of each other," he answered with a lazy bitterness.

For a long time there was a silence in which their separate thoughts seemed to be hanging over them in the darkness, crossing and recrossing invisibly like strong-winged nocturnal birds. That soundless, unseen combat, that ghostly battle of hostile thought seemed to her more sinister for the nearness of their bodies. There was no end of it ; there could never be an end. The strength of her will was wasting itself in the dark air. If it went on much longer she would have no power left with which to speak. After a long struggle she forced her thoughts to her lips.

" Are you awake, Dudley ? " she said.

" Yes. What's the matter ? " he answered. There was no sleep in his voice.

" He's not coming back," she said.

" Well ? "

" So I shall go to Stourford to-morrow."

A scornful laugh was all the answer he gave her. If he had risen and stormed at her she might have been happier.


# XI

## ULTIMATUM

NEXT morning at Stourford, in the big bow-windowed guest-room of blue and gold, beneath the wings of the gilt eagles that had sheltered her on the night of her betrothal more than fifteen years before, she found her Steven and came to life again.

" When once we are together," she had thought, " everything will be easy. I shall reason with him and give him more of my confidence. There's no need to be scared : when two people love each other as we do we're bound to understand each other. Besides, though he tries to make me forget it, he is really only a baby."

But Steven in the flesh was much more formidable than any Steven of her imagination. The surroundings of Stourford, which still, unreasonably, intimidated her, seemed to inspire him with a terrifying assurance. Against that background which dwarfed her into insignificance, he was no longer a baby amenable to caresses, but a considerable figure, perfectly at home, and aware, unfortunately, of his own importance.

Within five minutes of their meeting she knew that the scene of tender reconciliation, in which she had staged her prodigal's return, was to be modified by the change of setting. Nor was that all. During the twelve short hours through which they had been separated the very personality of Steven seemed to have changed.

It was as though certain elements in its composition, submerged or concealed at Alvaston, had suddenly risen to the surface, obliterating all those spiritual affinities with herself that she had cherished, proclaiming him, with quite alarming definiteness, a Hingston through and through. The transformation, alas ! was not merely spiritual. In his voice, in his eyes, in the very carriage of his body she recognized now what, before, the blindness of maternal love had hidden from her : a predominance of the Hingston strain that made him seem more alien to her than Ralph had ever been. For though his eyes were Ralph's as she had known them at their hardest, the voice, and the peculiar ruthlessness of spirit which coloured it, were obviously those of Lady Hingston herself. Even when he accepted her kisses and condoned her tears she knew that he did so because a tradition of intimacy constrained him, and that, at the core, he was as cold and stubborn as any steel that had ever left the works at Wolverbury.

With a faint heart she opened her losing battle :

" My darling, if you only knew what a dreadful time you've given me ! To leave me like that, without a single word ! "

" I'm sorry, mum. Of course, you know I'm sorry. I thought I explained that on the telephone. I couldn't tell you I was going. The brute had locked me in."

" Oh, Steven, how you hurt me when you talk like that ! You know as well as I do that you forced him to do it."

" Well, even if I forced him, he'd asked for it to begin with. I'm only sorry because it hurts you. And he *is* a brute all the same."

" Steven, I will not have you speak like that."

" In that case we'd better not talk about him, mum. I'm sure *I* don't want to. I've said I'm sorry. What more do you want me to do ? "

" Ah, if you meant it, it would be different ! You're not really sorry a bit."

He laughed. " Very well then, mum, I'm not sorry. I told you hundreds of years ago, that I hate the sight of him. If you want to know the truth, I meant every word you heard me say to him last night, and I'd say it again to-morrow. I think he's a brute, and I think he's a mean brute, and I think you're silly to put up with him in the way you do. Oh, mum, why can't you *see* how impossible it is ? "

" Oh, Steven, why can't you see that it's you, just you, who are making it impossible ? "

" I don't see anything of the sort," he told her. " *I'm* perfectly all right, thank you, as long as he leaves me alone."

" How dreadfully selfish you are ! You're not my boy. I can't imagine what's happened to you. You don't seem to realise, darling, that it's I who have to suffer."

"Of course I don't, mum darling, because it isn't true. You don't *have* to suffer. You can just get out of it, like I did."

"Oh, Steven, Steven, you're simply talking childishly. My dear, you know nothing about it."

"It's no good calling me a child, mum," he answered resentfully. "At any rate I'm old enough to know jolly well when I've had enough. If you choose to go on putting up with it it's your own fault. It won't make any difference to me."

"What do you mean, Steven?"

"I should have thought anyone could see what I mean. I mean that, after that, I'm not going back to Alvaston. I'm not going to see that beast again. It's no good talking. I've made up my mind."

"You mean," she said, "that you've had your mind made up for you by other people. I'm surprised at your being so weak, Steven. When I said you were childish I was right."

His fair brow flushed with annoyance. She knew him. She had pricked his pride. Quick to seize her advantage, she poured delicate scorn on his malleability :

"You think you're so clever, my darling, and really they're just making a little fool of you. If you want to know why, I'll tell you. Your grandmother has never forgiven me and Mr. Wilburn for marrying—heaven knows why, for it's none of her business—and now that she's got hold of you she's using you to spite us and make trouble between us. You think I'm silly, darling; but I'm not so silly as not to know who's put all these wicked ideas into your head. She's much more clever than you are . . ."

"Mother . . ." He stopped her. "You can't talk like that about grandma. Really you don't know her."

"Don't know her?" she smiled. "My darling, I knew her long before you were born.'

" But all the same, mum, behind her back . . . It isn't sporting . . ." He paused, a little bewildered and suspicious. Clare felt she was winning.

" Not sporting ? Then is it sporting of you to speak as you have spoken of Mr. Wilburn ? "

" Oh, but that's different," he cried. Her appeal to logic had betrayed her. " Good Lord, there's no comparison ! You know I've hated him ever since I can remember. Even at Uffdown I hated him. I shall go on hating him as long as I live ; and if I can, I shall take jolly good care I never set eyes on him again."

" Your father made him your trustee, Steven. You can't alter that."

" Oh, yes," he cried, " of course I know all about that. I can't imagine what father was thinking about when he did it. He must have changed a good bit since then, I should think. A lot of good father's money does me for all I can see of it ! But, anyway, money doesn't matter. There's plenty of money here. I can have what I want here without going down on my knees for it."

He began to soften a little, as though he felt compelled to take pity on her. " You see, mum darling, it's all as good as settled. I had it out with grandma last night. She came and sat on my bed and talked, just like you do. She was awfully sweet about it ; you've no idea how sweet she was. She quite agreed with me that I couldn't go on living at Alvaston after last night, and that all this business about going to Oxford is rubbish. She says that I can stay here, you see, until I leave Rugby. That won't be very long. Lots of fellows leave when they're sixteen. And then, you see, it'll be so awfully convenient. The only thing I really care for is engineering. I can start right away at Wolverbury and go over there with grandpa every morning. You see it all works out splendidly, doesn't it, dearest ? "

" Splendidly," she echoed. " But where do I come in ? "

" Why, couldn't you come and live here too, mum darling ? There's lots of room."

" Oh, Steven, you *are* a baby ! What did I tell you ? " She had to laugh at him. " Of course I couldn't."

" Well, then, at Uffdown," he added quickly. " The Beresfords' lease is up at the end of this year. If you went back to Uffdown we could be together."

The plot lay deeper than she had imagined. He was playing the part assigned to him with almost uncanny skill. She must go gently, gently.

" Who told you that . . . about the Uffdown lease ? " she asked him, with a persuasive sweetness.

He hedged at once. " I don't remember. Somebody must have told me. I think I must have known for a long time. What does it matter, anyway ? "

They were teaching him to lie to her. In everything except things that were connected with Stourford he had always been truthful.

" Are you quite sure," she said, " that grandma didn't tell you that ? " He shook his head. " Last night ? " she persisted.

He feared her questions. " Mother, you're at it again ! Even if it *were* grandma I shouldn't tell you."

" Oh, Steven ; and you used to tell me everything ! "

He remained silent.

" Oh well," she said at last, " it doesn't really matter. It sounds very ingenious, all this about Uffdown, but, of course, it's out of the question." She took him in her arms. " My darling, we shall have to keep that as one of our own private dreams. But now we must hurry up. Mummy has a taxi waiting from the junction. If it goes on ticking away much longer we shall all be ruined." She kissed him, long and tenderly. " Come along, my sweet. We shall have to catch the eleven-fifty to be back for lunch."

He started away from her as if he felt he had given her his kiss on false pretences.

"Mother, I'm not coming back to Alvaston, if that's what you mean. I can't."

"Steven, you break my heart. That means that you don't love me."

"Love you? Oh, mother, of course I love you. I love you dreadfully. Only . . ."

"Only it doesn't matter to you how much you hurt me! Steven, if you don't want to come of your own accord I can't make you. That is the terrible thing—that you don't really want to . . . with me."

"Oh, mother, it isn't that. You know it isn't. But with him there . . ." He flared up again : "I can't and I won't ! Oh, mother ! " He hesitated. "If you would only talk it over with grandma, or even Auntie Vivien, I'm perfectly sure . . ."

"No, no," she answered hardly. "It's no good talking any more about it. If you don't come with me now you'll never come."

"But, darling, that's nonsense. Really it is," he assured her.

"It isn't." Her voice was sadly, strangely self-possessed. "Give me my cloak, Steven. I shall have to hurry."

"Here it is, darling." He put it over her shoulders, a little bewildered by her sudden composure. She thanked him, formally, as though he were a polite stranger in a theatre. "If I say another word," she thought, "I shall be done for."

Without so much as a good-bye she hurried from the room. Along the soft carpeted corridor he pursued her ; but she did not turn to look at him. Down the wide staircase she went. In the hall the butler saluted her.

"Good morning, Parker," she said, with a sudden, bright smile. She ran down the steps to the waiting taxi before Parker could compose his dignified limbs to open the door for her, surprising the driver out of the intricacies of a racing almanac.

" You'll have to drive fast," she said, " or we shall miss the eleven-fifty."

" All right, ma'am. Don't put yourself out. We shall do it. There's no hurry," he assured her as he got down to crank the engine.

No hurry ! That was all he knew about it. " I don't think I can hold out another minute," she thought. The engine started up with a frantic roar. Steven, who had stood for a moment on the terrace, puzzled and disorientated by her swift determination, came racing down the steps. He jumped on to the running board of the taxi, leaned over and kissed her. She felt the heat of his kisses ; her own face was as cold as ice.

" Oh, mother, mother," he said ; but she could not trust herself to speak. Vivien, aroused by the rattle of the taxi engine, was hurrying after them with violent gestures of recall. Clare waved her hand to her as she spoke to the driver : " Go on please. You needn't wait ! " The clutch went in with a bang ; the car lurched forward. Still waving and smiling, Clare could see the look of astonishment on Vivien's face as the taxi gathered speed down the slope of the drive.

" It's over," she thought, triumphantly ; " it's over ; I've escaped "—though from what, or into what, she had escaped she couldn't say. It was strange that the physical breakdown from which she had felt so urgent a need to flee did not take place. Sitting bolt upright in the swaying taxi, whose rattle gave an impression of reckless speed, she saw the pageant of golden elms unfolding, mile on mile, in the still September air against the bases of the autumnal hills. Once on a time she had never tired of watching those familiar shapes. This morning their loveliness left on her mind no more impression than they would have made on a fogged plate. It was not until the taxi's tire-studs skidded on the cinder-strewn roadway abreast of the junction entrance that her bemused and shattered mind recovered its consciousness. With something of the mechanical affability that she had given to Parker she paid and thanked the driver and stepped into a slow train that came puffing in from the south. And even then, embarked on the final stage of her empty return to North Bromwich, she found herself unable, or rather obstinately unwilling, to think of what had happened, or what she was going to do about it.

Since the dawn of the age of motor-cars, six years before, she had never travelled in to " town " from Stourton Junction by rail. Now, as the slow train picked its way round the blighted margin of the black-country, with the huge spoil-heaps of Mawne on the right, the abominable desolations of Wednesford and Wolverbury on the left, and, hazed by eternal smoke, yet always sinister and dominant, the motionless headgear of the Fatherless Bairn mine behind her, her mind made arbitrary choice of a single memory with which the scene was connected : the journey that she had made on the day of her last return as a schoolgirl from St. Monica's to Pen House.

As the engine puffed up the incline to Mawne Road Halt her heart ached with a peculiar poignancy. It was on this platform, in the dusk of a March evening, that she had first seen Ralph and loved him, sixteen years ago. It seemed to her that this slow, backward journey was symbolical ; as if all the time between—and that was half her life—had been nothing but a single isolated incident toward which that long-forgotten journey, now so clearly remembered, had been taking her ; and that this present journey in the reverse direction, represented a definite withdrawal, the closing of the circle within which that incident—Ralph,

Uffdown, Steven ; the sum of her life's romance—had been enclosed.

One after another the joys that it contained—Ralph, Uffdown, Steven—had been stolen away from her. Now, at this moment when the circle closed, she was going out of it alone and naked, even as she came. There was something significant, almost sacramental, in the way with which the train stopped duly at its halts, hammering into her mind, station by station, the inevitable stages of her return to what she was, her abnegation of all that she had been. It came to rest at last under the smoky dome of the North Bromwich station, discharging her, dazed by the accomplished doom, into a scrambling, indifferent crowd.

" Where shall I go now ? " she thought. " It's all finished. I have nowhere to go."

Certainly not to Alvaston. After the nightmare of yesterday the vision of that empty, desecrated house in the Halesby Road filled her with horror. " I suppose I should go and lunch somewhere," she thought. But she was not hungry ; and the picture of Alvaston matrons wolfing pastries at Battie's made her sick. Climbing the station hill she found herself at the eastern end of Sackville Row, and with the sight of its wide cleanliness, the idea of Ernest Wilburn came into her mind. He was the only real friend that her new world had given her.

" If I could sit and talk with him a little," she thought, " I might come back to reality."

And though reality was the last thing that she wanted, the desire for Ernest's homely company was so appealing that she soon found herself climbing the steps that led to the office of Wilburn, Wilburn and Wilburn.

Outside the opaline landing-door she hesitated. She couldn't very well ask for Ernest without seeing Dudley, and, at that moment, the very thought of Dudley filled her with panic. " But I *must* see him," she told herself, and, driven by a need for companionship stronger than any scruple or convention, she entered the outer office.

Grosmont, the clerk, received her with his usual moonlike impassiveness. Mr. Ernest, he said, was in London, but expected back that afternoon for an appointment at three-thirty.

" If you know what train he's coming on," she suggested, " I might meet it."

But Grosmont seemed proud of knowing nothing about his employers' private movements. It was possible, he hazarded, that Mr. Ernest might travel by the luncheon-car ; but as two railway companies were running luncheon-cars in competition he'd no idea at which station Mr. Ernest would arrive. Perhaps Mrs. Wilburn would leave a message ?

Clare had no message to leave. As she was asking Grosmont to find out for her the time of the train's arrival, the door of the inner office opened and Dudley emerged. He smiled with quick surprise to see her waiting there.

" I've just this minute finished my snack of lunch," he told her. " You're lucky to find me with half an hour to spare. Come in and tell me all about it."

She obeyed him. It hardly seemed worth while explaining, and she had not the strength to escape. As he closed the door behind them, he turned and kissed her tenderly. She did not return his kiss, but sat down with a sigh. He was in such unusually high spirits that, even when he took his seat behind the shabby desk opposite to her, he didn't guess that a ghost had entered his room. He sat there with a beam of sunlight striking across a grey, ill-shaven face on to the dusty sleeve, the dusty desk-top, four dead-white drumming fingers.

" Well, well, my child," he said. " You're back much earlier than I expected. Have you brought home the prodigal ? "

He was so blandly exhilarated that, if she hadn't known him so well, she might have imagined that he had been drinking. For a moment she faced him in silence. Then suddenly, it seemed to her as if, in her new nakedness, her way had been made plain ; as if all the deferences and reservations with which, since childhood, her intercourse with him had been complicated, trammelled her mind and tongue no longer. She found herself speaking as she had never spoken to him before, with a freedom, an honesty, that she herself accepted with amazement. Her words issued as something apart from herself. They had a life of their own, uncoloured by fear or passion or pity. Pity . . . That was the treacherous emotion that she feared ; he was so grey and dusty in his black office clothes ; the skin of his cheek so lax and stubbly in the shaft of sunlight. But the words that came from her now were beyond pity.

" Dudley," she said, " I want to know about the Uffdown lease."

" Uffdown ? " he repeated. " How curious that you should mention it ! I'd made a note of it only this morning. The Beresfords have no option of renewal and are getting a bit restless. As they're so keen, I don't see any reason why we shouldn't raise the rent for a second term. But that's by the way. You haven't told me about Stourford. . . ."

He smiled. Encouraged by her unexpected return, he was prepared to be amused.

" The lease expires—when ? " she continued.

" At Christmas. You remember you went out in December, five years ago. It was rather an unusual period ; but Beresford was a bit unsettled about his Argentine interests, and we accommodated him. I think he would like to renew for the usual seven. But why do you want to know ? "

" Uffdown is mine ? " she said. " I can do what I like with it ? "

" It's yours. of course. until Steven is twenty-one."

" Then you mustn't renew the lease," she answered. " I'm going to live there."

" To live there ? What on earth do you mean ? Clare, are you mad ? "

" Steven will not come back to Alvaston. I can't live without him, Dudley. If he won't come to me I must go to him. It's been bad enough already. After last night I can't stand any more of it."

His grey cheek stiffened into gooseflesh in the sunbeam. The white, strong fingers came to rest on the desk-top. That was the only sign of emotion which he showed. And when he spoke, the tone of his question was almost colloquial.

" You mean that you want to leave me, Clare ? Isn't this rather fantastically sudden ? "

" It's not that I want to leave you, Dudley," she answered. " I can't have both of you. And if I have to choose, I must choose Steven."

He watched her narrowly, dispassionately, as he must have watched hundreds of clients in his time. And when he spoke next, his words came ready-made out of the vocabulary of habit.

" Let us consider this carefully," he said.

Carefully ! Of a sudden, behind her mask of words, her heart laughed out at him. Even this vital, soul-rending business he was treating as a " case ! " From the very beginning that was how he had treated her. If, at that moment, he had abandoned his moderation, if a word of passion had escaped him, he might have carried her off her feet, he might have filled the world for her and won her. But no. He considered her carefully ; and she despised him in her heart.

" I have considered everything," she answered. " The position seems quite clear in my mind."

He smiled at her with his faint, legal superiority. " Suppose we examine it more closely," he replied. " I gather

that you've been to Stourford.   Steven wishes to stay there
And the Stourford people, even if they haven't put him up
to this rebellious attitude, are ready to back him in it.   You
asked him to return to Alvaston, and he refused.   Very
good.   The legal position isn't as simple as you imagine.
You are his mother, and I am his trustee.   During his
minority he is entirely in our hands.   It is for us, not for
him, to decide where he shall live.   Legally we can compel
him to return to Alvaston.   If there is any nonsense we can
assert our rights."

"No, no," she told him, "it's no use doing that.   My
only anxiety is that Steven should be happy.   I've tried to
make him happy in Alvaston, and I've failed.   It's not my
fault, nor yours nor anyone else's.   You don't understand
him, Dudley.   That's not new.   It's been going on for
years.   He would be quite happy at Uffdown."

"Are you also taking your orders from Stourford ? " he
asked sharply.

"No.   I've not spoken to anyone there about it."   The
suggestion, which had been calculated to wound her, left
her unmoved.   "I only know that that's what I've got to
do.   I've scarcely thought about it."

"Then let me suggest," he answered ironically, "that
it's time you did.   The case has other legal aspects.   I
should like to know, for example, exactly where you think
I'm going to come in."

"Where do you come in now ? " she asked him
wearily.

"I happen to be your husband," he reminded her.

"Yes, yes, I know.   But what does that really mean ?
I never see you for more than an hour or two in the day.   If
it's a housekeeper you want—well, Mrs. Marple understands
you better than I do.   If it's a wife . . . Do you think we
need talk about that ?   For the last year or so we haven't—
what do they call it ?—lived together, have we ? "

He flushed slightly. In Clare he hadn't anticipated such directness.

" You're throwing my age in my face, Clare. That's hardly kind of you. I'd rather imagined that you, with your exalted ideals, placed marriage on a higher level than that. I know that you're a young woman, and that I am not a young man. But there's such a thing in marriage as companionship."

" Perhaps . . . But you've never given it to me, Dudley."

" You've never suggested that. Clare, I thought you were happy."

" No, no, my dear Dudley, you didn't ; you've never thought about it at all."

" There you're unjust. It's true that I'm not a man of many words ; but the fact remains that I love you."

She shook her head. " I daresay you imagine you love me. You believe it because you've taken it for granted so long. You're used to my being there ; but if I went away you wouldn't miss me. That's the whole difference : I *should* miss Steven. He's all my life, Dudley, even when he isn't there. That's why I want you to let me go to Uffdown."

" You began by threatening, not asking," he reminded her. " Why should I let you go ? " he demanded. " Of course I shall do nothing of the sort. The idea's preposterous."

" Even if you won't let me, it'll make no difference. I shall go in any case."

" That is what's technically known as desertion."

" Well, then, can't you divorce me ? " she suggested eagerly. " That wouldn't matter a bit."

He laughed. " Clare, you're fantastic ! I suppose you think a divorce would be a good advertisement for me ? Upon my soul I can't guess what's in your head."

" There's nothing—I promise you—nothing but what

I've said. Only that I want Steven. If I could have had him at Alvaston, I shouldn't want to go. But I can't have him happily ; and so I must."

He stared at her in silence for a moment. Then, suddenly, he rose and put his hands on her shoulders. His eyes stared into hers with a look which she had never seen in them before. His face was pale and agonized as he spoke :

" I want to know exactly what this means, Clare, tell me truthfully : there isn't anything behind this—there isn't anyone else ? "

" Oh, Dudley," she cried, " do you know me as little as that ? "

He released her. " No," he said. " I believe you. I'm sorry I suggested it."

And yet his apology, strangely, moved her less than the momentary flash of jealousy that had evoked it. Then he began again in level, judicial tones :

" You appear to have made up your mind pretty firmly," he said. " Perhaps you will tell me what your immediate plans are ? Unfortunately there's hardly time to discuss them now. My client is due. We had better talk it over this evening at home."

The new horror of Tudor House which had filled her since the sufferings of last night overwhelmed her. Whatever she might do, she knew she could not return to it.

" No, that's impossible," she said, " by the time you get home I shall be gone."

Until that moment he had not realized the extent of her determination. Now that it dawned on him, the ironical seriousness with which he had listened to her left him. His jaw was set ; he towered above her with a terrifying prepotence.

" Enough of this nonsense ! " he said. " You'll oblige me by going home at once. I shall expect to find you there at half-past six."

The gust of anger that shook him brought tears to her eyes.

" It's no good, Dudley," she said, " I shan't be there."

He stared at her, incredulous. " Do you think," he said, " that I'm the kind of man to be intimidated by this conspiracy ? Do you think that you can afford to treat me with contempt ? Either you're mad, or else there's more in this than what you've told me. In any case, I'm not in the habit of surrendering my rights without fighting for them. Are you determined to fight me, Clare ? " She could not answer him. " Then where do you propose to go to-night ? " he pressed her. " You'd better answer that."

" I don't know," she told him, pathetically, truthfully. " I think I shall probably go to Aunt Cathie's."

" Very well. I hope you realize the seriousness of what you're saying. If you don't, I can promise you that you soon will. If you force me to fight," he threatened, " I shall hit hard. I shan't spare you. Remember that ! "

" Oh, Dudley," she cried, " don't you see that I can't help it ? "

With that cry, something of the anguish that was in her soul must have found its way into her voice, which before had been the vehicle of a cold, somnambulistic impersonality. It had the effect of moving him, swiftly, strangely. The cruel anger that whirled through Wilburn's brain stopped dead, like the wind in the heart of a tornado. He stretched out his arms to her in a gesture of appeal.

" Clare, Clare," he cried, " my darling ! "

" Dudley, I can't, I can't," she repeated helplessly ; but even as she spoke he came toward her and crushed her in his arms, covering her face, her eyes, her lips with kisses of a violence which she had never known in him before. " I wouldn't hurt you, Clare, for the whole world," he whispered. " Clare, Clare, my child, I love you. God ! Don't you know it ? "

She only knew that however much he loved her now it was too late. Her heart was stone. For his poor sake she hoped he might misunderstand her silence, her impassivity. A discreet knock on the door cut short his ardours. He stood away from her with a flushed, unnatural face. In a moment he was himself again.

" Come in," he said, while Clare hurriedly tidied her disordered hair.

The clerk Grosmont appeared. " Sir Joseph Astill is here, sir."

" Ask him to come in."

Sir Joseph Astill entered, effusive, but robbed by the steep stairs of his last aspirates. Dudley went smiling to meet him ; his manner was unusually gracious, almost debonair.

" Good afternoon, Sir Joseph. I hope I've not kept you waiting ? It isn't often that we're surprised with our wives in town. You know each other, don't you ? "

" I've 'ad that pleasure," Sir Joseph gasped and smiled.

" Well, Clare, good-bye. At half-past six, then ? " Wilburn reminded her.

## XII

### FIRST CIRCLE

AT half-past six Clare's train was running westward. But this time, as she retraced her course, the station names which earlier in the day had been beaten in on her mind with the finality of nails hammered into a coffin succeeded each other in a crescendo of hopefulness : Winsworth, New Bromwich, Astbury, Dingley Regis, Mawne Road Halt. With each of them in succession she felt the grime and heaviness of Alvaston rolling away from her. The woods of Mawne drooped over beside the track. The little train careered and rattled down the gradient as though a breath of clean air had gone to its head. Clare heard the familiar sigh of Westinghouse brakes. Wychbury! At last . . .

" No Jabez waiting for me this time," she thought. For Jabez, that frail and homely old man, had tottered long ago into his grave in Wychbury churchyard; and the victoria, its curved shafts uplifted, stood moth-eaten and felted with dun dust in the cobwebbed coach-house. A strange, red-necked young porter, pounced on her ticket and handed her back half of the " return," which she had taken automatically. As she left the station-yard she tore the pasteboard into fragments, and the gesture pleased her by its symbolic recklessness. Never again, she thought, never again!

The new young porter didn't know her. Nobody knew her. This anonymity was encouraging. It gave her the feeling that she had left her old self behind her, that not only in imagination she was beginning life all over again. The rumble of the train, the instrument of her liberation, died away toward Worcester on its appointed course. It seemed to her as if it had dropped her, haphazard, in space, in darkness; yet sweet, sweet and familiar was the dusk through which she climbed the hill toward Pen House. Odours of childhood, released by the hush of twilight, rose through the limpid air, so sappy that she could have believed that spring was in the woods as well as in her heart. Their freshness purged her of all the stale and sterile airs of the Halesby Road. She inhaled them luxuriously, deeply, till the blood tingled in her cheeks. She was more happy than she dared to be.

On the brow of the hill the doctor's Wellingtonia-spires shot up into the sky. The drive gate swung and clicked as it had clicked on nights when Ralph had stood and watched her shadow disappearing. Now that old Jabez pruned them no more, laurels and lilacs narrowed the little drive; its surface, no longer worn by the victoria's wheels, was overgrown and softened by damp-smelling moss; out the window of the dining-room, yellow with lamplight, beamed, as before, its placid welcome. It was as though, through all those years, the low-browed house had been asleep and waiting her return. " But I mustn't wake it," she thought, entering, on tiptoe the narrow hall, breathing its faintly musty odour of beeswax and folded umbrellas and old oak. Only the clock at the foot of the stairs was awake to her presence. Although she couldn't see it, she heard its pendulum ticking like a slow, aged heart. " So here you are again. You will excuse me if I go on with my business," it seemed to say.

Through that familiar darkness Clare moved without hesitation. She opened the dining-room door. There, in her low sewing-stool, opposite the doctor's arm-chair, Aunt Cathie sat, slim and little, with her knees pressed tight together, her spectacled eyes concentrated on a book that she held at arm's length. Her hair was of a yellowish whiteness, very different from the silver of Lady Hingston, and through the thinning edge where it retreated from her forehead, her scalp showed shiny in the lamplight, just as the doctor's bald skull used to shine. Her cheeks were lax and puckered, dusted with a soft grey down; her mouth was old and gentle and resigned. " She is only fifty-five," Clare thought; " yet how she has aged ! " It seemed to her tragic, on this day of her new birth, that people should ever grow old. Her heart was full of love and pity for Aunt Cathie.

She spoke. Aunt Cathie looked up suddenly. Out of repose her face resumed its usual earnestness.

" Why, Clare, whatever are you doing here at this hour ? "

" I've come to supper, dearest."

" I'm afraid you'll have to put up with a boiled egg. Thirza's in bed, poor old thing. Her legs are troubling her, and she has a touch of bronchitis. She's becoming a real anxiety," Aunt Cathie added cheerfully, as if she were proud of having such a thing in the house again. " But what arrangements have you made about getting back ? " she said. " I hope you've ordered a cab. You know we're not grand enough for telephones in this part of the world. Sit down and tell me what is the meaning of this honour. Be careful ! Don't lose my place. I shall never find it again if you do. Yes, *Romola*," she admitted. " I've begun that book six times at least, and this year I'm determined to finish it. But before we talk, Clare, I think you'd really better settle about your cab."

" I'd like to stay the night if you can have me, dearest," Clare said.

" To stay the night ? Clare, something has happened. Tell me."

" I'm afraid I'm going to hurt you, Aunt Cathie darling."

" What does that matter ? I'm used to being hurt. I expect I can bear it."

But Clare, for all that, could see that Aunt Cathie was frightened. She had taken off her spectacles and was looking at her with mild, apprehensive eyes. She seemed so little, so worn, so old, that even before Clare began her story she felt convicted of brutality. " I think I'd rather sit on the floor," she said ; and there, at Aunt Cathie's feet, she plunged forth right into the tale of her troubles : the nightmare of Alvaston, Dudley's coldness, Steven's ineradicable dislike, the miseries that had culminated in the storm of the night before.

Aunt Cathie listened dumbfounded.

" Oh, Clare," she cried at last, " why did you never tell me about all this before ! I know Dudley's nature so well. I understand him. If you had come and told me, I'm sure I could have put it right."

" No. no," she answered, " nothing could have put it

right. It was wrong, if we'd only known it, from the beginning."

" And you've left Steven at Stourford ? "

" Yes. You may know Dudley, Aunt Cathie, but you don't know *him*."

" Steven, indeed ! In my day, Clare, children obeyed their parents. It's your duty to take him away from Stourford at once . . . for his own sake. You have no right, Clare, to take sides with him against your husband."

" I knew it was no use talking to you, dearest," Clare sighed. " You see everything from Dudley's point of view. You make a god of him. I only wish to goodness you'd married him yourself."

Aunt Cathie flushed quickly : " What a fantastic idea ! I'm not the marrying kind. But Dudley, it seems to me, is the principal sufferer in all this. In *my* day marriage was a serious thing ; and people like myself continue to regard it as such. The scandal, Clare ! I don't suppose you've ever thought of that. For a professional man to be abandoned by his wife ! His practice is bound to suffer."

" People will soon forget."

" People have longer memories than you think. And then, this plan of going back to Uffdown. . . . Don't you realize, Clare, that's just what the Hingstons want ? Are you so blind as not to see that you're playing into their hands ? "

" I can't help that. I only care about Steven. I'm going to Uffdown of my own free will."

" To say nothing," Aunt Cathie continued, " of the extremely awkward position in which you're placing *me*. Dudley's my oldest friend ; and it looks as if I'm harbouring you."

" Well, dearest," Clare explained, " if you feel like that— if, really, you don't want me, or are afraid to have me—I'd better go somewhere else "

" That's merely stupid," Aunt Cathie answered sharply.
" Where else could you go ? No married woman can stay
alone in an hotel. You know that just as well as I do.
Though, in these days . . ." She hesitated ; and when she
spoke again her voice was hard. " You're not suggesting,
are you, that you might go to Stourford ? I'd rather see
you dead than there, Clare, and that's the truth ! No,
I suppose you'd better stay here until you come to your
senses. It's eight o'clock. If we're going to have any
supper, we'd better begin to prepare it."

She rose and bustled off toward the kitchen. Clare
followed her. She felt like a scolded child, dogging Aunt
Cathie's footsteps helplessly into the mean, familiar pantry
and out of it. Aunt Cathie kept on muttering to herself,
taking no notice of her, throwing her irritation, as was her
wont, into a futile and resentful activity.

" One thing at least I beg you," she said impressively,
" and that is not to let Thirza know what has happened.
On the whole I think it would be better if she didn't know
that you are here. She's almost as old-fashioned as myself,
and in her present condition the shock might kill her."

And Clare remembered how, when she was a child, Aunt
Cathie had brandished the threat of disaster to the doctor
in her face. " She's just the same as ever," she thought.
She wondered if, unknown to themselves, people really
never changed, or whether it was only in backwaters such
as this that human personality lay preserved and suspended
for ever in unalterable shapes, like that ship in the bottle on
the kitchen mantelpiece.

Certainly the influence of the place lay heavy on her that
evening. The little train, with its backward journey, had
done its business to some purpose. Sitting at the supper-
table, watching the precision with which Aunt Cathie sliced
the top from her boiled egg and dipped a finger of toast
into the yolk, she felt as though her own dangling legs could

scarcely reach the floor. She sat there, tongue-tied and submissive, like a schoolgirl in disgrace, awed by the admonitions of an atmosphere whose potency took less count even than did Aunt Cathie of all the years between. By the time they had finished their meagre supper and cleared the table with every meticulous movement of the old routine, she felt that she could bear it no longer.

" I'm tired to death," she admitted at last. " You see, I was up most of last night. If you don't mind, I think I'd better go to bed."

" It's only a quarter-past nine," Aunt Cathie reminded her sternly. For ten o'clock was " bed-time " at Pen House.

" I shall have to make my bed up," Clare suggested. " You needn't trouble to help me, dearest. I know where everything is."

But Aunt Cathie, once offended, determined to continue her martyrdom to the bitter end. Heroically she dived into the dark, sweet-smelling linen cupboards and pulled out sheets and pillow-slips ; but nothing that evening went right, and Clare, in her eagerness to help, increased the confusion.

" Thank you very much," said Aunt Cathie, coldly ; " but I'd much rather you wouldn't touch things, Clare. I know exactly where everything is—it just so happens that I can't put my fingers on what I want—and I've realized that if you want things done in your own way, you must do them yourself. The doctor always used to say the same."

Yet Clare, helplessly watching, saw how the unusual exertion tired her, and knew that for all her obstinacy Aunt Cathie's strength was not what it had been. Gradually the elation that she had felt in her first moments of release faded away from her ; this house, so old, so quiet, so cynical, so full of ghosts, revealed its spuriousness. " I'm afraid I shall never bear to stay here," she thought.

" I think that is all," Aunt Cathie panted at last, punching the pillows into shape as though she hated them ; " so, if you're tired, I'd better say good night and get back to my book. Thirza must have her Benger's at half-past nine. If I go to bed before ten I shan't sleep a wink." She edged away as if she feared the possibility of a scene ; but Clare, knowing what this composure cost her, followed and took the frail, gaunt woman in her arms, pursued and haunted, as she did so, by the memory of another embrace.

" Don't judge me too hardly, Aunt Cathie, dearest," she pleaded.

" Don't judge you ? My dear child, there's no question of judgment," Aunt Cathie answered bitterly. " In *my* day we had standards. In *my* day, when people made their beds they were forced to lie in them. It seems I'm out of date. Apparently times and customs have changed. Apparently . . ." She gave a little cry of pain.

" Dearest . . . what's wrong ? "

" Nothing." She laughed uneasily. " Nothing. . . . You held me so tightly that you hurt my . . . my chest. I've always been tender there, you know, just over the heart."

" Oh, I'm so sorry, dearest. I didn't mean to be rough."

" It's of no consequence ; you needn't apologize," Aunt Cathie answered, as though she were annoyed to have been betrayed into such weakness. " Now, if you're really tired, you'd better stop gossiping and go to bed," she went on briskly. " Good night. Sleep well. Breakfast at half-past eight as usual."

Yet, when she was gone and Clare was left alone with the monstrous candle-shadows, she could not help remembering not only the cry but the twinge of pain that had narrowed Aunt Cathie's eyes and sent the blood from her cheeks. It wasn't until she held Aunt Cathie in her arms that she had realized just how thin, how fragile she had become. Now she remembered also the sinister pallor that had shocked her as Aunt Cathie sat reading in the lamplight. " She wasn't like that when I saw her three months ago," she thought. " I believe there's really something the matter with her. I must talk to her seriously about it to-morrow." Yet, though she consoled herself with this determination, the pain in Aunt Cathie's eyes still haunted her as she fell asleep.

## XIII

### INTERIM

AND now, in defiance of all other preoccupations, the pressure of her personal problems overwhelmed her. It was impossible, as she had guessed, to stay much longer at Pen House. In spite of Aunt Cathie's forced briskness Clare knew that the incubus of old Thirza's illness was almost more than those thin shoulders could bear without the added weight of another, and so uncomfortable a guest. On the subject of Clare's dissensions with Wilburn her divided loyalties kept Aunt Cathie distressfully and obstinately silent. Clare saw she was suffering, and that her own presence at Wychbury aggravated her distress. She also knew, from hints that Aunt Cathie dropped at table, that she was in correspondence with Wilburn and kept him informed of all that was happening at Pen House. An official letter, signed by Ernest, informed her that the matter of the Uffdown lease was being dealt with according to her instructions. If she had not been so enormously relieved by it she might have been piqued by the apparent unconcern with which Dudley treated her departure.

From the moment when an exchange of telegrams between him and Aunt Cathie informed him of her refuge, he might as well have been dead for all she heard of him. In any other man such silence might have been taken for acquiescence; in Dudley, whose slow determination she knew so well, this silence was a little sinister, leaving her to imagine the careful machinations that lay behind it.

From the cruelty of this suspense she had no release, except in Steven. Now that she was so near, she no longer grudged him the happiness that he so obviously found at Stourford. Each day, throughout the rapidly-dwindling holidays, she braved Aunt Cathie's disapproval by visiting the hostile camp where Lady Hingston, tactfully silent for once in her life, but frankly unable to disguise her satisfaction, would gladly have overwhelmed her with kindnesses that came, Clare couldn't help thinking, a little late in the day. At Stourford they were evidently determined that she should walk on velvet; so far from grudging her Steven's company, as they had always done, they conspired to thrust it upon her, even urging him to go with her when his inclinations drew him in other directions.

This calculated generosity disarmed her; and, indeed, those few, rare days of the Indian summer, so eagerly snatched from beneath the shadow of Wilburn's incalculable mood in the detachment of her own isolation, were among the most precious that she had ever lived. In them they wandered far and wide, she and Steven together; and it seemed to her as though she had almost recaptured the enchantment of the time when she and Ralph had first been lovers. With an added completeness; for Ralph, in their most precious intimacy, had been, at best, a miraculous stranger; while Steven, removed from unhappy Alvaston, was her very own—how much her own she had never realized until this glad reunion.

In the old days at Uffdown he had been merely a baby; at Alvaston the consciousness of his dormant hostility to Wilburn had constrained them both; now, in the sweet conspiracy of their escape, she found in him the companionship that she had always hoped for, but never yet achieved.

His eyes were quick to see the things that she loved most; his tongue anticipated hers in sudden turns of phrase; his moods of pensiveness or gaiety kept pace with hers; his open mind displayed a mirror of her own. In this so-different being, whose eyes and voice were the eyes and voice of Ralph, she found a community of thought and sense that Ralph had never given her. "He is mine," she thought; "at last he is mine! Blessed am I among women." There on the brown top of Pen Beacon, Clare's heart sang its *Magnificat*.

When the last evening of the summer holidays came they found themselves at sundown near the end of the ridge where a spur sweeps downward into the Uffdown coppices. Over vast distances the sinking sun dispersed like molten metal among the hills of Wales; but, at their feet, within a seeming pebble's throw, the beloved house lay floating in its pool of greensward.

For a long time they sat and contemplated the Beresfords' slow-rising smoke in silence.

"When I come back from Rugby at Easter," Steven said, "I shall find you there."

"Yes, darling," she told him, "I heard from Uncle Ernest yesterday. I'm afraid the Beresfords were rather annoyed at giving up their lease."

"I'm not surprised at that," he murmured. "Stourford's all very well in its way—I mean they're awfully kind and all that—but Uffdown's the place where we really and truly belong. Do you think it's because I was born there I feel like that, mum?"

"I don't know, Steven. Places are curious things, and houses even more so. You're talking just like your father. I'd no idea you felt like that about Uffdown."

"I didn't know that I did, mum," he admitted frankly, "until I saw it like this. But now I feel as if it's the only place that matters to me at all. When once we get there,

I'm certain I shall never want to leave it. Don't you feel a bit like that, mother ? "

" Indeed I do, my child. And I hope you never will."

" Well, that's a bargain, mum," he answered gaily. " We'll never leave it again."

" Never again ! " she assented. Yet when they had kissed good-bye at the Stourford lodge-gates and she had stood and watched him running up the drive, pausing to wave to her, then running on again until the dusk received him, that hollow word returned to haunt the melancholy emptiness of his departure.

On the hillside her return to Uffdown had seemed to give her an answer to all her doubts, to offer her all the permanence for which she was seeking. Now, in the dank autumnal dusk, her " never " took on colours of ill-omen. There was no such thing as " never " in this life. In a little more than six years, she reflected, Steven would be of age. In the ordinary course of events he would marry ; and, on the day of his wedding, she would be as homeless as she was at this hour. Six years ! Not very much more than the length of the Alvaston nightmare which had passed, as nightmares seem to have passed when we look back on them, in a flash of thought. " And then, whatever will happen to me ? " she asked herself.

Only the screams of little hunting owls answered her question. The chill exhaled by night-breathing woods was in her bones as she toiled up the steep lane to Pen House. Its lamp-lit window was a beacon of slender encouragement through that lonely night.

Aunt Cathie met her in the hall with a long, preoccupied face that brightened momentarily as she kissed her.

" Well, have you said good-bye to him ? " she asked, but her thoughts were elsewhere.

" Yes, we walked back to Stourford. I'm thankful to say that he's a lot braver than his mother."

" Ah, it's easy to be brave when you're young," said Aunt Cathie sadly. She paused. " I think I ought to tell you, Clare," she began with difficulty, " that I've had a wire from Dudley. He's coming here to supper to talk things over. He didn't say if he wanted me to tell you ; but I thought, on the whole, you had better be prepared."

The announcement threw Clare into a panic at once. " Aunt Cathie, I'm sorry to hurt you. I can't possibly see him. To-night of all nights ! Just when I've said good-bye to Steven ! "

" I think," said Aunt Cathie, " that Dudley has shown remarkable delicacy by waiting until Steven was gone. Far be it from me to advise you, Clare, much less to argue with you ; but, really, I don't see how you can refuse to see him if you're here when he comes. It's not fair to Dudley ; and it isn't fair to me. Besides," she went on, " however strongly you may feel about these differences of yours, which I, for one, can't pretend to understand, I *do* think, in common justice, you might allow Dudley to state his case, and define his position."

" My dearest, I *know* his position," Clare told her. " He's been defining it every day for the last five years. His case is a perfectly reasonable one from his point of view. But I'm not reasonable, and so it's no good his stating it."

" It may be," Aunt Cathie urged, " that he only wants to discuss business. He's Steven's trustee. It's obvious that he can't go on letting things drift in this ridiculous, equivocal fashion. You mustn't forget, the poor man has his rights."

" If it's a matter of business he can just as well write to me. I've had one letter about Uffdown already. Ernest signed it."

" Oh, *that* was what it was about," said Aunt Cathie, eagerly, her caution overcome by the solution of a mystery that had troubled her for a week. " You needn't see him alone, Clare," she continued, renewing her persuasions.

" However unpleasant it may be, I'm perfectly prepared to be present at your . . . interview."

" My dear, I know I've given you enough trouble already. You've been an angel. I can never thank you enough. But if my not seeing Dudley is going to worry you, I think I'd better go away before he comes."

" Oh, Clare, you're so impulsive ! Just like your mother ! You take my breath away. Really, I give you up. Why, where on earth could you go at this time of day ? "

" I don't know, dearest. Surely the world's big enough ? "

" You're not thinking——" Aunt Cathie hesitated.

" Of Stourford ? No, no. That's the last place in the world I should think of."

At eight o'clock, when Dudley reached Pen House, the car which Clare had hired in Wychbury deposited her and her luggage on Ernest Wilburn's doorstep. His butler-valet, Knight, received her as though the visits of ladies in distress were part of his daily routine. But Mr. Wilburn, he informed her, was not in " town," he had left North Bromwich that morning, and given no particulars of his movements.

" If you could let me know where a wire would find him ? " Clare timidly suggested. But Knight, however much he may have known, was too well trained in that mysterious employment to give away a syllable.

" I suppose he's in London, as usual," Clare thought ; and there passed through her mind a vision of those questionable haunts in which, according to Aunt Cathie, Ernest had been " seen." It was this spice of wickedness in Ernest that had made him so humanly attractive ; but, at this moment, she wished him as virtuous as Dudley.

" Perhaps you would like to leave a note for him, madam," said the resourceful Knight. " Or shall I ask him to ring up Tudor House immediately he returns ? "

To ring up Tudor House ! It was evident that, so far,

Dudley had succeeded in concealing the scandal of her departure. If anyone knew about it, Knight would surely have known.

With a happy renewal of confidence she asked him if he would call a taxi for her. At the moment she had no idea where she was going for the night. Probably it was the unconscious association of Ernest's name that made her tell the driver to take her to the Grand Midland, where they had often lunched together.

With a sense of overwhelming shame she passed through the revolving doors in Sackville Row and whispered her name to the booking-clerk. Even if it were familiar to him, he showed no signs of ever having heard it before ; and when the discreet, plush-cushioned lift conveyed her secretly to her room on the third floor, she felt, for the first time, as if she had left the censorious world behind her.

Next morning early, having scribbled a note to Ernest, she set off into Devonshire, hiding herself in a fishing village, on the southern horn of Torbay. She had chosen the place for no other reason than that a photograph of its harbour had caught her eye and held it in the railway carriage that had transported her to Wychbury. There, in a trawler's house that overlooked the anchorage where, every night, red sails came in to roost like homing birds, she settled down into a life more peaceful than any she had known for years.

On that Atlantic shore autumn was bland and kindly, its air still tempered by the warmth of summer. Behind the little port lay a broken country in which every combe held some gentle secret of its own ; a cressy watercourse, a white, thatched cottage, a fruiting orchard already heavy with the scent of pomace. Its leisureliness, its slow peace acted as a sedative on her ruffled spirit and changed it, so that, at last, she could scarcely recognize the distraught and hunted creature who had hidden herself in the hotel at North Bromwich. It seemed to her that she must have suffered more than she knew to have acted with such extravagance. Now, even if Dudley had proposed to visit her, she felt that she could have faced their meeting without alarm.

But Dudley did not propose to visit her. It was nearly a month since she had left Alvaston, and, so far, he had not vouchsafed her so much as a line. She was almost beginning to worry herself by imagining what was happening when a wire from Ernest asked her to book a room for him over the week-end at the local hotel.

His arrival betrayed her into a pretty excitement. She waited for him on the little platform like a young girl meeting her lover; her heart leapt as she saw his smiling face at the first-class carriage-window. Evidently he had no intention of playing the heavy brother-in-law. He came, indeed, in the gayest of holiday spirits, curiously, ridiculously urban in his elegant town-clothes, determined to temper his unpleasant mission with as much enjoyment as he was capable of extracting from her company.

" I've never seen you in such good form," she told him.

He smiled at her: " My dear, this life's so short that I believe in making the most of it."

' You have no business to say that life's so short," she told him. " It seems to me that you're younger every time I see you."

" Well, that's encouraging, Clare. But you never know . . ."

For the first two days of their holiday he did not even mention Dudley's name. It was only on the last evening of his stay, when, on a high ledge of limestone edged with thrift, they sat inhaling the almond scent blown seaward from hidden beds of ladies'-tresses orchis that he arrived at the purpose of his visit.

" Dudley has been talking to me about your joint affairs," he began abruptly. Clare drew her breath; between them and the misty lazuline water gulls were wheeling and crying.

Their screams gave voice to her heart's restlessness. "I gather from the fact that I find you still here that you've quite made up your mind ? "

" Yes, I am going back to Uffdown in January. I suppose that is all right ? "

" Perfectly. We gave the Beresfords notice at Michaelmas according to your instructions. No doubt the office will see the business through. But even now—I only suggest it because, down here, you've had an opportunity of thinking things over by yourself—you realize that it's not too late to go back to Alvaston ? "

" Ernest, I thought you knew better than anyone else the life I lived there ? "

" Yes, yes. I know quite well. So, if you'll believe me, does Dudley. Of course he didn't imagine it would end like this. But he's extremely reasonable. He has great qualities, Clare."

" I never denied them."

" And, of course, he wants you back."

" I can't go back, Ernest . . ."

" You know he won't ask you. He's far too proud for that. I must say I admire him for it."

" I've always admired him . . . some parts of him. But this isn't a question of admiration. Steven and he are incompatible, and Steven comes first. Dudley can live without me—he's done so, comfortably, for years—but I can't live without Steven. That's natural, isn't it ? Steven is all my life."

" I know. I only hope he won't disappoint you."

" Ernest, whatever do you mean ? "

" Nothing. I take it back. You're going to be very happy, Clare. You deserve to be happy."

" It was a mistake . . . our marriage."

" Yes. Principally, I think, because it came too late. That is the only kind of mistake I've ever avoided making."

He paused, then continued, gently : " If you don't mind I think I'd better tell you what Dudley asked me to say. He thinks, and I quite agree with him, that your question is too indefinite. We're lawyers, you see. As a matter of habit we like to know that everything is in order."

" You mean he wants a judicial separation ? "

The old, easy amusement came back into his eyes. " Why, my dear child, whatever are you talking about ? A judicial separation is what you get from a magistrate when your husband beats you. Dudley's never done that."

" I'm sorry. I didn't know. What *does* he want ? "

" An ordinary deed of separation—a civil contract—to regularize the equivocal position. Dudley's sense of fairness demands that you should make any conditions that occur to you. There are things, for instance, like joint banking-accounts to be put in order. It's better that your interests should be represented by some disinterested third party. He asked me to suggest—it's only a suggestion— James Veale, the solicitor whom the Hingstons now employ. If you wish to consult him, his address . . ."

" I don't," Clare interrupted him. " Please, Ernest, I want to make one thing clear at any rate : the Hingstons have nothing whatever to do with this. It's only fair to both of us to say that I haven't been influenced by them. Will you tell Dudley that ? "

" Of course I'll tell him if you wish it. I believe what you say ; but I warn you that Dudley won't."

" He ought to believe me, Ernest."

" I quite agree. But being a man and your husband he finds it hard to believe that any woman, and you particularly, could leave him of her own accord. Let the poor fellow have the consolation of his Hingstons. It won't hurt any-one."

" You must be very fond of him, Ernest."

" I am. I'm very fond of both of you. I think I under-

T

stand you both as well. However, let's get back to that deed of separation."

" I've nothing to say about it. I don't want anything . . . only to be free. Tell me what you advise."

" I don't think I'm the right person to advise you."

" But I want you to. Won't you ? "

" Very well. If you're quite satisfied I'll do what I think just."

" You know I trust you, Ernest."

" Yes, Clare. D'you know, it's a very embarrassing thing to be trusted ? However . . . I think that's all."

He was silent for a moment. The sun had almost disappeared ; the shrieks of the wheeling herring-gulls subsided ; the lilac limestone cliffs went dead and grey ; the scent of that ivory orchis faded from the air as the land grew cool.

" I shall miss you, Clare," he said at last. " I believe I shall miss you every bit as much as Dudley will. Our music, our talks, our little lunches together."

" Why do you say that, Ernest ? Is there any reason why, just because I'm leaving Dudley, we shouldn't be friends ? "

" No, that's no reason," he answered, " but there may be others. Life is extremely complicated, as I think I told you before. All sorts of things may happen. Don't let's talk about them."

They walked back in silence toward the little town. Clare had arranged that he should sup with her at her lodging, but when they reached the door he would not enter.

" I think, if you don't mind," he said, " I'll change my plans. It's a long journey round by Bristol to North Bromwich. If I take a car from here, I can catch the London express at Newton Abbott and reach town by midnight."

She found it difficult to hide her disappointment. It

seemed to her that there was something sinister in his change of plans.

" Why do you want to go to London, Ernest ? " she asked.

He stared at the unexpectedness of the question. " Will you think me rude if I don't tell you, Clare ? "

She saw that the moment of confidences had passed, and made the best of it. Within ten minutes of their reaching the hotel his car was ready. Then kissing her abruptly, he mounted beside the driver and was gone.

## XIV

### UFFDOWN AGAIN

SHE would have been content, she told herself, to stay on in Devonshire till the beginning of the new year, when Uffdown would be ready to receive her. As long as Steven was at Rugby, it didn't very much matter how or where she spent her time, and the surroundings of that placid little port accorded with the suspended mood of expectation in which her only excitements were Steven's weekly letters.

One morning toward the end of November, when autumn had broken at last beneath the fury of the south-west and bare-poled fishing-smacks shuddered and danced like corks on the long grey swell that swept the outer harbour, the red-bearded postman who staggered out along the road to the headland like a battered, over-laden freighter, brought her a rain-soaked letter from Ernest that changed her plans.

The Beresfords, it seemed, had decided to winter abroad and were ready, if she so wished it, to vacate Uffdown at the beginning of December. " I think you will be glad to get this news," Ernest wrote in postscript," because, as you see, it means that you will be able to have Steven with you at Uffdown for the Christmas holidays. Wire me at once if you would like the Beresfords to go."

So, in the first week of December, Clare returned to Uffdown.

For three days before her arrival Mrs. Bissell and the faithful Ellen had been busily removing the last traces of the Beresfords' occupation ; yet, as she approached it, through the pale gold of a frosty afternoon, she felt almost frightened to see what desecrations might have marred her vision. So precious to her heart, so sacramental seemed this moment of return, that she gave the servants no notice of her coming, and drove up from Wychbury station alone.

She stopped the station cab at the gate. The shrubberies on either side had been allowed to overreach the drive making the whole approach seem shrunken and ignoble. That was what happened with strangers, who didn't really care ; she would have to talk seriously to Waldron about it. A faithful soul, but probably a little too old for the job. She couldn't bear the idea of getting rid of anybody whom Ralph had engaged. Not only the shrubberies . . . The drive lay inches deep in beech-mast. One couldn't hear one's own steps ; one went like a ghost through a silence that seemed unnatural in daylight. December, of course. The month, above all others, in which life seemed to be suspended, the tide of sap at its ebb. " There's not a living thing awake to welcome me," she thought ; " not a leaf, not a bird. The place has been asleep ever since I left it."

Through the mouth of the beech avenue the flank of the house appeared. Clare stopped and gazed at it through the tears of joy and pride that came to her eyes, unreasonably elated to find that it had not changed, that it still stood there waiting for her, serene and patient as when she first had seen it. And yet, when she compared its actuality with the vision that had scarcely ever been absent from her mind it seemed to her that through all those years she had exaggerated its size. If it were as dear as ever, it wasn't half so impressive as she had imagined. It was a little old country house that had shrunk, like dear Aunt Cathie, with age. Perhaps, after all, poor Waldron wasn't responsible for the narrowness of the drive ; for now that the front lawn came into view, she saw that this, too, was much smaller than she had pictured it, and that Waldron had not been idle, since the turf was newly-mown and swept clean of the last offending leaf.

There, on the further side of it, where the grey hedge of rosemary bounded her rose-garden, the rockery, which she and Waldron had planted between them, no longer showed an outline of sandstone boulders. It lay there, an irregular, grey-green mound, completely smothered by sheets of alyssum, aubretia, and all the other living things that they had planted so lovingly. A single gleam of pale lavender lit the green. What could it be ? she wondered ; and, glad of any excuse to postpone the moment of intolerable emotion which lay in wait for her on the threshold, she stepped aside over the crisp, frozen lawn to find that this lavender gleam came from a clump of *Stylosa* iris which, in her presence, had never yet consented to flower. She knelt down beside them, reverencing their beauty, inhaling their faint scent, grateful for the fidelity—there was no other word—which these sweet things that she had planted showed by their flowery welcome. And there, beside them, half hidden in frost-nipped leaves, lifted the waxen petals of black hellebore and wintry stars of cushion saxifrage, each telling her that the part of herself which she had left buried there was not only living but wide awake ; that Uffdown, for all its momentary strangeness, was still its lovely self ; that all its seeming changes were nothing but a reflection of the changes in her own soul.

Standing entranced beside the rosemary hedge, whose grey-green leaves, thoughtlessly crumbled, released the perfume of so many and such poignant memories, she induced herself, at last, to overcome the shyness that inhibited her desire to re-enter the house. Over the length of the lawn its serious windows surveyed her kindly, complacently awaited her approach. There was no sign of any life, other than that of its own ghostly consciousness, behind them.

" Thank heaven nobody knows," she thought, " that I am here. If Ellen or anyone else opened the door for me I know I should make an exhibition of myself. I can do nothing but pray to goodness that it isn't locked."

Cautiously, almost guiltily, she stole across the intervening turf. Upon the drive her footsteps woke the absolute silence by a crunch of gravel that sent her forward on tiptoe. Gently she turned the brass door-knob ; smoothly, as if some ghostly hand had moved it, the heavy door swung inward. The homely, aromatic scent of Uffdown, that was like no other, filled her nostrils and stole into her mind. From the wide stairway the eyes of Ralph's portrait, amused, and only faintly critical, smiled down on her. She gazed at them until they were blurred so that she could see them no more.

" I have come home," she thought, " I have come home . . . at last."

Not a breath, not a sound. She and the house of memories alone together.

She took off her fur-coat with a sigh and sat down in the sweet, consoling silence, more deeply moved than she could even imagine, yet strangely, humbly happy. She sat there for a long time with closed eyes, only opening them, from time to time, to assure herself that this peace was true, bidding her turbulent heart be still, assuring herself over and over again that she was not dreaming. Warmth and a slow content caressed her silently, there was no sound, no stir except the settling of the fire. And still she was drowsily thankful that nobody knew she was there.

If they will leave me alone a little longer," she thought, " I shall be able to deal with anything."

It seemed as if they were going to leave her alone for ever. The hall grew so dim that she could no longer invoke the assurance of its familiar shapes. Suddenly she was startled by the contact of something cold and wet that made her snatch her hand away. There, at her side, blinking upward at her with the plaintive confidence of age, she saw the red eyes of a small rough-haired terrier.

" Oh, Sly," she cried, " you dreadful dog ! How you did startle me ! "

Sly yawned at her and wagged a languid tail. " So it *is* you, after all. Whatever are you doing here again ? " he seemed to say.

" You poor little thing, how old you've grown ! " she cried. And then, as though her soul had found some object for the physical expression which it had been seeking, she picked the ridiculous creature up and hugged it in her arms. For Sly, by some mysterious alchemy of the imagination, was part of Steven, and lay, indeed like a baby in her arms, limply accommodating herself to those embraces because any resistance to them might give her poor rheumatic joints a twinge. But Clare, as she felt the warmth of the little old dog in her arms, found, suddenly, that the worst had happened ; that between the murmured endearments which came to her lips, she was crying, for no reason, like a child.

A noise on the stairs ; a flurry of rapid footsteps. Then the sharp practical voice of Vivien :

" Ellen, come quickly. I do believe we've let the fire out. Why, Clare, *Clare*, my *dear !* Whenever did you arrive ? We haven't heard a sound. We were busy upstairs. Ellen, she's here ! Did you ever know anything like it ? "

" It didn't really matter, Vivien dear. Sly did the honours."

" Yes, poor old thing ! We're rather sorry for ourselves,

aren't we ? " She glanced down at Sly, who, suddenly released, was performing an intimate toilet on the floor, exactly where Clare had placed her. " You might have let us know the time of your train, Clare, Vivien continued. " Ellen will go to the kitchen and see about some tea at once."

" Yes, miss," said Ellen, from whose red face a twitching smile of welcome had not yet faded, while Sly, whose senile intelligence had grasped the comfortable word kitchen, just too late, stood staring resentfully at the baize door that swung behind her.

" And now, Clare," Vivien went on, " for goodness' sake, let's have some light on the scene."

That desire for brightness was so like Vivien ; there were no half-tones, and never had been, in all her character. As she switched on the light and came smiling toward her, Clare felt a little shock at the change in Vivien's appearance. Brusque, downright, swiftly efficient she had always seemed. But now the frank good-nature, which differentiated her from her mother and gave her the lovable quality that Lady Hingston lacked, had declared itself in a spreading of her figure which made her, although she was still under forty, look middle-aged, and allowed the masculine strain that had always been inherent in her to appear. The very voice in which she spoke was deeper, and, as their lips met, in one of her swift kisses, Clare felt the brushing of a palpable moustache.

" Now, *do* sit down and tell me all about it," Vivien said.

" My dear, there's nothing to tell you. Only that it was sweet of you to come over and help like this."

" Well, well," said Vivien, " I know what servants are, and I've a weakness for proving that I can be domestic when I want to. At the last minute I got a note from Miss Weir. She wanted to put the place in order for you herself, but apparently she was seedy."

"Aunt Cathie? You don't mean that she is really ill? I've had her on my conscience. I didn't like the look of her when I went down to Devonshire. But then, her letters were so awfully cheerful that I supposed she was better again."

"At any rate, my dear," Vivien assured her, like an elder brother, "you mustn't worry your head about her now. You've got to settle in here, and you can't do two things at once."

"No. But I think I'll go to Pen House to-morrow. What is your news, Vivien? Tell me about Stourford."

"Stourford?" Vivien repeated with a little laugh. "Why, just the usual excursions and alarms. They say that steel is slumping. Mother knows more about it. I'm merely a farmer in these days. Mawne's badly hit already. There's even some talk about a reconstruction. I suppose our turn, at Wolverbury, will come next. Then Mawne has a scandal of sorts as well. You remember Edward Willis? A queer lad, Edward. . . . It seems he's mixed up somehow with the manager's wife: a Mrs. Stafford, rather a dashing party. Unfortunately we're not in a position to throw stones. George and Eleanor are having some sort of trouble at Wolverbury. Since little Harold died they've never hit it off. Mother, of course, is furious with Eleanor."

"Eleanor's a queer, cold creature, Vivien."

"So, for that matter, is George. I'm sorry for both of them. I always told you that Ralph was the only one of us who wasn't just a little mad. But, really, Clare, upon my soul, all you married people seem to be the same in these days. I don't say it's your fault. There's somthing in the air just now that makes you all restless and discontented. I don't pretend to understand it. I'm only glad that my animals at Stourford are less fanciful in their marital arrangements. They don't seem to mix them up with soul-searchings. And I thank my stars, too, that I never let mother bully me into marrying anybody. Life's far too strenuous for me to have time for that sort of thing ! "

Clare smiled. How often, in the past, and how foolishly, had her match-making instinct amused itself by trying to think of a husband for Vivien ! And, if she had found one, how sad a mistake it would have been ! There was even something a little enviable in the bluff, whole-hearted independence with which Vivien had shaped her life to such a satisfactory end. She was above the weaknesses of her sex. It mattered nothing to her that she had lost her figure, that the faint down which once had lent a dashing air to her dark and sanguine face, had turned into something much more definite. She didn't have to consider things of that kind. " But if I had been like Vivien," Clare thought, " I should never have had Steven ; and if I hadn't Steven I might just as well cease to exist." And with the thought of Steven she became almost unconscious of Vivien's presence in the excitement of imagining the joy of his return. Wherever she went with Vivien that evening, traversing the recovered Uffdown, room by room, Steven went with her, smiling where she smiled, rejoicing where she rejoiced, ecstatic as herself in the air of paradise regained.

On the morrow, despite her busyness, she found time to drive over to Pen House ; for the letter which Aunt Cathie had compelled herself to send to Vivien remained as a focus of disquietude in her mind : a disquietude that changed itself into positive fear when in the dim light of the little dining-room Aunt Cathie, or rather the shadow of Aunt Cathie, came forward to greet her.

" My dearest," Clare said, " Vivien told me that you had told her you were seedy, but I'd no idea you were as ill as this. You never said a word about it in your letters."

" I hope I'm not in the habit of complaining unnecessarily, Clare," Aunt Cathie answered tartly. " I consider it merely decent that people should keep their little ailments to themselves. The doctor could never put up with folks that made an exhibition. Besides, I'm not *ill*—not in the very least. You don't seem to realize that I'm not as young as I was, and having Thirza bedridden for such a long time as this is rather a tax on me."

" But, my darling, that's nonsense. You've gone so dreadfully thin. I could pick you up like a feather."

" I hope you'll do nothing of the sort," said Aunt Cathie, with a feeble flash of her own prim humour. " I told you how rough you were when last you kissed me, and I always did hate being mauled about. Now, please don't talk about that any more. You're becoming far too personal. I'll make a cup of tea in the kitchen, and you shall tell me all about Devonshire and how you found Uffdown. I'm very glad that Miss Hingston was able to take my place. She seems to be settling down into a nice, practical creature, which is more than anyone could expect, remembering her mother."

All through the afternoon Clare had the feeling that Aunt Cathie was edging away from her, as though she were as tender as she was fragile and feared to be touched. At tea she ate more than usual and almost ravenously.

" You see I haven't lost my appetite," she said, with an excusing smile.

" I think," said Clare, returning to her attack, " you ought to see a doctor."

" My dear Clare, please don't be argumentative. They say that everyone at forty is either a fool or a physician. Please realize I'm fifty-five, and not a fool. Remember also that I'm a doctor's daughter, and able to understand myself far better than a stranger. I'm merely rather fatigued, as is quite natural, with looking after Thirza."

" In that case, darling, you ought to have a nurse to relieve you."

" A nurse . . . in *this* house ? Do you suggest that I'm

incompetent ? And don't imagine, please, that *that* would relieve me ! I know what modern nurses are, my dear. They expect to be treated like royalty and live on the fat of the land. I shouldn't be able to call the house my own, and at *my* time of life that isn't convenient to me. Oh no ! "

" If you would let me," Clare suggested humbly, " I'd love to bear the expense."

" The expense is nothing, thank you," said Aunt Cathie superbly. " I'm glad to say that my breweries are doing very well just at present." Since the Fatherless Bairn disaster Aunt Cathie no longer acknowledged Messrs. Astill's proprietorship of their own business. " The whole point is that if we had a nurse in the house, I should be nothing but a domestic in general service. No thank you, my dear ! "

" But, darling, suppose you got another servant ? That would relieve you of the housework and leave you free to look after Thirza. Perhaps, on the whole, that's a better plan."

Aunt Cathie shook her head impatiently. " It's no good trying, Clare, to teach me my own business. I'm not going to have any strange young girls poking their noses into every nook and corner of *my* house. In any case I'm afraid poor Thirza isn't long for this world. Her memory's almost gone. In fact I was going to suggest that it's hardly worth while your seeing her. I'm glad to say she does still recognize me ; but that's about the sum of it."

By the end of the afternoon Clare had exhausted all her persuasions. Frail as she was, Aunt Cathie could still resist her. The only authority to whom that stubborn spirit seemed likely to submit was Dudley. Dudley, no doubt, would " take the matter up " like any other case that might be submitted to him, deal with it methodically, tie it in a bundle with red tape, and file it in one of his shabby safes for future reference. But Dudley, at that moment, was the last person in the world of whom Clare wished to ask a favour. " I think I'd better mention it to Ernest to-morrow," she decided. For, on the next day, Ernest Wilburn was coming over to Uffdown to complete the deed of separation which he had prepared.

It wasn't only for this reason that Clare looked forward eagerly to Ernest Wilburn's visit. Within her narrowed world his was the human companionship that she prized most. She wanted to see him for himself—the suddenness of their last parting had left an uncomfortable flavour—but, even more, she wanted to show him Uffdown, and, perhaps, herself, the lost soul whom he had found and comforted in the desert of Alvaston restored to the kingdom that was hers by right and custom.

" Do come," she had written, " early enough to see the house and the garden by daylight. If you turn this into a business visit and nothing else I shall never forgive you." And all through the day, as she and Ellen moved about the house trying to reimpose the stamp of her own personality wherever traces of the Beresfords remained, she was seeing things not only through her own eyes but through Ernest's, and feeling the warmth of his approval even before it was spoken. It was only when she came to think of Uffdown in terms of Ernest's appreciation that she realized how great a part it had played already in their queer friendship. For Ernest, despite the growing preference for modern art which had made him dump his Madox-Jones' cartoons on the grateful municipality was really, at heart, an eighteenth century gentleman ; there was an intellectual scepticism in his culture that explained his isolation from the artistic life of North Bromwich and his ready acceptance of herself, not as the wife of his brother, but as a spirit already unconsciously moulded by the gracious influence of Uffdown. In the same way it was their unrecognized affinity with Uffdown that had made his Alvaston rooms so grateful to her in contrast with the mid-Victorian Gothic of Tudor House.

He came, urbanely, characteristically, with a forty-horse-power Daimler, whose softly-sighing sleeve-valves seemed to respect the Uffdown silence, and an enormous bouquet of his incomparable carnations.

" Oh, Ernest, you must have spoiled your greenhouse to bring me all these," she reproved him.

He smiled and shook his head. All through their tour of inspection he was grave, formal, almost silent. It made no matter. His silence was more understanding than the speech of others. She did not even need to look for approval in his eyes ; she knew when it was there. When the light faded and they sat together in a dusk through which they could scarcely distinguish each other's faces, he delivered his verdict.

" It is all exceedingly beautiful, Clare," he said, " and you are part of it. Perhaps I ought to have said that it's part of you—a part which I hadn't quite realized before, but which explains a great deal of the rest. Now that I've seen you here, I shall never think of you anywhere else. It's a good memory to take away with me."

" To take away with you, Ernest ? What do you mean ? I hope you're not going to desert me now that you've been here once ? "

He would not answer her directly. " You know, Clare, there are some beautiful things that it's better to see only once."

" You're mysterious, Ernest. We're such good friends ; and yet you've never given me any of your confidence . . . about yourself, I mean. It isn't that I'm asking for it. Don't think that. Only . . . there are obligations in friendship. It can't be all one-sided. You've done so much for me—I think you saved my reason in Alvaston— and I have done absolutely nothing in return."

" My dear, you've done a great deal in return," he told her. " The fact that I see you here to-day, so happy, so radiant, is quite enough. I've told you more than once that life is complicated. Sometimes the complications are amusing ; sometimes they aren't. But in any case—I'm brutally frank about it—I don't want a scrap of sympathy, and just because you're so sympathetic you'll understand me. You'll have to forgive my habit of walking by myself. It's in our blood. You've seen exactly the same thing in Dudley. It happens to be the only defect of mine that he shares. And, talking of Dudley, don't you think we'd better get our business over ? I have the documents here. Suppose you read them over before dinner. Then we can talk of pleasanter things afterwards."

Before she could answer him he rose and switched on the light which cut across the vague strands of sympathy that the dusk had woven between them like a sword. He sat down close beside her, and at an infinite distance.

" Perhaps you would rather I read it to you ? " he said.

" Is there any real necessity for that ? "

" Yes. Even though it hurts you, you mustn't sign anything you haven't read."

" Very well then," she said. " Please read it."

She closed her eyes to listen ; and his voice, its tones adapted to the legal phraseology, so obliterated all his other unlikeness that it seemed to her as if Dudley himself were speaking.

" That is the end of it," he said at last, becoming himself again. " To execute this deed you must put your forefinger on the wafer—that little red spot—and say : ' I deliver this as my act and deed.' "

" Those actual words ? "

" Yes."

" I deliver this as my act and deed," she repeated.

" Now sign."

She signed.

" That is all, Mrs. Wilburn. I've finished with you."

They dined alone at the table which she had so carefully prepared, in a soft candlelight that scarcely penetrated beyond the oval of the table. She had chosen a meal that her lunches with him assured her he would appreciate, and brought up from Ralph's choicest bin a bottle of port. When he complimented her on the cooking and the vintage it made her glow with pride. In his quiet way he had so established himself in her mind as an arbiter of taste that his approval elated her. This supper was a significant festival, the celebration of her return to Uffdown, and there was no one in the world with whom she would rather have shared it than Ernest. She told him so.

" But before I go," he said, " I want you to play to me."

" And I want to play *for* you," she said. " I have all your Wolf. You shall sing me *Anakreon's Grab.*"

" No, we won't talk of graves this evening, much less sing of them. To-night I'm a listener."

" What shall I play, then ? " she asked, as they entered Annabel Ombersley's drawing-room.

" In this room, I think, Scarlatti. Yes, certainly Scarlatti. And treat your piano as if it were a harpsichord."

She played him a little suite of Scarlatti, and then, as his silence approved, passed on, of her own inspiration, to the Italian Concerto of Bach. She felt that she had caught his mood ; that all their music that evening should be grave and light-hearted at once. From Bach she passed to Rameau and Couperin. He listened without comment. Only the smoke of his cigar, slow-coiling, showed that he was alive. And the room listened too. The night was full of listeners, and herself so entranced by the ghostly dance of her fingers tripping through that maze of gay old tunes, so nimble-witted and passionless, that it gave her a start when she found his hands upon her wrists.

" I'm afraid my time is up," he said, in a voice that she didn't know.

The phrase that she was playing faltered ; her fingers finished it tamely, of their own accord.

" You mean that you're going already ?  Oh, Ernest dear, what a pity !  It isn't to London this time, Ernest ? "

" To London ?  No.  Not London this time.  You've played most wonderfully to-night, Clare."

" I know I've played well," she admitted.  " I was enjoying listening to myself ; which means that it wasn't really *I* that was playing.  I'm quite reasonable, but dreadfully, dreadfully excited.  That's partly your fault, and because I'm happy.  I wish you weren't going so soon, Ernest.  I haven't had time to thank you for all you've done for me."

He smiled.  " Don't thank me, Clare.  Now I must say good night."

He bent over her and gave her his usual, formal kiss, so gently, so modestly that she flung her arms about his neck and kissed him in return.  " Dear Ernest," she said.

He took her arms from his shoulders and pressed both hands in his.

" Good-bye, my child," he said.  So quietly . . .

" Don't go just yet," she pleaded.

" I ordered my car to come round at ten o'clock.  It's waiting now."

" You never told me that.  How shabby of you ! "

" Don't trouble to see me out.  It's bitterly cold.  Really I'd rather you didn't, Clare . . . to-night."

She consented ruefully.  " I shall play to your dear carnations when you've gone.  Next time . . . ? "

For answer he waved her a kiss from the doorway.

He went, as she stood transfixed, with the smile of parting on her lips, and, as she did so, the interrupted phrase of the Rameau Sarabande resumed its gentle course and went on wandering through her mind.  Nothing could still it but that she should go back to the piano and give the ghostly little tune the life for which it clamoured. And so, since the mood of music was on her, she sat down again and played straight on from the point at which his hands placed on her wrists had arrested it. Indeed, his presence and his parting had both been so quiet that it almost seemed as if he had never left her, and, when the Sarabande was finished, she went on playing as though he were still there, trying to imagine, against the unconscious flow of music, what in the world had made him so strange that night.

" I like him so much," she thought, " and yet he's just as incomprehensible as Dudley. He's been an angel to me, and yet I mayn't thank him. A strange, inscrutable race ! If I were a fool, or very young, I suppose I should imagine he was in love with me. But when a man is in love with you, however self-contained he may be, he doesn't kiss you like that. Poor darling, I wonder if he's ever been in love. . . . But I am glad," she told herself, " that I did kiss him in my own way, after all. Even though it may have been that which frightened him away."

She laughed to herself as she closed the lid of the piano. The room was curiously quiet, as though the old music had lulled it into a doze. The scent of Ernest's pale-stalked carnations wandered through it. Lingering before them, she had a sudden feeling that something in connection with him had been forgotten. " Aunt Cathie," she thought. " I never asked him to speak about her to Dudley. I shall have to write to Ernest about it. To-morrow . . . not to-night."

## XV

### ERNEST

A GAY, crisp winter morning at last. Over the silvered fields the light came dancing ; freed from the tangle of bare beech-boughs it threw the delicate shadow of Ernest's carnations upon the first page of her letter. *Dear Ernest,* she had written, " *In the hurry of last night I quite forgot to speak to you about* . . . With a startling jangle the telephone-bell exploded. Vivien, perhaps, with some new offer of help.

" Is that you, Clare ? " she heard.

" Oh, Ernest, how lucky ! My dear, I was just writing to you."

" It isn't Ernest. Dudley Wilburn speaking."

" Dudley ? I'm sorry. Yes ? "

Her heart sank as she listened. It was the first time that she had heard his voice for more than ten weeks. She couldn't imagine what she ought to have said ; but, whether her answer had been right or wrong, he didn't wait to consider. His voice, made unmaterial by distance, went on grating :

" Ernest was with you last night ? "

" Yes, he had dinner here."

" At what time did he leave you ? "

" At ten. Five minutes past ten, I think, exactly."

" Did you notice anything extraordinary about him . . . about his manner, I mean ? "

" No. I don't think so. He was just like he always is."

" He didn't say anything to you about himself . . . his plans ? "

" No, I don't think so. He never does. Why do you want to know, Dudley ? What is the matter ? "

The silence was so long that she thought they had been cut off. Then, suddenly, the voice of Dudley grated out again :

" I'm sorry to have to tell you. He's dead. Between seven and eight this morning. He shot himself."

" Dudley ! " The sunlit writing-table swam away from her as she clutched it. She must have mistaken the words —unless those ordinary sounds had some new meaning.

Perhaps some trick of hearing. . . . "What did you say dear?" The word slipped in by habit. "I don't quite understand."

"Shot himself." The voice repeated brazenly. "With a revolver. Between seven and eight."

"Dudley, it's impossible," she cried. "Whatever can it mean?"

"I don't know yet. It may have been an accident. I'm afraid it wasn't. I have my suspicions . . . unfortunately. I only wanted to know if he told you anything. I'll let you know later."

"Oh, Dudley, you poor thing!" she answered.

But there was no reply.

The new housemaid came into the breakfast-room and advertised her presence by a clatter of china and vigorous sweeping of crumbs. The lawn began to lose its hoary silver as tree-shadows retreated. Old Waldron hobbled over the drive with his stiff besom, and doffed his hat toward the figure of his mistress sitting in the window. Clare did not see him. The flame of the mounting sun was in her eyes. She had not even the initiative to avoid it. Her mind was full of questions, vain, unanswerable, questions that reached out helplessly into a void in which the figure of Ernest Wilburn smiled at her, as always, with his faint, kindly, non-committal smile. Even in life he had never answered her questions. Perhaps it was because he could give them no answer himself but this last, terrible, eternal negative. "Life is extremely complicated," she heard him say. "Sometimes the complications are amusing, sometimes . . . they aren't. But, in any case, I'm not wanting sympathy."

Why had he made that so clear, even to the very last? What cruel shyness, obstinacy, had denied her the privilege of giving what she would so willingly have given. If he had trusted me, she thought. If he had only given me a chance of understanding, we might, between us, have found some other way. Oh, Ernest, Ernest, why ever didn't you trust me ? But no voice from the shadows answered her appeal. There was nothing of Ernest left for her in the world but the memory of slow smiles and rare, formal kisses, a sorrowful spirit, tenuously persisting in phrases of music that died as they were born, the vanishing odour of carnations that paled and faded on her writing-table.

No other word from Dudley. There was an inquest, reported in the *Courier :* the usual verdict. " He was as sane as I am," she thought. A notice addressed in the queerly, unclerical hand of Grosmont invited her to attend a funeral. How Ernest would have smiled if she had accepted ! Through all that week she could not bear to see a soul ; for the woman who moved about her daily business was not herself, and the answers that she gave to those who questioned her came lifeless out of the unresponsive distances in which her mind was wandering.

And then with a detonation that shook the business world of North Bromwich, already uneasily facing the slump in iron, more heavily than any catastrophe since the flooding of Fatherless Bairn, the Wilburn wreck, in all its sinister magnitude, stood revealed. It was Lady Hingston who carried the news triumphantly to Uffdown.

" You may thank your stars, Clare," she said, " that you're out of it by the skin of your teeth. Of course I always knew that something of this kind would happen. I've told my husband so again and again. As I always say, the most dangerous people in this world are the prigs. All our worst labour agitators at Wolverbury are chapel deacons, or elders, or something or other, and the Wilburns were just of the same sanctimonious brand."

" I don't think anyone can say," Clare contended, " that Ernest Wilburn ever pretended to be better than he was. I never knew a man less priggish in my life."

" Fortunately, I knew nothing of him but his unpleasant reputation," Lady Hingston admitted. " However, Dudley Wilburn's a prig if ever there was one."

" But Dudley," Clare maintained, " has nothing to do with the smash, In everything that's come out so far it seems that all the speculations and defalcations, or whatever they call them, were made by Ernest. As far as I can see there was nobody in the world more astonished by what happened than Dudley himself. I think, at least, you might do him so much justice. You can't condemn him just for the sake of making your theories about priggishness work out."

" Ah, there you go again ! " Lady Hingston scoffed. " Even now that you've got away from him the man still fascinates you. You're quite beyond me, Clare. Talking of Dudley Wilburn's saintly innocence ! It doesn't make matters better to say the man's a fool. To begin with, he isn't one. You can't be a Methusaleh—I mean a Socrates —one day and an idiot the next, just to suit your convenience. And if he *is* a fool, I'd like to know what sort of difference that makes to poor old maiden ladies and widows and retired colonels whose savings Ernest Wilburn threw away on gold-mines, and pearls for his grinning actresses. Of course it's all very fine and large to pretend to be loyal— though heaven only knows what you've got to be loyal about ! —but wait till you know the whole truth of the matter. Before it's over you and Steven may find yourselves without a penny, and then you'll smile on the other side of your face. You'll be telling me that Mr. Hooley's a saint next ! Wilburn, Wilburn and Wilburn, indeed ! As far as I'm concerned, one Wilburn's as bad as another. If I were you I should want to change my name."

" How delighted she would be," Clare thought, " if we were left with nothing ! "

Fortunately there seemed to be no probability of that, for the increasing lack of sympathy between the two brothers had divided the unlucky ship into two watertight compartments, and though the credit of the firm as a whole had been pledged by Ernest, the securities that Dudley handled remained intact. Even in the turmoil of the wreck Dudley had remembered her sufficiently to send her a hurried note of assurance that the Hingston trust and Aunt Cathie's breweries were safe.

*If you have left anything that you value at Tudor House,* he wrote, *you had better remove it. I shall probably have to file my petition in bankruptcy, and later, if things are sold, it may be difficult to discriminate between what is yours and what is mine. Of course the Deed of Separation simplifies matters, though as it was executed so very little time before my partner's decease my creditors may claim the balance of our joint account ; in which case I shall have to ask you to wait a little time before I can make you restitution of the sum involved . . .*

The very impersonality of this letter troubled her. Its formal phrasing—*my partner's decease . . . the sum involved*—aroused her compassion more acutely than a more intimate appeal could ever have done. It gave her a vision of the broken man, consistently scrupulous even in the midst of disaster, that made her ashamed of the vague suspicions—they had never, thank heaven, been more than vague—which she had harboured against him. In this catastrophe, the final test of the steadfastness and probity that she had always admired, the full measure of his strength and stature revealed themselves, while the sneers of Lady Hingston and the more cautious innuendoes which reached her from other quarters gave him, in her eyes, a touch of heroism, and filled her with an emotion in which pride was stronger than pity.

In place of the image of Ernest, mysteriously fading with his flowers, that of Dudley now began to haunt her imagination. Even when she comforted herself with the thought of his independence she remembered a hundred small things in which he had been dependent on the care that she had given, and which Mrs. Marple, with the best of intentions, would be unable to supply. In the days of his strength she had scarcely considered them ; but now that he was fighting for his life they became important, and the fact that she could no longer provide them when most they were needed was magnified in her mind until it showed plainly as an act of despicable treachery on her part.

Wherever she went the picture of Dudley's loneliness pursued her. Not even the prospect of Steven's home-coming could drive it from her mind. It troubled her so persistently that she knew that she could have no peace until she had squared her conscience. However she argued the matter, through busy days and sleepless nights, there seemed to be no way out of it. At last, when she could stand the strain of the silent struggle no longer, she found her solution.

On the spur of the moment, acting on an instinct which she distrusted even as she surrendered to it, she ordered the new car and drove, without preparation, to North Brom-wich. " I shall be able to decide what I'm going to say on the way in," she thought ; but, almost before she knew what she had done, Halesby and Tilton had dropped behind and Bissell was feeling his way through the traffic toward Sack-ville Row. She told him to wait outside the office. " I've no idea how long I shall be," she said.

The block of offices had a derelict air, as if every other firm in the building had been killed by the Wilburn catastrophe. The well of the stairs was dank and stony as a vault. The three Wilburns on the door of the office were like the *stele* in a desecrated tomb, their melancholy persist-ence gave her a shiver. She knocked ; but the moon-faced Grosmont did not open to her. After a long silence ghostly shoulders loomed against the opal, and when the door opened they were Dudley's.

Confronted with his haggard face her courage left her.

He did not even smile.

" May I come in ? " she said.

He let her pass in silence. The staleness of the office air, that she knew so well, seemed horribly intensified. He led her to his room without a word or a sign. His face was blank, emotionless, as though all power of feeling had been crushed out of it. Her heart bled for this cold, strong man. He sat and gazed at her over a desk snowed under with papers. She felt that whatever she said she could not hurt or heal him. No new weight could distress this tired Atlas, nor any power on earth lighten his burden. He waited for her to speak. She put out her hand to him, but he did not touch it.

She felt her whole face quiver in spite of herself as she began to speak :

" Dudley," she said, " I couldn't answer your letter. Words seemed impossible. It was very kind of you to write."

" My letter ? " he repeated. " Ah, yes. You haven't done anything ? I think, as far as the bank's concerned, it will be all right. They have been most considerate —my creditors, I mean—on the whole."

" No, no," she said. " I wasn't thinking of that. I really came to-day because I couldn't bear it any longer. I want to say something to you. If it seems too utterly childish and unpractical—well, I think you know me well enough to forgive me. It's about the Deed of Separation that I signed for Ernest. I want to know if there's any way of undoing it ? "

" Undoing it ? Whatever do you mean ? "

" I mean that at a time like this I oughtn't to leave you. I can't bear to think of you going through it alone. I know that I can't do much ; but anything that I can do, I feel I must."

" Your sense of duty," he began . . .

" No, no. It's more than that, Dudley, far more than that. I want to say to you that if you wish it, if it will make things easier in any way whatever—it doesn't matter a bit how small it is—I'm ready to come back to Alvaston."

" To Alvaston ? The house is for sale next week. If you drove in this morning you might have seen the notices."

" I didn't look. I couldn't bear to look. But wherever you are it makes no difference. If you want me, I'll come."

He shook his head slowly.

" Isn't it rather late in the day to talk like that, Clare ? You've just established yourself at Uffdown."

" That makes no difference. Of course I shall have to keep on Uffdown. I can send Steven to Stourford for his Christmas holidays, and leave the Bissells in charge. And then "—she hesitated—" then, afterwards, if you will allow me to make some sort of division in my life, I could spend the term-time with you, wherever you are, and the holidays with Steven at Uffdown."

At the mention of Steven's name she saw his mouth harden. He rose and, for a moment, stalked the room in silence.

" Let us be honest, Clare," he said at last. " You don't want to come back to me. Answer me truly."

" I don't want to leave you, Dudley, if I'm of any use to you."

" That's quite another matter."

" You have only to say the word : to tell me that you want me."

Now he, in his turn, evaded her : " I don't want you to immolate yourself. Enough happiness has been sacrificed already on this altar."

" I should be happy, Dudley, if I felt I was helping you."

" I don't believe it. There's no more happiness here. I'm a broken man."

" All the more reason. But I don't believe that either.

No man was ever broken by lies. There's nobody who can say a word against you."

" How do you know ? A good many hard words have been said."

" They make no difference. I don't believe them."

" Well, thank you for that at any rate." He smiled for the first time. " God bless you, Clare. Go back to Uffdown and be happy."

" I don't want to, Dudley."

He teased her : " To be happy, or to go back to Uffdown ? My dear, you don't know *what* you want. That's why I think you'd better trust me to know what's best for you. Go back to Uffdown."

" That means you don't want me, Dudley," she answered, almost bitterly.

It meant that the conscientious struggles which had brought her to that point had been wasted, that she had found her match in generous renunciation. He saw that she was piqued ; his habitual wisdom contrived, by a change of tone, to smooth her ruffled pride.

" The question of wanting or not wanting you doesn't arise. I'd like you to understand my position, Clare. At the present moment I'm fighting for my life : that's what my professional reputation means to me. The struggle is so intense, and, unfortunately, so doubtful, that however much I wanted you I couldn't afford to weaken myself by a moment's distraction. I need every spark of energy I possess in every moment of the day. You can help me best, in fact, by leaving me alone. Don't take it hardly, Clare. I'm only being honest with you. As soon as the house is sold I shall go into lodgings in Alvaston. All I want, for the moment, is somewhere to sleep. Don't worry about me either. Until this business came I'd no idea how many loyal friends I had : old Astill, Walter Willis, even the bank —they're all out to help me. There's just a thin chance that

I may be able to meet my obligations with their help. It's touch and go. I can't say more than that for the present. But in any case you'll realize that my hands must be free. That's why I can't accept your very brave . . . your very generous offer."

He paused. Clare knew him well enough to see how much the words had cost him. She knew, indeed, that there was no more to be said. He watched her gravely as she put on her furs. She felt he was only waiting for her to go.

" Promise me," she said at last, " that if you want me you'll send for me ? "

" Yes, yes, I promise," he answered.

She put up her face to him. Solemnly, he kissed her.

# XVI

## AUNT CATHIE

THREE days before Steven's return for the Christmas holidays old Thirza Rudge died in her sleep. The news was brought over to Uffdown before breakfast by Ellen's father, the black-smith. Clare drove him back to Wychbury in the car, flushed with the importance of his mission.

" I can't say I like the looks of your auntie either, Miss Clare," he informed her, with a kind of macabre satisfaction.

She found Aunt Cathie up and dressed in her best, seated, like a passenger waiting for a train, in the fireless dining-room. There were no tears in the hollow eyes that stared out of her grey, drawn face. Her mind was calm, and strangely self-possessed. She spoke of Thirza's death as she might have spoken of a stranger's.

" It would have made no difference to anyone but me," she said, " if she had died a year ago. Yesterday, for the first time, she didn't know me. She thought I was her daughter, the one that married the gardener. It may seem heartless, Clare; but, really, I feel nothing. Only most dreadfully tired. I hadn't even the strength to lay the fire. I wonder if you'd be so kind as to ask Ellen to set it now ? "

" I'll do it myself, darling."

" No, no, ask Ellen. She understands my ways. Thirza's daughter and her husband should be arriving by the ten o'clock train. Ellen will give them some breakfast and see that they're comfortable. You'd better take my keys and put out some tea. Ellen will find everything else they need in the larder, I think. There's bacon; and if the bread is stale she can toast it."

" Ellen is quite reliable. You needn't worry your head about details like that. I'm going to leave her here and take you back to Uffdown."

" You can do what you like with me now," Aunt Cathie sighed. " I think," she added, as though she had made an important discovery, " I must have overtired myself."

Ellen was squatting down in front of the fireplace spreading her great hips. The sticks began to crackle; she put on little lumps of coal one by one.

" I see you've not forgotten my ways," said Aunt Cathie approvingly. " Turn back the hearthrug, Ellen. This coal spits so."

The cheer of the fire seemed to warm her spirit a little. When Thirza's daughter and her husband arrived from the station she insisted on seeing them at once. They came in, bobbing and diffident, humble survivals of the old tradition of service.

" I leave the arrangements entirely to you," said Aunt Cathie grandly. " But all the expense will naturally be mine. Your mother was a very faithful servant. The doctor would have wished it."

At mid-day, leaving Ellen behind in charge, Clare put Aunt Cathie in the car and drove her back to Uffdown.

She went like a lamb. All the old, flashing spirit seemed to have faded out of her. She didn't even resent the suggestion that she should go to bed and rest, though she protested vigorously against the proposal that Clare should help her to undress. " No one has ever done *that* for me," she said, " and no one ever shall. I may be old, Clare, but I like my privacy."

She was so stubborn about it that Clare felt she must be trying to hide something.

" I'll ring the bell to let you know as soon as I'm in bed," Aunt Cathie said.

It was nearly forty minutes before the bell rang. When Clare reached the bedroom she found Aunt Cathie propped up against the high pillows like a doll ; a little slip of a woman in a high-necked calico nightdress with stiff lace trimmings. Everything about her seemed to have shrunk, except her great black eyes that followed Clare suspiciously wherever she moved. In contrast with the snow of linen sheets the skin of her face and of her long, bony forearms seemed drab rather than white. Her hands, lying limp upon the coverlet, showed the peculiar opacity of sickly leaves. Her lips were tense, constricted. There was no colour in them. Old Thirza's illness had seemed gentle and, somehow, natural, permeating her whole organism, as death invades a tree ; but Aunt Cathie's eyes, so lively in contrast with her wasted body, filled Clare with terror. She felt them watching her, but dared not meet them. At last she compelled herself to make an admission.

" I've telephoned Dr. Boyd to call here on his round," she said.

" Why ? Is there anybody ill in the house ? " Aunt Cathie asked innocently.

" My dear, I can't be happy unless someone sees you."

" If you're thinking of me, you might have saved yourself the trouble," Aunt Cathie answered after a long pause.

" I have no need of advice. If I had wanted him, you may be sure I should have sent for him myself."

" Aunt Cathie, you can't go on fighting against it for ever."

" I'm not fighting. I have *reasons* for not wishing to see him."

" There can't be any reason for not seeing a doctor when you're ill."

Aunt Cathie completely disregarded this contention, as though it were beneath contempt.

" I have no confidence in young Mr. Boyd," she declared. " I've made a point of avoiding him when he came to see Thirza."

" My dear, he can't be as young as all that," Clare protested. " He was over thirty when Steven was born, nearly fifteen years ago."

" The doctor always maintained that medical men should be married. I entirely agree with him. If I've *got* to see a doctor "—she began to waver—" I'd much rather consult an elderly man. My case," she added, with conscious superiority, " is not an ordinary one."

She paused, obviously expecting Clare to show no ordinary interest in the mystery ; but Clare was too thankful for the admission that Aunt Cathie had a case at all to think of anything else. Disappointed by her reaction to this announcement Aunt Cathie continued in a hurt voice :

" You don't seem interested, Clare. So I'll say no more about it. As a matter of fact I've been suffering, for the last year or so, from a troublesome pain "—the black eyes swept the room suspiciously as though in search of some irreverent eavesdropper—" a troublesome pain in my left . . . *bosom*." Her voice sank to a whisper on the embarrassing word ; but, once having spoken it, she became triumphantly communicative : " Now, perhaps, you remember the evening when you kissed me, and I asked you not to be rough with me ? That was the reason. And now, perhaps, you'll also understand my disinclination to consult a young, un-married man like Dr. Boyd ? "

" I don't understand," Clare told her, " how you have had the wickedness to let this go on for a year without consulting anybody. That is quite unforgivable."

" You seem to forget," said Aunt Cathie with dignity, " that I am not a married woman like yourself. In *my* day, we were led to understand that modesty was a matter of importance. Besides "—her thin lips trembled—" I am naturally rather nervous—my headaches, the doctor always said are the signs of a nervous temperament—and I thought if it were something serious I'd rather not know."

" My darling ! "

" However "—Aunt Cathie accorded Clare's emotion the tribute of a wan smile—" now that poor Thirza is off my hands I feel more free to go into the matter. All this con-versation has made me hot. You might open the window a little. I like fresh air. I've never been used to being mollycoddled."

As Clare lifted the sash obediently the intermittent explosions of the doctor's two-cylinder engine rose from the drive. She broke the news of his arrival as tactfully as she could.

" Well, since he's here," said Aunt Cathie resignedly, " I suppose, out of sheer politeness, I shall have to consult him. Please see that none of my underclothes are in sight, and open the window wider."

" If you really feel awkward, dearest, I'll stay with you," Clare suggested.

" I think it would be more becoming for you to wait in the dressing-room. I'll call you if you are wanted. You'd better receive the doctor on the landing."

He came upstairs three steps at a time, for his list was a long one that morning, and as Clare saw him she felt a comforting renewal of the confidence which women feel for the man who had piloted them through the pangs of childbirth. Boyd had not aged ; his hands were as supplely strong, his smiling eyes as penetrating as ever. The bloom of grey on his close-cropped temples made him look even cleaner and more efficient. He nodded, with quick understanding, when Clare told him of Aunt Cathie's unreasonable shyness. He smiled—" I know these old maids : trust me to be tactful ! "—as he entered the room.

Clare, as she waited, listening to the rumour of voices— Aunt Cathie's, at first staccato, and then more voluble ; the doctor's, pitched, as always, on that quiet, confident tone—stood with her mind suspended between alternations of hope and dread, between sounds that seemed too normal for seriousness and sinister silences. At last Boyd came to the door and called her in. " She'd like to see you," he said, " before I go."

Aunt Cathie's ashen cheeks were flushed with two dabs of colour ; her eyes communicated an unconfessed relief. She smiled nervously, like a young girl newly-kissed, as she spoke :

" My mind is greatly relieved, Clare. Of course the doctor's scolded me for not seeing him before "—she smiled, almost archly—" but he's quite set my mind at rest on the one point that had been worrying me. He says that there's no question of an operation . . ."

" Absolutely none," the doctor confirmed.

" . . . and as for this tiresome pain . . ."

" I'm going to send her some medicine to relieve it. Or rather, if you don't mind, Mrs. Hingston—Mrs. Wilburn, I beg your pardon—Bissell will fetch it from the surgery. What Miss Weir needs most, at the present moment, is sleep. The medicine will help that too."

" I hope," said Aunt Cathie anxiously, " there's no opiate in it ? The doctor felt very strongly about that. My father. I mean."

" Your father was quite right, Miss Weir," Boyd answered solemnly. " One of the wise old school. I shall never forget him."

He smiled, and Aunt Cathie smiled back, as at a personal compliment ; but when Clare and he had reached the landing his face changed ; its youth, its confidence left it ; it was heavy, as with the suffering of all the world. " I'm sorry, Mrs. Wilburn," he said.

" What is it ? "

" Cancer."

" Doctor ! You told her there was no question of operation ? "

" There isn't. It's inoperable. Six months ago we might have done a Halstead : removed the breast and the great pectoral muscle. But now the poor old lady's in a bad way. I could see that from the moment I set eyes on her. That cachectic . . ."

" Cach . . . ? "

" I'm sorry. Cachectic. That greyish yellowy colour which always means advanced malignant disease. She must have suffered terribly already. I haven't seen her for months, you know. Whenever I called on Mrs. Rudge, she kept out of the way. Stupidity . . . ! "

" Modesty, doctor. She was fearfully shy. If you only knew how she fought against being examined even now ! "

" It's a terrible price to pay for modesty, Mrs. Wilburn."

" Can nothing be done ? "

" Nothing whatever." He paused awkwardly. " Of course, if you would like some other opinion . . ."

" No, no. I trust you absolutely. As for the pain . . ."

" We shall relieve that, as much as we can. If it is any consolation to you to know it, I don't think it'll be very long."

" It's terrible to think that she's to die of cancer."

" Nobody dies of cancer in these days, Mrs. Wilburn ; she'll die of morphine poisoning. I suppose you'll keep her here ? She has no one else to look after her at Pen House ? "

" Not a soul in the world but me. She's a lonely woman. Of course we must keep her here. There's only one thing . . . "

" Yes ? "

" It isn't infectious, is it ? I'm thinking of Steven."

" No. Steven's all right. Don't trouble your head about him. Of course you realize that she doesn't know what's wrong with her ? I've called it simply a neglected *mastitis*, and said that it may be rather difficult to heal. Good-bye. You won't forget the medicine ? At first you'll treat it as a sleeping-draught ; but if she shows signs of acute pain you won't withhold it."

The first effect of the morphine was to make Aunt Cathie talkative.

" I don't think much of his medicine," she said ; " it's far too palatable, as the doctor always said, to be efficacious. However, I feel already that the rest is doing me good. My mind is clearer. What with poor Thirza and one thing and another I've been in a muddle for weeks. And, funnily enough, the pain's gone easier too." In this detached euphoria she began to approve of Dr. Boyd. " I must admit," she said, " that he's improved out of all recognition. He has none of the bedside manner that the doctor disliked so. You feel, when he speaks to you, that he's telling you the whole truth. I hate a doctor who hedges about his diagnosis. A doctor, I always think, should call a spade a spade. I'm delighted to find he shares your grandfather's opinion about the abuse of opiates, too."

When Steven returned from Rugby at Christmas Aunt Cathie was still in bed. For a whole week she had been agitating herself about the necessity of going back to Pen House ; but when, one afternoon, she took advantage of Clare's absence to " try her legs " she was discovered by

Ellen in a condition of dignified helplessness on the dressing room floor.

"The strain of nursing poor Thirza," she admitted, "must have taken far more out of me than I ever imagined. It's strange for *me* to be behaving like an invalid. The doctor always said that, apart from my headaches, I was as strong as a horse. The only mistake I made, Clare, was letting you bring me over here. I'd no intention of abusing your hospitality to this extent."

"My dear," Clare told her, "I'm only thankful that I managed to get hold of you. I couldn't have been happy to leave you like this at Pen House."

"I do hope that Ellen can be trusted to air everything and see that all the windows are shut when she leaves the house. I feel disgracefully lazy leaving all these details to other people. By the way, when she next goes over, I wish you'd ask her to look for a book that I left on the doctor's reading-table in the dining-room. It's *Romola*, by George Eliot. Ellen can't be expected to carry that in her head, so tell her it's a red book with gold lettering, and a little paper-knife of wood from the Mount of Olives to mark the place where I left off. There's no time so convenient for reading as convalescence."

But when the book came, Ellen had removed the paper-knife for fear of breaking it, and Aunt Cathie couldn't find her place.

"However, it's of no consequence," she said. "I may just as well begin at the beginning. I've always understood that the book was a classic, and the test of a classic, I'm told, is one's ability to read it again and again."

When the spring came in on the heels of one of the bitterest Februarys within memory, the red-bound book lay still unfinished at Aunt Cathie's bedside.

"The print is rather small for my eyes," she explained, and the paragraphs are so long that I'm ashamed to say

1 sometimes get lost in them. On the whole, I think I'd better leave it till I get back to Pen House. I shall regard it as a treat in store for me. At present I'm just enjoying the rest."

Although she was careful to explain how comfortable they made her at Uffdown, her thoughts continually swerved back on Wychbury, like tired birds flying home at sunset. Week after week she spoke of her return as though it were a matter of days, and gave Clare heart-breaking instructions about the preparations for her home-coming. " I think," she would say, " that you'd better get Ellen's brother to do some gardening by the day. Now that the evenings are lengthening out he'll work for more hours. The doctor always had early peas planted in the first week in March. You have to remember that the Pen House garden is exceptionally mild. I'm sorry to trouble you, Clare ; but when I came here I didn't imagine for one moment that I shouldn't be back in time to see to the planting myself. I must have been far more exhausted by poor Thirza than I dreamed. If I go on like this I shall end by imagining that there's really something wrong with me. However, I'm confident that Dr. Boyd would tell me if there were."

As time went on she became more and more pathetically anxious for Clare's company, and would call her to account for the hours she spent away from her, with something of the doctor's old impatience ; but when Clare came to her, as often as not the energy of that impatience had spent itself, so that she lay back on her pillows exhausted, assuring herself of Clare's presence from time to time by a lazy opening of her eyes, whose black pupils were now contracted to pin-points by the beneficent drug. And Clare, sitting silently by the window, listening to the tender courting-songs of thrush and willow-wren, would feel, as she smiled to meet Aunt Cathie's glances, an ineffable sadness which crushed, at the very moment of its birth, the joy of spring.

Death, coming nearer and nearer, quietly, like a creeping shadow . . .

If that were all ! But death is so ghastly a guise ! For now those cells gone mad were mastering the wasted tissues, rioting, proliferating in Aunt Cathie's virgin body with a strength that seemed more appropriate to generation and birth than to decay and death. And now the growth, once stony, exfoliated like a foul flower. There came a new horror of soaked dressings : blood and corruption. A nurse's work. . . . But Aunt Cathie wouldn't hear of nurses. Clare was the doctor's granddaughter : no excuse for squeamishness ! And while Clare shuddered and went pale with nausea, Aunt Cathie contemplated the evil monstrosity with a bland disinterest.

" I think it looks like closing at last," she would say. " The doctor always said I had wonderful flesh to heal."

Clare tried to close her eyes to this growing horror ; she told herself that she had been acquainted with death before. She remembered the day of her grandfather's death at Pen House ; how its suddenness had caught her, in the guise of a silence, yet scarcely checked the ecstasy with which her heart beat in the memory of Ralph's last kisses. And then, a few years later, Ralph had died. But that was in Africa, thousands of miles away. She had never pictured Ralph dying ; never, in the word's physical connotation, imagined him dead. He had gone from her like a dream. She knew that she had lost him, but never questioned how. At last the memory of that dream had almost faded. Ernest . . . That was another matter. With him, for the first time she had felt death real, and closed the eyes of her mind on horrors that imagination suggested. From too crude a realization of that tragedy her anxiety for Aunt Cathie had saved her. But now—it was almost as if some stern power were determined to make her face the facts that she had evaded—Aunt Cathie lay dying slowly before her eyes.

Sitting and watching at the windows of that sad room it seemed to her that the miracle of spring, which unfolded its beauty beneath them, was nothing but an elaborate mockery, a mirage flashed devilishly before eyes that could never possess it. She knew, now, that all the loveliness with which it had ravished her heart in youth was phantom. She knew that the only certain thing in life was death ; not the theoretical death whose mention claimed the momentary deference of a lowered voice and shadowed eyes, but the stark, monstrous, unanswerable, personal thing that soon must claim Aunt Cathie, and, only a little later in the vast scale of time, herself.

" It's merciful," she thought, as the spring evenings closed, " that, when we are young, there's some defect in our minds, which makes us incapable of realizing the meaning of what we see. Perhaps, when we're old, there'll be something else that makes us incapable of caring."

But Clare was neither young nor old ; and on her, in that terrible, unprotected moment, there descended a crushing sense of helplessness, which made her ask herself what was the good of it all, and wonder why, if this were the end, she had ever been born.

She remembered Mr. Darnay. The figure of Mr. Darnay, with his lank, red hair and prominent, emotional eyes rose out of the past to answer her. Ah, words, words, words . . .

" When I was young and religious," she thought, " death had no meaning to me, and so I had no need of religion. But now that I need religion, or something else, to make life seem significant, I'm far too old, too practical, too cynical to believe what I used to believe. A lost religion's like a dead love : you can't revive them honestly. You'd have to do it in secret, pretend to hide what you're doing from part of yourself. And that isn't playing the game. It wouldn't come off. And yet, if one's to make life possible, one *must* believe in something. Perhaps, after all, it doesn't matter so very much what . . ."

What did Aunt Cathie believe in, now that she lay there, slowly sinking toward the abyss ? Perhaps it was only ignorance of the truth that made her go on talking even now of trivial things : the sowing of peas in the south border of the kitchen-garden, her holding in Messrs. Astill's business —" my breweries," as she called them. Evidently there was some ultimate tribunal to which she referred the morality of her interest in the liquor-trade, for more than once she had returned to the subject, defining her responsibility :

" If people want alcohol, as the doctor used to say, they'll get it somehow or other ; and beer, I believe, Clare, is quite the most innocuous form of it. So if they choose to muddle their heads by drinking too much of it on Saturday night, I really don't see that *I* can be held responsible ; I honestly don't consider that anyone can put the blame on *me*."

" Of course not, dearest," Clare agreed emphatically.

It struck her suddenly : she knew Aunt Cathie's religion. Aunt Cathie still believed in the doctor. As time went by she quoted his judgments more freely than ever. Yet, curiously enough, she didn't now quote Dudley Wilburn, who used to share the hard old man's status of divinity. Never, since the moment of her arrival at Uffdown, had she mentioned Dudley's name ; and, though that seemed strange to Clare, she was thankful for it ; for if Aunt Cathie had been persistent she could not have refused to talk about him. Indeed, beneath her fantastic irrelevances, Aunt Cathie was very cunning.

One afternoon old Susan Abberley, the only visitor whom Dr. Boyd permitted, came over to visit her and left Aunt Cathie curiously disturbed and talkative by regaling her with all the gossip of the neighbourhood, including an account of Edward Willis's love-affair with the manager's wife at Mawne and the divorce between George and Eleanor Hingston that was now impending. Aunt Cathie seemed a little hurt that Clare had not kept her informed of these events, but even more alarmed at the course the world, bereft of her super-intendence, was taking. " It seems to me," she said, " that everything is changing for the worse. I am not squeamish, Clare ; the doctor always brought me up to be exceptionally broad-minded ; but the way people seem to be behaving is past my comprehension. In my days right and wrong were clearly defined, and people with any claims to decency or good-breeding respected them. But now it seems, they merely follow their inclinations. I'm not at all surprised by what has happened at Wolverbury ; after all, George Hingston's his mother's son ; but, really, I shouldn't have expected it of the Willises. They may be vulgar, but they were always *moral* people. However, it seems it's the same all the world over. Susan Abberley's cousin in London has told her things about the Socialists and the night-clubs, as they call them, that she positively can't repeat. It really looks to me as if the world were going mad. What's in the towns to-day will reach the villages to-morrow. I tremble to think of poor little Wychbury left to the mercies of a man like Mr. Pomfret."

" Which reminds me, dearest," said Clare ; " Mr. Pom-fret called here to enquire after you to-day."

" Mr. Pomfret enquired after *me ?* Well, all I say is : he must be going mad as well ! Of course he may have known that I was indisposed ; but I've never heard of him calling on any sick person who hadn't a title unless they were dying . . ."

" My dear Aunt Cathie, how can you speak of such things ? " Clare protested.

Aunt Cathie did not answer her. It seemed almost as if the dreadful word had thrown its shadow on her mind, unexpectedly, even as she spoke it. For the rest of the evening she lay quite still and quiet. only stirring to reach out in the half darkness for a dose of the medicine which she still affected to despise. When Clare was out of sight she could sometimes hear her groaning. Not even her Spartan repression of all feeling could hide the pain that twisted her features now.

" Can you do nothing more to relieve her ? " Clare asked the doctor. " Not only for her sake, but for mine ? "

" You can go on increasing the dose," he told her. " That is the trouble with morphine : it loses its effect."

" And this is what you doctors call *Euthanasia !* "

" My dear Mrs. Wilburn, we have to flatter ourselves sometimes."

" Why can't you make it stronger still ? "

" She's already taking a dose that would kill you or me."

" How long will it last, doctor ? Oh, I know you can't say."

He made a gesture of impotence : " God knows ! "

" If God knew, doctor, he'd be more merciful. Do you believe in God ? "

" I don't know what I believe in, Mrs. Wilburn."

" Neither do I."

" Suppose we call it humanity," he suggested.

" You see it at its worst, its feeblest."

" Also at its noblest. I'll tell you something curious. Do you know, I've never in my life seen an unhappy death-bed ? Pain, yes. But spiritual unhappiness never. At the very last there's always a sort of . . . clearing. It can't be quite as dreadful as we think."

" But the pain, doctor ? "

" Ah, yes . . ." He shook his head.

When Easter came she knew that she could not have Steven at Uffdown. It gave her some small satisfaction to know that he was disappointed to go to Stourford instead. Sir Joseph had arranged to take him over to the works at

Wolverbury every day. In any case, she reflected, she would only have seen him in glimpses. However much she loved him, she could not now have done him justice, for all the threads of her life seemed to be drawn in and concentrated upon that one sad room and the little, shrinking figure in the bed.

Almost before she had become aware of his arrival at Stourford Steven was gone again. It amazed her to think that time which, moment by moment, seemed to drag so heavily, was passing at all. Yet, while she stayed suspended, outside time, in a closed chamber filled and dominated by the sense of Aunt Cathie's suffering, the poignant gaiety of spring had subsided into summer's opulent drowsiness.

And still, in Aunt Cathie's body, indomitable life burned on, though now she was so weak that she seemed content to lie almost for days without speaking, sunk in nepenthal dreams. But the morphine, which set its seal upon the workings of her mind seemed powerless any longer to moderate her pain. That was a thing apart, malignant, uncontrollable, declaring itself in groans and in grimaces that seemed to have an existence independent from that of the dazed body through which they expressed themselves, even when it slept.

One evening still and breathless in late summer, Clare snatched an hour to walk with Steven above the Sling fishponds on his way back to Stourford. When she returned to Uffdown, and stole on tiptoe into Aunt Cathie's room, she was aware, even as she entered, of a strange lightening in its atmosphere. She found Aunt Cathie lying with her eyes wide open. There was a calmness in them that she had not seen before; the brows were no longer constricted, nor the mouth set with pain; the whole of her wrinkled face looked smooth and untroubled with a sweet, an almost childish innocence. When Clare came near to her she smiled faintly, and moved her hand. Clare took the hand in hers and sat down beside her. Aunt Cathie swallowed, moistened her tongue and spoke :

" You've been . . . a long time . . . away. I thought you . . . were never . . . coming . . . Sylvia."

The little fingers closed feebly on Clare's. She could not speak. With her head turned aside, she felt the cold tears tracking down her cheek. Aunt Cathie's fingers moved again, as if to reassure themselves of her presence. Clare sat there motionless, holding them, until it grew quite dark. It came so quietly, that ending, that she never knew the hour at which it came.

That night, as Aunt Cathie had prophesied, the world went mad. It was the fourth of August in the year nineteen hundred and fourteen.

# BOOK SIX

## VALLEY OF ARMAGEDDON

# THE AGE OF IRON

THAT night, when Clare stood alone in the garden at
Uffdown, dazed by the moment—so long expected and
even hoped for, yet, in its actuality, so devastating—of Aunt
Cathie's death, she heard the silence shudder and break
beneath sinister sounds. One after another, like the voices
of great liners feeling their way through fog, the syrens of
the black-country filled the sky with their howling. Others
had heard them. At the angle of the drive she saw the
shapes of Bissell and old Waldron standing and listening.
White aprons fluttered out ; the maids had joined them.
One of them suddenly caught sight of her ; their voices
were hushed. Out of respect for herself or for her sorrow,
Bissell, by right of seniority, came over and touched his cap.

"Is that you, Bissell ? What is it ? " she asked him.

"I don't rightly know, ma'am," he admitted ; "but
Waldron and me think it's likely this war that's in the papers
has broken out. It's the bulls, over Wolverbury way.
Waldron, he says, they acted like this on Mafeking night.
Well, well, if it is, I've had my fill of wars. South Africa
was good enough for me. But I reckon, from all I hear,
these Germans have been asking for a lesson, and Bobs'll
give it them, him and Kitchener, don't you have no fear.
But I'm sorry, ma'am," he added respectfully, "that they
should act like that on this sad night."

He lingered, out of politeness. They stood together on
the dewy lawn and there, in the northern darkness, the
"bulls" bayed at each other, like a pack of monstrous

bloodhounds scenting their prey, clamouring, with one voice, for the red dawn for which they hungered : the death and the culmination of the age of iron that had made them.

"Ay, there goes Mawne," said Bissell familiarly, as a nearer monster flung its echoes along the hills. "You might bet old Mr. Willis wouldn't be behindhand. They say it was the Franco-Prussian war as made him what he is. Well, ma'am, these wars they come and go, but it don't seem to make a power of difference to Wychbury. We don't take much notice of that sort of thing in these parts."

In Wychbury they prided themselves that they didn't take much notice of anything. They put up their shutters, out of habit, for Aunt Cathie's funeral. They had known Miss Weir and respected her, although she was a queer 'un. But wars . . . well, wars were a matter for soldiers and best not meddled with. They knew all about them already. They " minded " well that business in South Africa, fifteen years ago, with the dirty Boers. A few scatter-brains that ought to have known better had joined the yeomanry. Some of them, like young Squire Hingston, had left their bones there, and serve 'em right for not knowing when they were well off at home ! Others, like Mrs. Hingston's Bissell, had had more luck than they deserved, and come back with a couple of medals and a calabash pipe. No sense to talk about wars with the harvest coming along and labour scarce already. Old Parson Pomfret, he hit the nail on the head in his Sunday sermon. *Business as usual :* that was the ticket for them.

Clare heard that sermon. It was the first time that she had been to church for many months ; but, somehow, the thought of Aunt Cathie had made her want to go there —that and the fact that Steven was with her ; and, though she found it difficult to identify herself with the queer " churchy " strain he'd picked up at Rugby, she hated, just now, to lose a moment of his company.

" It is the duty of every one of us, here in Wychbury,"
said Mr. Pomfret, " to show the outside world an example
of steadiness. Under no circumstances must we lose our
heads. It is not for every one of us to shoulder a rifle in
Flanders, deeply as we may feel. Remember, my friends,
that all of us—every shopkeeper, every farmer, ay, and every
labourer, can best show his patriotism at this moment by
persevering with his daily task in the situation of life to
which it has pleased Almighty God to call him, and humbly
praying to the God of Battles for the safety of our brave
boys and their gallant allies in the sure and certain knowledge
that, come what may, He will defend the Right. And now
to God the Father, God the Son, and God the Heawly
Gheawost . . ."

Amid shuffles of relief Mrs. Pomfret, at the organ, played
the first bars of God Save the King. Later on, during the
collection, the congregation sang Kipling's *Recessional*.

Recessional . . . !

" I should love to know what they're doing at Stourford,"
said Steven, as they hurried out into the village atmosphere
of Sunday roasts. " They seem to be in the middle of it
there. Grandpapa's been on the telephone with the
Admiralty half the week. You feel that something's happening every minute. I'm lucky, aren't I ? If it had been
term-time at Rugby we shouldn't have heard a thing."

" Do you want to go over there this afternoon ? " she asked
him, a little jealously.

" Well, if you don't mind awfully, dearest," he said.

At Stourford, which turned its back on the yellowing
Worcester cornfields, they were, indeed, more nearly in
touch with reality. For Stourford looked northward to
Wolverbury and Mawne and all the black-country, where
war meant money. Already, in spite of the moratorium
and sudden food-scares, the price of Hingston's Deferred
had risen twenty per cent. on the private market. Even

Mawne, that vast concern that had seemed, a month ago, to be dying of its own inflation like a blown sheep, was on its feet again. Within two days of the declaration of war the Willises had restarted two furnaces which had been damped down in early summer.

Indeed, from the top of Pen Beacon, where Clare and Steven wandered in the peerless evenings of that entranced August, the whole wide basin of the black-country seemed to have burst into a fiery bloom which flourished as though its roots had tapped in triumphant desperation the eternal fires beneath its mine-riddled crust. " Business as usual " might be good enough for Mr. Pomfret and Wychbury. " Business as usual " was the disease from which the black-country had lain dying. " Business a good deal more than usual " was what they wanted, and what they got.

Not only such vast and complicated organisms as Mawne and Wolverbury, those iron-ribbed, iron-toothed, iron-hearted monsters that the industrial age unwittingly created for its own destruction. The mad wind out of Europe fanned humbler fires. In every ramshackle works that forged or stamped or cast or rolled or drilled or moulded metal, in all these humbler workshops, whose submerged activities Clare had discovered during her lonely perambulations of North Bromwich, the hidden flames leaped into an intenser life. No fuel like gold to keep them roaring. So the astonished Midlands gasped and clutched at the uncoffered wealth of a century rained upon them, encouraged by fate's ironical largesse to imagine that they were " doing their bit." For that was before the grim days of the New Armies. . . .

It was natural enough that Steven should want to go to Stourford. To him, at least, this war was a romantic diversion, a tale of adventure translated to the plane of everyday life. Clare had known war before and suffered by it ; but, now that Aunt Cathie had gone, there was only one love through which she could be wounded, and Steven, thank heaven, was too young for wars to touch—so young, so eager, that, in her maternal ruthlessness, she smiled at his excitement, as though the spectacle which diverted him were a nursery battle of tin soldiers rather than that dread reality of blood and iron. And when he came back from Stourford with a full equipment of maps and flags on pins with which to mark the movements of the iron-grey wave, she thought not of the shattered forts of Liège and Namur, the flames of Louvain, the blood-soaked pit-mounds of Mons, but of days at Uffdown, distant as a dream, when Aunt Cathie had moved her flags across the symbolic yellow of the Orange Free State.

In those days victory had been qualified by fear. Now, as the sinister line bent and sagged southward, no fear clutched at her heart. She had lost so much that there was only one more thing to lose, and that, thank heaven, was safely by her side.

When the retreating line of Union Jacks and tricolours gave their jump forward from the Marne to the Aisne, Steven returned to Rugby. She left the big map hanging on the wall in his bedroom. The tiny pennants stayed, appropriately, where they were. For herself she had no interest in them any more. In her heart there was an emptiness where Aunt Cathie and Steven had been, and nothing, for the moment, seemed to fill it.

For Wychbury, as Bissell had suggested, and, even more than Wychbury, Uffdown, was curiously isolated from the distracted world. The hospital trains, roaring northward from the Channel ports to North Bromwich, discharged no maimed convoys on the Wychbury platform. Two months had passed before Clare had seen a single wounded man. For all she knew of its actuality the great war might have been raging on the South African veld. Yet gradually, imperceptibly, as her own hurt healed, the consciousness of forty million souls made potent by intense emotion broke through the barriers that surrounded her and swept her along with it.

A single incident forcibly confirmed her enlightenment. One night, as she lay in bed, half reading, half thinking of Steven, her ears became aware of an unusual sound. At first she thought it was only the wind-swept rumour of one of the great munition trains that threaded the darkness with fire, roaring southward, like one great shell, with their deadly freight. Night after night she heard them passing, launched from the furnaces of their origin to the Flanders front. But this train was coming over the hills from eastward, gradually growing louder, until its engines were throbbing and drumming overhead. It seemed to hover there in the blackness, threatening, before it died away ; and a little later, one after another, like the bouncing of enormous metal spheres, she heard the echoes of five monstrous detonations.

" One of them Zepps," Bissel excitedly informed her next morning. " I reckon he must have steered by the furnaces at Mawne. A pretty old mess they say he's made there, and then he dumped the stuff that he'd got left at Stourford. They say there's a hole in the park you could put a house in."

" There's nobody hurt at Stourford ? " she asked anxiously.

" That I can't say for certain, ma'am. Nobody that I've spoke to seems to know the rights of it. But, sure enough, they're dirty old things, ma'am. You could hear him coming over like a darned bum-beetle."

That morning, as of duty bound, Clare hurried over to Stourford. The hole, which you could put a house in, gaped in the park a hundred yards from the front door steps. Lady Hingston was contemplating it triumphantly when she arrived. She seemed to consider it as a signal compliment to the importance of Stourford as if it had been a telegram from the Kaiser himself.

" Of course it was deliberate," she maintained. " The Germans realize that Wolverbury's a thorn in their side. Five hundred tons of shells in a single month go from our works. They probably knew, as well, that we intend to turn Stourford into a hospital."

Both she and Vivien wore the blue uniform of officers in the V.A.D. It suited Lady Hingston to perfection ; its severity emphasized her neatness, her hardness, her fire. In this atmosphere of militarism she had found, at last, the proper sphere for her uncompromising hatreds. Never had her personality seemed more keenly, more vividly hawklike, or to tell truth, more clean in its efficiency. Like a strong-winged peregrine she wheeled and hovered above the field of battle, an incarnation of all that was most steely and ruthless in the spirit of Wolverbury.

The excitements of her new pastime seemed to fill her with an unusual brisk, good humour, a comradeship of sisters-in-arms, a battlefield freemasonry that abolished, in a single glance, all the differences that had ever lain between them. She swept Clare in to luncheon with her : " You won't get much to eat," she warned her cheerfully. " We consider it our duty to set an example of economy. We have to do our bit in little things, you know. If the war lasts as long as Kitchener thinks, we may all go short of food before we've finished. We have to teach our people the meaning of sacrifice. Isn't that so, general ? "

The general, a fragile, weak-kneed old gentleman with three rows of ribbons, who had dashed down from the War Office to Wolverbury on a visit of inspection, agreed. " If there were more like you, Lady Hingston ! " he sighed, as he rolled the admirable Stourford Chablis round his tongue.

Suddenly Lady Hingston unveiled the cause of her good humours.

" I want you, Clare, to let me have Pen House for some of my Belgian refugees : a very superior family of seven.

The place is empty, so it may just as well be used. It's providential that you came over this morning: I was going to write to you. I'll take you round to see them this afternoon."

The car whirled Clare back through the lanes towards Wychbury. At her side Lady Hingston kept up the clatter of a machine-gun: " My Belgians, my wounded officers, my V.A.D.s, my canteens." Clare only awaited the moment when she would speak of " my war." And that, she thought, wouldn't be as inappropriate as one might think. Already last night's visitor had found its place in the proprietary lists as " our Zeppelin." The car stopped with a shudder in front of a red-brick cottage, where, presently, six bewildered Belgians, including a melancholy gentleman with a Leopoldine beard, stood struggling in the barbed-wire entanglements of Lady Hingston's French: " *Ma belle-fille vous a tres gentillement offert une maison, n'est ce-pas? C'est du propre !* "

The bearded gentleman bowed confused acknowledgments: " *Pardon? C'est du propre?* " he repeated.

" *Oui, du propre.*"

He found it difficult to understand why the loan of a house should be considered a dirty trick, not realizing that his benefactress had merely meant to imply that the house was Clare's own.

" You see," Lady Hingston confided in an undertone, " these people are Walloons; they only speak Flemish, probably; that is the reason why they're rather slow in understanding my French. Why should he gape at the word ' *propre* '? That isn't complicated? I never have to repeat a word with Marguerite." She could not resist the opportunity of showing off her captives and her idioms. *Ce pauvre, monsieur, a vu son propre frère mourir ventre à terre avec un coup de baionette Boche. C'est épatant, n'est-ce-pas. Sale cochon !* " And now, Clare," she continued,

" you had better dash back to Stourford for tea. Probably you'll see George."

They left the melancholy father in a state of benevolent mystification. " *Courir ventre à terre,*" he could have understood. It was true that he had seen his brother killed with a bayonet thrust ; but " *épatant* "—there was nothing particularly splendid about it ; and as for calling the poor martyr a dirty pig . . . !

Clare, for her part, was almost as mystified. The prospect of meeting George had never before been held out to her as an attraction ; but when they reached Stourford she soon realized why he had become one in his mother's eyes ; for George, although he still devoted himself, by special arrangement of the War Office, to the works at Wolverbury, appeared on the steps in the uniform of a Territorial captain. For the creation of a " war atmosphere " it was desirable that as many uniforms as possible should be seen in the streets. No uniform, of course, could ever have made George Hingston look a soldier ; but, even so, the associations of khaki gave to his mean figure an air of gallantry. It was flattering to feel that there was at least one soldier in the family.

Clare had not seen him since the day of little Harold's funeral at Wolverbury. Naturally, bearing in mind the painful history of his matrimonial difficulties, she carefully avoided all references to Eleanor. It amazed her to hear Lady Hingston enquiring how poor Eleanor was ; but a whisper from Vivien informed her that Eleanor had re-established her credit at Stourford by losing two brothers, regular soldiers, in the hammering of Le Cateau.

" Mother feels strongly," Vivien told her, " that at a time like this there's no place in life for domestic differences. It would be too terrible if George divorced her just now when he's gone into uniform, so we're all of us pretending that there was nothing wrong between them. You know that

the Mawne scandal has blown over as well ?   Yes, Edward
Willis has enlisted in the Royal Fusiliers."

Lady Hingston pricked up her ears.  " What was that,
Vivien ? "

" I was telling Clare that Edward Willis has enlisted as
a common soldier, mother."

" A common soldier !  I do wish, Vivien, you wouldn't
make use of a term like that.   There are *no* common soldiers
nowadays.   The time for social differences is past, and anyone who is tactless enough to remember them is going to
prejudice recruiting.   As I was telling Lord Alfred Powys
yesterday, we're all in the same boat together.   It'll be time
enough to think about things like that when we've won the
war.   The more we concentrate now, the sooner it'll be
over."

Before the afternoon was finished she had swept Clare
away into the rose-garden and lectured her on her duties
to herself, the family and the nation.   " I hope," she insisted, " that you've made all the men who work at Uffdown
register under Lord Derby's scheme ?   I was shocked, the
other day, to see Bissell going about without a badge.   It is
up to people in our class to show an example through our
servants.   *Noblesse oblige*, as I was saying to the Lord-
Lieutenant.   I think you should teach them to practise
economy too.   With all the money the country's spending
it's quite possible, in the near future, that wages may be
reduced.   And temperance.   You might let them know that
the King himself has decided to go without his glass of beer.
Equality of sacrifice : that is the point you must make them
realize.   My husband, although I say it, is an example to
everyone.   He has more energy than George and all the
younger men put together.   Contracts are coming in so fast
that he's scarcely time to sign them.   I only hope the
Government will have the decency to recognize his services.
As the General was saying at lunch to-day—I don't know if

you heard him ?—' If there's one man in England of whom it can be said that he's winning the war, that man is Sir Joseph Hingston ! ' When high officials from the War Office talk like that there must be something in it."

Clare assented ; yet, when she came to think of it, the General didn't seem to have committed himself very deeply.

" But now, Clare," Lady Hingston continued, " I feel it my duty to talk to you about yourself. I know that we have been out of sympathy for some time. That's all forgiven and forgotten, isn't it ? I know too, that, like many other people whom I won't mention, you've been going through a hard and troublesome time. Of course I realize that you were devoted to Miss Weir, and that you'll take some months to get over losing her. But a time like this, when there's so much to be done, is not one in which to give way to grief. You're young, Clare ; and when people so much older than yourself are throwing every ounce of their weight into the war, you have no right—I'll put it as strongly as that—to be self-centred. So now that we're fitting up the hospital here, I feel that you have an opportunity of falling in beside us. The County Director has authorized forty beds. I stipulated that our patients should be officers, so that there's no reason to fear anything unpleasant about them, though I'm sorry to say that at first we shall only have lightly wounded cases. You've no idea how the work will take you out of yourself."

" Of course I am ready to do whatever I can," Clare assured her.

" Well, then, that's settled," said Lady Hingston triumphantly. " In the meantime you'd better see that those poor Belgians get comfortably into Pen House. There's no one who can speak French to them but myself, and heaven only knows I haven't time for everything."

## II

### WOLVERBURY

A FORTNIGHT later the Stourford Auxiliary Hospital for Officers was opened. Like a wisp of straw Clare found herself sucked into the current. Confused, at first, and a little disorientated by the division of her life between Uffdown and Stourford, she soon discovered herself to be bobbing along with the others on a stream that was flowing heaven knew where, but which offered her, at least, the consolation of knowing that all her fellow-voyagers knew and cared as little about their destination as she did.

She began to see wounds objectively. At first she had *felt* them, every one, as a stab, a shiver in the back of her own thighs. In a little while the smell of antiseptics, the sight of blood-stained dressings, the sudden, unsentimental hospital companionships became as much a part of her life's routine as ever Uffdown had been. The convoys of wounded officers came and went. They seemed to her, most of them, astonishingly young. To them, at least, the spacious ways of Stourford were heaven. Within its wards these damaged men in khaki, whose talk was decorated with the new idiom of the trenches, expanded into a free, deliberate gaiety that made the war which had maimed them seem, at this comfortable distance, like a childish adventure.

They had no use, these boys, for the high-sounding abstractions that rolled with such righteous conviction from Lady Hingston's tongue. They didn't talk about equality of sacrifice or ordeal by battle. And if they brought with them to Stourford the humour of the trenches, they left the trenches' horror and heroism behind them as unpleasant memories which, even when a wound stabbed suddenly, it was their business to forget. Clare did not know the dark abysses that opened to them in their dreams, the fears, the hauntings, so desperately repressed.   So simple they seemed, so jolly, so patient, so companionable, so unconscious of any honour in their wounds or any credit in themselves, that, little by little, most of the vague horror that the word " war " had suggested to Clare since the nightmare of South Africa vanished from her mind, until, at last, the state of war in which the world was living began to seem as normal to her as if she had never known the meaning of peace.

Poor Lady Hingston shed her heroics less easily.   In its early stages she had been so convinced that the war was her personal affair, that she, through Wolverbury, was winning it with every shell and howitzer which left the works, with every labourer on the estate whom she had compelled to enlist, that the very pit which the Zeppelin had bombed into the park was a certificate of patriotism, that she still found it difficult not to be intense.

" The thing that shocks me in ' my ' officers," she complained, " is their lack of seriousness.   This morning Captain Blake was poking fun at his divisional general.   I'm sure they treat their superiors very differently in Germany. War is a serious matter, and should be treated as such."

" You ought to have been born a Prussian, mother," Vivien suggested.

" What ?   I . . . a Prussian !   How *can* you say a thing like that, Vivien, even in joke ?   Prussianism, as you know perfectly well, is the very thing above all others that we're out to destroy."

The young men joked about her militarisms more freely than Vivien ;   and yet, Clare noticed, they all respected her, realizing, perhaps, that she was prepared to sacrifice herself to the rigidity of discipline that she imposed on them ; knowing that, in a time like this, she was a woman to be proud of ;   admiring her frankness, her energy, her generous integrity, and, over and above all these, a certain quality that, whether it were typically Prussian or typically English (and

it was both) might fairly be summed up in the word aristocracy—the last in the language that Clare, or anyone else,
would ever have dreamed of applying to anything connected
with Stourford !

And still the war dragged on.   If Clare had not thrown in
her lot with Stourford's, she realized now that she would
have been utterly isolated from all the life with which she
was familiar.   Of all the men who had worked at Uffdown
only old Waldron was left.   In the fields round Wychbury
breeched and gaitered women led the horses to plough and
harrow.   Mr. Pomfret pursued his social avocations with
a brigade of cavalry in Ireland.   The submerged and vaguely
tragic figure of Edward Willis came to the surface and sank
away again somewhere in tropical Africa.   Even Dudley
Wilburn, his threatened bankruptcy bridged and salved by
the moratorium, had been seen in khaki, attached, in a legal
capacity, to the Southern Command.

The shortage of officers declared itself in the change of
types that filled the beds at Stourford and the removal of
the exemption that had allowed George Hingston to continue
his work at Wolverbury.   A healthier, more human George
appeared at intervals on leave from an intensive course of
gunnery on Salisbury Plain.   The hopes, the ardours of
nineteen-fifteen relapsed, of very inanition, into a sort of
dogged automatism.   People no longer speculated when the
war would end.   There seemed to be no reason why it
should ever end at all.

And, if it never ended, what about Steven ?

Steven was now seventeen, and still at Rugby.   In another
year, if still the war went on, he too must be sucked, automatically, into the vacuum of destruction, and all the sooner
by reason of his training in the Officers' Training Corps at
school.   It seemed incredible ; yet now the officers whom
the central hospital dumped on Stourford were many of
them little older than he.   And now that beds were scarce,

the cases that came to Stourford were no longer gay convalescents but pitiful creatures torn and shattered by missiles of an increasing, devilish ingenuity. They were the lucky ones; the mutilated dead Clare never saw; but, in each convoy of ravaged youth, her imagination pictured, beneath swathed bandages, the limbs, the face of Steven, and her heart sickened not with pity but with fear.

Now, week after week, he bombarded her with impatient letters. Why did she keep him kicking his heels at Rugby, passive and useless, when he might be " doing his bit " in the workshops of Wolverbury ? He had always wanted to go to Wolverbury in any case, and this was the time, above all others, in which he might make himself useful.

Because, she told herself, at Rugby he was safe. But Rugby would not be safe for very much longer. If he stayed there the net might close about him. At Wolverbury, performing " essential services," and under the personal protection of Sir Joseph, he might spin out the duration of the war, as, up to a point, his Uncle George had done. The end, alas ! must be the same ; for now, in the spring of nineteen-sixteen, George had joined his battery in Flanders. Afraid of leaving things any longer to chance, she took the worn Sir Joseph into her confidence.

" Of course you'd better let him come to Wolverbury," Sir Joseph told her. " To begin with, he'll be happier and less restless there. We shall work him hard. Although we mustn't talk about such things, I've reason to believe that there'll be a big offensive this summer. The odds are we shall smash the German line, and when once that's done your anxiety will be over. But, even if it came to the worst, I think I have enough influence to keep him at home. I didn't keep George ? Well, that was George's fault. Poor George has never got over that business of Eleanor's. He had a feeling of humiliation in staying in Wolverbury, and when they asked for him I think he jumped at the chance of leaving. But the very fact that George is in France will strengthen our hand if they want Steven. Of course one can't be sure ; but the fact remains that the War Office owe me a little consideration, and Steven, when all's said and done, is the only heir I have after George."

So Steven left Rugby, and Clare knew not only the relief of feeling that he was safer at Wolverbury, but the joy of having him with her again. It was even thrilling to feel, when they met, that he at Wolverbury and she at Stourford were active units in the same monstrous machine. Beneath the pressure of work and the incalculable menace of separation that still hung over them, the hours they snatched together at Uffdown were precious as the stolen meetings of lovers.

The new Steven, who came home to her from Wolverbury with the pallor of the machine-shops on his cheeks, hands made callous by habitual contact with hard metals, and clothes to which there clung a faint odour of steel and oil, was very different from the passionate child who, less than three years before, had scrambled away from her over the outhouse roof at Alvaston. He had grown tall and lanky, so tall that his shoulders stooped of their own weight and in spite of her corrections. His colour had lost a little of its freshness, for the poor war-food had denied his body support when most it was needed ; and the peculiar droop of his shoulders gave his attitude a curious resemblance to that of George. Physically he was still a Hingston, but Ralph Hingston no longer. Now it was only in his eyes and in his voice that Ralph came back to her : never in the movements of his body or mind. For, strange though it seemed, this loose-limbed youth was older in every way than Ralph had ever been. Ralph, till the day of his death, had been a child, and Clare had loved him for it ; this son of hers was a man before his time.

" Perhaps," she thought, " it is the hardness of these

war-years that has aged him ; perhaps the whole human race is growing older with experience. Though I'm his mother, I sometimes feel as if he were the parent and I the child. When I was seventeen I was a positive baby beside him."

He took his work at Wolverbury with tremendous seriousness. All the Hingston passion for machinery which had skipped a generation in Ralph re-appeared more strongly than ever in him. The neatness, the efficiency of each new mechanical triumph enchanted him. His room at Uffdown was littered with drawings of ideas that came to him ; even when Clare and he were together his mind withdrew itself into a world of calculated mechanical exactitudes where she could not follow him ; and when she played to him, in the spring evenings, as she had always done ever since he was a child, the music that he demanded of her was usually Bach, whom he loved not, as she did, for his exalted beauty, but for the mathematical ingenuity of his counterpoint. She loved him in these days perhaps more desperately than ever, but the actual points of contact between them were limited to their common passion for Uffdown and the instinctive devotion of mother and child. At times she wondered if he were not a little inhuman. But he was Steven, and therefore that was impossible.

Paradoxically, the only hereditary feature that he seemed to have derived from her was one which she herself had irrevocably lost : her instinct for religion. And there again, try as she might, she could not follow him ; for the religion of her youth, which the vanished Miss Boldmere and Mr. Darnay had taught her, had been essentially an emotional state. If she had ever submitted it to reason, the inherited scepticism of the Weirs would certainly have shaken it. But Steven's religion, like everything else that engrossed him, was curiously deficient in emotion. Given the premises, which his reason seemed incapable of questioning, his processes of thought became as rational as a problem of chess. His bookshelves were crowded with volumes of religious history; his mind concerned with academic arguments in which the authority of the fathers, of whom Clare had never heard, was of more consequence, because more complicated, than that of the gospels. He called himself an Anglo-Catholic. As luck would have it, Mr. Pomfret's *locum tenens* at Wychbury was of the same doctrinal persuasions—even in religious matters one couldn't be too particular in war-time—and Steven, surrendering to an influence that flattered his pre-conceived ideas, applied his Hingston obstinacy to religious matters, completely satisfied that the Great Schism was more important than the Great War.

She could not follow him; but as long as he continued to love her, she felt she could bear his disappointment in her lack of fervour. Rather than lose his company she joined him in his religious observances, trailing down with him to Wychbury at unconscionable hours, prepared, most willingly, to grant him the Great Schism as long as the Great War should leave him unscathed. She was even content to see him thin and hollow-eyed, in the hope that, if Sir Joseph's protection failed him, his frail and over-grown physique might save him from the recruiting officer's hands.

For the present, at any rate, he seemed safe; but there were evil moments. One Sunday in May she found him uneasily preoccupied with the day's casualty list. She dared not ask him what was wrong, but later, as they were walking home from church, he unbosomed himself.

"I got a bit of a shock this morning, mum," he told her. "Two fellows that I knew quite well at Rugby have been killed and another wounded. The chap that's wounded was in my house. Last year he used to sleep in the next bed to me. He was practically the same age as I am. It's odd how a thing like that'll set you thinking."

" Thinking of what, Steven ? " she asked him timidly.

" Thinking of one's own position and all that."

" My dear, your position's clear enough, surely ? Nobody can say you aren't doing your duty at Wolverbury, working yourself to death in the way you do."

" Oh, I work hard enough. My conscience is clear about that. But it's so beastly *safe*, mum. There isn't even a Zepp to bomb us nowadays. I'm just as safe at Wolverbury as if there weren't a war at all. While these poor chaps, and that fellow Sanders especially . . . Oh, I don't know . . ."

" It isn't your business to know, Steven," she maintained. " It's not for you to decide what kind of service you're to perform. It isn't for you to judge where you're most useful. If they want you to stay at Wolverbury you must stay there. If they want you to fight they'll tell you soon enough. That is the meaning of discipline."

" Oh yes, that's all very well," he answered gloomily, " but if you've got a conscience you can't help hearing it. It isn't only those Rugby fellows I'm thinking of. There was a chap who used to work beside me in the machine-shop, a cheerful little beggar with red hair named Harris. He used to come in pert as a robin every morning from Dulston. He'd got a wife and three kids as well. A first-rate mechanic, mind you, worth half a dozen of me. Well, yesterday morning he didn't turn up as usual. I asked the foreman about him, and he told me the poor little devil had got his papers. He had to go at a moment's notice, the same as the rest of them. It's not fair, mum."

" If you asked your grandfather, I'm sure he could get him back."

" Grandpapa can't fight for every workman who's called up. I'm not suggesting that they hadn't a right to call him ; they're ' combing out,' as they call it, all the time. But what I know is wrong is that they didn't comb me first. I'm ten years younger than him. I haven't got a wife and three kids in Dulston."

" You have a mother, darling," she reminded him.

" Oh, how illogical you are, mum ! You're not dependent on me."

" Would you feel happier," she asked him, " if we got this man Harris—was that the name ?—back ? "

" I don't know that I should. There are dozens of others. They're preparing for this break-through that everyone's talking about. It isn't particularly Harris that worries me. It's the whole principle. The more I think about it, the more rotten I feel. And I've got to face it."

A far cry floated over the moving meadows, mockingly sweet above the swaying, sorrel-rusted grasses.

" Listen . . . the cuckoo, Steven darling ! " she said.

" That only makes it worse ; I wish the brute would shut up," he told her.

They walked on in silence. She knew that it was no good arguing with him in his present, obstinate mood. That evening when he had gone to bed dog-tired, she telephoned to Sir Joseph at Stourford.

" I want to speak to you about a man named Harris, a work-mate of Steven's. He's just been called up, and Steven's horribly upset about it. I wish to goodness you could get him back."

" They go in batches," the weary voice of Sir Joseph answered her. " We haven't time to protest in individual cases ; it's quite mechanical ; as long as our own numbers are kept up, we've no cause to grumble and the recruiting authorities resent our interference."

" So Steven said. This man worked next to him. He lives at Dulston and has a wife and three children. Steven's most frightfully disturbed about him."

" Steven's all right," the tired voice answered her. " He

has no reason to worry. I can promise you he's perfectly safe."

"My dear, it isn't that. It's his wretched conscience. He feels he ought to have gone in the other man's place."

"That's sheer stupidity. You ought to tell him so."

"Tell him? You ought to know Steven! When once he gets an idea like that into his head . . ."

Silence. And then: "What did you say the man's name was?"

"Harris. He works in the machine-shops. Number four, I think."

"Very good. I've made a note. I'll see what can be done. Good night, Clare."

Ten days later Steven informed her that Harris had returned to work.

"I hope that's set your mind at rest, darling," she said.

He looked at her suspiciously. "I believe you got on to grandpapa about him."

"What does that matter, as long as he's back again?"

"It doesn't solve the problem, mum. As a matter of fact it makes it rather worse. We have no right to decide who shall be killed and who shan't be killed. It only means that some other poor devil has had to go instead of him. It may be someone who can be spared less easily than Harris. You may have made it more unjust than ever."

"Oh, Steven, you're perverse. Will nothing satisfy you?"

"Mum, I can't bear injustice."

"But, darling, isn't the whole war horribly unjust? You can't put an end to injustice without stopping the war. Do, do be reasonable!"

"We have no right to be partners in an injustice. You can't get away from it, mum, I ought to have gone."

"And what about *me*?" she cried. "Mustn't I be considered?"

He smiled solemnly and kissed her. He was old.
incredibly old. He left her cry unanswered. "I'm afraid
I can't make you see the point," he said.

Three weeks later, with July, the Somme offensive
opened. That evening George Hingston was blown to
atoms beside his gun.

## III

### PEDWORTH

*He that killeth with the sword must be killed with the sword*

. . . At Wolverbury, although the Union Jack above the
office buildings was half-masted, the black smoke-pennons
flew from the chimney-stacks as bravely as ever ; the furnaces
breathed their monstrous sighs, the dynamos hummed, the
great mills went on rolling ; in the machine-shops wheels
spun and belting writhed incessantly. By night as by day,
with never a break between the eight-hour shifts, the six
tall furnace towers, like gigantic hearts, pumped molten
metal into the last capillaries of these works that nourished
the Flanders front with steel and Stourford with gold. It
needed more than the death of a Hingston to stay their
functioning, to check the gigantic inertia, to break a rhythm
which, once established, seemed as little amenable to human
interference as the war itself.

In those days, indeed, a universal fortitude was needed.
Up till that moment the Midlands had been gorged with
gold. Now, when the North Bromwich City battalions hung
like torn rags upon the barbed wire of the Somme, they knew,
for the first time, the taste of their own iron, the scorching
of their own fires. Those black days found them subdued,
bewildered, and rather pitiful.

At Stourford they took their blow with an admirable
fortitude. It was as much as they could do to cope with

the flood of human wreckage that the Somme hurled back on them. When Mr. Parker, of his own initiative, hauled down the flag on the central tower to half-mast, it was Lady Hingston who, with a quite unusual consideration for his feelings, ordered him to run it up again.

"I don't want my officers to be depressed," she said. "I appreciate your sympathy for us, Parker, but it is Sir Joseph's wish that everything shall go on here just the same." It was a new materialization of the dead tag—*Business as usual*.

"I think," she told Vivien, "that we had better ask Eleanor to come over and stay with us for a bit and bring Enid with her." But Eleanor, the proud, cold Eleanor, refused them. They didn't realize, in the absorption of their own grief, that the man for whom George would have divorced her, lay buried within a mile of George's broken battery. "Well, she must go her own way, I suppose," said Lady Hingston, regretfully.

Through all those devastating days Clare found her mother-in-law curiously mild and sweet. Although she went about her hospital work as efficiently and vigorously as ever, the hardness of Lady Hingston's face was softened by a gentle transparency, a blandness which resembled that which may be seen in the faces of convalescents ; and when Sir Joseph came home from Wolverbury at night she treated him no longer merely as the mouthpiece of her own dominant personality, but as a human being whose suffering might be mitigated by the consciousness of her own. At evening time, when Clare saw Sir Joseph walking arm-in-arm with Lady Hingston through the rose-garden, she felt so sorry for him that she could have cried ; for George and he, in their inarticulate way, had understood each other, and this was an emergency that could not be met by the signing of a cheque.

Yet, though her heart bled for the Stourford people—poor

George had always been far too unreal for her to be sorry for him—it was the reaction of George's death on Steven that more nearly concerned her.

On the first evening he had told her : " Uncle George is killed." From that moment onward he had not uttered another word about it ; but from his face, so dour and dark and pre-occupied, she knew that he was pondering this or some other dangerous thing in secret. At times this sinister silence became intolerable. Fearing to take it seriously she made a joke of it and offered him a penny for his thoughts.

He shook his head. " I'm not thinking of anything in particular, mum," he said.

" I want to know about it all the same," she told him. " You never speak a word to me in these days. There must be something wrong with you."

He answered almost sullenly : " You needn't worry about *me*. I'm all right."

" I shall ask Dr. Boyd to see you next Sunday," she said.

" Oh, don't be silly, mum. I tell you I'm all right. I wish to goodness you'd leave me alone."

" My darling, I have eyes to see for myself. You're just tired out. I know you've been working yourself to death."

" I'm not working harder than anybody else at Wolverbury ; don't mention my work and death in the same sentence ; Wolverbury's a rotten, cushy job compared with anything they're doing in the trenches."

" Oh, Steven, will you never get that bee out of your bonnet ? "

He turned away and buried himself in the evening paper ; but when the autumn came she knew that the hidden thing in his mind was what she had feared.

" Do you realize, mum," he said, " that I shall be eighteen next week ? "

" Of course I do, my child ; I've reason to remember it."

" I've written to the Head and asked him to recommend me for a commission."

" Oh, Steven, Steven, are you determined to kill me ? "

" Mother, you have no right to put it like that. You've made me ashamed of myself for long enough as it is. For heaven's sake do try to play the game."

" The game . . . ! " It was no time for juggling with words. She hardened herself.

" If you've done that," she said, " I shall get your grand-father to stop it."

He turned on her fiercely : " You make me hate you, mother ! "

" I can't help that," she answered.

" Oh, do be reasonable ! "

" When you're at church this evening I shall go to Stourford."

" Then I shall come with you."

" It won't make any difference. I know what your grand-father thinks already."

" If I enlist under another name you won't be able to stop me. They're only too glad to get fellows of my age," he threatened.

" You've made such a wreck of yourself already that they won't accept you. But, anyway, your grandfather will stop it. You don't seem to realize that now George is gone, he's only you left."

" Oh, that rubbish ! His twopenny-ha'penny title ? Things like that don't count in these days."

But things like that did count. Within a fortnight the application which Steven had sent from Wolverbury was returned to him. She saw him open the long buff envelope at the breakfast table. He took out the official letter, then flushed and crumpled it, and threw it in the fire and left the room. She saw no more of him for the rest of the day ;

but, even though she knew she had wounded him, her heart was triumphant.

" You'd better leave it all to me," Sir Joseph told her ; " for another year or so, you'll have no reason to worry."

" And in another year," she thought, " this nightmare will be over." Everybody, including Sir Joseph, told her so. The Germans were retiring on the Hindenburg line. In April, when the Uffdown meadows were rich with cowslips and snowy blackthorn blossom drifted into the hill combes, America came in. The banners of that spring swept on to victory. Only in Russia the grip of winter tightened.

It seemed that time, the ally on whom she had most counted, was failing her. With summer the pressure of the war grew more strangling than ever. She tried to lose herself in the activities of Stourford. She had a feeling that by her own infinitesimal expenditure of energy she was bringing the end perhaps a little nearer ; but when, each Saturday, she returned to Uffdown and to the estranged, pre-occupied, overwrought face of Steven, she realized that each of these visits was a milestone bringing her not to the end of terror, but toward its true beginning.

" My year is out. Now you can't stop me, thank God ! " he told her triumphantly.

At least it was still worth trying ; but now it seemed as if her one hope, Sir Joseph, had abandoned her.

" I've talked it over with Steven," he said, " and the boy's set on it. He's brooded over the matter so long that it's become a mania. There's a streak of obstinacy in him that reminds me of poor Ralph. It seems to be mixed up in his mind with religion—though where he gets that from, goodness only knows. Of course he's young and more imaginative than most of us, which makes him feel the humiliation of not being in uniform, though he wouldn't confess it. On the whole I think we'd better let him take his commission. That doesn't imply any immediate danger

They don't send out untrained officers as they used to, so I think you can safely count on five or six months in England."

" And then ? " Clare asked.

" And then . . . Why, then we shall have to see what we can do. I've no doubt at all I can get him a staff billet that'll give him the satisfaction of feeling he's ' in it ' without much of the danger. You realize, my dear Clare, that I'm as deeply interested as you are. The last of my name. Not that the name's of much consequence as far as I'm concerned ; but his grandmother feels more strongly about these things than I do, and she agrees that we must do everything in our power to . . . to . . ."

Sir Joseph hesitated ; it was his habit to express himself in acts and figures rather than in words ; except at board-meetings, when his speech was typed out for him by his secretary. However, if Lady Hingston agreed, there was no more to be said about it.

" I've been thinking," said Clare, " that with his experience of engineering Steven might go to Woolwich. If he went there the training would last longer, wouldn't it ? "

Sir Joseph shook his head. " As far as that goes his plans are all cut and dried already. I could have got him a commission in the Greys or the Royals ; but he wants to join the Worcesters."

" An infantry regiment ? He never said a word about it. That's too dreadful ! "

" Well, I, for one," said Sir Joseph pontifically, " am all for territorial patriotism. As far as that goes I'm with him. But it seems that that man Harris, whom we talked about last year, is in the Worcesters, and Steven wants to join him."

" He never told me that Harris had been called up again."

" Didn't he ? The boy's extraordinarily secretive." He took Clare's hand and patted it absent-mindedly. " Cheer up, my dear, it won't be nearly as bad as you imagine. Steven'll be happier in khaki, and you'll be happier too."

Indeed, he was right. Together with his oiled Wolverbury overalls, Steven seemed to have shed the heaviness that had oppressed them both ever since he left Rugby. During his last two days at Uffdown during which he was accustoming himself to the feeling of uniform before joining the third line battalion of the Worcesters at Crown Hill he was so full of gaiety and affection that she scarcely knew him. His bowed shoulders straightened themselves, his dull eyes brightened ; his likeness to George and to his grandfather gave place to his old, long-treasured resemblance to Ralph, which, though she rejoiced in it, Clare found a little sinister, remembering the days when she and Ralph walked together through the fields at Uffdown on the eve of his sailing for South Africa. In these walks with Steven there was the same perilous, high-pitched gaiety, the same ominous significance in chance words and little things. She tried to match his happiness, his adventurous excitement ; but all the time her heart was crying against the injustice with which fate had deployed against her love the hate and anger of two wars.

" As soon as you are settled in at Plymouth," she told him, " I shall join you."

" I don't know if they'll like it, mum," he demurred, with a schoolboy's anxiety to insist on his own manliness " and I'm sure everybody'll miss you most terribly at Stourford."

" You sound as if you don't want me to come, Steven ? "

" Oh, mum, don't be so foolish ! Of course I want you. Only, now that Auntie Vivien's in France, there's nobody in the family there but grandmama."

" Whether they want me or not, darling, I shall come to you."

A week later she had made her arrangements to join him at Crown Hill. An hour before the train left Wychbury a telegram stopped her; he was leaving Crown Hill that evening for an Officers' School of Instruction at Pedworth on Salisbury Plain. " But I shall go there, just the same," she decided; for now each moment seemed more precious than ever.

It was late in the evening, after a villainous cross-country journey, when the train of the little military railway deposited her on the Pedworth platform. It seemed that she was the only woman and the only civilian aboard it; the carriages were crammed with men and officers travelling on pass, returning from leave or joining their third-line units. As the train crawled into the station they shouldered their equipment and swarmed out over the platform like a football crowd. The air was dank and smelt of smouldering incinerators, the darkness almost complete; for the station lamps were bleared with paint as a precaution against aerial attacks; on all the enormous length of platform no porter could be seen.

Thanking her stars that she had travelled light, she picked up her dressing-case and began to drag it towards the exit. Was ever a platform of such fantastic length, or night-black downland so bleak and desolate as this? She paused, exhausted, and dumped her baggage on the cinders. The station buildings seemed distant enough in themselves; beyond them there was no other sign of life.

" I shall probably have to sleep in a waiting-room," she thought. " If I had stayed until to-morrow Steven would have met me. I've only my silly self to thank for this ! "

As she stood panting she heard a rapid step on the cinders behind her. A tall figure in a trench-coat loomed out of the dank air and abreast. He gave her one glance and stopped in his stride; his hand came up to the salute.

" Won't you allow me to help you with your luggage ? "

The words were nicely shaped, the voice was cultured; although she couldn't see the marks of his rank, she knew he was a gentleman and accepted gratefully.  He swung the dressing-case away from her and made off so rapidly that she could hardly keep pace with him.

" I've no idea," she said, " how far the village is from the station.  I came here quite suddenly, at a few minutes' notice.  Perhaps you can tell me if I can get any kind of conveyance ! "

" It's doubtful," he answered, " if you haven't ordered one. I suppose you've booked a room somewhere ?  There isn't a village in the ordinary sense of the word.  This part of the Plain is all War Department property, you know."

" I'm afraid I've made no arrangements," she told him. " I imagined that near a big camp like this there must be an hotel."

" There is an hotel, ' The Thatched House,' but I happen to know that it's full.  Of course you may get lodgings in one of the shops. . . ."

He paused dubiously.  As they passed under one of the bleared lamps he shot a sudden, keen glance at her.  She saw that he was a man of middle age, with clean-cut soldier's features and a clipped moustache which might have been grey or only fair.  His face was the exact counterpart of his voice.  Instinctively she classed him as a regular of the old Army who had served in India ; why, she couldn't say. Apparently he, too, was satisfied with his momentary survey, for when he spoke again his voice was friendly as well as polite.

" If you'll excuse my asking you, what are you doing here ? "

" I've come to see my son.  He's in the Worcesters."

" The Worcesters ? " he asked with some surprise.

" Yes, he's attached to the Officers' School of Instruction."

" Ah, yes, I understand.  We must see what we can do for you."

A red-capped sergeant of the Military Police saluted at the wicket. He seemed to know her conductor.

" Are there any taxis about, sergeant ? " he asked him.

" No, sir. I can't rightly say that I've seen one."

" You don't happen to know if Siviter's is full ? "

" I can't say I know that either, sir," said the sergeant, as if he would have given anything in the world to oblige. " There's no harm in trying, sir," he added encouragingly.

Another line of bleared lights trickled down the hill-side. The road was a quagmire of unmetalled chalk cracked by crevasses in which the wheels of heavy transport wagons had foundered, pitted with pools of water. On one side a pavement fronted a series of brick-built stores and tin shanties from which blurred lights shone out through steaming windows ; on the other bare downland sloped away into utter darkness. Steadily, depressingly, a fine rain descended which shot the luminous projections of the shop-lights with threads of silver and glistened like dew upon the overcoats of the soldiers who slouched along the pavement out of very boredom with their collars turned up. The pavement was so shiningly treacherous that Clare lagged behind her escort. He stopped and waited for her.

" I can't apologize too much for giving you all this trouble," she told him.

" It's no trouble at all. I only hope these people can put you up. This is the place. It isn't much to look at, but I think it may be your only chance, so you'd better look inside and see if they can take you. I'll wait outside with the baggage until you tell me what you've settled."

A glass door, blurred with rain-splashes, opened to the ping of a shop-bell It showed her a narrow strip of wet, mud-trampled linoleum, a counter crammed with buns, confectionery, ravaged joints of ham and sad-coloured beef, half hidden by backs clothed in damp khaki and the red cropped necks of soldiers. Beyond, the metal-topped tables

of a little eating-house, where other soldiers sat stolidly
devouring round slices of meat that covered their plates like
limp pancakes. The air of the place was tepid, moist and
stagnant, made sickening by the odour of damp serge and
ham and beef and steaming cocoa. The red-necked soldiers
stared at her as she entered, but went on eating with open
mouths, or swilled down the food they had masticated with
gulps of hot fluid. To see the serious way they went about
it one would have thought that the British Army was starving.
Among them a giggling girl, in a soiled apron, flitted hither
and thither, excited and made self-conscious by the greedy
looks of so many male eyes. Seeing no chance of ever
breaking through to the counter Clare intercepted her.

" I want to know if you can put me up for the night," she
said.

" Well, really, I can't say," said the young girl jauntily.
" Missis," she screamed, " this lady wants to know if she
can have a bed."

A heavy woman, with a lardy, spotted face, and lank hair
that looked as if it had been dressed with ham-fat, deserted
the counter to come and scrutinize Clare. She wiped her
hands slowly on a cloth that seemed to be saturated in the
composite odour of the shop. She looked Clare's sables up
and down as if there were something discreditable about
them.

" Have you been to the ' Thatched House ' ? " she said,
with a jerk of her head.

" I was told at the station that it was full."

" I know it is," said the fat woman darkly, " and we're
full too, by rights."

" If you could suggest my trying anywhere else . . ."
Clare began, with a sinking heart.

" There *is* nowhere else," said the woman laconically.
" As a matter of fact I've got one bed to spare, but you'll
have to share the room with an Australian lady."

" I think," Clare said, " if you don't mind . . ."

" You'd better take it while you've got the chance," the woman advised her. " I suppose you have some luggage ? "

" My luggage is outside."

The woman grunted her approval. " That'll be ten shillings for the night," she said. " They always pay in advance." Clare took out her purse and paid her. " But you understand," the woman continued, " it's only for one night ? I have two other ladies coming in to-morrow."

" I suppose your Australian lady won't object ? " Clare asked, adopting the shopkeeper's idiom.

" She can like it or lump it," said the woman shortly. " You'd better bring your luggage in ; we shut at nine. It's number five. You'll see the number on the door."

Faint-hearted, yet thankful, Clare found her companion on the pavement.

" Please don't wait any longer," she said. " It's all right. I can't tell you how grateful I am for your kindness. No, please, don't carry it any further. I can take it in myself."

He smiled. " What nonsense ! Of course I'll carry it up for you."

She followed him in, through the reek of wet serge and viands, to the farther end of the shop. A couple of soldiers rose uneasily to attention, their cheeks bulging with food ; the rest contented themselves with gaping at him as they had gaped at her. Now, through the steamy light, she saw that his moustache was not fair but grey. In his blue eyes there was a humorous twinkle, as though he enjoyed the joke of the adventure. He opened a door of varnished deal and preceded her up a steep and narrow staircase.

" What number ? " he asked her, over his shoulder.

" Number five."

" That must be on this floor. Yes, here we are."

He put the luggage down and smiled at her. It was a frank, companionable smile ; his mouth was rather big, the teeth strong and regular. She was thankful, under the awkward circumstances—yet why should they be awkward ?—that he hadn't offered to take the luggage into the bedroom. She felt herself conscious of his masculinity ; almost as if she had taken an infection from the giggling girl downstairs. This moment of silence was painful. She held out her hand, to end it, with a renewal of thanks.

" You're lucky to have found a lodging," he told her. " A new territorial division came in yesterday for their final training. I shall tell your son you've arrived to-morrow morning."

She stared in surprise. She didn't remember having told him her name.

" Forgive me," he said. " I couldn't help reading the name on your labels. I haven't made your son's acquaintance yet. I expect he's reported his arrival to my adjutant. You see I happen to be commanding the School of Instruction. Which means, I hope, that we shall meet again."

He took her hand, saluted gravely, and retired, leaving Clare to survey her precarious lodging.

Two beds, thank heaven ! The room was so dark that, for a moment, she didn't realize that one of them was already occupied by the Australian lady, who announced her presence by suddenly striking a match and staring at her from under a mass of tousled reddish hair.

" Helleaw boy ! " she said. " Oh, I *am* sorry : I thought it was Jack."

Apologetically Clare explained her presence.

" Oh, that's all right," said the Australian lady hospitably. " Please make yourself at home. Though I *do* think Mrs. Siviter might have warned me you were coming, don't you ? But all these people are just the saime. It's your money they're after. That's all they think about."

Within five minutes of unpacking Clare was in possession of all the Australian lady's life history. She came from

Toowoomba, in Queensland, a bonza spot ; her " boy " from Brisbane. He had been wounded three times in Gallipoli, and was doing a course of machine-gun training at Pedworth. Pedworth was not a bonza spot compared with Toowoomba, and as for Siviter's ! Talking of hotels, you ought to see the Wentworth. You know, there's something heawmely about Australia ; the folks are all more chummy like down under. And then this ceawld ! She shivered dramatically. Jack—that was her husband, although, mind you, she could have had the pick of all the lads in Brisbane—had brought her a couple of blueys from the barracks to stop her being frozen. Blueys, you kneaw —those grey-blue blankets that they use on the stations. Australian wool was the best wool in the world. It tickled you to death to see these tiny little English sheep. If Clare could see the sheep out on Jack's station ! When the war was over she ought to go to Australia. Sydney harbour . . . God's own country . . . If it wasn't for the rabbits and the bush-fires and the prickly-pear. But then, the cochineal beetle would settle all that. . . .

A knock at the door. Before anyone had time to answer it Mrs. Siviter came panting into the room, suggesting that Clare should go downstairs for some supper. The shop was closed, the room free. She couldn't offer much, but suggested a slice of her ham, which was all right, and a cup of cocoa. The very idea was sickening ; the fumes of ham and cocoa had followed in Mrs. Siviter's wake up the stairs. Her aura was a feast in itself. Clare declined.

" You never told me," Mrs. Siviter complained, " that you were a friend of Colonel Hart's. To oblige the colonel I'd have turned out of my own bed."

The thought of Mrs. Siviter's own bed was not inviting, but Clare thanked her. She went. Far into the night the Australian lady, poor dear, went on explaining the attractions of Queensland, like an emigration agent. Whenever her supply of interesting information failed her, she dived back into Sydney Harbour. So often that Clare wished she had been drowned in it.

His name was Hart, Colonel Hart. In some vague way the sound was familiar, though how or where, for the life of her, she couldn't remember. An attractive creature. All Dudley's strength, without any of Dudley's heaviness; all Dudley's keenness, without Dudley's reservations. A certain hardness . . . yes, but a supple hardness; more vital, more quick, more adaptable than Dudley's. Poor Dudley, that he should be used like a stiff yardstick to measure men by! It wasn't fair; it was inevitable. And this man, although he hadn't shown it in anything he said, had a sense of humour lurking in his dark blue eyes. And sensibilities . . . that was the real difference.

" It's funny," she thought, " that I should go on thinking about him like this. But then, it's obvious that he must have liked me too, or else he wouldn't have hoped that we should meet again."

That was a conventional fashion of speech, and yet, since he was Steven's commanding officer, there might be something valuable in knowing him after all. For Clare his position was invested with incalculable powers. All Steven's destiny lay in this man's hands. A word from him might mean the difference between Pedworth and Flanders. In these days life and death, like kissing, went by favour, and if he became a friend . . . She could not pursue the line of reasoning further; it petered out beneath the remembered gaze of Colonel Hart's eyes. Whatever else she might read in them, one thing was certain : a man with eyes like those was incorruptible. And yet . . .

" But honest, you can't say you've lived until you've seen Sydney Harbour, dear," the Australian lady was saying.

*See Naples and die.* . . . Yes, once she had seen Naples. Pale rosemary creeping over the rocks at Capri : tall rosemary standing by the Uffdown roses. But Uffdown was further away than Sydney Harbour now . . . and Capri further still.

## IV
## SCHOOL OF INSTRUCTION

NEXT morning early, out of the smell of oilcloth in Mrs. Siviter's bedroom Clare escaped to the desolation of the restaurant downstairs. Her breakfast table was a desert island in a tidal waste of wet linoleum, over which the little maid moved crabwise, with swab and bucket, distributing the trampled mud of the night before, while the landlady herself, in a mauve dressing-jacket, sat at her desk and counted over the last evening's takings.

In such a carnal atmosphere it was impossible to eat, though Mrs. Siviter condescended to leave her accountancy and make suggestions.

" You never had a bite of supper last night," she said. Now, why don't you try a slice of our *alamode?* I'll cut it for you myself."

At the risk of offending her Clare declined. The air was already full of *alamode* to the point of saturation. But Mrs. Siviter continued to press her with small-talk and comestibles.

" Don't spare the butter, Mrs. Hingston," she said. " It's real Dorset, none of your rationed margarine. Those food-cards, we don't take any notice of them in these parts. I get as much as I like to ask for. You see, the contractors know I supply the officers' messes. Twenty-one pounds ought and sevenpence. No, I can't say the war's done *me* out of anything but sleep, and even if it had, we mustn't complain. People have got to put up with what they get in these days. Which reminds me, Missiser . . . Hingston, if you want to stay on here to-night I dare say I can manage all right ; I'll put the other lady off."

" But surely that's hardly fair ? " Clare suggested.

" Oh, fair be damned, if you'll excuse the word," said Mrs. Siviter. " Just hark at me ! That comes of being with soldiers. What I mean to say, as long as the beds are full it makes no odds to me who fills them, and seeing that you're a friend of the colonel's . . ."

" I don't think I could do that," Clare persisted. Another five minutes, let alone another night, of Siviter's would have been enough for her. " I have the whole of the day in front of me. My son and I will try to find a permanent lodging of some kind."

" Well, you can *try*," said Mrs. Siviter discouragingly. " And if you don't succeed I can always turn some other lady out. I expect you'll come back to me."

She waddled to the kitchen with the bags of counted money bunched in her apron. The little maid stood waiting with her bucket to submerge the island on which Clare was seated. Removed from the excitement of a room full of men she looked pale and dispirited.

" I've finished ; you can come here now," Clare told her. Braving the barrage of cook-house odours that separated her from the door, she passed precipitately into the reviving air of a brilliant winter morning.

During the night the low clouds had rained themselves out, so that now the shallow fold of downland in which Pedworth lay was roofed by a sky of unusual brightness and purity. Or so, at least, it seemed to Clare ; for even at Uffdown the chimneys of the black-country vitiated the upper air, while here the very openness of the plain, whose contours swelled away to southward smooth and unbroken as veld or pampas, seemed to reflect the radiant clarity of the sky, expanding at once the lungs and the imagination , so that even the broken roadway with its mud crevasses, the mean string of shanties and jerry-built shops which had been sown there like a catch-crop to profit by the war's emergencies, seemed dwarfed and negligible against the vast virgin spaces in which they were set.

On such a morning, beneath such a crystalline sky, there was no place for gloom or foreboding. The spirit of the plain was free, adventurous, and almost gay. Even those sinister reminders of the deadly activities with which it was connected, the crescent of red-brick barracks which housed, at that moment, more than ten thousand troops in training, exhaled that atmosphere of freedom from economic cares and domestic responsibility, that sense of abundant health and cleanliness which is man's compensation for the grimness of war.

At the bottom of the slope that fell from the station Clare struck the old road leading south to Salisbury, an ancient, peaceful highway, dominated by the bare branches of gigantic elms. The valley was threaded by a little river, a winterbourne whose waters nourished meadows of a startling green. Beyond it, the thatched, flint-walled cottages of the original village of Pedworth and its square church tower nestled, unconscious of wars or of any outer life, beneath the last wave of the opposite downland. A butcher's cart from Amesbury stood waiting at a garden gate. The housewife, in a blue-speckled overall, scrutinized the weighing of her Sunday dinner, while her husband, a sandy-whiskered pensioner in khaki trousers, pitchforked rubbish on to a garden bonfire whose vertical smoke filled the air with homely autumnal savours. The scene was as leisurely and undisturbed as Uffdown itself. Here in the very heart of war's tornado there was peace.

Clare waited until the woman had ceased her gossip with the butcher then asked her the way to Fontenoy Barracks where Steven was quartered. It was not that she had any hope of seeing him that morning, but because even the building that sheltered him was precious to her.

"Straight on up the hill, ma'am," the cottage-woman told her, "and you'll come to the road that runs through all the barracks. You can't miss Fontenoy. They run in alphabetical order. Fontenoy's the School of Instruction, isn't it, Joe?" she called to her husband. The gardener straightened himself and saluted. "School of Instruction for Orficers . . . that's right."

"You see my husband's an old soldier," the woman explained. "He knows exactly what units are in the barracks. I might be living in London for all *I* know about it. Things change so quickly here since the war. Straight on, ma'am, you can't miss it."

She spoke so quietly, so politely, she was so cleanly and deft, that Clare imagined she must be some kind of superior servant who had married and drifted into this backwater. The red-brick cottage, with its fillings of flint, looked so neat and homely under its thatch, the garden was so trim and tidy, the woman's speech so decent and refined, that a sudden impulse made Clare linger and speak to her.

"You haven't, by any chance, two rooms to let?" she said.

"No, ma'am, I'm sorry I haven't," the woman told her. "There's a great shortage of rooms in Pedworth just now. I have a medical officer and his wife here at present, and as he's on home-service I expect they'll stay here for some time. Though, of course, you never know."

"Can you suggest my asking anywhere else?"

"I'm sorry, ma'am, I can't. I get that question put to me every day."

"I suppose it's quite impossible to find a furnished house?"

"I think you'll find it difficult, madam," She shook her head "Now wait a minute though . . ." She called to her husband. " Joe, didn't you tell me last night that Major Waring was leaving Number Four Staff Colony ? "

" That's right. He's got a move to the Northern Command," the man replied.

" Well, if this lady wants to take it, what must she do ? "

" War Department Estate-Agent at Wilston. Captain Hamley. The one we pay our rent to. I doubt if the lady'll get it, there's a lot of competition for those bungalows, but there's nothing like trying."

" And where is Wilston ? " Clare asked eagerly.

" Over the plain, Amesbury way. You go through Bulford," the woman told her.

" Thank you so much. I'll go there this afternoon."

The bright morning seemed full of an added hopefulness as she climbed the slope toward the barrack-road. On her left the glittering steeple of the garrison church took the sun ; beyond, a clean, wide strip of tarmac swept in a crescent before the officers' messes, very different from the muddy morasses with which the stories of Lady Hingston's wounded had made her associate the Plain. One after another the alphabetical barracks received her. In Albuera the horses of the Scots Greys and Royals were whinnying and stamping. From Blenheim a body of lank slouch-hatted Australians, laden with full equipment, marched out in column of fours. Some of them smiled at her as they swung by, as though on such a morning it was pleasant to set eyes on a pretty woman. She liked their lean brown faces ; she was proud to see the brass " A's " that marked their Anzac service. A gay band, playing *Sammy* moved in front of them. She didn't realize that these smiling men were marching to the station : a draft of cannon-fodder for the Flanders front. At the gates of Corunna a grizzled brigadier stood talking to a group of red-hatted staff-officers. With a flash of surprise Clare recognized the general with whom she had lunched at Stourford. In these military surroundings he seemed a hundred times more impressive. She dared not bow to him. From behind Dargai emerged a straggling line of men in blue, convalescents from the hospital behind it. And then came Fontenoy. . . .

The building was in no way different from its fellows, a long, two-storeyed, red-brick suburban house with freestone facings. The lack of curtains gave its wide bow-windows a look of severity. For all the signs of life that it showed it might have been empty ; yet Steven was there, and that was enough for her.

" I wonder," she thought, " if I could send a message to him. Yet why should I send a message ? He might not like it ; and Colonel Hart promised me he'd let him know that I was here. During the morning, in any case, he's sure to be busy. I don't suppose I've any right to be here at all."

She stood in the roadway, waiting, unable to tear herself away. Smart N.C.O.'s went past her with a swagger and momentary glances of curiosity that made her conscious of her sex. A cavalry officer on a bright chestnut trotted by. Beneath the uplifted sky she heard a mournful blare of trumpets, practising cavalry calls. Over the down, toward Amesbury, an angry stutter of machine-guns. Above, so high that they seemed to be hovering rather than flying, an echelon of Handley-Page bombers from Upavon dotted the sky. The thunder of their engines descended on her in falling waves through the still air. Against this background of warlike sounds the sunny silence of Fontenoy seemed vaguely sinister. In such a world the sun should not have been shining.

" I had better go back to Siviters and wait for him," she thought ; but, as she turned to go, the door of the officers' mess swung open ; a tall figure in a trench-coat emerged and came toward her over the semi-circular sweep of drive. Feeling like an eavesdropper she quickened her pace and hurried on with lowered eyes ; but the long strides of the other overhauled her. Then, suddenly, he turned and looked, and she saw that it was Steven.

" Mother," he cried, " whatever are you doing here ? I was going to the village ; I might have missed you."

She held out her arms to him, expecting him to kiss her, then quickly realized the impropriety of her gesture.

" My darling, I didn't imagine you'd be free till the afternoon. I only wanted to see your quarters for myself."

" I don't suppose you have any business here at all," he answered, rather crossly.

" I'm sorry, dearest." She saw him as a schoolboy again, a schoolboy anxious not to transgress unimaginable codes ; and yet there was nothing of the schoolboy in his appearance. The week of service at Devonport had stiffened him and straightened his shoulders ; he looked stronger and healthier in every way, and, curiously, older. She realized, of a sudden, that he had begun to grow a moustache. Now that the embarrassment of finding her unexpectedly had subsided, he became himself again.

" Of course it's lovely to see you, mum," he told her ; " but really you shouldn't have come here before I told you. It's just like you to rush down here without waiting for me to make arrangements. The colonel told me this morning what a mess you were landed in last night. You seem to have made a conquest, by the way."

" He was extraordinarily kind, if that's what you mean."

" I bet he was. He seems to me a topping fellow. What's more, he's an old Rug, which makes a lot of difference. He sent for me this morning and told me you'd come. He says that you can't possibly stay on at Siviter's. He's left me free for the day to find some rooms for you."

" How splendid ! " She told him what she had heard about the Staff Colony bungalow.

" It sounds all right," he admitted. " The only question

is whether it's worth while for so short a time. I gather the school is shoving out officers pretty quickly. I'm fit for General Service, you know."

" Oh, Steven, don't even speak of it ! " she begged him.

" That's all very well, mum, but it has to be considered. I haven't come to settle for life on Salisbury Plain. Still, if you think it's worth while, we'll get a car and drive over to Wilston. What a ripping day ! "

They walked together through the water-meadows toward the station. His spirits were so high, the day so brilliant, that she soon forgot his sinister suggestions. All the moodiness that had weighed on him for the last year at Uffdown had disappeared ; the oily pallor of Wolverbury had vanished from his cheeks. At last he was happy ; and even though the cause of his happiness threatened hers, she was glad of it. And she was proud of him : of his strength, his manliness, which the sober uniform seemed to accentuate. Walking beside him it gave her a strange thrill of pride to see him take the salutes of the soldiers that met them on the cinder path that crossed the meadows.

The brilliant morning held. A Ford car, hired at a fantastic expense, rattled them out of the woods of the Pedworth valley to the open plain ; a dun expanse, cloud-dappled, like a tidal sea whose muddy waves rolled north and west to smooth hills crowned with pale clusters of hutments or systems of trenches whose chalk parapets gleamed through the distance like thawing snow. Among the barrows of the stone-age the red flag of a range was flying. They pulled up, waiting while rifle-shots cracked like whips ; then slowly bumped forward through the New Zealand lines at Sling, an outpost of the permanent camp of Bulford.

And now the desert became quick and populous with activity. On every " square " bodies of men were drilling. Clare heard the bark of staccato commands, the thud of grounded arms, the rhythmical tramp of heavy boots on gravel, the symphony of multitudinous bugle-calls whose overtones floated like high and melancholy echoes in the still air. Close by the roadway a group of New Zealanders of the Auckland battalion were busy with bayonet-practice, plunging their steel into the bellies of straw-stuffed Germans, whose heads some fanciful Maori must have painted with features that resembled those of South Sea gods or devils. A wicked string of mules danced past them warily ; the last, a dun-coloured demon fresh from the Argentine, let fly with a parting kick that struck the near wing of the car. The chauffeur stopped and swore at the corporal in charge ; the air grew thick with oaths until Steven ordered him to drive on.

Here, in the heart of the camp, they could only steal forward by a few yards at a time, the road was so congested with bodies of troops route-marching or moving to the ranges, with convoys of grey-hooded M.T. lorries swaying over the uneven surface as though they must capsize, with level-crossings of the military railway, with road-gangs, making good the surface that another month of such pitiless use would destroy. At a turning in the middle of Bulford a red-capped policeman waved them back. Wedged in a block of waiting traffic they watched a battery of howitzers cross the road ; the great grey monsters rolled past with their mouths gaping at the sky, where fighting-planes went droning by like hornets, and those melancholy overtones of bugle-calls fused and lost themselves in space.

To Steven all these sights and sounds were an excitement ; part of the apparatus of the great new game in which he was engrossed. They gave him, Clare supposed, the sensation of being " in it " at last. He was proud and eager to explain the technical significance of everything he saw, to make her free of the new world that he had attained.

She listened, she smiled, she humoured him ; but, deep

in her heart, this revelation of the activities and accessories of war distressed her. They seemed, somehow, themselves more actual than their results, of which she had seen enough, heaven knew, in the wards at Stourford ; there was something appalling in the strength, the liveliness, the concentration of all these instruments of death, the intense singleness of purpose that co-ordinated the movements of every element in this conglomeration of men and of materials. While Steven was thrilled to recognize each scattered unit of the machine in which he himself had become a part and rejoice in its shining fitness for its appointed function, she saw, instead, the waste to which the bulk of this panoply must come , the moments when the silvery fighting planes must crash downward in sheets of flame ; the agony of dumb, mangled horseflesh ; the broken iron, the shattered human bodies.

There, where war seemed most gay and gallant, its terror dawned on her with a definiteness that imagination had never been able to paint. She was shaken and thankful when the last huts of Bulford were left behind, when the acrid smell of incinerators was driven from her lungs by the clean river-air of the Avon valley.

The agent, a captain in the uniform of the A.S.C., received their enquiries cheerfully.

" You seem to have struck a lucky patch," he said. " I've two officers on my waiting-list for the Staff Colony bungalow. The first has got a transfer to the Curragh ; the second has written me this morning to say that he's found another house in Sidbury. So there you are ! As soon as Major Waring vacates the bungalow you can have it."

" When does he go ? " Clare asked.

" To-morrow as ever is. You'd better see him at once, or rather his memsahib ; you'll probably find it convenient to take over the furniture he's hired from Andover. I'd better jot down your name and the other particulars. Hing ston ? That sounds familiar. You're not by any chance related to the Hingstons of Stourford ? I spent a month there in Lady Hingston's hospital in nineteen-sixteen."

Clare told him who she was.

" Why, now I come to think of it," he said, " of course I recognize you. This war has made the world smaller than ever ; the whole of England's like a family party. I'm awfully glad that I've been able to fit you in. I hope for your sake you'll have as comfortable a time as I had at Stourford."

" Another conquest, mum," said Steven gaily as they drove away. " You seem to be having a great success in these parts."

## V

### STAFF COLONY

THREE days later Clare was established in number four, Staff Colony. There must have been something ironical in the agent's wishes that she might be as comfortable there as he had been at Stourford. The Staff Colony consisted of a series of six double huts, walled and roofed with galvanized zinc, which had been erected by the War Department to house the architects and foremen engaged in building the permanent barracks of Pedworth during the military renaissance that followed the Boer War. That they had continued to stand there for eighteen years was a miracle, for the wooden frames that sustained them were crumbling with dry-rot. In front, but separated from them by a strip of weedy garden, ran the main road to Salisbury. Beyond the road, a rank of bare-branched but magnificent elms consumed the upper air, revealing, between rough trunks mossed with moisture, vistas of the water-meadows through which the winterbourne trickled, a cinder-path, pointing to the blue slate roof of the Corunna officers' mess, and, lifted above another screen of elm-trees, the bare knoll of downland that sustained the red-brick Gothic of the garrison church, whose spire detached itself from the pale, chalk-bloomed slopes of the hills that separated the Pedworth valley from the rolling plain toward Bulford.

In spring, Clare thought, or early summer, the huts of the Staff Colony might make a pleasant setting for a picnic existence. In spring the elms would make a filigree of golden leaf; in summer, green shade. But now, in the depth of a winter sterner than any she had known at Uffdown, in an air that nightly closed on the bare downs with a grip which froze the very water in the makeshift bathroom, she could not even think of spring. And even if she could have thought of spring she dared not. There was no knowing what the spring might bring her. She was living from day to day, like all the rest of the women in Pedworth. And all her days were the same. . . .

Comfort, of a sort, she had ; for as soon as the bungalow was theirs the invaluable Ellen had arrived from Uffdown. " You'll never keep a servant here," Clare's Staff Colony neighbours had told her ; " the soldiers are after them like flies round treacle ; it turns their heads in no time, there's simply no holding them."

But Ellen was different. Her homely bulk and the memory of Jim Moseley's treachery were formidable enough to keep the boldest of N.C.O.s at bay. It flattered Ellen to know that Clare was dependent on her ; she liked to feel that number four was superior in comfort, in cleanliness, in every possible kind of distinction, to the rest of the Staff Colony. She scrubbed the dirt-blackened floors and waxed them ; she washed the curtains to shreds and sucked the stuffing out of the hired furniture with her vacuum cleaner. In her few moments of leisure she conducted a campaign of back-chat with Beazeley, Colonel Hart's batman.

For Colonel Hart had kindly sent Beazeley to help them, to draw Steven's rations from the quartermaster's stores and wheel down his allowance of coal and kindling-wood. Beazeley was a mild-mannered, respectful fellow, in civil life a butler, whose feet had rotted in the trenches like water-logged roots. In a little while he seemed almost as much a member of the family as Ellen.

And so, for that matter, did Colonel Hart.

From the beginning Hart appeared to have taken a liking to Steven ; a liking that Steven returned without hesitation ; and this in itself was enough to ingratiate him with Clare. In any case she was prejudiced in his favour. She couldn't forget his quick, spontaneous kindness on the night of her arrival. Beyond all this, she admired his physical presence ; his dignity, his courtesy, his directness, his air of wholly unconscious breeding, the tactful good-humour that had won the difficult hearts of Steven and Ellen by such different means.

She felt—she had felt from the moment of his first visit—that this was a man who could be trusted ; that, whatever he did, the purity of his motives was not to be questioned. She accepted him, confidently, at his surface value. She accepted him, unashamedly, for another reason : the fact that Steven's immediate destiny and all her own happiness lay, for the moment, in his hands. Sometimes the frankness of his eyes made her wonder if it was not unfair to conceal the ulterior motives that, even if she had not admired Hart as she did, would have compelled her to please him ; but, little by little, their triple intimacy became too precious for her to risk its destruction by such revelations. And, perhaps, she thought, he knew. As long as Steven didn't know, she had no reason to worry herself.

And Steven, so far at least, suspected nothing. That Hart had been at Rugby prejudiced him in his favour. To a young subaltern so much condescension on the part of an

admired commanding officer was flattering. Added to this
the fact that Hart was a regular with a brilliant career
behind him, that he was an inspiring teacher, and that all
the School of Instruction united in voting him a first-rate
man at his job and a damned good fellow as well was
sufficient to appeal to all the boy's instinctive hero-worship.
For Steven, in spite of his queer streaks of maturity, was
still a schoolboy, and the atmosphere of an army in training
is merely an extension of that of a public school. Within
a few weeks Clare saw him deferring to Hart as he had never
deferred to anyone else in his life.

" It is a splendid influence for him," she told herself.

At first she had only known Hart as a helpful friend whose
influence commanded the services of the admirable Beazeley,
and whose experience instructed them in the difficulties of
camp-life. The calls that he made at number four were
brief and businesslike. When the day's work was over—
and the dark winter evenings made them short—he would
" drop in " with Steven to see how things were going and
take what Ellen called a cup of tea. They would sit together
in the firelight and talk of unimportant things ; the war-
rumours that drifted through from G.H.Q. in Salisbury,
the small domestic gossip of the camp. Clare liked to see
them there, the boy and the man, sitting like father and son
in the hired chairs from Andover. She felt that she and
Steven were honoured by Hart's notice ; for in the narrow
military sphere of Pedworth the crown and stars on his
shoulder-strap counted for more than in the outer world.
It pleased her to see the respect that everybody, from Mrs.
Siviter onward, showed him ; it gave her a feeling of his
importance when Steven called him " sir."

But gradually, as Hart's presence grew more familiar,
their relation became more intimate. They spoke of Uffdown, of Stourford, of all the homely things that seemed so
distant from the closed circle of garrison life—so distant, and

therefore so pathetically desirable. Hart listened sympathetic-ally as though he understood and shared their nostalgia, until it seemed to Clare as though he were part of that life as well as this ; as though he were no stranger of a few weeks' acquaintance, but an old and well-tried friend ; until, at last, it seemed as if he would have been as much at home at Uffdown as in this bleak lodging on Salisbury Plain. And yet though he identified himself so cleverly with her life and Steven's, she noticed that he hardly ever spoke of his own. She found it queer and provocative, this one-sided intimacy. In everything else he was so extraordinarily open. She would have liked, as a matter of interest, to have broken through his reserve, but dared not do so, for she was still a little afraid of him.

One evening, when she had begged him to stay to supper, and they sat talking over the admirable coffee that Ellen made them, Hart gratified Steven's curiosity in all things military by telling them of the advance on Kimberley, in which he had won his D.S.O.

" I stopped a bullet at Magersfontein," he told them. " It's still there, lodged somewhere uncomfortably near my heart. That's why the W.O. keep me kicking my heels at Pedworth. With a little luck I should have got a division in France by now."

" If I were you, I should be thankful for it," Clare said.

He smiled. " Our points of view are different. You see, I'm a soldier. As it is, my career began and ended in South Africa."

Clare asked him, suddenly, if ever he had been in Bloem-fontein. He looked at her strangely.

" Of course I've been in Bloemfontein. How queer ! Why did you never ask me that before ? Now that you speak of it, I remember something."

" My husband—Steven's father—died there during the war. Enteric. He was an officer in the Yeomanry."

She listened to the detachment of her own voice with wonder. It was years since she had spoken of Ralph to anyone, even to Steven.

"Of course. I know. I was staff-captain, acting as brigade-major of his brigade. Do you realize that it was I who wrote you a letter of condolence?"

"Yes, I remember it quite well. I think we must have remembered almost at the same moment."

His eyes surveyed her curiously, as though he were trying to visualize her as Ralph Hingston's wife. She knew what he was thinking. It was uncanny, the way in which she was beginning to read his thoughts.

"Yes, I was dreadfully young," she told him. "Too young. . . . When Steven was born I was only eighteen. It was ten years later when I married again."

His blue eyes, black in the firelight, seemed to be demanding further confidences. She said no more. She saw that Steven was getting restless. The subject distressed him. Although, at this distance, Clare herself could speak of Dudley Wilburn without embarrassment, her consideration for Steven constrained her never to mention his name if it could be avoided. Seeing that Hart was anxious to know more, he rose, with a sudden awkwardness from his chair.

"If you don't mind, sir," he said, "I must be going. I promised to do 'orderly dog' for Braithwaite to-night; he's made an exchange with me for Tuesday."

"One moment, and I'll come along with you," Hart told him.

"No, no, sir. Don't do that. Mother will be lonely. I wish you'd stay with her a bit."

"May I?" he asked her.

"Of course you may, if you won't be bored," she said.

In silence they watched Steven buckle his belt and struggle into his British warm. He came across to Clare and kissed her twice. The fact that Hart was watching this embrace made her curiously shy. She knew that she was blushing, though why she couldn't imagine. When Steven had gone there was a long and awkward silence. She racked her brain in desperation to find some other subject with which to break it, but, all the time, she knew he would not allow her to do so. At last he spoke, as though the age-long interval had not existed.

"Well, it was ten years later when you married again."

"I married an old friend of the family. Steven's trustee. I admired him enormously. But Steven . . ."

"Steven didn't ? "

"He's funny in that way, you know. He's full of instinctive likes and dislikes. And awfully loyal. If he dislikes a person I can do nothing with him. If he takes a fancy to anyone they can do no wrong. You realize that he's taken an enormous fancy to you ? "

"I'm complimented. I hope I can live up to it. But do go on."

She hesitated. She had a feeling that she was being dissected, analyzed. She resented the process, and yet it gave her pleasure, as though it were cleansing her mind of old discomforts.

"There's really no reason why this should interest you, Colonel Hart," she said.

"There are a thousand reasons, my dear Mrs. Wilburn," he answered, echoing, with faint mockery, her formal address. "But if it hurts you to talk about it, don't for one moment . . ."

"It doesn't hurt me," she declared. "It's good for me to talk about it. My second marriage was not a happy one. Steven to begin with. Then there were other complications . . ."

She paused. For a moment he could not answer her, for Ellen had entered the room to take away the coffee things. She gave a start when she saw that Steven had gone and that

Clare and Hart were sitting alone in the firelight. Clare felt an unspoken criticism in her cautious movements, a shyness, like that which had overwhelmed her while Hart watched her kissing Steven. Evidently Hart was unconscious of both alike. As soon as Ellen had closed the door with a too-tactful deliberation, he spoke again.

" Complications ? The name of Wilburn is familiar. I seem to remember something . . ."

" No, no, that wasn't his fault." Her spirit rose suddenly in defence of the absent Wilburn. " There was a scandal, as you know, but he had nothing whatever to do with it. I don't believe there was ever a man more scrupulously honest than my husband. But everything was impossible. You have no idea how utterly hopeless an unhappy marriage is."

He shook his head slowly. " Ah, don't I ? I know for myself how heavily one has to pay for that kind of mistake."

"You too ? I'd no idea," she encouraged him, softly. It thrilled her when he responded to her encouragement.

" I was a subaltern in Malta," he told her. " It was ages ago, before the Boer war. She was Maltese. When they are young the Maltese girls are quite amazingly lovely. I thought that honour—whatever you like to call it—compelled me to marry her. As a matter of fact it didn't. That was the first unpleasant part of the story. The rest was rather more unpleasant than the beginning. To put it mildly, twenty years of hell. Don't talk to me about unhappy marriages ! "

His face was hard and lined. It seemed as if all his suffering had been renewed and concentrated in this confession. She was so sorry for him—yet what could she say ?

" There were no compensations ? You had no children ? "

" Yes, one. A girl. Miranda. She's two years younger than Steven."

Sixteen. Which meant that four or five years after this

disastrous marriage . . . Clare flushed and hesitated, ashamed of the trend of her own thoughts which, of themselves, seemed to be exploring indecent intimacies. To cover her confusion she asked abruptly : " And your wife ? "

" She died two years ago. In Malta. It was fortunate for both of us."

" That sounds very terrible."

" Yes, yes ; but not more terrible than it was. Even after two years I haven't quite got over it. The shock . . . the relief. You remember the Bastille prisoner in Dickens ? "

" *Buried how long ?* "

" *Almost eighteen years.*"

" *You had abandoned all hope of being dug out ?* "

" *Long ago.*"

" Something like that. Three parts of me are only just beginning to live. During the last month I've begun to feel myself coming to life again. Slowly, painfully . . . But I needn't tell you. You probably know as well as I do what it feels like."

" I can imagine," she told him gently, " though my case, of course, was infinitely less dreadful than yours. And my husband is still alive."

He stared at her, repeating, incredulously : " Your husband is still alive ? "

" Yes. We are merely separated. Although we don't see each other we are—how shall I put it ?—we're quite good friends."

He gazed at her in silence for a moment ; then spoke, with difficulty :

" I had imagined, quite unreasonably, that you were a widow. You always wear black. I thought . . ." He paused again. " The fact that neither you nor Steven had ever mentioned your husband made me . . . You see, I simply took it for granted. . . ."

" We don't. I suppose it's a kind of tacit agreement. I'm sorry. . . ."

But why should she be sorry ? she wondered.

" No, no. It's I who owe you an apology. I've trespassed on your sympathy—that's partly your fault for being so patient with me—by introducing you to the skeleton in my cupboard. I hope you'll believe that I'm not in the habit of thrusting my private affairs on people ? To tell you the truth, I haven't spoken about them to anyone for years."

" I feel it an enormous privilege," she told him. " If you regret having told me it will hurt me dreadfully."

" You know that I wouldn't hurt you for the world. I know what it means to be hurt. I'm a very lonely man, Mrs. Wilburn."

" You have your daughter to think of."

" Ah, yes. As you have Steven. But the woman's relation to her child is different from a man's. I feel that that isn't enough for me. I don't know. I suppose it is. It should be. I wonder . . ."

Once more he relapsed into silence. For a few moments they sat together quietly on either side of the fire. Physically the distance between them was the same as before. Spiritually it seemed to Clare as if it had stretched into infinity, and she knew that it was not she who had withdrawn herself from him.

Suddenly, almost brusquely, he rose from his chair and excused himself. Within the space of a few moments the intimacy which had given her the sensation of a warm human relationship had dissolved into the formality of a first acquaintance. She knew of no word, no action by which she could recreate it. For one second, on the wooden doorstep he hesitated ; she was conscious of the shattered aura regathering itself between them under the cold stars. His firm and formal handclasp annihilated it again. He thanked her for the supper she had given him and went. She stood at the door and watched his tall figure receding into the mist that shrouded the cinder path. And when the darkness hid him she felt as lonely as if his going had severed her last link with humanity. She was always lonely when Steven spent the night in barracks. . . .

## VI

### SUSPENSE

It was the gesture, she told herself, of a shy man, so unaccustomed to sympathy that hers had scared him. No doubt he would soon get over his shyness, and then the intimacy to which they had attained would be all to the good. For even if his experience of marriage were more bitter than hers, they still had a great deal in common.

But a week passed, and then another, and though they sometimes met on the roads or in the grounds of the big house which had been turned into an Officers' Club, those cosy fireside afternoons that she had shared with him and Steven were not renewed. It began to look as if Hart were avoiding her; and this troubled Clare, for she feared that in some way unknown to herself she had offended him and was anxious, for other, more urgent reasons, not to lose his friendship.

She approached the subject timidly through Steven. " You never bring Colonel Hart back to tea with you nowadays," she said. " We used to enjoy his visits, didn't we ? I can't think why he should suddenly desert us like this."

" I'm sure there's no particular reason," Steven told her. " The School's been enlarged and he's up to his ears in the job. He's a topping fellow, mother : as keen as mustard, and always up to some new stunt or other. As a matter of fact it's a rotten shame that they haven't given a man like that a command overseas."

" He's just the same to you ?   I mean, his manner hasn't changed ? "

" Good Lord, no !   But I'm nobody.   I don't suppose he's even aware of my existence."

" I wish you'd ask him to come to tea again, darling.   You might tell him from me that we miss him.   It seems funny for us to go on accepting his kindness and then to see nothing of him."

" I think it would be rather nerve for me to ask him like that.   After all, I'm only a subaltern and he's my C.O.   If he wants to come here, you can be jolly sure he'll invite himself."

" If you won't ask him, darling, perhaps I'll write to him."

" Oh, Lord, mum, don't do that ! " Steven advised ; " he's far too busy to answer letters from people like us. The wretched man has to sign his name five hundred times a day."

" My dear, you talk as if Colonel Hart were some sort of royalty !   Of course I shall write to him."

And yet, when she came to face it, she didn't, although, as she continued to brood on his defection, it seemed to her increasingly perverse and unreasonable.   If he were going to desert her like that, he really shouldn't have made friends so quickly.   When Christmas was over, and the days began to lengthen, she felt it more keenly than ever.   For all she saw of Steven she might almost have stayed at Uffdown. The training of the School of Instruction was intensive, and now that the light allowed it, their exercise took them much further afield, so that when Steven returned to her in the evening, he was usually dog-tired and more ready to sleep than to talk.

To divert herself she hired a tin-kettle piano from Andover ; but somehow, since the day of Ernest Wilburn's death, the music which she associated with him was charged with too many mournful memories for consolation.

Its slender beauty seemed empty and trifling against the warlike sounds that surrounded her ; the drone of planes which filled the sky from dawn to sunset ; the plaintive overtones of cavalry trumpets, echoed from the hillside behind Albuera ; the eternal crackle of machine-gun practice ; the dull detonations of heavies on the ranges at Rolleston.

And music now had other associations. She knew the meaning of those gay military bands that played a sprightly march on their way to the station. Week after week the drafts went swinging by. The bands marched back in silence to the barracks ; but the men who had marched behind them never returned. There was yet another horror associated with music. During the winter of nineteen-seventeen the epidemic of influenza which had swept the world brooded with particular virulence on the hutments of the Plain. Within a month the hospital at Dargai was extended by two hundred beds in which the New Zealanders from the Sling depot lay dying like flies. The road from the mortuary to the military cemetery ran immediately in front of the Staff Colony, and the last of the great elms, exactly in front of the windows of number four, marked the level at which the cortèges halted for a moment before the band struck up its funeral music and the slow march through Pedworth village began.

If they had played the *Dead March* in Saul or Chopin's *Marche Funèbre*, this funeral music might have been more tolerable ; but the march that all the bandmasters in Pedworth had united to choose was a brazen barbarity charged with the horror and the sombre pomp of death without any of its consolations. In Clare's early days at Pedworth she had sometimes stood with a set face at her window watching the slow march begin ; but now there was at least one funeral a day—sometimes there were five or six—and the repetition of that barbaric music became a torture against which she could not close her ears.

That muddy road, and, beyond it, the vista of the isolated Pedworth valley, wholly given over to the machinery of death, began to weigh upon her. Beneath the brisk and spurious liveliness of the camp she was aware, unceasingly, of the identical end toward which its activities were tending ; the cemetery on the hillside beyond the Pennings, or the ruthless, mechanical slaughter of the Flanders front. Three months had passed, and Steven's course was drawing to a close. The time moved swiftly, pitilessly, as though determined to bring all things to their end . . . except the war. There seemed to be no help for her, unless, like so many other women, she could accept the consolations of her own fortitude.

No help. She must go through with it. The only thing of importance was that Steven must not suffer with her. Steven, thank heaven, was in the best of spirits. Though Hart might work his limbs till they were tired, the hard life of the Plain was aimed at producing a physical perfection. He had left the smoke of Wolverbury a pale and tired stripling. Two months of Pedworth had re-established him. Now he was not only as tall as Ralph had been, but heavy and well-muscled. His health, his abounding strength filled her with a pride that was mingled with foreboding. They closed, it seemed, his only avenue of escape. If he could have taken the prevalent influenza—mildly—she would have thanked heaven for it.

One evening he came back to the Staff Colony languid and flushed.

" I think I must have got a bit of a chill," he told her.

She took his temperature ; it was a hundred and two. She sent Beazeley with a note to Dargai, summoning Captain Jerome, the medical officer attached to the School of Instruction. He was away on week-end leave. In his place came the Registrar of the Hospital ; the serious Major Ingleby in whom she recognized not only the son of the chemist in Halesby, but also the President of the Standing Board for Officers. If Steven were ill, it was Major Ingleby who would have to " board " him. As a new friend and accomplice he might some day be more useful, more powerful even than Colonel Hart. It was a piece of luck. She prayed that he might find that Steven was really ill. . . Really, but not *too* ill.

" It's influenza . . . no doubt about that," he told her. She saw the flag-draped gun-carriages ; she heard the muffled drums. " But there's nothing to worry about yet His lungs are quite clear. All you need do for the present is to keep him warm and well fed. Yes, yes ; a little aspirin if you like."

Her anxieties once relieved, she kept Major Ingleby talking in the little dining-room. This was a heaven-sent opportunity of confirming their acquaintance. She wanted to make him realize, behind the shabby, hired furniture, that it was the heir of Stourford whom he was attending. That ought to impress a man who came from Halesby. She set about her machinations without a scruple :

" You realize that we are neighbours, Major Ingleby ? We must often have seen each other, without knowing it when we were children. I often heard my grandfather, Dr. Weir, speak with admiration of your father."

He received her flatteries with the dry reserve of a man suspicious of patronage in the friendliness of social superiors who are aware of his humble origins. If she had counted on Stourford appealing to his snobbishness she was mistaken.

" But now that you've been here once," she pressed him, " I hope we shall see more of you. I feel, don't you, that we Midlanders ought to hang together. Of course you'll have another look at my son to-morrow ? "

" To-morrow, yes. The day after, his own M.O. will have returned. But don't, for heaven's sake, worry yourself, Mrs. Wilburn. There's no need to be anxious."

Anxious !

" An attack like this is bound to pull him down ? " she asked eagerly.

" Naturally. This year the type of infection's a severe one."

" I suppose it'll be months and months before he's fit again ? Fit for hard work, I mean ? " She meant " fit for General Service."

" That depends entirely on the course of the case. No doubt he'll want a little leave to put him straight again."

" He'll have to be boarded ? "

" Yes." He took pity on her. In spite of Stourford she was a charming woman. " When he comes before me, I'll see what I can do for him," he said.

" How kind of you ! I'm so thankful that Captain Jerome was away on leave."

" That's hardly polite to poor Captain Jerome," he laughed.

" Ah, but you know what I mean ? "

She wondered if he really knew what she meant. She didn't care if he did. She was prepared to expose herself to any humiliation if only Steven might be saved.

The influenza ran a normal course. For five days the fever ran high ; on the sixth it began to fall, and with the extinction of that unnatural flame Steven's weakness declared itself. He began to realize, for the first time, that he had been ill. He became querulous and rebellious against his own weakness.

" I ought to go back to the School to-morrow," he told her. " This means that I'm losing the continuity of the course. It's a bit of damnable luck. It won't be easy to catch up again."

" What does it matter, darling ? " she consoled him. " It's merely silly to fight against illness. You'll only worry yourself into a relapse by straining to make up for lost time."

" I wish I could talk to Colonel Hart about it," he said. " I do think he might have come to see me."

" I think he's been wise to keep away from the infection," she told him, repeating the argument with which she had already consoled herself. " I know he's been thinking about you quite a lot. Major Ingleby told me that he was enquiring particularly every day. And Beazeley has told Ellen too."

" I think, if you don't mind doing it for me, mum, I'd like you to write and ask him to come along. I'm sure he couldn't object to that."

" Of course I'll do that if you want me to."

As he dictated the letter she felt a curious pleasure in being compelled by him to do what modesty had restrained her from doing on her own account. Although she had originally set out to please Hart because of his importance as Steven's possible protector, it was for herself that she had missed him. The romantic appropriateness of their first chance meeting ; the kindnesses by which he had made her his debtor ever since ; the astonishing ease with which their little party of three had achieved a happy intimacy, had made her more dependent on him than she realized. In her life at Pedworth he filled the place that Ernest Wilburn had so disastrously vacated ; the office of a man, a little older than herself, who was prepared to offer his companionship, his experience, his advice, as a tribute to her beauty and her personal charms without any suggestion of a romantic relation.

They sent the letter to Hart by Beazeley that evening. Next day, in a state of fluttered expectation, she waited for his answering visit. Of course, Steven told her, they couldn't expect to see him before the end of the day's work ; but, as soon as lunch was over, she left Steven to go to her bedroom and make what was, for Pedworth, an unusually elaborate toilet before the distorted reflections of the mirror hired from Andover.

It did not seem to her that there was any coquetry in these preparations. She merely felt that in the stress of Steven's illness she had rather " let herself go." Yet, when she came into his bedroom, she was glad to know that Steven noticed the change. " By Jove, mum, you haven't half made yourself beautiful ! I wondered what you were up to," he said.

He, too, was in brighter spirits that afternoon ; not only in the expectation of Hart's visit, but because the sun, for once, was shining, and his natural resilience answered to warmth like that of a frost-pinched seedling. He begged her to open the window wider. Although no flowers were in bloom, the February air was charged with a perfume of spring that the unusual sunshine released from waking grass and purple hedgerow-twigs. Down from the elm-tops the song of a missel-thrush came dropping so clearly that they could almost have believed him a blackbird. They sat there talking and listening until the water-meadows swam with evening gold.

Suddenly Clare heard the crunch of rapid steps on the cinders and blushed. To hide her blushes she hurriedly began to put the room in order. Ellen would answer the knock on the door that followed ; but Ellen, perversely, was taking in washing from the clothes-line at the back, and Clare was forced to open the door herself, not, as she had expected, to Hart, but to a clean-shaven, white-haired major, in chaplain's uniform, who asked her, without raising his eyes, if this were Mr. Hingston's.

The face meant nothing to her, but the voice in which the question was asked carried her back abruptly through twenty years. " I am the senior chaplain," it was saying, " my colleague, Mr. Medway, who is attached to the School of

Instruction, asked me to visit Mr. Hingston in his absence. . . ."

" But surely you are Mr. Darnay ? " Clare exclaimed.

The senior chaplain suddenly raised his eyes. " And you ? Why . . . Clare ? Whoever would have dreamed it ! And how stupid of me ! It's all so long ago that the name had ceased to mean anything to me. So it's your boy I've come to see ? Well, well, it's a strange world ! "

He took her arm as they walked along the passage. The Mr. Darnay of Wychbury would never have permitted himself such a liberty ; but Father Darnay of the St. Ibrox Mission in Mayfair, the hero of innumerable exalted spiritual flirtations, had held the hands of so many duchesses with such incomparable discretion that Clare's arm had no more terrors for him.

The slender fare of Cowley had evidently suited Father Darnay ; the lean, red-headed zealot whose violence had been such a thorn in Mr. Pomfret's comfortable flanks had found, in plump middle age, a suave and white-haired urbanity that even Mr. Pomfret might have envied. He was now so completely a citizen of the polite world, his manners were so easy, his very uniform marked by an asceticism so expensive that Clare was not in the least astonished to learn, by implications which he dropped in passing, that he had lately been chaplain to the Brigade of Guards. Not that this social distinction could ever affect his relationship with such an old friend as herself. His manner prayed her to realize that his visit was in no way a condescension. The Anglican Church, it assured her, was, above all things, democratic : that very evening, he let slip, he was dining in his own quarters with a sergeant and a private of the Tenth Hussars. . . .

Steven knew all about him, for he had read all those famous tracts in which Father Darnay, meeting the scientists on their chosen ground, had proved, in their own language, that Anglican dogmas were not only compatible with modern science, but essential to its proper understanding. Medway, the chaplain at Fontenoy, had told him, as a thrilling secret, that Father Darnay was coming to Pedworth. And here, within forty-eight hours of his arrival, this hero of modern controversy was sitting at his bedside.

" There's no man living, sir," he blurted out shyly, " whom I'd sooner have met than yourself."

Darnay affected to laugh at his enthusiasms ; he knew how to deal with flattery ; he was used to it ; but Clare could see that he was pleased for her to hear the compliment.

" Come, come young man, you'll make me conceited if you talk like that ! It's odd that you never knew that your mother and I were such old friends. Those funny old days in Wychbury . . . poor little St. Chad's ! We were all very humble then, and probably much nicer than we are now. As soon as you're up," he told them, " you must come and see me in my quarters ; we'll have long talks together. That will be tremendous fun."

Those long talks hadn't been fun in Clare's day. Apart from music, she and Mr. Darnay had never spoken of anything but religion ; but now it seemed as if religion were the one subject in the world that Father Darnay wished to avoid. When Steven tried to draw him toward it he hedged with an urbane, persistent politeness. It was obvious that this life which had once been permeated by one unruly enthusiasm was now discreetly divided by watertight bulkheads into compartments in which religion, politics, society, science, and all its other components were separated from each other as neatly as the details of his admirable wardrobe. Father Darnay had no more intention of mixing theology with his tea than sergeants with his duchesses. And though he had come to visit Steven it was obviously Clare in whom he was more interested.

" I want you to tell me all about yourself," he said. " We

can talk about this dear Steven when I've got over the shock of seeing you. Some of your history I've heard, now I come to think of it, from poor old Mr. Pomfret. Yes, he served under me at Aldershot. The war's been full of queer reversals like that." He chuckled softly. " Dear me, dear me ! And then your music ? Do you remember the Mass in B Minor, Clare ? And Miss Weir's indignation ? That Papist stuff ! "

" Aunt Cathie died three years ago, poor darling," Clare told him. His brows contracted into an appropriate sympathy.

" Ah, well, God rest her soul. She was a good woman, I believe."

" A wonderful woman, and just as brave as she was good," Clare maintained. For as the figure of Aunt Cathie faded her halo grew always brighter.

" And then the Stourford people ? " Father Darnay continued. " I suppose Sir Joseph goes from strength to strength ? I noticed his G.B.E. in the *Gazette*. And Lady Hingston ? And George ? His wife was a Pomfret, wasn't she ? "

" George was killed on the Somme."

" Indeed ? Poor fellow ! He left a son, of course ? Twins, surely ? "

" They lost their boy some years ago."

" Really ? How very unfortunate ! But surely, in that case . . . ? " His eyes returned to Steven with a renewal of interest. Ellen came blundering in and interrupted him.

" Colonel Hart," she announced.

Clare rose to meet him. " I'm so glad," she said. It made her happy to see him, to find him just the same as ever ; and yet she was sorry that they had not met alone.

She introduced Father Darnay : " The new senior chaplain, one of my oldest friends." The two men shook hands ;

and from that moment she knew not only that they disliked each other, but that she herself was somehow involved in their dislikes. Sitting within the triangle composed by them and Steven she felt a curious renewal of the atmosphere of Tudor House when the cross-fire of unspoken hatreds had withered her. She tried, heroically, to make the best of it ; but knew that she could not influence the situation. She knew that if she were forced to take a side, the side would be Colonel Hart's. There was something in the manliness, the directness of the soldier that made the priest's fine brain and social cleverness seem rather flimsy ; his outline grew blurred and indefinite against Hart's steel-cut clearness. And Father Darnay, his dim eyes growing hazy behind the gold pince-nez which gripped his long, thin nose, seemed to guess what she was thinking ; for, of a sudden, like a small-part actor fading into the background of the stage when the " lead " appears, he excused himself and rose to go.

" No, please don't trouble to see me out," he protested in a voice that seemed unusually affected and high-pitched. " Now that we've renewed our acquaintance I'm sure we shall see a lot of each other. Old friends . . . you know the rest ?

He took her hand and held it, as though he were anxious that Hart should realize the intimacy.

Of course she couldn't let him go like that ; he made it seem so clear that he had been driven away. Alone with her in the passage he recovered himself.

" I'm glad to see," he told her, " that you have brought up Steven in our old tradition. I feel that there are very potent influences working against us in Pedworth ; that was partly the reason why the Chaplain-General sent me here. Now that I've found you again I know that I shan't have to celebrate Mass in an empty church like my predecessor. It'll be like those queer old days at St. Chad's. And when you want to see your old confessor you'll find him just the same. But I mustn't keep you from your other guest any longer."

He left her before she could explain to him that she hadn't confessed for years. When she returned to the bedroom she found Steven explaining to an unenthusiastic audience the significance of Father Darnay's arrival.

" You see, sir, he's not like an ordinary padre. Before he was ordained he took a first in science at Cambridge. You should read his books on science and religion ; he's one of the most distinguished men in the Church to-day. Nobody will realize what an enormous privilege it is for us to have him here at all."

He couldn't see, it seemed, that Father Darnay was the last person on earth whom Hart wanted to talk about. Clare came to Hart's rescue quickly ; he was so restless that she feared lest Steven's enthusiasms should drive him away, and she was determined, before he went, to get to the bottom of the change of atmosphere that had arisen between them.

" I wish you could convince Steven that we shan't lose the war because he's had influenza," she said.

" Mother will never realize the meaning of lost time," Steven interrupted impatiently. " I'm afraid it means I shall have to begin the course all over again. And my job. sir, is to be with the battalion, isn't it ? "

" Your first job, my dear boy, is to make yourself an efficient officer. They don't want half-trained platoon-commanders in France. And even before you think of that it's your duty to get fit again."

" I knew you'd tell him that," Clare answered eagerly. " He's dreadful ; he gets so excited ; he's been going on like this for the last three years, Colonel Hart."

" I'm afraid the new padre and I have excited him even more than usual," said Hart, " so I'd better be going." He rose and laid a firm hand on Steven's shoulder. " For the moment your job's an easy one. Get well quickly. And then we'll see what we can do for you."

But Clare was not going to let him go as easily as that. When she drew him aside into the darkened dining-room he took it for granted, perversely, that she wanted to continue talking about Steven's illness.

" Ingleby and I have discussed the matter together," he said. " He's a sound man, and agrees with me that in spite of all his keenness the boy isn't as strong as he looks. He's too emotional ; takes everything far too seriously. I hope this Father Darnay won't get hold of him. As soon as he's back again I shall have him boarded. At present he's only fit for service at home."

" You mean that you can keep him at Pedworth ? " The joy nearly choked her. " I can scarcely believe it. Oh, Colonel, how can I thank you ? "

" There's nothing to thank me for," he answered, almost harshly. " I'm doing my duty, which is to send out officers with minds and bodies fit to stand the strain of active service, and as much knowledge of their job as I can cram into them in a quite inadequate time. If Steven fulfilled these conditions there'd be no alternative : he'd go to his unit to-morrow wherever it was." He changed the subject abruptly ; Clare's mind could not keep pace with him, it was so bewildered with gratitude and relief. " I hope that Beazeley's behaving himself ? " he asked.

" Beazeley ? Oh, Beazeley's a treasure. It's too good of you to spare him in the evening. I feel "— she hesitated—" I only feel that we've no right to make use of him as we do."

" No right ? What do you mean ? My dear Mrs. Wilburn, I'm sure he enjoys it. Beazeley's the kind of fellow who is born in service ; and I, being used to a sort of bachelorhood, don't need his attentions."

" That's not quite what I meant to say ; and what I *do*

mean isn't exactly easy to express. Will you forgive me if I put it clumsily?" she begged him. For she saw that his mood was difficult, as though, for some reason, Father Darnay's presence had set his nerves on edge and made him shy of this solitary interview. "It seemed to me—of course I may be quite wrong—a little strange that while you send your servant to help us you never come to see us yourself any more. It almost looks as though you avoided us."

"Well, here I am at last," he said, with a laugh which implied that he still refused to take her seriously.

"But it's true, isn't it, that you have avoided us?" she persisted.

"That is an awkward question, Mrs. Wilburn. Better ask me another."

"I haven't another to ask," she answered truthfully. "If you don't want to answer me, I can't make you."

"No, you can't make me," he repeated, smiling.

"And yet," she went on, "I want you to realize that— quite apart from all questions of gratitude—we've missed you. I felt, I couldn't help feeling, that there had been a misunderstanding somewhere."

"If there's been any misunderstanding," he answered quickly, "I take the blame for it. And if I thought for a moment that I'd hurt you . . ." He paused, as though he couldn't trust himself to say more, and turned away from her. Then, suddenly, he continued : " Your honesty has put me to shame, Mrs. Wilburn. Probably my experience of women has been unfortunate ; it makes me suspicious. . . ."

"Suspicious? Of *me*? You suspected . . ."

"No, no, I suspected nothing. It's the wrong word again. I want to be as honest with you as you have been with me. Forgive me if my honesty seems brutal." Again he hesitated. "When last I was here," he continued, "I made a mistake. I've not been used to sympathy for a long time ; and when I found it in you I began to talk about myself. One oughtn't to talk about oneself ; it's indecent. As soon as I'd gone I knew what an ass I'd made of myself. It struck me that you might think I was asking for your pity, which was the last thing in the world I meant to do."

" No, no. I was sorry for you ; but that wasn't your fault."

" And then there was something else. At the end you happened to mention that your husband was alive. I'd imagined, to speak quite frankly, that you were a widow. My own disasters have rather—how shall I put it ?—have rather tightened my code in matters of that kind. I saw at once that I'd been coming here too often."

" Too often ? "

" Surely you understand ? The character of my interest in Steven and yourself might be mistaken. For myself it wouldn't matter a brass farthing. But . . . well, to put it shortly, this is a garrison town ; women are talkative, and I felt that you might suffer by it."

" Why didn't you tell me that before ? " Clare asked him gravely.

" I couldn't. You're far too good to be troubled even by the suggestion."

" I should have suffered much less if you'd told me."

" Well, now, at any rate, you understand ? "

" I understand. But still I think you were over-scrupulous. I'm not a young and inexperienced woman. Colonel Hart."

He laughed to hear her estimate of her own charms : " My dear Mrs. Wilburn ! "

" If there were any suggestion of my protecting myself —how vulgar it all sounds !—I'm capable of doing so. As it is, there's no question of anything but a very charming friendship ; a friendship that I value more than anything else in Pedworth. Why shouldn't I admit it? And then, with Steven, there's something else as well. You've no idea how he admires you, Colonel Hart. . . ."

" He might easily have found a better object for his admiration than an elderly dug-out like myself."

" That doesn't affect the genuineness of his feelings . . . nor of mine. I think you're far too humble about yourself in any case; and as for your scruples . . ." She paused. " Won't you take it from me that there's no reason in the world why we shouldn't be friends? "

For a long time he was silent. She felt as though he were searching beneath her frankness for some hidden coquetry, and his hesitation, far from offending her, only made her more anxious to reassure him.

" I think we are both behaving rather ridiculously," she added. " After all this is the twentieth century; we're not Victorians."

He smiled. " I'm not sure that you haven't hit it exactly : that's just what I am. For better or for worse."

They laughed together. His laughter brought him a little nearer to her, and she took courage again : " You haven't answered my question," she reminded him.

" No, you're quite right, there's no reason why we shouldn't be friends."

" So you'll come to see us, just as you did before? " she persisted.

" Just as before," he repeated. " I apologize."

" No, no, you'll spoil it all if you do that."

He took her hand and pressed it, and left her without another word.

" What have you two been talking about? " Steven demanded when she rejoined him. " You sounded as if you were quarrelling."

She laughed : " Don't be so inquisitive, my darling." Her spirits were as high and fluttered as those of a young girl returning from a secret assignation. It pleased her to tantalize him and mock his seriousness.

" You know I don't trust you, mum. You're always plotting against me behind my back. What is it now ? "

But she wouldn't tell him. Three weeks later he was boarded by Major Kennedy and relegated, in spite of his protests, to the Home Service category.

" I believe you're partly responsible for this," he grumbled " it'd be just like you to go and butt in."

Flushed with the first-fruits of her victory she could afford to smile at his ill-humour. And there were compensations even for Steven. No sooner had he returned to duty than a General Order announced his appointment as Assistant-Adjutant to the School of Instruction, a post that associated him with Hart more closely than ever. " If he makes himself indispensable to the School," she thought, " there's no reason why he shouldn't keep it till the war is over." She wondered if some idea of the same kind had made Hart give it to him, and was glad of any circumstance that strengthened their relation.

For now that the old intimacy was re-established, Hart's friendship and his vivid, reassuring presence had become a vital part of Steven's life at Pedworth.

## VII

### TORRENTS OF SPRING

SUDDENLY Spring came in with banners flying. It ran, like fire, along the Pedworth valley, lighting the purple shoots of the sallows with pale flame, kindling a glow of crimson in the high elm-blossom, till all the air seemed softened and warmed by its passage. Even the outlines of the stark woods on Sidbury grew mellow in distance with the swelling of invisible leaf-buds ; and though, as yet, the dun expanses of the Plain showed no quickening of colour. the sea-born billows of cumulus that warm winds drove above them caught up Clare's heart by their very height and purity, challenging her to leave the sodden valleys, to taste on her lips and in her lungs the new and vital air that gave their movement its stupendous energy. The very aeroplanes, once so sinister, seemed to exult more bravely in their dizzy evolutions. Day after day, through floods of sunlight and veils of silver rain, the south-west swept the land, carrying on its wings wave upon wave of migrants, till every gust seemed charged with notes of intoxicating sweetness ; the whole green world drowned in a bath of song.

Three months. The very definiteness of the period of Steven's reprieve made its ecstasies more poignant ; the threat that there might never be such another compelled her to drain the ultimate sweetness of this miraculous draught. Such beatific combinations of beauty and security might not come her way again ; she determined to accept them without reservation, as though they were sure to last for ever.

And Steven was happy too. When once he realized that his obstinacy was powerless against the medical board's decree, he had resigned himself to a gentler, convalescent mood. The board had recommended that his duties should be light ; and now that th ..rain of the intensive course of training had been relaxed into a routine of office work, he began to take his mission at Pedworth with a less deadly seriousness.

He was more reasonable and more contented, in fact, than he had ever been since the beginning of the war. Practically, his new duties at Fontenoy were those of private secretary to Hart ; and since, with the continued expansion of the School, the Colonel had been relieved from his teaching by the appointment of wounded subordinates, fresh from

France, so that his activities were limited to advice and administration, it came about that he and Steven were free to make the most of that rare season.

In their new intimacy the boy and the man had struck up a fast friendship. Before this, his hero-worship for Hart had made Steven shy. Now that they worked together his admiration became subordinate to an affection such as he had never shown for any human being but Clare herself. It was so different in kind that she could not be jealous of it. Indeed, it delighted her; for, to tell the truth, she knew that her son had always been a little inhuman, and there was no man living with whom she would rather have seen him intimate; for now that the cloud which lay between them had lifted, her liking and admiration for Hart's sterling qualities matched Steven's own. It seemed, in fact, as if he were supplying the influence, half brotherly and half paternal, which she had hoped to give Steven when she had married Wilburn; as if, in Hart's manly and sensitive comradeship, Steven were finding something that Wilburn, at his best, could never have afforded. And she was thankful, not only for Steven's sake.

For Hart had kept his promise. Now that the time and place of their labours coincided, it seemed only natural that he and Steven should return to her when these were over. With the coming of spring their quiet tea-times and firelit talks gave place to a companionship more active. The whole life of Pedworth had taken on a holiday air. The wave of the influenza epidemic had spent itself; the hateful funeral music no longer struck up in the roadway outside her door; and though the drafts went tramping to railhead with the same dread frequency, the sprightly music mocked her no more, for she knew that Steven would not go marching with them. Her heart, from the very persistence of its presence, had grown callous to the horror of war. London might cower in panic beneath night-flying Gothas. Here, where war forged its weapons, was nothing but confidence, peace and comfortable plenty.

At first they played tennis or badminton in the covered courts of the officers' club. Then, as the evenings lengthened, they moved further afield : up the green valley of the Pedworth winterbourne to its head-waters under Savernake ; over the downs to westward, where the hill-top cities of hutments were lost below long horizons which restored the wide depressions of Plain between them to an older, pastoral peace. Over those downs a man might walk from dawn to sunset and meet no fellow-man, but, perhaps, a shepherd emerging from his wheeled hut to gaze into the mud-trampled lambing-folds. They were all old men ; no young shepherds were left ; and the downs were empty, in that season, of all life but that of strutting rooks or here and there a mad hare bounding from its form or sitting bolt upright like a kangaroo to watch them ; for all the ewes were folded now, and the shepherds tending them day and night.

Plaintive and heart-softening in those days were the weak voices of lambs. From the bare down, with nothing of life in sight but the swellings of the stone-men's barrows and sunken trackways, perhaps older than those, Clare stopped to hear the wind-blown murmur of hidden folds. It was not the distressful bleating of flocks driven on dusty highways that came to her, but a sound beautiful and serene, that spoke of fulfilment. Then she, and Hart, and Steven, would set their course toward it, till the down sloped away, and they could see the trim squares of the folds. They would stand by the hurdles, and watch the new-born lying limp and pitiful, scattered where they had fallen, like flakes of cloud ; and older lambs, who trotted, weak-kneed, at their dams' tails, or shook their silly heads, or leapt sideways for no reason ; and stubborn weanlings, who bent their knees and splayed hind-legs to thrust their greedy muzzles upwards into their mothers' udders as they ran.

These, and the warblers that thrilled the valleys with their love-songs at dawn, the larks that trilled unseen, roofing the Plain with tremulous, daylong ecstasy, the swelling buds, swung catkins, the flying pollen of wind-mated blossom—all these and each claimed and found kinship with the tender emotions that trembled into birth within Clare's heart. Her heightened sensitiveness embraced them eagerly, knowing their impermanence ; yet never was beauty more remote from tears. Not even at Uffdown twenty years before. Not even with Ralph. She wondered if Steven knew what she was feeling. She hoped, she felt, unreasonably that Robert Hart did.

He was responsible, in part, for her fuller understanding. She had always counted herself a country girl, with eyes and ears alert, and had wondered at the slowness, the lack of country-sense, which separated Wilburn from her. But Hart's ears and eyes was more acute than hers. He missed nothing ; he knew everything—not merely the notes of birds, the movements of all shy, wild downland creatures which he followed with a skill that a poacher might have envied, but the least traces they left behind them when they had gone : the trail of a hungry vixen in the dew ; the form of a leveret ; the false-nests smoothed in the fallows by the love-dances of lapwings who wheeled and swooped above their olive-dappled eggs with anxious, cat-like cries.

" However do you manage to see all this ? " Clare asked him.

" The habit of observation. I'm a soldier. In the African bush I've been hunter and hunted at once, and little things of this kind meant the difference between life and death. It's easy enough, when once you've learnt to use your eyes."

It was not only that he saw such things ; he recognized and treasured the beauty in them and compelled her to see it with his eyes. When the wailing lapwings saw that they meant no ill he made her watch the miracle of the birds' alighting, the swift parabola of the *volplane*, with frail legs trailing, and then the run along the ground, so delicate that the creature seemed to belong neither to earth nor air : the folding of the spread wings.

" I think," he said, " that this is the loveliest movement in nature. All the plovers have it."

It was even more precious to love things than to know them. It made an end of loneliness.

" I feel," she told him, " that you are more English than anyone I've ever known."

He smiled at her ; his whole face glowed with pleasure.

" If you'd tried all your life you couldn't have paid me a greater compliment than that. England means more to me than anything else in life. Partly, perhaps, because I've spent so much of my life away from her. You and Steven, both of you, are extraordinarily English."

" Claerwen is Welsh. I used to like to think that I came —some part of me—from Radnorshire."

" And I am Shropshire. Radnor's an English county. Spiritually, we're near neighbours, people of Severn-side. What was your other name ? "

" Lydiatt," she told him.

" Lydgate, the monk of Bury. As English as Chaucer or Langland."

It was the first time she had realized that he had any interest in literature. Later, he showed it in ways that astonished her. One day they walked across the down to tea at the old inn at Everley.

" It was here that Cobbett stayed," he told her. " He called it the nicest and pleasantest inn in England. It was near here that he saw his field full of hares. Now he was an Englishman if you like ! "

Clare had never heard of him. And so, that evening, he brought down from the barracks Cobbett's *Rural Rides*.

They read it aloud together, taking turns ; and this was only the first of many books that they read, all of which seemed, in some way, reflections of Hart's own spirit and the spirit of the land in which they were living : Hardy and Hudson, Barnes and Housman ; a contrast most curious to the books that her other literary mentor, Ernest Wilburn, had lent her.

She was not ungrateful that Ernest had made his exotic reading part of her experience ; and yet, in Hart's more homely and more tranquil taste she found a simplicity of feeling nearer to her own. In those long evenings of reading at the Staff Colony, and in the little festive meals that Ellen cooked for them, she began to lose the shyness with which Hart's own shyness had infected her. Their party of three seemed curiously complete and natural ; it was as if they had known and understood each other all their lives. Within the comfortable aura of Hart's tobacco-smoke there grew an atmosphere of domesticity such as she had not even tasted alone with Steven at Uffdown. Sitting with them, air-drugged and soothed by the drone of voices, her mind would lose touch with the content of what the men were reading and wander away into pleasant and idle speculations.

" Our life would have been like this," she thought, " if Ralph had lived. Steven and Ralph and myself at peace together."

For now, at a distance of twenty years, the figure of Ralph had assumed a traditional shape embodying perfections that she never stopped to question, probably because, in her heart of hearts, she knew how questionable they were. She knew that the real Ralph had been nothing but a healthy, callow young Philistine adorned and exalted by her ideal love. If she had dared to think, she would have known that Ralph would have felt lost and even bored in their company ; he would have needed a hand of bridge to keep the evening alive ; for the library at Stourford—in which Vivien played badminton and Sir Joseph kept his cigars—was representa-

tive of the Hingstons' literary tastes. And as for her music
. . .

There, as a matter of fact, Hart's almost too-perfect
sympathies showed a lacuna. Except on those rare evenings
when Steven's mood demanded that she should play Bach
to him, the piano that she had hired from Andover remained
unopened. Music of itself meant little to Hart. He liked
old English songs ; but that was because their words had
moved him by their associations in distant lands : he liked
to listen while she played ; but that was because it was she
who was playing. And though she regretted this blind spot
in his aesthetic equipment, she felt it was atoned for by the
honesty with which he admitted it. Most men would have
hedged, or qualified the defect with excuses.

It seemed, after all, that in her music she was compelled
to go through life alone. None of the men with whom she
had been intimate, save only Ernest Wilburn, had been able
to share it with her. Ernest Wilburn and Darnay. And
Darnay, as it happened, was becoming an incongruous
element in their life at Pedworth.

In spite of his social preoccupations with the Reserve
Regiments of Cavalry he often found time to " drop in "
at the Staff Colony. Primarily, no doubt, he was after
Steven ; for even if Steven were not in the Greys or Royals,
he was heir to one of the wealthiest baronetcies in the Midlands, and, what was more important, likely to use his
coming wealth in support of the Anglican faith. Moreover,
such promising proselytes were rare at Pedworth. But it
wasn't only Steven whom he came to see. He had counted
on Clare to make one of the little band of devout women
which gave a basis of genuine faith to the formal religious
exercises of the Garrison Church. It piqued him to find that
she had deserted the path of grace in which he had planted
her footsteps twenty years before ; her backsliding was
a matter that affected his personal prestige ; he waited for

an opportunity to catch her alone, and took her to task for it. Something of the ancient zealotry gleamed through his gold-rimmed pince-nez as he attacked her.

" I have been here three weeks," he said, " and yet I've never seen you at my early celebrations."

In the old days he would have called them Masses.

" My life is a busy one, Father Darnay," she told him.

" That's no excuse. You know it's no excuse. When I was working in the East End the women would bring their babies to the Mission rather than forego their duties. No, no, Clare ; that won't do."

" You're quite right. I would rather tell you the truth," she said. " Soon after you left Wychbury I had a great blow. My husband died in South Africa. It was an awful cruelty. I couldn't get over it, couldn't reconcile myself After his death I lost all belief in religion."

" If you had remembered my teaching that should have strengthened your faith. There is no grief that real faith cannot console. Why didn't you write to me ? I'm sure I could have helped you to recover it. I'm afraid you didn't cry."

" I did. Later, when I was unhappy for other reasons, I tried hard. I found myself, quite by accident, near St. Jude's. In North Bromwich, you know. It looked like Providence. I went in, prepared for a miracle. It was a dreadful failure. Shall I hurt you very much, Father Darnay, if I tell you that it all meant nothing to me ? "

" You are hurting yourself," he assured her. " You do not realize the happiness you were missing."

She sighed. " And yet," she said, " I'm very happy now. I believe I'm happier than I've ever been in my life."

He shook his head solemnly. " You think so. Yes. But that is a very dangerous state of mind, more dangerous, I'm afraid, than you realize. Heaven has a summary way of dealing with the illusion of happiness that goes with spiritual pride. To-day you think you are happy. Only wait! You're a young woman, Clare. The future is veiled from us. Many things may happen. I'm afraid you'll find yourself unprepared to meet them. The war is not over."

His sombre tone disturbed her.

"What are you threatening, Father Darnay? There's something in your mind. Tell me more clearly."

"The war is not over," he repeated. "I'm thinking of Steven."

"Don't even speak of it for God's sake!" she begged him.

He smiled with distant satisfaction. "I've frightened you? That shows, my child, how precarious this boasted happiness is. I beg you, Clare, to come back to us for your own sake."

"That wouldn't be fair. I should be deceiving you and myself if I came back to you."

"Perhaps. But unless you make a beginning you'll never come at all. The will to believe would be more than half the battle. I beg you to believe me."

"You're trying to frighten me, Father Darnay. That's not my idea of religion. I should feel myself heathenish and primitive if I were driven to accept your God through fear."

"*The fear of the Lord is the beginning of wisdom,*" he quoted. "You're wrong. A religion that isn't terrible is no religion. If you don't believe in the vegeance of God, you might just as well not believe in Him at all." He changed his tactics suddenly. "It seems a pity," he said, "that old friends like ourselves should differ. It's waste of time to argue on matters that are beyond argument. Suppose you come just for the sake of old times? You'll be giving great joy to Steven as well as me. It's a pity that two people who care for each other as deeply as you and he should be separated in the most important thing of all.

Suppose you come with him to the early celebration to-morrow? Provided, of course, that you're in a state of grace."

"I can't. I'm very sorry, but I can't," she told him. "It's too late."

"It's never too late," he said. But he knew he was defeated. As he stood there and stared at her, she saw a purple tide of colour rising above his white collar-band ; his face went red, to his shelving forehead and the tip of his long nose ; his eyes blinked, his mouth twitched with annoyance, and when he spoke the last shreds of urbanity were gone.

"I think I know the meaning of this," he thundered in his pulpit voice. "You've tried to deceive me, Clare ; but I'll tell you the truth. This is the influence of Colonel Hart. An infidel. A notorious infidel. I've heard of him before. Meadows, his own chaplain, has told me. No, don't protest ! " He waved her words aside.

"I must protest. What you've said is unjust, untrue ! Colonel Hart has nothing whatever to do with my feelings. I respect him more than any man on earth."

"That is the kind of respect, if I may say so, that you might decently reserve for your husband."

She disregarded his taunt ; her loyalty was on fire in Hart's defence :

"You shall not drag his name into this. I won't allow it. Whatever his views may be they have nothing whatever to do with mine."

"In that case the general opinion of the camp appears to be mistaken."

"Do you mean anything by that, Father Darnay ? " She flushed quickly.

Retreating before her anger he recovered his suavity :

"No, not what you suggest. Please acquit me of that. I take your word for it."

" It seems you've already taken other people's. Please tell me what you've heard."

" Pedworth's a small place. Idle people will talk. It's natural . . ."

" It's damnable in this case, Father Darnay ! "

" I'm glad to hear you say so," said Father Darnay, rather confusingly. " Of course I believe what you tell me. But there again "—he paused—" if you'll allow me to say so, I think your position is less secure, more dangerous, than you imagine. And there again, I feel that I might be of use to you."

" Of use ? How ? Where ? " She couldn't see what he was driving at. The insult of the suggestion which he had made and withdrawn still made the blood tingle in her ears. She couldn't bear to listen to him any longer.

" When I feel that I need your help, Father Darnay," she said, " I'll tell you."

He could not deny himself the satisfaction of a parting shot : " I hope you won't leave it too late."

" The Colonel is right," she thought ; " he wants to have the last word, like a woman. He's more like a woman than I am. His arguments : so illogical ! "

But when he had gone she was disturbed not by his arguments, but by the scandalous talk at which he had hinted. Her first impulse was to tell Hart everything. On second thoughts she decided that she could not do so. He was too big, too honest, to be troubled with such ignoble tattle ; so scrupulous that, if she breathed a word of it, he might feel himself compelled to leave her again. The only people really concerned in this gossip were herself and Dudley. She would write to Dudley at once and warn him against it. Since Dudley had joined the army as Judge Advocate-General, attending court-martials all over the Southern Command, their correspondence had been much more friendly ; he had even suggested calling on her if his duties brought him to Pedworth. She would write and say how glad she would be to see him and make some allusion to this other business in a postscript. He would see through her postscript. She could hear his laugh. *Qui s'excuse s'accuse*. Better say nothing. Perhaps she might say something to Steven ? That, too, was ridiculous. Apart from that one strained interview during his illness she had scarcely spoken to Hart except in his presence. After all she felt that she was worrying herself over trifles. Even Darnay had withdrawn his veiled accusation as soon as it was spoken.

But Father Darnay had not finished with them yet. Between himself and Hart there was more than a religious antipathy. He regarded Clare as his convert, and was as jealous as none but a celibate could be. Abandoning his attacks on her, he began to concentrate them on Steven, courting the boy with flatteries that played upon his religious emotional side with a skill that would have undermined a loyalty less firmly established than that which attached him to Hart.

When Steven began to introduce the subject of religion into their evening discussions Clare knew what was afoot. She longed to warn Hart that Steven's challenges were inspired by Darnay ; she was frightened lest Hart's very candour might create a breach. But even here Steven's habit of deferring to his colonel robbed Darnay's indirect offensive of half its malignancy ; and Hart, if she had known it, was capable of defending himself with greater reserves of tact than she had given him credit for. She was amazed at the smiling virtuosity with which he denied his enemy's emissary contact. His charity, his good-humour, his infinite reasonableness were, of themselves, disarming.

" I see it's no good, sir," Steven complained. " You won't take me seriously."

" I take you so seriously, my dear boy, that I decline to argue with you. Besides, if you only knew it, we're on parallel lines. If we went on arguing for ever we should never meet. But our direction's the same. And, if you come to think of it, the only essential difference between us is in the points from which we start. And that's a small one. We've far too much in common for serious disagreement."

But with the middle of March, when the first northward nightingales began to nest along the borders of the beech-woods, the subdued, idyllic life of the Pedworth valley was shaken by repercussions of a blow that made all differences seem trivial. The front of the Fifth Army cracked and was hurled back on Amiens with the grinding pressure of a disintegrating ice-floe. Even as the waves of that miraculous spring drove westward in a foam of sloe-blossom the grey wave of destruction swelled behind them. The end of the war was coming, they told her. It seemed to Clare as if it might be the end of the world. The three months of reprieve were nearly over.

## VIII

### VICTORY OF FONTENOY

" I've asked for a board at once," Steven casually announced. " Anyone with half an eye can see I'm fit again. They're turning fellows out of hospitals and sending them back to France, I have no right to be doing office-work."

" You have no right to decide what you're to do," Clare protested. " It's a soldier's duty to take the orders that come to him."

" And stick to a cushy job till he's ' combed out ' ? You ought to know me better than that, mother ! "

She did ; and she knew it was idle to argue with him. The question wasn't arguable in any case ; by every canon of reason and human dignity he was right. In those days lives of men were of small account. But for her the emergency transcended reason or dignity. Already he had set in motion the monstrous machinery that would drag him away from her. She would have thrown herself, gladly, into the mangling cogs if, even for one moment, such a sacrifice could have stayed their revolutions.

Her thoughts turned first to Sir Joseph. A wire to Wolverbury? Impossible : three weeks ago the Government had sent him to America to organize vast new contracts for munitions. And even if he had been at Wolverbury she knew that in days like these his hands were tied. If Steven had stayed at Wolverbury he might have held him ; but Steven in the army was another matter. Two years before his influence might have counted. To-day the clamour of the press against civilian machinations made it of no account.

She thought of Major Ingleby. No help there. She felt that her attempts to ingratiate herself with him, to establish a kind of prophylactic intimacy had failed. Since the afternoon when she had set out to charm him he had evaded her invitations. Perhaps, like most Halesby people, he was suspicious of Stourford ; perhaps those inscrutable, incorruptible eyes of his had already guessed what she was after. As President of the Standing Board for Officers he must be well versed in every variety of veiled persuasion.

As for Steven, no plea but that of military exigency could save him ; that plea could be urged by no one but Hart. And there, thank heaven, she seemed to see a glimmer of hope. He had told her, a hundred times, how invaluable Steven was to him; how Steven's conscientiousness had made him an integral part of the School's efficiency. And, even if military reasons were not valid, the personal claim remained. Their intimacy, she told herself, had been of no ordinary kind. They three had been so happy, so free, so honest with each other, and Hart himself was so full of understanding that surely he couldn't fail to realize the devastation from which, with a little effort, he could save them both. The more she thought of him, of his wisdom, his generosity, the surprising tenderness that tempered his strength, the surer she felt that she could count on him at the last for an act of mercy and of salvation.

"If I can only catch him by himself," she thought. "When Steven isn't there, he'll be bound to listen to me. He's so good, so sympathetic, that he must see what this means and have pity on me."

She waited, distracted and tremulous, for her opportunity ; but when Steven stalked in late from Fontenoy that evening Hart did not come with him.

"What have you done with Colonel Hart ? " she asked him.

"The Colonel ? I left him up to his eyes in work. The whole show's in a ferment. We're sending a draft of thirty officers off to-morrow. I should have stayed in the office till midnight if he hadn't shoved me off."

That evening Steven was so preoccupied with his subdued excitement that he scarcely spoke to her. When dinner was over he left her to go routing in the spare-room for his overseas kit. His every moment seemed full of sinister purpose. She sat alone in the dining-room, pretending to read ; through the still night she heard the stutter of engines under load, the clank of couplings. Even in darkness, below the nightingale-haunted beechwoods, the stream of reinforcements hurried out of Pedworth. From beyond the winter-bourne, where the uncurtained windows of the barracks glowed through the fog in a bleared crescent, came an unusual rumour of voices, sharp words of command and a clatter of mallets.

"They're running up marquees at Dargai," Steven explained. "The general hospitals are overflowing. Two hundred wounded coming in here at midnight. Ingleby told me. My board, by the way, is fixed for Friday morning. I don't expect they'll waste much time over it."

He prowled about the house like a caged animal. She wished to heaven he could settle down to something.

" You know my battalion's in Gough's army ? " he said. " I can't help thinking of the fellows I met at Plymouth. A topping lot they were. If it hadn't been for that cursed influenza I should have been with them ! "

If it hadn't been for that cursed influenza he might have been lying on his face in the mud of St. Quentin. On Friday morning. Three days. Thank heaven there was still time !

In the middle of the night, when the beams of ambulance headlights swept one after another across her window, she heard his naked footsteps padding down the wooden passage. She slipped out of bed and lit a candle and called to him : " What are you doing, darling ? Is anything the matter ? "

" The blessed convoy wakened me," he told her, " and I couldn't get to sleep again. I went to get a book. Don't worry about me, mother ; I'm all right."

He smiled ; but his smile did not reassure her. She wanted to kiss him and take him into her bed and cuddle him as she had done when he was a tired child at Uffdown. But his eyes told her that she was rather a nuisance ; that he really wished to God she'd leave him alone. She stole back to her bed and lay there wakeful until the last ambulance of the convoy had rumbled on its way to Dargai and a chiff-chaff began its seesaw among the elm-buds.

Another day. . . . That evening Steven was later than ever. Again Hart failed to appear. The hours were slipping by, and she had done nothing. Ellen came in, her plump cheeks blotched with crimson, the tail of a moist handkerchief protruding from between pearl blouse-buttons.

" It's Beazeley, ma'am. He'd like to say good-bye to you, if he may make so bold."

Then Beazeley, a little the better for a spot of beer, hobbled in and stood to attention in the dining-room door.

"I'm glad to have served you, madam, and downright sorry to leave. It's these here drafts," he explained. "I suppose we C3 chaps have got to take our turn with the rest of them. They say it's good for everyone to have a change now and then, and as long as my old trench-feet don't go and give out . . . Yes, madam. Garrison duty abroad. I think that's what they call it. Egypt, or Salonika, madam, I expect. We're being issued with sun-helmets."

Those drafts. . . . Pedworth was emptying itself precipitously like a mill-pond with sluices lifted. They couldn't spare the bands to march them to the station now; but, as the troop-trains steamed out, Clare could hear them singing "Home Fires." Distantly, like the lowing of beasts in cattle-trucks. If Beazeley went, with his poor twisted feet, what chance had Steven—what chance had anyone?

Steven came in. "Do you mind if I leave you, mum? I promised to go round and have coffee with Father Darnay at Albuera."

He took it for granted that she didn't mind. From the moment that the date of his board was settled, she seemed to have been thrust into the background of his thoughts. Even when he was with her she couldn't get at him; for all the joy she had of him he might have been gone already. He pulled on a trench-coat: "Don't wait up for me." He went without kissing her.

"How can he leave me like that," she thought, "when the time is so short?"

Lonely, she wandered back to the dining-room; the ration-coal burned noisily; the stuffing of the hired furniture smelt staler than usual. If only, by some providential chance, Hart would come, and find her alone!

Through the half-closed door of the kitchen she heard the ungainly sound of Ellen sobbing. For Beazeley, no doubt. She should have sympathized, she supposed; but the sound only irritated her. She felt that she couldn't stay in the

house another moment.　She needed fresh air and darkness
to cleanse her mind.

She put on a mackintosh and stepped out into the evening
drizzle.　In another moment she was crossing the meadow
by the cinder-path that led to the barracks.　A subdued
light yellowed the rose-window of the Garrison Church.　No
help for her there, whatever Darnay might say !　From
the back of Corunna a strident voice called numbers, mad
numbers, one after another, without sense or order.　The
troopers of the Royals were playing " house."

She passed the new marquees in the parade-ground of
Dargai.　What pain, what brutal injustice lay within them !
The thought of all those mangled bodies made her shiver.
She hurried past them into the outskirts of Fontenoy.　Low,
at the back of the officers' mess, lay the office hut of iron
and asbestos in which Hart and Steven worked.　White
light illuminated the windows of opal glass.　She imagined
that Hart was sitting inside, perhaps alone.　It seemed to
her that some power more valid than conscious volition had
brought her there.　" I can say that quite truthfully," she
told herself.　Yet why should she look for excuses ?

She stood by the dripping lintel and knocked softly ; no
sound answered her.　The silence was discouraging ; but
now she had once begun she could not draw back.　She
opened the door and entered the outer office.　It was empty,
but hot to suffocation with the fumes of a red-hot stove.
Deal tables, stained with ink ;　two covered typewriters ;
innumerable files of " returns " and buff-coloured sheaves of
official documents.　She crossed the room, and knocked
again at a second door.

" Come in ! "　The voice was Hart's, as brisk and cheery
as ever.

She entered.

" My dear Mrs. Wilburn !　Whatever in the world ? "
His face grew anxious.　" Nothing wrong with Steven ? "

" No, no." She smiled faintly. " Nothing wrong at all. I happened to be passing by accident. I saw your light and blundered in like a moth."

" On a night like this ! Whatever are you doing, wandering about the barracks ? Where's Steven ? "

She couldn't keep pace with his questions. " Steven's at Albuera . . . with Father Darnay. I felt particularly wretched." His face clouded. " I went for a walk. And then . . . I found myself here."

He eyed her so narrowly that she felt as if she had been caught in a fabrication. She blushed guiltily. Couldn't he take her word ?

He put an office chair for her. " At any rate, there's no reason why you shouldn't sit down."

She thanked him. She sat facing him. From the other side of his table he continued to watch her curiously, as though he were still dubious of her explanation. He seemed to be waiting for her to tell him the real reason of her visit. There was no reason. Yet now that she was face to face with him she knew she would have to speak, though this formal background made him more unapproachable than she could have believed ; he was no longer the human friend of their happy walks, but an official abstraction, a steely, impersonal component of the machine that she dreaded.

" I'm afraid I'm disturbing you," she began.

" I feel myself honoured. You've never been here before."

" But now that I *am* here," she said, with the flimsiest pretensions to speaking casually, " I should like to talk to you about Steven. I've been expecting, hoping to see you for several days."

He pointed to the mass of documents that cumbered his table. " You see how little chance I've had of catching sight of you. The position's pretty desperate, you know.

Probably worse than we think. And I'm the last link in a chain that stretches to Amiens."

" I know ; the news is dreadful. It won't bear thinking of." The words meant nothing. Somehow she must begin. She plunged forthwith. " Steven has asked for a board. He told you ? "

" His application went through this office. I approved and forwarded it."

" There was no need for him to do that. They gave him three months' Home Service, didn't they ? And his time isn't up yet."

" There was certainly no *need* . . . if you like to put it that way. On the other hand he's as fit and fitter than most of my officers. He knew that perfectly well ; and I agree with him that he did the right thing."

His eyes challenged her to dispute it. She felt it more tactful to submit :

" Ah, by those standards of course he was right," she said. " I know it was splendid of him. And yet . . ." she hesitated. " Colonel Hart, I'm afraid I'm not a Spartan mother. I know I'm going to make you despise me. I want to ask you, as a friend : is there no way of stopping it ? "

" Since you ask me as a friend, Mrs. Wilburn, thank heaven there isn't," he answered, with a deliberate hardness of tone. She had to pretend that she didn't understand what he implied. She pushed on bravely :

" I was wondering," she said ; " I was wondering if you could drop a hint to Major Ingleby. About his board, I mean."

She knew by his eyes that the suggestion had pained him.

" You know that I can't interfere with Major Ingleby's department. I have nothing to do with the medical side. And if I had, I assure you it would make no difference. Major Ingleby is a conscientious officer. You can be sure that the findings of the board will be just. If Steven is fit for General Service, they'll say so."

" And then ? "

She challenged him to tell her the brutal truth. His blue eyes met hers firmly : " Why, then, he'll be put at the disposition of the War Office. His course under me is completed. I've finished with him."

" Colonel Hart," she began ; then stopped. Her hand fell, with a little gesture of despair, upon the desk within inches of his. She saw his face ; it was drawn, unusually old ; the grey hair, receding, gave to his brows a look of narrow obstinacy. But his eyes suffered ; she believed there were tears in them. The fingers of the brown hand close to hers were clenched. She felt a sense of premature triumph, seeing that already her wordless emotion had moved him ; but when she opened her lips to continue he broke in on her :

" No, no," he said, in a low voice, " please don't—for God's sake don't ask me any more."

" I must," she said desperately, " I must. You know what this means to me ; you can't help knowing. You've seen something of our life together ; you realize that he's the only thing that matters in it." Her lips trembled as she spoke ; tears trickled down her cheeks ; she excused herself, but was glad of them :

" If I disgrace myself," she pleaded, " please take no notice of me. I want you to understand that it's only because . . . because I admire and trust you, because I believe you can appreciate what I'm feeling, because you're so different from everybody, that I dare ask you. There's no one else in the world to whom I would speak like this."

He shook his head sadly. He raised his hand and let it fall in a gesture of impotence. " But supposing," she persisted, " supposing . . . don't look at me so strangely— I can't bear it . . . supposing he's passed fit for General

Service—after all, perhaps he won't be—supposing, then, you could say, quite truthfully, that he was useful to you ? You've told me often how splendidly he's worked. If you could say that he is doing something that nobody else could do as well ? If you could let them know that your work will suffer ? "

" It wouldn't be true," he answered heavily. " There are dozens of lightly-wounded officers in England who could do what he is doing."

" But still, you might strain a point ? There are other reasons." She marshalled them hurriedly : " It isn't an ordinary case. I'm not merely a mother pleading for her child. He's the only boy in the family, the heir to the baronetcy. His uncle, George Hingston—I told you, didn't I ?—was killed on the Somme. Surely that counts for something ? If Steven goes as well . . ."

" I realize exactly what it means to them. Unfortunately the case is not extraordinary at all. It's far too common."

" But, perhaps, a word from you . . . a word to the General ? "

" The General has nothing to do with him. As soon as he's passed fit he no longer belongs to this command. Automatically."

" To-morrow, then ? " she pleaded. " While he's still under you. Before the board is held ? "

" He's asked for the board himself. And I've approved. It's passed out of my hands."

" You say so, yet nothing but your miserable red tape . . ."

" Mrs. Hingston, I'm a soldier." He laid his hand upon a heap of papers. " Here is the order for his board from headquarters. I have to obey it. There's no alternative."

" But I know there *are* alternatives," she cried ; " don't tell me that ! Why should Steven be treated differently from others ? There are plenty of men as fit as him in

England. Who keeps them here? The papers say that the War Office is full of them."

" That may be. This isn't the War Office. I'm careful to have no *embusqués* under my command."

" He isn't an *embusqué*. He's longing to go. He's been longing to go ever since the war began. What difference would it make if he stayed or went? Answer me honestly!"

" To the war? Nothing. To me . . . everything."

He spoke so dully, so resolutely that a sense of impending failure drove her to her last resort. If neither argument nor persuasion could move him, something still remained. She threw herself, incontinently, on his mercy.

" My life," she said; " you know what it has been. You've suffered like me; so you can understand: you're the only soul on earth that knows how bitter it's been. So little happiness! First Ralph—you knew him yourself; isn't that strange? And then South Africa. I was only a girl. Then all the wretchedness of my second mistake. I broke away from it to get Steven; he was all that mattered. And now this other war. As soon as ever I've seen a gleam of happiness this monstrous thing comes on to me again! Isn't it cruel, isn't it horribly wrong that two wars, one after another, should rob a wretched woman of all she has on earth, twice running in one short lifetime? And when I try to escape it, you say I'm not playing fair. It's a sort of game with you . . ."

" No, no. I'm in deadly earnest. It's no game."

" Deadly," she echoed. " That is the right word. How well I know you! You soldiers are all the same: you can't do this and you can't do that and you can't do the other! What do your rules and regulations mean to me? There's no rule of God or man I wouldn't break with open eyes to keep this one bit of happiness that I'm fighting for!" She gasped. " It isn't only happiness; it's life. If Steven goes they'll kill him—like they killed his father—and that will kill me too. I'm like a drowning woman, Colonel Hart. You sit and watch me going under, and comfort yourself with the thought of books of regulations. You, whom I've trusted, you whom I've admired so much ! The only real friend I've found in this cruel place ! For the sake of all those happy times we've had together—for my sake, not for Steven's, oh, Colonel Hart, have pity, have pity on me ; don't let me go down utterly ! His life . . . that's what I'm asking you for, I know it's in your hands. You can't deceive me. I know that you could save him for me this moment if you wanted to. A word from you . . . your name on a bit of paper. There must be some way ; there *is*—I'm sure of it. Oh, for the love of heaven, pity me, pity me ! "

She stretched out her hands toward him. He took them in his. Swept by the torrent of her tears she clutched at them as though indeed she were drowning. She was sobbing her heart out, spent and prostrate over the deal table. He came round to her and took both her arms in his hands. She shuddered, abandoned herself blindly to his support. His hands seemed so strong that she felt a tremor of hope.

" Tell me," she sobbed, " that you won't forsake me ? You'll save me just this once ? I shall never, never ask you anything else."

" I would give my life for you," he muttered, " and you know it."

She clung to him more closely : " Then prove it . . . for heaven's sake prove it ? "

" In any way but that."

" How can you torture me with cant ? "

" If I did what you ask, I could never look you in the eyes again."

The solemnity of his tone struck her as fantastic. As if it mattered to her whether he could look at her ! The same old shibboleths : honour, honour, honour ! She would trample on his honour and show him how she despised it ; she would fling back his twopenny honour in his face !

"Ah, if that's all," she cried bitterly, "if it's only *that* . . ." She paused, at a loss for some more adequate taunt. He faced her, pale, unutterably sombre.

"Only that ? To me it means everything. If it had been anyone but you ! "

"More cant ! " she cried. "How can you say that when you crucify me like this ? "

"How ? " he laughed shortly. "Because I love you. Now do you understand ? "

"Oh, what are you saying ? " she cried. "What are you saying ? "

The words took her breath away. His hands loosened from her arms. He moved away from her, and stood with blank eyes staring at the office window. Her panic ceased. A curious numbness had fallen on her whirling thoughts. Her mind was like a dark pool in the silence ; a dead and motionless deep under a stillness more awful than storm. Emerging out of that stillness she turned slowly toward him. Once more their eyes met ; and still she could not speak. But the space between them was charged with an emotion unimaginably intense. Through the grey blank of her mind there floated unbidden, not thought, but a phrase of music, the motive of the love-potion in *Tristan*. How long they gazed at each other thus she could not say. Without a word, pathetically, she reached out her hand to him. Without a word he took it ; he bent and kissed her fingers.

"I'm sorry," she said. "I didn't know. I had no right to ask you.'

"It's a bad business," he said. "If I'd done what you asked you'd never have forgiven me. And now, again, you'll never forgive me. So there we are ! It's a bad business. Don't think too harshly of me. These things, heaven knows, are beyond our control. Forgive me."

"There's nothing for me to forgive on my side," she said. "I'm glad you told me. I understand. I see that you were right. I want you to know that I respect you more than I can say. It isn't often that one meets . . . a man of honour."

"Don't call me that for God's sake," he entreated. "Anything but that ; the word's a mockery now. This is the end of the most precious thing that has ever happened to me. Of course you didn't know. I shouldn't have told you . . . but there seemed to be no other way. And now it's over. I must pay for my happiness. One pays for everything sooner or later." He paused. "I suppose there's nothing more to be said, except, perhaps, good-bye."

He began to fold up his papers with mechanical precision. She watched his movements in silence. There was a dreadful loneliness in them. His face was grey ; his shoulders were bowed like those of a stricken man. The pain that was in him stirred her numb mind to motion. "I ought to hate him," she thought, "and yet I'm only sorry. He is the best friend I've ever had ; nothing can change it. There's nobody like him, nobody in the world. Isn't it cruel, isn't it just like life that when I need him most I should have to lose him ? I don't want to lose him . . . I can't do without him ! He and Steven together . . . Ah, it's too cruel ! "

He had finished with his papers. He took down his forage-cap and coat, and turned to her with something of his old, brave alertness. She saw that it was demanded of her that she, too, should be brave.

"Unless you would rather I saw you home," he said, "I think I'd better leave you. You can stay here as long as you like ; you won't be disturbed, I'll come back later and see that the office is locked."

She shook her head. "I think I'd better go now. No,

don't come with me, I'd rather you didn't. I can find my way."

She felt that both of them were dangerously near to tears. If they went on facing each other in silence any longer she couldn't answer for herself. And if he gave way . . . She pulled her strength together to say good-bye; but the nervous movement of her hand toward him passed unnoticed; he would not, or dared not take it.

" Before I go," she said quickly. " I want to thank you. For myself and Steven as well. I don't know what we should have done at Pedworth without you."

He shook his head : " No, don't do that, I beg you. It's you who have taught me the meaning of heaven on earth. We've cancelled our bargain, but I shall always remain your debtor."

He held the door open for her. She passed out with lowered eyes and hurried round the corner of the office, out of sight of him. The lights of Fontenoy still gleamed through a mist of rain. A melancholy bugle, in the lines beyond it, sounded the Last Post.

Suddenly, as though a circuit had fused, they were all extinguished. The night was dark as death, but she was glad of its darkness, for the light had compelled her to keep her emotions in hand. Now that it had gone, and no one could see her, she needn't attempt to control them any longer. There, stumbling blindly onward through the thin rain, she surrendered herself to such a fit of weeping as she never remembered. She went on through the dark crying at the top of her voice, like a lost child. She did not know where she was going ; if only she could get it over before anyone saw her it wouldn't matter if she wandered out on to the open Plain. And that was what she was doing. She realized it as she stumbled on the parados of a trench which the Greys had dug in the down behind Albuera. Still shaken by gusty sobs like a storm buffeted tree, she sat on the heap of wet chalk and cried aloud, until, from very exhaustion, she could cry no more. And then, for the first time, she was able to think : not rationally nor consecutively, but in gusts that burst on her mind and shook it, as those gusts of weeping had shaken her body.

"He is right," she thought, "he is right ; if he had betrayed his trust the betrayal would always have haunted us. He loves me. I didn't know. He has no right to love me. It's terrible, and yet it shows how fine he is never to have spoken. Why did I think of *Tristan?* How strange that was ! He knows he shouldn't have told me. How could he help it ? It was I who forced him. If he hadn't told me I should have thought he was merely cruel ; and he wasn't cruel at all, he was wonderful. As if it mattered what he was ! It's over. I must put him away from my mind."

"My life is over too. Steven is going. It's empty, empty ; and nobody else can fill it. It's no good struggling any longer. There's only one end. This war is stronger than anything else in the world. It goes on and on ; nothing can stop it. I was a fool to think that I could do anything. I have to take my part in it like the rest. Thousands on thousands of women with broken hearts all over the world ; I'm only one of them. Why should I be less brave than all the rest ? I could be braver, perhaps, if I weren't quite so lonely. Nobody that cares for me at all. The Stourford people have never cared. Dudley . . . ? No ; he can't help me. Ellen ? Poor Ellen's devotion ! That isn't what I want. Nobody really but Steven ; Steven and Robert Hart, but I mustn't think of him. I must be brave ; I must, I *must* be brave. For Steven's sake, of course I must be brave. If only I could be brave ! God help me ! . . . God help me ! "

Her mind went on repeating the words mechanically, as though the formula had a magical virtue of its own. Its ridiculousness in her own case suddenly dawned upon her.

" How can I call on God to help me like this when I've ceased to believe in Him ?   Perhaps it's because of that that I feel so utterly helpless and such a coward ? "

Her mind circled back in a dizzy sweep to Uffdown.  She was standing with Dr. Boyd outside the room where Aunt Cathie lay dying.  She heard herself ask a question : " Do you believe in God ? "

" I don't know what I believe in, Mrs. Wilburn."

" Neither do I."

" And yet," Boyd answered, " we *have* to believe in something."

That was the trouble.  She believed in nothing ; and now that her world was crashing round her, stood naked and helpless.  A little while before, in the pride of her love and happiness, she had scorned the consolations that Father Darnay offered her.  The voice of Father Darnay seemed to rebuke her.

" There's no grief that real faith cannot console," he was saying.  " I'm sure I could have helped you to recover what you have lost.  For your own sake, Clare, I beg you to come back to us."

" I can't, I'm very sorry.   It's too late."

" It's never too late."

" Not even now ? " she thought.  That was difficult to believe.   Yet Darnay was wiser than most men and believed what he said.   Steven believed it.   Others, millions, believed it ; millions had believed for centuries in the efficacy of prayer.   Prayer hadn't stopped the war any more than Ford with his peace-ship.   God had willed otherwise ; but supposing, after all, there were something in it ?

She saw Hart smiling charitably at her credulity.  Hart was an infidel : a notorious infidel, Darnay had called him.  She had never dared to discuss such things with Hart ; but he was usually right.  Hart was an infidel because he was so much stronger than other people ; that very evening she had cause to know and to rue his strength.

" If he were going to be left alone, as I am," she thought ; " if he were going to lose the one thing that has made life worth living for twenty years, he might think differently. And if I could believe, as I used to do, that praying wasn't just waste of breath ; if, instead of struggling like this, I could surrender myself to something . . . someone in whose justice and mercy I had faith, I might be . . . No, not happy ; perhaps less utterly abandoned. If only I could force myself to believe," she thought. " I *want* to believe ; but if I forced myself it would be no good."

And again it seemed in the darkness as though Darnay were speaking to her : " Unless you make a beginning you'll never come at all. The will to believe would be more than half the battle."

" Too late," her heart repeated. " How can I possibly begin again ? "

The black night gave no answer. For the moment the rain had ceased. She had been walking for half an hour without the least idea where she was going. Suddenly she struck a road that she did not recognize, made darker than the open Plain by over-arching branches of elms. Their shadow told her that she must have reached the valley, though at what level she could not possibly guess.

" I must hurry back," she thought, " or Steven will be home before me and ask questions. If I see a light in a window I'll knock and find out where I am."

And there, at the bend of the road, a haze of light appeared to comfort her. Encouraged, she quickened her pace and hurried toward it. A low wall bounded what she imagined must be a garden ; she felt her way along it till she reached a little gate. The moisture-laden air was harsh with the odour of yews ; beyond the black yew-shadow she made out the profile of a squat, square tower. Her garden was a graveyard; that faint light penetrated the chancel window of South Pedworth church.

A miracle? Her heart was ripe for miracles.

" Of course it can't possibly be open," she thought; and yet it was with eagerness that she unlatched the gate and made toward the porch. Her fingers groped for a latch; as she lifted it the heavy door swung open before her, revealing the Norman arches of a narrow nave, and beyond a little box of a chancel where, above the middle of the altar, a hanging oil-lamp burned dim over a veiled tabernacle. Seeing it, she remembered how Steven had told her that since the Chaplain-General objected to any practice so contentious as continuous reservation in the Garrison Church, Father Darnay had made arrangements with the Vicar of Pedworth to reserve the consecrated elements on his own altar.

As Clare's hand left it the door closed behind her of its own weight, discreetly as though some silent power had determined to isolate her in the awe and quietude of that lonely place. Her heart was beating as she stole on tiptoe up the dim nave. There was a feeling of suspense in the stone-cold air through which she moved as quietly as a dream wandering through the mind of a man in sleep. She came to the altar steps. The hanging light burned steadily before the tabernacle, and, as she gazed at it, a strange, hypnotic calm descended on her, as though invisible fingers smoothed her rain-wet brow and pressed upon her swollen eyelids. A cloud of peace, of resignation enveloped her; the old, lost sense of ecstatic surrender, stole through her mind. " It cannot be true," she thought; yet clutched at it desperately, lest it should fade away from her. Its flame burned in her soul, subdued, but unwavering as the suspended light. She fell to her knees, unknowing; she stretched out her arms in adoration and entreaty toward the Presence. There were no words to shape her prayer or paint her humiliation. There seemed to be no need for words. There, on the icy flags, she lay spent and submissive, strangely, miraculously at peace.

# IX

## LUCASTA

WHEN Steven came back from Albuera he was shocked to find that his mother had gone to bed. Usually, however late he might be, she waited up for him, if only to kiss him good night, and her absence suggested that he had been heartless in leaving her that evening, when their time together was running so short, to discuss the legitimacy of Queen Elizabeth's birth under the Bull of Pope Pius V with Father Darnay at Albuera. And though Darnay had quite convinced him that Gloriana was a bastard and her father's adulterous passion for Anne Boleyn the devil's own device for splitting Western Christendom, which was exactly what he wanted to believe, he felt a little guilty as he stood outside her door and whispered to see if she were awake.

Clare heard him, and held her breath, but made no answer. For the moment her heart was too deeply stirred for her to risk the shock of another emotion. She heard him go away, imagining that she was asleep. But next morning, when he emerged from his bedroom, he found her up and dressed before him.

" Are you going to the Garrison Church this morning ? " she asked him.

" Yes. I'll be back for breakfast as usual," he told her.

" I think I'd like to go with you, darling, if you don't mind."

He stared at her incredulously, with more surprise than pleasure. " Of course I'd love you to come with me," he said. The change in her attitude was so sudden that he didn't know how to deal with it. He had a feeling that this was not the mother he knew. They crossed the meadow arm-in-arm and in a silence that was almost awkward. " I imagined it would bring me nearer to him," she thought, " but he looks at me as curiously as if I were a stranger." And while they knelt together under the astonished eyes of Father Darnay the strangeness of this new problem disturbed his devotions.

Clare, too, was in a state of mind that made the whole proceeding seem unreal. The ecstasy of the night before had faded from her, though something of the calm remained ; and even this calm was different. Her heart was subdued and weak, as though it had been shaken to exhaustion ; her mind feeble, though almost pathologically clear ; her hands trembled as she held them out to receive the wafer which Darnay, mumbling his formula, placed in her palm. Beyond her own emotion she was so conscious of his that it marred the integrity of her devotions.

When the communion was over Darnay slipped out from the vestry to intercept them. In his eagerness she found a curious resemblance to that which he had shown her in the old days of St. Chad's. He drew her away from Steven and spoke in a low voice :

" I can't tell you how much happiness you have given me this morning, though I know that your own joy will be even greater. I asked no questions because I concluded that everything was all right."

" All right ? " she answered, a little puzzled.

" I mean, I gathered you were in a state of grace. But before you communicate again I think somebody had better hear your confession—either the Vicar of Pedworth or myself."

" I'll come to you to-day, Father," she said, " if you will hear me."

He fixed the hour at once. " I need hardly tell you what a great relief this is to me," he said.

" To me also. I hardly understand it."

" Don't try to understand it. God is merciful."

That afternoon, as Darnay had appointed, she confessed to him—not in the heartily official atmosphere of the Garrison Church, but in the dim little chancel that had witnessed her reconversion ; and once again, in the spoken word, she felt the release, the satisfaction of a complete surrender. His apprehension of what she had evidently suffered made Darnay gentle with her ; the questions that he asked her were general and not too searching. When it was over she felt grateful that he had not referred to Hart. She had been careful not to mention Hart's name herself, not only because she knew she had nothing to confess, but because she felt a debt of loyalty to him and considered that the confidence he had made her was sacred. Yet, as she parted from Darnay she couldn't help remembering those old confessions that he had heard at St. Chad's, when, with a similar reservation, she had shielded Ralph.

" But that was different," she argued. " I was in love with Ralph, and I'm not in love with Robert Hart. That he should have fallen in love with me is tragic. Father Darnay would call it more than that : an unforgivable sin. Yet even Father Darnay would have to respect his honesty if he knew what it had cost him ; and my own conscience is clear ; I've certainly never tried to make him love me."

For the moment the ardours of her new conversion intoxicated her ; they enabled her to seem courageous, and almost serene when Major Ingleby's board passed Steven fit for General Service ; to assure him that the attainment of his ambition was not a selfish triumph at her expense.

" My name has gone through to headquarters. I put the letter up for the Colonel's signature myself," he told her.

"Everything in the army moves infernally slowly; but now, any day, I must be prepared to get my orders."

She smiled, and wondered at the braveness of her own smile. " Let's try to make the most of what's left to us, darling," she said.

" Oh, mother, you are a brick ! " he cried, impulsively kissing her.

And that was her reward. A meagre reward, she couldn't help thinking in moments when the old feebleness assailed her. Now that his course was finished, and Hart had chosen another secretary in anticipation of his going, Steven was freer than he had been for months. The eagerly expected orders didn't come. A whole week passed, and then another, without them. The respite was so surprising that Clare began to wonder if Hart, repenting of the pain he had given her, had wavered, and fallen to her suggestions. " How wonderful that would be for us ! " she thought. Yet now, in spite of the joy that a reprieve would have given her, she knew that she would be disappointed if Hart had fallen. Her veneration for his integrity made her feel that this was impossible.

And yet she couldn't be sure. Since that night in the office behind Fontenoy she had not seen him. Now, when Steven's increased freedom and the mild spring weather allowed them to retrace their steps in walks over the downs toward Everley and through the beechen ridgewoods where pools of hyacinth reflected a fleeting blue, Hart no longer made one of their party.

She missed him. She dared not even admit to herself how much she missed him. Not only for his cheery company, but for the alertness and knowledge that had made each walk an adventure and the homely security of their evenings together. Now, if they found in their wanderings a flower that they couldn't name, or heard the note of a bird that puzzled them, they felt, at once, the loss of his company.

For herself Clare dared not speak of it ; but Steven, in his ignorance, had no such compunctions.

" Why ever isn't the Colonel with us ? " he would say. " I can't think what's come over him. He sits and stews in the office day after day ; I simply can't drag him out. To look at him you'd imagine he'd something on his mind ; but of course one can't ask questions."

" At any rate, you can tell him how much we miss him," she said.

" I shouldn't have given him the loophole," she thought, when she remembered it afterward. " He might mistake my meaning ; it's not fair to him."

And yet she wanted to see him, if it were only to have the opportunity of confessing the miracle by which, on the night when she left him so tragically, her woes had been resolved. Of course, being what he was, he wouldn't understand the meaning of the change in her ; and yet it seemed a pity that he, who had seen her at her weakest, should not have the chance of realizing how brave she could be.

Something on his mind, Steven said. . . . No doubt he was suffering because he felt that he had hurt her by his rigidity. If she could see him only once she could reassure him and set his mind at rest. Why, the very fact that she, whom he admired so much, had found this new, miraculous source of comfort, might make him realize, if only a little, the error which Father Darnay deplored in him. Trying to convince herself of the genuineness of this pretty casuistry she remembered the early days at St. Chad's when she had seriously considered the project of converting Ralph to her religious persuasions. That project had collapsed, fairly abjectly, on the first night of her married life when Ralph with a benevolent impatience had watched her pray. And Hart, heaven knew, was a harder nut to crack than poor, simple Ralph !

But whether the reasons with which she squared her conscience were valid or no, the fact remained that she wanted to see Hart. His absence multiplied and enlarged the virtues that she had always seen in him, and, strangely enough, considering the scruples of her new religious phase, his unexpected, scandalous avowal made him, if anything, more interesting to her than ever. For the sin, after all, was glossed by the compliment to herself implied in it, and the nice sense of honour that had made him refuse his protection to Steven would equally protect her from the embarrassment of his love. He was thinking, no doubt—poor man !— that by that rash confession he had lowered himself for ever in her eyes, and suffering accordingly. Yet it was flattering that he should suffer for her sake, and suffer so unnecessarily. The thought of that noble, melancholy figure distressed— if not her conscience, at least her instinct of kindliness. She wanted to let him know that she didn't think any the worse of him for his avowal ; that she respected him as much as—or more than ever. And again, apart from all right or reason, she wanted to see him.

In the end, since all the hints that she sent him through Steven seemed powerless to remove his doubts, she determined to write to him. The task was not so easy as she imagined. For a long time she wavered between the idea of a friendly note ignoring the passionate scene at Fontenoy or that of a direct appeal to his kindness. The affected innocence of the first might give him an impression of coquetry and frighten him ; the second, by reason by its very frankness, would be more difficult to refuse.

*Dear Colonel Hart*, she wrote :

*Are you never coming to see us again ? I want you to know that we miss you more than you can possibly imagine. Friendship, after all, is such a rare thing, and ours has always been such a happy one that it seems to me a crime to let it slide because of anything that has happened. I'm afraid you're*

*under the impression that what you said offended me.  Please
don't think anything of the sort.  It's just the other way round.
I realize now that you were absolutely right about Steven ;
you saved me from doing something that I should always have
regretted.  As for the other confidence you gave me, I only feel
that you did me a great honour, and want to show you that
I am trying to be worthy of it.  Let us both forget everything
that we said the other night and begin again.  If you don't
come to see us as usual to-morrow, I shall feel dreadfully
disappointed, and hurt as well.*

She waited anxiously for a reply to her letter ; but none
came.  In the old, happy days Beazeley had been their
messenger ; but Beazeley, with his sun-helmet, was now
dodging submarines off the coast of Portugal.  That morning Steven lunched at Fontenoy, and so she had no news
from him at mid-day.  She moved about the house all
morning, restlessly putting the shabby room in order as
though she were preparing for some distinguished visitor.
" I'm like Aunt Cathie," she thought.  Of late she had
often caught herself in moods and movements that called
Aunt Cathie to mind and made her smile.  She wondered if
Ellen noticed them.  " The truth of the matter is," she
thought, " I'm middle-aged.  At this time of life one
begins to show one's family characteristics, although it's
difficult to believe that one's growing older."

Soon after lunch Father Darnay dropped in.  Now that
the old relationship was re-established he treated the Staff
Colony house and Clare herself with a kind of proprietary
interest.  He liked, over Ellen's excellent coffee, to luxuriate
in his sense of power and prove to Clare how deeply she was
honoured by casual—too casual allusions to the great ladies
whom he frequented in Mayfair.

That afternoon he settled down to a longer talk than usual ;
a letter from his friend, dear Lady Clun, had put him in

a good humour. He talked of her, and of the Powys family in general, with a gentle, feminine familiarity designed, at once to assure Clare of her equal participation in that illustrious sisterhood and underline the exclusiveness of his own society. Clare listened, but felt she was less interested than she ought to have been. If Father Darnay prolonged his visit indefinitely he would be almost certain to collide with Hart. She was determined to restore the atmosphere of their friendship ; the presence of anyone other than Steven, who was part of it, would make that difficult : the presence of an element so definitely hostile as Darnay would ruin it entirely.

It seemed wrong that these two men, whom she respected equally, though with different parts of her mind, should be incompatible ; yet so it was, and now that the imminence of their collision overshadowed her, she couldn't help feeling anxious to save Hart, not Darnay, from the unpleasantness of meeting. It didn't strike her that Darnay needed her protection ; and this was queer, for when she came to contrast them, the personality of Hart in its sane robustness made Darnay's teacup refinements look curiously false and unsubstantial. Removed from the mystery and awe of what he represented, she felt that the priest could not hold a candle to the soldier ; and every moment of his company made Hart's superiority as a friend and a human being seem clearer.

" If he won't go of his own accord," she thought, " I shall have to tell him that Colonel Hart is coming, and then he'll be scared."

She didn't want to do that ; for, so far, she had tactfully excluded Hart from their conversation as well as from her confessions. It relieved her more than she would have dared to admit when Darnay told her that he was going to tea with the General's sister. " A charming woman," he told her, " and a saint as well. You don't mean to tell me you've never met Lady Sybil ? " He threw up his hands : " But that's ridiculous ; I must look into it," he said, knowing as well as Clare did that he had no intentions of doing anything of the kind ; for one of Father Darnay's rules was that his sisters in Christ should never be given opportunities of comparing notes.

He went ; and with his departure the old restlessness of anticipation returned. Now that the moment of meeting grew nearer she was half afraid of what she had desired. How should she meet this man now that she knew he loved her ? She had begged him to forget everything that had been spoken at Fontenoy. An agreement of that kind looked simple enough on paper, yet, when they met and spoke, each word and glance would carry with it a suggestion of the thing forgotten. It was easy to propose that they should begin again ; but no convention could change their real natures ; unless she were careful the new beginning might lead to an identical end. The prospect was so frightening that she almost regretted her letter and was ready to recognize the wisdom that had prompted Hart to avoid her. Perhaps he would still be wise enough not to come. But if he didn't come . . .

As the hour of dismissal grew nearer she stood at the window looking out over the meadow to catch the first glimpse of him and Steven crossing the cinder-path. At this time of the day a steady current of khaki set from the barracks in the direction of the village shops ; among so many men in uniform it would be difficult to pick out the two figures that she expected, or perhaps one only ; for the path that had once lain open in all its length was now concealed in part by a screen of bursting elm-buds. Yet no sooner had they reached the edge of the meadow than she recognized them : Hart with his swinging stride, long, lean and soldierly, and Steven, with his less disciplined carriage, walking beside him. Her heart fluttered triumphantly.

" He's coming," she thought ;  " he's coming after all."

Standing alone at the window she blushed so hotly, so unreasonably that shame compelled her to retire into the dim depth of the room.

" I'm behaving ridiculously," she told herself ;  " but I can't help it.  If I had known it was going to disturb me like this I wouldn't have taken the risk.  Perhaps when he's actually here it will be easier."

She stood at the back of the room, calculating the moments which it would take them to cross the meadow and reach her door, and all the time her heart was beating away like a restless string-figure, above which the blended overtones of bugle-notes from the down behind Blenheim came to her with a melancholy reminder of a page of music which she had often played for Ernest Wilburn.

" *Nicht Hornerschall tont so hold . . .*" the bugles whispered.  And with a shudder she realized that the memory that had drifted into her mind was the beginning of the second act of *Tristan :* Isolde and Brangaena waiting in that fateful woodland for the hero's coming.

" An ominous fancy," she thought, and thrust it away from her ;  but still, in uncontrollable levels of thought, the stream of music that the Blenheim bugles had started pursued its sweet and feverish course through her mind, dragging unwilling words to wed its phrases :

> *Bist du mein ?   Hab ich dich wieder ?*
> *Darf ich dich fassen ?   Kann ich mir trauen ?*
> *Endlich !   Endlich !*

The door swung open.  A trample of footsteps in the hall.  Steven was speaking :

" Let me take your coat, sir.  I'll hang it up.  Mother's in the drawing-room."

*Endlich . . . endlich !*  At last !

Hart came into the room. She smiled ; held out her hand to greet him :

" I'm so glad you've come."

" It was kind of you to ask me. I thought . . ."

He was silent. And Clare was silent too, though, through her mind, unchecked, relentless, the hurried passion of the great love-duet surged onward.

" Won't you sit down ? " she was saying. " You look tired."

Tired and worn and undefinably tragic. No wonder Steven had said there was something on his mind !

" It is my fault," she thought. " How can I atone for it ? He is so good, so loyal, I owe him so much ! It's wicked that I should have added to his unhappiness ; but how, without making matters worse, can I tell him what I feel ? "

She could say nothing ; do nothing. Those maddening bugles had made the whole atmosphere of their meeting unreal and impossible. Her frightened tongue took refuge in bald commonplace. He answered her in the same strain ; commonplace danced like a shuttlecock between them ; yet whatever words they spoke were only symbols concealing others : " I love you," on his side ; " I am so sorry," on hers. " Why did you ask me to come here ? " he seemed to be saying ; " you know that I couldn't refuse you ; yet what end does it serve except to flatter you and to give me pain ? "

Steven came in, providentially, to interrupt this heart-rending game. His abundant spirits shattered the spell that bound them.

" Isn't that tea made yet, mum ? I don't know about you, sir ; but I'm as hungry as a lion."

He sat between them munching sandwiches. Obviously unconscious of the tension that he had relieved he began to talk of what was uppermost in his mind, his overseas orders,

" It's typical of the way they do things," he was saying. " They give you to understand that the whole front's smashing up for want of officers ; but when a fellow's passed fit they keep him hanging about at a loose end in Pedworth. Surely they ought to have had time to get it through by now, sir ? "

" Whether they've had time or not is no business of yours," Hart told him. He stole a glance at Clare to see how she was taking it ; she knew he was ready to feel the pain that the subject would give her. She smiled, to show him that he need have no fear, and was proud of her smile ; for that was what she wanted him to see.

" In any case they're bound to come through in a day or two," Steven continued. " The only problem that remains is what to do with mother."

" Your mother can look after herself, Steven darling," she told him.

" That's all very well, mum," he persisted, " but you're bound to feel a bit lost at first. I think you ought to go straight back to Uffdown and forget all about it, messing about the garden. Don't you agree with me, sir ? "

" My dear child," Clare protested, " I couldn't possibly go back to Uffdown."

The very idea of it filled her with horror ; the loneliness, the associations of that sweet place desolate.

" Well, if you feel like that," he went on, " I don't think you could do better than stay here for a bit. You're used to the place and there's always something happening. You'll be able to play tennis at the club and have Father Darnay to tea and go for walks with the Colonel." He turned to Hart : " If I leave mother here, sir, you'll look after her, won't you ? "

Hart smiled, but did not speak. Clare pitied him. What could he say ? But Steven, enchanted by his plans for her future, did not see the glance that passed between them nor wait for Hart's reply. He ran on quickly : " In any case, mum, you've promised me you won't go to London. If you went there you'd be bound to get mixed up in an air-raid ; and Pedworth's just about the safest place in England. The Colonel's likely to stick on here for donkey's years, so you two can just carry on, so to speak, till I come back again. The old war can't roll on for ever. I don't mind betting this is a topping place in summer. You'll have all sorts of fun. This chalky stuff is bound to be stiff with orchises and things like that. I say, you don't look very thrilled about it, either of you ! "

" Don't worry, darling," she told him. " *Sufficient unto the day . . .*"

" That's all very well, mum ; but I should like to feel you were settled, and the Colonel being here like this is a perfect God-send. He'll cheer you up like anything, and see that you don't get into mischief. I shall feel quite happy if I know that you're in his hands. So that's a bargain, isn't it, sir ? "

Hart had to answer him : " My dear boy, your mother will do what she feels like. You can't make plans as far ahead as that. Of course, if she stays here . . ."

He hesitated. Whatever would he say ? How skilfully he might have meant to deal with this uncomfortable charge Clare never knew. A knock on the outer door cut short his answer. Whoever could it be ? Not Father Darnay, who was safely—though figuratively—in the bosom of Lady Sybil. They waited, with teacups suspended, listening while Ellen stumped along the passage. They heard her speaking : " Good afternoon, sir. Well, this *is* a surprise ! " No stranger, anyway. Ellen flung open the door.

" Captain Wilburn," she announced.

A sudden scowl of amazement settled on Steven's face Clare, blushing crimson, rose and went to meet the new-comer. Actually it was Dudley ; grey, ponderous and singularly unmilitary in his captain's uniform. He entered with a slow and heavy smile. Before Clare knew what she was doing habit compelled her to put up her face to him. He kissed her, and again the colour that had momentarily left her cheeks flowed back into them because she was aware that Robert Hart had seen. If anyone had a right to kiss her it was Dudley; and yet she felt that the instinctive gesture might be interpreted as one of coquetry rather than of surprise.

"I had a court-martial at Bulford," he explained. "I had to get back to North Bromwich to-night. Pedworth cuts out two sides of a triangle; so I thought, as I was almost passing your door, I'd drop in to have a look at you. How are you, Clare? You're looking remarkably well, and so is Steven."

"We're both of us very well, Dudley," she said.

Listening to him, her ear, attuned to the clear-cut speech of Hart and Steven, detected, for the first time, and with surprise, the ignoble intonations of the North Bromwich accent. "He never used to talk like that," she was thinking, "not when we were married . . ." and then, of a sudden, realized that Hart had not been introduced.

"Oh, I'm so sorry," she said, and blushed more deeply than ever. "Dudley, I don't think you know Colonel Hart."

"But I'm pleased to meet him," said Wilburn, shaking hands. "I've heard of him more than once at Southern Command Headquarters."

Clare watched their meeting uneasily. She felt a personal anxiety that Wilburn should shine, that all his old qualities, different from Hart's yet no less admirable, should appear, if only for her sake. But Dudley was not in a shining mood that afternoon; unless, indeed, he had changed. Though there could not have been as much as ten years between them he seemed, in comparison with Hart, an aged man. His face, made grey by a sedentary life, looked lax and lifeless beside Hart's bronzed features ; his hair, or what was left of it, was uniformally white and wispy ; his figure, stalwart as she remembered it, had gone painfully to seed : an elderly, flabby, slovenly man, with an undeniable paunch and that too dreadfully evident North Bromwich twang in his speech !

And when he settled down to eat, stirring his tea with a movement as persistent and irritating as a habit-spasm, each word that he spoke only increased the contrast between his dulness and the other's alert mind. She had known for long enough that Dudley, at his worst, could be heavy on the hand ; but never, till that moment, had she suspected that he was a bore.

The talk was left to the two men; for Steven, whose old dislike had subsided into a disinterested neutrality, was dumb. " You don't seem to be worried much with court-martials here," Wilburn was saying. " I suppose the other Judge Advocate-General from Salisbury attends to most of them. But all the same, on my few visits to the Plain, Colonel Hart, I always seem to have heard of you."

What had he heard ? Was it possible that these words concealed a knowledge of the gossip at which Darnay had hinted ? Had Dudley chosen them more cleverly than she imagined ? Was this the real reason of his visit ? Evidently no ; for still, between gulps of tea, his voice went droning on :

" As a matter of fact this is my first visit to Pedworth. If my wife hadn't been here I shouldn't have done more than hurry through it. For the most part they keep me moving about less comfortable places. However, I mustn't complain. It's a privilege for an old man like myself to be made useful in these days."

So, platitude after platitude. Was it that he had changed, or only herself ? And all the time, behind those alert eyes of his, she seemed to be reading through into Hart's mind.

" Is it possible that she could ever have married this man ? " he was thinking. " He wasn't like this when I married him," her heart protested. Yet now she was ashamed of him, and doubly ashamed of her shame.

It didn't surprise her when it seemed that Hart could bear it no longer. He rose to go, and though she tried to persuade him to stay, excused himself. It was poetic justice that Dudley, dropped from the clouds, should have spoiled their meeting ; for now that she had recovered from the first embarrassment of Hart's arrival she felt that with another opportunity of solitude she could have found her tongue. In a desperate attempt to make amends she went to the door with him.

" You understood my letter ? " she whispered. " Of course you did. Otherwise you wouldn't have come. I hope that means that you're not going to desert me ? I can't afford to lose such a good friend as you."

He smiled gravely as he took her hand. " You know quite well that I am always at your service, and always shall be."

It was evident that during her absence the conversation between Dudley and Steven had not prospered. They both looked infinitely relieved by her return, though Wilburn was already fidgeting with his watch.

" A charming fellow, Hart," he began by saying. " I'd heard someone speaking of him, curiously enough, the other day. What is his job, exactly ? "

" The School of Instruction. He's Steven's C.O.," she told him.

" Ah, that explains his visit."

Did it need explaining ? " He's been a very good friend to us ever since we came here." Evidently it did.

" A married man ? " Wilburn continued innocently.

" A widower," she answered. Why was he so persistent ? Or was it only her conscience that made him seem so ?

" Another victim, Clare ? " he asked, with a little laugh.
Steven got up in a hurry and bounced out of the room.

" I see our young friend's sense of humour hasn't developed," said Wilburn blandly.

" He's very touchy on anything that affects me. I'm glad he is."

" But really he might have understood my little joke." He looked at his watch again. " I'm afraid I must be going."

He rose and placed his two hands on her shoulders. He stood and gazed into her eyes, and shame for her shame in him grew more acute than ever ; he was so worn, so aged, so softened of his old hardness, and, when he spoke, so curiously humble. " My dear, I'm very glad to have seen you," he said. " You didn't mind my coming ? "

" Of course I didn't, Dudley," she lied bravely, while her heart ached for him and for the unhappy past.

" And I'm glad now to see you for a moment alone. Apparently all goes well. What about Steven ? "

" He's waiting for overseas orders, expecting them any minute. Please don't talk about it."

" What are you going to do, Clare, when he goes ? "

" I don't know. I'd rather not even think."

" Uffdown ? "

" No, no, not Uffdown. I couldn't bear it."

He paused. " If you ever feel too lonely," he said, " remember you still have a husband who's always at your service."

" Oh, Dudley, I know, I know. . . ."

The identical words ! Strange that on Wilburn's lips they moved her so much less deeply than on Hart's. He was wise enough to see that she could say no more.

" Well, well, I must be moving," he said abruptly. " At any rate let me know wherever you are, and don't be shy to ask for my help if I can be of any use to you. Good-bye, my child."

He kissed her quickly, almost as though he were shy of *her*, and went.

## X

### SECOND TRANSIT OF MARS

NEXT day, in the middle of the morning, a smart young orderly knocked at the door and handed Ellen a note in an official envelope. Clare heard them speaking on the doorstep : " From Colonel Hart," he said. " The staff-sergeant didn't say nothing about an answer."

" Well, then, you'd better wait a moment, hadn't you ? " said Ellen, opening the drawing-room door and handing on the note to Clare.

Whatever could Hart be writing about ? she wondered. Her name on the envelope was in Steven's hand, and Steven's the scribbled chit on a strip of buff-coloured paper inside it.

*Orders have just come through. Report embarkation officer at Southampton forthwith. That means this evening. I can easily get a train from Salisbury. Have ordered a taxi, and shall be back early for lunch. Love. Steven.*

She read the scribble through and through, as if she hadn't understood it. Heaven knew she understood it well enough ! The dazzling content was filling her brain to the exclusion of everything else, burned in with monstrous letters of fire like a Broadway sky-sign, shaping, reshaping itself over and over again. She stood and stared at the paper like an idiot. The smart young orderly on the doorstep announced his impatience by a fruitless throat-scraping that recalled her to herself.

" Ellen ! " she called ; and when Ellen presented herself : " Thank him, and tell him that there's no answer, please."

It was bravely done. She flattered herself that her voice, her face had shown no signs of the terror that was destroying her. " If I can keep it up as well as that," she thought, " it will be all right."

She had to keep it up. She knew that if once she didn't it would be impossible to recover. As long as she need not face anyone or force herself to speak it would be easier. She hoped to goodness that Ellen hadn't guessed what it was all about ; for if she had done so—and Ellen was capable of an uncanny penetration—she would doubtless consider it her duty to sympathize. Ellen, in fact, was so dangerous that Clare spent most of the morning avoiding her, carrying her numb heart and its burden from room to room in a pretence of busyness, telling herself that she must and could be brave, desperately hoping that her own persuasions could give her strength.

" And even if my will fails me," she thought, " prayer can surely help me. If I believe in the wisdom of God's guidance, if I surrender my life and Steven's into His hands He cannot abandon me."

But when, having locked the door of her bedroom, she knelt and prayed, it seemed that her spirit had lost a little of the confidence, the sense of security that before had sustained her. The flattering miracle of South Pedworth Church was losing some of its virtue ; for even when she concentrated her whole soul on the idea of God's mercy, creeping closer and hiding herself under the shadow of His wings, another and a vaster shadow pursued and enveloped her, threatening the light toward which she yearned. However close she crept, however steadfastly she set her eyes on that which she worshipped, the powers of doubt assailed her with pictures of anguish and death and incredible mutilation that threatened to invade her mind and fill it.

" This is the final test of my faith," she thought. " If I fail now I shall have only myself to blame. I've been too confident. It seemed so easy at first, so miraculously simple, that when I should have been humble I've been proud. I've taken to myself the credit that I should have given to God's mercy. I acknowledge my fault. What more can I do? Oh, God in Heaven, what more? "

In the midst of this extremity of anguish Steven arrived. She heard him go into the drawing-room and call her, then hurry along to the kitchen and ask Ellen where she was. She rose from her knees and rapidly sponged her eyes. The sight of her harrowed face and dishevelled hair in the cracked mirror was frightening; it would never do for him to see her like that; but before she could restore herself he was turning the handle of the bedroom door.

"Whatever are you doing there, mum? Why have you locked the door?"

"One second, darling," she begged him. "I'm coming at once."

For that moment, if never again, now let God help her! A smile belied the suffering in her face as she emerged.

"So there you are," he cried. "I've scarcely a moment for lunch. The train leaves Salisbury at three-fifteen, so I've ordered the taxi for half-past one."

"Then we'd better eat at once," she answered calmly.

He was so busy and excited stowing away the haversack full of accumulated rubbish that he had cleared out of Fontenoy that he scarcely had time to notice how she looked or what she said. She was thankful for anything that could distract them during those intolerable moments. She smiled and helped him, and even joked a little; but all the time her heart was breaking . . . breaking.

"We'd better shove the whole lot into this suitcase," he said. "It's quite impossible to sort out all these books and papers. I'll look at them when I come back to Uffdown."

To Uffdown! How did he manage to be so confident? Was he deliberately, bravely, playing her own sad game, or did the buoyancy of youth absolve him from the terror that held her ?

" Even if his confidence is real," she thought, " he can't help feeling how dreadful it is to leave me. I won't believe that he's as heartless as that."

And yet, though the thought wounded her, she was grateful ; for if Steven had shown a sign of weakness it would have been all up with her. No doubt he knew the danger to both of them of being serious, and suffered, poor darling, as deeply as herself.

Providentially the voice of Ellen called them to lunch.

" I don't suppose I shall get another meal before Southampton," he told her. He ate as heartily as if there were no other thought in his mind, and pretended not to notice that she was eating nothing. All through the meal he kept up a flow of careless talk :

" It's funny that when one's been expecting a thing for weeks it should take one by surprise like this. I had to scramble like the deuce to finish a return for the Colonel this morning. By the way, he's promised to look in this evening, just to have a ' dekko ' as he calls it, and see that you're all right. I wish you wouldn't be so beastly shy of him, mum ; you're so jolly serious you put the poor chap off his stroke. I don't think I've ever known anybody I liked so much. You're lucky to have a man like that to look after you when I'm gone. And Father Darnay . . . Good Lord ! I've never said good-bye to him ! You might make my apologies and all that ? I've asked him to come and stay with us at Uffdown some day, and have another look at St. Chad's. I doubt if poor old Pomfret'll be glad to see him ; he must have got a little of his own back at Aldershot. But don't forget to give him my message when he rolls up again."

He stopped suddenly. They heard the grating of a brake-ratchet in the road outside.

Steven crumpled his napkin and rose from the table

" That's the taxi," he said. " I told the beggar I'd give him beans if he came late. Ellen ! " he called. " I wish you'd chuck my valise into the car."

Ellen came blundering out of the kitchen. They could hear her dragging the heavy canvas along the wooden floor of the corridor.

" I mustn't stay, mother. There's no time to lose."

" Steven, my darling ! "

He took her in his arms. She clung to him wildly. " My darling, my little darling," she was mumbling.

He kissed her lips. It seemed as if that kiss would never end. Her soul went with it ; her body was empty, empty. . . .

" Don't come to the door, mum," he was saying ; " I'd rather you didn't."

His fingers slipped away from hers. He was gone. From the garden path she heard his voice, speaking to Ellen :

" Good-bye, Ellen. We'll soon be back at Uffdown."

" Good-bye, Master Steven. God bless you and keep you ! "

The engine of the car started up with a roar. She heard the swish of the wheels passing the window ; and then another sound, a pitiful wailing. Ellen had begun to cry out in the garden. She couldn't bear to hear it. Above all to see it. Her soulless body was precipitated along the corridor to her bedroom ; a dead hand turned the key.

Prostrate on her bed in that awful solitude, incapable of thought or prayer or any feeling whatever, her empty, shattered body spent itself in tears and gasps and uncouth howlings that seemed to have no connection with her annihilated self. In that soulless, animal desolation her body had no relation to time or place. She didn't know, she didn't care, where or even who she was. The world was blank as chaos, a darkness in the midst of which pain glowed and faded timelessly like a white-hot nebula.

At times, in the distance, she seemed to hear Ellen speaking to her. It was idle to speak, for there was no one to answer ; no woman, only a core of pain and a sound of hoarse weeping.

And then, of a sudden, when she had ceased crying for sheer exhaustion, a hesitant tapping on the door maddeningly penetrated that deadly silence. So, dazed and inchoate, her body obeyed and struggled to meet it.

" What is it ? " she whispered.

" The Reverend Darnay would like to see you, ma'am," Ellen answered.

" Tell him I can't see him. I can't see anybody."

A gust of something like anger, the first stimulus that had reached her numbed brain for hours, swept through her. Darnay, with his plausible formulas ; the treacherous assurances of his frail mysticism, shrivelled and wrinkled now like premature seedlings at a touch of frost ! Who was his God ? The God of battles who, in two generations, had lain in wait to annihilate all that she loved best ! She stood there, swept by hatred, like a disappointed savage ready to burn the idols that have betrayed him. But even that spurt of emotion was too much for her, and as soon as Darnay's polite voice had died away, she relapsed into the nothingness from which it had roused her, lying on her bed face-downward like a dead man abandoned in battle.

Suddenly, once more, as when the drumming of a thundershower ceases, she found herself alive again : alive, but a little mad. For the moment she had forgotten her grudge against Darnay. The pendulum of her distracted mind swung backward to Robert Hart.

" At any rate *he* has not deceived me," she thought. " He had the courage to face things as they were ; he didn't lead me into that fool's paradise ! "

But though her feelings suffered this revulsion in Hart's favour, in contrast with the failure of the unfortunate

Darnay, the prospect of actually meeting him face to face filled her with an equal alarm. She remembered, of a sudden, that he had promised Steven to visit her that evening ; the very idea of an encounter with anyone so intimately connected with Steven threw her into a panic. Of course she could refuse to see him, as she had refused Darnay ; but that would only increase her agony by other complications. She felt, like a poisoned rat, the need to escape from all things and persons that had seen her sane and happy. Even the presence of Ellen, poor soul ! was now intolerable.

" I must go away," she thought. " I must go away somewhere . . . anywhere. I can't . . . I can't bear to set eyes on anyone that I know. I think I should die or go mad if I saw anyone or stayed here."

Moved by a rapt and urgent automatism she found herself turning out her wardrobe and packing a suitcase. The very idea of escape encouraged and distracted her. For one mad moment she had the idea of following Steven to Southampton, of trying to catch one more glimpse of him before he embarked. The plan was as futile as fantastic. She abandoned it. She looked at her watch and found that it was half-past five. In another half-hour Hart would be free to visit her. It was sheer luck that he had not arrived already. If she were ever going to escape she must set about it at once ! Yesterday, she remembered, Dudley had caught a train at five-fifty.

She stepped out into the corridor with her packed suitcase and called Ellen. Ellen came running to her, her honest face tear-stained and full of awe.

" I'm going to catch a train in a few minutes, Ellen."

" You're never going ? Good gracious, ma'am ! Am I to come with you ? "

" No, you'll stay here until I let you know. If you want anything specially, ask the Colonel."

" I don't like the thought of your going alone, ma'am, the

way you are. Not all of a rush like this. Couldn't you wait till to-morrow morning, ma'am ? "

Of course the woman thought she was quite mad. Perhaps she was right. What did it matter anyway ?

" No. no," Clare told her. " I've got to go at once. Don't worry, Ellen, I'll write to you. You can pack up everything ready to go to Uffdown."

" If you'll stay one moment, ma'am, I'll get you a spot of tea. You've not had a bite of anything since breakfast. You'd ought to keep your strength up now Master Steven's gone off, and the kettle's on the boil."

" Well, hurry up then."

Any excuse was good enough to get her out of the way. As soon as her bewildered face had disappeared Clare picked up her bag and went. Up the dishevelled garden, over the open down, toward the station on the crown of the rise. When she trudged upward, heavily laden, through the coarse grasses, and paused, at last, for breath, she saw the red-brick crescent of Pedworth barracks lifting above the elms, the long, smooth ramparts of the Plain behind it. Small specks of men were moving across the meadow on the cinder-path. Perhaps Hart was among them. As she picked up her baggage and moved on she was thinking : " This is the end of Pedworth ; I shall never see him, nor the barracks nor the Plain again. We were so happy. What does it matter ? This is the end of everything."

The train stood steaming in the station. The guard impatiently called her to hurry up. Without a ticket she jumped into a third-class compartment full of soldiers. The men made room for her with a touching courtesy. They didn't know that they had a dead woman with them.

Over the trench-scarred down a blood-red sunset gleamed from the windows of hutments dumped on the hilltops like fortifications of the Stone Age. The train crept slowly past the debauched villages that edge the Plain. At Ludgershall they turned her out on to a long platform scattered with patient soldiers and their packs. A train from the south roared in. That meant North Bromwich and Uffdown. She felt that she would have died if she'd gone to North Bromwich. Anyway, she was on the wrong side of the line. A moment later another train pulled up beside her. She entered it, and, a little later, found herself in Andover.

An elderly porter, with a kind face, offered to carry her bag. "Where are you going, ma'am?" he asked her. "I'd better label it."

She didn't know where she was going; only that she was going away.

"When does the next train start?" she enquired, to his amazement.

"The up-express is due in now," he told her. "If you haven't got a ticket I'll book one for you."

He took it for granted that she was going to London. Why not? There was no better place in which to bury herself. The porter was very gentle with her; perhaps he was used to seeing women in her case. She gave him her purse without another thought.

And, then, once more she found herself in a third-class carriage of the express. It whirled her desperately through the dim Hampshire woodlands, with a rhythmical roar that was like the throbbing of drums. She sat in her place with blank eyes staring in front of her. By Woking the sky was dark. At last Waterloo. . . .

Another porter suggested finding a taxi. "The beggars are scarce to-night," he confided to her. He took her bag and advanced down an infinite length of platform in search of one. Suddenly, to the astonishment of both of them, the station lights went out.

"What is it?" she asked in the darkness.

"We're used to that," he told her. "I reckon it's one of these air-raids. Them blasted Gothas!"

An air-raid ! Suddenly she remembered her promise to Steven. Only the day before she had promised him that she wouldn't go to London for fear of them. And here she was, in the very thick of it ! Whatever would he think of her ?

She pulled the porter's arm. " I've changed my mind. I mustn't stay here. Find out if there's another train to the west."

He pulled out a ragged timetable and looked at it in the glow of a standing engine's furnace.

" There ought to be one for Exeter and Plymouth in another ten minutes," he said. " We'll just step round to the platform and see if she's running."

A long black train stood waiting . " Don't much look like it," said the porter. He called through the darkness to a passing inspector :  " Is the nine-twenty running ? "

" No more trains out to-night. All service suspended."

" It looks like you've got to stay here, ma'am," said the porter. " I reckon we'd better find that taxi after all."

She followed him down a tunnel that was like a mine. At the bottom of it the traffic of a street moved blindly. No lights in the shops or houses. No light at all but a glimmer in the rear of passing omnibuses. And not a sound ; all the impatient motor-horns were quiet, as though they hoped to slink by unheard beneath the night-flying terror ; a shadow that she would never have imagined to be that of a taxi crept near them ; the porter jumped for the step.

" Hurry up, ma'am, he's got to keep moving or he'll be run into from be'ind."

" Can you take me to Smith's Hotel in Dover Street ? " she gasped.

" Now you're asking ! " said the driver humorously. " Come along, lydy, it's a sportin' charnst ! "

She scrambled into the cab ; the porter thrust her luggage in after her ; she opened her purse to tip him, and, feeling in the darkness, found nothing but treasury notes. She gave him one. Whether it was of a pound or ten shillings made no difference. He fell behind. The taxi went creeping on through the darkness.

Suddenly the window that separated her from the driver was lowered. A cockney voice—he was only a voice—faintly laden with beer, but kindly :

" Put down the extra seat, lady, and sit up close to me. It'll be company for you like. What with one thing and another, these old air-raids they're a regular nuisance. Very annoying they are ! " She obeyed him gladly.

" That's the ticket," he said over his shoulder, " now we can have a bit of a talk. Yer can't move above two miles an hour in this here dark."

For a moment Clare distrusted his familiarity. Ellen had lately been full of white slave traffic scares ; stories of sinister taxis in which unsuspecting females had been driven to houses of ill-fame, pulled out and gagged and chloroformed and ruined—that was Ellen's word—before they knew where they were.

" But how foolish of me," she thought, " that kind of thing doesn't happen to middle-aged women with grown-up sons like myself. We shall probably be blown to pieces in another half-hour anyway." And the taxi-driver, for company's sake, went on to freeze her blood with a personal story of the Gothas' last visit :

" When the lights went out, I said to Beat—that's my wife—we're for it, old girl. That's what I said. You'd better come down into the yard. These top floors can cop it easy."

" What kind of yard ? " Clare wondered. It struck her suddenly that it might be the yard of a mews.

" But not a bit of it," the driver went on cheerfully. " You see, to tell you the truth, she'd only been confined like the week before. ' You taike the kids, Jim,' she says.

' If the devils '—excuse the word, lydy—' if the devils gets me that's that.' Like a bloomin' 'orse with the stable on fire she was ; no moving of 'er ! So I ups with the kids and carries them downstairs to the yard and covers 'em up with straw. There was a chap naimed Charlie what does the washing at night to look after them. Then back I went to Beat, and sat down by 'er and 'eld 'er 'and. But the blarsted Gothas—if you'll excuse the term—never got no nearer than Sarthend, they tell me ; so it was all for nothing, as you might say. Nor, if you ask my straight opinion, they won't to-night. Not they ! "

As the streets grew narrower the darkness became even more impenetrable ; and all the time the beery voice kept up its monologue, like that of a patter comedian, determined to entertain her. The form of diversion was not tactfully chosen, embracing, as it did, the surgical details of how the driver had lost his leg at Wipers in fifteen and been blown up, later, by an aerial bomb in the hospital at Ee-taples ; but the will to divert was none the less kindly. She was amazed, when after nearly an hour of tortoiselike progression, she found herself triumphantly deposited at the door of the hotel in Dover Street which she and Steven had frequented during their week-ends in town. She thanked the driver and gave him another of her notes. He seemed surprised when she refused the change.

" You've been extremely kind to me," she said.

" Well, lydy, in a manner of speaking, I'm a family man," he told her, by way of explanation.

Inside the doors of the hotel the manager himself received her. He seemed, like the porter and the taxi-driver, made intimate and humanized by the common danger. He shook hands heartily, as though she were an old and valued friend.

" Well, Mrs. Hingston, this is a surprise ! You're all alone ? Then where is Captain Hingston ? "

He always gave Steven two degrees of brevet rank.

" He's sailing for France this evening," she answered.

" Dear, dear, is . . . that . . . so ? " said the manager. " Allow me ! "

He took her bag, to the evident scandal of the porters, and conducted her to her room in person. On the first floor, he told her, one was reasonably safe.

" Anything that I can do for you," he said, as he retreated.

There was nothing he could do for her, nothing that anybody could do for her. With a kind of devoted automatism she undressed and crept into bed. She blew out the candle which was the only light allowed her, and lay, with eyes wide open, miserably waiting for the first bomb to fall.

" How angry Steven will be with me," she thought. " I must have been quite mad. If I am killed to-night I shall only deserve it."

She saw the dark channel, and a troopship crossing the submarine-infested waters to Havre.

" Oh, Steven, Steven," her heart cried. " Oh, Steven, my darling . . ."

When she awoke next morning it surprised, but scarcely cheered her, to find that she was still alive.

# BOOK SEVEN
## CLAERWEN

# WYSHFORD

By one of those coincidences that only the captious reader of fiction finds incredible, the news of Sir Joseph Hingston's elevation to the peerage, announced in the birthday honours, and the wire from the War Office reached Clare on the same June morning. For two months, ever since her retreat from the populous desolation of London, she had been working in a convalescent hospital at Overbury in Gloucestershire, where Joyce Wilburn, encountered by chance on the pavement of Piccadilly, was acting as house-surgeon; a pleasant, modern country-house, embowered in rose-gardens and tufted elms, with the wide outlet of the Vales of Evesham stretched beneath it.

It was in the middle of the morning that Mrs. Payne, the commandant, brought in her telegram to the dressing-room where Clare and the sister-in-charge were swallowing a hurried cup of tea.

" The boy is waiting in case there's an answer," Mrs. Payne said softly; and waited too; for in those days one never knew what a wire might contain, and she herself had a son at the front in the Canadian Army. Clare opened the envelope hurriedly. It was not the first time that she had known such an intolerable moment; for Lady Hingston, now Lady Wolverbury, had an inconsiderate habit of conducting all her most trivial correspondence by telegram. Mrs. Payne and the sister watched her anxiously. But this time the wire was shorter than any of Lady Wolverbury's, and much more to the point.

" He's wounded," Clare gasped, " he's wounded ! " Her heart added : " Thank God ! He's safe. . . ."

" Let me look, nurse," said the sister with brisk officious-ness. She took the telegram from Clare's trembling fingers and read the message out loud for Mrs. Payne's benefit :

" *Regret to inform you*—what a waste of words !—*Second-Lieutenant S. Hingston seriously wounded*. Well, that's first rate ! "

*Seriously* . . . How seriously ? When once the tumult of fear and gratitude had subsided, there was no other question in Clare's mind.

The sister was a mass of information : " Seriously ? There's nothing to worry over in that. You see there are three degrees : slightly, seriously and dangerously. If they call it serious it may only be a little more than slightly, and at any rate it isn't dangerous, or they'd have said so. Why, nurse, you're white as a sheet ! Sit down and have another cup of tea."

The commandant, a plain and motherly woman, patted Clare's shoulder : " Sister's quite right. There's nothing to worry about now. You're sure to hear more particulars in a day or two. He'll be over in England in no time. Serious means ' blighty ' for certain. I'll send the boy away, and I think you'd better take the afternoon off to get over it."

Clare thanked her gratefully. That afternoon she wandered away over the dome of Bredon Hill, which rose, amid plantations of vivid larchwood, immediately behind the house. For a long time she could not set her mind on anything. It was vexed by the alternation of two phrases : he's safe ; he's wounded ; that followed each other like waves, one buoyant, exulting, the other bewildering and full of noisy confusion ; for, in spite of all the sister's assurances, that dark word " serious " had a sinister sound, speaking, if not of danger, of pain and unthinkable mutilations.

Yet, in the end, the sense of relief outweighed all others. In that warm wind that swayed the pines on Bredon there rose again, miraculously, undeniably, the life and hope that had left her for dead, two months before, in the deserted bungalow at Pedworth. She sat on the summit of the hill bemused, suspended, while, like a ravishing narcotic, the warm flood of returning life stole through her body, unsealing her frozen senses, loosening the chains that bound her spirit one by one till it seemed as though the tired and anxious body were not large enough to contain it, till it soared heavenward, tremulously, like a rising lark. Larks? The whole sky was alive with their torrential music; it rained down on her in a stream of silver. She hadn't realized before that there were skylarks in Overbury. How should a dead woman realize anything? Nor yet had she realized what now burst upon her with such bloom and freshness as if it had been newly born, like the red admiral that sunned its powdered wings on a head of hemp agrimony, the incomparable homely beauty of that essential England which lay beneath her: southward the towers of Gloucester, aspiring stone made blue and filmy as cloud; the billowing blossom of the Vale of Evesham lavished at her feet; northward, where the horizon thickened against the smoke of the black-country, the Clents; two shadowy undulations, Pen Beacon and Uffdown, the twin geniuses that had inspired her childhood and her love. Two months before she had said goodbye to beauty; and beauty, returning now to welcome and to reflect the ecstasy of life new-born in her, moved her to such depths that her eyes failed for tears.

And when, restored and confident, she descended to Overbury, in a mild sunset mellowed by chiming bells, another wire was waiting for her, this time from Steven.

*Am at Wyshford Abbey*, it said. *Don't worry. Longing to see you.*

"I was burning to open it," the sister confided. "Thank

goodness it's nothing worse. You never know, you know."

Nothing worse indeed ! Clare hurried off with her wire to Mrs. Payne.

" Wyshford Abbey ? That's not far from Salisbury ; it belongs to the Earl of Bemerton," the commandant told her. " I'm sure it's out of the question getting there to-night— a long cross-country journey. And in any case they probably wouldn't let you see him. To-morrow morning. Yes, yes, of course we can spare you. We must. Naturally I shall be sorry to lose you after so short a time ; but if your son needs you I shall understand."

Joyce Wilburn was a little less complacent. " If you only knew, my dear Clare, what a blessed nuisance you fond mothers are ! However, I suppose I'm not in a position to understand your sentiments." Joyce had never married, and spoke with a shade of bitterness that didn't spare herself ; but Joyce, for all her affectation of brusqueness, was softer than she had ever been at Tudor House. There had been some man or other in India. And during those two months at Overbury, she had atoned, in her deliberately clumsy way, for many of the petty wrongs that she had done to Clare in Alvaston. It was Joyce who got up early next morning to wake her with a cup of tea . . . but not for one moment would she admit that her kindness was anything but an accident.

In a fever of glad impatience, Clare left the Overbury car at Cheltenham station. The train moved with an excruciating slowness ; it climbed the scrap of Cotswold so laboriously that Clare felt it could never reach the crest, then sauntered idly southward, stopping to exchange a word of gossip with every village station it encountered. The very strain of continued anticipation was exhausting, and Clare who had spent the whole night in fervent imaginings, dropped off to sleep in her corner.

When she awoke it seemed to her that the country through

which the train still ambled was familiar. Vast folds of arable clothed in blue-green wheat, streaked with spills of charlock and flagrant poppies ; horizon lines of downland, as pale and velvety as though the chalk itself had flowered minutely like a mossy saxifrage, lifting, at last, into a huge domed hilltop crowned with beechwoods. When last she had seen that shape the woods were almost leafless, but she knew it at once for Sidbury, the northernmost bastion of Salisbury Plain, and, with the sight of it, all the coloured memories of Pedworth returned to her.

All memories of Pedworth ; but, overpoweringly, memories of Robert Hart. During her penance at Overbury she had not dared to think of him, much less to write and risk a letter in return. In some obscure and atavistic way she had associated him with a taboo. It was not that she admitted a shadow of guilt in their relationship ; his attitude toward her had been far too correct for that ; yet, on the plane of instinct which is beyond reason, she felt some mystical connection between her conduct with regard to him and Steven's safety ; as if it were not merely impious but dangerous to have any contact with him during Steven's absence. She couldn't explain the feeling : there it was. But now, when Steven was home again and relatively safe, there seemed to be no more need for inhibition. In retrospect, the joys of their life at Pedworth, that had been so perilous and high-pitched, took on an aspect of serenity in which the memory of Hart's frank friendship was among the most precious. Now, as the train passed Savernake and skirted the edge of the Plain, revealing landmark after landmark with which Hart was associated, she allowed his figure to assert its old spell over her mind.

" How glad he would be," she thought, " to know that Steven is home again ! It's a shame that he can't share the relief, the happiness."

For, in the back of her mind, she was sure that Hart

would have held himself responsible if Steven had been killed. This homecoming was the reward, the vindication of his integrity.

" I must write and tell him as soon as I get to Wyshford," she thought. " Perhaps he will come over and see us there some day ; it can't be very far. That will be like old times, we three together." The reaction from her severity was carrying her to an opposite extreme. It didn't strike her now that Hart's company might be dangerous to either's peace of mind ; she was happy, and unshared happiness was of little value ; she could afford to be generous, and she felt that she had treated Hart rather badly.

But now the spire of Salisbury pierced the sky. Her heart grew eager for Steven, nothing but Steven. A car from the station carried her out along the straight, avenued high road to the west. A stone bridge spanned a chalk-stream with emerald trailing poa-grass swimming in smooth flats beneath it. Then the grey gatehouse of Wyshford, a court-yard bounded on four sides like a cloister, and the sober, undecorate front of the Abbey itself.

She told her taxi-driver to wait, and rang the house-bell. They showed her in to a high hall, hung with the armour of St. Quentin. The High Constable of France faced her with his lance raised. The hall was permeated by a sweet and faintly aromatic odour as of strange woods or pot-pourri. A visitor ? Mr. Hingston ? But first she must see the matron. And there, within the Elizabethan shell, was a cloister in-deed ; part of the ravished Abbey which he of St. Quentin, the first Earl of Bemerton, who doubtless knew a good place when he saw it, had made his own. An acquisitive race they seemed, these Bemertons ; for all the cloister was lined by statuary that had found its patina under bluer skies. It was a long way, the servant apologized ; one had to walk round two sides of a square to reach the steps that led down to the hospital wards. Their footsteps echoed over stone flags ; the marble heroes and emperors surveyed them as they passed ; like Mignon, Clare remembered in *Kennst du das Land ?* " Down here ! " A rounded archway, a groined roof. A sweep of shallow steps ; a long tunnel of a corridor with many numbered doors ; and here no odours of pot-pourri or sandal-wood, but one more sinister, the faint acridity of iodine which she had learned to recognise at Stourford.

" This is the matron's office, madam. If you'll wait a moment next door, I'll tell her you're here."

The cool and stony silence was monastic. Clare told herself that she must be patient ; and yet it seemed strange that any formality in the world should keep her from Steven when he was lying so near. A kindly voice soon summoned her : " Mrs. Hingston ? Won't you come and wait here for a moment ? The doctors are just ' boarding ' him, reporting on his wound. I expect you'll be glad to hear exactly what they think of him."

A slender, youngish woman, with a pale and delicately-moulded face ; her eyes were almost violet, and lovely, Clare decided. She spoke very rapidly, almost as if she were shy of visitors. It seemed strange to Clare that the matron shouldn't wear uniform, but a linen skirt and a jersey of plum-coloured silk.

" That's very kind of you," she murmured. " You are the matron ? "

" No, no," the woman smiled quickly ; " I'm the commandant. Here comes the doctor. Now you'll know everything."

The figure of an officer in major's uniform, carrying a sheaf of papers, filled the doorway. Clare stared at him, and he stared back at her. It was Major Ingleby. He smiled and held out his hand :

" Why, Mrs. Hingston, I was wondering when you'd come."

"I see you're old friends," said Lady Bemerton tactfully, "and so I'll leave you in Major Ingleby's hands. If your son's not comfortable, you'll be sure to tell me? The matron, I'm certain, will find you a room in the village somewhere."

She left them, almost before she had finished speaking. "An amazing woman," Major Ingleby explained, "and such a sportsman! There isn't a voluntary hospital near the Plain to compare with Wyshford. The officers adore her, and so do I ; that is a secret, mind you ! But now you're wanting to know everything about your son ? " He smiled ; he was much more friendly than he had ever been at Pedworth. "Well, first of all let me tell you that his fighting days are probably over."

"Thank God for that ! " Clare whispered.

"He stopped a piece of high explosive just below the knee. Smashed up the tibia ; but the joint isn't involved. You may thank your stars for that ; the knee-joint's the devil. Apart from accidents—of course we don't make promises—apart from accidents there's no danger. A bit of shortening perhaps, but that needn't worry him. The board's decided that he won't be fit for service for six months. That's only an approximate figure, you understand. These cases are sometimes slow. It depends entirely on the amount of suppuration. And now that I've told you the good news you'd better come and see him."

She followed Ingleby into another vaulted chamber, with windows opening on an expanse of cedar-shadowed turf of an incredible smoothness. He moved diagonally toward a screened bed near the window. "I've brought a present for you, Hingston," he said gaily, and pushed her inside the screen.

"Hello, mum, is that you ? " said Steven's voice.

"My darling . . . my darling ! "

The ecstasy of that moment atoned for everything she had

suffered . . . everything! It was so poignant as to be almost unbelievable; she was thankful for the screens that concealed her emotion from other eyes. He was lying on his back, most strangely quiet; an enormous cradle protected the wounded leg. His face, she saw with a pang, was pale from loss of blood and definitely older; but for all the marks of strain, his eyes and mouth were more contented than she had ever seen them. Even the old petulance had vanished from his lips. A fantastic idea shot through her brain : " He looks just like a woman who has had a baby."

But now, while her tremulous lips were on his face, he began to talk in a subdued voice of all that had happened. His wound? No, it didn't hurt much. A kind of dull ache, as if the leg didn't properly belong to him. It had been like that from the moment when he was hit. As if, to begin with, somebody had smashed it with a crow-bar.

" I went down like a ninepin," he said, smiling. " I had to look to be certain it was still there; the leg, you know. A chap in my platoon, a fellow from Wychbury, stuck on the emergency dressing. It was bleeding like billy-oh. And then our M.O. gave me a couple of morphine tablets under my tongue. After that I felt as right as rain, rather pleased with myself than otherwise, though I thought the blighters would put the lid on me on the way to the clearing-station. A lot of heavy stuff coming over. One of the stretcher-bearers stopped one in the head, poor devil. The crumps were making that area pretty unhealthy. And then . . . well, there's no more to say about it. Here I am, and very nicely thank you! I've had quite enough of war for a day or two."

" Thank heaven you say that."

" Well, anyone who doesn't is a liar, mum, and that's that. Still, I can honestly say I wouldn't have missed it for anything. If I'd stayed on hanging about at Pedworth I should have felt an awful waster."

His voice was weakening as he talked ; but though she begged him to lie still for a moment, his mind was too full to let him be silent.

" How's Uffdown ? " he asked. " Of course, how silly of me ; you've been at Overbury. And how's the Colonel ? We must get him over here. I should like to see his jolly old face again. I often used to think of him in France, you know. Especially when I saw birds and things like that. You've never heard a golden oriole, have you ? And Camberwell Beauties, as common as tortoiseshells with us ! Pedworth's a jolly place when you come to look back on it. I shouldn't half mind being stationed there again. But everything one had lived through seemed like that in France. At a distance, a real distance you know, all life seems much of a muchness ; it flattens out, like a hilly country when you're flying." He asked her if she'd yet seen Lady Bemerton. " A topping woman. Just like a man to talk to. I don't mean that ; she's just as feminine as they make 'em." He chuckled. " I wish you could have heard the fellow over in that corner. A splendid chap, a captain in the Warwicks, he's lost an arm or something. He calls her ' the countess ' to us, and ' ma'am ' when he speaks to her. He's been giving me no end of hints on the 'olesale grocery trade. Which reminds me, we shall have to be no end of careful, shan't we ? Have you seen this ? "

He handed her a copy of the *Daily Mirror*, from the middle of which the wholly undistinguished face of the new Lord Wolverbury looked out at her as though the photographer had caught him in a moment of puzzled shyness at his new elevation.

" Won't grandmama just be on the top of herself ? " Steven chuckled. " It's rather fun for us, too, when you come to think of it. It'ld feel a bit queer to sign oneself Wolverbury,' wouldn't it ? I suppose it comes natural to people like the Bemertons. Still, every family has to be founded sometime, even though we happen to be a bit late in the field."

Behind the screen a soft voice breathed : " Excuse me . . . Do you mind very much if I take this away ? "

She took the answer for granted and carried the screen away with her. A tall and slender girl, in V.A.D. uniform. Even in that short moment Clare could see that she was dazzlingly pretty, with eyes that were a dark gleam, a profile that but for the straight nose was classical, blue-black hair, a skin whose creamy darkness was permeated by the flush of health as the colour of a ripe peach glows through its bloom. A peach, or even an apricot, Clare was thinking ; for there were tones of copper blended beneath, and the bloom was part of the skin's own lucent texture, not that of face-powder. A specimen fruit, Clare thought, and a foreign fruit as well ; there was a delicacy, a poise, a fineness in all her movements that was not a usual attribute of English girlhood, as though she had devoted hours of practice to their perfection : or rather as though the inherited instincts of some old civilization had given a dower of maturity to a youthful shape ; for this creature could not be older than seventeen, or eighteen at the most.

And if Clare's eyes and mind had been busy Steven's had not been idle.

" I say, mum," he whispered, " did you notice that girl ? "

" She's rather pretty, isn't she ? "

" Pretty ? That's not the word. She's absolutely stunning ; she takes one's breath away."

Clare glanced at him quickly ; his face was all on fire. A sudden uneasiness clutched at her heart. It was one of Steven's peculiarities that he didn't notice girls. She had often teased him about it at Pedworth, half rallying him on his indifference and half testing him ; for it gave her a pleasant sensation to feel that she herself was the only woman in the world for him. But now Steven was taking notice with a vengeance ; there was no need to tease or encourage him. Indeed, she had a vague feeling that encouragement would be dangerous. How had this change come over him in two short months ? She knew that the asceticism of the trenches was a polite convention : hadn't the papers been full of outcries against certain " facilities " provided behind the lines ? Of course she must realize that he was a child no longer ; and yet—and yet this obvious disturbance, the hot cheeks, the urgent whisper, warned her that a new interest might soon dispute the absolute possession on which she prided herself. Clare's own reaction to it was swift and unmistakable :

" Yes, she's a pretty girl," she repeated doubtfully, " although, of course, I never admire that type. They mature too early, you know, and go off dreadfully quickly. She sounded English ; but don't you think there's something rather foreign about her ? "

" I don't know. She doesn't look French. I never saw anything to touch her in France. She never came into this ward yesterday. I suppose she doesn't belong here. I jolly well wish she did ! "

She mocked him. " Poor dear ! We'll see what Lady Bemerton can do about it. But really, Steven darling, you must be a little light-headed. I assure you she isn't as attractive as all that."

" Attraction's a funny thing, mum, isn't it ? You can't define it. It's curious that very few girls really attract me. But that one does."

Well, he was candid anyway ; and the uncomfortable subject died a natural death with the arrival of the matron, a plump, soft-spoken, gentle woman in pince-nez, who chatted with them for a moment, tactfully concealing the real object of her visit which was to take Clare away.

That evening, in the Bemerton Arms at Wyshford, a comfortable inn asleep amid the murmur of the clear waters that flowed round it, Clare had time to ponder on the events of the day. It was wonderful to think that Steven's wound was less severe than she had dreaded ; to know, for certain, that he was sleeping safely within a few hundred yards of her, and, as Major Ingleby had insisted, in such careful hands. " I ought to sleep like a child to-night," she told herself ; and yet, as she surrendered her body to the seductions of the vast feather-bed, the most persistent of all the remembered visions that rose before her was that of the slim, dark girl whom Steven had admired.

" The queer thing is," she thought, " that though I didn't say so, I was almost as much attracted as he was. There's something familiar about her face ; I've seen her before. And yet I'm positive that I haven't seen her before. What can it be ? But in any case I've no earthly reason to worry about her. To begin with, she doesn't belong to Steven's ward ; and even if Steven falls in love with her—as I'm sure I should, if I were he—it doesn't mean that I'm going to lose him. All wounded soldiers fall in love with their nurses. There's safety in the very number of them. If I treat the matter seriously I shall only make it worse : I suppose it's time he fell in love with somebody. But if, after all this time, I've found him only to lose him . . . ? That," she reflected, " is where the influence of an older man, like Colonel Hart, would come in. I'm glad that Steven is so anxious to see him. No doubt Major Ingleby will tell him that we're here."

In the confusion of thought that eddied upon the verge of sleep the figures of Hart and of the dark, slim V.A.D. were strangely blended.

Next day, when she penetrated the aromatic cloisters of Wyshford and entered Steven's ward, her lovely rival was standing at his bedside. Stephen was in higher spirits than ever.

" So here you are at last ! " he said ; " I thought you

were never coming. I've got a surprise for you, mum. Allow me to introduce Miss Hart. *Now* do you understand why we stared at her yesterday ? What do you think of that for a coincidence ? "

The slim girl held out her hand to Clare and blushed. Yes, she was radiantly lovely, there was no denying it. And modest, too, Clare thought, unless she knew how blushes suited her powdered blooms and made them come to order. Even as it crossed her mind Clare rejected the ungenerous thought. This girl was far too young for such guiles to be possible. It was true that her instinct for poise made her look in the distance like an older woman, but when her eyes met Clare's, she saw that the face was as innocent as a child's. Her speech was charming, low-voiced, with each word beautifully and delicately formed, recalling the fineness that she had always admired in Hart himself.

" When last I heard of you," Clare said, " I think you were in a convent. I'd no idea you were working here."

" I'd no idea," Steven echoed, " that she even existed. The Colonel never breathed a word about her. I shall have a bone to pick with him over that when he comes to see us."

" I've only been here three weeks," the girl answered softly. " I hope you'll manage to make him come. He's dreadful. I never see him. And Pedworth's so near."

" Get mother to write to him," Steven suggested. " He'll do anything for her."

" Will he ? " The dark eyes swept Clare critically.

" Of course he won't. My son's exaggerating. We were all great friends at Pedworth," she explained.

" I think," said the girl, " that I had better be going. Matron will tick me off like anything if I'm caught gossiping. Do you mind ? "

" Of course I don't," Clare told her.

" *I* do ; I mind most awfully," Steven added.

" But he shouldn't have minded a bit," Clare thought,

" when I was with him. It was tactful of the girl to see that she was *de trop*. Now that she's gone, perhaps we shall be able to talk of something else."

But not a bit of it ! For the present there was only one subject for Steven.

" She's called Miranda," he told her. " A topping name don't you think so ? She isn't really a V.A.D. Only a sort of probationer. She's just seventeen."

" Of course, she's a mere child. I don't think it's wise of the Colonel to let her work here. With all these men she'll have her head turned in no time."

" But, my dear mother," Steven reminded her, " at her age you yourself were as good as married."

" Ah, that was twenty years ago. In those days people married earlier than they do now."

" I can't imagine," he said, " why the Colonel never mentioned her."

" He did, to me," she told him.

" I know. That's what's so shabby of him," he answered jealously.

" Really I don't see why you're so excited about it."

" Why ? She's so frightfully pretty. I think she's marvellous."

" She's striking, I admit. Her mother . . ."

Clare stopped. She wanted to tell him that Miranda's mother had not been a success and that she came from Malta, but realized that she had learned this under the seal of confidence.

" Yes, mum ? Her mother ? What do you know about her ? "

" Nothing, darling. I was only going to say that her mother died some years ago."

" Well, anyway, that has nothing to do with her looks. You must confess she's lovely ? "

"I feel what I told you before. It's the kind of beauty that doesn't wear very well."

He laughed. "I can see that you've been determined to crab her from the beginning. Can't I admire a girl? Surely you're not jealous, darling?"

"Steven, don't be ridiculous! What an idea!"

But she was jealous soon, and not without reason. Whenever she came to see him, Steven was full of Miranda. When once, for forty-eight hours, the matron transferred her to another ward, he was as moody and cross as a child whose favourite toy has been locked away from him; so difficult and distracted that, if it had been in her power, she would have sacrificed herself and given him his toy again; but no sooner had Miranda returned than he became himself.

It wounded her to feel that his happiness was dependent on another woman, even on one so innocent and inoffensive as this dark-eyed child. She wanted to talk to someone else about it; not to complain, but just to arrange her thoughts. The ideal counsellor would have been Miranda's father; but ten days passed before Hart came to see them.

When he did come unexpectedly, on a blazing midsummer afternoon, they had wheeled Steven out over the lake of smooth lawn into the shade of an enormous cedar. The air was utterly still; not a blade stirred. Beneath the silvery stone of the Palladian bridge the river spread itself soundlessly in shining flats. All the grey loveliness of Wyshford, that peerless house, seemed rapt into a dream of its own beauty, secure, inviolable within its boundaries of lucent water and wooded hills. There was no sound but the sighing of the cedar, a cool, aerial music borne by invisible movements of air through its vast fans, or, distantly, so far that they only served to point the silence, the woody click of a bat, thin cries and laughter, from the pitch where Lady Bemerton was playing cricket with her children.

"Uffdown is peaceful," Clare was thinking, "but this

is an older peace. Arcadia . . ." And she thought of Philip Sydney walking with his sister on cool evenings between the walls of yew.

It was Steven's voice that aroused her from this dream.

" Why, here he comes ! The Colonel. She's coming with him. It's the first time I've seen her out of uniform."

In Steven's mind she knew there was only one " she." Over the shaven turf, advancing with the long strides that she knew so well, Hart came toward them, Miranda fluttering in pale muslin at his side ; and the pang that Steven's words had given her was drowned in a flush that recognized the recovery of something that she had been loth to lose. Miranda had taken her father's arm as they approached ; the glow of pleasure and excitement transfigured her ; his height and wiry strength seemed proper foils to her more delicate fire ; but though Miranda laughed with Hart her eyes were for Steven, as Clare's were for Hart.

" He is just the same," she thought triumphantly. " He hasn't changed a bit. Of course it's only two months since I saw him ; yet those two months have seemed an eternity. How happy and how proud he looks to-day, and how thankful, thankful I am to see him happy ! "

Hart took her hand and pressed it without a word.

" At last," she said. " We thought you were never coming to see us."

He laughed : " My prison grows more close than ever. How jolly to see you again, and Steven too ! How are you, my son ? I needn't ask. Ingleby's told me. You're one of the lucky ones."

" It's topping to be together again like this, sir ! " said Steven. He turned to Miranda. " Are you off duty this afternoon ? How splendid ! We can invite you to tea. I shall be able to wait on you for a change. You'll have to behave yourself ! "

She flashed a smile of amusement at Steven and dropped

him a curtsey. She seemed extraordinarily soft and delicate in her sprigged muslin, as if that filmy tissue were part of the lithe body which it scarcely concealed. Yet, though she smiled at Steven and made him know that she was aware of his presence, a ravishing coquetry, disguised as modesty, kept her always away from him and at her father's side, listening, with an attention that was almost embarrassing, to every word that passed between him and Clare.

" I wish to goodness she wouldn't stick to us so," Clare thought. " She's only hanging on to her father like that to excite Steven. The child is a positive minx. I have to choose my words all the time. She makes me self-conscious."

But Hart, at any rate, was not self-conscious. She had never before in her life known him more natural. It made her realise the relief that Steven's safety must have given him. During those dead months at Overbury no doubt he had suffered, knowing, in spite of the conviction that he had acted rightly, that if Steven were killed, she would blame him.

" Since we have suffered apart," she thought, " we should be happy together. His friendship means far more to me than I ever imagined. Now that we have met again I mustn't lose him . . . I can't afford to lose him." For she knew, by now, that the time was coming when she must lose Steven. " He is bound to fall in love with somebody," she told herself. " It's no use fighting against that. If it's not this child, it's certain to be some other."

When they had laughed and gossiped over tea beneath their cedar, feeling an urgent need to speak with Hart alone —for their one meeting after the night at Fontenoy had been marred by Dudley's visit—she suggested that they should explore the yew-tree garden on the western side of the house.

" I say, you'll leave Miranda with me, won't you ? " Steven entreated.

So now it was " Miranda ! " Of course Clare would leave her ; she had never intended doing anything else ; yet even the fulfilment of this plan demanded a sacrifice, for though Miranda was soft and demure as a rabbit—a little too demure, Clare thought, for safety—she could see by Steven's eyes that he was on fire.

" I'll make myself responsible for her good behaviour," he laughed ; but as soon as she and Hart had turned their backs Clare knew that the two children were speaking in whispers.

They were walking together, she and Hart, along the high yew alleys which the feet of dead poets had trodden before them ; for all that water-guarded island of Wyshford is holy ground. And now that they were alone at last Clare had nothing to say to him. It was enough, she felt, that they should be together ; and Hart, on his side, seemed equally contented with their silence and the sweet air ; for this was the month of roses. They came, at last, to a seat in the midst of a pavement, on whose stone flags the shadows of yew and cypress fell with a blackness of velvet. Such quietude, such beauty, in Hart's company seemed almost intolerable.

" I have been wanting to tell you," she said, " ever since last I saw you, how right you were. I'm very grateful. Please believe me when I say so."

" Of course I believe you. All the time I couldn't help wondering if you were thinking hardly of me. The thought of it has rarely been out of my mind."

" No, no, you were right. I knew it long ago. And now providence has proved it."

He smiled.

" If you like to put it that way, you may."

" Major Ingleby says six months. That's a long time isn't it ? "

" It's a long war. But in six months I feel sure it must

be over. By now there are over a million Americans in France ; the end has begun."

" We've said that so often ; but this time I suppose you're right. You're likely to stay on at Pedworth till the end ? "

" I imagine so. They seem to find me useful."

" Then I hope we shall see more of you ? "

He was silent. Now that the others were no longer with them, the old reservation appeared, and yet he was too honest to make excuses. It seemed to be left to her to force his hand by an admission.

" Colonel Hart, I shall take it very hardly if we don't. We have so many happy memories behind us. It will seem a dreadful pity if we can't."

" You know," he said, " that you're asking for something that will be very difficult ? For me, I mean. Perhaps not at all for you."

" Is it so awfully difficult as all that ? Is it impossible that we should just be friends ? "

" My dear," he said, " if I didn't know you, I should think you were playing with me."

" But you know that I'm doing nothing of the kind ? "

" I know ; but somehow that doesn't make it so much easier."

" Last time I asked you to do something for Steven's sake. This time it's for my own. I don't want to lose you."

" We'll see," he said after a long pause. " But if I throw my hand in, all of a sudden, you won't blame me, will you ? "

" I shall never blame you," she told him.

A deep bell in the Abbey campanile tolled the hour. Its sound was the signal for his going to catch the 'bus that ran from Salisbury to Pedworth. Already the river-breeze had brought a chill into the air, and when they returned to

Steven and Miranda it was time for the wounded man to go indoors, and time, too, for Miranda to fly and change her muslins for going on duty.

" You'll come again soon, sir, won't you ? " Steven said. " Mum hasn't given me the chance to get a word with you."

" That's what you say," Clare thought, " but I know that you've been only too glad to get me out of the way. And now, when you beg him to come again, you're only hoping to do the same thing ; you're only hoping to have Miranda to yourself." Yet, knowing how charily Hart kept her company, she was glad to hear Stephen adding his persuasion to hers. " Why don't you try to fit it in with Miranda's free afternoon, sir ? " he said, disarmingly.

Hart smiled, half promised. Clare saw him to the lodge and then returned to say good night to Steven, although, for all it meant to him, she might have spared herself the trouble. The boy's head was spinning with Miranda. Whatever he might say—and his exaltation made him even more attentive than usual—Clare knew quite well that his thought —if, in that divine ferment, thought were possible—was far away from her ; his ears strained for the sound of a soft voice in the echoing cloister, his eyes for the first opening of a door.

" Poor darling," Clare thought, " he's badly hit. These boy and girl affairs are very desperate ; but very rarely serious, thank heaven ! "

Indeed, that evening, as she returned to her inn, she was preoccupied not so much with Steven's abject surrender to Miranda in muslin as with the curiousness of her own relation to Miranda's father.

" If it were anyone but you," he had told her frankly, " I should think that you were playing with me."

" If it were anyone but he," her heart replied, " he might think that I was throwing myself at him."

Which meant not only that they were both extraordinary people, but that they understood each other.

" And that is all one can ask at our time of life," she mused as she sat before her mirror, in a scent of white jasmine, brushing out her hair. " How grey I have gone in the last two months," she reflected. She hadn't had time to notice her greyness at Overbury. " In my mother's time, at this age, I should have begun to wear a lace cap with mauve ribbons in it. When one's as grey as I am it's no use pretending to be young any longer. To think that I'm older now than Aunt Cathie was when first I remember her ! How soft and delicious poor little Miranda looked in her sprigged muslin ! It's difficult to believe that I was ever as young as that."

Next day, when she went to visit Steven, Miranda was not in evidence. A hard-faced middle-aged sister with a red nose wheeled him out to his post beneath the cedar. Clare teased him gently. " It's much healthier for you," she said, " to have two nice plain women like us to look after you. You'd run a temperature if you saw too much of Miranda."

He took her seriously. " That's just what you *would* say, mother ; you're absolutely wrong. Miranda helped with my dressing yesterday. Her hands were as light as . . . as feathers."

" Don't be so touchy, darling. I'm only teasing you."

" Then I wish you wouldn't. Not about her. I want to tell you something, mum. I'm going to marry that girl."

She laughed uneasily. " Steven don't be ridiculous You've only known her for ten days."

" That makes no difference."

" It does. It means that you can't possibly know your own mind."

" I do, mother. I always do. It's my peculiarity. You ought to realize that by now."

" You're so young, and so is Miranda. You're a pair of children."

" She's no younger than you were when you married father."

That was unanswerable. She began again : " I suppose you realize that your guardian and the Stourford people may have something to say about it. Particularly now . . ."

" Stourford be damned, mum," he answered hotly. " It's no business of theirs. Or Mr. Wilburn's. Besides, in fifteen months I shall be of age."

" Exactly. That's rather my point. You're in too great a hurry. It'ld be much better not to think any more of it till then."

" I can't think of anything else, mum," he confessed. " I've got it badly. What have you against her ? I wish to goodness you'd tell me."

" Nothing, my child. Of course I've nothing against her."

" Then what on earth is all this nonsense about ? "

She hesitated. " My darling, perhaps it's that I don't want to lose you. So soon ! Just when I've got you back again."

" That's quite ridiculous. You'll never lose me. Miranda knows that as well as I do. She simply adores you."

" How do you know that, Steven ? "

" We've spoken about it."

" Already ? " Her heart sank. " At any rate, promise me one thing. Don't say any more till I've talked it over with the Colonel."

" You needn't do that. I wrote to him last night."

" Oh, Steven ! How fast you go ! And what about Miranda ?

" She loves me too, darling. We understand each other perfectly."

An inspiration came to her : " Of course, if it's gone as far as that she'll have to leave Wyshford. The hospital rules are very strict in that way."

His face fell : " Good Lord, I'd never thought of that."

" I'm afraid you haven't thought of anything, my child."

" Lady Bemerton's a dear. I'm sure she'd understand. And anyway there's no reason why she should know."

" If the Colonel and I consented to an engagement we should have to tell her."

" That's downright mean, mum, and not a bit like you. You wouldn't say that unless you disliked Miranda."

" I don't do anything of the sort, darling. You've no right to suggest it. I merely think, as any reasonable person would, that you've been extremely precipitate."

Extremely precipitate ; was that Aunt Cathie's voice ?

" You're both of you frightfully young. You're under age, and Miranda's a positive baby. A number of people are interested, although you only think of yourself : the Colonel, myself, and Dudley, who's still your guardian."

" I never imagined you'd turn rough like this, mum," he said ruefully.

" My darling, I'm *not* turning rough ; I'm only trying to show you . . ."

She wasn't quite sure herself what she was trying to show him or what she was fighting for. But she knew she was fighting now with her back to the wall. And Steven was ready to give back as much as he took. He lay there staring at her with all the Hingston obstinacy in his blue eyes ; Ralph reincarnate—how well she knew that look !

" Whatever you do or say," he told her, " will make no difference. You may take it from me, mum, I'm going to marry that girl."

## II

### ACTION AND REACTION

WITHIN a few days the battle had begun and Stourford opened fire with a tremendous salvo.

*My dear Clare*, Lady Wolverbury wrote :

*This morning I have received an* amazing *letter from Steven. Who is this girl? The name sounds like an actress. All kinds of shady women are nursing in these days* as I have reason to know. *I cannot imagine how you, being on the spot, could possibly have allowed things to go so far. Of course you must tell Lady Bemerton about it at once and have her moved away from him. The girl I mean. It seems to me that Steven is either* quite mad, *or else he completely fails to realize his future position, which amounts to the same thing, though I'm quite sure this creature and her father*—whom Steven says is a friend of yours—*are perfectly aware of it. His grandfather and I have talked it over and decided that since you have brought this on yourself you must act strongly.* (1) *Get the woman removed from the hospital.* (2) *If that can't be done, get Steven moved.* (3) *Destroy all letters that come for him after this has been done. Those people are sure to pester him. Please let me know at once when these instructions have been followed.*

*I'm afraid I haven't had time to answer your letter about the peerage. Thank you all the same. It was the* least *they could do. When the history of the war comes to be written everybody will realize, as Mr. Lloyd George says, that if anyone won it,* he *did. I mean your father-in-law.*

> *Yours affectionately,*
>
> *Margaret Wolverbury.*

*P.S.—I notice that Steven says the girl's father is a colone. I suppose that means " temporary " ?*

*P.SS.—Please tell Steven when next he writes to me to address me as " The Lady Wolverbury," not " Lady Wolverbury." He ought to have known better. This is important. I enclose a cheque from his grandfather.*

Clare smiled as she began to disentangle the sense of this letter from the underlinings whose thickness symbolized the urgency of Lady Wolverbury's feelings. It pleased her to know that Steven, to use his own slang, had " put the wind up " Stourford ; she welcomed her mother-in-law as an ally, however capricious, though she couldn't help feeling hurt that, characteristically, they had thrown the blame on herself. Yet, when she reached the suggestion that Miranda, and even more, Miranda's father, had been influenced by the thought of Steven's inheritance, she ceased to smile. It seemed to her that they, and not the Stourford people, had been wronged by an unpardonable vulgarity. A " temporary " colonel, indeed ! And even if he had been " temporary," what had that to do with it ?

Another letter from Dudley, scribbled on the back of an army-form :

*Dear Clare,*
*Thanks for your letter (undated). I heard from Joyce that you had gone to Wyshford, and hope that Steven is as well as can be expected. I gather he's all right, since he's managed to fall in love. As to any action under the deed of trust, I need hardly say that I shall be guided by you entirely. What do you want me to do ? I'm all over the Southern Command, but the N.B. address will always find me.*
*Yours affect'ly,*
*Dudley Wilburn.*

They were all affectionate ! What *did* she want him to do ? She couldn't say ; she couldn't even think till she and Robert

Hart had talked it over together. Hart's own response to
Steven's letter was laconic.

*Dear Mrs. Wilburn,*

*I expect Steven's told you that he wrote to me. If I can*
*possibly get away I should like to see you on Friday afternoon*
*at 4.30. At the Bemerton Arms : not at the Abbey. And*
*don't tell Steven.*

*Yours always,*
*Robert Hart.*

Even if Hart hadn't warned her she wouldn't have told
Steven, and yet she knew beforehand that she would find it
difficult to invent a pretext for leaving him alone on the
afternoon of Friday ; for Steven, who was always acute,
had now become suspicious. Shopping in Salisbury was
the excuse she gave him, and his ready acceptance of it was
two-edged ; although it freed her it showed that, on occasion
—or rather on all occasions when Miranda was about—her
company was not as precious to him as she had imagined.

She waited for Hart in the inn garden. A narrow, cobbled
pathway, bordered by clove-scented stocks and springing
hedges of sweet-peas, ran straight to an arbour of trellised
roses which overhung the river, a three-feet depth of swift,
pellucid water through which one could see the tremor of
a black trout's fins holding the current, and shadowy grayling rising from the gravel like ghosts. Clare sat there
watching them, as much disturbed by the mere fact of Hart's
coming as by his uncomfortable mission. At half-past four,
to the stroke of the Abbey clock, she saw his tall shape
moving down the path toward her.

" How punctual you are ! " was all she could say to him.

" It's the 'bus that was punctual," he said as he sat down
beside her. " I hope you're not dreadfully upset by all
this business ? "

Upset ? Why should I be upset ? Are you ? "

" I've used the wrong word as usual. I should have said surprised."

" Ah, that is different. Surprised, yes. Although it isn't very surprising after all."

" Steven's a charming boy, and Miranda, though I say it, is not wholly unattractive."

" She's positively lovely. But they hardly know each other, and both of them are awfully young, aren't they ? "

" Of course. That is the point. I had six pages from Miranda as well as Steven. She's got it just as badly as he has, poor darling ! "

" Don't say ' poor darling ' ! It's wonderful for both of them to be young and in love. The most wonderful thing, I suppose, that happens to anybody."

" Yes, there's no doubt about that. One feels it poignantly as one grows older."

His voice grew strangely tender. That wasn't what she wanted.

" Well, what are we going to do? " she said, abruptly. " It's your affair as much as mine. I preferred to do nothing without consulting you."

" You mean you wanted to do something very—drastic ? "

" I don't know what I *ought* to do. You must tell me. I want them to be happy, most of all. Will they be happy ? You know her . . ."

" Ah, I can't tell you that. There's something else in your mind. You're keeping something back from me."

" You're right. I'm sorry. I've had a violent letter from my mother-in-law. They're very perturbed. You don't mind my telling you this ? Steven's his grandfather's heir."

" Miranda's not good enough ? I see." His calm voice hardened. " And is that all ? "

She was forced to answer him : " No, that's not all. If I tell you the truth. You'll think me fiendishly selfish, I can't bear losing Steven. I simply can't face it."

She lowered her eyes before the compassion in his. " My dear," he said, " if I tell *you* the truth, you'll think me fiendishly brutal; some day you'll have to lose him, if that's what you call ' losing.' It's a law of nature."

" I know. I know. But not just yet . . ."

" Just yet ? Surely there isn't any question of just yet ? They're children, as we've agreed. Miranda particularly. Steven is practically the first man that she's set eyes on. They're both in love ; but we can't pretend for a moment that they know their own minds."

" Steven does. He says so, and I believe it. He's frightfully definite ; he always has been. You remember . . . that other business ? And if we cross him . . ."

" I quite agree with you. That is the danger. His obstinacy would force him into anything. Much better let things take their natural course."

" But not an engagement ? " she asked anxiously, thinking again of Stourford.

" Engagement ? Of course not. In a year's time, perhaps ; if they still feel the same."

" Yes, yes. I'm so thankful that you agree with me. You've taken an enormous weight off my mind."

" I'll get hold of Miranda this evening and talk to her. If I go now I may catch her." He rose and took Clare's hand to say good bye. " This is a strange business, isn't it ? " he said, " when you come to think of it. Even if we two had wanted to avoid each other fate wouldn't have allowed it. There's a sort of poetic justice in the situation. One can't help feeling it."

" No. It's all very strange," she answered him. " And very fortunate. If it had been anyone else it would have been much more difficult for me."

" Do you really think that makes it easier ? You're lucky." He broke from the subject abruptly. " D'you know there's a kingfisher's nest somewhere under this bank ? "

" No. How can you tell ? I often sit here. I've never seen them."

" If you watch carefully I'm sure you will. I can smell it distinctly."

They leaned above the fence that bounded the garden together. She loved him when he talked of small things like that ; it made her feel as if they were children together as they had been in those spring days at Pedworth. He pressed her hand suddenly. " Good-bye, don't worry," he said, and was gone.

Five minutes later the chambermaid came running down the garden with a wire from Stourford.

*No answer to my letter*, it said : *telegraph at once if you have done what I suggested. Wolverbury.*

She crumpled it up and tossed it into the water. " No answer, thank you, Marion," she said. The telegram went gaily down the slide of water, under the bridge and through the hatch into the Abbey gardens.

This summary treatment of Lady Wolverbury's command was symbolical. The letter from Stourford had infected her with something of its own alarm. That was because she had received it alone ; and now she was no longer alone. The consciousness of Hart's sympathy, however difficult or dangerous it might be for him to give it her, had filled her with a vicarious strength and confidence. That final moment of silence in which they had leaned together over the sliding water had given her a momentary glimpse of happiness the memory of which still thrilled her. Although he hadn't said so, she knew that he still loved her ; and even if she couldn't return that love, its mere existence was an armour against the new loneliness that she dreaded.

When she had told him that this strange business was fortunate she had scarcely realized the meaning of her own words. Now that he had gone it was plain to her : they meant that even if Steven didn't change his mind and married

Miranda, the common interest of the marriage that robbed her of Steven would draw Hart closer to her.

" When the war is over," she thought, " and we go back to Uffdown, it will be more difficult than ever for him to see me. But if Steven is engaged to Miranda and Miranda's at Uffdown nothing could seem more natural."

The thought that she was willing to sacrifice Steven's happiness for Hart's friendship distressed her. " But there is no reason why he shouldn't be happy with her," she told herself. " She's young, she's beautiful, she's simple, they love one another : what more can I ask ? Now that he's evidently so impressionable, if once I thwarted him, out of sheer obstinacy he might make an awful mistake."

By the time that she came to see Steven next day she was so far reconciled to Miranda as a form of insurance that if he had pressed it and Hart had agreed she would even have acquiesced in an informal engagement.

She found him, as it happened, in a white suppression of fury.

" I've had a stinker from grandmama," he said. " Somebody must have written to her as well as me, and sent her off into the deep end. Was it you ? "

" No, darling, of course it wasn't," she answered truthfully.

" She's sprung a fit over it, anyway. She's out for blood. I want to know quite plainly, mum ; which side are you going to take ? "

" I'm taking no sides, my darling. I know better."

He seemed almost disappointed. Already he was cleared for action and wanted fighting. Miranda was all injured loveliness and innocence, and he her champion.

If it was fighting he wanted he could have counted on The Lady Wolverbury. Ten days later, out of the fog of war that brooded over Stourford, the first blow of a counter-offensive was launched. There came, from the Medical

Headquarters of Southern Command an order transferring
Second-Lieutenant Hingston to an auxiliary hospital in the
neighbourhood of North Bromwich.

" But this is monstrous," Steven protested to the medical
officer.  " I haven't asked for a transfer."

" Then somebody else must have asked for it," he was
told.  " The War Office policy is to get all convalescent
officers as near as possible to their own homes.  It's a
fatherly provision."

" Grandmotherly," said Steven bitterly.  " I say, doctor ;
I really don't want to leave here.  Can't you say I'm not
fit to be moved ? "

" Impossible, my dear boy.  You are."

" Supposing I sprung a temperature ? "

" I know those temperatures, if you were going to do
that you shouldn't have warned me.  I've made arrangements for you to go at the beginning of next week by
motor-ambulance."

Steven grew desperate.  At once he tried an appeal to
Lady Bemerton.  But Lady Bemerton was far too good
a soldier to question orders from high authorities.  Perhaps
she suspected : the matron was no fool.  In the violence
of his frustration Steven turned on Clare.

" Mother, you promised me you weren't taking sides.
I'll swear that you have something to do with this."

" My darling, I've told you I haven't.  I think you might
believe me.  Do you imagine I want to go tearing back to
North Bromwich just when we're so happily settled here ? "

She war speaking the truth.  She didn't.  For the
scatter of Lady Wolverbury's blunderbuss had hit her too,
by putting a hundred miles and more between her and Robert
Hart.  Now she had a double grudge against her mother-
in-law ; her sympathy for Steven surprised him so much that
he refused to believe it was genuine.  A coldness grew
between them for which she had only one consolation : the

knowledge that the Stourford missile was a boomerang which might return to its sender with unexpected violence.

For this antagonism aggravated the boy's infatuation to a tragic degree. Miranda was all paradise to him. He rose in hot rebellion against the flaming swords that separated them. The wrong had been done not merely to him but to her goodness, her loveliness. The invisible enemy should feel his revenge. To Clare, since she, unhappily, was visible, he gave a foretaste of that uncomfortable process.

During those last few days at Wyshford he made her suffer. She did not mind suffering ; that was a mother's privilege. What hurt her more was to know that Steven was suffering too. It was an agony to see his set mouth, his brooding eyes, to hear his short-spoken irritable words ; to know that all the time one thought in which she had no share consumed him. When Miranda came near, so pallid and composed, with never the shadow of a smile on her young lips, Clare felt it her duty to disappear and leave them together. They were such children, so serious ; they loved each other so. She began to scheme to give them moments together. But Steven didn't appreciate her scheming ; he wasn't even aware of it.

The day of parting came. They set off northward together in a big Vauxhall ambulance. As ironical fate would have it their way took them through Pedworth, past the very door of the Staff Colony bungalow where she had said good-bye to him. There lay the meadow and the cinder path ; through heavy foliage of July the crescent of barracks showed itself. Steven, although she tried to arouse remembered enthusiasms, would not even look at them. That was a world in which there had been no Miranda. It did not interest him. But Clare was not only interested but moved as well, for that was the world which Miranda's father still inhabited. She strained her eyes to catch a gleam of the red-brick façade of Fontenoy. She saw, with curious dispassionateness, the small, square, ivied tower of South Pedworth church. She thought of Father Darnay. Quite kindly. What would *he* think of her ?

As the road climbed, the whole mass of Fontenoy disclosed itself. The ambulance, roaring up the slope on low-gear, dragged them away from it.

" He is my friend," she thought. " There is no one like him." She dared not think : " He loves me."

Late in the afternoon, tired out and jolted to a pulp, the car deposited them on the doorstep of Steven's new hospital : a gloomy Victorian country house named Warshill on the heights above Bewdley.

" This is his country," she thought. " Real Severn-side. That is the Forest of Wyre, those are the Clees, and that is Shropshire."

Once more the impersonal medical mechanism received Steven from her. At the last moment, when they carried him in, he handed her a letter to post with a pencil message scribbled on the back of the envelope. He had written it to Miranda that morning before leaving Wyshford.

" You'll be sure to catch the evening post ? " he implored her.

" Of course I will."

Even as she promised, the devil, disguised as Lady Wolverbury, tempted her to destroy it.

At Warshill they were perilously near home ; a half-hour's drive from Stourford. Lady Wolverbury had chosen the strategic position with care, and proposed, immediately, to descend and inspect her handiwork. To save the situation Clare insisted on visiting Stourford first.

From the new drive gates, on which the substitution of a baron's coronet for that of meaner quality which had been allowed for in the architect's original design, was, happily, not noticeable to any but those acquainted with the Hingston family history, Clare was made conscious of an ascendant magnificence ; though, looking at the castle towers with gracious memories of Wyshford in her mind's eye, she might have guessed that Jones & Co., of North Bromwich, not Inigo, had put his heart into the stucco. That fabric seemed to totter a little beneath its accumulation of honours. But Lady Wolverbury herself could have assumed an unlimited number of strawberry leaves without flinching. Whatever might happen to the rest of the world, it was evident that the war had suited her.

"Well, Clare," she began, with a dangerous suavity. "As you appear incapable of answering my letters and telegrams, I've been forced to take the law into my own hands."

"And much good may it do you !" Clare thought. She said : "I hope you're satisfied ? "

"At any rate, I've got him under my eye, and out of this girl's clutches. Please tell me about her."

Clare did. She made the most of Miranda ; a little more, in fact, than there was to be made. Her canonized version should have brought a blush of shame to the cheeks of the most hardened grandmother.

"That's all very pretty," snapped Lady Wolverbury ; "but what about her family ? "

"She has none. Only a father," said Clare with deliberate wickedness.

"I know that already. Some kind of colonel, isn't he ? "

"The very best kind," Clare told her. "He's a great friend of mine."

"You make friends very quickly. You always did. And what does Dudley Wilburn think ? "

"I really don't know. I haven't asked him. They've met ; but that's no reason why he should think anything."

"I can see by your attitude that you approve of this . . . this . . ."

" No, no. I neither approve nor disapprove. I only realize that Steven's like Ralph. If you cross him he digs his hind legs in. History's merely repeating itself. He'll feel it a point of personal honour to marry her if you don't leave him alone."

" I'm not in the habit of leaving things alone," said Lady Wolverbury, with undeniable truth. " If I'd left things alone, where would you all be to-day ? You'd be a German subject at this moment if your father-in-law had left things alone. I see that you're totally lacking, like everybody else, in moral courage. In that case I shall be forced to act independently. Kindly oblige me with this Colonel what's-his-name's address."

Point-blank she refused it.

" I begin to see that this is a conspiracy," said Lady Wolverbury darkly. " However, you'll gain nothing by that. My friends at the War Office will soon give it to me, together with the gentleman's history. Perhaps he'll prove more sensible than you are. Tell Steven I'm coming to see him to-morrow."

Next day, according to plan, the cohorts of Stourford came down like wolves on the fold. Clare carefully absented herself from that alarming interview. For the twentieth time in her life she had washed her hands of Stourford ; she knew that, in Steven's present mood, he was able to fight his own battles. Indeed, now that she had survived the first shock of his infatuation with this sudden stranger she was inclined, for reasons of policy as well as from inclination, to let the affair take its course. " For if he tires of her," she thought, " or if she disappoints him, he'll be gladder than ever to come back to me ; and if he marries her, at least that will make it easier for me to keep my friend." And now Lady Wolverbury's malignity, embroidered by Steven, and awakening corroborative memories of her own past wrongs, was making her neutrality waver in the lovers' direction ; the more decidedly since Lady Wolverbury's tongue had spattered some of its venom on Hart.

Steven resented this as much as she did. She felt proud of his loyalty ; and Steven, quick to realize that she was veering to his side, infected her, by force of repetition, with his indignation against the slurs that Stourford cast on the wronged, the absent, the idealized Miranda. Their separation only intensified a passion, which spent itself, fortunately for everyone, through the safety valve of flaming love-letters. His confidence in Clare was now so far restored that he showed her passages in these compositions. To her prejudiced eye they seemed entirely marvellous. His father had never written her letters like that. And as for poor Dudley Wilburn . . . She wondered what kind of love-letters Robert Hart would write.

By the beginning of October Steven's wound was healed. He walked with her, on crutches, through the gardens of Warshill, made gloomy by the mid-Victorian passion for blue, exotic conifers. Westward, imagination found release in the shining Severn, the distant mossy expanses of the Forest of Wyre, and the Clees, reared up like thunder-cloud beyond it. The doctor said that in another month he would be fit for some light form of duty. But now, as everyone agreed, the German line was beginning to crack, and war had diminished terrors. As soon as he left hospital he was certain to be given a longish period of Home Service ;, which meant that they might easily find themselves back at Pedworth. Steven would jump at anything that brought him nearer to Miranda.

And then, in mid-November, just as they were returning to Uffdown for his statutory three weeks' leave, the Armistice came. Even at Warshill, seven miles west of the black-country, Clare heard the works' bulls howling at midday as, once before, she had heard them at night. By now they had their bellies full of war !

" Well, that's the end of the army for me," Steven told her triumphantly. " I can soon get grandpapa to have me demobbed. The War Office'll be glad to get rid of me; they've no use for us Home Service duds."

It did her good to see him at Uffdown, still limping slightly, but radiantly happy to be in mufti again. He seemed to have found a new and vivid interest in everything about the house. He was looking at it, she knew, through Miranda's eyes.

" I think I shall arrange to be away next week-end, mum," he said ; " so don't ask anyone over to see me."

" But my darling," she protested, " we've only just come home ! "

" I've booked a room at the pub at Wyshford," he told her. " I'll be back on Tuesday. You'll come and meet me at Worcester, won't you ? "

She accepted the sop that he offered her, knowing that she was lucky to get it. During that empty week-end her old jealousy troubled her. As penance—for the light which Father Darnay had rekindled had survived the extinction threatened during those black hours at Pedworth—she walked down twice to church at Wychbury and sat in the lonely Uffdown pew meditating on the reminders of her past inscribed on the fly-leaves of psalters and Prayer Books.

By Tuesday evening she stood waiting for him with renewed humility on Worcester platform.

As soon as he climbed down from his carriage she knew that something had happened. " They've quarrelled," she thought. " Poor darling ! " Since his return from France she had often seen anger and frustration in his eyes, but never quite this gravity. He was so grave that she dared not question him.

The express rolled on and left them waiting for the slow train that stopped at Wychbury.

" Let's go and look at the Cathedral," he said. " I haven't seen it for years : I've almost forgotten it."

They took a cab and drove down Foregate Street to the Close. Then, arm-in-arm, they sauntered slowly toward the great north doors.

" I wanted to speak to you, mum," he said, " before we got home. I've done something that I'm afraid you mayn't approve of."

He stopped, as though he found it difficult to continue without encouragement.

" I can't say anything, my darling," she answered timidly, " till you've told me what it is."

" Miranda and I were married yesterday. By special licence. In Salisbury. Are you very angry, mum ? "

" Oh, Steven . . . what can I say ? "

" Nothing, I suppose. If you hate me for not telling you, I can't help it. Grandmama's responsible for that."

" You didn't tell the Colonel ? "

" Of course not. We weren't taking any risks. But he knows now. Miranda's expecting him at Wyshford this afternoon."

" What about Stourford ? "

" It's no business of theirs. They can like it or lump it."

" They're bound to make trouble if they can, Steven. Are you sure it's all right ? Your age, I mean, and Miranda's ? I know nothing about the law."

" Neither did I. I couldn't find out without giving the show away ; so I put down my age as twenty-one. It's only twelve months difference, and I had to do it."

" Surely that's dangerous ? However could you dare ? Mayn't that make it illegal ? "

" No, that's all right. I happened to know about that. When once you've pulled it off, the law can't touch you. In any case we're married in the eyes of God. Mother, you haven't even wished me happiness ! "

" Oh, Steven, you've taken my breath away. Give me a little time. I can't quite realize it. Of course I wish you every happiness that heaven can give you, my darling."

" Then you've made me happier already," he said, as he kissed her.

They walked through the great church like lovers, or children, in silence and hand-in-hand. Clare's mind was too dazed to be aware of any of its beauties. The thing was still incredible. " It is over," she thought; " I have lost him. And yet we are in this strange place together and his hand is in mine." Beyond this mute stupefaction a sense of the anger of Stourford bulged like an anvil-headed thundercloud. It made her frightened for him and Miranda and herself.

" You will have to tell them," she said, with sudden irrelevance.

" Let them find out for themselves."

" But Miranda ? "

" That's all settled. She'll stay at Wyshford till the hospital closes. Now that we're safe we neither of us mind waiting. Of course, if you feel bound to tell them, you must do so."

" I couldn't possibly face her. I shall have to write."

" I leave it to you, mother."

He was extraordinarily complaisant. After those passionate months she could scarcely recognize him in his new state of serenity and contentment. His sweetness, his gentleness, his consideration for her were unbelievable ; this was an active happiness ; it seemed to radiate part of its own warmth.

At Wychbury Bissel met them with the brougham, for both the Uffdown cars were still laid up. He smiled to welcome them.

" You're looking worlds better for your outing, Mr. Steven, sir."

They sat in the car, still holding each other's hands.

The very air seemed to hold breath that evening ; the rubber tyres rolled softly over a felting of new-fallen leaves that a storm had laid ; the smell of the wet lanes and the gurgle of brimmed dykes were sweet in the twilight. Stirred branches shed thick drops on the roof of the landaulette as though it were raining still. A race of ragged cloud drove scudding across a pale sky drenched in hidden moonlight ; but as they entered the drive at Uffdown the moon's face cleared and showed the house standing like a silvery ghost and all the sweep of the lawn rimed with spent raindrops, more lovely, in that moonlit dream, than Wyshford with all its glory. Its beauty stabbed Clare suddenly to the heart.

" I shall never see it again like this," she thought. " It was part of my life—in some ways the loveliest and most stable part of it—and now I must say good-bye. When he brings Miranda here I shall be only a stranger. It will stay here for ever ; but God knows where I shall go. I wonder how many other women, in its lifetime, have felt the pang of parting as I do now ? "

A drift of memories flickered through her brain. She remembered the day on which Ralph had first tricked her into finding Uffdown. They stood with bodies close together, by the rosemary hedge : " Well, what do you think of it," Ralph was saying. " Will it do ? " Again she was standing on the verge of the orchard, old Waldron waiting with his cap in his hand ; and Ellen running, running with a wire from Bloemfontein. Another day, more recent, the first of her freedom, when, from the slopes above, Steven and she had watched the Beresfords' straight smoke ascending : " So that's a bargain, mum," he was saying ; " we'll never leave it again." " Never again," she had repeated.

Now, as she hurried upstairs to her room, the eyes of Ralph's portrait saw that she was crying.

When the news broke on Stourford two days later there was the devil to pay.

" We must stop it," Lady Wolverbury screamed through the telephone. " If we take it to the House of Lords it must be stopped. Tell me at once, Clare : where did they spend the night . . . or *didn't they ?* I hope to heaven they didn't ! What ? You don't know ? Not *important ?* Find out at once. It's vitally important ! "

They had. With the utmost publicity, at the County Hotel in Salisbury.

" We shall fight it all the same," said Lady Wolverbury. The experience of the war had taught her to imagine that all British institutions, the law included, were pliable beneath the weight of heavy metals which Wolverbury could bring to bear on them ; she thought that she could whistle Steven out of matrimony as easily as she had snatched him from Wyshford. She encamped herself, like a victorious army, in the offices of poor Sir James Veale, the head of the firm who handled Wolverbury's legal business, and instructed him, in five minutes, exactly how to act. He wasn't quite clear, he told her, in what capacity she was instructing him. The capacity of an outraged grandmother would hardly do.

" You may take it from me, Sir James, that I'm acting for his lordship." She forgot, for the moment, that she wasn't talking to Parker. " Lord Wolverbury accepts my views of the matter, as is natural."

" I see," said Sir James.

It seemed that Lady Wolverbury was instructing Lord Wolverbury to instruct her to instruct him . . .

" But, unless I'm mistaken—of course I'm open to correction—your grandson's affairs are in the hands of two trustees : his mother and my colleague, Dudley Wilburn ? Any action that may be taken lies with them."

Lady Wolverbury told him, briefly, what she thought of both of them.

" Oh, really ? " said Sir James. " Dear me ! You don't

say so ! " His office was, structurally, a model of discretion. It was doubtful if the walls had ever witnessed such fluency of slander.

" I gather," he said at last, when the waves had subsided, " you'd like me to state your views—in a slightly modified form—to Mr. Wilburn ? "

" Make him understand that we'll take it to the House of Lords." Lady Wolverbury was convinced that his peers would do the saviour of their country justice.

" I think," said Sir James, with an air of ineffable cunning, " I think—d'you know ?—we'd better keep that up our sleeve."

As soon as he was delivered from the armies of occupation, he took one of the quill pens, which he still affected for private correspondence, and wrote to Dudley.

*My dear Wilburn,*
*Lady Wolverbury appears to be somewhat disturbed by Steven Hingston's marriage. She seems a little hurt that you and his mother have taken no action in the matter. I presume from this that everything's all right. You might just let me know if that is so, in order that I may set her mind at rest. I hope soon to hear that you've been demobilized. That running about the country must be very irksome.*

*Sincerely yours,*
*Jas. Veale.*

At the other end of the line his lordship sustained the forefront of the battle. It opened, with the regularity of a German " evening hate," at the exact moment of his arrival from Wolverbury, and closed, precisely, with Lady Wolverbury's eyes. It was unfortunate—for Lady Wolverbury—that this excitement should have coincided with an activity that kept him, every evening, later at the works : his crowning achievement which was to make the name of Hingston remembered in the black-country. Part-ownership was in the air ; and Hingstons, who always moved a little in front of the times, had been unloading their war-inflated stock on their workmen in the form of a bonus. Now that the war was over and peace opened vistas of illimitable prosperity to every maker of armaments, Lord Wolverbury and his directors had decided to go one step further in the direction of social regeneration by offering the bulk of their personal holdings and those of their friends for purchase, on preferential terms, to the workmen who had made Wolverbury what it was. They had only to look at the works—more than a square mile of them—to see for themselves a running concern that was as sound as the British Empire, and, incidentally, paid much bigger dividends. In Wolverbury and Dulston there was a great liquidation of War Bonds. At last the thrifty workman was entering into his kingdom. As a tribute to Joseph Hingston's acumen it should be remembered that when, a year later, Walter Willis tried the same game at Mawne, he was exactly six weeks too late. But Walter Willis, with all his opportunities, had remained plain Walter Willis. And that, said Lady Wolverbury, was Mrs. Willis's fault. . . .

From the moment when she had figuratively thrown the telephone receiver in Clare's face and literally thrown a pair of shoes at Marguerite, Lady Wolverbury had severed diplomatic relations with Uffdown. The letters with which, through the office of Veale and Co., she kept up a long distance fire on Dudley Wilburn, Clare, and even Steven himself, made no impression on anything but Sir James's ledgers. Steven was married, and that was the end of it. By mid-December the thunder of battle had subsided into a sulky silence ; and Lord Wolverbury, having completed his altruistic labours, returned to Stourford, by cautious stages, on an earlier and then a yet earlier train.

And as for Uffdown . . . For the moment Clare had Steven to herself ; she knew she could ask no more.

## III
## THE THIRD GREAT WAVE . : :

STEVEN was beginning to take Uffdown seriously. Between the excitements of his week-end visits to Miranda he found a new distraction in putting the war-worn estate in order. In the present depression of the Stourford barometer his old enthusiasm for the Wolverbury works had somewhat subsided. His army life had awakened a latent taste for riding, much to the satisfaction of Bissell, who had only become a mechanic in spite of himself; and now, since walking tired his wounded leg, Steven would spend the greater part of the day on horseback, setting out over the neglected fields, where the scutch-fires smouldered, returning at nightfall, tired and weather-beaten, to drowse, as his father had done before him, over the fire in the hall.

It seemed to Clare that he was growing every day more like the Ralph whom she had known in the first serene contentment of their marriage. Sometimes when she came into the hall unnoticed and saw him sitting over an unread newspaper, with his gaitered legs outstretched, the likeness would catch at her heart with a queer poignancy, the more so when he began to talk, in Ralph's own voice, of all the daily business of the farm that now engrossed him.

And all the time, as she knew well, he was only thinking of the day on which he might bring Miranda home. Although he rarely mentioned her name, she realized that all the suggestions which he made for putting Uffdown in order were only planned to please Miranda's eyes ; and though she helped him with all her will and an appearance of sympathy, she felt like a prisoner under sentence of death condemned, by a refinement of unconscious cruelty, to turn her hand to the digging of her own grave.

" I should like to have everything ship-shape before Christmas," he told her.

For already it had been decided that Miranda and her father should come and spend Christmas at Uffdown. Hart's leave was limited ; but Miranda, since the Wyshford hospital was closing down, would stay on indefinitely.

" I want her to get accustomed to the feeling of the house, mum," said Steven.

" As soon as she sets foot in it," Clare thought, " I shall cease to belong here. But if I let him see how much I feel it I shall only spoil his happiness." So she threw herself with all her strength into Steven's anxious enthusiasms, consoled by the knowledge that Miranda was not coming alone. " I can bear it more easily," she thought, " if the Colonel is with me. He'll know how I feel without my telling him, and, even if it's for the last time, it will be a joy to show him everything that we've talked about so often."

On Christmas Eve, when the Harts came up from Salisbury, she found herself as flustered and impatient as Steven himself. Steven drove down with Bissell to meet them at Wychbury station, while Clare, to overcome a restlessness that made confinement intolerable, went out, with gloves and scissors, to clear the thickets of Michaelmas daisies, whose vigour had overreached old Waldron's failing strength. Behind them, among the ill-pruned rose-bushes, she found a single silvery bloom of *La France*. She picked it, lovingly, remembering how and when she had seen it planted. " I shall never pick another rose at Uffdown," she thought. When the car drove up and she hurried across the lawn with a beating heart to greet them, she found herself covering her confusion by giving it to the radiant Miranda.

" The last," she said ; " I'm afraid it's the very last."

And Miranda, with no suspicion of the hidden meaning— of which, indeed, Clare herself had been unconscious until the words were spoken—took her and the rose together to her young breast.

" How lovely ! " she said. " How sweet you are . . . both of you ! "

Clare kissed her, smiling, overwhelmed by the generosity with which her unpremeditated gesture had been taken ; and Steven stood by, smiling at them, aglow with love and pride.

" Steven will take you to your room," Clare said, " and I will show the Colonel his."

The lovers left them together, talking in low, excited voices. Clare and Hart followed in a sedate silence. At the foot of the stairs he paused to gaze up at Ralph's portrait.

" That is your husband ? " he said. " Of course. I remember him."

The boy in the picture and the man on the stairway faced one another. " I wonder what they are thinking ? " she asked herself. Ralph's eyes, for once, didn't tell her. She saw, for the first time in many years, that the picture was nothing but painted canvas ; dead, painted canvas facing the living man. Strange . . .

" He was only a boy," she said softly. " I think he was younger in most things than Steven is now."

" But you loved him, didn't you ? "

" I don't know." The monstrous word was spoken. " I suppose I did. I think I was too young myself to know the meaning of love then."

What was she saying ? What treachery was this ? Her eyes met Hart's in a long look that frightened her. They proceeded in silence to his room.

That night, soon after dinner was over, the lovers left them.

" You don't mind, mum, do you ? " Steven joked her. " I haven't set eyes on my beloved wife for a week, and want to show her my study. I know I can trust the Colonel to entertain you. We shan't see you again ; so we'd better say good-bye. Good night, sir."

He took Hart's hand and kissed his mother. It seemed

to Clare, looking beyond Steven's shoulder, as though Miranda's soft mouth hardened at that kiss ; and yet when her turn came to be kissed good night Miranda was as soft and shy as ever.

When they had gone a curious quietness fell on Annabel Ombersley's room. It seemed, for the moment, as if Hart's powers of entertainment had been overrated. They sat and stared at the fire without a word to say for themselves until the pressure of unspoken thought became too heavy for the silence to bear.

" I'm glad you came," Clare said at last. " I thought, perhaps, you wouldn't. I wanted you to see Uffdown—*my* Uffdown—before it quite ceased to be mine. The whole place, and this one room particularly, has been a very intimate part of my life."

" It was difficult ; it's still difficult," he answered. " And yet I wanted to come here more than I can possibly tell you. I knew what this place meant to you, and anything that is even remotely connected with you interests me. Interest's the wrong word. But you know what I mean. And now that I've seen it," he went on slowly, " I realize how absolutely it suits you. You're part of it ; you're like a tutelary spirit. You give it its life, its extraordinarily gracious life— and it's given you your dignity, your repose. D'you realize you're the most restful person I've ever known in my life ? "

She shook her head : " You're thinking of me too kindly. Because I'm not really restful at all. I'm a mass of dreadful unrest and . . . contradictions. I'm just as bad as ever I was at Pedworth. That night at Fontenoy you saw me as I really am."

" No, no," he said. " You're not fair to yourself. That night was different. We've agreed to forget it, anyway. But now that I've seen you here I can't help feeling that it's a crime that you should ever leave Uffdown."

Her eyes smiled her thanks for his understanding.

" We mustn't allow ourselves to think of it," she said. " I've got over the worst of it now. I have to realize that I'm a dowager and make a dignified retirement. The only thing that really matters to me is that Steven and Miranda should be happy." She demanded his assurance : " They will be happy, won't they ? "

" You've only to look at them to see that they're happy now," he answered. " I've been wondering, for a long time. What are you going to do with yourself ? "

" I don't know. I haven't liked to think of it. Steven had a wild idea. He wanted me to stay on here for a year or two. Miranda has had no experience of housekeeping. He was anxious that I should break her in to it, so to speak. And Miranda agreed. But somehow . . . It wasn't merely that it would be prolonging the agony—of going away, I mean. I felt, in any case, it wouldn't work. The risk would be too great."

" And of course you're right. It takes a very young head to suggest an arrangement of that kind. Miranda may be an angel—as a matter of fact she's not ; she's just a child—but even an angel would fall under those conditions. I suppose "—he hesitated—" there's no question of your going back to your husband ? "

" To Dudley ? Never. That wouldn't work either. He's really a bachelor, and always has been. He has a housekeeper who understands him perfectly. At a distance like this we're excellent friends. I'm using the word conventionally : I don't mean real friendship. I couldn't talk to him, for instance, as I'm talking to you now."

" He's a good deal older than you ? "

" Eighteen years."

" You will have to think about it soon . . . where you are going."

" I know. You must make me face it in spite of myself. What are *you* going to do ? "

" That's almost as difficult to answer. My soldiering s over. I have a house, you know, on the border of Shropshire. Up in the hills between the Clees and the Teme. It belongs to a sort of cousin of mine : Arthur Powys."

" How strange ! You never told me. I've met Lord Arthur at Stourford, and I've been to fish with Ralph in his water on the Teme."

" Hingston was a fisherman ? Steven isn't, is he ? My cousin rarely comes to Dinsop. He's an old man now. I haven't seen him for years. But my land marches with his, and I often fish his water. I suppose I shall turn into a regular old soldier, fussing about the land and writing indignant letters which the *Morning Post* won't print. Books and the country. That's all that's left for a retired soldier-man like me. It might be worse. Anything's better than Leamington or Cheltenham."

" You shouldn't talk like that," she told him. " I know that you've led an active life. But you'll always be active. D'you know, I don't believe you'll ever grow old."

" My dear, I'm forty-eight."

" And I'm thirty-eight. Steven's just twenty. I'm nearly as old as you are."

He laughed. " At my time of life ten years make a big difference. To-night you look like a girl."

She flushed with pleasure. She knew that the greyness which had stolen on her unperceived at Overbury had used her gently. Steven had told her so a hundred times.

" And yet," she said, " I may soon be a grandmother. That is a milestone, isn't it ? One has to admit it : I have to realize that what I imagined was my life is over."

" You have no right to talk or even think like that. It isn't worthy of you. You're not cowardly . . ."

" Oh, but I am, I am ; I'm an awful coward. I'm frightened, I'm desperately frightened of being lonely. It's the one thing I've been frightened of all my life."

He gazed at her unhappily. " My dear Mrs. Wilburn," he began.

" Don't call me that. It hurts me. Why not ' Clare ' ? After all," she smiled faintly, " now that you're one of the family I think you might."

When he obeyed her and spoke her name his voice was terribly moved : " But what does it matter ? " she thought ; " it's just as bad for me."

" Clare, there's no reason why you should be lonely," he was saying." You know, in your own heart, that you're more loved than most women."

" I know," she answered ; " of course, I know. I'm a wretched coward. As Dudley used to tell me, I want to have it both ways ; and you can't. Only," she begged him, " you must help me, Robert. If you were to desert me, I don't know what I should do."

" Clare, Clare, why need you ask me ? " he answered in a low voice.

She bowed her head and sat for a long time in silent, tumultuous thought. The French clock on the mantelpiece broke into a breathless little chime. Its sugary gong struck twelve.

" It's midnight," she said. " Whoever would have believed it ? Time for the grandparents to be in bed ! " She rose to pour whisky and soda for him. She raised the glass, smiling above it, and sipped : " I drink to you, Colonel Hart," she said. " A Happy Christmas ! "

Indeed, at that moment, she had all the happiness that she wished him ; but when they had parted on the landing and gone their ways, he to the big spare room that had once been Aunt Cathie's, and Clare to another, on the eastern side of the house, above the drawing-room, which she had chosen when she insisted on surrendering her own to the bride, her courage failed her a little. The room was strange to her ; for over twenty years at Uffdown she had occupied none but that to which she had returned with Ralph at the end of their honeymoon ; and though the lichened roof of Uffdown covered both, this new room, with its unfamiliar shape and orientation declaring themselves through the darkness, made her feel anywhere but at home. This feeling, combined with a restless groundswell which was all that was left of the day's stormy emotions, made it impossible for her to sleep. Lying with closed eyes, it seemed to her as though her too-active mind had been transported not merely to another bedroom but to a new element, even a new dimension, in which the landmarks that had always guided her processes of thought and sensation, even though habit discounted their existence, had been mysteriously removed ; so that all life seemed as strangely shaped and orientated as her physical surroundings.

" I know I shall never sleep a wink," she thought. " Whatever can I do to compose myself ? "

She looked at the luminous hands of her travelling clock. It was half-past three. At least four hours of empty darkness yawned before her. She slipped on a dressing-gown and stole downstairs to the room which she and Hart had left three hours before. Softly she opened the Bechstein and sat down before it.

" Of course it will be no good," she thought. " I haven't been able to play with any heart since the night when Ernest was here."

Yet when she began to play the first thing that came into her head, the suite of Scarlatti which Ernest's memory had suggested, she found, to her amazement, that her disused fingers were alive again. The gay notes leaped and trilled and fell again like silvery cascades and fountains in a formal garden.

She held her breath to listen to them, transported by the elegance of their slightly faded gaiety, ravished by the thin delicacy of their trilling.

" My music is coming back to me," her heart sang, " it's coming back ! "

Daring more greatly, yet still doubtful, she passed from Scarlatti to Beethoven, from Beethoven to Bach. She played Busoni's arrangements of the organ fugues. There, on the Himalayan peaks of eternal music, she knew that out of the disintegrating past one joy, at least, was saved. " No more," she thought, " after that ! " And yet, as she closed the lid of the keyboard her hand hesitated. She lifted it again and played, as she stood, with one foot groping for the pedal, that one, that tragic phrase which had haunted her in the office at Pedworth : the motive of the love-potion in Tristan.

" *Mein die Halfte.*" The words ran through her mind. "*Verrather ! Ich trink' sie dir !* " And then an echo : " I drink to you, Colonel Hart."

She smiled. Then, pulling her dressing-gown round her with a shiver, she switched off the light and returned to her room ; this time to sleep.

Next morning, with tired eyes, she faced Hart over the breakfast-table. They were alone ; for Steven, surprisingly, had hurried off his bride to the early communion service at Wychbury. The monitory shadow of Father Darnay reminded Clare that she should have gone with them ; and yet, that morning, her conscience reacted sluggishly.

" It's funny," she thought ; " when I have love or music, religion seems to mean less to me ; which shows, I suppose, that with me they must all be part of the same thing, and if one is missing, I have to have the other. But that's a dreadful confession ! "

In those days people were beginning to listen to the teaching of Freud. She heard Hart's voice :

" You're very serious this morning. What are you thinking about ? "

" Not only serious but rude. I was thinking about religion. Those two children. . . . You know, of course you know—what am I saying?—that curious side of Steven? *Is* Miranda religious?"

He smiled. "At present, evidently. Miranda is very adaptable."

"If she adapts too much, Steven will bore her. The Council of Trent and that sort of thing."

"She's in love with him. That's the one unfailing antidote. I always thought that you were the same as Steven. I imagined that you had stayed behind as a compliment to a pagan visitor. At Pedworth I seem to remember . . ."

"Yes. Sometimes I've been religious. When I was a young girl. And then, again at Pedworth. Now . . . I don't know. I suppose if I'd been religious I should have gone with them. At any rate I must go to church this morning."

"You sometimes feel a need for it?"

"No, not exactly that . . ."

"You mean that it crops up now and then, like influenza? That's awkward. Supposing, at any time, your religion was opposed to something that you wanted very much to do. I wonder what would happen?"

She answered him honestly: "I really don't know."

He looked at her narrowly. "Clare, you're a curious woman. Perhaps . . ." he went on; but whatever he may have been going to say the arrival of Steven and Miranda saved her from cross-examination. They sat down to their late breakfast with an enormous appetite. The immobility of convalescence had thickened Steven's figure. By the side of the slim Miranda he looked as robust and determined as a lusty young bull; yet, as she watched him, finding a present standard of comparison in Hart's spare, concentrated strength, Clare wondered if this robustness were not, perhaps, a little gross; if the determination were really no more than obstinacy; if, now that the influence of her own spiritual refinement were withdrawn, he might not slide too easily into the purely physical existence toward which, at the time of his death, his father had been tending.

" In some things," she thought, " he is very easily influenced. If Miranda were a woman of character and sensibility, if she had anything of her father in her, there's nothing that she couldn't do with him."

But Miranda, as Hart had admittea, was primarily adaptable. For the present she was content to follow Steven's lead ; and the lead that Steven gave her was one in which her own physical nature would happily acquiesce. For now, as Clare examined Miranda's beauty no longer masked by the severity of her nurse's uniform, she realized its essential voluptuous laxity. It seemed that Miranda had shed, deliberately, all the resemblances to Hart that Clare had imagined in her. This child, this woman—for marriage had already subtly aged her—was really an alien, an Oriental. The languorous glooms of her olive-shaped eyes should have shown themselves between kohl-darkened lids above a *yashmak*. As Clare sat gazing at her and wondering, the girl became aware of her scrutiny, looked up, and smiled ; but Clare knew that the melting eyes had more than an innocent friendliness behind them, and the smile, for all its quick brilliance, was sly.

" Of course the child is delicious," she thought. " I'm giving way to a subconscious jealousy ; I'm acting like a traditional mother ; I'm forgetting that Robert is her father."

But however hard she tried she couldn't forget the story of Miranda's mother, or the reservations that Hart had always betrayed when he spoke of Steven's marriage. And when the idea of jealousy returned to her, she knew that it was Miranda, rather than herself, who suffered from it.

That instinctive hardening of the soft mouth which she had glimpsed the day before when Steven kissed her was only the first of many sinister symptoms. Whenever Steven paid her any of the small attentions that had become hers by right of habit if for no other reason, Miranda's dark eyes were aware of them ; whenever Steven called her " darling," a shadow of anxiety clouded Miranda's face ; whenever, in the business of Christmas, they snatched an intimate moment for each other, Miranda waited with a smiling but ill-veiled impatience, watching Steven's movements with greedy eyes, reclaiming him with an air of triumphant possession.

It seemed as if all Miranda's guile, and all the blandishments to which Steven surrendered so abjectly, were deployed with the one object of enveloping him to suffocation in the amber-scented mystery of her own presence. And though, in her contacts with Clare, she remained as sweet and yielding as a lump of Turkish delight, it was evident that this suave exterior concealed a core of unyielding opposition to everything in Steven's surroundings that Clare held precious or sacred. She betrayed it, particularly, in her attitude toward those old friends, Ellen and Bissell. " I am only waiting," her dark eyes seemed to say. " Wait till you're gone, and then see what I'll do with him and with Uffdown ! "

" Although she's so stupid in many ways," Clare thought —it had come to that !—" in others she's remarkably subtle. She knows the power of her beauty and uses it cleverly. When once I'm gone poor Steven won't have a dog's chance. Whatever can I do about it ? "

She knew that she could do nothing. And yet, in calculating the lesser of two evils, Miranda's desire to possess and segregate Steven rewarded Clare with the compensation of Hart's company. With a generosity of questionable origin Miranda set herself to throw them together.

" It must be dreadfully boring," she conceded, with sweet reasonableness, " for you and father to see us always spooning. It isn't my fault, I promise you ; but Steven's incorrigible, aren't you, darling ? Really, out of sheer decency, I think you ought to conduct your ridiculous love-making in private."

Then Steven, smiling, but almost foolishly complaisant, would be dragged away to Annabel Ombersley's drawing-room, which Miranda professed to adore and daily dese-crated by spasms of ragtime, played with the loud pedal and a sketchy bass, to which Steven listened as though it were the music of the spheres. And Clare, when she could bear the irritating echoes no longer, would seek, with Hart, the healing silences of the wintry woods.

One afternoon, when a boisterous night had scoured the sky and a pale December sun emerging washed the still countryside with tenuous amber, they found themselves walking hillward through the Sling valley. The wistfulness, the relief of nature in this calm interval was mirrored in Clare's mind. It was so fugitive, and therefore so precious, that she dared not marr it even by thinking of what they had left behind them. It was enough for her to be alive and moving through the sweet air with the companion of her choice. They walked together, vigorously but in silence, each conscious of the other's presence and each content. Clare knew so little whither they were going that it came as a surprise to her when, on the summit of Uffdown at the edge of the pinewood, the glory of that incomparable pros-pect burst upon them : from Cotswold to the sandstone bluffs of Brecon, from Charnwood to the blue dome of the Forest of Dean ; all the vast basins of Severn and Wye and Avon ; all the sweet heart of England stretched beneath and around them, and they alone, possessing, worshipping, at the same shrine. The creak of a cart-wheel in the Sling valley dissolved their silence. It was Hart who spoke:

" *The lines are fallen unto me in pleasant places ; yea, I have a goodly heritage.*"

" You can quote scripture glibly," she told him ; " yet Steven would say that you have no religion."

He waved his arm in a wide sweep. " *This* is my religion, Clare, and I thank God for it. Humbly, I assure you, in spite of all the pride I have in it. The earth that bore me and all my forebears. Its own beauty; the courage, the patience, the goodwill, the piety of the men who have lived in it. When I think of England that is what I mean."

There, with the silent plains and hills for witness, he began to talk of England and his faith.

" No doubt you may call me narrow and insular," he told her. " Perhaps it's because I've travelled so widely that I feel so strongly. I've seen great mountains, Clare; the Alps, Himalaya, the Drakensberg; I've scorched and shivered in the Libyan desert; and yet, wherever my body might be, my heart was here. When you come back to it out of those fiery places, it's just a haze of blue woodland. Then the green bursts on you in a wave of birdsong. Not London . . . London's a capital; it belongs to nobody; I hate it as Cobbett, who had far less reason, hated it. But this, to me, will always be the essential England. Mercia, the heart of England, where its blood flows purest. Only this morning I listened to old Waldron talking to you. That was the speech I knew when I was a boy, the words in which the dreams of the English first took shape.

> *In a summer season, when the sun was softest,*
> *Shrouded in a smock, in shepherd's clothing,*
> *In the habit of a hermit of unholy living,*
> *I went through this world to witness wonders.*
> *On a May morning on a Malvern hillside*
> *I saw strange sights like scenes of Faerie . . .*

" That's Langland—Piers Plowman "—he pointed—" there's Cleobury, where he was born; and there is Malvern, where the vision came to him. That shadow—yes, only a ripple, North of Cotswold—is Edgehill: Shakespeare was born beneath it. And even to-day . . . There's Elgar, Houseman, Masefield. Small names, perhaps, but greatly English, whatever else they may be. . . ."

Clare smiled at him : " I'll give you another text, Robert : *No doubt but ye are the people, and wisdom shall die with you.*"

"Of course. I deserve it," he admitted, "and yet I can't go back on my belief. No man who isn't a patriot deserves to have a fatherland. What's more, in a larger sense we *are* the people. The day when our race goes under will be Europe's Götterdämmerung. Because . . . because the things we stand for, even if we don't always achieve them, are all that matters. The cult of liberty, mercy, justice, gentleness. Ben Jonson knew what he was talking about when he called the author of King Lear gentle ! "

Strange love-making, maybe. Yet, as he stood and glowed before her, Clare's spirit caught fire from the faith that was in him and loved him for it.

" Do you remember, once before," she asked him, " how I told you—I think it was on the downs by Everley—that you were more English than anyone I'd ever known ? You're a great Englishman, Robert."

" My dear, I'm a great windbag when once I get going on that theme. It's my King Charles's head. You must make allowances."

" I had never realized England at all till I saw it through your eyes," she said. " I'm grateful."

When they returned to Uffdown, in time for tea, Steven was waiting for them in the hall in a state of mild agitation.

" We're for it, mum," he told her. " A telephone message from Stourford. His lordship and her ladyship are driving over ; to make the peace. Influence of Christmas, no doubt. I suppose we shall have to kiss and forgive all round."

And ten minutes later, before they had time to adjust their minds to the occasion, the Stourford Rolls-Royce came stealing up the drive, putting the lichened bricks of Uffdown to shame with its lucent coachwork. When they entered, the sight of its occupants gave Clare a shock. The four years that had passed since last she saw him had dealt more heavily with her father-in-law than she could have imagined. Joseph, Lord Wolverbury, had never been physically impressive; the strain of winning the war and skimming the cream from the shares of Hingstons Limited before he got rid of them had reduced his pasty plumpness to the desiccation of a pre-dynastic mummy; but Lady Wolverbury, whose persistent modishness when she " went out " made all her sixty-eight years seem but as yesterday, was swifter, younger and more effective than ever. With her matchless faculty for pretending that nothing had happened when nearly everything had, she greeted Clare as though they had only parted the night before, and on the best of terms.

" Well, Clare," she said, " how are you ? We thought we'd run in and have a look at you as we were passing this way." Her black eyes swept the hall as if to make sure that nothing in it had been altered without her permission, and lighted, with a gleam of triumph, upon Hart. " Ah, *that* is the man I want to talk to," she said, and held out her white-gloved hand.

Clare blundered into an introduction : " Colonel Hart."

" I feel," said Lady Wolverbury, completely disregarding her and enveloping Hart in a thin ghost of her once-radiant smile, " as if we had always known each other. I ought to explain. Your cousin, Arthur Powys, was a member of my husband's directorate for years. I always look on him as one of my best and oldest friends. We were talking about you only yesterday at his nephew's, Lord Clun's. I hadn't the remotest idea that you were connected with him," she added with devastating honesty.

" I don't suppose you had, Lady Wolverbury," Hart answered with a gleam of wickedness. " As a matter of fact, although we're excellent friends and have been, ever since I was a boy, our cousinship is—how shall I put it ?—dangerously remote."

" He's very fond of you, anyway, and that's enough for me," Lady Wolverbury admitted. She took Hart by the arm with an old lady's privileged coquettishness. " I quite approve his taste. And now," she said, " I want you to show me Miranda." She knew by the smile of amusement at her audacity which Hart could not suppress that she had carried it off.

Miranda was brought forward, assayed, apparently approved ; and Steven, whose grievances had inclined him to be frosty, was thawed at once by the warm stream of blandishments that made Miranda blush so prettily. The old lady's manner begged his pardon with an appealing childishness that he couldn't refuse. " You mustn't be cross with me ; it was only my little way," she seemed to be saying ; and when she had pinched his ear, and playfully kissed him, her triumph—or perhaps the tabloid of thyroid extract which she gulped down with her tea—released her tongue, for Hart's benefit, in a dizzy and scandalous display of aerial acrobatics, while her husband, who knew the whole bag of tricks and, anyway, hated holidays, instructed the wide-eyed Miranda, sitting shyly beside him, in the commercial properties of Vanadium steel.

Later, as soon as she had satisfied herself that Hart had succumbed to her usual methods, Lady Wolverbury turned her private attention, in a very different mood, to Clare.

" Why didn't you tell me from the first," she whispered, as she took her aside, " that this man was Arthur Powys's cousin ? "

" I didn't know myself," Clare told her, honestly.

" Naturally. You wouldn't. You go through life with your eyes shut. I suppose you've no idea who the girl's mother was ? "

" None in the least." She felt that she owed the lie to Hart and Miranda too.

" H'm, that's a pity. She's not her father's type. Of course she's attractive, very. No style. But then, no modern girls have that. And she won't last ; that colouring never does. All right until she's forty. *Et puis la déluge.*" The gender slipped inevitably. " However," Lady Wolverbury went on, " by that time she'll have had a family. I suppose there's nothing yet ? "

" Really . . ." Clare began, " I haven't . . ."

" Of course you haven't ! You're just as dreamy as ever. Miranda isn't dreamy ; I can promise you that. Her eyes are as sharp as needles ; she's listening now. I wish you'd ask her one thing, Clare, as soon as I've gone : not to wear diamonds—imitation ones—in the daytime. And don't let Steven give her any real ones either. As soon as I've got her in hand I'll teach her to dress." She raised her voice suddenly : " Miranda, darling ! " And Miranda, assuring Lord Wolverbury how interesting it all was, came obediently to her side.

" I want you to come and stay at Stourford," Lady Wolverbury cooed. " Of course, if you're not tired of him, you can bring Steven with you. And I shall hope to see you all at dinner to-morrow night. Your father particularly."

" I'm sorry," said Hart. " They haven't finished with me yet. To-morrow I shall be going back to Pedworth. Of course I'm leaving Miranda behind me. I've finished with *her*."

" Well, Steven and Miranda, anyway. Clare can do as she pleases."

And Clare, as it happened, could also take a hint.

Next day, after lunch, while Steven and Miranda were

" resting," she drove down with Hart to Wychbury station to see him off.

" I wonder if you know how much I shall miss you," she said.

He shook his head : " At least we have something to remember. We may see each other sooner than we imagine."

When she returned to Uffdown the house was deserted. Steven and Miranda had already started for Stourford without so much as leaving a message for her. She took her tea in solitude. Her mind was with Hart ; she could not settle to anything. Without him Uffdown seemed a wilderness. Not even the calm of Annabel Ombersley's drawing-room could soothe her. It's friendly ghosts had all been frightened away by the alien spirits whose symbol was the pile of ragtime sheet music untidily strewn upon her suffering piano. In all the house there was no spot that she could feel verily her own.

" I have no business to be here any longer," she thought. " Although he wouldn't like to admit it, Steven would be far happier without me. Whenever he even looks at me, her eyes are on him."

While she sat alone in the firelight of the darkened hall a sudden determination crystallized in her brain. She rang for Ellen, and told her that she was going to pack.

" You're never thinking of going away to-night, ma'am ? "

" No, but to-morrow morning early. I want to be ready to start. Mr. Steven and his wife are staying for several days at Stourford. I shall be leaving in any case, and it seems a good opportunity to get the packing over while they're away."

All through the evening, with a short break for dinner, they toiled among trunks and wardrobes in the room that had once been hers and Ralph's and was now Miranda's. The very distraction and confusion were grateful to Clare. When it was over she went, in her dusty tiredness, to ring up Stourford. The melancholy voice of Parker answered her.

"Good evening, ma'am; and, if you'll allow me to say so, a Happy New Year."

*Ice-pudding or meringues, madam?*

She thanked him. "I want to speak to Mr. Steven," she said. "And, Parker . . ."

"Yes, madam?"

"You needn't tell him who it is."

A moment later Steven came to the telephone. His voice was flurried. She knew she had disturbed him.

"Good lord! It's *you*, mum! Whatever's the mystery?"

"I wanted to tell you, darling. I'm going down to Brixham to-morrow. You remember? The place in Devonshire where I went before."

He was concerned. "I say, mum, this is rather sudden, isn't it?"

"I need a rest. I want to think things over. Don't worry about me. I'm feeling a bit lonely."

Thank heaven, he couldn't see how her lip trembled! There was a long silence before his troubled voice came through:

"You make me feel a beast, mum. If it's like that we'd better come home to-morrow."

"No, no, my child; you'd better do nothing of the sort. Go back and enjoy yourself. We have to get it over somehow, darling. Better begin by degrees."

"Miranda will be awfully sick about it."

She smiled. Was it possible that he believed what he said?

"Give her my love. Tell her that Ellen will look after her. She'll enjoy trying her hand at housekeeping. You'll have great fun over it. I'll write and tell you what's happening to me as soon as I get there. Good-bye. Be happy!"

He couldn't leave it at that. " I say, mum. Tell me honestly. There's nothing else ? "

" Of course there isn't. I've told you already ; I'm tired."

He wavered. " It only struck me . . . it looks a bit queer, you know."

" Nonsense, my child . . . You're married. You don't want a chaperon."

" Well, after all I suppose you've got to do what you like . . ."

A young lady at North Bromwich, immersed in the law-reports of the *News of the World*, awoke to the fact that she was in charge of a telephone-line and justified her existence abruptly by cutting them off. Clare thanked her, from the bottom of her heart.

## IV

*Dear Robert* (she wrote to him, barely three months later), *I wonder if you will be very angry with me for what I've done. I do hope you won't. In any case it's happened more by chance than anything. You know that I couldn't bring myself to Steven's wild idea of going back to Pen House. It's a gloomy place in any case, and for me it's far too full of memories and . . . ghosts. I wanted a small house in the country, not too near to Uffdown but near enough—you'll know exactly what I mean. So I asked Dudley, who's always in touch with house-agents, to get some friends of his to send him a list of possibilities. It seems that houses are dreadfully scarce just now : small ones at any rate. When Dudley had weeded them out he sent me particulars of two. One of them was quite impossible, in a frightful hole. The people told me that a brook runs into the cellars every winter. And the other—this is the point at which you're going to be angry with me !—is a place called Ashfurlong—you must know it, less than two miles from your beloved Dinsop. Robert, it's no good being angry with me ; it's too late ; I've taken it on a seven years' lease.*

*The house is a darling, just big enough for me and Ellen and a chauffeur-gardener. It's right off the road ; you needn't ever see me if you don't want to ; but, all the same, I shall feel less lonely knowing that you'll be near me. That wasn't why I took it, I assure you. There seemed, for the moment, to be nothing else in the least suitable. I've made all sorts of plans already for the garden. There's a coppice behind it, absolutely full of birds. I wished you were with me when I went there, to tell me which was which. I can never remember ; you know what a fool I am. Joyce Wilburn, who's a doctor, drove over with me and inspected the drains. She says they're all right ; and Dudley approves of the house—or rather of the lease, which is what interests him most. He was very kind to me. I think he realizes how lost I feel with losing Steven. I told him, before we settled it, that you would be my neighbour. And now I am only longing to talk to you about it. I shall go in on Lady Day. Is there any further news of your demobilization ?*

*Clare.*

She waited a little anxiously for his reply, but, when he wrote, he was not cross with her. He had known Ashfurlong ever since he was a boy ; for more years than he cared to remember, he said ; he hoped she'd be happy there ; as for his demobilization, the movements of the War Office were mysterious : he wasn't of any use now that the school was disbanded ; it might come any day.

Clare threw herself, with all her strength, into the task of making Ashfurlong fit her desires. It was a small Elizabethan manor house full of good timber, with mullioned windows, string-courses of red-brick dog's-tooth, and

slender clusters of chimneys set diagonally. For all its age
it had none of Uffdown's graces. A homely, red-cheeked
old countrywoman, it seemed, beside a grand Augustan lady,
patched and powdered. And yet, to Clare, its very humility
seemed fit for a gentle dowager's retirement ; and the garden,
as she had told Hart, was soon to be a joy.

Beside the house lay deep herbaceous beds of cool black
loam, along the brink of which, when first she came to see
them, massed crocuses burned like the edge of a creeping
fire. And then the little lawn beyond, so cool, so secret ;
as quiet and shady as a forest clearing, narrowly running
into a distance of domed beeches, with the black boughs of
damson orchards on either side. For miles around there
stretched a wild brookland, so broken into hills and valleys,
so choked with oak-woods and hazel thickets which baffled
the twisting lanes, that it seemed impossible that she should
ever penetrate its last secrets, though Robert, no doubt,
knew every stream and coppice and stile by heart.

All through her preparations she was thinking of him,
submitting everything to his judgment, as she imagined it,
in ways that puzzled Vivien, who had come over to help her.
Clare knew that whenever a man's work was to be done she
could count on Vivien ; though at night, when they sat
together in a room that looked as though it had been looted
by a passing army and Vivien expounded her views on the
blessings of spinsterhood, she was often forced to smile.
" The one good thing about this place, Clare," Vivien would
say, " is that you'll have it to yourself with no men about
you."

Her only other visitor was Steven, a rather awkward
Steven, anxious to prove for his own satisfaction that if she
were burying herself in this wilderness instead of at Pen
House, it wasn't really his fault, much less Miranda's. His
embassy was made more difficult by the fact that when it
came to transporting furniture from Uffdown there were

several things to which, as he said, Miranda had taken a fancy. Clare's Bechstein was one of them. He asked for it, timidly.

"With the baby coming and all that," he suggested, "I feel as if it might be dangerous to cross her in anything she's set her heart on."

"But Steven, my darling," Clare protested; "Miranda's not musical."

"No, she isn't musical," he admitted dubiously; "but she likes to play."

"My dear, I'll give her another piano with pleasure and then she can play to her heart's content; but I really want my own."

He brightened up: "I say, that's topping of you, mum. I think, as a matter of fact, she'd prefer a pianola."

In Annabel Ombersley's drawing-room? The room was Annabel Ombersley's no longer.

"Very well, she shall have one," said Clare.

He left her, always, a little hurriedly, as though his visits endangered his reputation. He seemed to be putting on weight at an alarming rate. All the old military hardiness had left him, and his cheeks were liverish.

"It's obvious you're not getting enough exercise, darling," she told him.

"It isn't as easy as all that, mum," he answered. "The doctor's insisted on Miranda keeping quiet. She gets a bit nervy; she can't bear my leaving her. When this business is over I shall go back to the works at Wolverbury. Grandpapa's very keen on it, and so's grandmater."

From him, as well as from Vivien, Clare gathered that he and Miranda were very much in the bosom of Stourford. "No doubt," she thought, "the old lady's 'moulding' her." She remembered how, years before, George's Eleanor had warned her against an identical process. Was it her duty to warn Miranda? She wondered. No, no, Miranda was capable of looking after herself and would resent advice in any case.

By January the War Office had discovered that they were paying Hart for doing nothing. In the middle of May, when nightingales were in full song, he came to Dinsop.

He came across the fields through the May evening, in the hour when milky-white mist began to steal along the hedgerows and lay the cowslip's scent. Clare knew it was he, although he had not told her he was coming, as soon as his boots began to crunch along the drive.

" Well, Colonel, this *is* a surprise, upon my word ! " said Ellen cheerfully.

The low-roofed drawing-room was dim, pervaded by the vinous smell of other cowslips—Clare did not even rise to meet him or utter a word. Her heart was too full. She held out her hand to him.

" I thought you were never coming," she said at last. " I've been waiting."

" I reached Dinsop at five o'clock."

That was all he said, and yet it moved her with thankfulness to hear his voice. Whatever they said that night would sound inadequate.

" Of course you'll stay to supper ? " she asked him.

" I'd love to. Ellen seemed quite pleased to see me."

" She's always talking about you—you and Steven at Pedworth. You must come and see my garden before the light's gone."

" The sky will be light to-night. You know there's a new moon—the nightingale's moon."

They walked together in the garden, though she had forgotten everything that she wanted to show him. A land-rail was craking in the mowing-grass beyond the damson orchards. There was no other sound but that of their foot-steps falling on the moist grass and their voices, lowered, as though respecting the silence. They spoke of unimportant things, laughing softly together ; of everything but the secret joy that was in both their hearts ; and the grave beech-domes rose ghostly as the moon sank, and the dim shrubberies listened as though their converse were no more alien than a murmur of nesting birds ; until, as the dew fell thicker and the lawn darkened so that they could no longer see each other's faces, the tinkle of a ridiculous supper bell came to them from Ellen, standing white-aproned at the door.

Hart left her early ; for he had not even stopped to unpack his things at Dinsop. By then the night was of a soft but pitchy darkness.

" You must have a lantern," she said. " I'm sure there's one somewhere. You cannot possibly see."

" From Ashfurlong to Dinsop ? I know every step and stile of it. I could find my way between them if I were blind."

He went. When Ellen, as was her custom, came in to gossip under the pretence of taking orders, a smile still left its beauty on Clare's lips.

" Well, ma'am, the Colonel's looking fine, and no mistake. That man, he grows younger every day to my thinking."

" I expect he's happy, Ellen, to be at home."

" It's handy to have a gentleman like that near by. I shouldn't wonder if we see a good bit of him now summer's coming in."

" I shouldn't wonder if we do, Ellen," Clare repeated. " He's always been a very good friend to me."

" To say nothing of being a relation like," said Ellen, approvingly—" I'm sure it will take a great weight off Mr. Steven's mind."

For all practical purposes he was her only neighbour. Dinsop Court, Lord Arthur's gloomy Georgian mansion, stood waiting for a purchaser in bleak neglect ; Dinsop Vicarage had lain empty ever since the beginning of the war, the offices of its church being served perfunctorily by the Rector of its mother parish down in the Teme valley; the only other gentlefolks' houses in that lost and almost roadless triangle between Rea and Teme and Ledwyche were Clare's Ashfurlong and Robert's Dinsop Lodge. Another Mesopotamia, he called it. In Mesopotamia, Clare remembered, lay the Garden of Eden.

All through that summer it was Eden indeed. For a long time the people in the valleys failed to realize that their wild brookland had become reinhabited. The roughness of the lanes, which in five years of war-time had degenerated into mere torrent-beds, isolated them as completely as if they had been living on a Hebridean islet.

As Ellen had prophesied, they saw a good bit of each other. It was rarely that a day passed without their meeting; and though, deferring to a code which they accepted without admitting its necessity, Clare never visited Dinsop Lodge when Hart was alone, their days, serene or stormy, were spent in an open-air companionship that thoughts of propriety never invaded, walking and motoring and talking together—as Ellen declared—like brother and sister; until it seemed as though there were nothing in the life of either of them that the other did not share and understand.

And when they returned in the evening to the intimate quietude of Ashfurlong, as likely as not Clare would persuade him to stay to supper; or, even if she didn't, Ellen, with an old servant's privilege, would do so for her. For Ellen knew that her cooking was wasted on another woman, and liked, as she said, to see a man about the house, particularly a gentleman who appreciated the excellence of her kitchen and had the manners to say so. When supper was over, and the lamps lit, they would sit and read aloud; or, if the evening tempted, prolong their walk by gentle pacings to and fro along that secret lawn among the damson orchards. And then, at the early hour which country-people kept, the ritual of their first night's parting would be repeated in a calm confidence which filled the intervening darkness with the certainty that, on the morrow, they would meet again.

Although they loved each other, and knew it, the serenity of their relation was never broken by passionate words nor made intolerable by an embrace. It was a state too tender, too precious to both of them to bear the risk of such disturbance ; enough for each to know that the other had no thought nor aspiration beyond their small, closed world.

" This is the first time in my life," Clare thought, " when I have never been lonely."

In early autumn, when the Shropshire damsons ripened and bulging baskets of dusky fruit stood waiting for market-carts at every cottage gate, the ladies of the neighbourhood discovered Clare's existence, and the privacy of Ashfurlong began to disappear. They came up from the valleys in every historical type of conveyance, suspicious of a new-comer, but anxious, every one of them, to know all about her. Even in their tea-time conversation they conformed to a type.

" These dreadful roads ! I must say, you've really done wonders with Ashfurlong. You'll have to make a rock-garden next : I'll send you some plants. My dear Mrs. Wilburn, what delicious tea ! It's the nicest I've tasted for years. Of course I guess that you're musical. That must be a great consolation. But tell me truly, Mrs. Wilburn, isn't it awfully lonely ? "

" No, I'm not a bit lonely," Clare told them. " The days aren't long enough for all I have to do."

" Your husband doesn't come here often ? "

" His business keeps him constantly in North Bromwich."

" Now that Lord Arthur has deserted us there's really nobody near you. Except, of course, Colonel Hart. I hear he's returned. Probably you know him already."

"Yes. I've known him very well for a long time. He was my son's commanding officer on Salisbury Plain. My son married his daughter."

"Really?" The interest quickened. "But what an extremely fortunate coincidence!"

At the end of September, Miranda's baby was born mercifully, for Lady Wolverbury, a son.

"*Miranda is simply longing for you to see him,*" Steven wrote. "*Father Darnay is coming up specially for the christening. Unfortunately his mission work in London prevents him from staying at Uffdown; but you, of course, will stay with us for a day or two, and let the Colonel motor you over. I want you to see all my improvements. It's scandalous to think that you've not been at Uffdown since the spring. You simply won't know it.*"

"I suppose," she told Hart, "I shall have to go. You'll drive me to Uffdown, won't you, Robert? I'm rather scared. The longer you stay away from a thing the more difficult it is to face it."

"Of course I'll drive you over, but I won't stay there, unless you really feel you can't do without me. I think you're rather silly to be frightened, my dear."

"I know. I suppose it's what they call an inhibition. I can manage with Steven here; but there, somehow, it's different. Of course I won't force you."

They arrived at Uffdown on the morning of the christening. Nobody was there to receive them. Steven and Miranda, it seemed, had spent the night at Stourford. "Thank heaven they're away," Clare whispered to Hart. From the moment when the car entered the drive she had been overwhelmed by an unconquerable nervousness that made her afraid to open her eyes.

"The mistress said she hoped you'd make yourself at home, ma'am," a strange new butler told her.

The word was unfortunate. Poor Uffdown! As Steven

had warned her, she simply didn't know it. The dim, panelled hall now shone with a radiance of white enamel. The newly-upholstered furniture gleamed with purple and gold. On every side Miranda's opulent tastes proclaimed themselves in colours that shattered the place's old sedateness.

" Robert, it's dreadful," she gasped. " I simply can't bear it."

" You poor dear," he consoled her. " Think of Ashfurlong."

His sympathy made her feel guilty ; for he, by means of Miranda, was indirectly responsible for what wounded her. She was anxious that he shouldn't realise this.

" I mustn't be foolish," she told him. " It's only that I'm shocked at the suddenness of the change. She's awfully young and modern. I must make allowances. In any case she mustn't know what I think. I remember when first I came here how indignant I was at Lady Hingston's criticism ; and now I'm doing exactly the same as she did. I'm being nothing but a typical mother-in-law. It's her home : she's a right to do what she likes with it."

But when, consumed with curiosity, she opened the door of Annabel Ombersley's drawing-room and peeped inside, she found it more difficult than ever to contain herself. There, by the window where she had sat and played to herself so often, stood the new pianola, its top infested with uniformed photographs of officers whom Miranda had nursed at Wyshford ; a gramophone, with the lid open, and a heap of dance records in torn paper covers. Facing her, in the chair which Ernest Wilburn had occupied on the night before his death, a grotesque, enormous teddy-bear leered at her with beady eyes. Scattered on the floor, in chairs, and under the piano, a series of dressmaker's boxes disclosed the flimsy garments that Miranda habitually ordered on approval from London but rarely sent back.

Clare turned to Hart pathetically. " It *is* rather careless, isn't it ? I can't imagine what kind of maids she has got. Poor Ellen would be scandalized, wouldn't she ? "

And when she returned in a flurry from Stourford, Miranda was rather like her drawing-room ; a little blowsy and diffuse, in spite of her smart frock. Although, as Lady Wolverbury had prophesied, she was " going off " rapidly, *la déluge* had not yet come. She was fatter and more mature in every way, but still, from an Oriental point of view, a beauty. At least she was evidently beautiful to Steven, whose smiling glances followed her with a nervous fascinated persistence. He was anxious, Clare felt, that Miranda should appear at her best ; he showed her off, like an anxious matron conducting her fluffy Persian at a cat-show, determined to demonstrate, by strokings and endearments, that his darling was not only beautiful but innocent of claws or vices ; while as for spitting . . . But Miranda, purring and arching her back beneath his blandishments, continued to glance at Clare, with a dark, suspicious, feline detachment that quite belied her superficial complaisance.

" At any rate he's still happily in love with her," Clare thought ; " and that is really all that matters to me."

Lunch was a scramble of one rich dish after another. Unlimited champagne. Clare could have sworn that the butler had been drinking. No wonder, if this were Steven's ordinary fare, that Steven was putting on flesh. " You're eating nothing, sweetheart," Miranda cooed at him in her rich deep voice. Steven had already eaten three times as much as Hart. His face was pasty and formless ; his eyes puffed ; for the first time in his life he resembled his grandfather.

The butler autocratically bustled them into the car. Miranda laughed familiarly and made eyes at the chauffeur ; as a matter of habit she made eyes at everybody ; she liked to be popular with men.

" Where's Bissell ? " Clare asked Steven. " I haven't seen him."

" Bissell ? Did I never tell you that Bissell had left ? "

She knew by his shifty eyes that he had deliberately concealed it from her.

" Oh, Steven, what a pity ! He'd been with us so long."

" He'd been with you too long, hadn't he, Steven darling ? " said Miranda.

Steven laughed uncomfortably : " I think Miranda's just about hit it, mum. And Bissell, of course, was never a good mechanic."

At Wychbury church, baronial Stourford awaited them. Miranda, evidently, was all over old Joe Hingston, prepared to translate extremes of boredom into cheques ; and Lady Wolverbury was all over Miranda. Miranda had done her duty promptly and must be rewarded. There, too, stood Mr. Pomfret, gone rather brittle for the hunting-field, but just as boyishly hearty and vaguely aristocratic ; while Mrs. Pomfret, longer-toothed than ever, cantered up and tossed her plumes as she smiled above the baby. And there, urbane, yet delicately withdrawn from a scene where once his spirituality had not been appreciated, moved Father Darnay.

When Joseph Ralph Powys Hingston—the cousinship with the Cluns was not too remote for that—had, under protest, been made a Member of Christ, a Child of God, and an Inheritor of the Kingdom of Heaven, and Father Darnay had worked through the titles in order of precedence, he sidled up to Clare.

" How *are* you ? " he said, as though he had only just caught sight of her, pressing her hand with quite immoderate affection. " We haven't met or corresponded since you left Pedworth. I want to know all about you."

" There isn't much to know. I'm very well, thank you.

As well as a grandmother can expect to be feeling at her first christening."

" You're living in Shropshire now, Steven has told me."

" Just over the border.   Yes."

" Near Colonel Hart ? "   Clare scented an air of inquisition.

" Not very far away from him.   Isn't that nice for me ? "

The question was a bold one.   Father Darnay's principles struggled with the politeness which he owed to the occasion.   He evaded it neatly :

" If you had said : ' Isn't that nice for *him ?* ' you'd have given me a chance to tell you what I think about you." He changed the subject hurriedly : " What is your parson's name ?   I hope you're not worried with an Evangelical. Tell me ; it's possible that I may have heard of him."

" D'you know, I'm ashamed to say I've really no idea."

" And that," she thought, " will be put down to poor Robert.   How that man hates him ! "   But before Father Darnay could express his opinion of this enormity, Steven had snatched him from her.

That afternoon she did not see Darnay again.   In such confusion—for Lady Wolverbury had mobilized the whole neighbourhood—it was hard to speak to anyone.   The vestry and churchyard were full of people with whom she had no acquaintance and who evidently had no idea who she was either.   It was not until the tumult had subsided and the Uffdown drive had emptied itself of congregated motor-cars that she managed to get Steven for a moment to herself.

" Thank God that's over," he said, as he took her arm. " It's jolly to see you here again, the same as ever.   Too shabby of the Colonel to run away like that ! "

They walked to and fro over the gravel fouled by leaky crank-cases ; a smell of exhaust gases still clung to the drive. Steven was happy and affectionate ; he seemed less frightened of her at Uffdown than he had been, of late, at Ashfurlong. She wanted to speak to him again about Bissell; but dared not do so, for she knew that the subject would pain him. They spoke instead of small things that they remembered; of Sly, and poor Miss Pidgeon and Bo-peep.

"Poor Sly, we had to shoot her," he told her. "She was so blind that she got in everybody's way. Miranda was always treading on her. It really was dangerous. But little Bo-peep is still a pensioner. She's down in the paddock, and nearly as fat as I am."

They laughted together over many memories that seemed to turn him into a child again. Yet always, as they walked slowly to and fro, Clare had the feeling that they were not alone. At last a sudden instinctive impulse made her look up toward the house. A curtain in the window of the bedroom that had once been hers swung suddenly backward. She knew at once that somebody had been watching them. "One of those insolent new maids," she thought. "Not, surely, Miranda? Miranda couldn't be as jealous of me as that!"

And yet it was difficult to say of what Miranda wasn't jealous. That evening, over a dinner that was like a city banquet, she began to talk about Dinsop.

"I've no idea what father does there," she said inno-cently. "He must be bored to tears. I know I should be. I suppose you often go there?"

"I've only been there once—or twice, perhaps," Clare told her.

"Really? But I suppose you see a good deal of him all the same?"

"Of course I do." Whyever not be candid? "I see your father for a few moments nearly every day."

"I thought you would," said Miranda softly.

Her black eyes shot a meaning glance at Steven, as though she were underlining a point that they had already discussed.

" But she can't be jealous about Robert as well as Steven," Clare thought.

When dinner was over Clare moved, by sheer force of habit, in the direction of the drawing-room.

" Oh, are you going there ? " Miranda asked quickly. " I hate that horrid room. We hardly ever use it now. There won't be even a fire. We always sit here in the hall after dinner. It's so much brighter now that the panels are gone."

She plumped herself down among the gold and purple cushions, and was obviously in keeping with them. Steven stood dubiously at his mother's shoulder.

" I say, Miranda," he said. " If mum would like to, why don't we sit in the drawing-room this evening ? "

" I've told you, already, darling one, there's no fire."

" Then they can jolly well make one ! I don't see why we should pay these shoals of servants and not get what we want."

" Steven, don't worry," Clare begged him. " Of course we can stay here."

But Steven was in for a fit of obstinacy.

" Not a bit of it." He opened the drawing-room door and looked inside.

" Miranda, there's fire enough to roast an ox ! Come along, darling. Go on, mum, you go first."

Clare entered before him. She heard whispers behind her ; and then the sound of a precipitant rush upstairs.

" It isn't my fault," she told herself, " it really isn't ! "

She stood in the middle of the room, her eyes before her, looking at nothing. A heaped fire roared up the chimney. What extravagance ! Her eyes became aware of other eyes set on them : the black beads of Miranda's tawny teddy-bear.

" And really, of course," she thought, " I mustn't be hard on her. I have to remember she's only a spoilt child. How can I sympathize with the sort of mind that's interested in toy-animals ? No doubt she'll have her burst of temper and get over it. When she comes back I shall have to pretend that nothing's happened."

But Miranda didn't come back. The butler brought in coffee.

" You'd better leave it here. They'll be down in a minute," Clare told him.

From his manner Clare saw that he knew quite well what had happened.

It was odious for servants to be aware of things like that. Why didn't he go ? He moved about the room, methodically picking up Miranda's rubbish. Finally, with a gesture ridiculous in its solemnity, he picked up the teddy-bear by one ear and sat it on the piano.

Clare drank her coffee alone. " It must be worse than I imagined," she thought.

Far worse ; as Steven, descending three-quarters of an hour later with a white face and eyes that looked as if he had been crying, explained to her :

" I'm frightfully sorry, mum ; and she's sorry too. You see, the fact of the matter is, she's so dreadfully in love with me that she simply can't bear my doing anything for anyone else."

" You weren't doing anything for anyone else," Clare reminded him.

" I know. It's hard to explain. She thought I was going to move . . . but really, I know it's childish. And then that business about the fire upset her. She thinks you thought she was fibbing "—Clare *did*—" and considers that I let her down. She says I oughn't to have told you that there *was* a fire. I know it's illogical ; but then she *is* like that. She says she's always felt things deeply, ever since she was a child. And really, when she does get a fit like this, you can see how much she suffers. It's absolutely harrowing."

" Does she often get them ? "

" Not often. Just now and then. Only when she feels that I'm not considering her or when I cross her—without meaning to, you know—in something that she's set her heart on. As I was saying, whenever these fits come you can always trace it to her being so much in love with me. She's awfully frank about it too. She doesn't hide anything. She told me just now, for instance—you won't be angry, will you ?—that she couldn't help watching us all the time we were walking up and down the drive to-night. That's touching, isn't it, mum ? "

" It strikes me as rather distressing."

" It would be, if it weren't for the cause of it. But when she comes round again she's so dreadfully ashamed of herself that you can't help feeling you've been a brute to let her suffer."

" I'm afraid your coffee's cold, Steven. Shall I ring for some more ? "

" Oh, that doesn't matter, thank you, mum." He began to fidget. " I think, if you don't mind, I'd really better go up to her again. She'll be wondering what we're talking about, poor darling. I shall see you at breakfast. Miranda always has hers in bed. Do you mind very much, mum ? " His voice was pathetic.

" Of course you must go to her. Good night, my darling." She kissed him.

At the door he turned again. " Good lord, I'd forgotten ! She wanted me to bring Rupert back with me."

He picked the teddy-bear from the piano and thrust it under his arm.

" It isn't as if she hadn't a baby of her own," Clare thought. " I suppose I'd better go to bed as well."

This time they had given her Aunt Cathie's bedroom. It was a relief to enter it ; for it seemed to be the only part of the house that had not suffered from Miranda's improvements. Yet even that had lost its ancient quietness. Down in the kitchen beneath it the coarse voices of servants were celebrating Joseph Ralph Powys Hingston's christening in the remains of the baptismal champagne ; nearer, along the landing, she could hear the querulous monotone of Miranda's chatter and Steven's sympathetic replies.

" I suppose I had better try to read," she thought. " I hope to goodness they've left me a book of some kind."

She switched on the light. Yes, there was a single book on the bed-table beside her. She opened it where it was marked, at page seventeen, by an olive-wood paper knife. *The Shipwrecked Stranger*, she read. The first chapter of *Romola* . . .

Next morning she rose early and packed her dressing-case, determined, for Steven's sake as much as for her own, to set out for Ashfurlong before Miranda was up. Downstairs, as yet, there were no signs of breakfast ; so she crossed the wet lawn to take a hurried look at her old rock-garden. A call from Steven detained her. He came running after her, and they went on together, arm-in-arm. She broke her news gently :

" I'm going back to Ashfurlong this morning."

" Oh, mum, what a shame ! I promise you Miranda's as right as rain now. She'll be frightfully disappointed."

" You must come to see me at Ashfurlong one day soon and bring my grandson," she answered, evading that vexatious subject. " Why, Steven, there's something wrong here ? Whatever have you done ? "

" The rosemary hedge ? Oh yes, mum, we dug it out. It was always horribly straggly if you remember. Miranda couldn't bear the smell of it. We decided that what was wanted here was a splash of colour. I wish you'd advise us. We thought geraniums . . ."

" So that," Clare said to herself, " is the end of remembrance."

## V

## RAIN IN THE HILLS

FROM Wychbury she had wired for Hart to meet her at Tenbury station. He was there with his car, as strong and cheery as ever. They drove up to Ashfurlong almost in silence. Although he knew that something unpleasant had happened, he would not ask her any questions ; and Clare, for her part, made him no confidences ; much as she trusted him—perhaps because she trusted him so much—she felt it unfair to trouble him. For, after all, Miranda was his daughter. If she had complained he might have felt a responsibility that he didn't deserve, since the weakness and infatuation of her Steven had contributed an equal sha  to the disaster.

The first sight of Ashfurlong awaiting her in its intimate, rain-washed quietude with Ellen standing, all smiles, at the doorway to  welcome her, removed the last bitterness of Uffdown from her mind.

" This is my home," she thought ; " this is my new life ; here everything is peaceful and everyone faithful. It's time I realized this and forgot all the rest."

That evening at supper they laughed together over the discomforts of Uffdown and the air of pretentiousness that Stourford had thrown over the Wychbury christening. The whole experience now seemed so bizarre and remote that none of its distresses could touch them. By next morning Clare felt as if the continuity of her placid life at Ashfurlong had never been broken.

So autumn crept in peacefully and slowly ; a season of incomparable beauty in those wild woodlands. Lord Arthur came down to Dinsop Court to watch his guests shoot pheasants. Clare's orchards and shrubberies were a refuge for the driven birds. In the early morning she would hear the cocks' shrill trumpetings and see them trailing their splendid, burnished tails over the dewy lawn. Robert was shooting with his cousin's party and saw little of her ; but when she heard the shots crackling along the edge of the oakwoods like a *feu-de-joie*, she knew that he could not be far away from her.

On the last day of the shoot she received a note from Dudley.

*My dear Clare,*

*I don't want to trouble you, as you're perfectly aware, but under the circumstances I feel it my duty to write to you. This morning I received an anonymous letter with a North Bromwich postmark. Of course I always treat these things as I advise my clients to deal with them ; i.e. I burn them. But as your name was involved, I think it's only fair to tell you. The suggestion was that I should be anxious about your relations with Colonel Hart. I'm not, in the least ; please don't mistake my meaning. I know that Hart is a gentleman, and that you are perfectly capable of looking after yourself. But I think you ought to know that people—one person at any rate —are talking about you and trying to make mischief ; and in order that I may not appear as a foolishly complaisant husband and you as . . . something else, it may be well for you to be exaggeratedly prudent. It seems curious to be back in practice again. I jog along as usual with Mrs. Marple, and am rather thankful, as a matter of fact, that some of my " indispensable " friends have removed the greater part of my practice. Of course you needn't answer this. Whatever you were going to say, I quite agree with you. And if you're in real difficulty at any time, you know where to come.*

*Yours affectionately,*
*Dudley Wilburn.*

Although the letter was written with Dudley's characteristic detachment, Clare's heart went chill as she read it. She began to rack her brain for any memory that might suggest the source of these threats. The ladies from the valley who had called on her ? Truly, they were a trifle more interested than they need have been, and ready to prick up their ears at Hart's name ; but even though they might chatter among themselves, they were not the kind of people who would condescend to anonymity. Besides, for that matter, they had no motives of hostility. Then, Father Darnay . . . It was true that he disliked Hart, believing him to be the cause of her backsliding ; true, also, that the words which he had spoken at Wychbury might be regarded as significant. Yet Darnay, for all his aristocratic foibles, had a certain dignity. If he had felt himself compelled to write about Hart, he would surely have written to her. Miranda . . . ? Miranda, as she had seen, was jealous. That was the reason why Clare had given Steven up to her. There came the memory of a glance that had passed between Miranda and Steven at the dinner-table ; that soft voice breathing the words : " I thought you would." Yet even Miranda . . . No, it was too fantastic.

" I must tell Robert everything," she thought. " He's bound to come to supper this evening."

But, when he came, tired with his day's shooting and full of amusing observations on the comedy of Lord Arthur's guests, she hadn't the heart to spoil his happy humour by the mention of anything so sordid and disturbing as Dudley's letter. She tried, for his sake, to put it out of her mind ; but, tired as he was, his keen senses realized that something was wrong.

" Clare, you seem queer to-night. Something has happened. Why don't you tell me ? "

Although she was moved by the quickness of his sympathy, she put him off :

" Imagination, Robert. There's really nothing. It's

three days since you've seen me ; you've forgotten what I'm like."

With enormous effort she became herself again. However much she might suffer it was her duty to shield him. There were other reasons. At Pedworth she had learnt how quickly he reacted to the suggestion of any scandal that might affect her. Even if she wanted his support it would be dangerous to ask for it.

And, in any case, as Dudley assured her, there was nothing to worry about. The only right way of dealing with anonymous letters was to forget them. " I'll take his advice," she thought. " In future, I'll be exaggeratedly prudent." But hadn't she been exaggeratedly prudent already ? Hadn't she made a point of avoiding Dinsop Lodge ? Hadn't they both, by a kind of tacit agreement, renounced all words, all actions, retreated from all situations that might endanger the complete platonism of their affection ? " What more can I possibly do ? " she asked herself. " If Robert sees the least suspicion of change in my attitude he'll wonder what it means and call me to book for it. And then, out of sheer decency, I shall have to explain, which is certain to be disastrous ! "

A month passed, and then another. Winter came. At Christmas they made a little festival of their own at Ashfurlong. It was gay and homely and atoned for the discomforts of their Uffdown Christmas the year before. It pleased Ellen to treat them as if they were a pair of children. No children could have been more careless than they. Apart from one hurried visit from Steven in November they had heard nothing for months of Uffdown or Stourford. " They all seem to have forgotten us," Clare thought. " What a good thing ! " Indeed, the calm of Eden that Dudley's letter had disturbed was now as complete as ever.

One day in March, when daffodils were already blowing in certain secret meadows, Steven drove over from Uffdown by himself. Another of his lightning visits, she supposed ; but when he had backed his car into the barn that still served for garage, she saw that he had brought a suit-case with him.

" You don't mean to say you're staying the night ! " she said.

" I thought I would, if you'd have me, mum. I've started work at Wolverbury. I can get there directly to-morrow morning. I hope it isn't awkward ? "

" Of course I can have you, my child. I couldn't believe it."

" Something has happened," she thought. " She's hurt him, and he's come to me to be comforted." Her heart opened itself to him triumphantly. This was the moment for which she had been , . . no, not hoping . . . for which she had been prepared.

Although he pretended to be interested in everything at Ashfurlong Clare could see that his mind was distracted ; there was something in it which pride or shyness would not allow him to reveal. She tried to help him by mentioning Miranda. " If I show myself friendly toward her," she thought, " it'll be easier for him to speak out."

" Oh, Miranda's first-rate, thank you, mum. I think she wrote and told you there's going to be another ? "

Of course Miranda had done nothing of the sort ; but she let it pass.

" In that case I'm even more surprised that she could bring herself to spare you."

" As a matter of fact," he said, " it was she who suggested my staying the night. As a matter of fact," he began again, and then stopped suddenly. " Is there any chance of our seeing the Colonel this evening, mum ? " he asked.

" I think there's every chance. He'll probably drop in to supper. Why ? Have you something to tell him ? "

" No. I was only wondering," he told her, and relapsed into his mystery.

Perhaps he wanted to talk about Miranda to both of them poor dear! But when Hart arrived at dusk Steven was awkward and silent. She tried to help him out of his difficulty by being more lively than usual; and Hart, who always responded quickly to her moods, was soon at his best.

" Well, Steven, old fellow," he said as they settled down to talk after supper; " here's history repeating itself as it should do : we three together, just as we used to be at Pedworth—though you're a Justice of the Peace and your mother's a grandmother, and Dinsop, thank heaven, makes better sleeping than Fontenoy. Do you remember the evenings when we used to read old Cobbett ? "

" And the field of hares at Everley . . . or was it Upavon ? " Clare joined in.

" And the Dorset butter we used to smuggle in from Mrs. Siviter's back-door ? And the admirable Beazeley ? I wonder what's happened to Beazeley's trench-feet ! "

But Steven left Clare and Hart to do most of the talking. His trouble, whatever it was, kept him quiet till the Colonel had gone.

" Do you mind sitting up a bit, mum ? " he said at last. " I want to talk to you about something."

Thank heaven it was coming at last !

" Of course, my darling ; come over and sit near me."

" I think, if you don't mind, I'll stay where I am. It's about the Colonel."

" Whatever can you have to say about him ? "

" He comes here rather often, doesn't he, mum ? "

" Nearly every day. Now that I've lost you, Steven ; he's a great help to me."

" I'm sure he is. But do you think it's . . . wise ? "

" What do you mean, darling ? Surely you're not suggesting . . ."

" No, mum, of course I'm not. I only mean . . . I mean that other people might suggest . . ."

" You mean that other people *have* suggested, Steven."

" Well, yes. As a matter of fact, that's what I do mean."

" What people, Steven ? "

He hedged : " You really can't expect me to mention names, mum."

She felt she knew, in her bones, whom he was shielding. This time she had no mercy.

" I suppose you mean Miranda."

" I knew you'd say that ! " But he didn't deny it.

" In any case," she said, " I don't consider I need defend myself, Steven. But, apart from that, I'd really like to know what it has to do with Miranda."

" I wish you hadn't dragged Miranda into it, mum. However, since you have, I think it has a lot to do with her."

" How ? Tell me," she answered. She was as hard as steel.

He fumbled with his thoughts. She could see that he was obeying instructions faithfully, but wanted to spare her feelings as much as possible.

" Naturally it isn't pleasant," he burst out at last, " for her or me or anyone of the family to have a scandal hanging over our heads. After all, it isn't as if we're nobody. We have a certain position in the county, and people like us are supposed to set an example."

The voice was Steven's ; the words were recognizably Lady Wolverbury's.

" I see," Clare said, " you've done me the compliment of discussing this with your grandmother ? "

" I think," he admitted, " that Miranda may have mentioned it."

" I think," she repeated—it was hard to hold her anger— " that you might tell Miranda to mind her own business."

He flushed. But it was evident that he, too, was determined to keep his temper.

" It's no good talking like that, mum," he said. " You

can't discriminate between us. If Miranda feels anything, I feel it too."

" So it seems, my child," she said, unable to resist a shade of irony.

He quickly responded to a prick that had reached his pride.

" You talk as if you thought Miranda was running me. I assure you she's doing nothing of the sort. Not only the Stourford people : a number of your best friends feel exactly as we do."

" For instance . . . ? "

He couldn't let the challenge pass.

" For instance, Father Darnay."

" How long have you been discussing this in public behind my back, Steven ? "

" You have no right to put it like that, mum. Father Darnay's as secret as the confessional. I always ask his opinion on matters of conscience."

" Then what "—she spoke slowly—" what have you, and your conscience, and Miranda, and Father Darnay, and your grandmother decided that I ought to do, Steven ? "

" We think," he replied quite seriously ; " I think that you oughtn't to stay so near him as this. That's common-sense, isn't it, mum ? "

" You mean that you want me to give up Ashfurlong ? "

" Or give up seeing the Colonel. One or the other."

" The second is quite impossible. We're friends and near neighbours."

" Then you ought to leave Ashfurlong. I always wanted you to live at Pen House. It's ridiculous keeping a place empty like that."

She was silent for a long while.

" I hope Miranda . . . I hope you haven't said anything to the Colonel ? "

" I don't think she's said anything. I certainly haven't. Although I'm sure, if I did, he'd see the point at once."

Of course he would see the point ; that was the trouble. Clare threw up defences swiftly.

" I want you to promise me one thing, Steven," she said : " That neither you nor Miranda will say anything to him till I've thought this over."

" Of course I'll promise, mother darling," he said. He was glad of any chance to be kind to her. " You know, mum, I wouldn't have spoken of this to-night if it hadn't been for "—he hesitated—" if it hadn't begun to be beastly unpleasant for all of us. When a thing like that begins to affect the family reputation . . ."

" Steven, darling," she said, " has it never struck you that there may be things more important to me than the family reputation ? "

His face went suddenly white as if she had struck him.

" Good God, mum," he stammered ; " you don't mean to say that there's something in it ? "

She could not answer him. She was sorry she had spoken. The secret was not her own. She went on hastily :

" I suppose it hasn't struck you either that the one person whose business it really is is Mr. Wilburn ? "

The interposition of Dudley's name saved her from the consequences of her indiscretion.

" I suppose you're right in a way," he said with unexpected reasonableness. " It never struck me. Somehow, since I've no more to do with him now, it never occurred to me to think of him. But even if he approved of this . . . arrangement," he went on, " it wouldn't make it look any better from our point of view, would it ? "

She was silent. Her silence compelled him to make excuses. " I know—we all know—that it's only a matter of appearances. I don't want to hurry you or anything of that kind. It's only because we think so much of you, mum darling, that I've forced myself to . . ."

" I quite understand," she said. " Let's say no more

about it for the present, darling.   You've tired yourself out
We'd better go to bed."

Next day he hurried back early to Wolverbury.   When
Hart came round in the morning to say good-bye to him he
had already gone.

" Our son-in-law wasn't exactly on the top of his form
last night, was he ? " he said.   " He's an odd lad, Steven.
At Pedworth I used to try and persuade myself that he was
like you.   But he isn't ; and he gets less like you every day.
There's something mediæval about Steven, Clare ;  he's
a curious mixture of the paladin and the bigot ; he's the
kind of fellow whose conscience would make him do acts
of incredible gallantry one minute and burn witches the
next.   What was wrong with him yesterday ?   Nothing to
do with Miranda, I hope ? "

" No . . . not exactly.   I want to talk about it, Robert.
Let's go somewhere, a long way away, in the car and take
lunch with us.   Ellen will put up the basket."

That day, in the Teme valley, March was a very lamb.
They crossed the river by Little Hereford bridge, where
white-nosed bullocks stood knee-deep in a grayling-haunted
shallow.   They struck, at Woofferton, the main road of the
Marches, running north and south to Shrewsbury and
Hereford.

" Which way shall we go ? " Hart asked her.   " This is
your picnic."

" Wherever you like to take me."

He drove west, skirting, by ways that she had never seen
before, the wooded watershed of Leinthall and High
Vinnalls, dropping, at last, into the valley of the Lugg.   It
was still early when she saw before her a dome of mountain
that was like a pale cloud.   It blackened as they drew nearer ;
its shapes grew threatening ;   then, as the massive convolutions enfolded them, not threatening at all.   Green sheep-
walks flawed by moving shadows of cloud that raced to meet

them ; tracts of dead bracken from which winter rains had washed away the gold. The car went singing up an endless gradient ; the air was of a thin, intoxicating lightness ; the mountains became mere hills, for the road had climbed them.

" This must be Radnor Forest," she thought. She turned and asked him, as the wind rushed past them.

" Yes, we're in Wales," he said. " God, what a day ! I think we could almost see Plynlimon."

" Where are you taking me ? "

He laughed : " That is my secret."

In such exhilaration of swift air it seemed to her as though the car and themselves were alike possessed. Their speed never slackened, for the roads were clear. They shot ahead like an arrow launched into the blue of vast anonymous mountain masses, until the dark hills thrust out sprawling limbs to trip them, steep pitches roughened by waters colder and more impetuous than their Shropshire brooks. The jaws of a deeper valley gaped to receive them ; black crags, a pair of ravens wheeling and croaking ; and then, as though the wind had swelled to a hurricane, came a thunder of white waters shagging the face of an enormous dam.

" But this must be . . ." she began. He smiled ; his eyes were full of a childish gaiety :

" The North Bromwich waterworks. Can any good thing come out of Nazareth ? My secret's nearly out. Not quite. Give me five minutes."

The thunder of waters died away beneath them. They were skirting the shore of a wide lake that laughed and sparkled in wind and sunshine like a sea. An arched stone viaduct spanned it. They crossed and were hidden by shades of the primeval oak-forest that clogged the valley from which the waters came. The lake began to narrow through reedy marshland into the neck of an estuary. And there, by a wooden bridge where he brought the car to rest, a river died in a boiling caldron of boulders.

He took her hand and led her to the bridge where the tumbling water was veiled by a rainbow of spray.

" There's my surprise," he said ; " your Claerwen—your clear-white river, which North Bromwich impounded."

" My river," she murmured. " Poor Claerwen, lost in such deep waters ! "

How deep they were she had yet to tell him. They laid their lunch on a bank beyond the bridge. He was so happy that morning that it seemed a piece of gratuitous cruelty to tell him. When they had finished, and Hart had lit a pipe, she began.

He listened gravely. As she spoke the happiness faded out of his face.

" I suppose it was only to be expected," she told him. " The world is unhappy and jealous of all happiness. We were far too happy, Robert, to be left alone."

" But this is the first you've heard of it ? " he asked her keenly.

She couldn't lie to him. She told him about the anonymous letter that had reached Dudley in the autumn.

" I think it would have been kinder if you'd let me know," he said.

" I couldn't, Robert. I simply didn't dare risk it."

" Had Steven any idea that . . . we loved each other ? "

" I don't think so. I believe he was only concerned for the conventions."

" You didn't tell him ? "

" How could I ? That was your secret as well as mine."

For a moment she heard nothing but the boil of the river and the high distressful whistle of a buzzard drifting over. At last he spoke :

" Well, I suppose that's that. What are we going to do about it, Clare ? "

" What *can* we do about it ? I've been thinking all night."

" You mean that you want to leave the doing to me ? "

" What can I do ? " she pleaded. " I love you, my darling. I've found more happiness in loving and being loved by you than I've ever known before. This last year, while we've been together, has been the best thing in my life. I can't . . . I can't bear to think of living without you. You know that, don't you ? "

He took her hand. " It's almost too much to believe ; but I do know."

" And yet . . ." she hesitated. " And yet I can't help knowing that it's wrong of me. Don't misunderstand me, Robert. There can't be anything wrong with our love in itself ; there really can't be, can there ? But the consequences, my darling—that's what I'm thinking of. I feel that however innocent we are we haven't the right to give the distress that we've given to all these people. If Steven had spoken to you last night you'd have seen how upset he was for yourself. At first I was indignant, as you would have been. Afterwards I was merely wretched. Not because I loved you. Because our love was such a nuisance to everybody. You understand ? "

" I think I know what you mean, my child. And then ? "

" Then . . . Oh, Robert, what can I say ? I felt that we had no right at all to be selfish. We have no right to be happy at the expense of other people. We've had our happiness ; now we must pay for it. Only "—her voice was breaking—" I haven't the strength or the courage to do what I know is right by myself. I want you to help me, like you helped me at Pedworth. You're so much stronger and bràver than I am, Robert."

" You mean," he answered slowly, " that you want us to separate ? "

" Want ? Oh, my dear, I don't want anything but you ! "

" My dearest child, you know you can't have it both ways."

" Ah, don't say that ! " she begged him. " That's what Dudley used to say."

" It's the truth, my darling . . . If I went away from Dinsop—is that what you mean by helping ?—it would be easier for you ? "

" Still difficult and dreadful ; but much, much easier. Of course I don't think I could bear to stay at Ashfurlong if you went."

" Then why not go in any case ? "

" I can't. Don't ask me ! "

He meditated. Then his hand tightened on hers.

" What would you say, Clare, if I refused to go ? "

" I could say nothing. You know I couldn't. Don't even suggest it. It frightens me. Have pity on me for heaven's sake ! "

" Clare, Clare, you're putting an awful weight of responsibility on me."

" Only because I know you can bear it and I can't, Robert."

Again he was silent. When he spoke again the old directness and self-reliance had returned to his voice.

" It's a bad business ; I told you that at Pedworth. However, I suppose this is the end of it. As soon as we're back at Dinsop I'll make arrangements to clear off somewhere. Any excuse will do. Call it a fishing holiday. I'll go at the end of the week. Three days from now. How will that do ? "

He smiled at her, with a wise, brave tenderness.

" Oh, Robert, how you make me love you ! " she said.

He put out his hands to help her to her feet. As he drew her up toward him she came, with all her will, into his arms. For the first time in those three years they kissed. And then she began to cry, most desolately, elated, annihilated by what she had done.

Even as they turned eastward the wind rose behind them. The rainbow that shimmered above the river boulders had vanished ; the roar of the torrent was dull and threatening.

" Rain in the hills," he told her. " I'm afraid we may catch it."

The oak-woods shivered as they drove beneath them ; the mountains frowned on them with an angry darkness ; the waves of the Claerwen's lake were leaden black and capped with running foam ; leaping from the lip of the dam and flinging themselves into the abyss beneath as though some devil drove them. Clare felt as if she and her lover were flying in guilt from the same spite. The west wind whipped and harried them out of Wales ; it swept them over the crown of Radnor Forest like a witch's besom, as though it could not bear to be troubled with such contemptible rubbish. By the time they reached Presteign it had begun to rain in torrents.

Soaked and bewildered by stings and buffetings they came at last to the front door of Ashfurlong. The rain had slackened to a spitting drizzle through which, in the beams of the side-lights, the car's hot bonnet steamed.

" Well, ma'am, you haven't half caught it ! " said Ellen cheerily. " I reckon you, both of you, ought to have a mustard bath. Thanks be there's plenty of hot water this evening."

She took the luncheon basket from Clare.

" Well, isn't the Colonel coming ? There now, and I'd cooked a lovely supper for him ! "

" Too soaked to-night, Ellen," he answered gaily. " Thank you, all the same. Is that all ? Good night, Clare."

The car shot forward ; its lights described a rainy arc across the illuminated shrubberies. The motherly Ellen made way for her in the hall.

" Well, ma'am, you're drenched and blown and no mistake ! To see your face anyone'ld imagine you'd been crying. I don't know what both of you were thinking about not to put the hood up."

They had been thinking of nothing but love and pain. The rain and wind had washed away her tears as she shed them. In stormy darkness she must have been crying for hours.

Of course she couldn't eat Ellen's lovely dinner.

" You're chilled to the bone, ma'am," said Ellen, " and that's the truth of it. The Colonel didn't ought to have taken you so far, that he oughn't ! I'll put a couple of nice hotwater bottles in your bed at once."

" I shall be all right to-morrow, Ellen," Clare told her.

But when the morrow came she knew that she had been too confident. It was a torture to be at Ashfurlong alone and to know that Robert was still at Dinsop. Her heart ached emptily, continually with a pain that was like a dull toothache. There was no solace or rest for her anywhere. She tried to bring herself to work in the garden. Birds were singing ; the shrubberies rustled with their busy movements. All her green things gave thanks for the fallen rain ; the petals of her daffodils lifted from their ivory trumpets. All beauty of sound or form or colour wounded her ; for that part of her which answered to it had ceased to exist.

" It is only the first day," she told herself. " He has shown me an example. He has done what I asked him to do. I shall soon get over it."

" You know you will never get over it," another voice reminded her. " You have sent him away ; and now you might just as well be dead."

And the evening was a hundred times more intolerable than the empty day. When the lamps were lit Clare sat in a kind of stupor with a book on her knees. The solicitous Ellen hovered round her like a blundering moth.

" What's wrong with you, ma'am, is that you've taken a chill. And no wonder ! I thought the Colonel'ld be round this evening for certain. If he'd come I should soon have given him a bit of my mind. Perhaps he's caught it too. It's long past his time."

The mention of Hart was too much for Clare. She had forgotten that Ellen would need explanations.

" Why, didn't I tell you," she said, " that he was going away ? "

" Never a word, ma'am ! When did you say he was going ? "

" The day after to-morrow."

" Well, think of that ! But he's bound to look in for a moment before he goes."

That was what Clare was hoping. It seemed to her inhuman that he should abide by the letter of his compact. Inhuman ? Even cruel. " He might know," she thought, " how grateful I should be for one little moment."

But the second day passed, and still Hart did not come.

" If he loved me as much as I've thought," she told herself, " he wouldn't have been able to keep away."

Her mind brooded on his absence. She had asked for his strength, but not such strength as this. That night she sat up later than usual waiting for him. It seemed to her that he might postpone his visit till he knew that Ellen was in bed. She went upstairs in the small hours, but could not sleep before dawn.

When she awoke next morning the sun was shining.

" This is the last day," she told herself. " This morning he will come."

But the morning dragged through without him. By lunch-time her uneasiness had become a panic.

" I cannot let him go like this without a word," she told

herself. " If he won't come here I shall have to go to Dinsop."

She left the table hurriedly and took the path across the fields. Though March had not yet gone, this was April weather ; the green world stood wrapped in a pale crystalline radiance. When, out of breath, she reached the drive gates at Dinsop she saw the muddy roadway marked with recent motor tracks.

" He has gone," she thought. " He has left me ! What can I do ? "

With a failing hope that, even at the eleventh hour, she might catch him, she hurried along the drive and rang at the front door. The door-bell tinkled in a sinister emptiness ; it echoed in the emptiness of her heart.

A step on the stone flags. The door swung open. It was he.

" Clare ! What has happened ? What are you doing here ? "

She didn't know what she was doing there. She couldn't answer him.

" Come in," he said.

Without a word she entered. Without a word he followed her into the gun-room, where his strapped luggage and rod-case lay waiting for his departure. He closed the door behind them. " Clare . . ." he said.

With a little gesture of impotence she flung herself into his arms.

" How could you leave me, Robert ? How could you leave me ? "

" My love . . . my love . . ." His voice was broken, tortured.

" You were going away. I know you were going without seeing me. You say that you love me, and yet you can leave me like this ! Oh, Robert, Robert . . . ! "

" My dearest, what are you saying ? I can't understand

you. You ask me to help you ; you ask me to go away ; and then, when I'm fool enough to do what you ask me . . ." He could think of no way of dealing with this unreason that might not hurt her. Anything but that.

" If it had been anyone but you," she continued illogically. " If it had been anyone but you I think I could have borne it. But for *you* to go . . . to leave me . . . without a word . . . Oh, Robert, you couldn't," she sobbed, " you couldn't, if you loved as I do."

Little by little, within his arms, she recovered her self-possession.

" When were you going . . . Robert ? " she asked, her voice still shaken with sobs.

" By the two-forty-five. I've missed it."

" Thank heaven I caught you ! Now I shan't let you go. Oh, Robert, I've been through hell in the last two days. I knew I was a coward, but not such a coward as that. I've made another discovery." She smiled faintly. " I don't believe I've ever been in love before."

She kissed him, long and tenderly. Her kisses blinded his mind already disorientated by her swift change of tactics.

" But if I don't go," he said at last, " what shall we do ? "

" Need we do anything ? " she asked him innocently.

" This talk which has reached Steven must be pretty widespread. He's right, my child, in not wishing your name to suffer. And then there's another person, more deeply concerned than Steven : your husband."

" But Robert, Dudley wrote to me about that letter. He said, in as many words, that he trusted me. He knows me, darling."

" That doesn't make it any easier, Clare. We love each other. If we admit that, the position becomes equivocal : either you belong to him or you belong to me. Any position between the two is intolerable. For me, at any rate."

" I can never belong to anyone but you," she told him.
" Why can't we go on just as we were before, darling ?
Why should that be intolerable ? "

" Because I love you, Clare ; because I'm a man. Now
things can never be as they were before. For God's sake
let's be honest and try to face them."

" How can we be honest, how can we face them ? Tell
me."

" For me there's only one way. If Wilburn divorces you."

" Divorce ? "

He saw by her eyes that she had taken fright. Indeed,
the word was very terrible to her ; it recalled the horror of
Stourford at the time of Eleanor's affair ; the fanatical light
that shone in Steven's eyes whenever the sanctity of his
sacraments was in question ; it raised to the stature of her
girlhood the monitory figure of Father Darnay.

" But that is too dreadful," she said. " You don't understand. If I mentioned the word to Steven he'd go mad.
It's a thing about which Church people feel violently. They
don't even recognize it."

" It's the only way in which I can marry you. Don't
you see ? "

" They wouldn't consider that we were married at all.
A marriage of that kind's a mortal sin to them."

" But what will they think of us now, Clare ? Is that
any better. If it comes to that, they seem to have us both
ways."

She could not deny it. Yet surely, in divine justice,
there must be some other.

" Oh, can't we begin all over again ? " she implored him.

He shook his head. " Didn't we begin all over again three
days ago ? And where are we now ? My child, there's no
escaping it. We should find ourselves in the same position
in no time. Besides," he went on, " my thoughts of the
last few days have made a difference. I realize now what

a sad mess I've made of it. By my own codes of conduct I've behaved abominably. Knowing that I loved you, I should never have allowed you to come to Ashfurlong. I tried to atone to myself by going away from you. It couldn't be done—and thank God, it wasn't!—because you love me. But now, more than ever, it becomes a point of honour . . ."

Honour . . . oh, honour! They had settled that at Pedworth. He had been right; she admitted it. And now, for all her impatience, he was right again.

" Unless we can marry," he was saying, " we must make an end of it."

" What can I do ? " she asked him helplessly.

" You must write to Dudley Wilburn and tell him the truth."

" I don't think I can write. I'd rather see him."

" It's all the same. If you like I'll write to him."

" No, no. You'd better not do that. He's . . . funny, you know."

She felt a duty to protect him, though from what, precisely, she couldn't have said.

" I must think about it, Robert. I daren't promise you. I have to consider Steven . . . so many things. Oh, what have we done," she cried, " to deserve all this ? "

He answered her brokenly : " I don't want to hurry you."

" But promise me," she entreated, " that you won't go away ? As long as I just know you're near, it'll be all right. I won't expect to see you or anything of that kind. Robert, you'll promise me that, at any rate ? "

He promised ; there was nothing else for him to do.

## VI

### CLAERWEN

AMID the doubts and tortures of the succeeding days the thought of Steven haunted her. In the ecstasy of her Shropshire idyll she had tried to forget the pains and humiliations she had suffered at Uffdown. Now, when the whole course of her life was threatened by a cataclysmic deviation, she began to realize that something more integral in her being than a sense of duty would not allow her to neglect him. Time after time, when it seemed as though the path to happiness lay plain and open before her, the image of Steven rose and barred her way.

In any case he would be expecting to hear if she had yielded to the force of his objections.

" I can do nothing," she thought, " until I have seen him again. If only that didn't imply my going to Uffdown and seeing Miranda ! "

It came to her suddenly, as an inspiration, that he had started work at Wolverbury.

" Of course, I can send him a wire to the works," she thought, " Miranda need know nothing about it. I'll ask him to meet me at Battie's in North Bromwich for lunch to-morrow, and go in myself by the morning train."

The morrow, as luck would have it, was Thursday : North Bromwich market-day. The Teme valley train was full of her calling acquaintances, who trooped into North Bromwich, on special occasions, for the theatre matinees. Happily she escaped them at the station, but no sooner had she settled herself in a corner seat at Battie's to wait for Steven th n she found herself, once more, the object of their ingratiating smiles.

" I suppose," she thought, " they imagine that Robert will be meeting me."

For a long time it looked as if no one would meet her at all. Steven was twenty minutes late for their appointment. He came in flushed and obviously worried.

"I only got your wire by the merest accident," he told her. "Whatever made you address it to Wolverbury? Luckily they sent it after me. I've been in here all morning with grandpapa on 'change. I say, mum, tell me at once: there's nothing wrong, is there?"

She reassured him quickly. "I only want to talk to you."

"Well, thank the Lord for that. I thought something had happened."

She watched him wolfing his lunch, just like a schoolboy. She remembered the days when to lunch at Battie's had been one of his great treats. When he had finished, he looked at his watch.

"You're in a hurry, darling?"

"No . . . not exactly. I have to keep an eye on the time. Miranda's driving into town for tea."

"I'm glad you told me. I'd rather speak to you alone. Where can we talk?" Her Temeside friends were listening.

He could think of nowhere better than the Art Gallery. There, under the eyes of nobody but a commissionaire and numerous languid ladies by Burne Jones, they sat upon a shiny bench and talked it over.

"I've been thinking about what you came to tell me the other day," she said.

"Yes. I supposed it was that. I hated to have to speak about it."

"Poor darling! I'm sorry. Steven, I didn't tell you the truth."

His face grew anxious. "What do you mean, mum."

"I didn't tell you that the Colonel and I were in love with each other."

"Good God! That's pretty awful. Mum, you can't mean it!"

" I do, Steven. It is pretty awful, as you say. I had to tell you."

" I never thought that possible for a moment. We were such good friends. I thought it was only gossip. I can't believe it."

He was taking it even more hardly than she had expected. Her heart ached for him. But she went on steadily.

" So now the question arises : what can we do about it ? "

" Do ? Why, there's nothing to be done. Only to get over it."

" I can't get over it, Steven. I know. I've tried."

" You must, mum. Really. Nothing else is possible. Oh, why, in heaven's name, didn't you go to Pen House ? "

" Because . . . I must tell the truth . . . because, although he didn't know it, I was in love with him then."

" You take my breath away, mum." He went very white. " You'd better come home with us this evening, I think."

She shook her head. " My child, that would make it no better. There's only one way of happiness for either of us. We know ; we've proved it. And there's only one legal way in which to get that happiness. If Mr. Wilburn would divorce me . . ."

" Mother," he cried, " whatever are you talking about ? It isn't as bad as that. You must be mad ! The scandal's nothing. I could put up with that. Everybody has to at some time. But you . . . a Churchwoman ! You . . . a friend of Father Darnay's."

" You wouldn't like me to go away with him, Steven ? "

" Oh, mother, how can you suggest such things ? This is too terrible ! And as for divorce . . ." A flash of the old zealot's fire came from his eyes. " The law of God and the law of the Church are against it. The law of the land can say what it likes. That makes no difference. Before everything else you're a member of the Church, you're a citizen of

Christ. If you're divorced and marry the Colonel, in the eyes of Christ you'll be an adulteress."

" I seem to remember," she answered slowly, " that Christ himself was charitable once in a matter of that kind."

" That . . . that's beside the point," he maintained rather lamely. " You are a Churchwoman, baptized, confirmed, and married in the Church. The woman taken in adultery certainly wasn't. I'll tell you something, mother. It's awful ; but it's true. If you should really do what you've proposed, I should feel . . . I should feel that I never wanted to see you again."

" You're very cruel, Steven."

" It isn't cruelty ! "  He was ashen white and breathless. " I'm anxious that you shouldn't fall into mortal sin."

" What do you want me to do ?  I must do something ? "

" Come back with us to Uffdown . . . Pen House, if you like."

" I can't do that, Steven."

" Then go back right away to Mr. Wilburn. We have no right to forget that he's your husband."

" Steven, you're very generous all of a sudden ; really that sounds extraordinarily strange from you."

" I know it does.  But still I mean it, mother.  I'm trying not to be personal.  I'm trying to think of this business as Father Darnay would think of it.  I'm sure that's what he would say.  And I'm sure," he continued, " that's what I ought to say too.  When I was a kid I didn't understand these things.  I'm afraid I behaved rather badly to Mr. Wilburn.  When you're married you begin to see things differently.  I think we did wrong."

" It was for your sake I left him, darling," she reminded him.

" I know.  And that's why I feel a sort of responsibility. Because, mum, after all, marriage is a sacrament.  There's absolutely no getting away from that."

"You know that we have practically nothing in common?"

"That makes no difference, mother. You're his wife. This isn't a new idea. Ever since I've been married to Miranda I've been thinking of it. I wish you'd think of it too. It would be an enormous happiness to me if you went back to him. My conscience isn't easy as it is."

"But must I sacrifice myself," she thought, "to Steven's conscience?"

"I don't know what to say," she told him at last. "I had half meant to go and see Dudley this afternoon. I shall have to tell him anyway."

"Oh, mum," he cried, "I wish you would think of it. That would solve everything."

"I don't know what to say, Steven. I don't know what I can do."

"If only you'd leave it to God, mother, He would help you."

Ah, would He . . . ? They kissed and parted. He hurried away from her. Evidently he was frightened of missing a moment of Miranda.

"How simple it would be," she thought, "if I could see it all as he does. Life is amazingly easy for really religious people. And there's something in it; there *must* be something in it. I wonder what would happen if *he* fell in love. Would it all look as simple then? I wonder . . ."

Leaving the Art Gallery she passed the Municipal Buildings, turned into Sackville Row and proceeded mechanically in the direction of Wilburn's office. She mounted the stairs and tapped at the opaline door. A slovenly office-boy opened it to her cautiously.

"Mr. Wilburn?" he said. "Not in, miss," and would have shut the door again.

"When do you expect him?"

Behind the screen of the door the boy held converse with

another voice, as the result of which a freckled young man with a high collar appeared.

"Mr. Wilburn, I'm sorry, madam, is out. He very rarely comes here now on account of his indifferent health. Mr. Flower, his partner, will be in at five. Perhaps you'd like me to make an appointment?"

"I wanted to see Mr. Wilburn himself. Would you be good enough to give me his address?"

The clerk hesitated. "I'm afraid that's not usual, madam. What name, please?"

"Mrs. Wilburn."

"Some relative? Oh, well, in that case . . ."

He gave her a slip of paper with an address: 24, James Watt Street, Winsworth.

She knew nothing of Winsworth except that it was an unfashionable district lying somewhere on the low ground beyond the jewellers' quarter; and as for James Watt Street . . . ! She took a taxi that carried her downhill past the fried-fish shops of Blockley into a maze of stucco and grimed brick that the extension of the municipal tramways had left mouldering behind them like a desert city; streets that had once been respectable, and now survived as a sump into which the less successful of the middle classes subsided helplessly, as by gravitation. In one such street, a trifle more pretentious and therefore more gloomy than the rest, the taxi pulled up suddenly before a door upon whose fanlight she read the number 24 in figures of tarnished gilt.

She rang. A vision of frayed respectability answered her.

"Who would have thought of seeing you, madam?" said Mrs. Marple.

Could it be possible that this pitiful old woman had once been formidable?

"I've come to see my husband," Clare told her. "I was sorry to hear at the office that he isn't well."

" Not *well !* " said Mrs. Marple, with a flash of her old severity. " I'm afraid, ma'am, you'll find him very ill indeed. He's been fit for nothing ever since he came out of the army. If you don't mind I'll just put him tidy before you go in."

She disappeared. The narrow corridor smelt of cats and cabbage water. A clock, which Clare remembered at Tudor House, ticked slowly, resentfully, as though it hated the change. Mrs. Marple reappeared.

" Now he'll be glad to see you, ma'am, if you'll come this way."

Clare followed her, frightened by the prospect of what she was going to see.

Dudley was sitting up in a horsehair chair with a travelling rug wrapped about his knees. As she entered he looked up eagerly and smiled to greet her. That greeting, and the change, which was even more than she had dreaded, overwhelmed her. The big man seemed to have shrunk to half his former size. The hand which he stretched out to her was big and bony, but of a mortal whiteness. Emaciation had given his face a strange, thin-lipped refinement, and accentuated the shrewdness of his deep-set eyes. There was even a hint of ironical humour in his smile.

" Oh, Dudley, why didn't you tell me that you were ill ? " she said. She took the bony hand in hers and pressed it. At that moment there was nothing in her heart but awe and pity ; awe for the mark of mortality that was on him ; pity, reinforced by the memory of innumerable intimacies that his wasted face recalled.

" Yes, I've been rather rocky, lately," he admitted ; " but really there seemed no reason why I should bother you. Apart from this cursed weakness I'm quite comfortable. Sit down, my dear."

Still holding his hand she sat down beside him. She dared not look at him any longer ; her eyes were full of

tears. And all the time, as she pitied him and shuddered
at the meanness and discomfort that surrounded him, the
words of Steven went running through her brain : " Marriage is a sacrament ; we have no right to forget that he's
your husband."

No right. . . . But now there was no mere question of
right. To love and to cherish ; in sickness and in health.
. . . The desire for sacrifice, more potent than any sense of
duty, constrained her to devote herself to this broken,
pitiful man. Whatever bitterness their life together had
known was forgotten. She could remember nothing now
save the admiration, the idealization which once she had
given him, the trustful tenderness of those early years. She
could not forget the nights through which she had lain in those
poor arms. The very characteristic reticence with which
he had kept her in ignorance of his sad state affirmed his
nobility, his courage. All through the exalted moments of
her idyll at Ashfurlong he had suffered. He had a right,
an indisputable right, to ask that she should share in his
suffering. That sacrifice he had never demanded. She must
give it to him.

" Well, tell me all about yourself, Clare," he asked, with
a harrowing kindliness.

" There's nothing to tell. If there were, it would be of
no importance. Oh, Dudley, however could you deceive
me like this ? "

He smiled. " My dear child, I imagined that you were
happy. Why should you be bothered with my little ups and
downs ? I've had an uphill struggle during these last six
years. The war was a big break ; it spoiled my plans for
me. But now it's over. The last of the burdens that poor
Ernest left me with has been paid. Before, I was a slave.
Now, thank God ! I'm a free man. I've taken a partner.
That's merely a matter of form. In point of fact I've handed
over the practice to him. I've no responsibilities, and just

enough to live on. What can a sick man in his sixtieth year ask more than that ? "

Indeed, the thin, ascetic face was full of a strange serenity. The cloud of thought and preoccupation that she had always known had lifted from it.

" But, Dudley," she said, " my dear, this horrible house ! I can see you're starved for light and air ; for everything that an ill man needs. It's impossible ! It's more than I can bear to see you sitting here alone. At Ashfurlong it's spring. It might be winter here, for all you know of it. How can you ever get better if you stay here ? "

" I'm afraid I shan't get better, it's a question of albumin," he answered with a deadly quietness. " You mustn't make me discontented, Clare. It's what I'm used to ; I'm perfectly happy with it. I'm perfectly happy," he repeated mechanically, and then, with a gleam of his old manner : " I see you haven't changed, Clare. You'll never realize, as long as you live, that beggars can't be choosers."

" But, my dear," she protested, " this isn't your only choice. It's not like you to throw up the sponge in this way. If only, for once, you'd let me take you in hand, if only . . ."

He laughed and pressed her fingers : " Why, what would you do with me ? "

" You mustn't laugh at me, Dudley ! " His gentleness was killing her. " I mean . . ." She hesitated. " I mean . . . why can't you come back with me to Ashfurlong ? " She pressed him : " You've no idea how lovely it is. So quiet, and such sweet air . . . It would make all the difference to you. Now that the summer's coming . . . And I could look after you, Dudley. That's what I want to do. Now that the practice is sold, there's no reason in the world why you should stay in this ghastly Winsworth. Do, do think of it ! "

He shook his head : " My child, it's too late to think of things like that. I'm an old tree. It's dangerous to transplant me. No, no, it's much, much better to leave me as I am."

" Not even for my sake, Dudley ? " she entreated him.

"Not even for your sake, Clare. It's too late. I'd rather you said no more of it. Too late, too late. And now," he went on, with a changed voice, " let's talk of something else. It's cheered me up tremendously to see you. You're looking splendid. Tell me about Ashfurlong."

She could not bear to give way to him.

" What is the good of my telling you if you won't come there ? "

" I want to know about you. Everything. It will amuse me. Tell me about Colonel Hart."

What could she tell him ? How could she cheat this broken man with lies ? Besides, in the agony of that last hour, even Hart had become unreal. The old truth, if she told it to him, would be the truth no longer. But now, with something of the old keenness made curiously impersonal, his eyes were on hers. There was a look of divination in them.

" I wish you'd tell me," he said. " You may be quite sure that it won't hurt me. I wanted to ask you about the letter I sent you."

And now she knew that she could no longer refuse him. Sitting at his side, his hand still clasped in hers, she opened her heart to him, withholding nothing, telling him the whole history of her love for Hart from the black days of Pedworth onward to that of Steven's visit and her own panic-stricken quest at Dinsop. And it seemed to her, as if, in this man who had never understood her, she had at last found understanding.

He listened without a word until she had finished.

" I'm glad you've told me all this," he said when she had ended ; " although, as a matter of fact, it isn't news to me. Hart is a fine type. You remember I saw him once for a moment at Pedworth ? I knew, that afternoon, that you were in love with him. I was sorry for both of you. That's why I found it so strange to-day," he went on, " when you pressed me to come to Ashfurlong. Don't midunderstand me, Clare ; it made no difference. I know where I stand. I shouldn't have come in any case. But, knowing what I did, it struck me as curious that you should be ready to sacrifice yourself for an old man like myself."

The calm of his manner imposed itself upon her.

" We are none of us young any longer, Dudley. Robert is nearly fifty."

" I know he's not young. But you love him."

" Yes."

" And you don't love me. You've been very sweet to me, Clare ; but you've never loved me. Answer me truthfully."

She answered : " No."

" And love is the only thing that matters in this life. What are you going to do ? "

" I don't know, Dudley. I've never known. I wish to God you could tell me."

" There is only one reasonable way of dealing with the situation." He spoke to her as he would have spoken to a client. " And that is divorce."

" That is what Robert said. But when I mentioned it to Steven . . ."

" Steven's a bigot. You mustn't listen ·to him. My God, the stupidity, the inhumanity of these religious minds ! Listen to me, Clare ! " He spoke with a kind of bitter eloquence that wrung the last ounce of strength from his wasted body. " You love this man. As far as I'm concerned you have a right to love him. I'm happy that you should do so. Now that it's no longer possible for me, I know, as I've told you, that love is the only reality in this fantastic, ironical life. And standards have changed. The war has taught us something. This generation has seen the cruelty of life at its utmost. We've suffered, you and I and Hart and all the rest of us. And we know, or at any rate we ought to know, that no human being has the right to add to the world's suffering. It's a crime against life and against love, which is the best of life, to sacrifice either to the mouthings of a pack of priests The crime against life ! That's what I call the crime against the Holy Ghost : the unforgivable sin. And yet the same men tell you that God is Love . . . "

His vehemence carried her with him. The words had the authenticity of the ultimate hour ; he was so moved that the hand that lay in hers twitched and trembled.

" But, my dear," she cried, " if only you could have heard what Steven said ! He said, as a Churchwoman . . ."

" What is their church ? A system of traditions corrupted by time and brooding, morbid, emasculate, celibate fancies, with which they've hidden the essential humanity of Christ. That bitter, bloodless sterility ? A Churchwoman ? You were a woman before ever you were that ! The gift of life has been given to you. Live, Clare, live ! That is the only advice that a man from whom life is being taken away can give to you."

He paused, exhausted. She could feel the heaviness of his breathing. He saw the pain in her eyes.

" Don't worry," he said. " I'll be better in a moment. I've nothing more to say. I hope I've convinced you."

" I'm only thinking of Steven," she answered helplessly.

" You're wrong to think of Steven," he told her. " Be honest, Clare. You know that you've ceased to be the first thing in Steven's life. I told you, years ago, that that was inevitable. You wouldn't believe it. It shocked you. But, none the less, it's come true. It's waste of life to sacrifice yourself to something that's dead. Above all to his dead formulæ."

" I know you are right," she said, " though it kills me to

confess it. You have been wonderful with me, Dudley. But what can I do ? I don't know where to begin. I suppose you must divorce me. What do I have to do ? "

He laughed, as he had always laughed, at her innocence.

" How fortunate you are," he teased her, " to have a lawyer for a husband ! No, no, my child ; of course you needn't do anything. There's no reason in the world why you or Hart should bear the blame—such as it is. Of course, I shan't divorce you. It's you who'll divorce me. The only thing is," he ended ironically, " I think you'd better hurry up about it. Will you pass me that paper and pencil ? "

He began, without further ado, to draft a letter. He was like a kindly father instructing his child.

" To-night," he said, " when you get back to Ashfurlong, you'll send me this. *Dear Dudley* . . . I needn't read it. The sense is plain enough. It says that we've been separated for so many years and that you want me to come back to you. When I get this, to-morrow, I shall answer it, saying, as I've said this afternoon, that nothing will induce me to return. There's no necessity to give the reasons. You send these letters to my friend, James Veale. I shall also supply him with evidence of infidelity, which, of course, will be false, but quite categorical. Then you will ask James Veale to file your petition. You understand ? "

" But is it as simple as that ? " she asked him. " Isn't this rather what they call collusion ? "

" Of course. The laws under which we live are insane. Without collusion a large number of unhappy people would be chained to each other for life. We're acting as criminals and as rational people. The fact that we're criminals will compel us to be careful. Before James Veale has filed the petition you had better get rid of Hart. You'll have to send him away somewhere until the decree, which I won't defend, has been made absolute. Only one other precaution. You mustn't see me again." He looked at his watch.

" And now, if you want to get back to Ashfurlong to-night, you'd better think of going. I've even forgotten to offer you a cup of tea. I think we just have time, if you'll ring for Mrs. Marple."

She would not. She was so bewildered that she could think of nothing.

" In that case," he said with a smile, " there's nothing left but to say good-bye." He held out his arms to her. His eyes were strangely bright. There was a happiness in them that made him seem almost beautiful. He kissed her. " Good-bye, my child. Live, and be happy ! "

She picked up her bag and hurried from the room, through the mean hall, out into the meaner street. She walked and walked over the blue-brick pavements not knowing where she went until, of a sudden, she found herself on the North West Road, and a two-decked tramcar came clanging toward her on its way citywards. She waved to the driver, who turned his control. The wheels screeched on the rails. She scrambled aboard it. The conductor stood waiting for his fare.

" This goes to the Western station, doesn't it ? " she gasped.

" Yes, madam. Twopence, please."

Still crumpled in her hand was the draft letter that Dudley had given her. She folded it neatly and put it into her bag. Opposite her, on the tramcar window, a dark advertisement turned the glass into a mirror. She saw reflected in it the image of a small, neat, grey-haired woman with delicate hands, that clutched a bag of black watered silk and a blue tram-ticket, a gentle mouth, which had known sorrow, and happy eyes, that were still full of tears.

Fraita, Anacapri : 1924.

107, East 70th St., N.Y. : 1927.

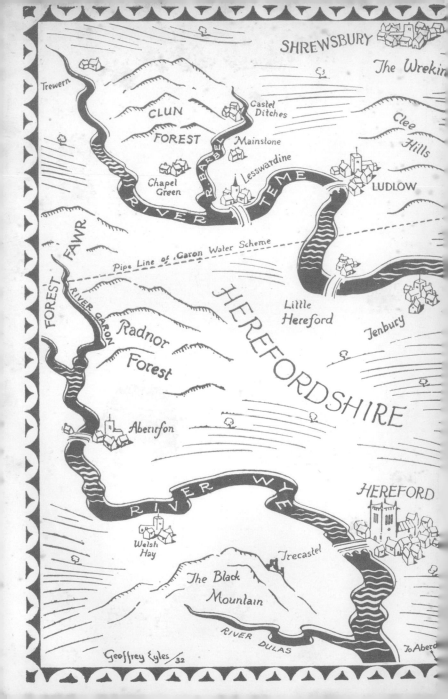